Text Book Of

DESIGN OF MACHINE ELEMENTS

For
Semester – VI
Third Year Diploma Courses in Mechanical Engineering Group

As Per MSBTE's 'G' Scheme Syllabus

Vinod Thombre Patil

B.E. (Mech.) M. Tech. (Energy Technology)
Vice-Principal and Head of Department – Mechanical,
S. H. Jondhale Polytechnic, Dombivli

N3263

DESIGN OF MACHINE ELEMENTS   ISBN 978-93-5164-306-7

Third Edition   : **January 2017**

©   : **Author**

Published By :

NIRALI PRAKASHAN

Abhyudaya Pragati, 1312, Shivaji Nagar,
Off J.M. Road, PUNE – 411005
Tel - (020) 25512336/37/39, Fax - (020) 25511379
Email : niralipune@pragationline.com

☞ DISTRIBUTION CENTRES

PUNE

Nirali Prakashan : 119, Budhwar Peth, Jogeshwari Mandir Lane, Pune 411002, Maharashtra
Tel : (020) 2445 2044, 66022708, Fax : (020) 2445 1538
Email : bookorder@pragationline.com, niralilocal@pragationline.com

Nirali Prakashan : S. No. 28/27, Dhyari, Near Pari Company, Pune 411041
Tel : (020) 24690204 Fax : (020) 24690316
Email : dhyari@pragationline.com, bookorder@pragationline.com

MUMBAI

Nirali Prakashan : 385, S.V.P. Road, Rasdhara Co-op. Hsg. Society Ltd.,
Girgaum, Mumbai 400004, Maharashtra
Tel : (022) 2385 6339 / 2386 9976, Fax : (022) 2386 9976
Email : niralimumbai@pragationline.com

☞ DISTRIBUTION BRANCHES

JALGAON

Nirali Prakashan : 34, V. V. Golani Market, Navi Peth, Jalgaon 425001,
Maharashtra, Tel : (0257) 222 0395, Mob : 94234 91860

KOLHAPUR

Nirali Prakashan : New Mahadvar Road, Kedar Plaza, 1st Floor Opp. IDBI Bank
Kolhapur 416 012, Maharashtra. Mob : 9850046155

NAGPUR

Pratibha Book Distributors : Above Maratha Mandir, Shop No. 3, First Floor,
Rani Jhanshi Square, Sitabuldi, Nagpur 440012, Maharashtra
Tel : (0712) 254 7129

DELHI

Nirali Prakashan : 4593/21, Basement, Aggarwal Lane 15, Ansari Road, Daryaganj
Near Times of India Building, New Delhi 110002, Mob : 08505972553

BENGALURU

Pragati Book House : House No. 1, Sanjeevappa Lane, Avenue Road Cross,
Opp. Rice Church, Bengaluru – 560002.
Tel : (080) 64513344, 64513355,Mob : 9880582331, 9845021552
Email:bharatsavla@yahoo.com

CHENNAI

Pragati Books : 9/1, Montieth Road, Behind Taas Mahal, Egmore,
Chennai 600008 Tamil Nadu, Tel : (044) 6518 3535,
Mob : 94440 01782 / 98450 21552 / 98805 82331,
Email : bharatsavla@yahoo.com

niralipune@pragationline.com | www.pragationline.com

Also find us on ⨍ **www.facebook.com/niralibooks**

Preface ...

I am glad to present the new edition of book entitled **"Design of Machine Elements"** for IIIrd year Diploma in Mechanical engineering as per the "G" Scheme code syllabus prescribed by MSBTE.

I have observed the students facing extreme difficulties in understanding the basic principles and fundamental concepts without adequate solved problems along with the text. To meet this basic requirement of students, sincere efforts have been made to present the subject matter with frequent use of figures and lots of numerical examples.

I am thankful to Mr. Dineshbhai Furia, Mr. Pradeepbhai Furia, Mr. Jigneshbhai Furia, Mr. Shashikant Patel, Mr. Santosh Bare, Mrs. Manasi Pingle, Mrs. Prachi Sawant of Nirali Prakashan along with their staff members for bringing this publication timely to the Market.

I must acknowledge special gratitude to Mr. Raosaheb Patil Danve (Hon'ble. Minister, Central Govt. of India), Mr. Ankushrao Tope (President, Matsydari Shikshan Sanstha, Jalna), Er, Rajesh Tope (Hon'ble Minister – Higher & Technical Education), Er. Sagar Jondhale (Director, Jondhale Educational Group), Mr. Pawar Uttamsingh (Ex. M. P., Jalna), Mrs. Aglawe Vimal (President, District Congress, Jalna), Mr. Aglawe M. R., (Designated Member, Maharashtra Revenue Tribunal, Aurangabad), Dr. Ram Reddy, (Principal, LRT College of Engineering, Mumbai), Dr. R. G. Tated (Principal, Sandip Foundation, Nashik), Prof. Shinde N. N. (HOD – Energy Technology, DOT, SUK), Prof. Hemant Sarje (Dean, Fabtech Technical Campus, Sangola), Dr. Nehte (Principal, Father Agnel), Prof. S. L. Pawar (HOD, E&TC DEPT, Fabtech Technical Campus), Prof. S. A. Magar (Assistant Professor, Vidyalankar, Mumbai), Dr. Pable M. J. (G. P. Bandra), Prof. R. K. Nandarage (Principal, S. S. Jondhale Polytechnic, Ambernath), Prof. Patil A. B. (Principal, IT, Ulhasnagar), Prof. Nayak (Principal, VPM, Thane), Prof. Ibrahim (Principal, Saboo Siddiqui Polytechnic, Mumbai), Prof. R. B. Sholapurkar, (Principal, Virar Polytechnic), Prof. Chavan Manoj (Principal, JMM Trust's Polytechnic, Shahapur), Prof. Nathe (Principal, G. P., Thane), Prof. Taskar (Principal, G.P., Mumbai),

❑❑❑

Chapter 1

INTRODUCTION TO DESIGN

About This Chapter

This chapter has weightage of 20 marks and assigned duration is 12 hours. In this chapter, we will learn machine design philosophy, procedures, design considerations, various types of stresses, stress strain diagram, creep curve, fatigue, S-N curve and endurance limit. Also we will study the factors considered in design such as properties of Engineering materials, designation of materials, stress concentration, and their properties, standardization and theories of elastic failure, ecology, societal consideration and concept of Product Design along with Ergonomics and Aesthetic considerations in design.

Statistical Analysis

Examination	Weightage of questions asked
S-09	16 Marks
W-09	20 Marks
S-10	22 Marks
W-10	24 Marks
S-11	20 Marks
W-11	24 Marks
S-12	28 Marks
W-12	30 Marks
S-13	30 Marks
W-13	28 Marks
S-14	28 Marks

1.1 INTRODUCTION TO MACHINE DESIGN PHILOSOPHY

Question

1. Define machine design. **(S-13)**

- Machine design refers to the creation of new and better machines alongwith updating the existing ones.
- As per the consumer needs, the machines are invented or modified by creating an idea in mind.
- The idea is then reformed in terms of dimensions and suitable drawings.

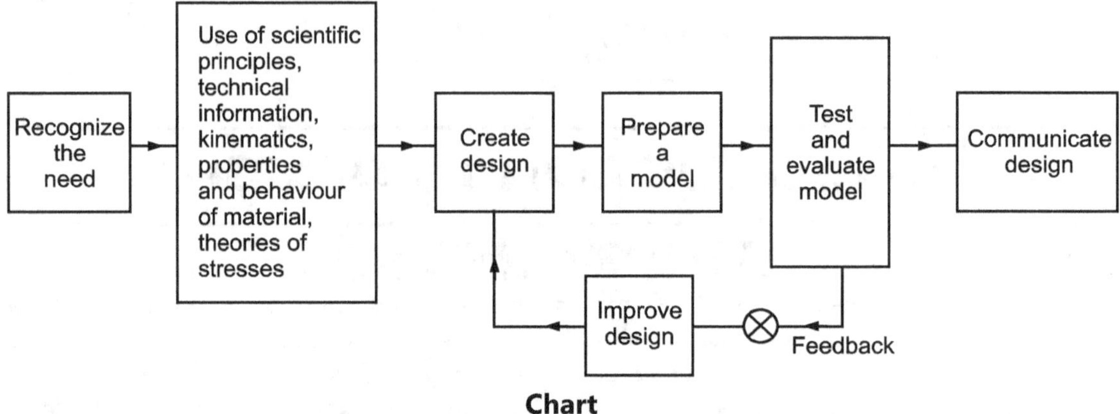

Chart

- Machine design is defined as *"the use of scientific principles, technical information and imagination in the description of a machine or mechanical system to perform specific functions"*.

1.2 GENERAL PROCEDURE OR STEPS INVOLVED IN DESIGNING A MACHINE COMPONENT

Questions

1. What are the steps involved in general design procedure ? Explain.

(S-09, 12, 13; W-10, 11)

2. List the steps involved in general design procedure. **(S-14)**

Steps in the Process of Designing a Machine Component :

1. **Recognition of need :** First of all, make a complete statement of the problem, indicate the need, aim or purpose, for which, the machine is to be designed.

2. **Mechanism :** Select the possible mechanism or group of mechanism, which will give the desired motion.

3. **Analysis of forces :** Find the forces acting on each member of the machine.

4. **Material selection :** Select the material best suited for each member.

5. **Design of machine elements :** Find size of each member by considering forces acting on the member and permissible stress for the material used.

6. **Modification :** Modify the size of member to agree with the past experience and judgment to facilitate the manufacturer. It may be necessary to reduce the overall cost.

7. **Detailed drawing :** Draw detailed drawing of each component and assembly of machine with complete specification for the manufacturing process suggested.

8. **Production :** The component as per the drawing is manufactured in the workshop.

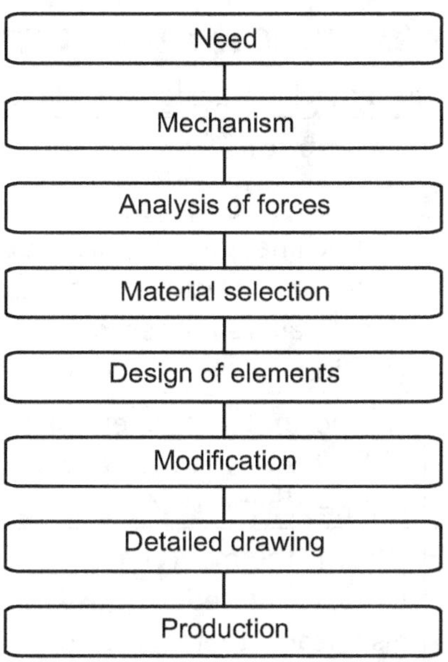

Chart : Steps involved in design process

1.3 GENERAL CONSIDERATIONS IN MACHINE DESIGN
(S-06; W-08)

(1) Type of loads and stresses caused by the load : The load, on a machine component, may act in several ways, due to which, the internal stresses are set up.

(2) Mechanism (Motion of the parts or kinematics of machine) : The successful operation of any machine depends largely upon the simplest arrangement of the parts, which will give the required motion.

(3) Selection of material : Designer should have a deep knowledge of properties of materials and behaviour under working conditions i.e. strength, durability, flexibility, weight, resistance to heat and corrosion, castability, weldability, hardenability, machinability etc.

(4) Convenient and economical features : The designed machine must be convenient to operate and cost wise economical for the customer.

(5) Use of standard part : The use of standard parts reduces the overall cost.

(6) Safety of operation : To avoid accidental hazards, care should be taken by designer.

(7) Workshop facilities : A design engineer should be familiar with limitations of his employer's workshop, in order to avoid the necessity of vendors.

(8) Number of machines to be manufactured.

(9) Cost of construction and assembly : As far as possible, the designed machine must be cheap and it should be easy to assemble.

(10) Frictional resistance and lubrication : Designer should provide necessary lubrication to the parts, where there is sliding, rolling and rotating motion.

1.4 BASIC DESIGN REQUIREMENTS

- Basic design requirements in machine design are explained as follows.

Sr. No.	Design requirement	Description
1	Strength	A machine part should not fail under the effect of the forces which act on it. It should have sufficient strength to avoid failure either due to fracture or due to general yielding.
2	Rigidity	A machine component should be rigid, i.e. it should not deflect or bend too much due to forces or bending moment acting on it.
3	Wear resistance	Wear is the main reason for putting the machine parts out of order. It reduces useful life of the component. Wear also leads to the loss of accuracy of machine tool. The wear resistance of the machine part can be increased by increasing the surface hardness, e.g. case hardening of gears and cams.
4	Manufacturability	Manufacturability is the ease of production, fabrication and assembly. The shape and material of the machine part should be selected in such a way that, it can be produced with minimum labour and material costs.
5	Safety	The shape and dimensions of the machine parts should ensure safety to the operators of the machine.
6	Standardization	A machine part should conform to the national or international standards covering its profile, dimensions, grade and material used.
7	Reliability	Reliability is probability that, a machine part will perform its intended functions under desired operating conditions over a specified period of time. Reliability is sometimes described as 'long term quality'. A machine part should be reliable, i.e. it should perform its function satisfactorily over its life time.
8	Maintainability	A machine part should be maintainable. Maintainability is the ease, with which, a machine part can be serviced or repaired.

- In addition to above, the other desired requirements are Operational safety, Repair and maintenance (Maintainability), Durability, Size and shape, Efficiency, Simplicity, Easy to assemble, Lubrication, Cost etc.

1.5 TYPES OF LOADS

Question

1. State four types of loads acting on a machine element.   **(S-13)**

- The external forces grouped together constitute *'load'* acting on the body.
- The load acting on a member can be classified as,

(a) Dead or Steady Load :

- It is the gradually applied load, which do not change in magnitude, direction or point of application with respect to time.
- It can be a force, torque or twisting moment, bending moment or combination of these.
- Example : Load acting on column or strut.

(b) Variable or Fluctuating Load :

- It varies in magnitude, direction or point of application with respect to time.
- It is also called as fatigue load, which may be (i) reversed (ii) repeated (iii) completely reversed.
- Examples : Force in I.C. engine valve spring, bending moment on rotating shafts.

(c) Impact Load :

- It is suddenly applied with initial velocity.
- Example : Blows of a hammer.

(d) Shock Load :

- It is applied or removed suddenly.
- Example : Leaf spring of automobile.

1.6 STRESS AND STRAIN

Stress :

Stress is defined as *'the internal resistive force per unit cross-sectional area of the body, when subjected to external load'*.

Mathematically, Stress $= \sigma = \dfrac{W}{A}$

Where, W = load acting on a body and, A = cross-sectional area of the body.

Its unit is N/mm^2.

Note that, $1 \text{ MPa} = 1 \text{ N/mm}^2$

$$1 \text{ kPa} = 1 \times 10^3 \text{ N/m}^2 = \frac{1 \times 10^3 \text{ N}}{10^6 \text{ mm}^2} = 1 \times 10^{-3} \text{ N/mm}^2 = 1 \times 10^{-3} \text{ MPa}$$

$$1 \text{ GPa} = 1 \times 10^9 \text{ N/m}^2 = \frac{1 \times 10^9 \text{ N}}{10^6 \text{ mm}^2} = 1 \times 10^3 \text{ N/mm}^2 = 1 \times 10^3 \text{ MPa}$$

Strain :

Strain is defined as *'the ratio of change in dimension to original dimension of the body subjected to external loads'*.

Mathematically, Strain $= \dfrac{\text{Change in dimension}}{\text{Original dimension}}$

It is unitless quantity.

1.6.1 Stress-Strain Diagram for Ductile Material
(Mild Steel)   (S-06, 08; W-07)

Questions

1. Draw stress-strain diagram for ductile material. Show different regions.   (S-09, 10, 12)
2. Draw stress-stain diagram for mild steel and state all points on it.   (W-12, S-14)

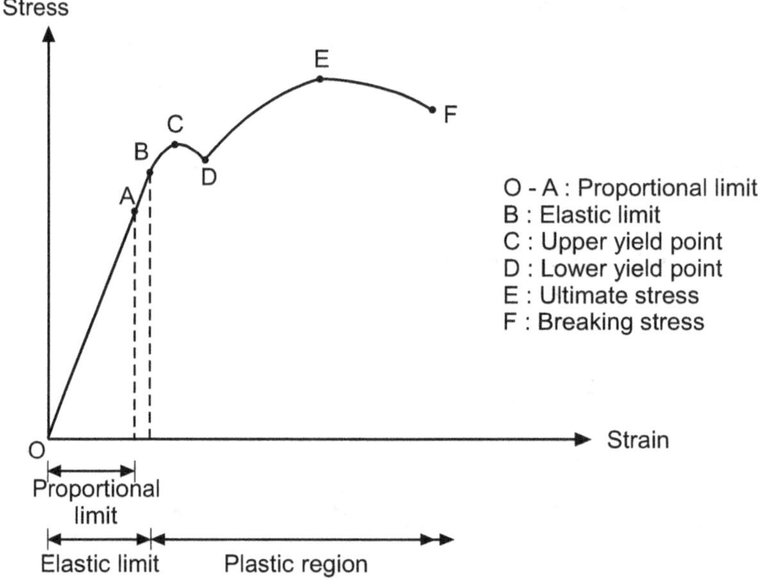

Fig. 1.1 : Stress-strain diagram for ductile material

Proportional Limit (O to A) :

• In the stress-strain diagram, O to A represents straight line, i.e. stress is directly proportional to strain obeying Hook's law. It is known as *Proportional Limit.*

Elastic Limit (B) :

• In the stress-strain diagram, point B represents elastic limit i.e. if the load is increased between points A and B, the body will regain its original shape, when load is removed. It means body possesses elasticity upto point B, known as *Elastic limit.*

• After point 'B', if load is increased, the body undergoes permanent deformation. This indicates the start of plastic stage.

Yield Point Stress (C and D) :

- In the stress-strain diagram, if the load is increased beyond point B, the body loses elasticity and reaches plasticity. The strain increases at a faster rate with any small increase in stress, until the point 'C' is reached and material starts yielding. This point 'C' is called as *upper yield point*.
- Further addition of small load drops the stress-strain diagram to point 'D', as soon as, the yielding starts. This point 'D' is called as *lower yield point*.
- The stresses corresponding to the two points 'C' and 'D' are called as *yield stresses*.

Ultimate Stress (E) :

- After the end of yielding, if the load is increased beyond point 'D', there is increase in stress upto point E. The maximum value of stress at point 'E' is called as *ultimate stress*.
- Simultaneously strain increases, which is followed by decrease in cross-sectional area of the specimen.

Breaking Stress :

- When the load is increased after reaching ultimate stress, neck formation takes place alongwith the further decrease in cross-sectional area of the specimen.
- The stress now decreases with increasing strain, till the specimen ruptures.
- Therefore, stress required to break away the specimen is less than maximum stress. So curve falls down from point 'E' to point 'F'. The stress corresponding to point 'F', where the specimen breaks, is called as *breaking stress*.

Formulae

$$\text{Yield stress} = \frac{W_{yt}}{A}$$

$$\text{Ultimate Stress} = \frac{W_{ut}}{A}$$

$$\text{Percentage reduction in area} = \frac{\text{Original area} - \text{Reduced area}}{\text{Original area}} \times 100$$

$$\text{Percentage elongation} = \frac{\text{Increased length} - \text{Original length}}{\text{Original length}} \times 100$$

Numerical Type No. 1 : "Tensile Test"

Problem 1.1 : *A mild steel rod of 12 mm diameter was tested for tensile strength with gauge length of 600 mm. Following observations were recorded. Final length = 800 mm, final diameter = 7 mm, yield load = 4 kN, ultimate load = 6 kN. Calculate :*

(a) *Yield stress.* (b) *Ultimate stress.*

(c) *Percentage reduction in area and percentage elongation.* **(S-11)**

Solution : Given data : $d = 12$ mm, $L = 600$ mm, $L_1 = 800$ mm, $d_1 = 7$ mm

$$\text{Yield load} = W_{yt} = 4 \text{ kN} = 4 \times 10^3 \text{ N}$$

$$\text{Ultimate load} = W_{ut} = 6 \text{ kN} = 6 \times 10^3 \text{ N}$$

Procedure : Original area $= A = \frac{\pi}{4}d^2 = \frac{\pi}{4} \times (12)^2 = 113.09 \text{ mm}^2$

(a)   Yield stress, $\sigma_{yt} = \dfrac{W_{yt}}{A} = \dfrac{4 \times 10^3}{113.09} = \mathbf{35.37 \ N/mm^2}$

(b)   Ultimate stress, $\sigma_{ut} = \dfrac{W_{ut}}{A} = \dfrac{6 \times 10^3}{113.09} = \mathbf{53.05 \ N/mm^2}$

(c)   (i)   % Reduction in area :

        Reduced area $= A_1 = \dfrac{\pi}{4} \cdot (d_1)^2 = \dfrac{\pi}{4} \times (7)^2 = 38.48 \text{ mm}^2$

$\therefore$ % Reduction in area $= \dfrac{A - A_1}{A} \times 100 = \dfrac{113.09 - 38.48}{113.09} \times 100 = \mathbf{65.97\%}$

   (ii)   % elongation $= \dfrac{L_1 - L}{L_1} \times 100 = \dfrac{800 - 600}{800} \times 100 = \mathbf{25\%}$

1.6.2 Stress-Strain Diagram for Brittle Material   (S-12)

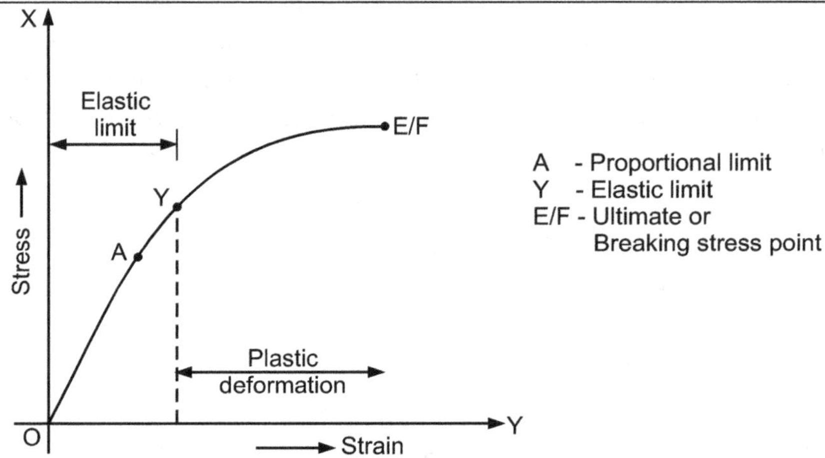

Fig. 1.2 : Stress-strain diagram for brittle material

- Brittle materials fail at relatively low strain.
- Consider a specimen of harder material like cast iron subjected to load. It will be observed that, stress is directly proportional to strain from point O upto point A. Thus, there is continuous elongation of bar, within this limit. This is called as *proportional limit*.
- In such materials, the elastic limit lies above proportionality limit. As shown in Fig. 1.2, elastic limit is from point A to point Y.
- After elastic limit, the curve shows permanent deformation, i.e. the material reaches plastic stage.
- Point E is the *breaking point*, at which, the specimen breaks or fails. Here breaking stress is almost equal to ultimate stress i.e. point F.
- Therefore, design of parts made of brittle material is based on ultimate stress.

1.6.3 Difference between Stress-Strain Diagram for Brittle and Ductile Materials

- Stress-strain diagram for ductile materials obeys the Hook's law within elastic limit, whereas in case of stress-strain diagram for brittle materials, the deviations from Hook's law begins very early.
- Stress-strain diagram for ductile materials shows that, there is always sufficient plastic deformation prior to failure, which is a warning well in advance, whereas stress-strain diagram for brittle materials shows that, fatigue cracks are not visible, till they reach the surface and by that time, the failure has occurred and the fracture is sudden.

1.7 TYPES OF STRESSES

Questions

1.	Explain the following stresses : (i) Transverse shear stress, (ii) Compressive stress.	**(S-10)**
2.	Explain bearing stress.	**(S-11)**
3.	Explain : (i) Transverse shear stress, (ii) Bending stress.	**(S-12)**

The different types of stresses are :

(1) Tensile Stress :

- *"When a body is subjected to equal and opposite axial pull forces, the stress produced is called as tensile stress".*
- Fig. 1.3 shows a circular rod subjected to axial tensile force W. The tensile stress induced is given by, $\sigma_t = \dfrac{W}{A}$

where,   W = Axial tensile force

A = Cross-sectional area of rod $= \dfrac{\pi}{4} d^2$, d = Diameter of rod

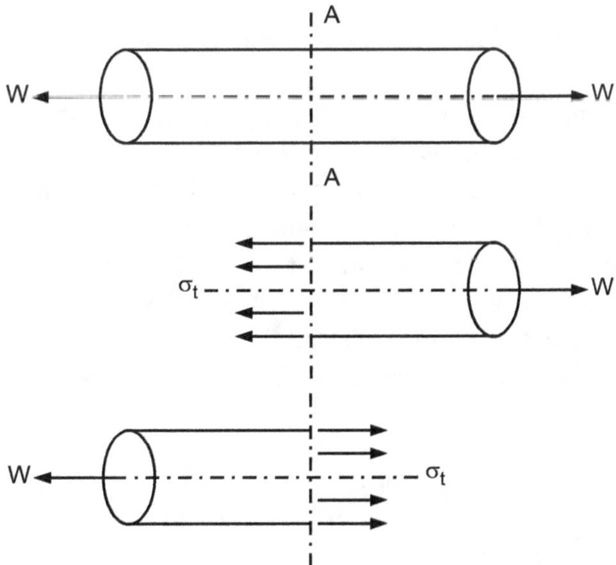

Fig. 1.3 : Tensile stress

(2) Compressive Stress :   (S-10)

- *"When a body is subjected to equal and opposite axial push forces, the stress produced is called as compressive stress".*
- Fig. 1.4 shows a circular rod subjected to axial compressive force W. The compressive stress induced is given by,

$$\sigma_c = \frac{W}{A}$$

where,   W = Axial compressive force

$$A = \text{Cross-sectional area of rod} = \frac{\pi}{4} d^2$$

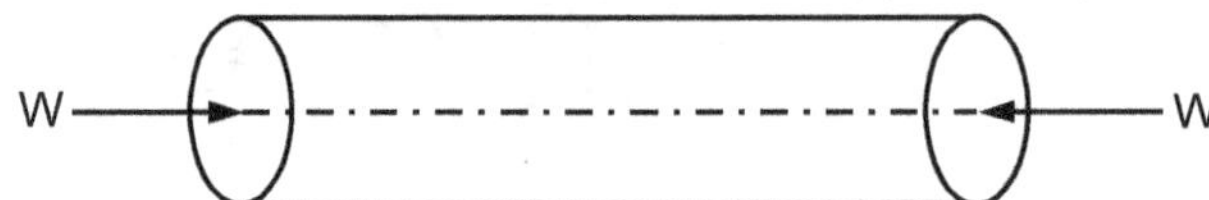

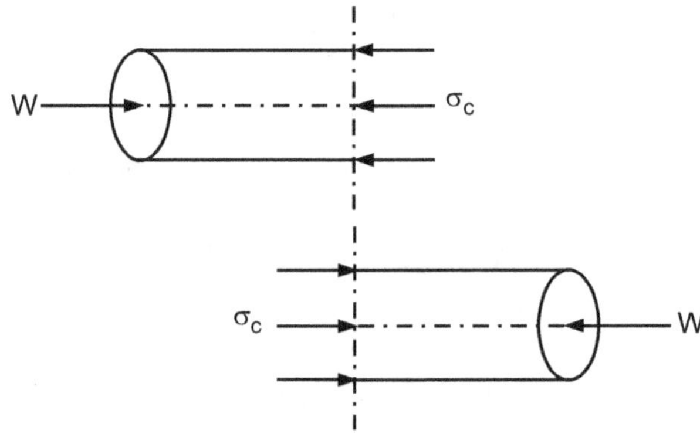

Fig. 1.4 : Compressive stress

(3) Bending Stress :   (S-12)

- *"When the beam is subjected to bending moment (M), the stress induced is called as bending stress".*
- Consider a straight beam subjected to bending moment as shown in Fig. 1.5. It is clear that, the upper fibres will be shortened due to compression, while the lower fibres will be elongated due to tension. Also, there is a surface, called *neutral axis*, where fibres are neither shortened nor elongated.
- Thus, the bending stress is nothing but, a tensile or compressive stress. The fibres above the neutral axis are subjected to compressive stress, whereas fibres below the neutral axis are subjected to tensile stress.
- The bending stress induced at extreme fibre i.e. at greatest distance from *neutral axis* is given by,

$$\sigma_{b\,max} = \frac{M}{I} \cdot y_{max}$$

Also,
$$\sigma_{b\,max} = \frac{M}{\left(\dfrac{I}{y_{max}}\right)} = \frac{M}{Z}$$

where, Z = Section modulus = $\dfrac{I}{y_{max}}$

I = Moment of inertia of cross-section

M = Bending moment acting in the beam

y_{max} = Distance of extreme (outermost) fibre from neutral axis.

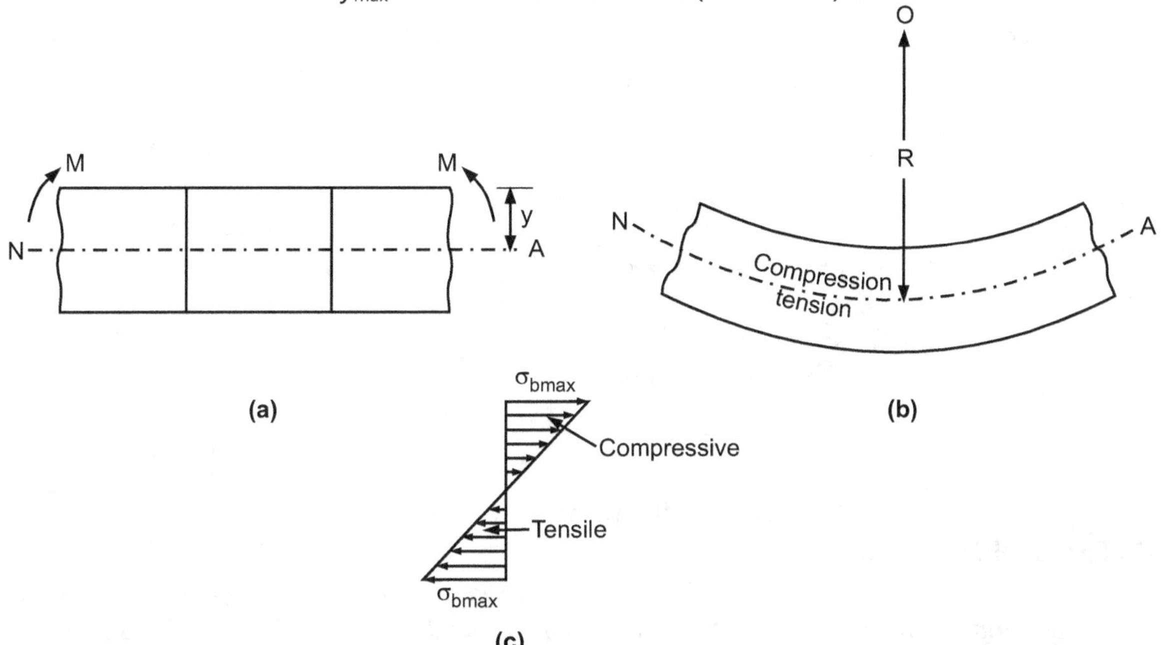

Fig. 1.5 : Bending stress

(4) Transverse Shear Stress : (S-10, 12)

- When a section is subjected to two equal and opposite forces acting tangentially across the section, such that, it tends to shear off across the section. The stress produced is called as *transverse shear stress*.

- Fig. 1.6 shows a riveted joint for two plates resting one above another, subjected to single shear.

- Transverse shear stress is given by, $\tau = \dfrac{W}{A}$

where, W – Force applied tangentially

A = Area of cross-section = $\dfrac{\pi}{4}d^2$ and d = Diameter of rivet

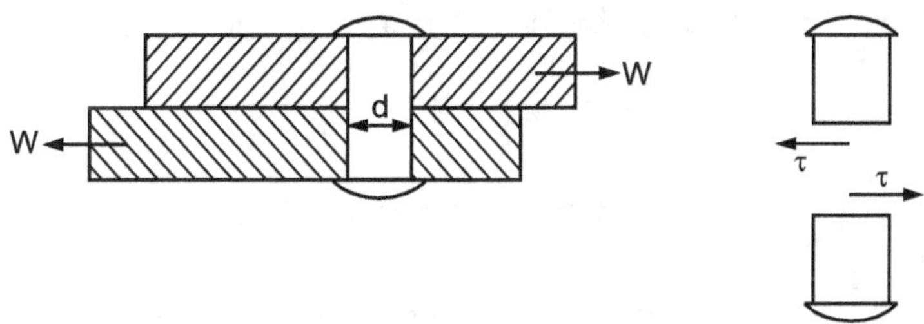

Fig. 1.6 : Single transverse shear stress

- Fig. 1.7 shows a riveted joint for three plates resting one above other, subjected to double shear.

Here,

$$\tau = \frac{W}{A} = \frac{W}{2 \times \left(\frac{\pi}{4} d^2\right)}$$

where,

W = Force applied tangentially

A = Area of cross-section

$$= 2 \times \frac{\pi}{4} d^2 \qquad\qquad (\because \text{ double shear})$$

d = Diameter of rivet

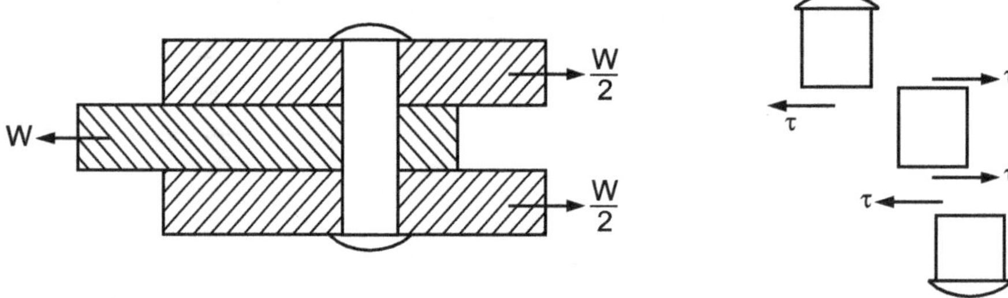

Fig. 1.7 : Double transverse shear stress

(5) Torsional Shear Stress :

- *"When a machine component is under the action of two equal and opposite couples i.e. twisting moment or torque, then component is said to be in torsion and the stress set up due to torsion is called as torsional shear stress".*
- It is zero at the neutral axis and maximum at outer fibres.

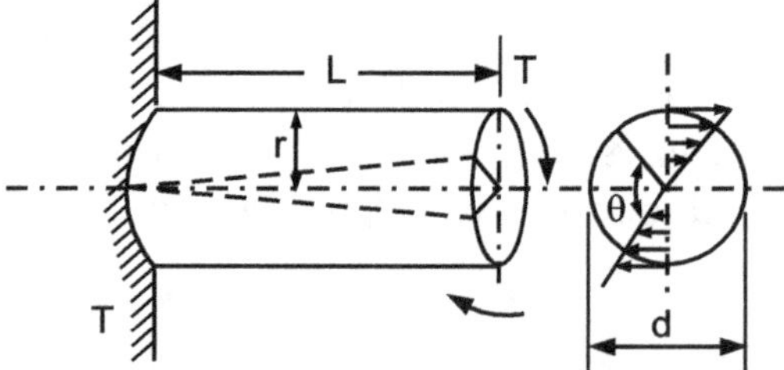

Fig. 1.8 : Torsional shear stress

- Consider a component of circular cross-section, 'd' in diameter, subjected to torque T, as shown in Fig. 1.8.
- Torsional shear stress is given by, basic torsion equation,

$$\frac{T}{J} = \frac{\tau}{r} \quad \text{i.e. } \tau = \frac{T \cdot r}{J}$$

where,

r = Distance of outermost fibre from neutral axis $= \dfrac{d}{2}$

J = Polar moment of inertia of cross-section $= \dfrac{\pi}{64} d^4$

(6) Crushing Stress :

- Crushing stress is defined as *'the localized compressive stress at the surface of contact between two components of a machine, which are relatively at rest'.*
- Here, there is no relative motion between the two components.
- Consider a riveted joints subjected to load W,

$$\sigma_{ck} = \frac{\text{Load}}{\text{Projected area of contact}} = \frac{W}{d \cdot t \cdot n}$$

where, d = Diameter of rivet, t = Thickness of plate

     n = Number of rivets

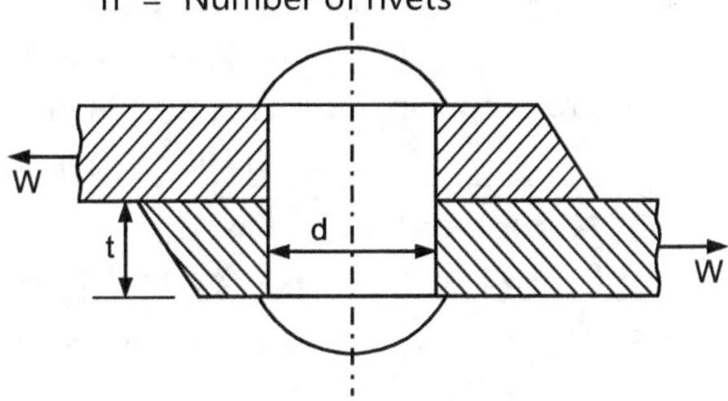

Fig. 1.9 : Crushing stress

- Other examples of crushing stresses are cotter joints, knuckle joint etc.

(7) Bearing Stress :   (S-11)

- Bearing stress is defined as, *'the localized compressive stress at the surface of contact between two members of a machine part, which have relative motion between them'.*
- The bearing stress is taken into account in design of machine elements like,
  - Screwed joint
  - Crank pin and large end bearings in I.C. engines.
  - Small end of connecting rod and piston pin etc.
- Referring Fig. 1.10. Let us consider a journal supported in a bearing subjected to load W, then bearing stress is given by,

$$\text{Bearing stress (pressure)}, P_b = \frac{\text{Load}}{\text{Projected area of contact}} = \frac{W}{l \times d}$$

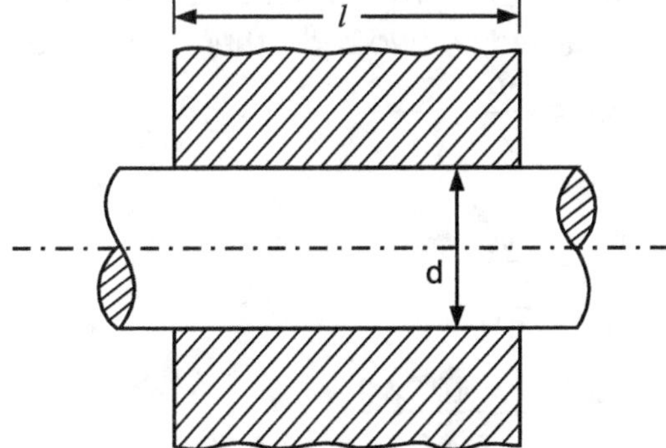

Fig. 1.10 : Bearing stress

1.7.1 Difference between Crushing and Bearing Stress

Sr. No.	Crushing Stress	Bearing Stress
1	Two machine components are in contact with each other.	The two machine members are in contact with a small lubricating film.
2	There is no relative motion between two parts.	There is relative motion between two parts.
3	Examples: (a) Screw and nut subjected to axial load. (b) Cotter inserted in a rectangular slot in cotter joint.	Examples : (a) Cross head and guide. (b) Pin in a knuckle joint. (c) Crank pin in bearing. (d) Fulcrum pin of lever.

Numerical Type No. 2 :
"Tensile Stress and Compressive Stress"

Problem 1.2 : *A load of 5 kN is to be raised by means of steel wire. Find minimum wire diameter required for safe stress of 100 MPa.*

Solution : Given data : $W = 5$ kN $= 5 \times 10^3$ N, $\sigma_t = 100$ MPa $= 100$ N/mm^2

Procedure : Let d be diameter of wire.

We have,
$$\sigma_t = \frac{W}{A}$$

$$\therefore \quad 100 = \frac{5 \times 10^3}{\frac{\pi}{4} \cdot d^2}$$

$$\therefore \quad d = 7.97 \text{ mm} \cong \textbf{8 mm (say)}$$

Problem 1.3 : *A press exerts a load of 2 MN. This load is carried by two rods of 2 metre length and supports the upper head of the press. Find : (i) Diameter of rods.(ii) Change in length of rods. Assume safe stress = 80 MPa, E = 210 kN/mm^2.* **(W-13)**

Solution : Given data : $W_1 = 2$ MN $= 2 \times 10^6$ N, $L = 2$ m $= 2 \times 10^3$ mm,
$E = 210 \times 10^3$ N/mm^2, $\sigma_t = 80$ MPa $= 80$ N/mm^2.

Procedure : As the load is carried by two rods, therefore, load taken by each rod is,

$$W = \frac{W_1}{2} = \frac{2 \times 10^6}{2} = 1 \times 10^6 \text{ N}$$

(i) Diameter of rods :

We have,
$$\sigma_t = \frac{W}{\frac{\pi}{4} d^2}$$

$$\therefore \quad 80 = \frac{1 \times 10^6 \times 4}{\pi \times d^2}$$

$$\therefore \quad d = \textbf{126.15 mm}$$

(ii) Change in length of rods :

We have,
$$\delta L = \frac{WL}{AE} = \frac{1 \times 10^6 \times 2 \times 10^3}{\frac{\pi}{4} \times d^2 \times 210 \times 10^3} = \frac{1 \times 10^6 \times 2 \times 10^3 \times 4}{\pi \times (126.15)^2 \times 210 \times 10^3}$$

$$\therefore \qquad \delta L = \mathbf{0.7619 \ mm}$$

Problem 1.4 : *A cast iron link as shown in Fig. 1.11 is required to transmit a steady tensile load of 45 kN. Find tensile stress induced in linked material at section A-A and B-B.*

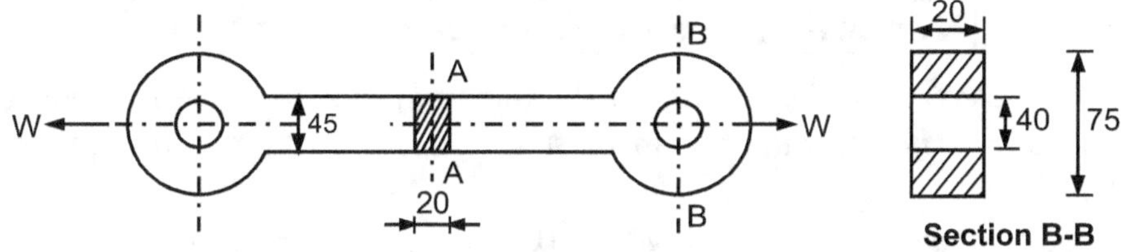

Fig. 1.11

Solution : Given : $W = 45 \ kN = 45 \times 10^3 \ N$

Procedure : To find tensile stress at section A-A,

$$\sigma_{t \ (A-A)} = \frac{W}{A} = \frac{45 \times 10^3}{45 \times 20} = \mathbf{50 \ N/mm^2}$$

To find tensile stress induced at section B-B,

$$\sigma_{t \ (B-B)} = \frac{W}{A} = \frac{45 \times 10^3}{(75 - 40) \times 20} = \mathbf{64.28 \ N/mm^2}$$

Problem 1.5 : *Reciprocating steam engine connecting rod is subjected to maximum load of 65 kN. Find diameter of connecting rod at thinnest part, if permissible tensile stress is 35 MPa.*

Solution : Given data : $W = 65 \ kN = 65 \times 10^3 \ N$

$$\sigma_t = 35 \ MPa = 35 \ N/mm^2$$

Procedure : Let d be diameter of connecting rod.

$$\sigma_t = \frac{W}{A}$$

$$\therefore \qquad 35 = \frac{65 \times 10^3}{\frac{\pi}{4} \cdot d^2}$$

$$\therefore \qquad d = 48.63 \ mm \approx \mathbf{50 \ mm \ (say)}$$

Problem 1.6 : *The diameter of piston is 300 mm and maximum steam pressure is 0.7 N/mm². If compressive stress is 40 MPa, find diameter of piston rod.*

Solution : Given data : $D = 300 \ mm$, $p = 0.7 \ N/mm^2$, $\sigma_c = 40 \ MPa$

Procedure :   Load on piston $= \frac{\pi}{4} D^2 \times p$

$$\therefore \qquad W = \frac{\pi}{4} (300)^2 \times 0.7 = 49.48 \times 10^3 \ N$$

We have, $\qquad\qquad \sigma_c = \dfrac{W}{\dfrac{\pi}{4} \cdot d^2}$

$\therefore \qquad\qquad 40 = \dfrac{49.48 \times 10^3}{\dfrac{\pi}{4} \cdot d^2}$

$\therefore \qquad\qquad d = 39.68 \text{ mm} \approx \textbf{40 mm (say)}$

Numerical Type No. 3 : "Shear Stress"

Problem 1.7 : *Determine the maximum thickness of plate, that can be punched in a hole of diameter of 20 mm, having ultimate shear stress of 0.40 kN/mm². The maximum load on punch is 0.25 MN.*

Solution : Given data : $W = 0.25 \text{ MN} = 0.25 \times 10^6 \text{ N}$, $d = 20 \text{ mm}$, $\tau_{ut} = 0.4 \text{ kN/mm}^2$ $= 400 \text{ N/mm}^2$.

Procedure : Assume factor of safety = 5

Thus, the permissible shear stress $= \tau = \dfrac{\tau_{ut}}{\text{F.O.S.}} = \dfrac{400}{5} = 80 \text{ N/mm}^2$.

We know that, $\quad \tau = \dfrac{W}{\pi \times d \times t}$

$\therefore \qquad\qquad t = \dfrac{W}{\pi \times d \times \tau} = \dfrac{0.25 \times 10^6}{\pi \times 20 \times 80} = \textbf{49.73 mm} \cong \textbf{50 mm (say)}$

Problem 1.8 : *Calculate force required to punch a circular blank of 60 mm diameter in a plate of 5 mm thickness. Ultimate shear stress of plate is 350 N/mm². Find force (W).*

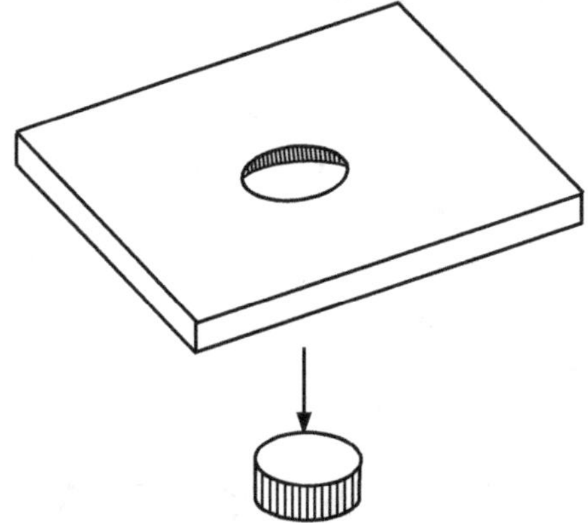

Fig. 1.12

Solution : Given data : $d = 60 \text{ mm}$, $\quad t = 5 \text{ mm}$, $\quad \tau = 350 \text{ N/mm}^2$

Procedure : We have, $\qquad \tau = \dfrac{W}{A} = \dfrac{W}{\pi \times d \times t}$

$\therefore \qquad\qquad 350 = \dfrac{W}{\pi \times 60 \times 5}$

$\therefore \qquad\qquad W = \textbf{329.86} \times \textbf{10}^\textbf{3} \textbf{ N}$

Problem 1.9 : *Circular rods of diameter 50 mm are connected by knuckle joint with a pin of 40 mm diameter. If pull of 120 kN acts at each end, find tensile stress in rod and shear stress in the pin.*

Solution : Given data : $D = 50$ mm, $d = 40$ mm, $W = 120 \times 10^3$ N

Procedure : Tensile stress for rod (σ_t),

$$\sigma_t = \frac{W}{A} = \frac{W}{\frac{\pi}{4} \cdot D^2}$$

$$\sigma_t = \frac{120 \times 10^3}{\frac{\pi}{4}(50)^2}$$

$$\sigma_t = \textbf{61.11 N/mm}^2$$

∴ Shear stress in pin (Pin subjected to double shearing).

$$\tau = \frac{W}{2A} = \frac{W}{2 \times \left(\frac{\pi}{4} \cdot d^2\right)} = \frac{120 \times 10^3}{2 \times \frac{\pi}{4}(40)^2}$$

∴ $\tau = \textbf{47.74 N/mm}^2$

Numerical Type No. 4 : "Crushing Stress"

Problem 1.10 : *Two plates of 16 mm thickness are joined by a double riveted lap joint, the rivets are 25 mm in diameter. Find the crushing stress induced both on the plates and rivet, if the maximum tensile load on joint is 48 kN.*

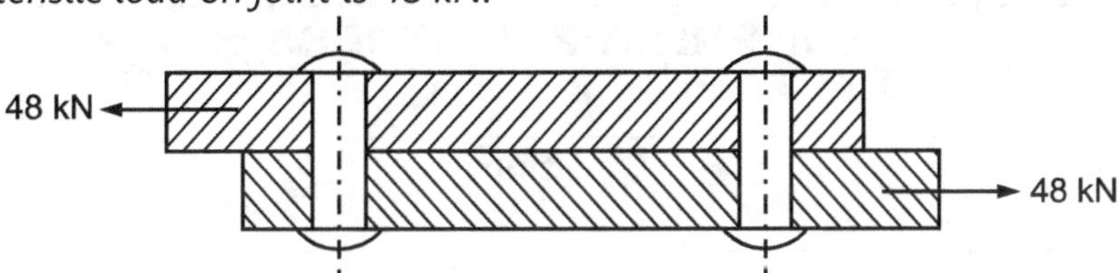

Fig. 1.13

Solution : Given data : $t = 16$ mm, $d = 25$ mm, $W = 48$ kN $= 48 \times 10^3$ N

Procedure : We have, $\sigma_{ck} = \dfrac{W}{\pi \times d \times t \times n} = \dfrac{48 \times 10^3}{\pi \times 25 \times 16 \times 2} = \textbf{19.09 N/mm}^2$

Problem 1.11 : *Find the maximum diameter of hole that can be punched in a M.S. plate 10 mm thick having ultimate shear stress of 220 N/mm². The allowable crushing stress in punch material is 350 N/mm².*

Solution : Given data : $t = 10$ mm, $\tau_{ut} = 220$ N/mm², $\sigma_{ck} = 350$ N/mm².

Procedure : Assume factor of safety = 5.

Thus, the permissible shear stress $= \tau = \dfrac{\tau_{ut}}{\text{F.O.S.}} = \dfrac{220}{5} = 44$ N/mm²

We know that, $W = $ Area under shear $\times \tau$

$$= (\pi \times d \times t) \times \tau = (\pi \times d \times 10) \times 44$$

$$\therefore \qquad W = 1382.30 \; d \qquad \qquad \dots (1)$$

Also, $\qquad\qquad W = \text{Area under crushing} \times \sigma_{ck}$

$$= \left(\frac{\pi}{4} d^2\right) \times \sigma_{ck} = \frac{\pi}{4} d^2 \times 350$$

$$\therefore \qquad W = 274.88 \; d^2 \qquad \qquad \dots (2)$$

Equating equations (1) and (2), we have

$$1382.30 \; d = 274.88 \; d^2$$

$$\therefore \qquad \mathbf{d = 5.02 \; mm \cong 6 \; mm}$$

Numerical Type No. 5 : "Bearing Stress"

Problem 1.12 : *A journal 25 mm in diameter supported in sliding bearing has maximum end reaction of 2.5 kN. Assuming allowable pressure 5 N/mm². Find length of sliding bearing.*

Solution : Given data : $d = 25$ mm, $W = 2.5 \times 10^3$ N, $\sigma_{bearing} = 5$ N/mm²

Procedure : We have, bearing pressure or bearing stress as,

$$\sigma_{bearing} = \frac{W}{d \times l}$$

$$\therefore \qquad 5 = \frac{2.5 \times 10^3}{25 \times l}$$

$$\therefore \qquad l = \mathbf{20 \; mm}$$

1.8 PRINCIPAL STRESS

Question

1. Explain principal stress.   **(S-11)**

- When the component is subjected to several types of loads simultaneously, it is necessary to determine the state of stresses under such conditions. For example, a transmission shaft is subjected to bending moment as well as twisting moment (torque) at the same time.

- *"The plane, on which, only normal stresses acts, but no shear stress, is called as principal plane. The magnitude of normal stress acting on the principal plane is called principal stress".*

- Consider an element of a plate subjected to two dimensional stresses as shown in Fig. 1.14 (b).

- In this analysis, the stresses are classified into two groups : (a) Normal stress, (b) Shear stress. Normal stress is perpendicular to area under consideration, while shear stress acts over the area. Refer Fig. 1.14 (c), showing the stresses acting on oblique plane.

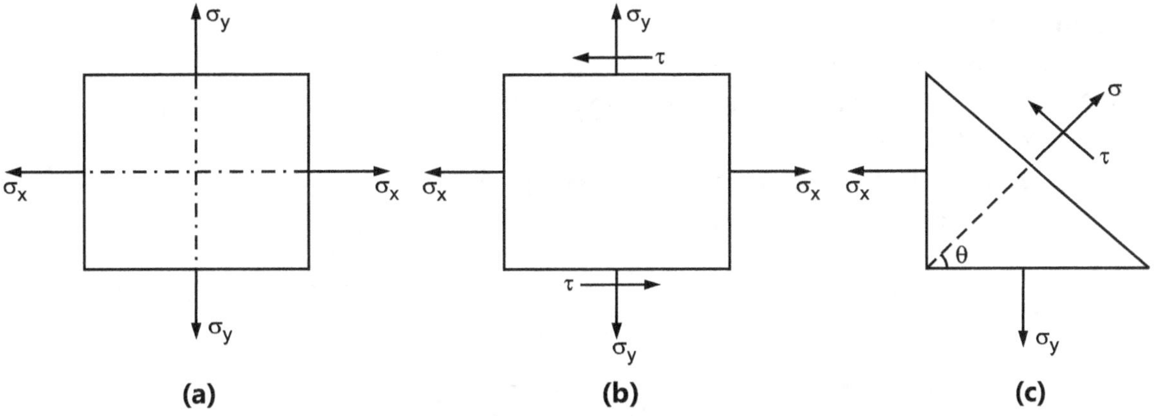

(a)   **(b)**   **(c)**

Fig. 1.14 : Principal stresses

- *"Major principal stress is the maximum value of normal stress acting on the principal plane, whereas, the minimum value of normal stress acting on principal plane is called as minor principal stress".*

Maximum principal stress,

$$\sigma_{t_1} = \frac{\sigma_x + \sigma_y}{2} + \frac{1}{2}\sqrt{(\sigma_x - \sigma_y)^2 + 4\tau^2}$$

Minimum principal stress,

$$\sigma_{t_2} = \frac{\sigma_x + \sigma_y}{2} - \frac{1}{2}\sqrt{(\sigma_x - \sigma_y)^2 + 4\tau^2}$$

The planes of maximum shear stress are at right angles to each other and are inclined at 45° to principal planes. The maximum shear stress is given by one half of the algebraic difference between the principal stresses.

$$\therefore \qquad \tau_{max} = \frac{\sigma_{t_1} - \sigma_{t_2}}{2} = \frac{1}{2}\left[\sqrt{(\sigma_x - \sigma_y)^2 + 4\tau^2}\right]$$

1.9 CREEP AND CREEP CURVE

Questions

1. Define creep.   (S-10; W-10)
2. What do you mean by creep ?   (W-12)

- *"When a component is subjected to constant stress at high temperature over a long period of time, it will undergo a slow and permanent deformation called as creep".*
- Thus, creep is defined as *'slow and progressive deformation of material with time under constant stress'.*
- Creep is a function of stress and temperature and becomes important for components operating at elevated temperature. For example : Bolts and pipes in thermal power plant.

Creep Curve :

- Fig. 1.15 shows an idealized creep curve.
- When load is applied at the beginning of creep test, instantaneous elastic deformation OA occurs.
- This elastic deformation is followed by creep curve 'ABCD'.
- Creep occurs in three stages.

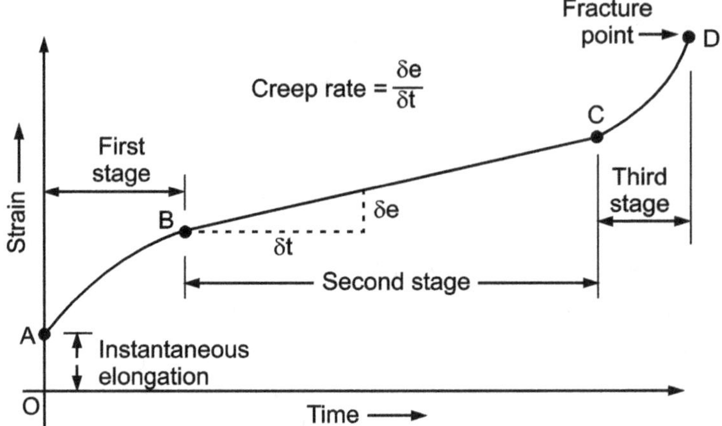

Fig. 1.15 : Creep curve

(a) First Stage :

- It is called as 'primary creep' shown by AB on the curve.
- During this, creep rate decreases i.e. slope of creep curve increases from A to B progressively with time. Hence, the metal strain hardens to support the external load.

(b) Second Stage :

- It is called as 'secondary creep' shown by BC on the curve.
- Here, the creep rate is almost constant. This stage occupies a major portion of the life of component.

(c) Third Stage :

- It is called as 'tertiary creep' shown by CD on the creep curve.
- During this, creep rate is accelerated due to necking and finally results into fracture at point D.

1.10 FATIGUE

Questions

1.	Define fatigue strength.	(S-10)
2.	What do you mean by fatigue failure.	(W-12)
3.	Define fatigue. Give one example of fatigue failure in machine component.	(S-13)

- When a material is subjected to repeated stresses, it fails at stresses below yield point stresses. Such a type of failure is called as *fatigue failure*.
- This failure is caused by means of progressive crack formations, which are, actually fine and of microscopic size. The failure may occur even without any prior indication.

- The fatigue failure begins with a crack at some point in the component.
- The crack is more likely to occur in the following regions :
    (i)   Regions of discontinuity, such as, oil holes or keyways.
    (ii) Regions of abrupt change in cross-section, such as, shoulder or steps.
    (iii) Regions of irregularities in machining operations, such as, machining scratches, stamp mark or inspection marks.
    (iv) Internal cracks in materials like blow holes.
- These regions are subjected to stress concentration due to presence of crack. The crack propogates with increasing number of stress cycles.
- A component with a crack, which is subjected to alternate tensile and compressive stresses is shown in Fig. 1.16.
- During first half of the cycle, there is tensile stress and the crack opens. During the second half of the cycle, there is compressive stress and crack closes.
- This opening and closing of the crack during each cycle continues and results in crack propogation.
- Finally the cross-section of the component is so reduced that, the remaining portion is no longer in a position to sustain the external force and it is subjected to sudden fracture.

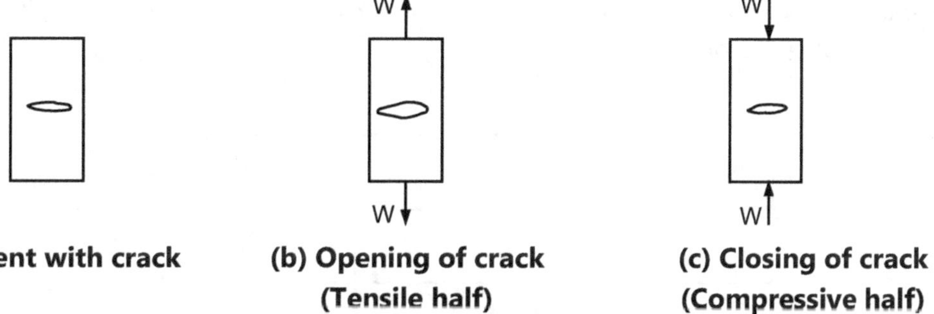

(a) Component with crack   **(b) Opening of crack**   **(c) Closing of crack**
(Tensile half)   **(Compressive half)**

Fig. 1.16 : Crack propogation

- The fatigue failure depends upon number of factors, such as number of cycles, mean stress, stress amplitude, stress concentration, residual stresses, corrosion and creep.

1.11 NOTCH SENSITIVITY

Question

1. Define notch sensitivity.   (S-13)

- **Notch sensitivity** is defined as, *'the degree to which, theoretical expected effect of stress concentration is reached'*.
- It is given by,

$$\text{Notch sensitivity} = \frac{\text{Increase of actual stress over nominal stress}}{\text{Increase of theoretical stress over nominal stess}}$$

1.12 ENDURANCE LIMIT

Questions

1. Sketch S-N curve and explain the term 'endurance limit'. **(W-09)**
2. Define endurance limit. **(S-10, 11; W-10)**
3. Draw S-N curve. **(S-11)**
4. Explain the term, endurance limit with S-N curve. **(S-14)**

- Consider a standard mirror polished specimen rotating in a fatigue-testing machine and loaded in bending as shown in Fig. 1.17 (a).
- As the specimen rotates, the bending stresses at the upper fibers vary from maximum compression to maximum tensile, whereas, the bending stresses at the bottom fibers vary from maximum tensile to maximum compressive.
- In other words, the specimen is subjected to completely reversed stresses. This is represented by time-stress diagram shown in Fig. 1.17 (b).
- A record is kept of number of cycles required to produce a failure at given stress and results are plotted in stress-cycle graph. Refer Fig. 1.17 (c).
- A little consideration will show that, if the design stress is kept lower than a certain value as shown by dotted line, the material will not fail, whatever may be the number of cycles. This stress, (shown by dotted line) is known as **endurance or fatigue limit.**
- **Endurance or fatigue limit is defined as** *'maximum value of completely reversed bending stress, which a standard specimen can withstand without failure, for infinite number of cycles of loads'.*

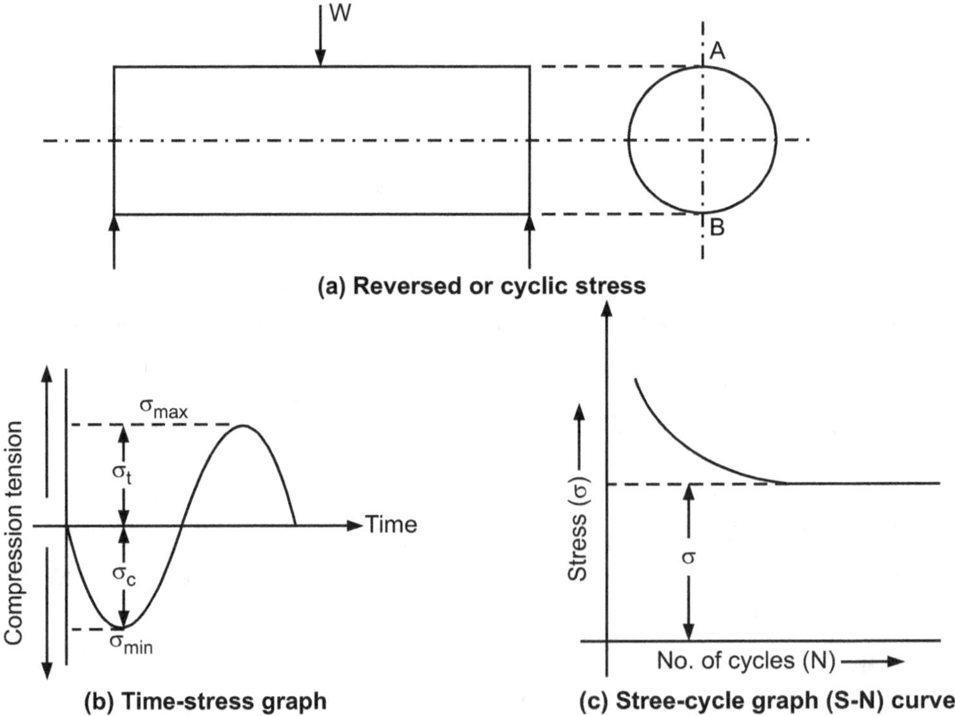

(a) Reversed or cyclic stress

(b) Time-stress graph

(c) Stree-cycle graph (S-N) curve

Fig. 1.17 : Endurance limit

1.13 DESIGN STRESS

While designing machine parts, it is desirable to keep the stress lower than the maximum stress, at which, failure takes place. This stress is known as *working stress* or *design stress*.

$$\text{Mathematically, Design stress} = \frac{\text{Maximum stress}}{\text{Factor of safety}}$$

1.14 FACTOR OF SAFETY

Question

1. Define factor of safety for ductile and brittle materials.   **(W-09, 12)**

- There are a number of parameters, which are difficult to evaluate accurately in design analysis, such as,

    (a) Uncertainty in magnitude of external forces acting on the component.

    (b) Variations in the properties of material like yield strength or ultimate strength.

    (c) Variations in the dimensions of the component due to imperfect workmanship.

- In order to ensure the safety against such circumstances, factor of safety is used.

- Factor of safety is defined as '*the ratio of maximum stress to the working stress*'.

$$\text{Mathematically, Factor of safety (F.O.S.)} = \frac{\text{Maximum stress}}{\text{Working or design stress}}$$

- In case of ductile materials, e.g. mild steel, where yield point is clearly defined, the factor of safety is based on yield point stress.

$$\text{Factor of safety} = \frac{\text{Yield point stress}}{\text{Working or design stress}} = \frac{\sigma_{yt}}{\sigma_t}$$

- In case of brittle materials, e.g. cast iron, where the yield point is not well defined, factor of safety is based on ultimate stress.

$$\text{Factor of safety} = \frac{\text{Ultimate stress}}{\text{Working or design stress}} = \frac{\sigma_{ut}}{\sigma_t}$$

1.14.1 Factors to be Considered While Selecting Factor of Safety

Question

1. What is factor of safety ? State factors governing selection of factor of safety.

     (W-12, 13; S-13)

1. Reliability of properties of material and change in these properties during service.
2. Reliability of applied load.
3. The certainty as to exact mode of failure.
4. Extent of stress concentration.
5. The extent of initial stresses set up during manufacture.
6. The extent of loss of life, if failure occurs.
7. The extent of simplifying assumptions.
8. The reliability of test results to actual machine parts.

1.14.2 In What Cases, the Value of Factor of Safety is Taken High ?

1. Analysis of loads with respect to magnitude and nature is difficult to estimate.

2. Impact loads and accidental loads.

3. Non-uniformity in material.

4. Corrosion and high temperature.

5. Reliability of parts.

6. In case of possibilities of accidents and damage to property and life due to design failure.

1.14.3 In What Cases, the Value of Factor of Safety may be Taken Low ?

1. No damage to property and life in case of design failure.

2. Less frequently used parts.

3. Analysis of loads with respect to magnitude and nature is easy to estimate.

4. Past knowledge of working conditions and strength of similar parts is known.

5. In case of failure, little time and low money is needed for rectification.

1.14.4 Why the Factor of Safety is High in Design Subjected to Uncertain Environments ?

- There may be different environmental conditions at the time of use than those assumed at design stage.

- For example, the machine component may be subjected to high temperature situations or corrosive atmosphere.

- Therefore, the factor of safety chosen for certain machine component should be increased considering the environmental conditions, otherwise, it will reduce the strength of component.

- This factor depends on type of loading.

Table 1.1

Type of load	Factor of safety
Static load	1.5 to 3
Variable load	3 to 6
Impact/shock load	6 to 12

1.15 STRESS CONCENTRATION AND ITS CAUSES

Questions

1. What is stress concentration ? Illustrate any four methods to reduce it with neat sketches. **(S-09, 10, 12, 13; W-10, 12)**
2. What is stress concentration ? State its causes. **(W-09)**
3. Define stress concentration. List any four methods to reduce it with neat sketches. **(S-14)**

- Whenever the machine component changes the shape of its cross-section, the simple stress distribution no longer holds good. This irregularity in the stress distribution caused by abrupt changes of form is called as *stress concentration.*

- It may occur due to,

   a) Change in cross-section such as stepped axle, key-ways, grooves, threaded holes.

   b) Concentrated loads applied at minimum areas of machine parts, such as contact between gear teeth, a beam and its supports.

   c) Variation in mechanical properties of materials from point to point due to cavities, cracks or air pockets.

   d) Surface irregularities or poor surface finish.

- It occurs for all kinds of stresses in presence of fillets, notches, holes, keyways etc.

- Consider a member with different cross-section under tensile load as shown in Fig. 1.18. A little consideration will show that, the nominal stress is uniform in the right and left-hand sides, but in the region, where cross-section is changing, a redistribution of forces must take place.

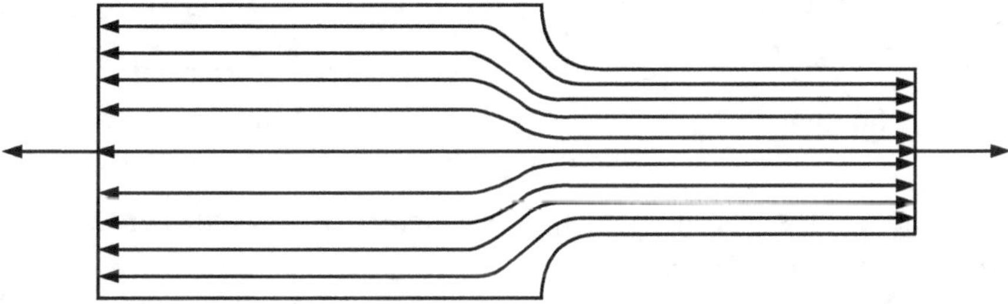

Fig. 1.18 : Stress concentration

1.16 METHODS OF REDUCING STRESS CONCENTRATION

(W-10; S-09, 10, 12, 14)

- The presence of stress concentration cannot be totally eliminated, but it can be reduced.

- To reduce stress concentration, various methods are adopted such as,

   (a) By fillets, undercutting and notches.

   (b) Additional notches and holes.

   (c) Reducing stress concentration in case of threaded members.

- Fig. 1.19 (a) shows that stress lines tend to bunch up and cut very close to the edges or sharp corner. For improvement, fillets may be provided as shown in Fig. 1.19 (b) and (c).

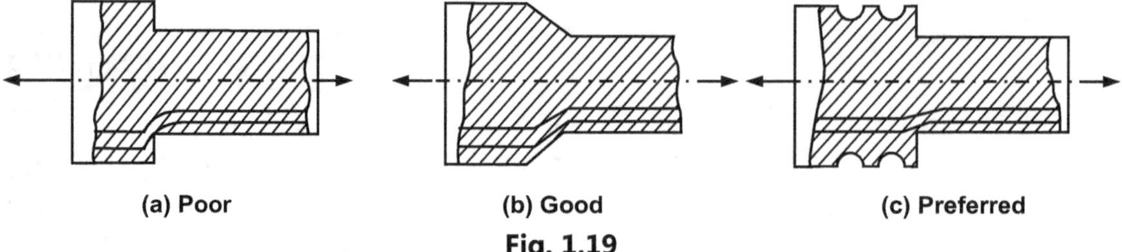

     (a) Poor   **(b) Good**   **(c) Preferred**

Fig. 1.19

- Fig. 1.19 (d), (e) and (f) show methods of **reducing stress concentration in case of cylindrical members with shoulders.**

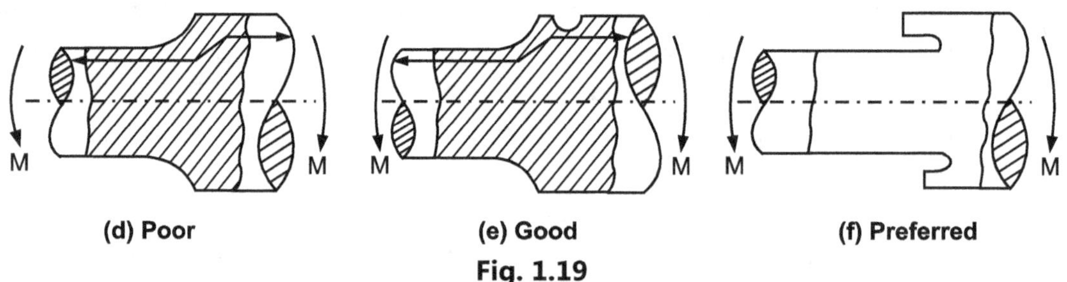

     (d) Poor   **(e) Good**   **(f) Preferred**

Fig. 1.19

- Fig. 1.19 (g) and (h) show methods of **reducing stress concentration in case of cylindrical members with holes.**

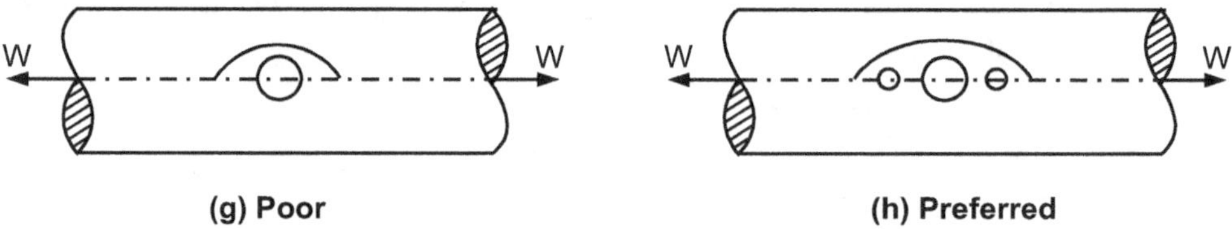

     (g) Poor   **(h) Preferred**

Fig. 1.19

- Fig. 1.19 (j) and (k) show methods of **reducing stress concentration in case of cylindrical members with threads.**

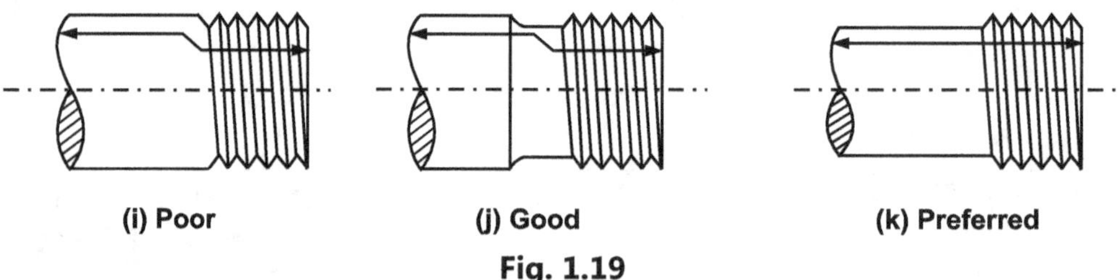

     (i) Poor   **(j) Good**   **(k) Preferred**

Fig. 1.19

1.16.1 Theoretical Stress Concentration Factor

- Theoretical stress concentration factor is defined as *'the ratio of maximum stress in member (i.e., stress at a notch or fillet) to the nominal stress at the same section based upon net area'.*

- It is given by,

$$\text{Stress concentration factor, } K_t = \frac{\text{Maximum or Ultimate sterss}}{\text{Nominal stress}}$$

- It is used in case of components made up of brittle materials subjected to static loading.

- Its value may vary due to,

  a) Type of loading i.e. dead load or live load.

  b) Type of forces such as tensile, compressive or torque or combined loading.

  c) Material used.

1.16.2 Fatigue Stress Concentration Factor

- The stress concentration factors may vary according to type of material, type of loads (tensile, compressive, bending, combined of them), nature of loading (steady or cyclic).

- When a material is subjected to cyclic or fatigue loading, the value of fatigue stress concentration factor is applied instead of theoretical stress concentration factor.

- This is due to the reason that, in fatigue loading, the effect of stress concentration is usually less than that predicted by theoretical stress concentration factor.

- The value of fatigue stress concentration factor (K_f) is less than the theoretical stress concentration factor (K_t).

- Fatigue stress concentration factor is defined as *"the ratio of endurance limit without stress concentration to the nominal stress"*.

- Mathematically,

$$\text{Fatigue stress concentration factor, } K_f = \frac{\text{Endurance limit without sterss concentration}}{\text{Nominal stress}}$$

- It is used in case of components made up of ductile materials subjected to fluctuating loads, where endurance strength is greatly reduced.

1.17 CONVERTING ACTUAL LOAD OR TORQUE INTO DESIGN LOAD OR TORQUE USING DESIGN FACTORS LIKE VELOCITY FACTOR, FACTOR OF SAFETY AND SERVICE FACTOR

- The design factor is not the factor of safety. It is used to take into account unknown contingencies and emergencies.

- It is a factor, which the designer uses to allow for unreliable material, the probable effects of unknown or accidental overloads, temperature effect, and stresses encountered during machining, assembly, transportation, intentional overloading, and the chances of failure leading to injury, loss of life, costly shutdowns and expensive repairs.

- It is also known as real margin of safety.

The various design factors are,

1. Velocity factor :

- This factor is considered in design of gears. It depends on velocity of operating gears. It is represented by 'C_v'.

- Permissible working stress is obtained as follows :

$$\sigma_{wp} = \sigma_p \times C_v$$

Here,

σ_{wp} = Permissible working stress

σ_p = Permissible stress

C_v = Velocity factor

2. Factor of safety :

- It is already discussed in article 1.14.

3. Service factor :

- Whenever power is transmitted from a prime mover to a machine through one or more intermediate mechanical elements like: shaft, coupling, clutch, gears, chain, or belt etc., sometimes there is momentary shock on these elements either due to a prime mover or a machine to be driven. This leads to a momentary high load (or torque) acting on these elements. This momentary load (or torque) is higher than the average load acting on these elements.

- Consider an example of electric motor driving the hoisting drum through a reduction gear box.

- At the beginning of operation, the torque required is much higher than the average torque required. In a design process, the torque (or load) calculated from the power is an average torque (or load), whereas for a shorter duration, the mechanical elements are subjected to high momentary torque or load. This high momentary load is accounted in design process by a factor known as *service factor* or *application factor* or *overload factor*.

- Thus, the service factor or application factor is defined as, *"the ratio of maximum load (or maximum torque) to the average load (or average torque)"*.

- If service factor is given in the problem, then find maximum torque as follows :

$$T_{max} = \text{Service factor} \times T_{average}$$

- All the above factors are considered for protecting machine parts in overloading condition and to increase their useful life.

1.18 PROPERTIES OF ENGINEERING MATERIAL

Question

1. Define brittleness and malleability. **(W-10)**

Mechanical Property :

It is concerned with the ability of a material to resist various types of loads. The mechanical properties are,

(a) Strength :

- Strength is defined as *"the ability of the material to resist, without rupture, under the action of external force causing various types of stresses"*.

- Strength is measured by different quantities. Depending upon the type of stresses induced by external loads, strength is expressed as tensile strength, compressive strength or shear strength.

- Tensile strength is the ability of the material to resist external load causing tensile stress, without failure.

- Compressive strength is the ability of the material to resist external load causing compressive stress, without failure.

(b) Stiffness :

- Stiffness can be defined as *"the property of material to resist deformation under stress"*. All materials deform to more or less extent, under stress.

- For a given stress within elastic limit, the material that deforms **least** is said to be **stiffest**.

(c) Elasticity :

- *"When the body regains its original shape on removal of external load, then the body is said to be elastic"*.

- All engineering materials are elastic, but degree of elasticity varies. Steel is perfectly elastic within elastic limit.

(d) Plasticity :

- *"When the body is permanently deformed under load and do not regain its original shape, when external load is removed, the material is said to possess plasticity"*.

(e) Ductility :   (S-08)

- *"The property of a material, which enables it to be drawn into wire under the action of tensile load, is called as ductility"*.

- Ductility is also defined as *"the ability of the material to deform to a greater extent before the sign of crack, when it is subjected to tensile force"*.

- Example : Mild steel, copper, aluminium.

- Ductility is a desirable property in machine components, which are subjected to unexpected overloads or impact loads.

(f) Brittleness :   (W-10)

- Brittleness is defined as, *"the property of material of breaking down under the action of load"*. It is opposite to that of ductility.

- A brittle material is that, which undergoes little plastic deformation prior to fracture in tension test. Cast iron is an example of brittle material.

- In ductile materials, failure takes place by *yielding*. Brittle components fail by *sudden fracture*.

(g) Malleability : **(W-10)**

- *"The property of a material, which enables it to be rolled into thin sheets, is called as malleability"*.
- It may be considered as a special case of ductility.
- Malleability is also defined as *"the ability of the material to deform to a greater extent before the sign of crack, when it is subjected to compressive force"*.
- The term malleability comes from a word meaning 'hammer' and in a narrow sense, it means the ability to be hammered out into thin sections.
- Example : Low carbon steels, copper, aluminium.

(h) Toughness :

- *"The property, which resists the fracture under the action of impact loading, is called as toughness"*. It is inversely proportional to heat.
- In other words, toughness is energy for failure by fracture. This property is essential for machine components, which are required to withstand impact loads.
- Tough materials have ability to bend, twist or stretch before failure takes place.
- All structural steels are tough materials.

(i) Hardness : **(S-08)**

- Hardness is defined as *'the ability of a metal to cut another metal'*. It is usually expressed in numbers. i.e. Brinell Hardness Number (BHN) and Rockwell Hardness Number (R_a).
- The following tests give hardness of a metal.
  1. Brinell hardness test.
  2. Rockwell hardness test.
- It usually indicates resistance to abrasion, scratching, cutting or shaping.
- Hardness is an important property in selection of material for mating parts, which rub on one another such as pinion and gear, cam and follower, rail and wheel and parts of ball bearing. Wear resistance of these parts is improved by increasing surface hardness by case hardening.

1.18.1 Difference between Malleability and Ductility

Malleability	Ductility
1. It is the ability to deform under compressive load.	1. It is the ability to deform under tensile load.
2. All malleable materials cannot be ductile.	2. All ductile materials are malleable.
3. It is desirable, when component is forged, rolled or extruded.	3. It is desirable, when component is formed or drawn.
4. It increases with increase in temperature.	4. It decreases with increase in temperature.

1.18.2 Difference between Ductility and Brittleness

Ductility	Brittleness
1. Ductile material deform to a greater extent before fracture in tension test.	1. Brittle materials show negligible plastic deformation prior to fracture.
2. Here, failure takes place by yielding.	2. Here, failure takes place by sudden fracture.
3. Energy absorbed by ductile specimen before fracture in a tension test is more.	3. Energy absorbed is negligible.
4. Examples : Steel, copper, aluminium.	4. Examples : Cast iron.

1.19 RESILIENCE, PROOF RESILIENCE AND MODULUS OF RESILIENCE

Question

1. Define resilience.   **(S-10)**

1.19.1 Resilience

- Resilience is defined as *'the property of a material to absorb strain energy while resisting shock or impact loads'*. This strain energy will be given up, when the load is removed.

- A resilient material absorbs energy within elastic range without any permanent deformation. This is desirable in case of spring materials.

1.19.2 Modulus of Resilience

- Resilience is measured by modulus of resilience.

- It is defined as *'the maximum strain energy stored in a member per unit volume, when loaded within elastic limit'*.

- It is required to stress the specimen in tension test upto elastic limit point.

1.19.3 Proof Resilience

- *'The maximum strain energy, which can be stored without being permanently strained'* is called as Proof Resilience.

- In other words, it is the maximum strain energy that can be stored in the body upto elastic limit.

1.19.4 Difference between Resilience and Toughness

Resilience	Toughness
1. It is the property of a material to absorb energy upto elastic limit.	1. It is the property of a material to absorb energy, when loaded till its fracture.
2. It is the ability of material to absorb energy within elastic range.	2. It is the ability of material to absorb energy within elastic and plastic range.
3. It is essential in spring applications.	3. It is required for components subjected to bending, twisting, stretching or impact loading.

1.20 FACTORS TO BE CONSIDERED FOR SELECTION OF MATERIAL IN DESIGNING MACHINE ELEMENT

Question

1. State any four factors that govern the selection of material while designing a machine components. **(W-11, 13)**

Following considerations are to be made, while selecting the material :

1. **Availability :** Material should be easily available in the market.
2. **Cost :** The material should be available at cheaper rates.
3. **Physical properties :** Like colour, density, thermal conductivity, melting point, magnetic properties and specific heat.
4. **Mechanical properties :** Such as strength, ductility, malleability, toughness and hardness.
5. **Manufacturing ease :** From the manufacturing point of view, castability, weldability, machinability, forgeability, surface properties are considered.
6. **Corrosion resistance :** Material should be corrosion resistant.
7. The properties of material should not change or deteriorate with time.
8. Suitability of material for working conditions in services.

1.20.1 The Materials Possessing Specific Mechanical Property

Table 1.2

Mechanical property	Material
Elasticity	Steel, Rubber
Ductility	Mild steel, Aluminium, Copper, Tin
Brittleness	Cast iron
Malleability	Lead, Soft steel, Aluminium

1.20.2 List of Machine Parts with Suggested Material

Questions

1. Recommend suitable materials for following components.
   - (i) Connecting rod.
   - (ii) Machine tool spindle.
   - (iii) Hydraulic cylinder.
   - (iv) Heavy duty gear. **(S-11)**
2. Suggest suitable material for the following machine parts :
   - (i) Crank shaft.
   - (ii) Helical spring.
   - (iii) Bushes for knuckle pin.
   - (iv) Lathe bed. **(W-11)**

Table 1.3

Machine parts	Suitable material
1. Crank shaft	Alloy steel like 35Mn2Mo28
2. Helical spring	Oil tempered carbon steel/ chromium vanadium alloy steel
3. Bushes for knuckle pin	Phosphor bronze, Grey C.I.
4. Lathe bed	Grey cast iron like FG150
5. Spring for I.C. engine valve	Carbon steel
6. Screw of screw jack	Carbon steel, low alloy steel
7. Nut of screw jack	Phosphor bronze
8. Bearing bushes	Bronze (Alloy steel)
9. Shaft	Mild steel
10. Body or casing of centrifugal pump	Cast iron
11. Balls for ball bearing	Chrome steel
12. Hydraulic cylinder	Plain carbon steel, steel casting or aluminium alloys.
13. Machine tool spindle	High quality steel.
14. Heavy duty gear	Ferrous metal.
15. Connecting rod	Drop forged heat treated steel.
16. Turbine blade	Chromium steel like 7Cr13
17. Clutch spring	Plain carbon steel with magnese like 60C4
18. Locomotive carriage or Wagon wheels	Fe 290 or FeE230, plain carbon steel
19. Closed coiled helical spring	Low alloy steel

1.21 DESIGNATION OF DIFFERENT MATERIALS

Questions

1. State the following material specifications.

 (i) FeE230, (ii) FG200, (iii) 35C8, (iv) X20Cr18Ni2. **(S-12)**

2. Explain the following material specification.

 (i) FG3000, (ii) X20Cr 18Ni2. **(S-14)**

1) Ferrous metals :

Magnetite	Fe_2O_3
Hematite	Fe_3O_4
Limonite	$FeCO_3$
Siderite	$Fe_2O_3\,(H_2O)$

2) Cast iron :

a) Grey cast iron :

FG200	Grey C.I. with tensile strength 200 MPa (N/mm^2). **(S-09, 12)**
FG300	Grey C.I. with tensile strength 300 MPa (N/mm^2). **(S-14)**
Examples	FG220, FG260, FG300, FG350, FG400.

b) Malleable cast iron :

WM400	White malleable cast iron with minimum tensile strength 350 N/mm^2 or 400 N/mm^2.
BM300	Black malleable C.I. with 300 N/mm^2 tensile strength.
BM320	Black malleable C.I. with 320 N/mm^2 tensile strength.
BM350	Black malleable C.I. with 350 N/mm^2 tensile strength.
PM450	Pearlitic malleable C.I. with 450 N/mm^2 tensile strength.

c) Nodular or spheroidal C.I. :

SG450/10	Spheroidal graphite cast iron with minimum tensile strength **450 N/mm^2** followed by **10% elongation**. **(W-09)**
Examples	SG800/2, SG400/15, SG350/18.

3) Steels designated on the basis of mechanical properties :

Fe290	Steel with minimum **tensile** strength of 290 N/mm^2.
FeE230	Steel with minimum **yield** strength of 230 N/mm^2. **(S-09, 12)**
Examples	Fe310, Fe330, Fe360, Fe410, Fe490, Fe540, Fe620, Fe690, FeE230, FeE250, FeE270, FeE310, FeE370, FeE400 etc.

4) Steel designated on the basis of chemical composition :

35C8	Steel with 0.35% carbon and 0.8% manganese **(S-09)**
60C4	Steel with 0.6% carbon and 0.4% manganese. **(W-09)**
Examples	30C8, 45C8, 50C4, 70C6, 75C6.

5) Free cutting steels :

10C8S10	Steel with 0.1% carbon, 0.8% manganese and 0.1% sulphur
Examples	14C14S14, 28C12S14, 40C10S18, 11C10S25, 40C15S12

- Instead of sulphur, P_b i.e. lead can be used.

6) Alloy steel :

They are designated as –

- Figure indicating 100 times average % of carbon.
- Chemical symbol for alloying elements followed by figure for its average percentage content multiplied by a factor as given below.

Element	Multiplying Factor
Cr, Co, Ni, Si, W, Mn	4
Al, Be, V, P_b, Cu, Ti, Zn and Mo	10
P, S and N	100

For example :

40Cr4Mo2	Alloy steel having 0.4% carbon, 1% chromium and 0.2% molybdenum.
20Mn2	Alloy steel having 0.20% carbon and 0.5% manganese.
40Ni2Cr1Mo28	Alloy steel having 0.4% carbon, 0.5% nickel, 0.25% chromium and 2.8% molybdenum.

7) High alloy steel :

They are designated as –

a) Letter X.

b) Figure indicating 100 times the percentage of carbon content.

c) Chemical symbol for alloying elements followed by a figure for its average % content rounded off to nearest integer.

d) Chemical symbol to indicate specially added element to provide desired properties.

Note :

   If it is not designated by X, then see chromium %. If it is written Cr13, Cr14 (i.e. more than 9), then it is a type of high alloy steel (stainless steel or heat resisting steel).

For example :

20Cr18Ni2	Alloy steel having carbon 0.20%, chromium 18%, and nickel 2%. **(S-09)**
15Cr16Ni2	Alloy steel having average carbon 0.15%, chromium 16%, nickel 2%.
45Cr9Si4	Alloy steel having carbon 0. 45%, chromium 9% and silicon 4%.
X20Cr18Ni2	High alloy steel having carbon 0.20%, chromium 18%, Nickel 2%. **(S-12, 14)**

8) High speed tool steel :

They are designated as,

1) Letter XT.
2) Figure indicating 100 times the average per cent of carbon.
3) Chemical symbol indicating alloying elements in their average %.
4) Chemical symbol to indicate specially added element to attain desired properties.

	C%	Si%	Cr%	W%	V%	Co%	Mo%	Mn%
XT72W18Cr4V1	0.72	---	4	18	1	---	---	---
XT72W18CoCr4V1	0.72	---	4	18	1	4	---	---
XT125W10Co10CrMo4	1.25	---	4	10	---	10	4	---
XT90W6CoMo5Cr4V2	0.90		4	6	2	5	5	---

1.22 ALLOY STEEL

Alloy steel is defined as *'steel to which certain alloying elements other than carbon are added to improve the mechanical properties'*. The alloying elements are **nickel, molybdenum, chromium, vanadium, manganese, silicon, tungsten** etc.

Examples :

a) Invar :

It is nickel alloy steel containing 36% nickel, which has negligible coefficient of expansion. It is largely used in measuring devices.

b) Nickel Chrome Steel :

It is used to combine hardness with high strength. It improves anti-corrosive property. It is used for motor crankshafts, axles and gears.

1.23 FREE CUTTING STEEL (W-08)

- They contain more sulphur and phosphorous than any other carbon steel. Due to presence of the two, the long chips in machining can be easily broken. This prevents clogging of machines and improves machining rate.

1.24 HIGH SPEED TOOL STEEL

- They are used for cutting the metals at much higher rate than any other tools.
- During the rapid cutting, considerable heat is generated and ordinary tools may loose hardness. But in high speed tool steels, tungsten is added as chief alloying element, which retains the hardness at high temperature.

1.25 ROLE AND ADVANTAGES OF STANDARDIZATION

Question

1. Explain the term 'standardization' with its advantages (any four). (W-11)

- Standardization is defined as *'the process of establishing standards so as to minimize the varieties in the characteristics'*.
- Standard is a set of specifications, defined by a certain body or an organization, to which various characteristics of a component, a system, or a product should conform. The characteristics include materials, quality, dimensions, shapes, tolerances, surface finish, materials, method of testing, method of use, method of packing and storing etc.

- The purpose of standardization is to establish the norms intended to achieve uniformity, specified quality, interchangeability, safety, and to put reasonable limit on the variety.
- In India, BIS is responsible for evolving all types of technical standards.

Standards used in design are,

1. Standards for material, their mechanical properties and chemical composition.
2. Standards for dimensions of commonly used machine elements.
3. Standards for fits, tolerances and surface finish of machine elements.
4. Standards for engineering drawing of components.

Categories of Standards:

Based on the defining body or organization, the standards can be divided into three categories:

1) Company Standards :

- These standards are defined or set by a company or a group of companies for their use.

2) National Standards :

- These standards are defined or set by a national apex body and are normally followed throughout the country.
- The examples are standards prepared by :
    - Bureau of Indian Standards (BIS)
    - American Society of Mechanical Engineers (ASME)
    - American Gear Manufacturers Association (AGMA)
    - American Welding Society (AWS)
    - American National Standards Institute (ANSI).

3) International Standards:

- These standards are defined and set by an international apex body and normally followed all over the world.
- The examples are standards prepared by :
    - International Standards Organization (ISO)
    - International Bureau of Weights and Measures (IBWM).

Benefits of Standardization :

1. It helps in manufacturing the components quickly and economically.
2. It saves effort of design engineer to design and manufacture new machines, as standard components are readily designed by experts.
3. It helps in manufacturing the components on mass production.
4. Interchangeability of components is possible.
5. It ensures certain minimum specified quality.
6. Effective utilization of resources.
7. Easy and quick replacement of the components is possible.
8. It also contributes to ensure the safety.

1.26 IMPORTANCE OF DESIGN DATA BOOK FOR A DESIGNER

- When a designer wants to design and develop a product, he requires lot of information such as material specifications, physical and mechanical properties of materials, standards, different manufacturing processes, process specifications, empirical relations, tool data, details of standard machines such as motors, bearings etc.

- The standard dimensions of nuts, bolts, shafts, bearings are available in the design data book.

- Use of design data book makes easy for the designer to collect the above data.

- Also it saves the time of designer. So that design procedure becomes easy and quick.

1.27 PREFERRED NUMBERS SERIES

- Preferred numbers are an important tool, which minimize unnecessary variations in sizes.

- They help the designer in avoiding selection of sizes, in an arbitary manner.

- The complete range is covered by minimum number of sizes, which is advantageous to both producer and consumer.

- With the acceptance of standardization, there is need to keep the standard sizes or dimensions of any component or product in discrete steps.

- The sizes should be spread over wide range, and at the same time, they should be spaced properly. For example, diameters are to be standardized between 10 mm and 25 mm, then sizes should be 10 mm, 12.5 mm, 16 mm, 20 mm and 25 mm. This led to use of geometric series known as **preferred series**.

- It includes S5, S10, S20, S40 and S80 series.

- Each series has a series factor.

- The series factors are as shown in following table.

Table 1.4

Series	Multiplying Series Factor
S5	$\sqrt[5]{10} = 1.58$
S10	$\sqrt[10]{10} = 1.26$
S20	$\sqrt[20]{10} = 1.12$
S40	$\sqrt[40]{10} = 1.06$
S80	$\sqrt[80]{10} = 1.03$

- For establishing a series, first a number is taken. By multiplying this number by a series factor, second number is obtained. By multiplying second number by a series factor, third number is obtained and procedure is continued.

1.28 THEORIES OF ELASTIC FAILURES

Questions

1. State various theories of elastic failure. Explain maximum shear stress theory. **(S-09)**
2. Name different theories of failure and state its significance. **(W-09)**
3. State various theories of elastic failure. Explain maximum principal stress theory. **(W-10, 11)**
4. State the various theories of elastic failure. Explain maximum distortion energy theory. **(S-12)**
5. Name theories of elastic failure for combined stresses. **(W-12; S-13)**
6. Name the different theories of elastic failure and explain any one. **(S-14)**

- Theories of elastic failure provide a relationship between the strength of machine component subjected to complex state of stresses with the mechanical properties obtained in a tension test.

- Mechanical properties include yield strength, ultimate strength and percentage elongation.

- With the help of these theories, the data obtained in tension test can be used to determine the dimensions of the component, irrespective of nature of stresses, induced in component due to several types of loads simultaneously.

- The various theories of elastic failure are as follows.
    - (1) Maximum principal or Normal stress theory.
    - (2) Maximum shear stress theory.
    - (3) Maximum distortion energy theory.

(1) Maximum Principal or Normal Stress Theory or Rankine's Theory :

- According to this theory, *"the failure of machine part occurs, when maximum principal stress in a biaxial stress system reaches limiting stress of the material in a simple tension test. Therefore, factor of safety is taken into consideration".*

- According to this theory, we have Maximum principal stress as,

$$\sigma_{t\,max} = \frac{\sigma_{yt}}{F.O.S.} \qquad \text{(For ductile material)}$$

where, σ_{yt} = Yield point tensile stress

     F.O.S. = Factor of safety

Also, $\sigma_{t\,max} = \dfrac{\sigma_{ut}}{F.O.S.} \qquad \text{(For brittle material)}$

where, σ_{ut} = Ultimate tensile stress

- For ductile material, limiting stress is yield point tensile stress. For brittle material, limiting stress is ultimate stress.

- This theory is preferred for brittle material, as it considers possibility of failures only either in tension or compression. It ignores the possibility of failure due to shearing.

(2) Maximum Shear Stress Theory or Guest's Theory :   **(W-08)**

- According to this theory, *"the failure of a machine part occurs, when the maximum shear stress in a biaxial stress system reaches to a value equal to shear stress at yield point in a simple tension test".*

- According to this theory, considering factor of safety, we have,

$$\tau_{max} = \frac{\tau_y}{F.O.S.} \qquad \ldots (1.1)$$

where, τ_{max} = Maximum shear stress

      τ_y = Yield point shear stress

But, *shear stress at yield point is equal to half of yield point stress in tension.*

$$\therefore \quad \tau_y = \frac{1}{2}\sigma_{yt}$$

where, σ_{yt} = Yield point stress in tension

Therefore equation (1.1) becomes,

$$\therefore \quad \tau_{max} = \frac{\frac{1}{2}\sigma_{yt}}{F.O.S.} = 0.5 \times \frac{\sigma_{yt}}{F.O.S.}$$

$$\therefore \quad \tau_{max} = 0.5 \times \sigma_{t\,max} \qquad \left(\because \sigma_{t\,max} = \frac{\sigma_{yt}}{F.O.S.}\right)$$

This theory is preferred for ductile materials.

(3) Maximum Distortion Energy Theory :   **(S-12)**

- According to this theory, *"the failure of a machine part or member occurs, when the distortion strain energy or shear strain energy per unit volume in a biaxial stress system reaches distortion energy at yield point per unit volume as obtained from a simple tension test".*

- According to this theory, considering the factor of safety into account, we have

$$\sigma_{t\,max}^2 + \sigma_{t\,min}^2 - 2\cdot\sigma_{t\,max}\cdot\sigma_{t\,min} = \left(\frac{\sigma_{yt}}{F.O.S.}\right)^2$$

where, $\sigma_{t\,max}$ = Maximum principal stress

      $\sigma_{t\,min}$ = Minimum principal stress

      σ_{yt} = Yield point tensile stress

- This theory is mostly used for ductile material only.

1.29 DESIGN FOR SAFETY

- In olden days, the engineers gave first consideration to the functional and economic aspects of the new devices.

- After all, unless the devices made are functionally useful, they are of no further engineering interest.

- Furthermore, if a new device cannot be produced for a cost that is affordable by society, it is a waste of engineering time to pursue it further.

- The increasing engineering effort is now being devoted to broader considerations relating to the influence of engineered products on people and on the environment. Thus, safety is now the important aspect in machine design.

Steps Involved in Safety Considerations:

1) **To develop engineering competence in the safety area:**
    - It is done by cultivating an awareness of its importance.
    - Product safety is of great concern to various legislators, judges, insurance executives, and so on.
    - But none of these individuals can contribute directly to the safety of a product: they can only underscore the urgency of giving appropriate emphasis to safety in the engineering development of a product.
    - It is the engineer, who must carry out the development of safe products.

2) **Imagination and Ingenuity:**
    - The engineer must be imaginative and ingenious (intelligent and clever) enough to anticipate potentially hazardous situations relating to a product, which may happen.

1.30 ECOLOGICAL CONSIDERATIONS

- People inherently depend on their environment for air, water, food, and materials for clothing and shelter.
- In olden days, human-made wastes were naturally recycled for repeated use.
- When open sewers i.e. artificial underground conduit for carrying off sewage or rainwater and dumps were introduced, nature became unable to reclaim and recycle these wastes within normal time periods, thus interrupting natural ecological cycles.
- Traditional economic systems enable the products to be mass-produced and sold at prices that often do not reflect the true cost to society in terms of resource consumption and ecological damage.
- Now the society is becoming more generally aware of this problem. Legislative requirements and more realistic "total" cost provisions are having increasing impact upon engineering design.
- Certainly, it is important that, the best available engineering input go into societal decisions involving these matters.
- We can perhaps state the basic ecological objectives of mechanical engineering design rather simply:
    (1) to utilize materials, so that, they are economically recyclable within reasonable time periods without causing objectionable air, ground and water pollution and
    (2) to minimize the rate of consumption of non-recycled energy sources (such as fossil fuels), both to conserve these resources and to minimize thermal pollution.
- In some instances, the minimization of noise pollution is also a factor to be considered.

List of Suggested Points Under Ecology:

1. Consider all aspects of the basic design objective involved, to be sure that, it is *sound*.

2. After accepting the basic design objective, the next step is a *review of the overall concept* to be translated into the proposed design. For example, a modular concept may be appropriate, but specific components or modules are most likely to wear out or become obsolete. They can be replaced with updated modules that are interchangeable with the originals. The motor and transmission assembly of a domestic automatic washing machine is an example, for which, this approach would be appropriate.

3. An important consideration is designing for *recycling*. At the outset of a new design, it is becoming increasingly important that, the engineer considers the full ecological cycle including the disposal and reuse of the entire device and its components. Consider an automobile, in which, parts appropriate for reuse (either with or without rebuilding) should be made, so that, they can be easily removed from a junk car. Dismantling and sorting of parts by material should be made as easy and economical as possible.

4. Select materials with ecological factors in mind, like availability of the required raw materials in nature, processing energy requirements, processing pollution problems (air, water, land, thermal and noise), and recyclability.

5. Consider ecological factors, when specifying processing, like all kinds of pollution, energy consumption and the efficiency of material usage. For example, forming operations such as rolling and forging use less quantity of material (and generate less scrap) than cutting operations.

6. Packaging is an important area for resource conservation and pollution reduction. (i) Reusable cartons, and (ii) the use of recycled materials for packaging, are two areas receiving increasing attention.

1.31 PRODUCT DESIGN

- Product design deals with the conversion of ideas into reality and aims at fulfilling the human needs.

- Product design is defined as, *"the set of activities required to bring a new product concept or service to a state of market readiness."*

- This set of activities includes :

    1. Initial inspiration of new product vision.
    2. Business and technological feasibility study.
    3. Engineering design of the product.
    4. Evaluation or validation of the product design.
    5. Planning of manufacturing processes of the product.
    6. Planning for the distribution of the product into the market.
    7. Planning for the use of the product by consumer, and
    8. Planning for retirement of the product.

- Product design includes design of wide range of products, concepts, and services, which may be of engineering type or non-engineering type.
- The few examples of product design are: design of car, design of refrigerator, design of dress in the world of fashion, design of stadium etc.
- Mechanical engineering design is not the product design. It is just one of the areas of product design.

1.31.1 Importance of Product Design

- The product design is a very important stage and has an impact on following three major areas of the product competitiveness:

1. Product Cost:

- The product design consumes a small fraction of the cost of product (approximately 5%), while the other 95% of the cost of product is consumed by capital, material and labour.
- However, the decisions made in the product design stage influences about 70 to 80% of the final cost of the product. The decisions made beyond the product design stage can influence only about 20 to 30% of the final cost of the product.
- In other words, the final cost of the product is almost decided in the product design stage.

2. Product Quality :

- The second major impact of product design is on the product quality.
- The old concept of achieving the product quality by inspection is no more true. The inspection can have a limited influence on the product quality.
- The true quality, desired by the customer in respect of features and performance, has to be designed into the product. Therefore, the product quality mainly depends upon the product design.

3. Product Cycle Time:

- The third area, where the product design makes the difference, is the product cycle time.
- The product cycle time is the time required to bring a new product into the market.
- The use of new design and development tools, such as, computer-aided engineering, rapid prototyping etc. reduces the product cycle time.
- The reduced product cycle time not only increases the marketability of the product, but also reduces the cost of product development.

1.32 FEASIBILITY STUDY

- Feasibility study means scientific study to check the possibility of bringing the product into reality.

Types of Feasibility Study:

a) Technological feasibility study:

- The technological feasibility study determines the possibility of technological success of the product with existing technology and constraints.
- Consider an example of design of a solar powered car. In technological feasibility study, it is necessary to check the possibility of designing and manufacturing the car, which can totally work on the solar energy, with existing technology.
- If the product is technologically not feasible, there is no point in initiating the project.

b) Economical feasibility study :

- The economical feasibility study determines the economic worthiness of the product.
- The design team needs to explore the possibility of individuals, companies or society paying for the product, which can satisfy their needs.
- The product must be cost competitive, not only in terms of initial cost, but also in terms of running and maintenance cost.
- The solar powered car can be economically feasible, only, if it is cost competitive with the petrol/diesel cars, battery operated cars and hybrid cars.

c) Financial feasibility study :

- The financial feasibility study determines the financial capability of the company to take up the project and the expected financial returns for the company.
- The project may be meritorious from the technological and economical point of view. However, it cannot be implemented, if (a) it is difficult for the company to mobilize the funds for its implementation, or (b) it does not assure the returns for the company for an adequate duration.
- For example: If the company cannot mobilize the magnitude of the financial resources required for the solar powered car project, the project cannot be initiated irrespective of its merit.

d) Societal feasibility study :

- The societal feasibility study determines the level of acceptance of the product by the society and the various controlling government agencies.
- The product must be acceptable to society. In addition, it must get approval from various controlling government agencies.
- For example, before launching the project of solar powered car, it is necessary to find the acceptance of such car by society over conventional cars.

e) Environmental feasibility study:

- The environmental feasibility study determines the extent, to which, the product is environment friendly.
- Now-a-days, the customers prefer environment friendly products.
- In addition, there are strict rules and regulations in place for the protection of environment. Therefore, the product must be environment friendly and non-polluting.

- For example, while designing the solar powered car, it is necessary to take into account the rainy season, during which, the availability of sun light is inadequate and make the provisions accordingly.

1.33 CREATIVITY IN DESIGN

- Creativity is defined as, *"an ability to synthesize new combinations of ideas and concepts into meaningful and useful forms"*.
- A design engineer should possess creativity. Most creative ideas occur by a slow and deliberate process that can be cultivated and enhanced with study and practice.
- In a creative process, initially the idea is only imperfectly understood. It is followed by a slow process of clarification and exploration as the entire idea takes shape.

Steps to be Taken for Enhancing Creative Thinking:

1. Develop a creative attitude:
- To be creative, it is essential to develop a confidence that can provide creative solution to a problem.
- Confidence comes with small success, so one can start with small problems and build up self confidence with small success.

2. Unlock imagination :
- The questions like "Why" and "What If" should be questioned by the design engineer to unlock imagination.

3. Be persistent:
- Creativity requires hard work. Many problems will not be solved easily. So the design engineer should be persistent i.e. he should continue and try to do something to resolve the problem.

4. Develop an open mind:
- Design engineer should be always curious to receive new ideas coming from any sources.
- Even a simple suggestion has a potential to become a solution of the problem and hence suggestions should be encouraged all the time.

5. Suspend judgement at early stage:
- Creative ideas develop slowly and hence, critical judgment on the ideas should be avoided at an early stage.

6. Set problem boundaries:
- Proper definition of problem and its boundaries enhances creative process.

1.34 INTRODUCTION TO ERGONOMICS AND AESTHETIC ASPECTS

Questions	
1. Define the term Aesthetic and Ergonomics.	**(S-09, 10, 12, 13; W-11, 12)**
2. State the importance of Aesthetic and Ergonomic considerations in design.	**(W-09)**
3. What is ergonomics ? State its scope in machine design.	**(W-13)**

1.34.1 Ergonomics

- Ergonomics is concerned with optimizing the overall and detailed design of controls, operations, and maintenance interfaces between machines and men in both, normal and emergency working.

- At the same time, the man and the machine are interacting with environment, surrounding work place, all in terms of efficiency, reliability, safety on low cost-effective basis.

- This involves a knowledge of human characteristics such as :

    (a) Anatomy and physiology – structure and function of the human body, senses, mental processes.

    (b) Anthropometry – information on body size, field of movement, field of view, speed of response, forces that can be exerted.

    (c) Psychology – knowledge of the brain, nervous system and human behaviour.

    (d) Conditions that aid efficiency and comfort and avoid fatigue.

- Therefore, **ergonomics** is defined as *'the relationship between man and machine and the application of anatomical, physiological and psychological principles to solve the problems arising from man-machine relationship'*.

- The word 'ergonomics' is derived from two greek words – 'ergon' = work and 'nomos' = natural laws. Ergonomics means the natural laws of work.

- From design considerations, the topics included in ergonomic studies are as follows :

    (a) Anatomical factors in design of driver's seat.

    (b) Layout of instrument dials and displays panels for accurate perception by the operators.

    (c) Design of hand levers and hand wheels.

    (d) Energy expenditure in hand and foot operations.

    (e) Lighting, noise and climatic conditions in machine environment.

- Thus, the purpose of applying ergonomic information to design situations is to ensure that, the environments provided and the designs prepared offer the man the greatest comfort, advantages and safety.

- While designing equipments for human use, it is important to realize that, the man has only limited powers. Hence, the designer should design the machine to suit the man's health, happiness and effectiveness.

- **Ergonomics** can also be defined as *"a systematic study of the relationship between people and their occupation, equipment and work environment for the purpose of increasing human efficiency and removing those features of design, which tend to cause inefficiency or physical disability"*.

1.34.2 Importance of Ergonomics in Design   (W-13)

- It decreases physical and mental stresses.
- It helps to study the man-machine relationship.
- Working environment can be improved to increase human efficiency.
- Reliability, safety etc. can be improved on low cost-effective basis.

1.34.3 Aesthetics   (S-08, 13)

- **Aesthetics** is defined as *'a set of principles of appreciation of beauty'*. It deals with the appearance of the product.
- Appearance is the outward expression of the quality of the product and is the first communication of the product with the user.
- Although function, cost, safety and the physical aspects of ergonomics may be important in the initial stages of the design process, the appearance of a product is often a major factor in its sale-ability.
- An engineering design with good aesthetics will be pleasing to the eye and gives a visual impression of functioning efficiently.

1.34.4 Importance of Aesthetics in Design

- Each product is to be designed to perform a specific function or a set of functions for the satisfaction of customers.
- The parameters that are normally considered by the customer, while selecting the products are :
  1. Functional performance,
  2. Durability,
  3. Initial and running cost,
  4. Ability to withstand the adverse conditions,
  5. Service support available,
  6. Comfort to the user, and
  7. Appearance.
- In a present days of buyer's market, a number of products available in the market are having most of the parameters identical. Thus, the *appearance of the product* becomes a major factor in attracting the customer.
- This is particularly true for customer durables like : automobiles, domestic refrigerators, television sets, music systems etc.
- At any stage in the product life, the aesthetic quality cannot be separated from the product quality.
- The growing importance of the aesthetic considerations on product design has given rise to a separate discipline, known as *'industrial design'*.
- The job of an industrial designer is to create new shapes and forms for the product, which are aesthetically appearing.

1.34.5 Relation between Aesthetic and Ergonomics

- Ergonomics is the scientific study of the relationship between men and their working environment. Since the appearance of a design directly affects the relationship between product and user and can often improve the efficiency of an operation, aesthetic engineering may be considered as an important part of ergonomics.
- Knowing the terms ergonomics, aesthetics and their interrelation, we are able to understand more details about Ergonomic factors influencing the product design and the man-machine relationship.

1.35 MAN-MACHINE RELATIONSHIP

- Machine has separate identity in itself in machine design. However, it cannot perform well without man.
- Therefore, egronomists consider man-machine as a joint system, to perform combination of activities to obtain output from the given input.
- From display instruments, the operator gets the information about the operations of the machine.
- If he feels that, a correction is necessary, he will operate the levers or controls. This, in turn, will alter the performance of the machine, which will be indicated on display panels.
- The contact between man and machine in this closed-loop system arises at two places - **display instruments**; which give information to the operator, and **control**; with which, the operator adjusts the machine.

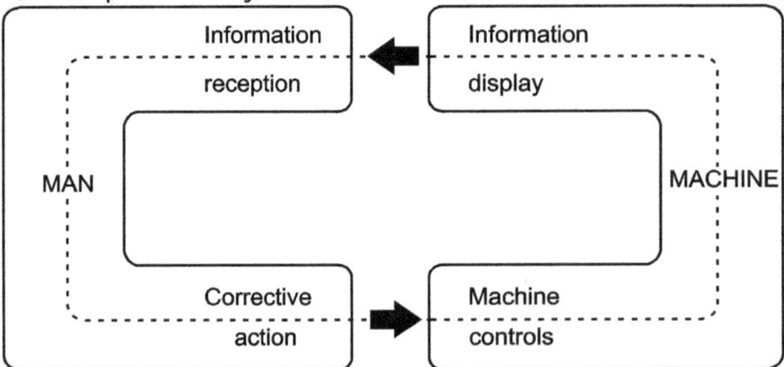

Fig. 1.20 : Man-machine closed loop system

1.36 ERGONOMIC CONSIDERATIONS WHILE DESIGNING A MACHINE

- Following are the major ergonomic considerations, in the process of designing a machine.

  (a) Design of displays. (b) Design of controls. (c) Environment and safety.

1.36.1 Design of Displays

- The displays are devices, through which, the man (user) can receive the information from the machine.

- A good display device is one, which allows the proper combination of speed, accuracy and sensitivity of display.
- Display devices can be mainly classified into two groups.

1. Qualitative Displays :

- The displays, which indicate only the condition or state without giving the values, are known as *'qualitative displays'*.
- The qualitative display or signal is used to indicate an 'on' or 'off' response such as valve open or closed, power 'ON' or 'OFF'.
- The examples of the qualitative displays are traffic signals and ON-OFF indicators.

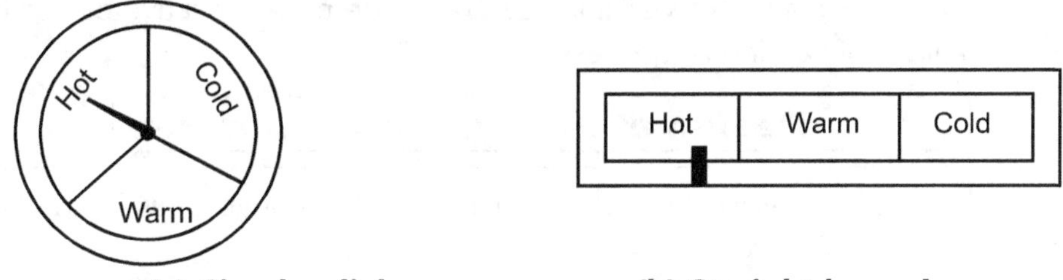

(a) Circular dial   **(b) Straight legend**

Fig. 1.21 : Qualitative displays

2. Quantitative Displays :

- When the user requires numerical information from the instrument, the displays used are called as *'quantitative displays'*. The information can be given as a 'digital display' or as an 'analogue display'.
- A digital display presents the information directly as a number and an analogue display does it by means of a scale and a pointer, whose position relative to the scale is analogous to the value, it represents.
- The examples of the quantitative displays are : voltmeters, ammeters, speedometers, watches, energy meters etc.

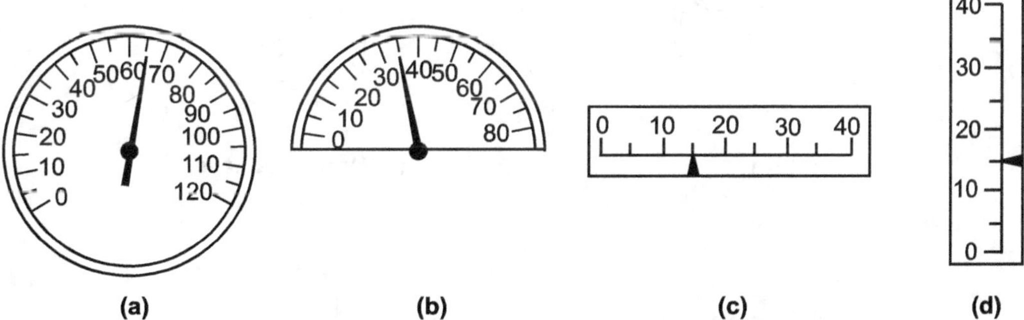

(a)   **(b)**   **(c)**   **(d)**

Fig. 1.22 : Quantitative displays

1.36.1.1 Ergonomic Considerations in Design of Displays

The ergonomic considerations in design of displays are as follows :

- The scale on the dial indicator should be divided in suitable linear progression such as 0-10-20-30.
- Number of subdivisions between the divisions should be minimum.

- The vertical figures should be used for stationary dials, while the radially oriented figures should be used for rotating dials.

- The height of the letters or numbers on displays should be $\geq \dfrac{\text{reading distance}}{200}$.

- The pointer should have knife-edge with a mirror to minimize parallax error.

- The numbering should increase in clockwise direction on a circular scale, rightwards on a horizontal scale and upwards on vertical scale.

- Distinction in display groups should be made with the help of colour, shape and size. Important displays, like warnings can be made more effective by use of flashing lights or a light of varying brightness.

1.36.2 Design of Equipment for Controls

- The controls are the devices, through which, the man conveys his instructions to the machine.

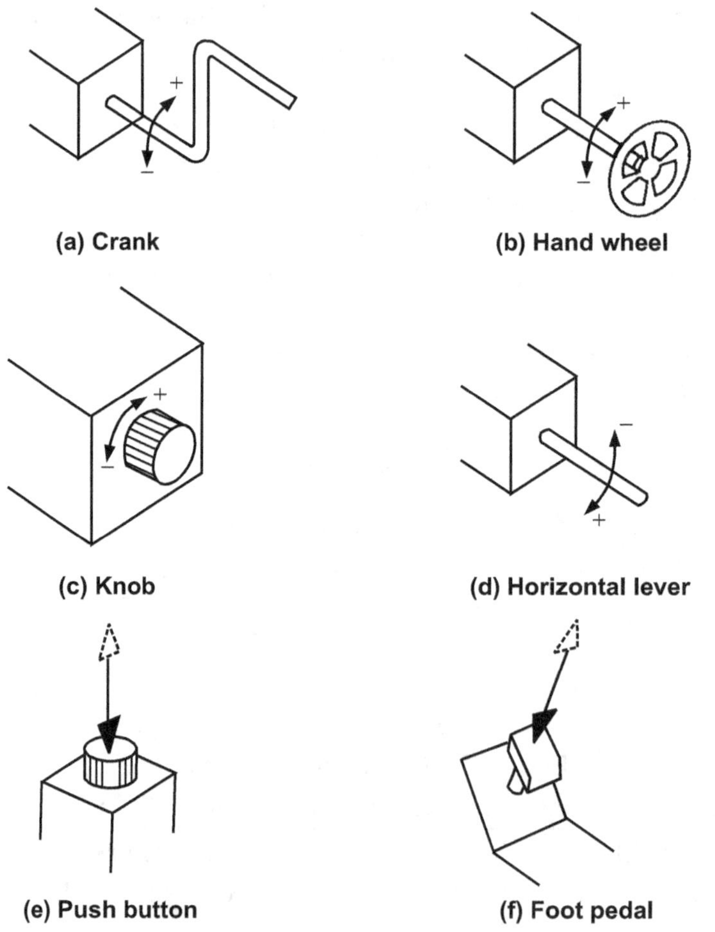

Fig. 1.23 : Equipment for control

- The selection of control device depends upon the following factors :
    - (a) The required speed of operation.
    - (b) The required accuracy of the control.
    - (c) The required operating force.
    - (d) The required range of the control.
    - (e) The required direction of the control.
    - (f) The convenience of the user.
- The control device is usually rotated in clockwise direction or moved to the right for 'on' or 'increase', but a different movement is adopted for special circumstances.
- The various types of controls used in machines are :
  Crank, handwheel, knob, levers, push button, foot pedal etc. shown in Fig. 1.23.

1.36.2.1 Ergonomic Considerations in Design of Controls

The ergonomic considerations in design of controls are as follows :

- The controls should be easily accessible and properly positioned.
- The control operation should involve minimum motions.
- The shape of the control device, which comes in contact with hands, should be in conformity with the anatomy of hands and feet.
- The control should be painted in proper colour to attract the attention.

1.36.3 Design of Environment and Safety

- The working environment affect significantly the man-machine relation. It affects the efficiency, health and safety of the operator.
- Varieties of functions are performed by human beings in industrial environment such as controlling, supervising, maintaining the work and equipment etc.
- The most important factors affecting efficiency of human being are heat, humidity, light, air movement, noise, acceleration including vibrations.

(a) Lighting :

- The amount of light required to enable a task to be efficiently performed depends upon the degree of precision required with the work, time allowed to see the task, reflective characteristics of the equipment involved and the sharpness of vision of human beings.
- The surrounding area including walls, ceiling, floor and other objects should be bright and more coloured than the workplace, where he should concentrate.
- Lighting should match the needs of the task as far as illumination is concerned.
- Glare often causes discomfort and reduce visibility of the task. Glare can be minimized or eliminated by careful design of lighting sources and their positions and changes in the texture of the working surfaces.
- Workers will become less tired, if the lighting and the colour scheme are arranged, so that, there is a gradual change in brightness.

(b) Noise :

- It produces three effects – annoyance, loss of hearing power and reduced efficiency at work.
- High pitched noise, interrupted and sudden noise, unexpected noise produces maximum discomfort than steady ones.
- Experimental studies indicate that, the workers do not work slower, when exposed to noise, but it appears that, loud noise causes them to be less accurate and liable to make mistakes and become accident prone.
- If the noise level is too high, it can be stopped at source by better maintenance of equipment, placing vibration isolating materials, pluging ears and providing sound insulating walls.

(c) Temperature :

- In order to perform task efficiently, the operator should feel neither too hot nor cold, but comfortable. The optimum air temperature for light work may range from 18°C to 23°C.
- When heavy work is done, the temperature should be lowered and when office work is done, it should be little higher.
- The radiant temperature comfort level is in between 16°C to 20°C and it is important to protect workers from radiant heat, when high temperature processes are used.

(d) Humidity and air circulation :

- Humidity has little effect at ordinary temperatures, but low humidity may cause discomfort through drying of the nose and throat.
- Air humidity and air velocity become important at high temperature, because they influence the amount of sweat, which can be evaporated from body surface to produce cooling effect.

Ideal Working Conditions :

Property	Range or value
Temperature	18°C to 23°C.
Relative humidity	30% to 70%.
Illumination level	Better than 200 lux (lighting intensity on floor/m^2).
Ventilation rate of air	6.6 m^3/hr at sea level per person and light work.
Noise level	Not to be more than 10 dB.

For work requiring higher level of skill and efficiency, temperature should be reduced, ventilation may be increased by a factor of 2 to 3 and illumination level may be raised by a factor upto 4.

1.37 CONSIDERATIONS IN AESTHETIC DESIGN

Questions

1. What are the aesthetic considerations in design.   (W-10)
2. State aesthetic considerations in design regarding shape and colour.   (W-12)
3. Explain the importance of shape and size in aesthetic design.   (S-11, 14)

The various aspects of the aesthetic design are discussed below :

1.	Shape (Form)	2.	Symmetry and Balance
3.	Colour	4.	Continuity
5.	Variety	6.	Proportion
7.	Size	8.	Contrast
9.	Impression and Purpose	10.	Style
11.	Material and Surface Finish	12.	Tolerance
13.	Noise		

1. Shape (Form) :

There are *five basic shapes* (forms) of the products, such as step, taper, shear, streamline and sculpture, as shown in Fig. 1.24. The external shape of any product is based on one or combination of these basic shapes.

(i) Step form : The step form is a stepped structure having vertical accent. It is similar to the shape of multistorey building.

(ii) Taper form : The taper form consists of tapered blocks or tapered cylinders.

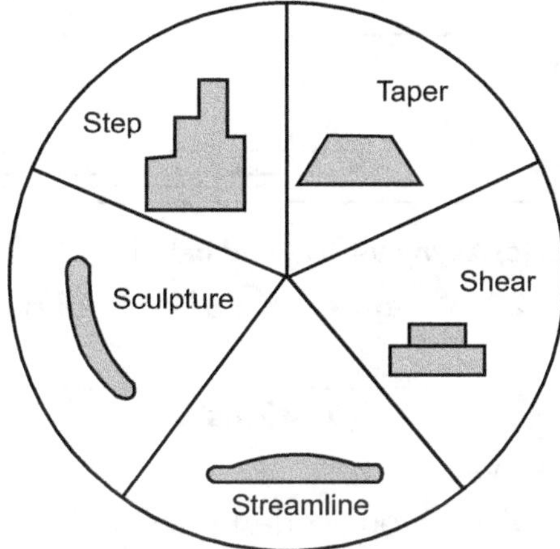

Fig. 1.24 : Basic types of product shapes (forms)

(iii) Shear form : The shear form has a square outlook.

(iv) Streamline form : The streamline form has a streamlined shape having a smooth flow as seen in automobile and aeroplane structures.

(v) Sculpture form : The sculpture form consists of ellipsoids, paraboloids and hyperboloids.

2. Symmetry and Balance :

- Most of the life forms in the nature are approximately symmetrical about at least one axis.

- The human eye is thus conditioned to see the things in symmetrical form and tends to reject asymmetrical shapes as ugly.

- Hence in many products, symmetry about at least one axis improves the aesthetic appeal of the product.

- However, whenever functional requirement demands symmetry, balance in the product improves the aesthetic feeling (Fig. 1.25).

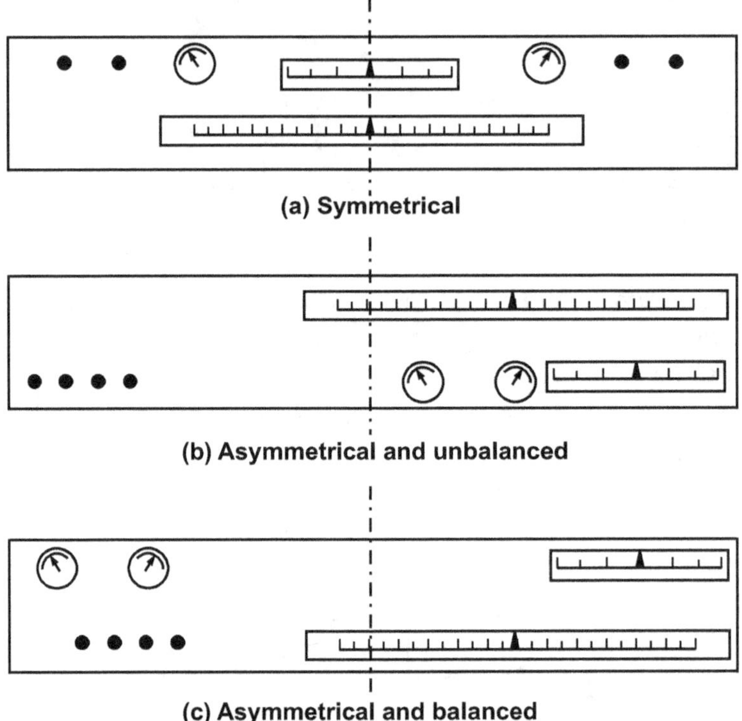

(a) Symmetrical

(b) Asymmetrical and unbalanced

(c) Asymmetrical and balanced

Fig. 1.25 : Arrangement of control panel

3. Colour :

Questions
1. State Morgan's colour code in Aesthetics.   **(S-13)**
2. State the meaning of following colour code in aesthetic consideration, while designing product : (i) Red, (ii) Orange, (iii) Green, (iv) Blue.   **(W-13)**

- *Colour* is one of the major contributors to the aesthetic appeal of the product. Many colours are linked with different moods and conditions.

- The selection of the colour should be compatible with the conventions. 'Morgan' has suggested the following colour code :

Colour	Meaning
Red	Danger, Hot
Orange	Possible Danger
Yellow	Caution
Green	Safe
Blue	Cold
Gray	Dull

4. Continuity :

- A product, which has good *continuity of elements*, is aesthetically appealing.
- For example, a fillet radius at the change of cross-section adds the continuity to the product and hence improves the appearance, as shown in Fig. 1.26.

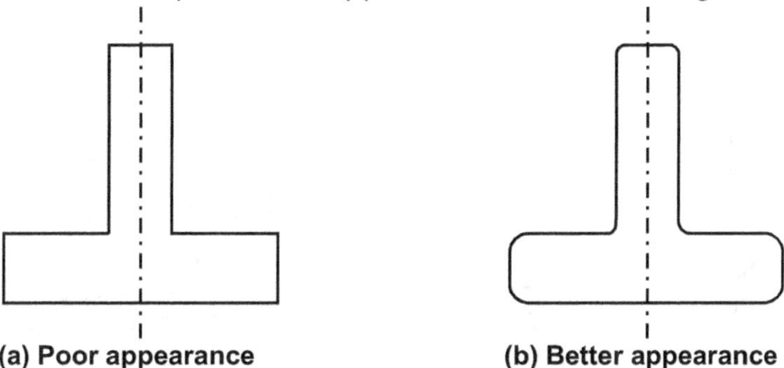

(a) Poor appearance   **(b) Better appearance**

Fig. 1.26 : Continuity

5. Variety :

- *Variety* is particularly useful, while marketing the range of products.
- For example, in case of consumer appliances, the functionally identical products are manufactured in a number of varieties by a single manufacturer.

6. Proportion :

- *Proportion* is concerned with the relationship in size, between connected items, or elements of items.
- The product, which is out of proportion, is not aesthetically pleasing.
- The spanner shown in Fig. 1.27 (a) satisfies the functional ability and is also easy to manufacture. But, it is out of proportion and hence poor in appearance.
- The spanner shown in Fig. 1.27 (b) is in proportion and aesthetically pleasing.

(a) Poor appearance   **(b) Better appearance**

Fig. 1.27 : Spanner

7. Size :

- Due to advancements in electronic fields, designers can use previously unaccepted housing for integrated items, so freeing them from many of design constraints.
- Now, design of telephone is an example of integrating the entire telephone circuitry in a single component providing good balance, proportion and ergonomic styling.

8. Contrast :

- *Contrast* is a distinction between the adjacent elements of the product, which have clearly different characteristics and functions.
- The contrast improves the appearance of the product.

9. Impression and Purpose :

- The product should give the *impression* of the satisfactory performance or *purpose*.
- The taper shape gives the impression of strength and stability as shown in Fig. 1.28 and 1.29 respectively.

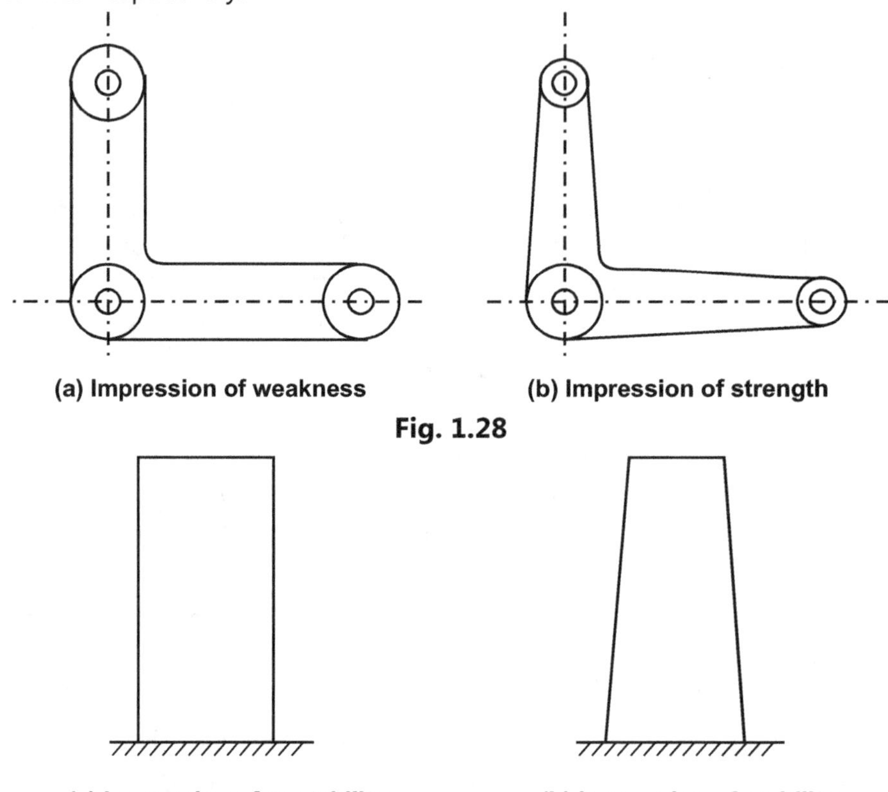

(a) Impression of weakness   **(b) Impression of strength**

Fig. 1.28

(a) Impression of unstability   **(b) Impression of stability**

Fig. 1.29

10. Style :

- *Style* is a visual quality of the product, which sets it apart from the rest of the functionally identical products.

11. Material and Surface Finish :

- The *material* and *surface finish* of the product contribute significantly to the appearance.
- The material like stainless steel gives better appearance than the cast irons, plain carbon steels or low alloy steels.
- The brass or bronze give richness to the appearance of the product.
- The products with better surface finish are always aesthetically pleasing.
- The surface coating processes like spray painting, anodizing, electroplating etc. greatly enhances the aesthetic appeal of the product.

12. Tolerance :

- Giving proper tolerance to the mating parts improve the aesthetic appeal of the product.

13. Noise :

- Unwanted noise is disturbing and is suggestive of some malfunction within the product and hence it greatly reduces the aesthetic appeal.

1.38 GUIDELINES IN AESTHETIC DESIGN

- For any product, there exists a relationship between the functional requirements and the appearance of the product.

- The aesthetic quality contributes to the performance of the product, though the extent of contribution varies from product to product.

- For example, the chromium plating of automobile components improves the corrosion resistance alongwith the appearance. Similarly, the aerodynamic shape of the car improves the performance as well as gives the pleasing appearance.

- The following guidelines may be used in aesthetic design (design for appearance) :

  (a) The appearance should contribute to the performance of the product. For example, the aerodynamic shape of the car will have lesser air resistance, resulting in the lesser fuel consumption.

  (b) The appearance should reflect the function of the product. For example, the aerodynamic shape of the car increases the speed.

  (c) The appearance should reflect the quality of the product. For example, the robust and heavy appearance of the hydraulic press reflects its strength and rigidity.

  (d) The appearance should not be at too much of extra cost, unless it is a prime requirement.

  (e) The appearance should be achieved by the effective and economical use of materials.

  (f) The appearance should be suitable to the environment, in which, the product is used.

Practice Questions

1. State the design consideration for selection of material of a part.

2. Give general procedure in machine design.

3. State general considerations in machine design.

4. Define following stresses induced in machine member with suitable example : (i) Crushing stress (ii) Bearing stress (iii) Torsional shear stress (iv) Transverse shear stress.

5. Draw stress-strain diagram for ductile material and brittle material and show clearly proportional limit, elastic limit, yield point, ultimate tensile strength.

6. Explain the term "stress concentration" of machine element.

7. Explain four remedies to reduce "stress concentration".

8. What do you mean by 'creep' ? Explain different stages of creep with graph.

9. Define any four properties of material.

10. Suggest the suitable material for the following machine parts : (i) Hydraulic cylinder (ii) Turbine blades (iii) Helical spring (iv) Bearing bushes.

11. Suggest the suitable material for the designing of following machine parts : (i) Crank shaft (ii) Helical spring (iii) Bushes for knuckle pin (iv) Lathe bed (v) Spring for I.C. engine valve (vi) Screw for screw jack.

12. Define endurance limit and draw typical S-N curve for steel.

13. State the meaning of following : (i) 30Ni4Cr1 (ii) SG400/12

14. Define factor of safety for ductile material and brittle material.

15. State the four factors to be considered while selecting the factor of safety.

16. Name different theories of elastic failure and explain any one in brief.

17. State maximum principal stress theory and maximum shear stress theory with their uses.

18. Define : (i) Ductility, (ii) Hardness.

19. Define 'ergonomics'. State areas covered under ergonomics.

20. List ergonomic considerations in design of display and controls.

21. Illustrate the role played by 'colour' in ergonomics and aesthetic design of products.

22. Discuss the aesthetic considerations in machine design regarding shape and colour.

23. Explain the term "aesthetic". Give the important features.

Problems for Practice

1. Determine the smallest size of the punch that can made to punch a 10 mm thick mild steel plate having ultimate shear stress as 0.3 kN/mm^2. The permissible crushing stress for the hardened punch is 1.3 kN/mm^2.   **(S-05, 08)**

                                                   (Ans. d = 2 mm)

2. Determine the smallest size of a hole that can be punched in 10 mm thick M.S. plate having an permissible shear stress of 39 N/mm^2, if permissible crushing stress for punch material is 24 N/mm^2. Sketch an arrangement.   **(S-07)**

                                                   (Ans. d = 65 mm)

MSBTE Questions and Answers

Summer 2013

1. Define machine design.   **(2 M)**

Ans. Refer Article 1.1.

2. State four types of load acting on a machine element.   **(2 M)**

Ans. Refer Article 1.5.

3.   Define fatigue. Give one example of fatigue failure in machine component.   **(2 M)**

Ans. Refer Article 1.10.

4.   Define notch sensitivity.   **(2 M)**

Ans. Refer Article 1.10.1.

5.   Write down steps involved in general design procedure.   **(4 M)**

Ans. Refer Article 1.2.

6.   State the factors governing selection of factor of safety.   **(4 M)**

Ans. Refer Article 1.14.1.

7.   State the meaning of stress concentration and state remedial measures on it. **(4 M)**

Ans. Refer Article 1.15.

8.   State the names of theories of failure.   **(4 M)**

Ans. Refer Article 1.28.

9.   State Morgan's colour code in Aesthetics.   **(2 M)**

Ans. Refer Article 1.37 (3).

10.   Define the following terms : (i) Aesthetics, (ii) Ergonomics.   **(4 M)**

Ans. Refer Articles 1.34.3 and 1.34.1.

Winter 2013

1.   State any four factors that govern the selection of material while designing a machine components.   **(4 M)**

Ans. Refer Article 1.20.

2.   What do you mean by 'Factor to Safety' (FOS)? Enlist your factors on which FOS depends?   **(4 M)**

Ans. Refer Articles 1.14, 1.14.1.

3.   A press exerts a load of 2 MN. This load is carried by two rods of 2 metre length and supports the upper head of the press. Find : (i) Diameter of rods, (ii) Change in length of rods. Assume safe stress = 80 MPa, E = 210 kN/mm^2.

Ans. Refer Problem 1.3.

4.   State the theories of failure under static load. Explain maximum stress theory and maximum shear stress theory with equations.   **(8 M)**

Ans. Refer Article 1.3.

5.   What is 'Ergonomics'? State its scope in machine design.   **(4 M)**

Ans. Refer Articles 1.34.1 and 1.34.2.

6.   State the meaning of following colour code in aesthetic consideration while designing product : (i) Red, (ii) Orange, (iii) Green, (iv) Blue.   **(4 M)**

Ans. Refer Article 1.37 (3).

Summer 2014

1.   List the steps involved in general design procedure. **(4 M)**

Ans. Refer Article 1.2.

2.   Name the different theories of elastic failure and explain any one. **(4 M)**

Ans. Refer Article 1.28.

3.   Explain the term, endurance limit with S - N Curve. **(4 M)**

Ans. Refer Article 1.11.

4.   Define stress concentration. List any four methods to reduce it with neat sketches.

(4 M).

Ans. Refer Articles 1.15 and 1.16.

5.   Draw the stress-strain diagram for mild steel and indicate clearly various key points on it. **(4 M)**

Ans. Refer Article 1.6.1.

6.   Explain the following material specification. (i) FG300 (ii) X20Cr18Ni2 **(4 M)**

Ans. Refer Article 1.21.

7.   Explain the importance of shape and size in aesthetic design. **(4 M)**

Ans. Refer Article 1.37.

❑❑❑

Chapter 2

DESIGN OF JOINTS, LEVERS AND OFFSET LINKS

About This Chapter

This chapter has weightage of 12 marks and assigned duration is 08 hours. In this chapter, we will learn about cotter joint, knuckle joint and turnbuckle. Also we will study design of levers; hand/foot lever and bell crank lever, design of C-clamp, offset links, overhang crank.

Statistical Analysis

Examination	Weightage of questions asked
S-09	22 Marks
W-09	20 Marks
S-10	12 Marks
W-10	20 Marks
S-11	16 Marks
W-11	16 Marks
S-12	24 Marks
W-12	26 Marks
S-13	24 Marks
W-13	24 Marks
S-14	22 Marks

2.1 INTRODUCTION TO MACHINE PARTS SUBJECTED TO DIRECT LOAD

- A **direct load** means a load, which produces the same kind of effect in the machine member all the time. It does not change its magnitude as well as direction so as to cause stress reversals in the material. The load may be tensile, compressive or shear. Therefore, for design of such members, it is essential to know the nature of load and area of member sustaining that load.

- The practical examples of machine parts subjected to direct load are :

  (1) Bolts used for securing cover to the engine cylinder.

  (2) Riveted joint for the tie rods.

  (3) Cotter joint to connect big end bearing of a connecting rod of steam engine.

(4) Knuckle joint.

(5) Screwed end of a piston.

(6) Turn buckle etc.

2.2 COTTER JOINT

Introduction :

- A **cotter joint** is a temporary fastening and it is used to connect two co-axial rods or bars, which are subjected to axial tensile and/or compressive forces.

- A **cotter** is a flat wedge shaped piece of rectangular cross-section and its width is tapered (either on one side or both sides) from top to bottom for an easy adjustment. The taper in cotter varies from 1 in 48 to 1 in 24.

- The cotter is usually made of mild steel and wrought iron.

2.2.1 Applications of Cotter Joint

Question

1. Write applications of cotter joints.   **(W-10)**

(1) Connection of the piston rod to the cross-head of a reciprocating steam engine.

(2) Valve rod and its stem.

(3) Strap end of connecting rod.

(4) Lewis foundation bolt and other cottered foundation bolts.

(5) Piston rod to the tail end (rod) in an air pump.

2.2.2 Types of Cotter Joint

There are three main types of cotter joints :

(1) Socket and Spigot cotter joint.

(2) Sleeve and cotter joint.

(3) Gib and cotter joint.

2.2.3 Advantages of Cotter Joint

(1) Quick to assemble and dismantle parts.

(2) Very high tightening force due to the wedge action developed, which prevents loosening of parts in service.

(3) The joint is simple to design.

(4) The joint is easy to manufacture.

2.2.4 Design of Socket and Spigot Cotter Joint

Question

1. Write any four strength equations in design of socket and spigot cotter joint with relevant sketches.   **(S-10, 12)**

- In a socket and spigot cotter joint, one end of the rods (say A) is provided with a socket type of end and other end of rod (say B) is inserted into a socket. The other end of rod, which goes into socket, is called as spigot. Refer Fig. 2.1.
- A rectangular hole is made in the socket and spigot.
- A cotter is then driven tightly through a hole to make the temporary connection between two rods.

Let,

W	=	Load carried by the rods.
d	=	Diameter of rod.
d_1	=	Outside diameter of socket.
d_2	=	Diameter of spigot or inside diameter of socket.
d_3	=	Outside diameter of spigot collar.
d_4	=	Diameter of socket collar.
t_1	=	Thickness of spigot collar.
t	=	Thickness of cotter.
b	=	Width of cotter.
l	=	Length of cotter.
a	=	Distance from end of slot to the end of spigot.
c	=	Thickness of socket collar beyond slot.
τ	=	Permissible shear stress for cotter material.
σ_t	=	Permissible tensile stress for rod material.
σ_{ck}	=	Permissible crushing stress for cotter material.

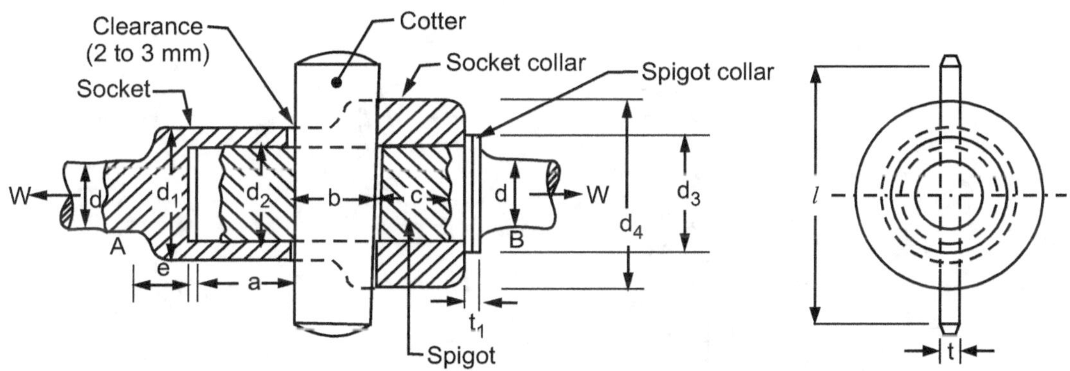

Fig. 2.1 : Socket and spigot cotter joint

Step I : Failure of rod in tension : The rod may fail in tension due to tensile load W.

We know that, Area resisting tearing $= \dfrac{\pi}{4} \cdot d^2$

Considering tensile stress,

$$\sigma_t = \frac{\text{Load}}{\text{Area resisting tearing}} = \frac{W}{\dfrac{\pi}{4} \cdot d^2}$$

Hence, diameter of rods (d) can be determined.

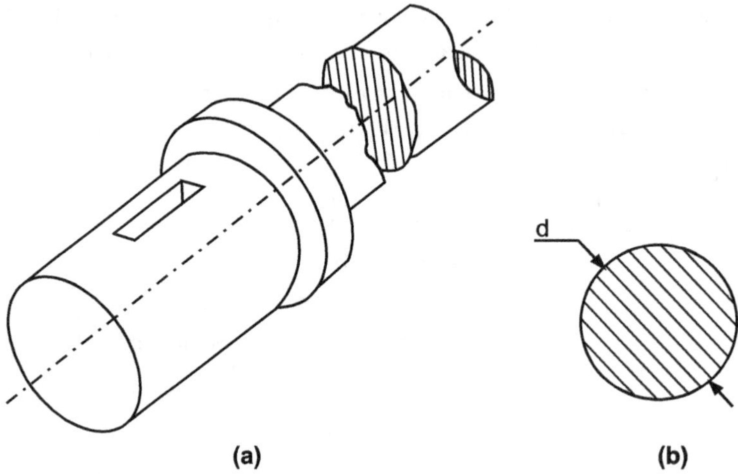

(a)   (b)

Fig. 2.2

Step II : Failure of spigot in tension across the slot (weakest section) : Area resisting

tearing of spigot across the slot $= \dfrac{\pi}{4} \cdot (d_2)^2 - d_2 \cdot t$

Considering tensile stress, $\sigma_t = \dfrac{W}{\dfrac{\pi}{4} \cdot (d_2)^2 - d_2 \cdot t}$

Assuming $t = \left(\dfrac{d_2}{4}\right)$, diameter of spigot ($d_2$) and thickness of cotter (t) can be determined.

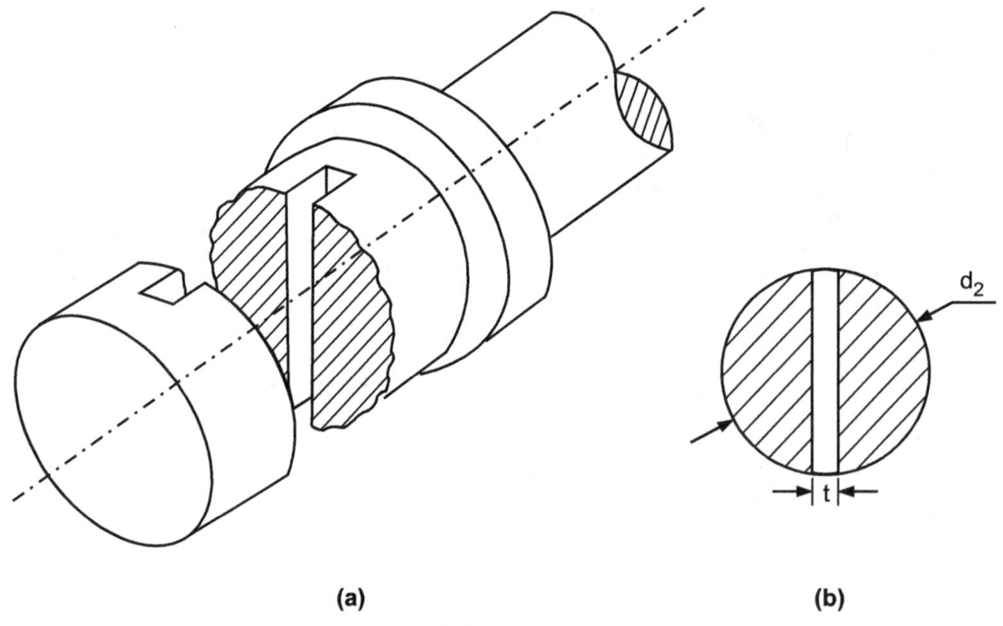

(a)   (b)

Fig. 2.3

Step III : Checking the spigot for crushing stress : The contact area between rod end (spigot end) at the slot and cotter shall be under crushing stress.

To check for safe crushing, the induced crushing stress should not exceed permissible crushing stress.

Area resisting crushing of rod or cotter = $d_2 \cdot t$

Induced crushing stress, $\quad \sigma_{ck} = \dfrac{W}{d_2 \cdot t}$ $\hspace{4cm}$ [Take $t = \dfrac{d_2}{4}$]

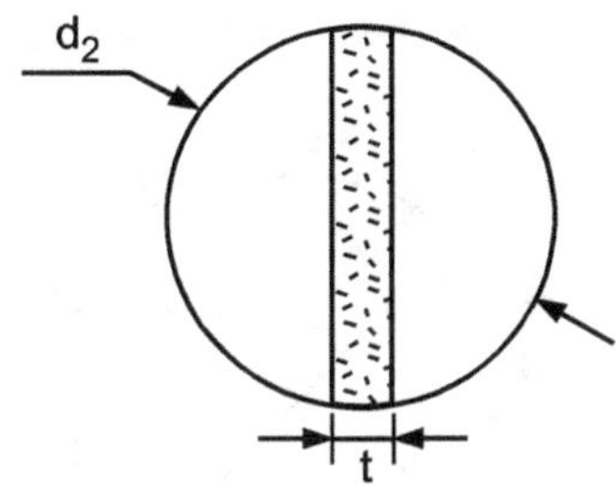

Fig. 2.4

If the induced crushing stress is less than permissible stress, we say that, design is safe.

Step IV : Failure of spigot end in shear (shear failure of spigot end beyond slot) : Due to cotter, the spigot end may undergo a double shear,

And area-resisting shear of spigot end = $2 \cdot a \cdot d_2$ $\hspace{3cm}$ (for double shear)

Considering shear stress, $\tau = \dfrac{W}{2 \cdot a \cdot d_2}$

Here, distance 'a' can be determined.

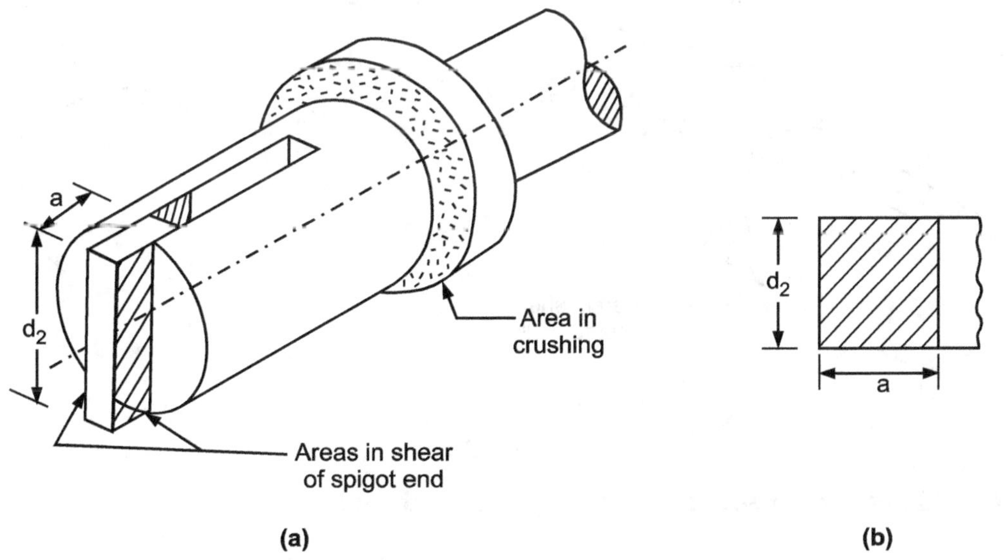

Fig. 2.5

Step V: Failure of spigot collar in crushing (with socket collar) :

Area resisting crushing of collar $= \dfrac{\pi}{4} \cdot [\,(d_3)^2 - (d_2)^2\,]$

Considering crushing stress,

$$\sigma_{ck} = \dfrac{W}{\dfrac{\pi}{4} \cdot [(d_3)^2 - (d_2)^2]}$$

Here, d_3 = outside diameter of spigot collar can be determined.

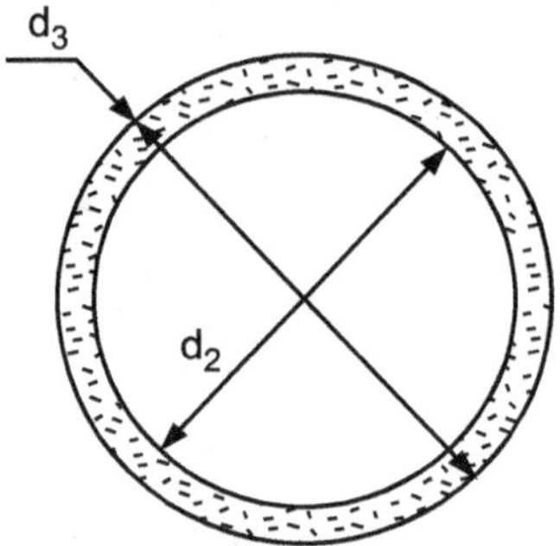

Fig. 2.6

Step VI : Failure of spigot collar in shearing :

Area resisting shearing $= \pi \cdot d_2 \times t_1$

Considering shear stress, $\tau = \dfrac{W}{\pi \cdot d_2 \times t_1}$

Hence, t_1 i.e. thickness of spigot collar can be determined.

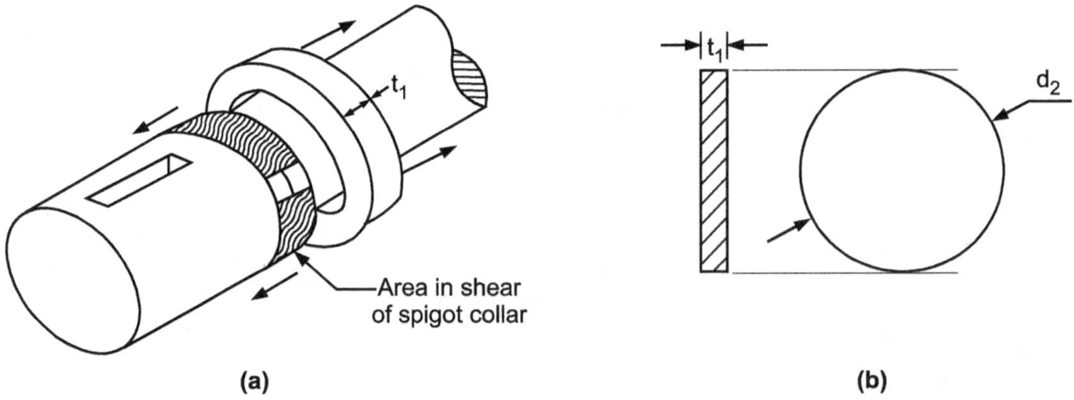

Fig. 2.7

Step VII : Failure of socket in tension across the slot :

Area resisting tension across the slot $= \dfrac{\pi}{4}\ \{(d_1)^2 - (d_2)^2\} - (d_1 - d_2)\, t$

Considering tensile stress, $\sigma_t = \dfrac{W}{\left[\dfrac{\pi}{4}\{(d_1)^2 - (d_2)^2\} - (d_1 - d_2)\,t\right]}$

Hence, d_1 = outside diameter of socket can be determined.

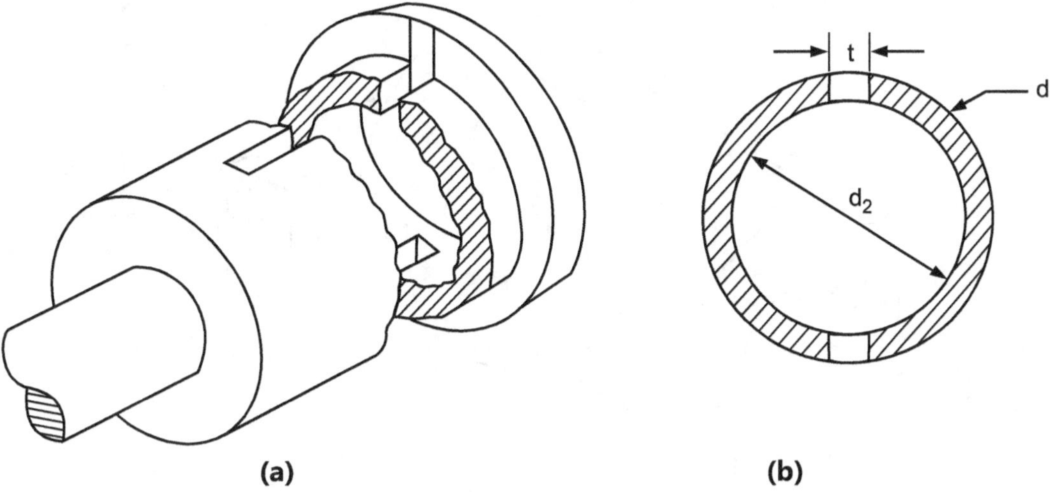

(a)   (b)

Fig. 2.8

Step VIII : Failure of socket collar in crushing :

Area resisting crushing $= (d_4 - d_2) \cdot t$

Considering crushing stress,

$$\sigma_{ck} = \frac{W}{(d_4 - d_2) \cdot t}$$

Hence, diameter of socket collar (d_4) can be determined.

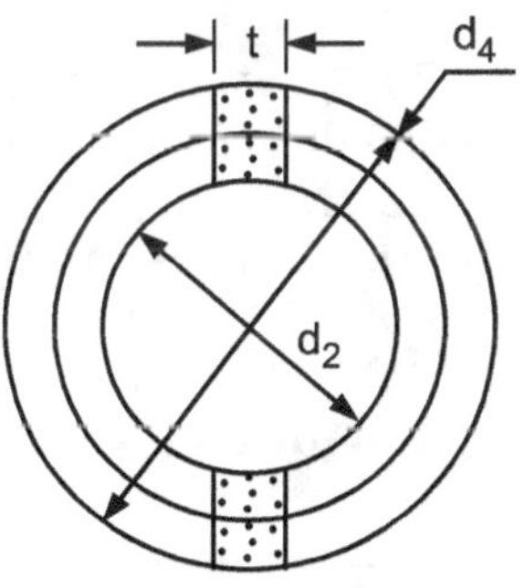

Fig. 2.9

Step IX : Failure of socket end in shearing :

Area resisting shear $= 2 \cdot (d_4 - d_2) \cdot c$ [For double shear]

Considering shear stress, $\tau = \dfrac{W}{2 \cdot (d_4 - d_2) \cdot c}$

Hence, distance 'c' i.e. thickness of socket collar beyond slot can be determined.

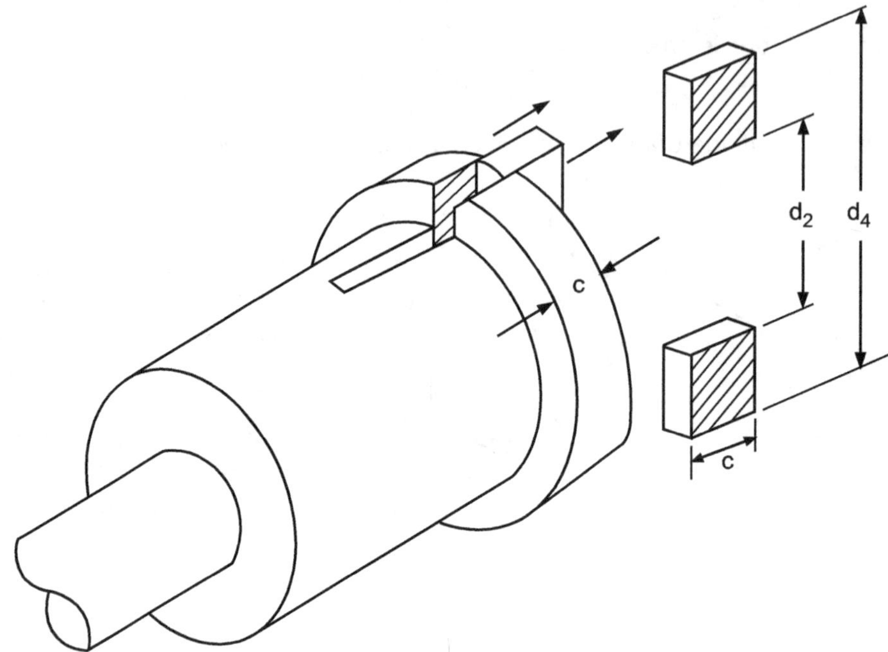

Fig. 2.10

Step X : Failure of cotter in shear : Cotter is in double shear.

$\therefore$ Area resisting shear $= 2b \times t$ [For double shear]

Considering shear stress, $\quad \tau = \dfrac{W}{2b \times t}$

Here, we can find the value of b i.e. width of cotter.

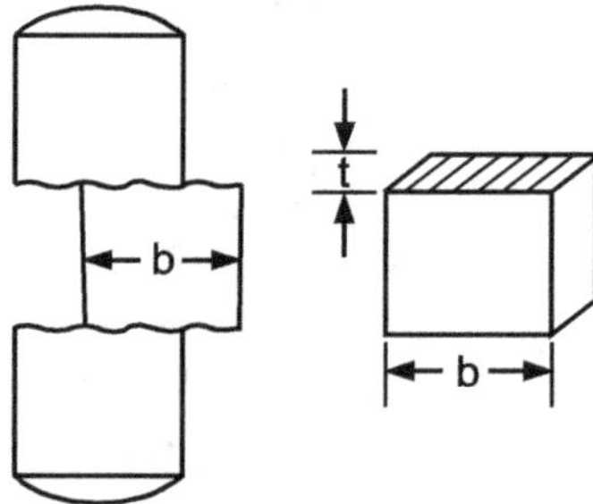

Fig. 2.11

Step XI : Take length of cotter = 4d.

Numerical Type No. 1 : "Socket and Spigot Cotter Joint"

Problem 2.1 : *A socket type cotter joint is to be designed for a load of 32 kN. Steel having the maximum permissible stresses as $\tau = 39$ N/mm^2, $\sigma_t = 56$ N/mm^2 and $\sigma_{ck} = 70$ N/mm^2 is used.*

Solution : Given data :

W = Load carried by roads = 32 kN = 32×10^3 N, $\tau = 39$ N/mm^2, $\sigma_t = 56$ N/mm^2 and $\sigma_{ck} = 70$ N/mm^2.

Procedure :

Step I : Failure of rod in tension : The rod may fail in tension due to tensile load W.

We know that, Area resisting tearing $= \dfrac{\pi}{4} \times (d)^2$

Considering tensile strength, $\sigma_t = \dfrac{W}{\dfrac{\pi}{4} d^2}$

$$\therefore \quad (d)^2 = \dfrac{4 \times W}{\pi \times \sigma_t} = \dfrac{4 \times 32 \times 10^3}{\pi \times 56} = 727.56$$

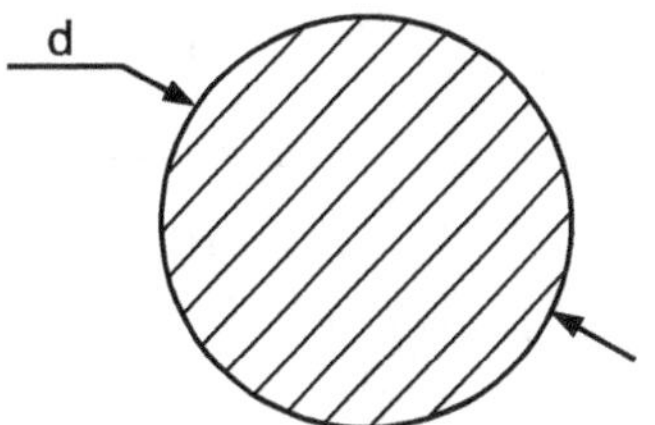

Fig. 2.12

$\therefore$ diameter of rod $= d = 26.97$ mm $\cong$ **28 mm (say)**

Step II : Failure of spigot in tension across the slot (weakest section) :

Area resisting tearing of spigot across the slot $= \dfrac{\pi}{4} \times (d_2)^2 - d_2 \times t.$

Where, d_2 is the diameter of spigot and t is thickness of cotter.

Considering tensile strength, $\sigma_t = \dfrac{W}{\dfrac{\pi}{4} \times (d_2)^2 - d_2 \times t}$

Take $\qquad t = \dfrac{d_2}{4}$

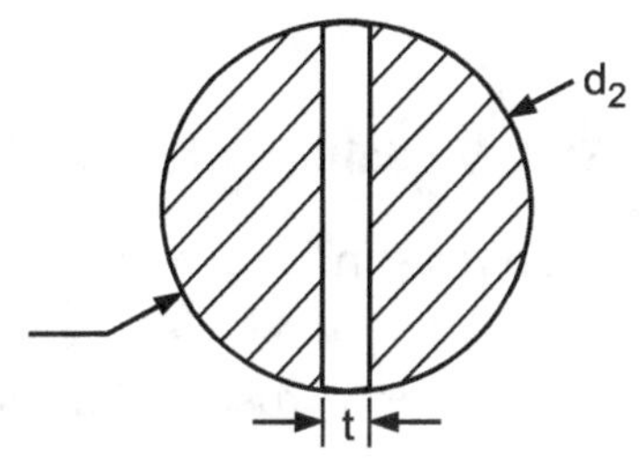

Fig. 2.13

$$\therefore \qquad 56 = \dfrac{32 \times 10^3}{\dfrac{\pi}{4}(d_2)^2 - d_2 \cdot \dfrac{d_2}{4}}$$

$$\therefore \qquad (d_2)^2 = \dfrac{4 \times 32 \times 10^3}{(\pi - 1) \times 56}$$

$$\therefore \qquad d_2 = 32.67 \cong \textbf{34 mm} \text{ and } t = \dfrac{d_2}{4} = \dfrac{34}{4} = \textbf{8.5 mm}$$

Step III : Checking the spigot for crushing stress :

Area resisting crushing of rod or cotter $= d_2 \times t.$

Induced crushing stress, $\sigma_{ck} = \dfrac{W}{d_2 \cdot t} = \dfrac{32 \times 10^3}{34 \times 8.5}$

Thus, $\qquad \sigma_{ck} = 110.73$ N/mm^2

As the induced crushing stress is more than the given permissible value of 70 N/mm^2. Therefore, the values of $d_2 = 34$ mm and t = 8.5 mm are not safe.

Now, let us find out these values by putting,

$$\sigma_{ck} = 70 \text{ N/mm}^2 \text{ in the equation as follows :}$$

$$\sigma_{ck} = \frac{W}{d_2 \cdot t}$$

$$\therefore \quad 70 = \frac{W}{d_2 \times \dfrac{d_2}{4}} \quad ; \quad \therefore d_2^2 = \frac{4 \times 32 \times 10^3}{70}$$

$$\therefore \quad d_2 = 42.76 \text{ mm} \cong \textbf{44 mm (say)}$$

$$\text{and} \quad t = \frac{d_2}{4} = \frac{44}{4} = \textbf{11 mm}$$

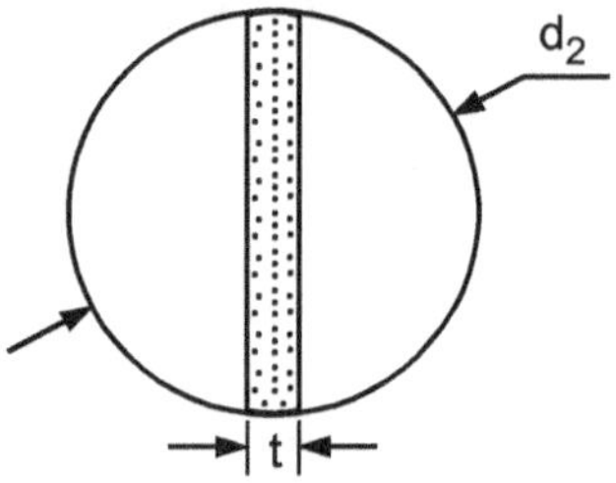

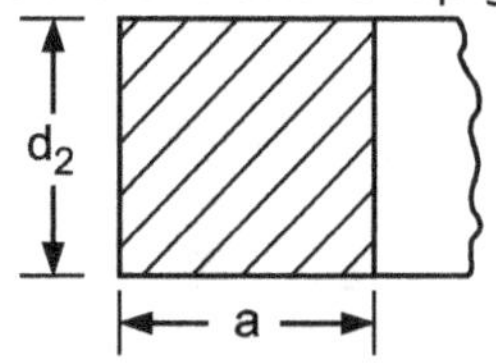
Fig. 2.14

Step IV : Failure of spigot end in shear : Due to cotter, the spigot end may undergo a double shear. Area-resisting shear of spigot end = $2 \times a \times d_2$.

$$\text{Considering shear stress, } \tau = \frac{W}{2 \times a \times d_2} \quad \therefore \quad 39 = \frac{32 \times 10^3}{2 \times a \times 44}$$

Thus, a = distance from end of slot to the end of spigot = **9.32 mm** $\cong$ **10 mm (say)**.

Fig. 2.15

Step V : Failure of spigot collar in crushing :

Area resisting crushing of collar $= \dfrac{\pi}{4} \left[(d_3)^2 - (d_2)^2 \right]$

$$\therefore \quad \text{Considering crushing stress, } \sigma_{ck} = \frac{W}{\dfrac{\pi}{4} \left[(d_3)^2 - (d_2)^2 \right]}$$

$$\therefore \quad 70 = \frac{4 \times 32 \times 10^3}{\pi \times (d_3^2 - 44^2)}$$

$$\therefore \quad d_3 = \text{diameter of spigot collar} = \textbf{50.18 mm}$$

$$\cong \textbf{52 mm (say)}$$

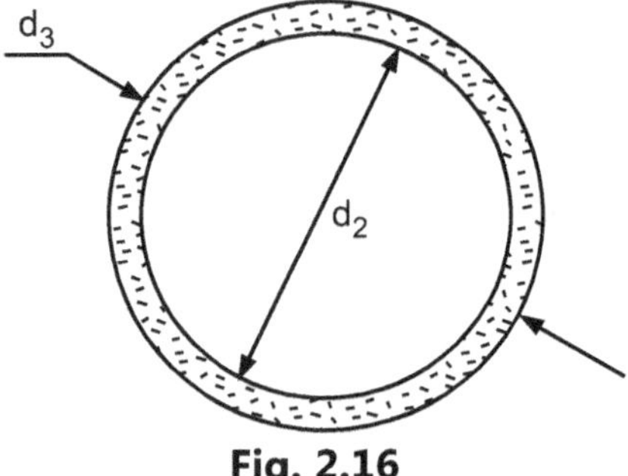
Fig. 2.16

Step VI : Failure of spigot collar in shearing :

Area resisting shearing $= \pi d_2 \times t_1$

Considering shear stress,

$$\tau = \frac{W}{\pi d_2 t_1}$$

$$\therefore \quad 39 = \frac{32 \times 10^3}{\pi \times 44 \times t_1}$$

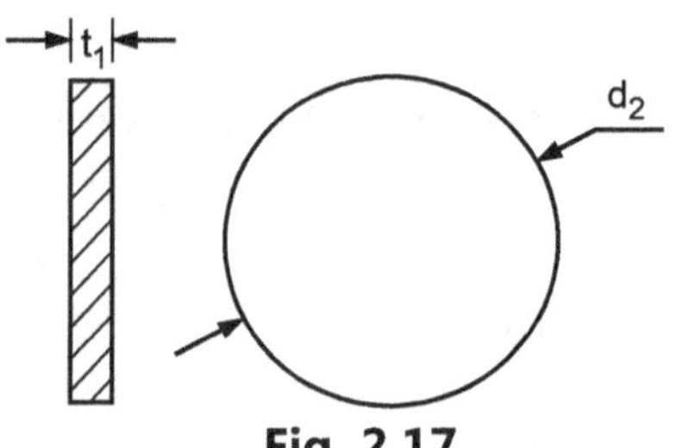
Fig. 2.17

Hence, t_1 = thickness of spigot collar = **5.93 mm**

$$\cong \textbf{6 mm (say)}$$

Step VII : Failure of socket in tension across the slot :

Area resisting tension across slot

$$= \frac{\pi}{4} \{(d_1)^2 - (d_2)^2\} - (d_1 - d_2)\, t$$

Considering tensile stress,

$$\sigma_t = \frac{W}{\frac{\pi}{4}[(d_1)^2 - (d_2)^2] - (d_1 - d_2)\, t}$$

$$\therefore \quad 56 = \frac{32 \times 10^3}{0.7853 \times [d_1^2 - 44^2] - (d_1 - 44) \times 11}$$

$$\therefore \quad 0.7853\,(d_1)^2 - 11 d_1 - 1607.76 = 0$$

$$\therefore \quad d_1 = \frac{-(-11) \pm \sqrt{(-11)^2 - 4 \times 0.7853 \times (-1607.76)}}{2 \times 0.7853}$$

$$= \mathbf{52.78\ mm} \cong \mathbf{54\ mm\ (say)}$$

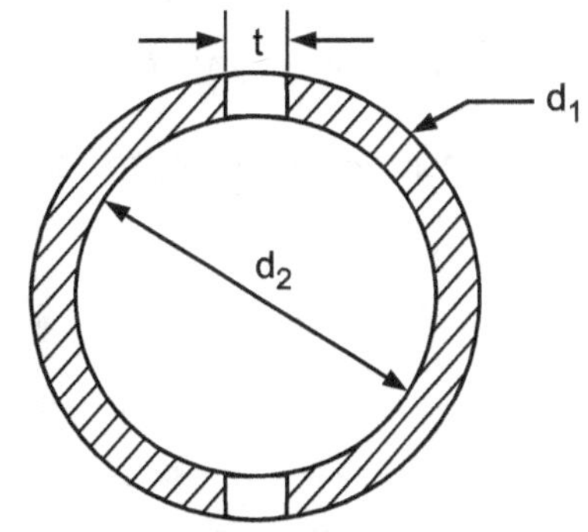
Fig. 2.18

Thus, d_1 = outside diameter of socket = **54 mm**

Step VIII : Failure of socket collar in crushing :

Area resisting crushing $= (d_4 - d_2) \times t$

Considering crushing stress,

$$\sigma_{ck} = \frac{W}{(d_4 - d_2) \times t}$$

$$\therefore \quad 70 = \frac{32 \times 10^3}{(d_4 - 44) \times 11}$$

$$\therefore \quad d_4 = 85.55\ mm$$

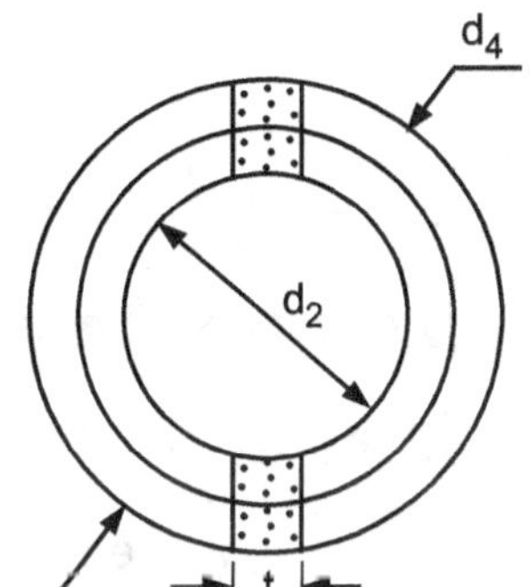
Fig. 2.19

Outside diameter of socket collar = d_4 = **85.55 mm** $\cong$ **86 mm** **(say)**

Step IX : Failure of socket end in shearing :

Area resisting double shear $= 2 \times (d_4 - d_2) \times c$

Considering shear failure,

$$\tau = \frac{W}{2 \times (d_4 - d_2) \times c} \qquad \text{[For double shear]}$$

$$\therefore \quad 39 = \frac{32 \times 10^3}{2 \times (86 - 44) \times c}$$

Hence, c = thickness of socket collar = **9.77 mm** $\cong$ **10 mm (say)**

Step X : Failure of cotter in shear : Cotter is in double shear as shown in Fig. 2.20.

Area resisting shear $= 2b \times t$ [Double shear]

Considering shear stress, $\tau = \dfrac{W}{2 \times b \times t}$

$\therefore \qquad\qquad 39 = \dfrac{32 \times 10^3}{2 \times b \times 11}$

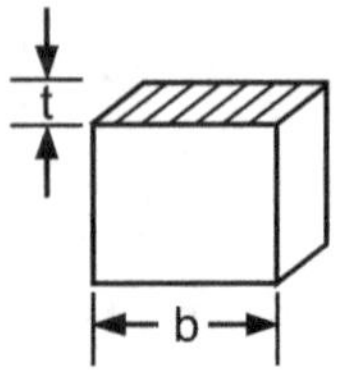

Fig. 2.20

Thus, b = width of cotter $= \mathbf{37.29} \cong \mathbf{38\ mm\ (say)}$

Step XI : Take length of cotter $= 4 \times d = 4 \times 28 = \mathbf{112\ mm}.$

Problem 2.2 : *Two C-40 rods of 40 mm diameter are to be connected by cotter joint. The thickness of cotter is 12 mm. Calculate the dimensions of the socket, if the maximum permissible stresses are 46 N/mm^2 in tension, 35 N/mm^2 in shear and 70 N/mm^2 in crushing.*

(W-13; S-14)

Solution : Given data : $d = 40$ mm, $t = 12$ mm, $\sigma_t = 46$ N/mm^2, $\tau = 35$ N/mm^2, $\sigma_{ck} = 70$ N/mm^2

Procedure : Step I : To calculate the load taken up by rods, considering tensile failure of rod, we have,

$$\sigma_t = \frac{W}{\frac{\pi}{4} d^2}$$

$\therefore \qquad W = \dfrac{\pi}{4} d^2 \times \sigma_t = \dfrac{\pi}{4} \times (40)^2 \times 46 = \mathbf{57805.3\ N}$

Step II : Consider failure of spigot in tension across the weakest section (slot) :

Area resisting tearing of spigot across the slot $= \dfrac{\pi}{4} \times (d_2)^2 - d_2 \times t$

where, d_2 is the diameter of spigot and t is thickness of cotter.

Considering tensile strength,

$$\sigma_t = \frac{W}{\frac{\pi}{4} \times (d_2)^2 - d_2 \times t}$$

$\therefore \qquad 46 = \dfrac{57805.3}{\dfrac{\pi}{4} \times (d_2)^2 - d_2 \times \dfrac{d_2}{4}}$ $\left[\text{Take } t = \dfrac{d_2}{4} \right]$

$\therefore \qquad (d_2)^2 = \dfrac{4 \times 57805.3}{(\pi - 1) \times 46}$

$\therefore \qquad d_2 = 48.44\ \text{mm} \cong \mathbf{50\ mm\ (say)}$

and $\qquad t = \dfrac{d_2}{4} = \dfrac{50}{4} = \mathbf{12.5\ mm}$

Step III : Failure of socket in tension across the slot :

$$\sigma_t = \frac{W}{\frac{\pi}{4} \times [d_1^2 - d_2^2] - (d_1 - d_2)\, t}$$

$$\therefore \quad 46 = \frac{57805.3}{0.7853 \times [d_1^2 - (50)^2] - (d_1 - 50) \times 12.5}$$

$$\therefore \quad 0.7853\, (d_1)^2 - 12.5\, d_1 - 2594.88 = 0$$

$$\therefore \quad d_1 = 65.99 \cong \textbf{66 mm (say)}$$

where, d_1 and d_2 are outside and inside diameters of socket respectively.

Step IV : Failure of socket collar in crushing :

$$\sigma_{ck} = \frac{W}{(d_4 - d_2) \times t}$$

$$\therefore \quad 70 = \frac{57805.3}{(d_4 - 50) \times 12.5}$$

$$\therefore \quad d_4 = 116.06 \text{ mm} \cong \textbf{118 mm (say)}$$

where, d_4 is outside diameter of socket collar.

Step V : Failure of socket end in shearing :

$$\tau = \frac{W}{2 \times (d_4 - d_2) \times c} \qquad \text{[Double shear]}$$

$$\therefore \quad 35 = \frac{57805.3}{2 \times (118 - 50) \times c}$$

$$\therefore \quad c = \text{Thickness of socket collar} = \textbf{12.14 mm} \cong \textbf{14 mm (say)}$$

2.2.5 Failure of Cotter in Bending

Question

1. Explain "Failure of Cotter in Bending".   **(S-13)**

- When the cotter is tight in socket and spigot, it is subjected to shear stress. But when it becomes loose, bending occurs. The forces acting on the cotter are shown in Fig. 2.21 (a).

- The load W between the cotter and spigot is assumed to be uniformly distributed over length d_2.

- The load between the socket end and cotter is assumed to be varying linearly from zero to maximum with triangular distribution. The cotter is treated as a beam as shown in Fig. 2.21 (b).

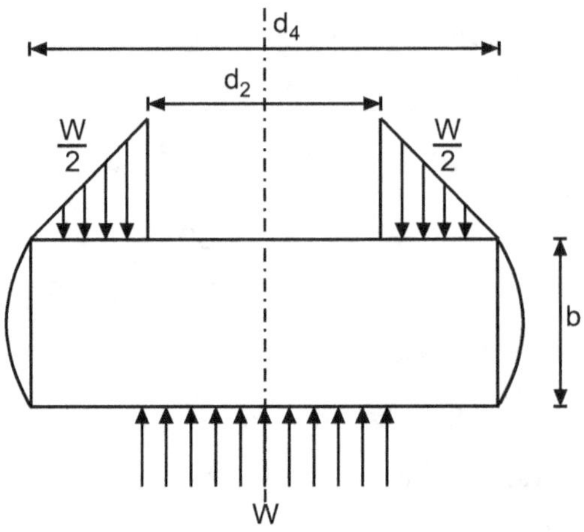

(a) Actual distribution of forces

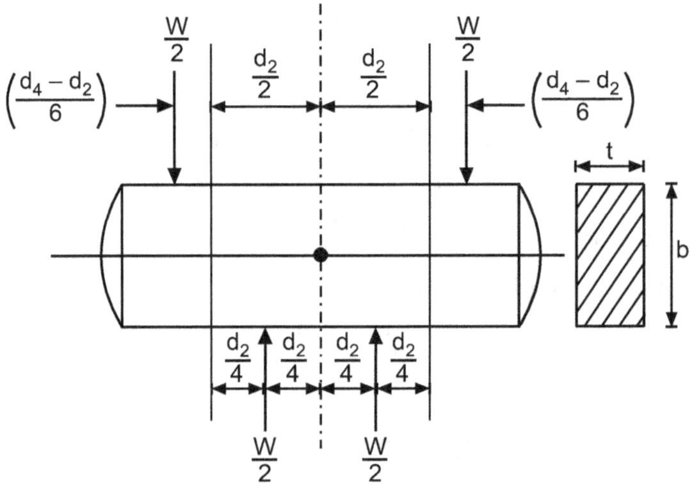

(b) Cotter treated as a beam

Fig. 2.21 : Failure of cotter in bending

The maximum bending moment at centre of cotter is given by,

$$M = \frac{W}{2} \times \left[\frac{d_4 - d_2}{6} + \frac{d_2}{2} \right] - \frac{W}{2} \times \left[\frac{d_2}{4} \right]$$

$$\therefore \quad M = \frac{W}{2} \left[\frac{d_2}{4} + \frac{(d_4 - d_2)}{6} \right]$$

Also,

$$Z = \frac{I}{y} = \frac{\frac{1}{12} tb^3}{\frac{b}{2}}$$

$$\therefore \quad Z = \frac{1}{6} tb^2$$

Bending stress is given by,

$$\sigma_b = \frac{M}{Z}$$

$$\therefore \qquad \sigma_b = \frac{\dfrac{W}{2}\left[\dfrac{d_2}{4} + \dfrac{(d_4 - d_2)}{6}\right]}{\dfrac{1}{6}\,tb^2}$$

Assuming suitable proportion like b = 3t or 4t, the dimensions of cotter may be calculated.

2.2.5.1 Reasons for Taper Provided on Cotter

Question

1. Why taper is provided to cotter ?   **(S-13)**

- Cotter is a flat wedge shape piece of rectangular cross-section and its width is tapered (either on one side or both sides) from one end to another.

- Reasons for providing taper are,

    (a) It helps the easy removal.

    (b) Due to it, cotter remains in its position.

    (c) It provides maximum friction area.

- Taper provided is usually between 1 in 48 to 1 in 24. Higher taper than this increases the risk of slipping back.

- Usually taper is provided only on one side, as machining taper on both sides is rather difficult.

- Also, taper provided is usually small, so that, self locking can be achieved. If taper is more and joint is subjected to variable loading, then, the cotter may be provided with some locking arrangement, so as to keep it in position.

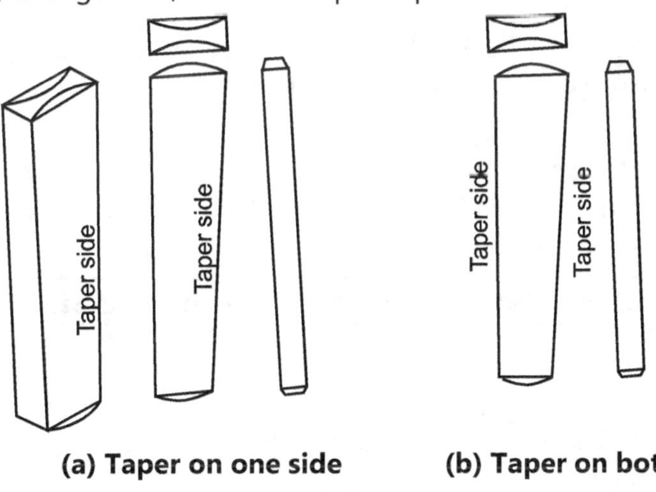

(a) Taper on one side   **(b) Taper on both sides**

Fig. 2.22

2.2.5.2 Difference between Cotter and Key

Key	Cotter
(1) Key is driven parallel to the axis of shafts.	(1) Cotter is normally driven at right angle to the axis of connected parts.
(2) Key is subjected to torsional shear stress and crushing stress.	(2) Cotter is subjected to crushing stress and shear stress.
(3) Key resists shear over longitudinal section.	(3) Cotter resists shear over transverse sections.

2.2.5.3 Purpose of Providing Clearance in Cotter Joint

- A clearance of 2 to 3 mm is provided between the slots and cotter.
- When cotter is driven in slots, the two rods are drawn together, until the spigot rests on the socket collar.

2.3 KNUCKLE JOINT

2.3.1 Introduction

- A knuckle joint is used to connect two circular rods, which are under action of tensile loads. A knuckle joint may be easily disconnected for adjustments or repairs.
- In knuckle joint, one end of one rod is made into shape of an eye and the end of the other rod is formed into shape of a fork with an eye in each of the fork leg. The knuckle pin passes through both the eye hole and the fork holes and may be secured by means of collar and taper pin as split pin.
- It allows relative angular movement of the rod in the plane about axis of pin.

2.3.2 Applications

Question

1. State four applications of knuckle joint.   **(W-09, 10)**

   (i) Used to connect links and structural members.

   (ii) Air brake arrangement on locomotive.

   (iii) Connections of valve rods and eccentric rods.

   (iv) Reversing gear mechanism in case of steam locomotives.

   (v) Remote controls of steam valves etc.

2.3.3 Advantages of Knuckle Joint

(i) Simple to design.

(ii) Easy to manufacture.

(iii) Due to less number of parts, the cost of the joint is less.

(iv) Reliability of the joint is high.

(v) Quick assembly or dismantling.

2.3.4 Design Procedure of Kunckle Joint

Questions

1. Draw neat sketch of knuckle joint and state its strength equations with failure diagram in tabular form. **(W-09, 11; S-10)**
2. Explain various failures to be considered in designing a knuckle joint along with necessary sketches and strength equations. **(W-12)**
3. Explain design procedure of knuckle joint with neat sketch . **(S-13)**

- Knuckle joint is used to connect two rods, which are under the action of tensile load. The rods may have their ends either coincide, or intersect and lie in one plane.
- It allows relative angular movement of the rods in plane about axis of pin.

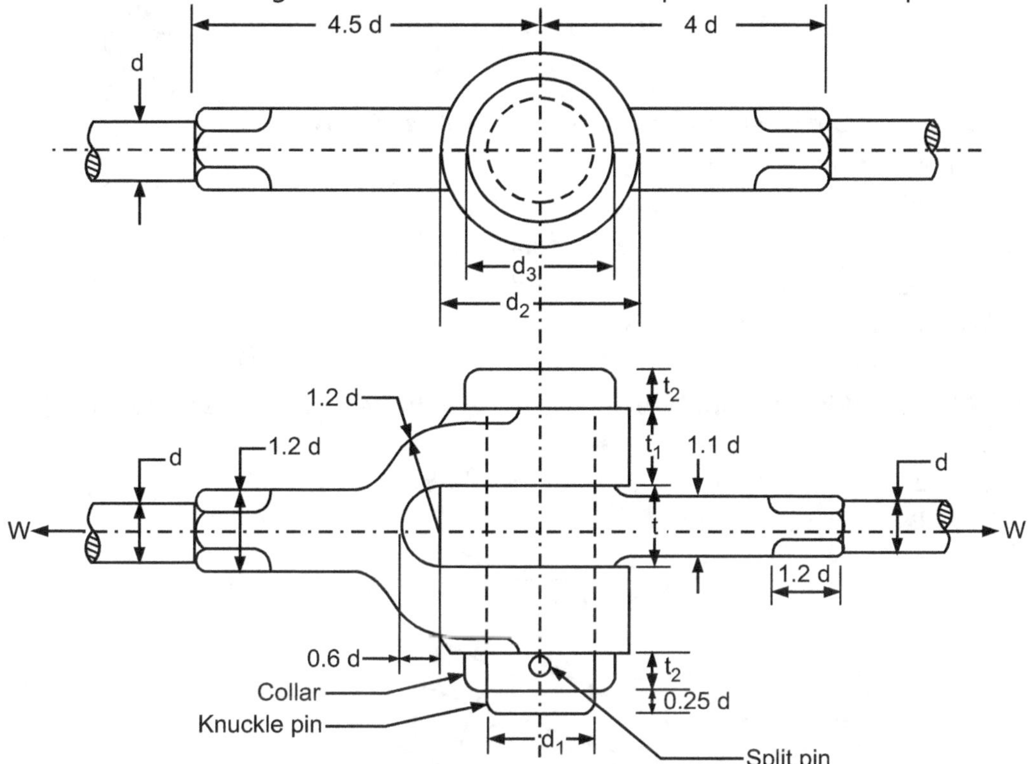

Fig. 2.23 : Knuckle joint

Let　　　　W = load carried by the rods,　τ = Permissible shear stress

　　　　σ_t = Permissible tensile stress　σ_{ck} = Permissible crushing stress

Step I : Failure of rod in tension : The rod may fail in tension due to tensile load W.

We know that, Area resisting tearing $= \dfrac{\pi}{4} \times (d)^2$

Considering tensile failure, $\sigma_t = \dfrac{W}{\dfrac{\pi}{4} \cdot d^2}$

Hence, value of d can be determined.

Step II (a) : Diameter of knuckle pin considering double shearing of knuckle pin :

Resisting area, $\qquad A = 2 \times \dfrac{\pi}{4} \cdot d_1^2$

Considering shear failure of pin,

$$\tau = \frac{W}{2 \times \dfrac{\pi}{4} \cdot d_1^2}$$

Here, value of d_1 can be found.

Value of d_1 should be kept minimum and equal to d for safe design.

$\therefore \qquad$ Use, $d_1 = d$

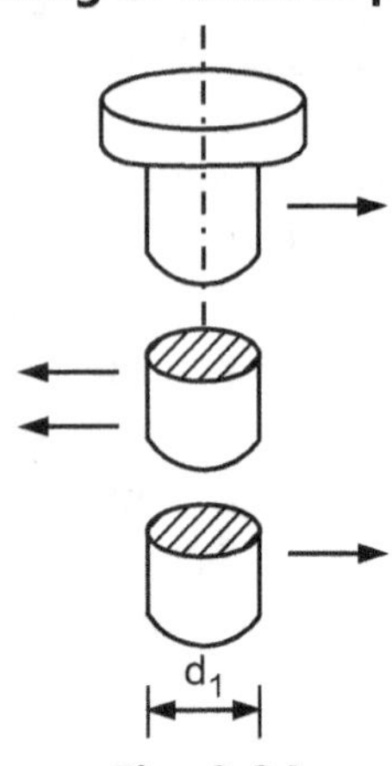

Fig. 2.24

Step II (b) : Fix the dimensions using empirical relations :

Diameter of pin $= d_1 = d$

Outer diameter of single or double eye $= d_2 = 2d$

Diameter of knuckle pin head and collar $= d_3 = 1.5\,d$

Thickness of single eye $= t = 1.25 \times d$

Thickness of fork $= t_1 = 0.75 \times d$

Thickness of collar pin $= t_2 = 0.5 \times d$

Step III : Checking the failure of single eye in tension across the slot (weakest section) :

Area resisting tearing of single eye across the slot $= (d_2 - d_1) \times t$

$\therefore$ Considering tensile failure,

$$\sigma_t = \frac{W}{(d_2 - d_1) \times t}$$

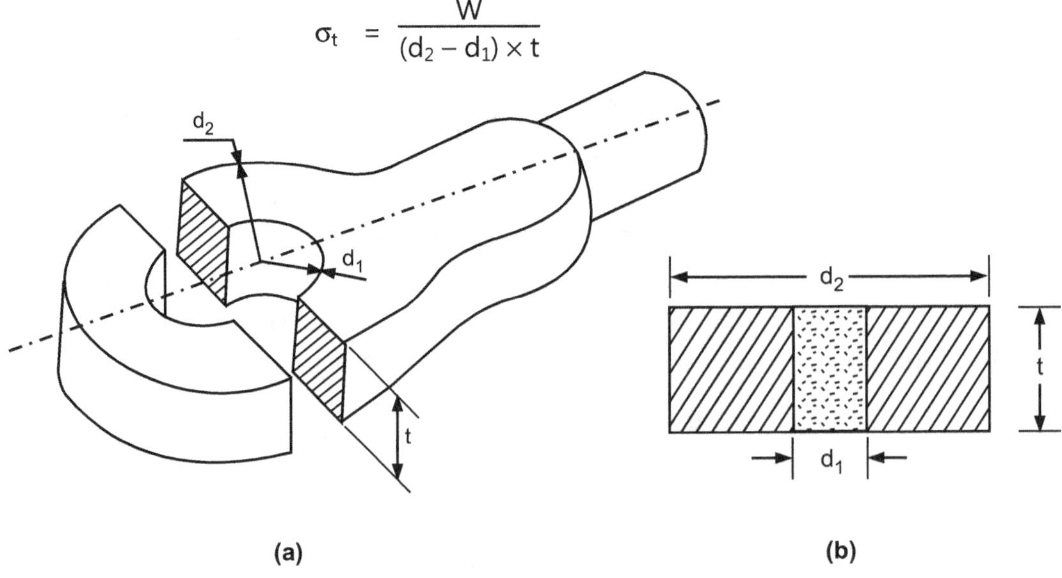

(a)   (b)

Fig. 2.25

Step IV : Checking the failure of single eye for crushing stress : Checking for safe crushing, included crushing stress should not exceed permissible stress.

∴　Area resisting crushing single eye $= t \times d_1$

∴　Induced crushing stress,

$$\sigma_{ck} \;=\; \frac{W}{t \times d_1}$$

Step V : Checking the failure of single eye in shear :

Area-resisting shear of single eye $= 2 \times \left(\dfrac{d_2 - d_1}{2}\right) \cdot t = (d_2 - d_1) \cdot t$

Considering shear failure,

Induced shear stress, $\tau \;=\; \dfrac{W}{(d_2 - d_1) \cdot t}$

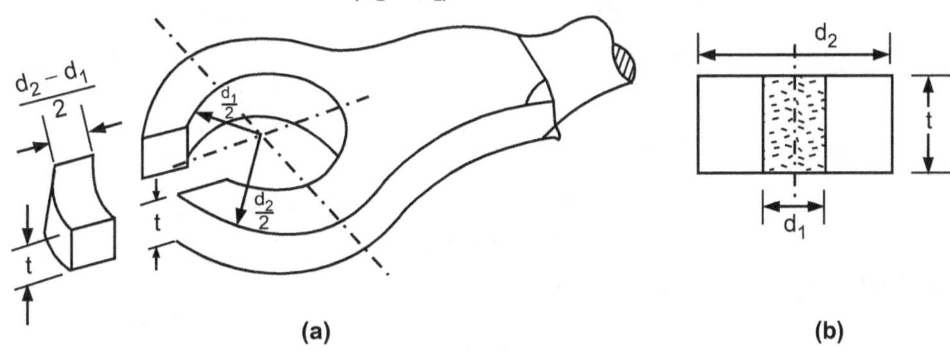

(a)　　　　　　　　　　　　　　　　　　(b)

Fig. 2.26

Step VI : Checking the failure of fork end in tension across the slot :

Area resisting tearing of spigot across the slot $= 2 \times (d_2 - d_1) \cdot t_1$

Considering tensile failure,

Induced tensile stress, $\sigma_t \;=\; \dfrac{W}{2 \times (d_2 - d_1) \cdot t_1}$

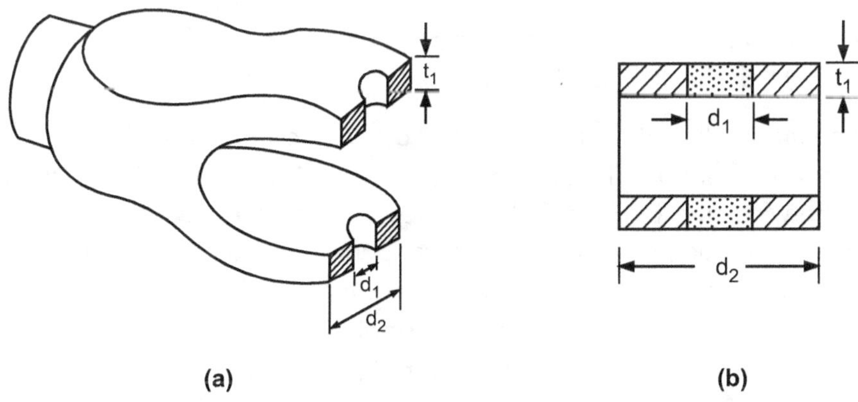

(a)　　　　　　　　　　　　　　　　　　(b)

Fig. 2.27

Step VII : Checking the failure of fork end in crushing : Checking for safe crushing, induced crushing stress should not exceed permissible crushing stress.

$\therefore$ Area resisting crushing of fork end $= 2 \times t_1 \cdot d_1$

$\therefore$ Considering crushing failure,

$$\text{Induced crushing stress, } \sigma_{ck} = \frac{W}{2 \times t_1 \cdot d_1}$$

Step VIII : Checking the failure of fork end in shearing :

Area-resisting shear of fork end $= 2 \times (d_2 - d_1) \times t_1$

$\therefore$ Considering shear failure,

$$\text{Induced shear stress, } \tau = \frac{W}{2 \times (d_2 - d_1) \times t_1}$$

Step IX : Checking the failure of knuckle pin in shear : Cotter is in double shear as shown in Fig. 2.28.

$$\therefore \qquad \text{Area resisting shear} = 2 \times \frac{\pi}{4} \cdot d_1^2$$

$$\text{Induced shear stress, } \qquad \tau = \frac{W}{2 \times \frac{\pi}{4} \cdot d_1^2}$$

Here, it can be checked, whether induced shear stress is less than permissible value or not.

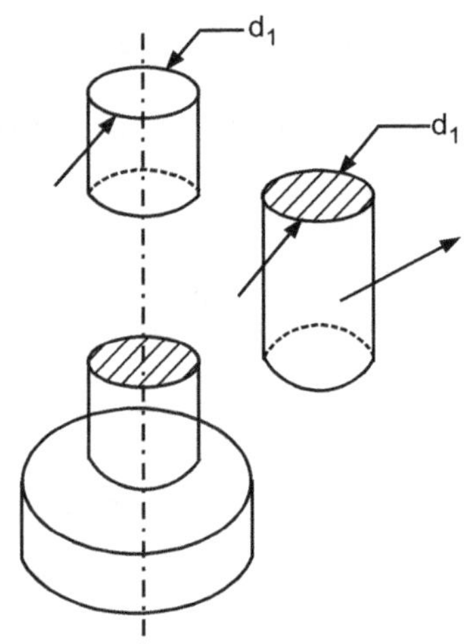

Fig. 2.28

2.3.5 Modes of Failure in Knuckle Pin

Question

1.   Explain with neat sketch, what are the modes of failure in the knuckle pin ?   **(S-12)**

(1) Failure of knuckle pin in shear : As the knuckle pin is in double shear, therefore cross-sectional area of pin under shearing $= 2 \times \frac{\pi}{4} \times (d_1)^2$.

$$\therefore \quad \text{Shear stress induced, } \tau = \frac{W}{2 \times \frac{\pi}{4} \times (d_1)^2}$$

From this equation, diameter of knuckle pin (d_1) can be obtained.

(2) In the above equation of designing knuckle pin, it is assumed that, there is no slack and clearance between the pin and fork and hence there is no bending of the pin. But, in actual practice, the knuckle pin is loose in forks to permit angular movement.

Therefore, the pin is subjected to bending, in addition to shearing.

Let t = thickness of single eye

t_1 = thickness of forks

If bending is taken into account, it is assumed that, the load on the pin is uniformly distributed in the middle portion (i.e. eye end) and varies uniformly over the forks.

Refer the Fig. 2.29. Maximum bending moment will be induced at the centre of the pin. It is given by,

$$M = \frac{W}{2} \times \left(\frac{t_1}{3} + \frac{t}{2}\right) - \frac{W}{2} \times \left(\frac{t}{4}\right) = \frac{W}{2} \times \left[\frac{t_1}{3} + \frac{t}{2} - \frac{t}{4}\right] = \frac{W}{2}\left[\frac{t_1}{3} + \frac{t}{4}\right]$$

Also,   Section modulus, $Z = \dfrac{\pi}{32} d_1^3$

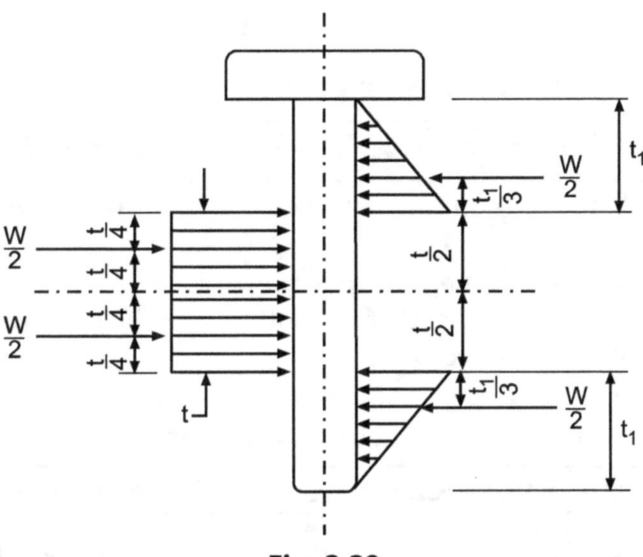

Fig. 2.29

∴   Maximum bending stress is given by

$$\sigma_b = \frac{M}{Z} = \frac{\dfrac{W}{2}\left[\dfrac{t_1}{3} + \dfrac{t}{4}\right]}{\dfrac{\pi}{32} d_1^3}$$

From this expression, value of d_1 may be obtained.

2.3.6 Reasons for Designing Knuckle Pin with Bearing Consideration

- Pin is designed on the basis of shearing consideration.
- From the figure, it can be seen that the knuckle pin is pressed against the eye and hole of fork.
- But as knuckle joint is not a rigid joint, instead, it is a flexible joint. It permits angular movement between the rods, as the knuckle pin is loose in forks. Also, it provides some turning movement of the fork and eye about the pin. Therefore, there is friction between the pin and the fork.
- Thus, the pin is subjected to bearing pressure. Therefore, knuckle pin is also designed considering bearing pressure.

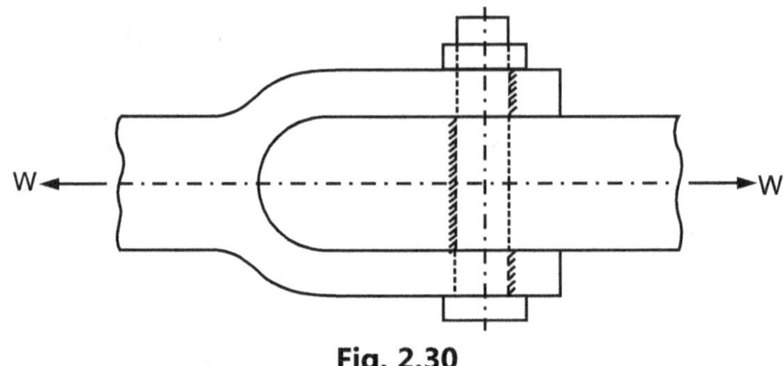

Fig. 2.30

2.3.7 Function of Split Pin in Knuckle Joint (S-13)

- Split pin (also known as cotter pin), is metal fastener having two tines, that are bent during installation.
- In knuckle joint, after inserting the knuckle pin into eye, the split pin is pushed into the hole of knuckle pin provided at the bottom and the two tines are bent, so that, it works as fastener of locking device.
- Its working is similar to a stapler or lever.
- It is made up of thick wire half circular cross-section.

2.3.8 Difference between Cotter Joint and Knuckle Joint

Cotter Joint	Knuckle Joint
1. Capable of taking both tensile/ compressive load.	1. Can take only tensile load.
2. Cannot permit angular movement between rods.	2. Can permit limited angular movement between rods.
3. Cotter is not subjected to bearing failure.	3. Knuckle pin is subjected to bearing failure.
4. Since there is no forked end, it is not known as forked pin joint.	4. It is known as forked pin joint.
5. Taper and clearance is provided in the cotter.	5. No taper or clearance is provided.
6. Cotter is rectangular in section.	6. Knuckle pin is circular in section.
Applications :	**Applications :**
(a) Cotter foundation bolt.	(a) Tie bar and roof truss.
(b) Big end of the connecting rod of a steam engine.	(b) Links of suspension bridge.
(c) Joining piston rod with cross-head.	(c) Valve mechanism.
(d) Joining two rods with a pipe.	(d) Fulcrum of the lever.
	(e) Links of bicycle chain.
	(f) Joint for rail shifting mechanism.

Numerical Type No. 2 : "Kunckle Joint"

Problem 2.3 : *A knuckle joint is to withstand a load of 30 kN. Design the joint, if permissible stresses are, σ_t = 56 N/mm², τ = 35 N/mm² and σ_{ck} = 70 N/mm².*

Solution : Given data : W = load carried by the rods = 30 kN = 30×10^3 N

σ_t = 56 N/mm², τ = 35 N/mm² and σ_{ck} = 70 N/mm².

Step I : Failure of rod in tension : The rod may fail in tension due to tensile load W.

We know that, Area resisting tearing $= \dfrac{\pi}{4} \times (d)^2$

Considering tearing failure in rod, we have,

$$\sigma_t = \frac{W}{\frac{\pi}{4} \times (d)^2}$$

$$\therefore \quad 56 = \frac{30 \times 10^3}{\frac{\pi}{4} \times (d)^2}$$

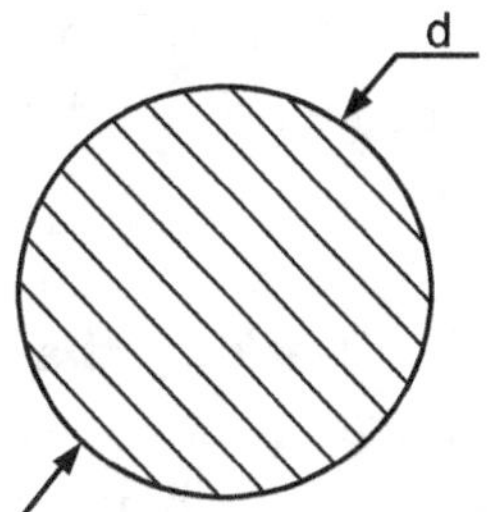

Fig. 2.31

$$\therefore \quad d = \textbf{26.11 mm} \cong \textbf{28 mm}$$

Hence, value of d can be determined.

Step II (a) : Diameter of pin considering shearing of pin :

$$\text{Resisting area} = 2 \times \frac{\pi}{4} \cdot d_1^2$$

$\therefore$ Considering shear failure,

$$\tau = \frac{W}{2 \times \frac{\pi}{4} \cdot d_1^2}$$

$$\therefore \quad 35 = \frac{30 \times 10^3}{2 \times \frac{\pi}{4} \cdot d_1^2}$$

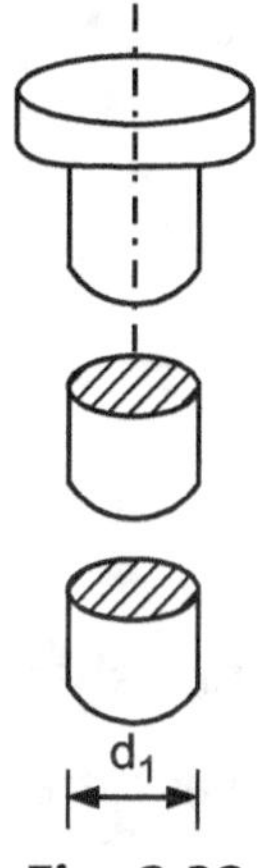

Fig. 2.32

$$\therefore \quad d_1 = \textbf{23.35 mm}$$

This diameter is also to be calculated using empirical relation in step II (b) for more safer design.

Step II (b) : Fix the dimensions using empirical relations :

Diameter of pin = d_1 = d = **28 mm**

Outer diameter of single or double eye = d_2 = 2d = 2 × 28 = **56 mm**

Diameter of knuckle pin head and collar = d_3 = 1.5d = 1.5 × 28 = **42 mm**

Thickness of single eye = t = 1.25 × d = 1.25 × 28 = **35 mm**

Thickness of fork = t_1 = 0.75 × d = 0.75 × 28 = **21 mm**

Thickness of single eye = t_2 = 0.5 × d = 0.5 × 28 = **14 mm**

Step III : Checking the failure of single eye in tension across the slot (weakest section) :

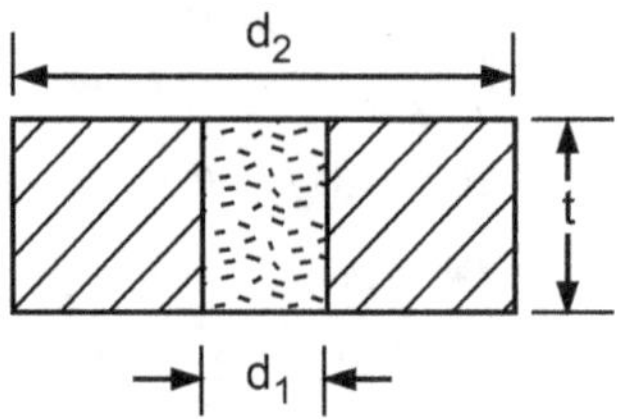

Fig. 2.33

Area resisting tearing of single eye across the slot $= (d_2 - d_1) \times t$

Induced tensile stress,

$$\sigma_t = \frac{W}{(d_2 - d_1) \times t} = \frac{30 \times 10^3}{(56 - 28) \times 35} = 30.61 \text{ N/mm}^2 < 56 \text{ N/mm}^2$$

Step IV : Checking the failure of single eye for crushing stress : Checking for safe crushing, induced crushing stress should not exceed permissible crushing stress.

Area resisting crushing of single eye $= t \times d_1$

∴   Induced crushing stress,

$$\sigma_{ck} = \frac{W}{t \times d_1} = \frac{30 \times 10^3}{35 \times 28} = 30.61 \text{ N/mm}^2 < 70 \text{ N/mm}^2$$

Step V : Checking the failure of single eye in shear :

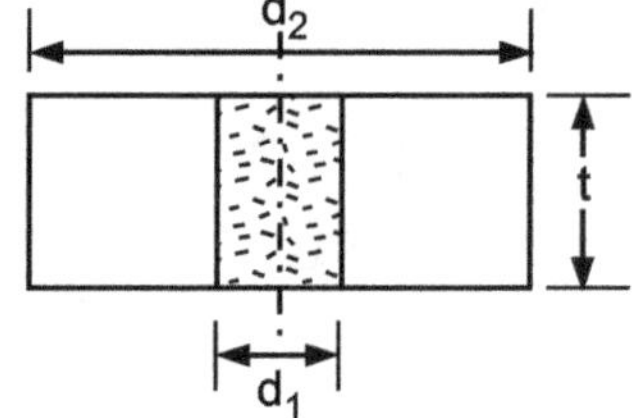

Fig. 2.34

Area resisting shear of single eye $= 2 \times \left(\frac{d_2 - d_1}{2}\right) \cdot t = (d_2 - d_1) \times t$

∴   Induced shear stress,

$$\tau = \frac{W}{(d_2 - d_1) \times t} = \frac{30 \times 10^3}{(56 - 28) \times 35} = 30.61 \text{ N/mm}^2 < 35 \text{ N/mm}^2$$

Step VI : Checking the failure of fork end in tension across the slot :

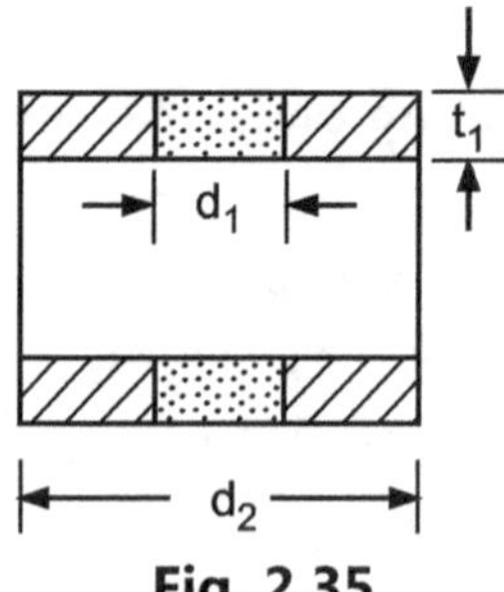

Fig. 2.35

Area resisting tearing of spigot across the slot $= 2 \times (d_2 - d_1) \times t_1$

∴ Induced tensile stress,

$$\sigma_t = \frac{W}{2 \times (d_2 - d_1) \times t_1} = \frac{30 \times 10^3}{2 \times (56 - 28) \times 21} = \mathbf{25.51\ N/mm^2} < \mathbf{56\ N/mm^2}$$

Step VII : Checking the failure of fork end in crushing : Checking for safe crushing, induced crushing stress should not exceed permissible crushing stress.

Area resisting crushing of fork end $= 2 \times t_1 \times d_1$

∴ Induced crushing stress,

$$\sigma_{ck} = \frac{W}{2 \times t_1 \times d_1} = \frac{30 \times 10^3}{2 \times 21 \times 28} = \mathbf{25.51\ N/mm^2} < \mathbf{70\ N/mm^2}$$

Step VIII : Checking the failure of fork end in shearing :

Area resisting shear of fork end $= 2 \times (d_2 - d_1) \times t_1$

∴ Induced shear stress,

$$\tau = \frac{W}{2 \times (d_2 - d_1) \times t_1} = \frac{30 \times 10^3}{2 \times (56 - 28) \times 21} = \mathbf{25.51\ N/mm^2} < \mathbf{35\ N/mm^2}$$

Step IX : Checking the failure of knuckle pin in shear : Knuckle pin is in double shear.

∴   Area resisting shear $= 2 \times \frac{\pi}{4} \cdot (d_1)^2$

∴   Induced shear stress, $\tau = \dfrac{W}{2 \times \frac{\pi}{4} \cdot (d_1)^2} = \dfrac{30 \times 10^3}{2 \times \frac{\pi}{4} \times (28)^2} = \mathbf{24.36\ N/mm^2} < \mathbf{35\ N/mm^2}$

As all the induced stresses are within permissible limits, hence the design is safe.

2.4 TURN BUCKLE

2.4.1 Introduction

- Turn buckle is an adjustable screwed joint used to connect two round tie rods.

- Two round tie rods are connected by means of a coupling known as a turnbuckle. In this type of joint, one of the rods has right hand threads and the other rod has left hand threads. The rods are screwed to a coupler, which has a threaded hole.

- The two threaded rods are under the action of tensile load.

- When the coupler is given a revolution, the ends of the rods either approach or recede from each other.

- The coupler is of hexagonal or rectangular shape in centre and round at both the ends to facilitate the rods to be loosen or tighten with the help of spanner (or rod) when needed.

- The turn buckle is made hollow in the middle to reduce its weight.

2.4.2 Purpose or Applications of Turn Buckle or Coupler

Questions

1. Explain the purpose of turn buckle. Explain its design procedure.   **(W-10)**
2. Give two applications of knuckle joint.   **(W-12)**

(i)   It is used to connect two tie rods and act as a coupling.

(ii) Due to coupler nut, it facilitates the rods to tighten or loosen with the help of spanner, when required.

(iii) It is used to couple two railway wagons.

(iv) It is used to connect links in mechanisms to transfer motion.

(v)   It is used to connect structural members like roof trusses.

2.4.3 Design Procedure of Turn Buckle

Questions

1. Draw a neat sketch of turn buckle and write the design procedure.   **(S-12)**
2. Write strength equations considered in design of turn buckle with neat sketch.   **(W-13)**

Design of Turn Buckle or Adjustable Screwed Joint for Round Ends :

Let, W = design load = $1.3 \times$ load carried by the rods

τ = Permissible shear stress

σ_t = Permissible tensile stress

σ_{ck} = Permissible crushing stress

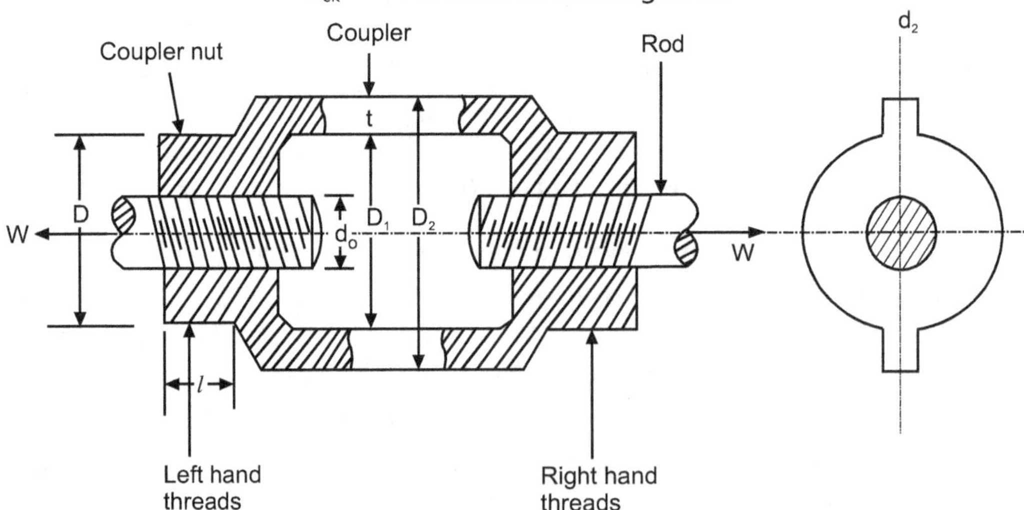

Fig. 2.36 : Turnbuckle or coupler

Step I : Failure of rod in tension : The rod may fail in tension due to tensile load W.

We know that, Area resisting tearing $= \dfrac{\pi}{4} \cdot d_c^2$

Considering tensile stress, $\quad \sigma_t = \dfrac{W}{\dfrac{\pi}{4} \cdot d_c^2}$

Hence, value of d_c can be determined.

From the standard table of square threads (Refer Appendix A) values of nominal diameter (d_o) and pitch (p) can be determined.

Step II : Considering the shear failure of threads at their roots :

Area-resisting shear $= \pi \cdot d_c \cdot l$

$\therefore \qquad$ Shear stress $= \tau = \dfrac{W}{\pi \cdot d_c \cdot l}$

Here, the value of 'l', i.e. length of coupler nut can be determined.

But in actual practice, length of coupler nut (l) can be taken as d_o to $1.25 d_o$ for steel and $1.5 d_o$ to $2 d_o$ for cast iron.

Step III : Checking the crushing stress induced in threads : Checking for safe crushing, induced crushing stress should not exceed permissible crushing stress.

Area resisting crushing of fork end $= \dfrac{\pi}{4} \times (d_o^2 - d_c^2) \times n \times l$

where, $\qquad\qquad n =$ number of threads per mm of length $= \dfrac{1}{\text{pitch}}$

$\therefore$ Crushing stress, $\quad \sigma_{ck} = \dfrac{W}{\dfrac{\pi}{4} \times (d_o^2 - d_c^2) \times n \times l}$

Step IV : Considering the tensile failure of coupler nut : Diameter (D) of coupler nut is found by considering tensile failure,

$$\sigma_t = \dfrac{W}{\dfrac{\pi}{4} (D^2 - d_o^2)}$$

Diameter of coupler nut is taken from $1.25\ d_o$ to $1.5\ d_o$.

Step V : Considering tensile failure of coupler : Outer diameter (D_2) of coupler is found by considering tensile failure of coupler,

$$\sigma_t = \dfrac{W}{\dfrac{\pi}{4} (D_2^2 - D_1^2)}$$

where, inside diameter of coupler $= D_1 = d_o + (6\text{ to }8\text{ mm})$

From the above equation, value of D_2 can be calculated.

In practice, the outside diameter of coupler (D_2) is taken as $1.5\ d_o$ to $1.7\ d_o$.

Also, Length of coupler $= 6\ d_o$ and thickness of coupler $= t = 0.75\ d_o$

Numerical Type No. 3 : "Turn Buckle"

Problem 2.4 : *The pull in the tie rod of an iron roof truss is 50 kN. Design a suitable adjustable screwed joint. The permissible stresses are 75 N/mm^2 in tension, 37.5 N/mm^2 in shear and 90 N/mm^2 in crushing.*

Solution : Given data : W_1 = load carried by the rods = 50 kN = 50×10^3 N

Let W = design load = 1.3 × load carried by the rods

$$= 1.3 \times W_1 = 1.3 \times 50 \times 10^3 = 65 \times 10^3 \text{ N}$$

σ_t = Permissible tensile stress = 75 N/mm^2

τ = Permissible shear stress = 37.5 N/mm^2

σ_{ck} = Permissible crushing stress = 90 N/mm^2

Step I : Failure of rod in tension : The rod may fail in tension due to tensile load W.

We know that, Area resisting tearing = $\dfrac{\pi}{4} \cdot (d_c)^2$

Considering tensile failure in rod,

$$\sigma_t = \frac{W}{\dfrac{\pi}{4} \times (d_c)^2}$$

$$\therefore \quad 75 = \frac{65 \times 10^3}{\dfrac{\pi}{4} \times (d_c)^2}$$

$$\therefore \quad d_c = \mathbf{33.21 \text{ mm}}$$

From the standard table of square threads, value of nominal diameter d_o and pitch can be determined.

$$d_o = \mathbf{42 \text{ mm}} \text{ and pitch} = p = \mathbf{7 \text{ mm}}$$

Therefore, $d_c = d_o - p = 42 - 7 = 35$ mm.

Refer appendix A of standard table for "square threads" at the end of text book.

Step II : Considering the shear failure of threads at their roots :

Area resisting shear = $\pi \times d_c \times l = \pi \times 35 \times l$

Considering shear failure,

$$\tau = \frac{W}{\pi \times 35 \times l}$$

$$\therefore \quad 37.5 = \frac{65 \times 10^3}{\pi \times 35 \times l}$$

$$\therefore \quad l = \mathbf{15.76 \text{ mm}}$$

But in actual practice, Length of coupler nut (l) can be taken as d_o to 1.25 d_o for steel.

$$\therefore \quad l = 1.25 \, d_o = 1.25 \times 42 = \mathbf{52.5 \text{ mm}}$$

Step III : Checking the crushing stress induced in threads : Checking for safe crushing, induced crushing stress should not exceed permissible crushing stress.

Area resisting crushing of fork end $= \dfrac{\pi}{4} \times (d_o^2 - d_c^2) \times n \times l$

Where n = number of threads per mm of length $= \dfrac{1}{\text{pitch}} = \dfrac{1}{7} = 0.1428$

Considering crushing failure,

$$\sigma_{ck} = \dfrac{W}{\dfrac{\pi}{4} \times (d_o^2 - d_c^2) \times n \times l} = \dfrac{65 \times 10^3}{\dfrac{\pi}{4} \times (42^2 - 35^2) \times 0.1428 \times 52.5} = \mathbf{20.48 \ N/mm^2} < \mathbf{90 \ N/mm^2}$$

∴   Induced crushing stress is less than permissible crushing stress. Hence, design is safe.

Step IV : Considering the tensile failure of coupler nut : Outside diameter (D) of coupler nut is found by considering tensile failure,

$$\sigma_t = \dfrac{W}{\dfrac{\pi}{4}(D^2 - d_o^2)}$$

∴ $\qquad D^2 = d_o^2 + \dfrac{W \times 4}{\sigma_t \times \pi} = 42^2 + \dfrac{65 \times 10^3 \times 4}{75 \times \pi} = 2867.47$

∴ $\qquad D = \mathbf{53.54 \ mm} \cong \mathbf{54 \ mm}$

Step V : Considering tensile failure of coupler : Outer diameter (D_2) of coupler is found by considering tensile failure of coupler.

$$\sigma_t = \dfrac{W}{\dfrac{\pi}{4}(D_2^2 - D_1^2)}$$

where, inside diameter of coupler $= D_1 = d_o + 6 = 42 + 6 = 48$ mm

∴ $\qquad D_2^2 = D_1^2 + \dfrac{W \times 4}{\sigma_t \times \pi} = 48^2 + \dfrac{65 \times 10^3 \times 4}{75 \times \pi} = 3407.47$

∴ $\qquad D_2 = \mathbf{58.37 \ mm}$

In practice, the outside diameter of coupler is taken as 1.5 d_o to 1.7 d_o.

∴ $\qquad D_2 = 1.7 \ d_o = 1.7 \times 42 = \mathbf{71.4 \ mm}$

Length of coupler $= 6 \ d_o = 6 \times 42 = \mathbf{252 \ mm}$

Thickness of coupler $= t = 0.75 \ d_o = 0.75 \times 42 = \mathbf{31.5 \ mm}$

2.5 LEVERS

2.5.1 Introduction to Levers

- A lever is a rigid rod or bar capable of turning about a fixed point called *fulcrum*. It is used as a mechanism to lift a load by the application of small effort.

- The ratio of load lifted to the effort applied is called mechanical advantage.

- Sometimes, a lever is used to apply force in a desired direction. A lever may be straight or curved and force applied on the lever may be parallel or inclined to one another. Lever works on the principle of moments.

- Consider a straight lever with parallel forces acting in the same plane as shown in Fig. 2.37. The points A and B, through which, the load and effort is applied, are known as load and effort points respectively. F is the fulcrum, about which, the lever is capable of turning.

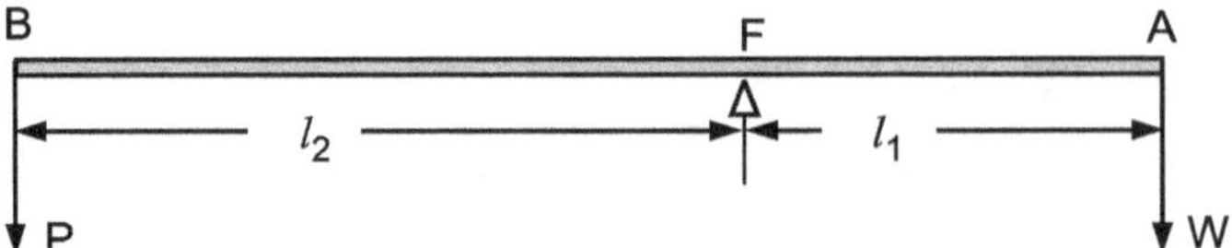

Fig. 2.37

- The perpendicular distance between the load point and fulcrum is known as *load arm* (l_1) and the perpendicular distance between the effort point and fulcrum is known as *effort arm* (l_2).
- Taking algebraic sum of moments of all forces about fulcrum and equating it to zero,

$$W \times l_1 = P \times l_2$$

$$\therefore \quad \frac{W}{P} = \frac{l_2}{l_1} = \text{Mechanical advantage}$$

$$\therefore \quad \text{M.A.} = \frac{W}{P} = \frac{l_2}{l_1}$$

2.5.1.1 Leverage

- Leverage is defined as *'the ratio of effort arm to the load arm'*, i.e. $\frac{l_2}{l_1}$. In order to lift a large load by small effort, the effort arm must be greater (longer) than the load arm.

2.5.1.2 Why Levers are Tapered at the Ends ? (S-08)

- Levers are subjected to bending moment and this bending moment is directly proportional to the distance of the load from the point, about which, bending moment takes place.
- Bending moment is zero at the point of application of load.
- So the resisting area at this point is minimum and maximum, where the bending takes place. So levers are tapered to avoid stress concentration.

2.5.2 Design Procedure of Hand Lever

Questions

1. Explain the design procedure of hand lever with suitable sketch. (W-12; S-14)
2. Draw a neat labelled diagram of hand lever and state how diameter of shaft and boss is calculated. (S-13)

Let,
$$P = \text{Force applied at the handle.}$$
$$L = \text{Effective length of lever.}$$
$$d = \text{Diameter of shaft.}$$
$$d_1 = \text{Diameter of shaft at centre of bearing.}$$
$$d_2 = \text{Diameter of boss.}$$

$$l_2 = \text{Length of boss.}$$
$$l_1 = \text{Length of key.}$$
$$l = \text{Overhang distance of bearing from the lever.}$$

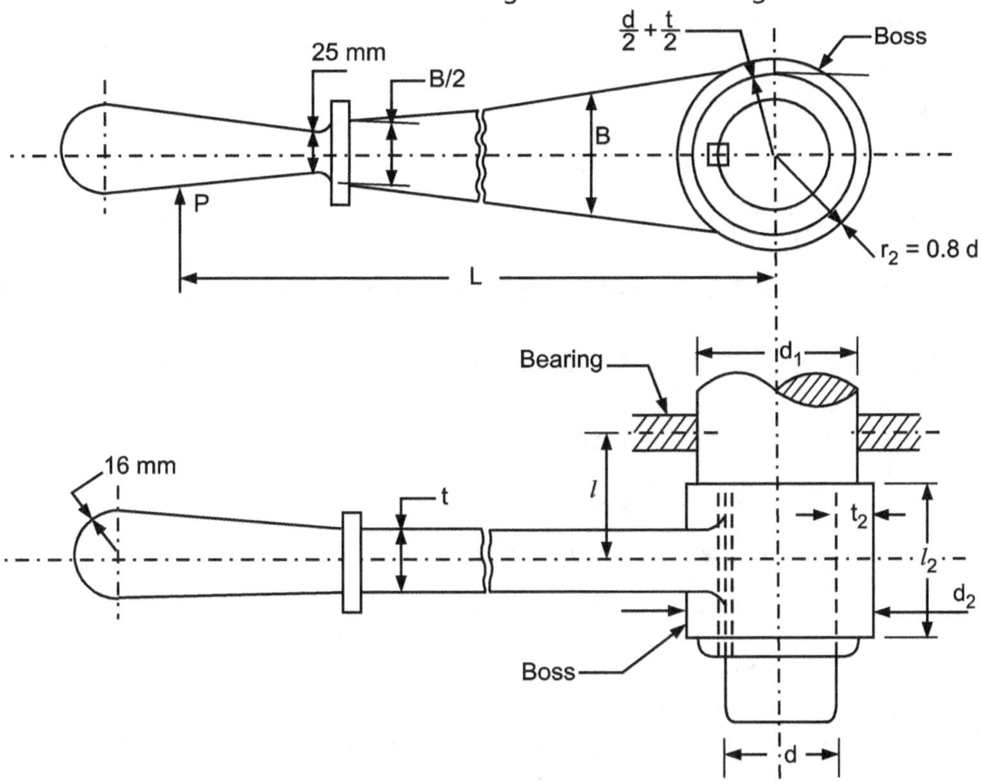

Fig. 2.38 : Hand lever

Step I : Considering shaft under pure torsion, we have,

$$T = \frac{\pi}{16} \cdot \tau \cdot d^3$$

But, twisting moment on shaft,

$$T = P \times L$$

∴   On equating, we have,

$$P \times L = \frac{\pi}{16} \cdot \tau \cdot d^3$$

∴   Diameter of shaft (d) may be obtained.

Step II : Using the empirical relations, fix the other dimensions as,

$$d_2 = 1.6d$$
$$t_2 = 0.3d$$
$$l_2 = d \text{ to } 1.2d$$
$$l = 2 \times l_2$$

Step III : Considering the shaft supported at the centre of the bearing under combined twisting and bending moment, we have,

$$M = P \times l \text{ and } T = P \times L$$

∴   Equivalent twisting moment,

$$T_e = \sqrt{M^2 + T^2} = \sqrt{(P \times l)^2 + (P \times L)^2} = P\sqrt{l^2 + L^2}$$

Also, equivalent twisting moment,

$$T_e = \frac{\pi}{16} \cdot \tau_{max} \cdot d_1^3$$

∴

$$P\sqrt{l^2 + L^2} = \frac{\pi}{16} \cdot \tau_{max} \cdot d_1^3$$

From here, value of d_1 = diameter of shaft supported at centre of bearings can be determined.

Step IV : Design of key : Let t_1 = thickness of key, w = width of key and l_1 = length of key.

After finding diameter of shaft (d), we can fix the dimensions for key as,

$$w = \frac{d}{4} \text{ and } t_1 = \frac{d}{6}$$

Considering shear failure of key,

We have,

$$T = (w \cdot l_1 \cdot \tau) \times \frac{d}{2}$$

∴   Length l_1 can be determined.

Also, length l_1 may be taken as length of boss i.e. l_2.

Step V : Considering bending failure of lever, we can determine the cross-section of lever near the boss.

Let t = thickness of lever near the boss and B = width or height of lever near the boss.

We have,

Bending moment on the lever = $M = P \times (L - r_b)$ and Section modulus = $Z = \frac{1}{6} \cdot t \cdot B^2$

where, r_b = Radius of boss = $\dfrac{d_2}{2}$

∴   Bending stress, $\sigma_b = \dfrac{M}{Z} = \dfrac{P \cdot (L - r_b)}{\frac{1}{6} \cdot tB^2}$

Width of lever may be taken as, B = 4t to 5t.

From this equation, values of t and B can be determined.

Numerical Type No. 4 : "Hand Lever"

Problem 2.5 : *A hand lever is 800 mm long from the centre of gravity of the spindle to the point of application of pull of 300 N. The effective overhang from the nearest bearing is 100 mm. If the permissible stresses in tension, shear and crushing are not to exceed are 66 N/mm² each, design the spindle, key, lever and boss. Assume the arm of lever to be rectangular having width as twice of thickness.* **(S-09)**

Solution : Given data : $L = 800$ mm, $P = 300$ N, $l = 100$ mm, $\sigma_t = \sigma_c = \tau = 66$ N/mm^2, $B = 2t$

Procedure for Designing a Hand Lever :

Let,

$$
\begin{aligned}
P &= \text{Force applied at the handle.} \\
L &= \text{Effective length of lever.} \\
d &= \text{Diameter of shaft.} \\
d_1 &= \text{Diameter of shaft at centre of bearing.} \\
d_2 &= \text{Diameter of boss.} \\
l_2 &= \text{Length of boss.} \\
l_1 &= \text{Length of key.}
\end{aligned}
$$

Step I : Considering shaft under pure torsion, we have,

$$T = \frac{\pi}{16}\tau \cdot d^3$$

But, twisting moment on shaft,

$$T = P \times L = 300 \times 800 = 240 \times 10^3 \text{ N-mm}$$

$$\therefore \quad 240 \times 10^3 = \frac{\pi}{16} \times 66 \times d^3$$

$$\therefore \quad d = 26.45 \text{ mm} \cong \textbf{28 mm (say)}$$

Step II : Using the empirical relations, fix the other dimensions as,

$$
\begin{aligned}
d_2 &= 1.6d = 1.6 \times 28 = \textbf{44.8 mm} \\
t_2 &= 0.3d = 0.3 \times 28 = \textbf{8.4 mm} \\
l_2 &= 1.25d = 1.25 \times 28 = \textbf{35 mm}
\end{aligned}
$$

Step III : Considering the shaft supported at the centre of the bearings, under the combined twisting and bending moment.

$$M = P \times l = 300 \times 100 = 30 \times 10^3 \text{ N-mm}$$

and

$$T = P \times L = 300 \times 800 = 240 \times 10^3 \text{ N-mm}$$

$\therefore$ Equivalent twisting moment,

$$T_e = \sqrt{M^2 + T^2} = \sqrt{(30 \times 10^3)^2 + (240 \times 10^3)^2}$$
$$= 241.867 \times 10^3 \text{ N.mm}$$

Also,

$$T_e = \left(\frac{\pi}{16}\right)\tau_{max} \cdot d_1^3$$

$$\therefore \quad 241.867 \times 10^3 = \left(\frac{\pi}{16}\right) \times 66 \times d_1^3$$

$$\therefore \quad d_1 = \textbf{26.52 mm}$$

Modifying the diameter of shaft at centre of bearing $= d_1 = \textbf{32 mm (say)}$.

Step IV : Design of key : After finding diameter of shaft (d), we can fix the dimensions for key as,

$$w = \frac{d}{4} = \frac{28}{4} = \textbf{7 mm} \quad \text{and} \quad t_1 = \frac{d}{6} = \frac{28}{6} = \textbf{4.67 mm}$$

Considering shear failure of key, we have,

$$T = (w \cdot l_1 \cdot \tau) \times \frac{d}{2}$$

$$\therefore \qquad 240 \times 10^3 = (7 \times l_1 \times 66) \times \frac{28}{2}$$

$$\therefore \qquad l_1 = \text{length of key} = \mathbf{37.10\ mm} \cong \mathbf{38\ mm\ (say)}$$

$\therefore$ Length of boss may be taken as length l_1 i.e. $l_2 = l_1 = 38$ mm.

Step V : Considering bending failure of lever, we can determine the cross-section of lever.

Let $\qquad\qquad\qquad t$ = thickness of lever near the boss.

and $\qquad\qquad\qquad B$ = width or height of lever near the boss.

We have, bending moment on the lever,

$$M = P \times (L - r_b) = P \times \left(L - \frac{d_2}{2}\right) = 300 \times \left(800 - \frac{44.8}{2}\right)$$

$$= 233.280 \times 10^3 \text{ N-mm}$$

$$\text{and} \qquad Z = \frac{1}{6} \cdot t \cdot B^2 = \frac{1}{6} \cdot t \cdot (2t)^2 = 0.67 \times t^3 \qquad (\because B = 2t)$$

$$\therefore \qquad \text{Bending stress, } \sigma_b = \frac{M}{Z}$$

$$\therefore \qquad 66 = \frac{233.280 \times 10^3}{0.67 \times t^3}$$

$$\therefore \qquad t = 17.407 \text{ mm} \cong \mathbf{18\ mm\ (say)} \text{ and } B = 2t = 2 \times 18 = \mathbf{36\ mm}$$

Problem 2.6 : *A hand lever is connected to the shaft. The length of lever is one metre and a force of 300 N is applied at its end. Determine : (i) The shaft diameter (ii) The dimensions of rectangular cross-section of the lever near the shaft (assume b = 3t). Assume allowable shear stress for shaft as 60 N/mm² and allowable bending stress for lever as 80 N/mm².*

Solution : Given data : $L = 1$ m $= 1000$ mm, $P = 300$ N, $\tau = 60$ N/mm², $\sigma_b = 80$ N/mm², $B = 3t$.

Step I : Considering shaft under pure torsion, we have,

$$T = \frac{\pi}{16} \times \tau \times d^3 = \frac{\pi}{16} \times 60 \times d^3 = 11.78\ d^3$$

But twisting moment on shaft,

$$T = P \times L = 300 \times 1000 = 300 \times 10^3 \text{ N.mm}$$

$$\therefore \qquad 300 \times 10^3 = 11.78\ d^3$$

$$\therefore \qquad d = \mathbf{29.42} \cong \mathbf{30\ mm\ (say)}$$

Step II : Using empirical relation, fix the other dimensions.

$$d_2 = 1.6\ d = 1.6 \times 30 = \mathbf{48\ mm}$$

$$t_2 = 0.3\ d = 0.3 \times 30 = \mathbf{9\ mm}$$

$$l_2 = 1.25\ d = 1.25 \times 30 = \mathbf{37.5\ mm}$$

Step III : Considering bending failure of lever, we can determine the cross-section of lever.

Let, t = Thickness of lever near the boss

B = Width or height of lever near the boss

We have, bending moment on lever,

$$M = P \times [L - r_b] = 300 \times \left[L - \frac{d_2}{2}\right]$$

$$= 300 \times \left[1000 - \frac{48}{2}\right] = 292.8 \times 10^3 \text{ N-mm}$$

and $$Z = \frac{1}{6} t B^2 = \frac{1}{6} \times t \times (3t)^2 = 1.5 \, t^3 \text{ mm}^3 \qquad (\because B = 3t)$$

$\therefore$ Bending stress, $\sigma_b = \dfrac{M}{Z}$

$$80 = \frac{292.8 \times 10^3}{1.5 \, t^3}$$

$$t = \mathbf{13.46} \cong \mathbf{14 \text{ mm (say)}}$$

and $$B = 3t = 3 \times 14 = \mathbf{42 \text{ mm}}$$

2.5.3 Design Procedure of Foot Lever

Let, P = Force applied at the paddle.

L = Effective length of lever.

d = Diameter of shaft.

d_1 = Diameter of shaft at centre of bearing.

d_2 = Diameter of boss.

l_2 = Length of boss.

l_1 = Length of key.

Step I : Considering shaft under pure torsion, we have,

$$T = \frac{\pi}{16} \cdot \tau \, d^3$$

But, twisting moment on shaft,

$$T = P \cdot L$$

$\therefore$ On equating, $$P \times L = \frac{\pi}{16} \cdot \tau \, d^3$$

$\therefore$ Diameter of shaft (d) may be obtained.

Step II : Using the empirical relations, fix the other dimensions,

$$d_2 = 1.6d$$

$$t_2 = 0.3d$$

$$l_2 = d \text{ to } 1.25d$$

$$l = 2 \cdot l_2$$

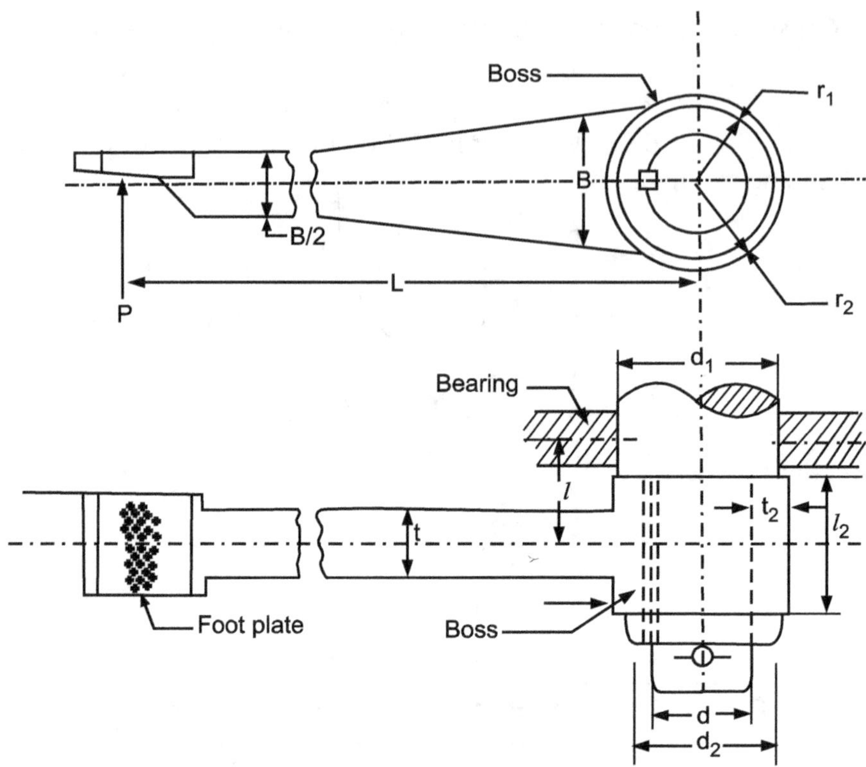

Fig. 2.39 : Foot lever

Step III : Considering the shaft supported at the centre of the bearing under combined twisting and bending moment, we have

$$M = P \cdot l \text{ and } T = P \cdot L$$

∴ Equivalent twisting moment,

$$T_e = \sqrt{M^2 + T^2} = \sqrt{(P \cdot l)^2 + (P \cdot L)^2} = P\sqrt{l^2 + L^2} \qquad \dots (2.1)$$

Also, equivalent twisting moment,

$$T_e = \frac{\pi}{16} \tau_{max} \cdot d_1^3 \qquad \dots (2.2)$$

On equating (2.1) and (2.2),

$$\therefore \qquad P\sqrt{l^2 + L^2} = \frac{\pi}{16} \tau_{max} \cdot d_1^3$$

From here, value d_1 = diameter of shaft supported at the centre of the bending, can be determined.

Step IV : Design of key : Let t_1 = thickness of key, w = width of key and l_1 = length of key.

After finding diameter of shaft (d), we can fix the dimensions for key as,

$$w = \frac{d}{4} \text{ and } t_1 = \frac{d}{6}$$

Considering shear failure of key, we have,

$$T = (w \cdot l_1 \cdot \tau) \times \frac{d}{2}$$

∴ Length l_1 can be determined.

Also, length l_1 may be taken as length of boss i.e. l_2.

Step V : Considering bending failure of lever, we can determine the cross-section of lever near the boss.

Let t = thickness of lever near the boss and B = width or height of lever near the boss.

We have, Bending moment on the lever $= M = P \times \left(L - \dfrac{d_2}{2}\right) = P \cdot (L - r_b)$

and Section modulus $= Z = \dfrac{1}{6} \cdot t \cdot B^2$

We have, $\sigma_b = \dfrac{M}{Z}$

∴ $\sigma_b = \dfrac{P \cdot (L - r_b)}{\left(\dfrac{1}{6}\right) \cdot t \cdot B^2}$

Here, width of lever may be taken as, $B = 4t$ to $5t$ and values of t and hence B can be determined.

Numerical Type No. 5 : "Foot Lever"

Problem 2.7 : *Design a foot brake lever from the following data :*

(i) Length of lever from the centre of gravity of the spindle to the point of application of load = 1 m.

(ii) Maximum load on the foot plate = 800 N

(iii) Overhang from nearest bearing = 100 mm

(iv) Permissible tensile and shear stress = 70 MPa (S-13; W-13)

Solution : Given data : $L = 1$ m $= 1000$ mm, $P = 800$ N, $\sigma_t = 70$ N/mm^2, $\tau = 70$ N/mm^2, $B = 3t$. (Assumed).

Procedure :

Let,
$$\begin{aligned}
P &= \text{Force applied at the paddle} \\
L &= \text{Effective length of lever} \\
d &= \text{Diameter of shaft} \\
d_1 &= \text{Diameter of shaft at centre of bearing} \\
d_2 &= \text{Diameter of boss} \\
l_2 &= \text{Length of boss} \\
l_1 &= \text{Length of key}
\end{aligned}$$

Step I : Considering shaft under pure tension, we have

$$T = \frac{\pi}{16} \cdot \tau \cdot d^3$$

But, twisting moment on shaft,

$$T = P \times L = 800 \times 1000 = 800 \times 10^3 \text{ N-mm}$$

$$\therefore \quad 800 \times 10^3 = \frac{\pi}{16} \times 70 \times d^3$$

$$\therefore \quad d = \textbf{38.75 mm} \cong \textbf{40 mm (say)}$$

Step II : Using the empirical relations fix the other dimensions,

$$d_2 = 1.6\,d = 1.6 \times 40 = \textbf{64 mm}$$
$$t_2 = 0.3\,d = 0.3 \times 40 = \textbf{12 mm}$$
$$l_2 = 1.25\,d = 1.25 \times 40 = \textbf{50 mm}$$
$$l = 2 \times l_2 = 2 \times 50 = \textbf{100 mm}$$

Step III : Considering shaft supported at centre of bearings under combined twisting and bending moment,

$$\therefore \quad M = P \times l = 800 \times 100 = 80 \times 10^3 \text{ N-mm and}$$
$$T = P \times L = 800 \times 1000 = 800 \times 10^3 \text{ N-mm}$$

$$\therefore \quad \text{Equivalent twisting moment,}$$

$$T_e = \sqrt{M^2 + T^2} = \sqrt{(80 \times 10^3)^2 + (800 \times 10^3)^2}$$
$$= 804 \times 10^3 \text{ N-mm}$$

Also, equivalent twisting moment,

$$T_e = \frac{\pi}{16} \cdot \tau_{max} \cdot d_1^3$$

$$\therefore \quad 804 \times 10^3 = \frac{\pi}{16} \times 70 \times d_1^3$$

$$\therefore \quad d_1 = \textbf{38.81 mm} \cong \textbf{44 mm (say)} \text{ (assumed more than diameter of shaft, d = 40 mm)}$$

Step IV : Design of key : After finding diameter of shaft (d), we can fix the dimensions for key as

$$w = d/4 = 40/4 = \textbf{10 mm} \text{ and } t_1 = d/6 = 40/6 = \textbf{6.67 mm}$$

Considering shear failure of key,

We have,
$$T = w \times l_1 \times \tau \times \left(\frac{d}{2}\right)$$

$$\therefore \quad 800 \times 10^3 = 10 \times l_1 \times 70 \times \left(\frac{40}{2}\right)$$

$$\therefore \quad l_1 = \text{length of key} = \textbf{57.14 mm} \cong \textbf{58 mm (say)}$$

Length l_1 may be taken as length of boss i.e. $l_1 = l_2 = \textbf{50 mm}$, but the key dimensions like b and t are to be modified for safe design.

Step V : Considering bending failure of lever, we can determine the cross-section of lever.

Let
$$t = \text{thickness of lever near the boss}$$

and
$$B = \text{width or height of lever near the boss.}$$

We have, Bending moment on lever,

$$M = P \times [L - r_b] = P \times \left[L - \frac{d_2}{2} \right]$$

$$= 800 \times (1000 - 32) = 774.4 \times 10^3 \text{ N.mm}$$

where, $\qquad r_b$ = radius of boss = $\dfrac{d_2}{2} = \dfrac{64}{2} = 32$ mm

Also, $\qquad Z = \dfrac{1}{6} t\, B^2 = \dfrac{1}{6} \times t \times (3t)^2 = 1.5 \times t^3$

We have, $\qquad \sigma_b = \dfrac{M}{Z}$

$\therefore \qquad 70 = \dfrac{774.4 \times 10^3}{1.5\, t^3} \qquad\qquad$ (Assume $\sigma_b = 70$ N/mm^2)

$\therefore \quad t = 19.46$ mm $\cong$ **20 mm** (say) and B = 3t = 3 $\times$ 20 = **60 mm**

2.5.3.1 Applications of Hand Lever and Foot Lever

Question

1. Write applications of hand lever and foot lever.   **(W-10)**
   (i) Handle of hand pump.
   (ii) Handle of punching machine.
   (iii) Lever of loaded safety valve.
   (iv) Bell crank lever used in railway.

2.5.4 Bell Crank Lever

2.5.4.1 Introduction

- In a bell crank lever, two arms of the lever are at right angles to each other.
- Such type of lever is used in railway signaling, Hart-Nell governors, and drive for air pump of condensers.
- The arms of lever may be rectangular, elliptical or I-section.

2.5.4.2 Design Procedure of Bell Crank Lever

Step I : Calculate the reaction at fulcrum, R_F :

$$R_F = \sqrt{W^2 + P^2}$$

[To calculate W and P, (if one of them is given), take moments about fulcrum and equate it to zero applying the condition of equilibrium]

Step II : Design of fulcrum pin :

(a) Let d = diameter of fulcrum pin and l = length of fulcrum pin.

Considering the fulcrum pin in bearing, we know that, the load on fulcrum pin is (R_F).

$\therefore$ Bearing pressure $= \dfrac{\text{Load}}{\text{Bearing area}} = \dfrac{R_F}{l \times d} = \dfrac{R_F}{1.25d \times d} \qquad$ ... [Assume $l = 1.25d$]

From here, l and d can be determined.

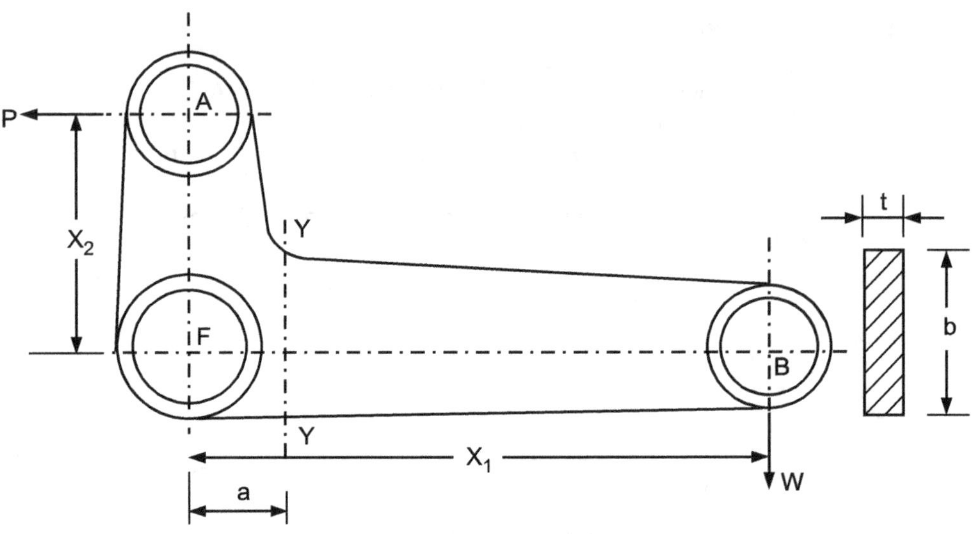

Fig. 2.40 : Bell crank lever

(b) Checking shear stress induced in the fulcrum pin. As the pin is in double shear,

$$\tau \;=\; \frac{R_F}{2 \times \left(\dfrac{\pi}{4} \cdot d^2\right)}$$

(c) A brass bush of 3 mm thickness is pressed into the boss of fulcrum as bearing surface.

∴   Diameter of hole in the lever = $d + 2 \times 3$. and Diameter of boss at fulcrum = $2d$

Step III : Design of pin at A : Checking whether the effort at A is close to the value of R_F. If it is, take same dimensions for pin at A as fulcrum pin.

∴ d_1 = diameter of pin at A = d, And, l_1 = length of pin at A = $1.25\, d_1$.

Step IV : Design of pin at B :

Let, d_2 = diameter of pin at B, And, l_2 = length of pin at B

(a) Considering bearing of pin at B.

We know that, the load on pin at B is W.

∴ $P_b \;=\; \dfrac{W}{d_2 \times l_2}$ [Assume $l_2 = 1.25\, d_2$]

From here, we can find d_2 and l_2.

(b) Checking the pin for shear stress. As pin is in double shear,

$$\tau \;=\; \frac{W}{2 \times \left(\dfrac{\pi}{4} \cdot d_2^{\,2}\right)}$$

(c) As end B is forked end, calculate dimensions, t_1, D and d_2 in the following manner.

Thickness of each eye = $t_1 = \dfrac{l_2}{2}$ and Inner diameter of each eye = $d_2 + (2 \times 3)$, where chilled phosphor bronze bush of 3 mm thickness is provided in each eye.

And   Outer diameter of each eye = $D = 2d_2$.

Step V : Design of lever :

Let t = thickness of lever at section Y-Y and b = width of lever at section Y-Y.

Taking distance 'a' from centre of fulcrum to Y-Y,

Maximum bending moment at Y-Y = $W \times (X_1 - a)$

and section modulus $= \dfrac{1}{6} \cdot t \cdot b^2 = \dfrac{1}{6} \times t \times (3t)^2$ [Assuming b = 3t]

$$\therefore \qquad \sigma_b = \frac{M}{Z} = \frac{W \times (X_1 - a)}{\dfrac{1}{6} \times t \times (3t)^2}$$

Here, we can find dimensions of lever b and t.

Numerical Type No. 6 : "Bell Crank Lever"

Problem 2.8 : *A right angle bell crank lever is to be designed to raise a vertical load of 6000 N at longer arm end. The arm lengths are 48 cm and 12 cm. The permissible stresses in shear and tension for the lever and pin material are 70 N/mm² and 81 N/mm² respectively. The bearing pressure of the pins is limited to 10 N/mm². Determine the salient dimensions of the pin. (Assume l/d = 1.25 for fulcrum pin and pin at two ends of lever).*

Solution : Given data : $W = 6000$ N, $X_1 = 480$ mm, $X_2 = 120$ mm, $\sigma_t = 81$ N/mm²,

$\qquad\qquad\qquad \tau = 70$ N/mm², $P_b = 10$ N/mm²

Procedure :

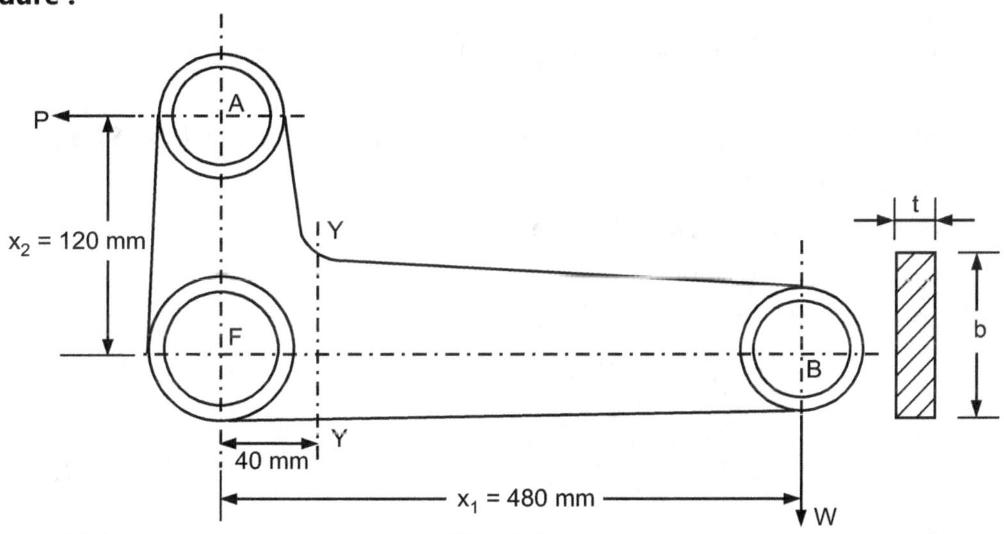

Fig. 2.41

Step I : Calculate the reaction at fulcrum, R_F :

Taking moment about fulcrum,

We have, $\qquad\qquad W \cdot X_1 = P \cdot X_2$

$\therefore \qquad\qquad 6000 \times 480 = P \times 120$

$\therefore \qquad\qquad\qquad P = \mathbf{24 \times 10^3 \ N}$

$\therefore \qquad\qquad\qquad R_F = \sqrt{W^2 + P^2} = \sqrt{(6000)^2 + (24 \times 10^3)^2} = \mathbf{24738.63 \ N}$

Step II : Design of fulcrum pin :

(a) Let d = diameter of fulcrum pin and l = length of fulcrum pin.

Considering the fulcrum pin in bearing, we know that, the load on fulcrum pin is (R_F).

$\therefore$ Bearing pressure $= \dfrac{\text{Load}}{\text{Bearing area}} = \dfrac{R_F}{l \times d} = \dfrac{R_F}{1.25d \times d}$ [Assume l = 1.25d]

$\therefore$ $10 = \dfrac{24738.63}{1.25d \times d}$

$\therefore$ d = 44.48 = **46 mm** and l = 1.25 × 46 = **57.5 mm**

(b) Checking shear stress induced in the fulcrum pin. As the pin is in double shear,

$$\tau = \frac{R_F}{2 \times \left(\dfrac{\pi}{4} \cdot d^2\right)} = \frac{24738.63}{2 \times \left[\dfrac{\pi}{4} \times (46)^2\right]}$$

$$= \mathbf{7.44 \ N/mm^2} < 70 \ N/mm^2$$

$\therefore$ Induced shear stress is less than given permissible value, so design of pin at fulcrum is safe.

(c) A brass bush of 3 mm thickness is pressed into the boss of fulcrum as bearing.

$\therefore$ Diameter of hole in the lever = d + 2 × 3 = 46 + 6 = 52 mm.

$\therefore$ Diameter of boss of fulcrum = 2d = 2 × 46 = 92 mm.

Step III : Design of pin at A :

As the effort at A is close to the value of R_F, take same dimensions for pin at A as fulcrum pin.

$\therefore$ d_1 = diameter of pin at A = d = **46 mm** and l_1 = 1.25d_1 = 1.25 × 46 = **57.5 mm**

Step IV : Design of pin at B :

Let d_2 = diameter of pin at B and l_2 = length of pin at B.

(a) Considering bearing of pin at B.

We know that, the load on pin at B is W.

We have, $P_b = \dfrac{W}{d_2 \times l_2}$

$\therefore$ $10 = \dfrac{6000}{d_2 \times 1.25 \times d_2}$ [Assume l_2 = 1.25 d_2]

$\therefore$ d_2 = 21.90 mm $\cong$ **22 mm (say)** and l_2 = 1.25d_2 = 1.25 × 22 = **27.5 mm**

(b) Checking the pin for shearing stress. As pin is in double shear,

$$\tau = \frac{W}{2 \times \left(\dfrac{\pi}{4} \cdot d_2^2\right)} = \frac{6000}{2 \times \left[\dfrac{\pi}{4} \times (22)^2\right]} = \mathbf{7.891 \ N/mm^2} < 70 \ N/mm^2$$

Thus, the induced shear stress is less than given permissible value, so design is safe.

(c) As end B is forked end, we can write,

$$\text{Thickness of each eye} = t_1 = \frac{l_2}{2} = \frac{27.5}{2} = \textbf{13.75 mm}$$

and inner diameter of each eye = d_2 + (2 × 3) = 22 + 6 = 28 mm, where chilled phosphor bronze bush of 3 mm thickness is provided in each eye.

∴   Outer diameter of each eye = D = $2d_2$ = 2 × 22 = **44 mm**

Step V : Design of lever :

Considering t = thickness of lever at section Y-Y and b = width of lever at section Y-Y.

Taking distance of a = 40 mm from centre of fulcrum i.e. section Y-Y,

Maximum bending moment at Y-Y = M = W × (X_1 – a) = W × (480 – 40) = 6000 × 440 = 2.64 × 10^6 N-mm

and Section modulus $= \frac{1}{6} \cdot t \cdot b^2 = \frac{1}{6} \times t \times (3t)^2 = 1.5 \times t^3$.   [Assuming b = 3t]

$$\therefore \qquad \sigma_b = \frac{M}{Z}$$

$$\therefore \qquad 81 = \frac{2.64 \times 10^6}{1.5 \times t^3}$$

$$\therefore \qquad t = 27.9 \text{ mm} \cong \textbf{28 mm (say)}$$

and $b = 3 \times t = 3 \times 28 = \textbf{84 mm}$

Problem 2.9 : *A bell crank lever having one arm 500 mm and another arm 150 mm is used to lift a load of 5 kN. The permissible stresses for lever and pin materials in shear and tension are 60 N/mm^2 and 80 N/mm^2 respectively. The bearing pressure on the pin is to be limited to 10 N/mm^2. Determine.*

(i) The diameter of pin.

(ii) The diameter of boss of the lever.

(iii) The dimensions of the rectangular cross-section of lever.

Solution : Given : W = 5000 N, X_1 = 150 mm, X_2 = 500 mm, σ_t = 80 N/mm^2,
          τ = 60 N/mm^2, P_b = 10 N/mm^2

Procedure :

Step I : Calculate the reaction at fulcrum, R_F :

Taking moment about fulcrum, we have,

$$W \cdot X_1 = P \cdot X_2$$

$$\therefore \qquad 5000 \times 150 = P \times 500$$

$$\therefore \qquad P = \textbf{1500 N}$$

$$\therefore \qquad R_F = \sqrt{W^2 + P^2}$$

$$\therefore \qquad R_F = \sqrt{(5000)^2 + (1500)^2} = \textbf{5220.15 N}$$

Step II : Design of fulcrum pin :

(a) Let

$$d = \text{diameter of fulcrum pin}$$
$$l = \text{length of fulcrum pin}$$

Considering the fulcrum pin in bearing, we know that, the load on fulcrum pin is (R_F). We have,

$$\text{Bearing pressure } (P_b) = \frac{\text{Load}}{\text{Bearing area}} = \frac{R_F}{l \times d}$$

$$\therefore \qquad 10 = \frac{R_F}{1.25d \times d} \qquad\qquad [\text{Assume } l = 1.25\ d]$$

$$\therefore \qquad 10 = \frac{5220.15}{1.25d^2}$$

$$\therefore \qquad d = \mathbf{20.43\ mm} \cong \mathbf{21\ mm}$$

$$\therefore \qquad l = 1.25d = 1.25 \times 21 = \mathbf{26.25\ mm}$$

(b) Checking shear stress induced in the fulcrum pin. As the pin is in double shear,

We have,
$$\tau = \frac{R_F}{2 \times \left(\frac{\pi}{4} \cdot d^2\right)} = \frac{5220.15}{2 \times \left[\frac{\pi}{4} \times (21)^2\right]}$$

$$\tau = \mathbf{7.53\ N/mm^2} < 60\ N/mm^2$$

∴ Induced shear stress is less than given permissible value, so design of pin at fulcrum is safe.

(c) A brass bush of 3 mm thickness is pressed into the boss of fulcrum as bearing :

∴ Diameter of hole in the lever = d + (2 × 3) = 21 + 6 = 27 mm

And Diameter of boss of fulcrum = 2 × d = 2 × 21 = 42 mm

Step III : Design pin at A : As the effort at A is close to the value of R_F, take same dimensions for pin at A as fulcrum pin.

$$d_1 = \text{diameter of pin at A} = d = 21\ mm$$
$$l_1 = 1.25\ d_1 = 1.25 \times 21 = 26.25\ mm$$

Step IV : Design of pin at B :

Let

$$d_2 = \text{diameter of pin at B}$$
$$l_2 = \text{length of pin at B}$$

(a) Considering pin at B in bearing, we know that, load on pin at B is W.

$$P_b = \frac{W}{d_2 \times l_2}$$

$$\therefore \qquad 10 = \frac{5000}{d_2 \times 1.25 \times d_2} \qquad\qquad (\because l_2 = 1.25\ d_2)$$

$$\therefore \qquad d_2 = \mathbf{20\ mm}$$

and
$$l_2 = 1.25\ d_2 = 1.25 \times 20 = \mathbf{25\ mm}$$

(b) Checking shear stress induced in the pin at B.

As pin is in double shear, Area resisting shear $= 2 \times \left(\dfrac{\pi}{4} \cdot d_2^2 \right)$

$$\therefore \quad \text{Induced shear stress,} \quad \tau \;=\; \frac{W}{2 \times \left(\dfrac{\pi}{4} \times d_2^2 \right)} \;=\; \frac{5000}{2 \times \left(\dfrac{\pi}{4} \times (20)^2 \right)}$$

$$\tau \;=\; \textbf{7.9577 N/mm}^2 < \textbf{60 N/mm}^2$$

Here, induced shear stress is less than given permissible value. So design is safe.

(c) As end B is forked end, we can write,

$$\text{Thickness of each eye} \;=\; t_1 \;=\; \frac{l_2}{2} \;=\; \frac{25}{2} \;=\; \textbf{12.5 mm, and}$$

Inner diameter of each eye $= d_2 + (2 \times 3) = 20 + 6 = \textbf{26 mm}$

where, chilled phosphor bronze bush of 3 mm thickness is provided in each eye.

and, Outer diameter of each eye $= D = 2d_2 = 2 \times 20 = \textbf{40 mm}$

Step (V) : Design of lever : Consider a section Y-Y at a distance of a = 25 mm from centre of fulcrum.

Let, t = thickness of lever at section Y-Y

and b = Width of lever at section Y-Y

Maximum bending moment at Y-Y $= P \times (X_1 - a) = 1500 \times [500 - 25]$

$$\therefore \qquad M \;=\; 1500 \times 475 \;=\; 712.5 \times 10^3 \text{ N-mm}$$

and   Section modulus $= \dfrac{1}{6} \times t \times b^2 = \dfrac{1}{6} \times t \times (3t)^2$ (Assume b = 3t)

$$\therefore \qquad Z \;=\; 1.5 \times t^3$$

We have, $\sigma_b = \dfrac{M}{Z} \;=\; \dfrac{712.5 \times 10^3}{1.5 \times t^3}$

$$\therefore \qquad 80 \;=\; \frac{712.5 \times 10^3}{1.5 \times t^3}$$

$$\therefore \qquad t \;=\; 18.10 \text{ mm} \cong \textbf{19 mm (say)}$$

$$\therefore \qquad b \;=\; 3t \;=\; 3 \times 19 \;=\; \textbf{57 mm}$$

2.6 LEVER SAFETY VALVE

2.6.1 Introduction

Fig. 2.42 shows a lever loaded safety valve used in steam boilers. The valve gets opened by steam pressure, when the steam pressure reaches a certain maximum valve, upto which, it is safe to operate. The controlling force for the valve is provided by weights put, at free end of the lever, which is provided at fulcrum by a pin to the toggle. In spring balance type of safety valve, the controlling force is provided by the spring attached at the end of lever.

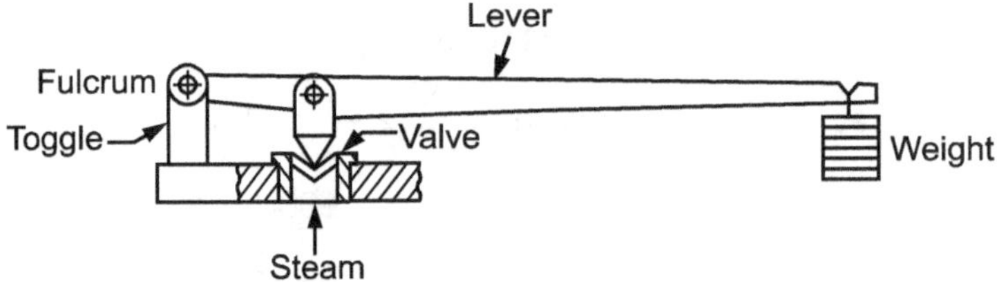

Fig. 2.42 : Lever safety valve

2.6.2 Design Procedure of Lever for Lever Safety Valve

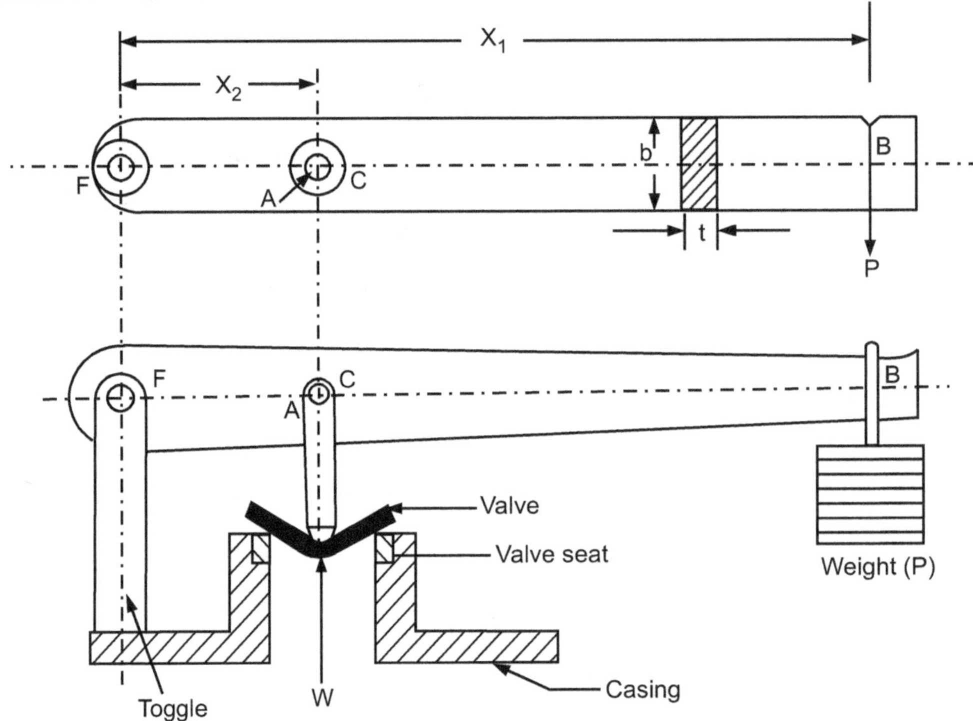

Fig. 2.43 : Lever for lever safety valve

Step I : Calculate the reaction at fulcrum R_F (which is acting vertically downwards)

$\Sigma F_y = 0$; $\therefore -R_F + W - P = 0$

$\therefore \qquad\qquad R_F = W - P$ $\qquad\qquad$ ... (2.3)

Now calculate, $\qquad W = $ Maximum steam load, at which, valve blows off, by using,

$\therefore \qquad\qquad W = \dfrac{\pi}{4} \cdot D^2 \cdot p$

where, D = diameter of valve, p = pressure of steam acting on the valve.

Now take moments about fulcrum,

$\Sigma M_{@F} = 0 \qquad \therefore P \cdot X_1 = W \cdot X_2$

Find P from above equation i.e. load at point B.

Put P and W in equation (2.3) to calculate R_F.

Step II : Design of fulcrum pin. i.e. pin at F :

Let, d_F = Diameter of fulcrum pin

       l_F = Length of fulcrum pin

Considering bearing of pin at F,

Bearing pressure, $P_b = \dfrac{R_F}{d_F \cdot l_F} = \dfrac{R_F}{1.25\ d_F \times d_F} = \dfrac{R_F}{1.25 \times d_F^2}$ (Assume $l_F = 1.25 d_F$)

From the above, diameter of fulcrum pin (d_F) and length (l_F) can be determined.

Step III : Checking the fulcrum pin for shearing : As the fulcrum pin is in double shear,

Induced shear stress, $\tau = \dfrac{R_F}{2 \times \left(\dfrac{\pi}{4} \cdot d_F^2\right)}$

Step IV : A gunmetal bush of 3 mm thickness is provided in the pinholes at A and F in order to reduce wear and to increase life of lever.

∴   Diameter of hole for fulcrum pin = $d_F + (2 \times 3)$.

and Outside diameter of boss = $2 \cdot d_F$.

Step V : Design of pin at A : Since load at F does not very differ with load at A, pin of same diameter may be used at A as that of F, in order to minimize number of parts and to facilitate the interchangeability of parts.

Step VI : Design of lever : Let us find out the cross-section of lever considering the bending moment near the boss at A.

Let,   t = thickness of lever and b = width of lever.

Maximum bending moment near the boss at A. i.e. at point C,

     M = $P \times BC = P \times (BF - AF - AC)$ in N-mm

where,   AC = Radius of hole of fulcrum pin

and Section modulus, $Z = \dfrac{1}{6} \cdot t \cdot b^2$

∴ $\sigma_b = \dfrac{M}{Z} = \dfrac{P \times BC}{\dfrac{1}{6} \cdot t \cdot b^2}$

Assuming b = 3t,

Here, we can find here dimensions of lever b and t.

Numerical Type No. 7 : "Lever Safety Valve"

Problem 2.10 : *A lever safety valve is 75 mm in diameter. It is required to blow-off at 1.3 N/mm². Design the mild steel lever of rectangular cross-section, if the permissible stresses are 70 N/mm² in tension, 52 N/mm² in shear and 24.5 N/mm² in bearing. The pin is made of same material as that of lever. The distance from the fulcrum to the dead weight of the lever is 800 mm and distance between fulcrum pin and the valve spindle link pin is 80 mm.*

Solution : Given data : D = 75 mm, p = 1.3 N/mm², σ_t = 70 N/mm², τ = 52 N/mm²,

     P_b = 24.5 N/mm², X_1 = 800 mm, X_2 = 80 mm.

Procedure : Step I : The maximum load, at which, the valve blows off is given by,

$$W = \frac{\pi}{4} \cdot D^2 \cdot p = \frac{\pi}{4} \times (75)^2 \times 1.3 = \textbf{5743.22 N}$$

Taking moment about the fulcrum,

$$P \times 800 = W \times 80$$

$$\therefore \qquad P \times 800 = 5743.22 \times 80$$

$$\therefore \qquad P = \textbf{574.32 N}$$

Calculate the reaction at fulcrum R_F,

$$R_F = W - P = 5743.22 - 574.32 = \textbf{5168.9 N}$$

Step II : Design of fulcrum pin. i.e. at F.

Let, $\qquad d_F$ = diameter of fulcrum pin and l_F = length of fulcrum pin

Considering bearing of pin at F,

$$P_b = \frac{R_F}{d_F \times l_F}; \quad \therefore \ 24.5 = \frac{5168.9}{1.25 d_F \times d_F} \qquad \text{[Assume } l_F = 1.25 d_F]$$

$$\therefore \qquad d_F = 12.99 \text{ mm} \cong \textbf{14 mm (say)}$$

and $\qquad l_F = 1.25 d_F = 1.25 \times 14 = \textbf{17.5 mm}$

Step III : Checking the fulcrum pin for shearing : As the fulcrum pin is in double shear,

$$\text{Induced shear stress, } \tau = \frac{R_F}{2 \times \left(\frac{\pi}{4} \cdot d_F^2\right)} = \frac{5168.9}{2 \times \left(\frac{\pi}{4} \times 14^2\right)} = \textbf{16.78 N/mm}^2 < 52 \text{ N/mm}^2$$

Thus, the induced shear stress is less than given permissible value. Design is safe.

Step IV : A gunmetal bush of 3 mm thickness is provided in the pinhole at F in order to reduce wear and to increase life of lever.

$\therefore$ Diameter of hole of fulcrum pin = $d_F + (2 \times 3) = 14 + 6 = 20$ mm

and Outside diameter of boss = $2 \times d_F = 2 \times 14 = 28$ mm

Step V : Design of pin at A : Since the load at F does not very differ with load at A. Therefore, pin of same diameter may be used at A as that of F, in order to minimize the number of parts and to facilitate the interchangeability of parts.

Step VI : Design of lever : Let us find out the cross-section of lever considering the bending moment.

Let, $\qquad t$ = thickness of lever and b = width of lever

We have, maximum bending moment near the boss i.e. at point C,

$M = P \times BC = P \times (BF - AF - AC) = 574.32 \times \{800 - 80 - (20/2)\} = 407.767 \times 10^3$ N-mm

$$\text{and Section modulus, } Z = \frac{1}{6} \cdot t \cdot b^2 = \frac{1}{6} \cdot t \cdot (3t)^2 = (1/6) \times t \times (3t)^2 = 1.5 \, t^3$$

$$\text{... [Assuming b = 3t]}$$

$$\therefore \qquad \sigma_b = \frac{M}{Z} \quad \therefore \ 70 \text{ N/mm}^2 = \frac{407.767 \times 10^3}{1.5 \, t^3}$$

$$\therefore \qquad t = 15.72 \text{ mm} \cong \textbf{16 mm} \text{ and } b = 3t = 3 \times 16 = \textbf{48 mm}$$

2.7 ECCENTRIC LOADING

- An externally applied load on a machine part is said to be **eccentric**, if its line of action is parallel, but does not coincide with the centroidal axis of machine part.

- The distance between the eccentric load and centroidal axis of component is called as *eccentricity* and denoted by 'e'.

- Examples : 'c' clamp, brackets, offset links, punching machine.

- Consider a short column of rectangular cross-section subjected to eccentric compressive load 'W' at a distance 'e' from the centroidal axis of column as shown. Refer Fig. 2.44 (a).

- Let us introduce two equal and opposite forces of magnitude W_1 and W_2, without altering the equilibrium of column. Also, $W_1 = W_2 = W$. Refer Fig. 2.44 (b).

- The force W_1 will induce a direct compressive stress over the entire cross-section of column. The magnitude of this direct compressive stress is given by,

$$\sigma_o = \frac{W_1}{A} = \frac{W}{A}$$

where, A = cross-sectional area of column. Refer Fig. 2.44 (c).

- The force W_2 and W will form a couple equal to '$W \times e$', which will induce bending stress.

- The bending stress induced on face AB will be tensile in nature, whereas, on face CD will be compressive. Refer Fig. 2.44 (d).

∴ Maximum bending stress induced at face AB and CD can be given by,

$$\sigma_b = \frac{M}{Z} = \frac{W \cdot e}{I/y} = \frac{W \cdot e \cdot y}{I}$$

where, M = Bending moment = $W \cdot e$

$$Z = \text{Section modulus} = \frac{\text{Moment of inertia}}{\text{Distance of N.A. from outermost fibre}}$$

$$= \frac{I}{y_t} \text{ or } \frac{I}{y_c}$$

Here, y_t and y_c are the distances of neutral axis from the outermost fibres from tensile and compressive faces respectively.

∴ Maximum resultant stress at CD,

$$\sigma_{max} = \sigma_o + \sigma_b = \frac{W}{A} + \frac{M}{Z} = \frac{W}{A} + \frac{W \cdot e \cdot y}{I}$$

For rectangular cross-section of width 'b' and thickness 't',

$$\sigma_{max} = \frac{W}{b \cdot t} + \frac{W \cdot e \cdot \left(\dfrac{b}{2}\right)}{\dfrac{1}{12} tb^3}$$

∴ $$\sigma_{max} = \frac{W}{b \cdot t} + \frac{6W \cdot e}{t\, b^2}$$

W
e
A
C
B
D
(a)
N
O
A
A
N
W
W₁
W₂
A
C
B
D
(b)
W₁ = W
A
C
B
D
(c)
σ₀
σ₀
O
M = W.e
A
C
B
D
(d)
Compressive face
Tensile face
σ_b
σ_b
O
W
M = W.e
A
C
B
D
(e)
σ_min = σ₀ − σ_b
σ_max = σ₀ + σ_b
=
=
+
=

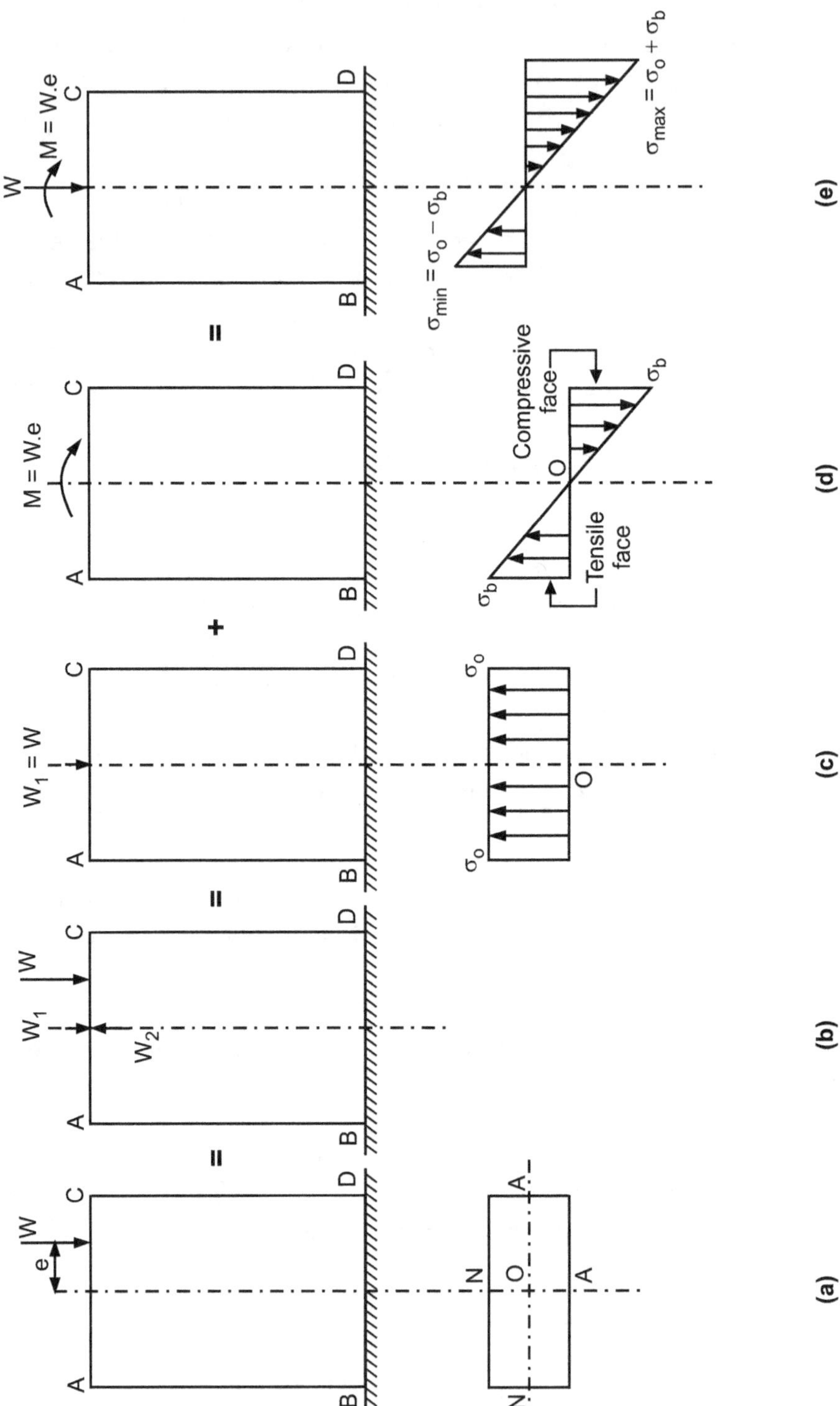

Fig. 2.44

Also, minimum resultant stress at AB,

$$\sigma_{min} \;=\; \sigma_o - \sigma_b \;=\; \frac{W}{A} - \frac{M}{Z}$$

$$\therefore \qquad \sigma_{min} \;=\; \frac{W}{A} - \frac{W \cdot e \cdot y}{I}$$

$$\therefore \qquad \sigma_{min} \;=\; \frac{W}{b \cdot t} - \frac{6 \cdot W \cdot e}{t\, b^2}$$

The resultant stress distribution diagram is as shown in Fig. 2.44 (e).

2.7.1 Design Procedure of C-clamp

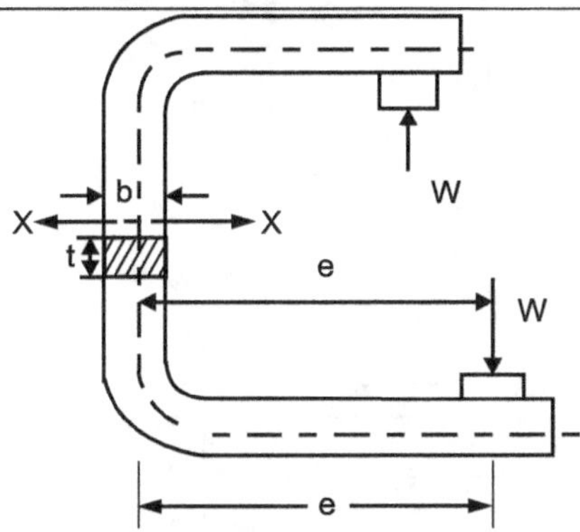

Fig. 2.45 : C-clamp

Step I : Considering the direct tensile load,

$$\text{Direct stress, } \sigma_o \;=\; \frac{W}{A} \;=\; \frac{W}{(b \times t)}$$

$$\sigma_o \;=\; \frac{W}{t \times 2t} \;=\; \frac{W}{2t^2} \qquad\qquad \text{(Assuming } b = 2t)$$

Step II : Due to an eccentricity, the section is subjected to bending moment. Therefore, bending stress will be induced in the clamp.

$$\therefore \qquad \text{Bending stress, } \sigma_b \;=\; \frac{M}{Z} \;=\; \frac{W \cdot e}{\frac{1}{6} t\, b^2} \;=\; \frac{6 \cdot W \cdot e}{t \times (2t)^2} \qquad\qquad (\because b = 2t)$$

$$=\; \frac{6 \cdot W \cdot e}{4t^3}$$

Step III : Maximum stress induced in C-clamp is given by,

$$\sigma_{tR} \;=\; \sigma_o + \sigma_b$$

$$=\; \frac{W}{2t^2} + \frac{6 \cdot W \cdot e}{4t^3}$$

Equating the above equation to permissible stress, we can find values of t and hence 'b'.

[**Note :** Ratio $\left(\dfrac{b}{t}\right)$ may be assumed from 2 to 4, if not given in the numerical.]

Numerical Type No. 8 : "C-clamp"

Problem 2.11 : *Design 'C' clamp frame for a total clamping force of 20 kN. The cross section of the frame is rectangular and width to thickness ratio is 2. The distance between the load line and neutral axis of rectangular cross-section is 120 mm and gap between two faces is 180 mm. Frame is made of cast steel. The permissible tensile stress for cast steel is 100 N/mm².*   **(S-14)**

Solution : Given data : $W = 20$ kN $= 20 \times 10^3$ N, $b = 2t$,

Safe tensile stress for C-clamp $= \sigma_t = 100$ N/mm²

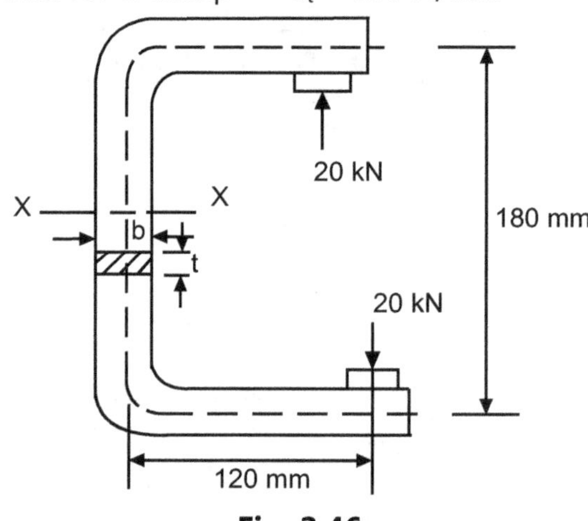

Fig. 2.46

Procedure :

Step I : Considering the direct tensile stress due to direct load,

$$\sigma_o = \frac{W}{A} = \frac{W}{(b \times t)} = \frac{20 \times 10^3}{(2t \times t)} = \frac{20 \times 10^3}{2t^2} = \frac{10 \times 10^3}{t^2}$$

Step II : Due to eccentricity in application of load, the section is subjected to bending moment.

∴   It will be subjected to direct bending stress , $\sigma_b = \dfrac{M}{Z}$.

But $M = W \times e$ and $Z =$ section modulus $= \dfrac{1}{6} t b^2$

$$\therefore \quad \sigma_b = \frac{W \times e}{\dfrac{1}{6} t b^2} = \frac{6 \times W \times e}{t b^2} = \frac{6 \times 20 \times 10^3 \times 100}{t \times (2t)^2} = \frac{3 \times 10^6}{t^3}$$

Step III : Total direct stress induced in c-clamp,

$$\sigma_o + \sigma_b = \sigma_{tR}$$

$$\therefore \quad \frac{10 \times 10^3}{t^2} + \frac{3 \times 10^6}{t^3} \leq 100$$

$\therefore \quad 10 \times 10^3\, t + 3 \times 10^6 \;=\; 100\, t^3$

$\therefore \quad 100\, t^3 - 10 \times 10^3\, t \;=\; 3 \times 10^6$

Use trial and error method.

$\therefore \quad$ By trial and error method, t = 32.14 mm $\cong$ **34 mm** and b = 2t = 2 $\times$ 34 $\cong$ **68 mm**

Problem 2.12 : *The load on 'C' clamp shown in Fig. 2.47 is 25 kN. Assuming that, clamp is made of cast steel and b = 3 t and e = 140 mm. The allowable stress in the material is 100 N/mm². Determine the dimensions b and t.*

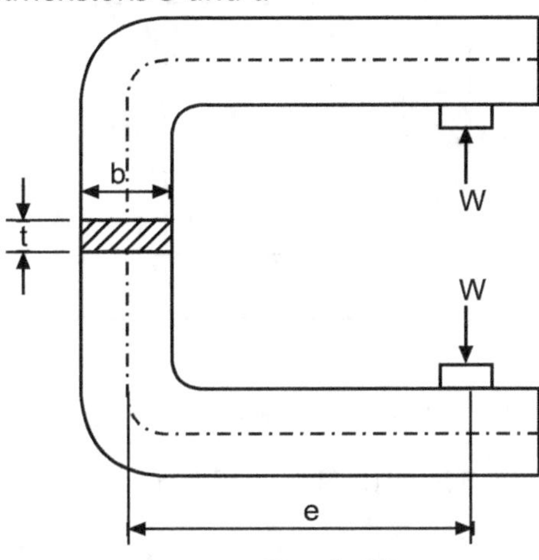

Fig. 2.47   (W-12)

Solution : Given data : $W \;=\; 25\,\text{kN} \;=\; 25 \times 10^3\,\text{N}, \quad b \;=\; 3t$

$e \;=\; 140\,\text{mm}, \quad \sigma_t \;=\; 100\,\text{N/mm}^2$

Procedure :

Step I : Direct stress : $\quad \sigma_o \;=\; \dfrac{W}{A} \;=\; \dfrac{25 \times 10^3}{b \times t} \;=\; \dfrac{25 \times 10^3}{3t^2} \;=\; \dfrac{8.33 \times 10^3}{t^2}$

Step II : Bending stress : $\sigma_b \;=\; \dfrac{M}{Z} \;=\; \dfrac{W \times e}{\frac{1}{6}\, tb^2} \;=\; \dfrac{25 \times 10^3 \times 140 \times 6}{t \times (3t)^2} \;=\; \dfrac{2.33 \times 10^6}{t^3}$

Step III : Resultant stress :

$$\sigma_{tR} \;=\; \sigma_o + \sigma_b$$

$\therefore \qquad 100 \;=\; \dfrac{8.33 \times 10^3}{t^2} + \dfrac{2.33 \times 10^6}{t^3}$

$\therefore \qquad 100 \;=\; \dfrac{8.33 \times 10^3 \times t + 2.33 \times 10^6}{t^3}$

$\therefore \qquad 8.33 \times 10^3\, t + 2.33 \times 10^6 \;=\; 100t^3$

$\therefore \qquad 100t^3 - 8.33 \times 10^3\, t \;=\; 2.33 \times 10^6$

Using trial and error method, we get,

$$t \;=\; 29.53 \cong 30\,\text{mm}$$

$\therefore \qquad b \;=\; 3t \;=\; 3 \times 30 = \textbf{90 mm}$

Problem 2.13 : *The spindle of a drilling machine as shown in Fig. 2.48 is subjected to a maximum axial load of 10 kN during operation. Determine the diameter of the solid cast iron column, if the permissible tensile stress is 40 N/mm². The distance between the axis of the spindle and the axis of the column is 350 mm.*   **(S-12)**

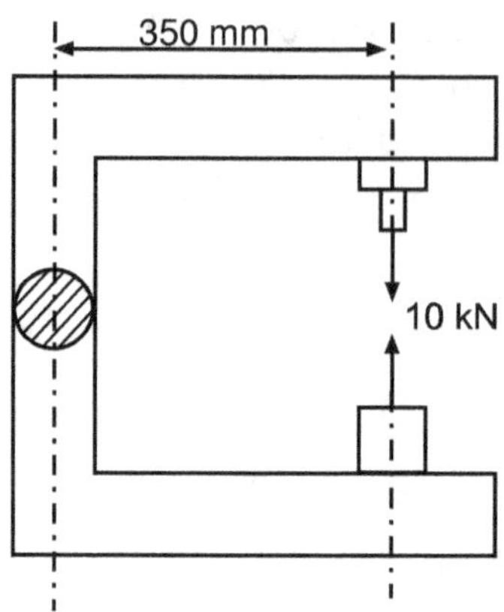

Fig. 2.48

Solution : Given data : $W = 10 \times 10^3$ N, $e = 350$ mm, $\sigma_t = 40$ N/mm²

Procedure :

Step I :   Direct stress : $\sigma_o = \dfrac{W}{A} = \dfrac{W}{\dfrac{\pi}{4}d^2} = \dfrac{10 \times 10^3 \times 4}{\pi \cdot d^2} = \dfrac{12732.39}{d^2}$

Step II : Bending stress : $\sigma_b = \dfrac{M}{Z} = \dfrac{W \times e}{\dfrac{\pi}{32}d^3} = \dfrac{10 \times 10^3 \times 350 \times 32}{\pi \times d^3} = \dfrac{35.65 \times 10^6}{d^3}$

Step III : Resultant stress : $\sigma_{t_R} = \sigma_o + \sigma_b$

$$\therefore \qquad 40 = \dfrac{12732.39}{d^2} + \dfrac{35.65 \times 10^6}{d^3}$$

$$\therefore \qquad 40 = \dfrac{12732.39\, d + 35.65 \times 10^6}{d^3}$$

$$\therefore \qquad 40d^3 - 12732.39\, d - 35.65 \times 10^6 = 0$$

By trial and error method, d = **97.34 mm** $\cong$ **98 mm**

Problem 2.14 : *Fig. 2.49 shows a hacksaw. The blade is assembled with tension of W = 320 N. The frame of hacksaw is made out of cold drawn steel, for which, yield point value in tension is 360 N/mm². Design a rectangular cross-section of U-frame at sections 'A-A' and 'B-B'. Assume factor of safety = 4 and b = 2.5 t.*

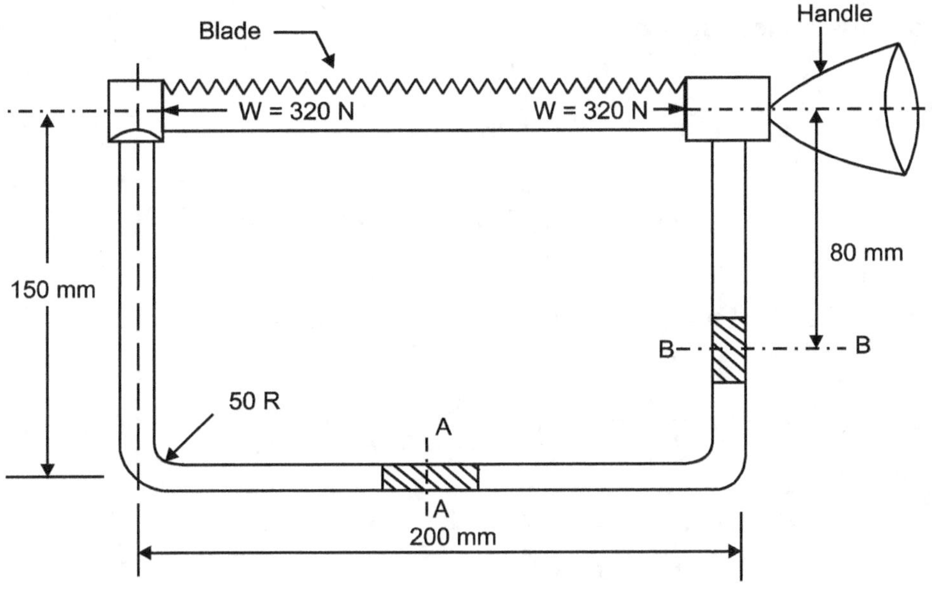

Fig. 2.49

Solution : Data given : $W = 320$ N, $\sigma_{yt} = 360$ N/mm^2, F.O.S. $= 4$, $b = 2.5\,t$

Procedure :

$$\left[\begin{array}{c}\text{Allowable stress} \\ \text{in tension}\end{array}\right] = \frac{\text{Yield point stress}}{\text{F.O.S.}} = \frac{360}{4} = \mathbf{90\ N/mm^2}$$

Section at A-A :

Step I : Direct stress :

$$\sigma_o = \frac{W}{A} = \frac{320}{b \times t} = \frac{320}{(2.5t) \times t} = \frac{128}{t^2}$$

Step II : Bending stress :

$$\sigma_b = \frac{M}{Z} = \frac{W \times e}{(1/6)\,tb^2} = \frac{320 \times 150 \times 6}{6.25t^3} = \frac{46080}{t^3} \qquad [\because b = 2.5t]$$

Step III : Resultant stress :

$$\sigma_{tR} = \sigma_b + \sigma_o \geq 90$$

$$\therefore \quad \frac{46080}{t^3} + \frac{128}{t^2} = 90$$

$$\therefore \quad 90t^3 - 128t - 46080 = 0$$

$$\therefore \quad t = 8.06 \text{ mm} \cong \mathbf{9\ mm\ (say)}$$

$$\therefore \quad b = 2.5\,t = 2.5 \times 9 = \mathbf{22.5\ mm}$$

At section B-B :

Frame is uniform in section throughout.

$\therefore$ Using same section at B-B, we should find the stresses induced at section B-B. These induced stresses should be within the permissible stress limit.

Use $b = 22.5$ mm and $t = 9$ mm.

Bending stress induced at section B-B,

$$\sigma_{b\,ind} \;=\; \frac{M}{Z} \;=\; \frac{W \times e}{\frac{1}{6}\,tb^2}$$

$$\therefore \qquad \sigma_{b\,ind} \;=\; \frac{320 \times 80 \times 6}{9 \times (22.5)^2} \;=\; \textbf{33.71 N/mm}^2 < 90 \text{ N/mm}^2$$

It is less than permissible stress.

In addition to bending stress, there is transverse shear stress.

We know, $\tau = 1.5\,\sigma_o$

$$\therefore \quad \tau = 1.5 \times \frac{W}{A} \;=\; 1.5 \times \frac{W}{(b \times t)} = 1.5 \times \frac{320}{(9 \times 22.5)} \;=\; \textbf{2.37 N/mm}^2 < 90 \text{ N/mm}^2$$

Hence, design is safe.

$\therefore$ At section B-B : Use $\;b \;=\; \textbf{22.5 mm}$

$\qquad\qquad\qquad\qquad\quad t \;=\; \textbf{9 mm}$

2.7.2 Design Procedure of Offset Links

An offset link in tension due to load 'W' acting on the load line is shown in Fig. 2.50. Here, Y-Y is the neutral axis of the rectangular cross-section of the link. Distance between load line and centroidal axis of the section is called as eccentricity 'e' and load 'W' is eccentric load.

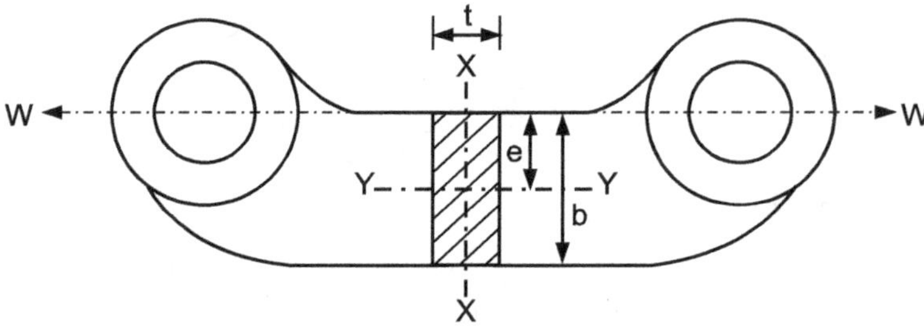

Fig. 2.50 : Offset link

Let,
- b — Width of rectangular section at X-X.
- t — Thickness of rectangular section at X-X.
- e — Eccentricity.
- W — Eccentric load on offset link [Tensile].
- σ_o — Direct tensile stress due to load W.
- σ_b — Bending stress

When load is eccentric, the cross-section will be subjected to both direct and bending stress.

Step I : Direct stress :

$$\sigma_o \;=\; \frac{W}{A} \;=\; \frac{W}{b \times t}$$

Step II : Bending stress :

$$\sigma_b \;=\; \frac{M}{Z_{yy}} \;=\; \frac{W \cdot e}{\frac{1}{6} \cdot tb^2} \;=\; \frac{6\,W \cdot e}{t\,b^2}$$

Step III : Maximum stress is obtained by,

$$\sigma_t \;=\; \sigma_o + \sigma_b$$

$$\therefore \qquad \sigma_t \;=\; \frac{W}{b \times t} \;+\; \frac{6W \cdot e}{tb^2}$$

where, $\qquad e \;=\; \text{eccentricity} = \dfrac{b}{2}$ $\qquad$ [for the given figure]

Equate the above equation to permissible stress for given material. Thus, we can find the values of b and t, using the relation between b and t.

> **Numerical Type No. 9 : "Off-Set Link"**

Problem 2.15 : *Design an off-set link for a load of 1000 N. Maximum permissible stress in tension for link material is limited to 60 N/mm². Assume for rectangular cross-section of link b = 3t.*

Solution : Given Data : $W \;=\; 1000 \text{ N}, \quad \sigma_t \;=\; 60 \text{ N/mm}^2, \quad b \;=\; 3t$

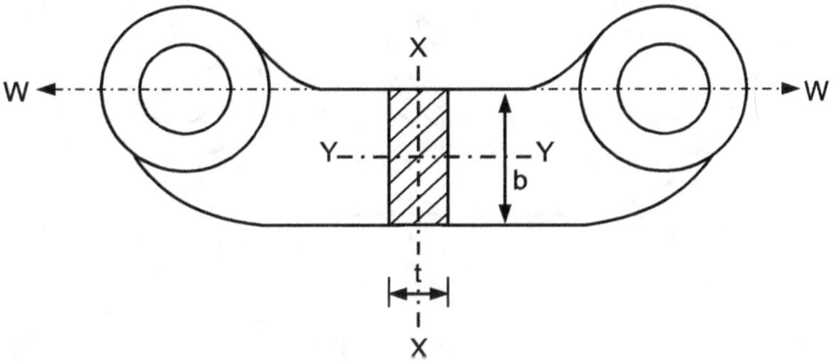

Fig. 2.51

Procedure : Step I : Direct stress :

$$\sigma_o \;=\; \frac{W}{A} \;=\; \frac{1000}{b \times t} \;=\; \frac{1000}{3t \times t} \qquad\qquad [\because b = 3t]$$

$$\therefore \qquad \sigma_o \;=\; \frac{1000}{3t^2}$$

Step II : Bending stress : $\;\sigma_b \;=\; \dfrac{M}{Z_{yy}} \;=\; \dfrac{W \cdot e}{\frac{1}{6} \cdot t \cdot b^2}$

$$\therefore \qquad \sigma_b \;=\; \frac{1000 \times \dfrac{b}{2}}{\dfrac{1}{6} \cdot t \cdot (3t)^2} \qquad\qquad \left[\because e = \frac{b}{2}\right]$$

$$\sigma_b = \frac{1000 \times 3t \times 6}{2 \times t \times 9t^2} \qquad [\because b = 3t]$$

$$\sigma_b = \frac{1000}{t^3}$$

Step III : Maximum stress is obtained by superimposing 2 stress diagrams.

$$\sigma_t = \sigma_b + \sigma_o \leq \sigma t_p$$

$$\therefore \quad \sigma_t = \frac{1000}{t^3} + \frac{1000}{3t^2}$$

$$\therefore \quad 60 = \frac{1000 + (1000/3)\, t}{t^3}$$

$$60t^3 = 1000 + 333.33\, t$$

$$60t^3 - 333.33t = 1000$$

By trial and error method, t $= $ **3.26 mm $\cong$ 4 mm**

$$\therefore \quad b = 3t = 3 \times 4 = \textbf{12 mm}$$

Problem 2.16 : *Fig. 2.52 shows an offset link carrying load 'W' in N. The safe working stresses for link material are σ_t = 20 MPa, σ_c = 80 MPa. Find the magnitude of load 'W'.*

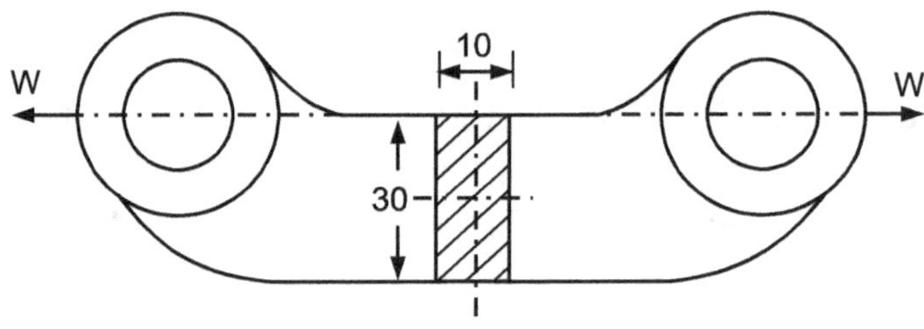

Fig. 2.52

Solution : Given data : $\quad t = 10$ mm, $b = 30$ mm, $e = \dfrac{b}{2} = \dfrac{30}{2} = 15$ mm

$$\sigma_t = 20 \text{ N/mm}^2, \quad \sigma_c = 80 \text{ N/mm}^2$$

Procedure :

Step I : Direct stress :

$$\sigma_o = \frac{W}{A} = \frac{W}{b \times t} = \frac{W}{30 \times 10} = \frac{W}{300}$$

Step II : Bending stress : $\sigma_b = \dfrac{M}{Z_{YY}} = \dfrac{W \times e}{\frac{1}{6} tb^2} = \dfrac{W \times 15}{\frac{1}{6} \times 10 \times (30)^2} = \dfrac{W}{100}$

Step III : $\quad \sigma_{max} = \sigma_t = \sigma_b + \sigma_o$

$$\therefore \quad 20 = \frac{W}{100} + \frac{W}{300}$$

$$\therefore \quad W = \textbf{1500 N}$$

Step IV : Also, $\quad \sigma_{min} = \sigma_c = \sigma_b - \sigma_o$

$\therefore \qquad\qquad 80 = \left[\dfrac{W}{100} - \dfrac{W}{300}\right]$

$\therefore \qquad\qquad W = \mathbf{12000\ N}$

Problem 2.17 : *A mild steel link, as shown in Fig. 2.53, by full lines, transmits a pull of 80 kN. Find the dimension of b and t, if b = 3t. Assume the permissible tensile stress of 70 MPa. If an unsymmetrical one, as shown by dotted lines, replaces the original link having the same thickness t, find new depth b_1, using the same permissible stress as before.*

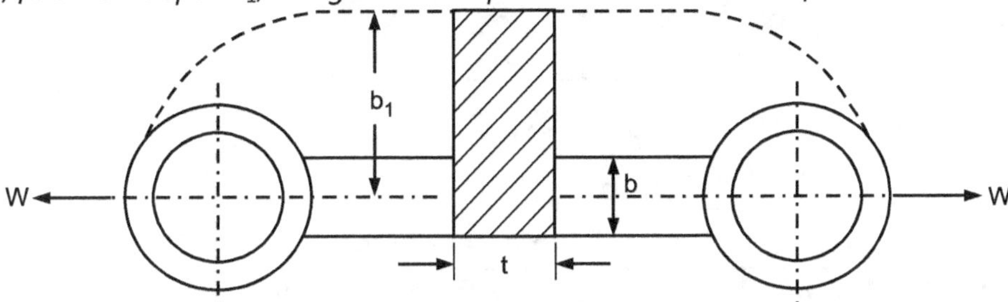

Fig. 2.53

Solution : Given data : W = 80 kN = 80×10^3 N, b = 3t,

Safe tensile stress for link = σ_t = 70 N/mm^2.

Procedure :

Case I : When the link is in the position shown by full lines, then it is subjected to direct tensile stress, which is given by,

$$\sigma_t = \dfrac{W}{A} = \dfrac{W}{(b \times t)} = \dfrac{W}{(3t \times t)} \qquad\qquad (\because b = 3t)$$

$\therefore \qquad\qquad 70 = \dfrac{80 \times 10^3}{3t^2}$

$\therefore \qquad\qquad t = \mathbf{19.51\ mm} \cong \mathbf{20\ mm\ (say)}$ and b = 3t = 3 × 20 = **60 mm**

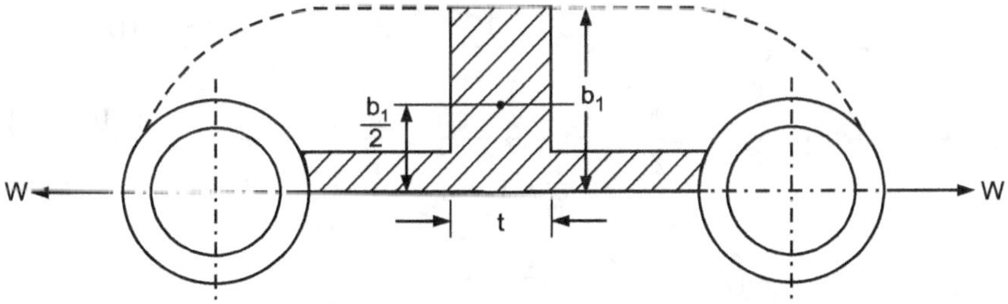

Fig. 2.54

Case II : When the link is in the position shown by dotted lines (Refer Fig. 2.54), it will be subjected to direct as well as bending stress. Here, the new depth will be b_1, but thickness will remain same, t = 20 mm.

The direct stress is given by,

$$\sigma_o = \dfrac{W}{A} = \dfrac{W}{(b_1 \times t)} = \dfrac{80 \times 10^3}{(b_1 \times 20)} = \dfrac{4 \times 10^3}{b_1}$$

The bending stress is given by,

$$\sigma_b = \frac{M}{Z}$$

But $M = W \times e$ and Z = Section modulus = $\frac{1}{6} tb_1^2$

$$\therefore \quad \sigma_b = \frac{W \times e}{\frac{1}{6} t b_1^2} = \frac{6 \times W \times e}{t b_1^2} = \frac{6 \times 80 \times 10^3 \times (b_1/2)}{20 \times b_1^2} = \frac{12 \times 10^3}{b_1}$$

Total stress induced in offset link $= \sigma_t = \sigma_o + \sigma_b$

$$\therefore \quad \sigma_t = \frac{4 \times 10^3}{b_1} + \frac{12 \times 10^3}{b_1}$$

$$\therefore \quad 70 = \frac{16 \times 10^3}{b_1}$$

$$\therefore \quad b_1 = 228.57 \text{ mm} \cong \textbf{230 mm}$$

Problem 2.18 : *An offset link subjected to force of 30 kN is shown in Fig. 2.55. If the permissible tensile stress is 55 N/mm^2, determine the dimensions of the cross-section of link.*

(W-08)

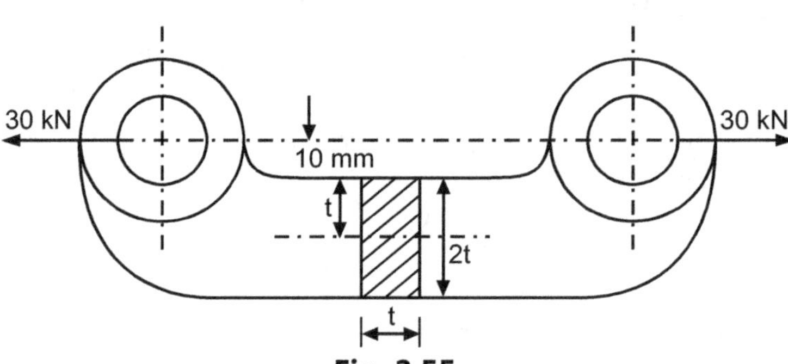

Fig. 2.55

Solution : Given data : $W = 30 \times 10^3$ N, $\sigma_t = 55$ N/mm^2, $e = (10 + t)$.

Step I : Direct stress, $\quad \sigma_o = \dfrac{W}{A} = \dfrac{30 \times 10^3}{t \times 2t} = \dfrac{30 \times 10^3}{2t^2} = \dfrac{15 \times 10^3}{t^2}$

Step II : Bending stress, $\sigma_b = \dfrac{M}{Z_{yy}} = \dfrac{W \times e}{\frac{1}{6} \times t \times b^2} = \dfrac{W \times e}{\frac{1}{6} \cdot t \cdot (2t)^2} = \dfrac{30 \times 10^3 \times (10 + t)}{\frac{4}{6} t^3}$

$$\therefore \quad \sigma_b = \frac{45 \times 10^3 (10 + t)}{t^3}$$

Step III : Total stress, $\quad \sigma_t = \sigma_o + \sigma_b$

$$\therefore \quad 55 = \frac{15 \times 10^3}{t^2} + \frac{45 \times 10^3 (10 + t)}{t^3}$$

Multiplying by t^3 on both side.

$$55t^3 = 15 \times 10^3 t + 45 \times 10^4 + 45 \times 10^3 t$$

$$\therefore 55t^3 - 60 \times 10^3 t - 45 \times 10^4 = 0$$

By trial and error method, $t = \textbf{36.28 mm} \cong \textbf{37 mm}$ and $b = 2t = 2 \times 37 = \textbf{74 mm}$

Problem 2.19 : *A symmetrical link shown in Fig. 2.56 carries load of 10 kN, breadth to thickness ratio is 4 : 1 and material used is 30C8 with yield strength 350 MPa, and factor of safety as 4. Find breadth (b) and its thickness (t), when the shape is modified to Fig. 2.57. Determine increase in breadth (b) and thickness (t).* **(W-09)**

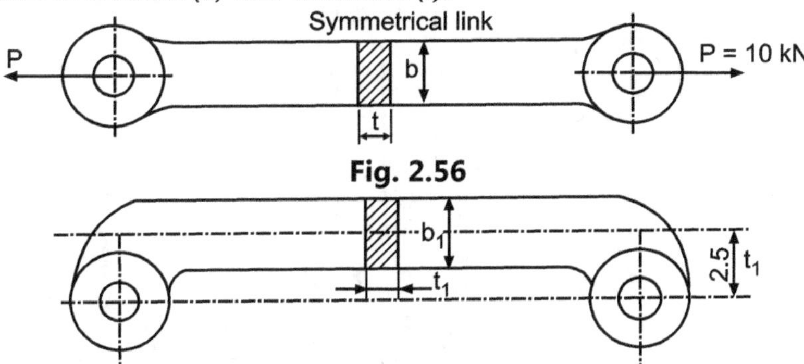

Fig. 2.56

Fig. 2.57

Solution : Given data : $W = 10$ kN $= 10 \times 10^3$ N, $b = 4t$.

Safe tensile stress for link $= \sigma_t = S_y/$factory of safety $= 350/4 = 87.5$ N/mm^2

Procedure :

Case I : When the link is in the position shown by full lines, then it is subjected to direct tensile stress is given by,

$$\sigma_t = \frac{W}{A} = \frac{W}{(b \times t)} = \frac{W}{(4t \times t)} = \frac{10 \times 10^3}{4t^2} = 87.5 \text{ N/mm}^2$$

Thus, $4t^2 = 114.285$, therefore, $t = 5.345$ mm $\cong 6$ mm (say) and $b = 4t = 24$ mm.

Case II : When the link is in the position as shown in Fig. 2.57, it will be subjected to direct as well as bending stress.

The direct tensile stress is given by,

$$\sigma_{t1} = \frac{W}{A} = \frac{W}{(b \times t)} = \frac{10 \times 10^3}{4t^2} = \frac{2.5 \times 10^3}{t^2}$$

Then bending stress is given by,

$$\sigma_b = M/Z$$

But $M = W \times c$ and $Z =$ Section modulus $= tb^2/6$

$$\sigma_b = \frac{W \times e}{tb^2/6} = \frac{6 \times W \times e}{t\,(4t)^2} = \frac{6 \times 10 \times 10^3 \times 2.5t}{16t^3} = \frac{9375}{t^2}$$

Total direct stress induced in offset link $= \sigma_t = \sigma_{t1} + \sigma_b$.

$$\sigma_t = \frac{2.5 \times 10^3}{t^2} + \frac{9375}{t^2} = 87.5$$

∴ $87.5\, t^2 = 11875$; thus, $t = 11.64$ mm $\cong 12$ mm (say)

and $b = 4t \times 12 = 48$ mm

∴   Thus, increase in width $= 48 - 24 = 24$ mm and increase in thickness $= 12 - 6 = 6$ mm.

Problem 2.20 : *An offset bar is loaded as shown in Fig. 2.58. The weight of bar is neglected. Find maximum offset, if allowable tensile stress is 70 MPa.*

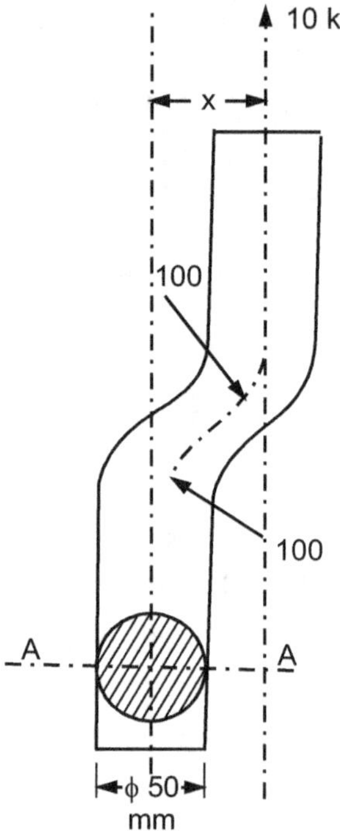

Fig. 2.58

Solution : Given data : $W = 10$ kN $= 10 \times 10^3$ N, $\sigma_t = 70$ MPa, $e = x$

Step I : Direct stress :

$$\sigma_o = \frac{W}{A} = \frac{10 \times 10^3}{\frac{\pi}{4} \times 50^2} = 5.092 \text{ N/mm}^2$$

Step II : Bending stress :

The maximum bending stress induced,

$$\sigma_b = \frac{M}{Z_{yy}} = \frac{W \times e}{\frac{\pi}{32} d^3} = \frac{10 \times 10^3 \times x \times 32}{\pi \times (50)^3} = 0.8148 \, x \text{ N/mm}^2$$

Step III :　　$\sigma_t = \sigma_o + \sigma_b$

∴　　　　$70 = 5.092 + 0.8148 \, x$

∴　　　　$x = \mathbf{79.66 \ mm}$

Problem 2.21 : *A mild steel bracket as shown in Fig. 2.59, is subjected to a pull of 2500 N acting at 30° to its horizontal axis. The bracket has a rectangular section, whose depth is twice the thickness. Find the cross-sectional dimensions of the bracket, if the permissible stress in the material is limited to 60 MPa.*　　**(S-09)**

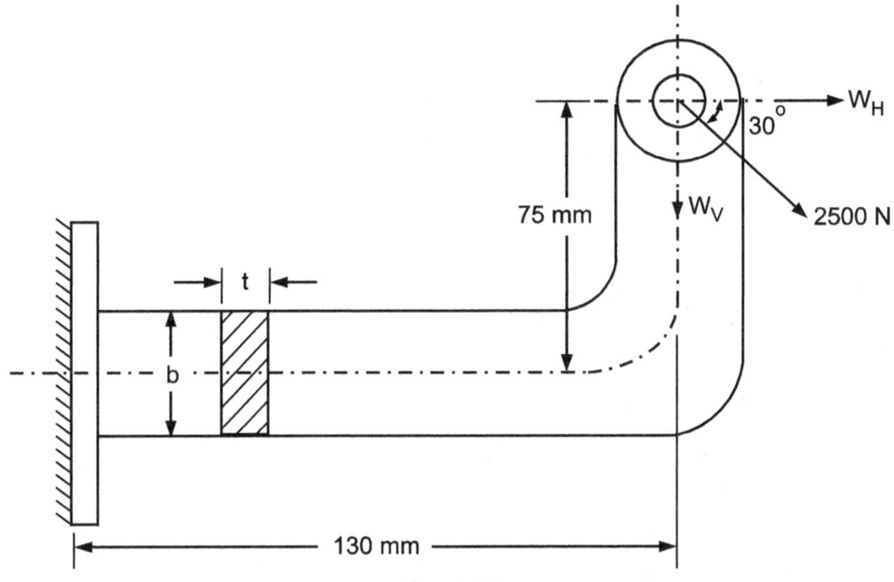

Fig. 2.59

Solution : Given data : $W = 2500$ N, $\theta = 30°$, $b = 2t$.

Safe tensile stress for link $= \sigma_t = 60$ N/mm^2.

Procedure : Resolving the load into two perpendicular components,

Horizontal component $= W_H = W \times \cos 30° = 2500 \times \cos 30° = 2165.06$ N

Vertical component $= W_V = W \times \sin 30° = 2500 \times \sin 30° = 1250$ N

(1) Due to horizontal component, bending stress will be induced in the link.

$M_H = W_H \times 75 = 2165.06 \times 75 = 162.3795 \times 10^3$ N-mm

$\therefore$ Bending stress, $\sigma_{bH} = \dfrac{M_H}{Z} = \dfrac{162.3795 \times 10^3}{\dfrac{1}{6}\,tb^2} = \dfrac{162.3795 \times 10^3 \times 6}{t \times (2t)^2} = \dfrac{243569.25}{t^3}$

(2) Due to vertical component, direct stress as well as bending stress will be induced in the link.

Direct stress $= \sigma_t = \dfrac{W_V}{A} = \dfrac{1250}{b \times t} = \dfrac{1250}{2t \times t} = \dfrac{1250}{2t^2} = \dfrac{625}{t^2}$

Bending moment $= M_V = W_V \times 130 = 1250 \times 130 = 162.5 \times 10^3$ N-mm

$\therefore$ Bending stress $= \sigma_{bV} = \dfrac{M_V}{Z} = \dfrac{162.5 \times 10^3}{tb^2/6} = \dfrac{162.5 \times 10^3 \times 6}{t \times (2t)^2} = \dfrac{243750}{t^3}$

Since the permissible stress is 60 N/mm^2,

$\therefore \quad \sigma_{bH} + \sigma_t + \sigma_{bV} = 60$

$\therefore \quad \dfrac{243569.25}{t^3} + \dfrac{625}{t^2} + \dfrac{243750}{t^3} = 60$

$\therefore \quad \dfrac{487319.25}{t^3} + \dfrac{625}{t^2} = 60$

$\therefore \quad 60t^3 - 625t - 487319.25 = 0$

$\therefore \quad t = 20.27$ mm $\cong$ **21 mm** and $b = 2t = 2 \times 21 =$ **42 mm**

Numerical Type No. 10 : "Overhang Crank"

Problem 2.22 : *The shaft of an overhang crank subjected to a force W of 1 kN is shown in Fig. 2.60. The shaft is made of plain carbon steel 45C8 and the tensile yield strength of 380 N/mm². The factor of safety is 2. Determine the diameter of the shaft using the maximum shear stress theory of failure.* **(S-11)**

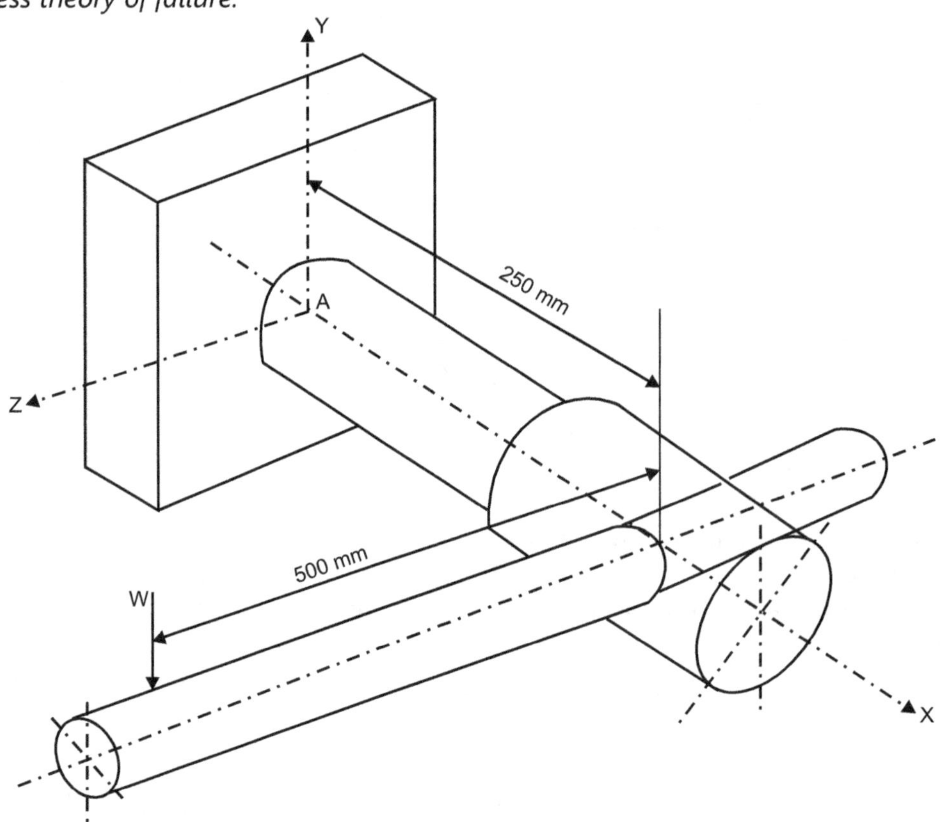

Fig. 2.60

Solution : Given data : σ_{yt} = 380 N/mm², W = 1 kN = 1000 N, F.S. = 2.

Procedure : According the maximum shear stress theory,

$$S_{sy} \; = \; 0.5 \, \sigma_{yt} \; = \; 0.5 \times 380 \; = \; \textbf{190 N/mm}^2$$

∴   The permissible shear stress τ will be,

$$\tau \; = \; \frac{S_{sy}}{F.S.} \; = \; \frac{190}{2} \; = \; \textbf{95 N/mm}^2 \qquad \ldots (1)$$

The stresses are critical at point A, which is subjected to a combined bending and twisting moment.

$$M \; = \; W \times 250 \; = \; 1000 \times 250 \; = \; 250 \times 10^3 \text{ N-mm}$$

$$T \; = \; W \times 500 \; = \; 1000 \times 500 \; = \; 500 \times 10^3 \text{ N.mm}$$

∴ $$\sigma_b \; = \; \frac{M}{Z} \; = \; \frac{250 \times 10^3}{\dfrac{\pi}{32} \cdot d^3} \; = \; \frac{2546.48 \times 10^3}{d^3}$$

$$\therefore \quad \tau = \frac{16T}{\pi d^3} = \frac{16 \times 500 \times 10^3}{\pi \cdot d^3} = \frac{2546.48 \times 10^3}{d^3}$$

According to maximum shear stress theory,

$$\tau_{max} = \frac{1}{2} \sqrt{\sigma_b^2 + 4\tau^2}$$

$$\therefore \quad 95 = \frac{1}{2}\sqrt{\left[\frac{2546.48 \times 10^3}{d^3}\right]^2 + 4\left[\frac{2546.48 \times 10^3}{d^3}\right]^2}$$

$$\therefore \quad d = \textbf{31.06 mm} \cong \textbf{32 mm (say)}$$

Problem 2.23 : *Find the maximum principal and shear stresses induced at the centre of the crankshaft bearing, if the overhang crank carries a tangential load of 20 kN at the centre of crank pin as shown in Fig. 2.61.*

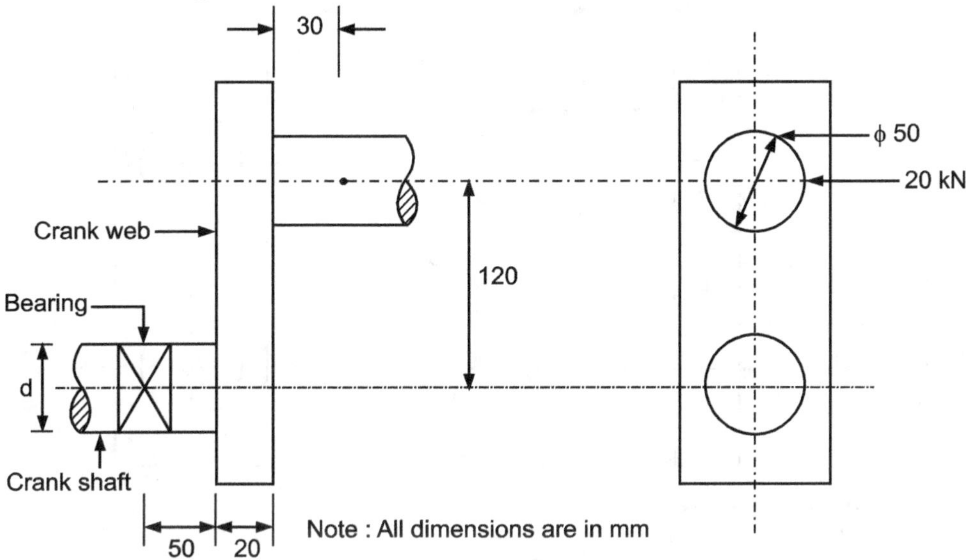

Fig. 2.61

Solution : Given data : W = 20 kN = 20×10^3 N, l = 50 + 20 + 30 = 100 mm,
     L = 120 mm, d = 50 mm.

Procedure : Torque transmitted at the axis of shaft is given by,

$$T = W \times L = 20 \times 10^3 \times 120 = 2.4 \times 10^6 \text{ N.mm}$$

Also, the bending moment induced in the crank is given by,

$$M = W \times l = 20 \times 10^3 \times 100 = 2 \times 10^6 \text{ N.mm}$$

The torsional shear stress induced in the crank,

$$\tau = \frac{16T}{\pi d^3} = \frac{16 \times 2.4 \times 10^6}{\pi \times (50)^3} = \textbf{97.78 N/mm}^2$$

Also, the bending stress induced in the crank,

$$\sigma_b = \frac{M}{Z} = \frac{M}{\frac{\pi}{32} d^3} = \frac{2 \times 10^6}{\frac{\pi}{32} \times (50)^3} = \textbf{162.97 N/mm}^2$$

According to maximum principal stress theory, maximum principal stress is given by,

$$\sigma_{max} = \frac{1}{2}\left[\sigma_b + \sqrt{\sigma_b^2 + 4\tau^2}\right]$$

$$= \frac{1}{2}\left[162.97 + \sqrt{(162.97)^2 + 4 \times (97.78)^2}\right] = \mathbf{208.76\ N/mm^2}$$

According to maximum shear stress theory, maximum shear stress is given by,

$$\tau_{max} = \frac{1}{2}\sqrt{\sigma_b^2 + 4\tau^2} = \frac{1}{2}\sqrt{(162.97)^2 + 4 \times (97.78)^2} = \mathbf{127.28\ N/mm^2}$$

Problem 2.24 : *Find the diameter 'd' of shaft, if 1.5 kN force acts at the crank pin. Take yield point stress as 600 MPa and factor of safety as 4. Use maximum shear stress theory.*

Solution :

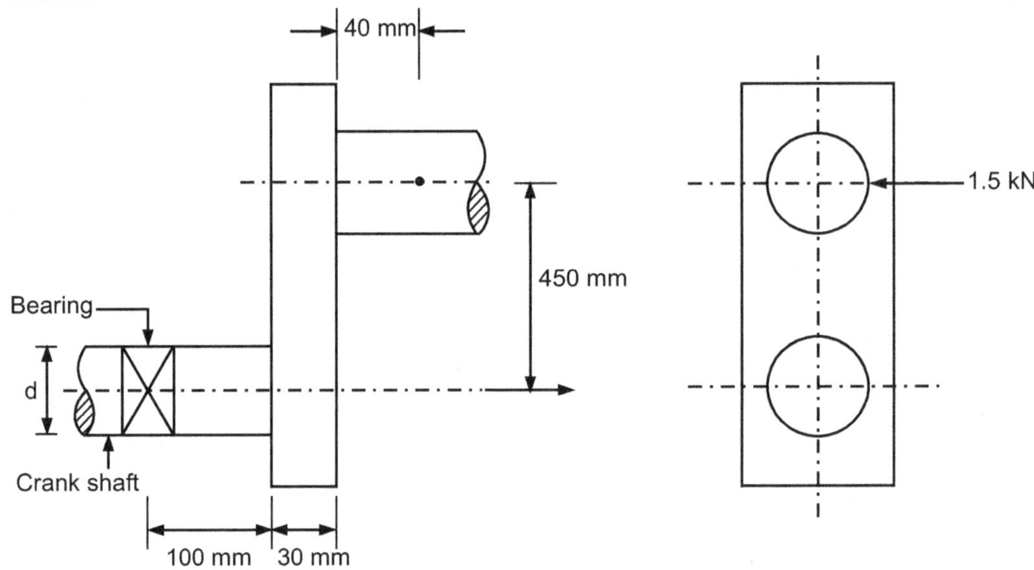

Fig. 2.62

Given data : W = 1.5 kN = 1500 N;　σ_{yt} = 600 MPa,　F.O.S. = 4,

l = 100 + 30 + 40 = 170 mm,　L = 450 mm.

Procedure : According to maximum shear stress theory,

$$S_{sy} = 0.5\ \sigma_{yt} = 0.5 \times 600 = \mathbf{300\ N/mm^2}$$

and allowable shear stress,

$$\tau_{max} = \frac{S_{sy}}{F.O.S.} = \frac{300}{4} = \mathbf{75\ N/mm^2}$$

Torque transmitted,

$$T = W \times L = 1500 \times 450 = \mathbf{675 \times 10^3\ N\text{-}mm}$$

Bending moment,

$$M = W \times l = 1500 \times 170 = \mathbf{255 \times 10^3\ N.mm}$$

Shear stress induced due to torque T is given by,

$$\tau = \frac{16T}{\pi d^3} = \frac{16 \times 675 \times 10^3}{\pi \times d^3} = \frac{3.438 \times 10^6}{d^3}$$

Also, the bending stress induced,

$$\sigma_b \;=\; \frac{M}{Z} \;=\; \frac{255 \times 10^3}{\dfrac{\pi}{32}\, d^3} \;=\; \frac{2.597 \times 10^6}{d^3}$$

According to maximum shear stress theory,

$$\tau_{max} \;=\; \frac{1}{2}\sqrt{\sigma_b^2 + 4\tau^2}$$

$$\therefore \qquad 75 \;=\; \frac{1}{2}\sqrt{\left(\frac{2.597 \times 10^6}{d^3}\right)^2 + 4 \times \left(\frac{3.438 \times 10^6}{d^3}\right)^2}$$

$$\therefore \qquad d \;=\; \mathbf{36.59\ mm} \;\cong\; \mathbf{38\ mm}$$

$\therefore$ The diameter of overhang crank shaft is **38 mm**.

Practice Questions

1. What is a cotter joint ? Explain with a neat sketch.
2. State various applications of a cotter joint ?
3. Discuss the design procedure of a spigot and socket cotter joint with a neat sketch.
4. Draw a neat sketch of cotter joint and write the various strength equations for its complete design.
5. Why taper is provided on cotter ? What is its normal value ?
6. Sketch two views of knuckle joint and write the strength equations showing failure sketches.
7. State the purpose of a turnbuckle. Describe its design procedure with a sketch.
8. Sketch an adjustable screwed joint for round rods and write the equations showing the strength of joint for most portable modes of failure.
9. Differentiate between 'direct stress' and 'bending stress'.

Problems for Practice

1. Design a cotter joint for a maximum load of 6 kN. The cotter joint parts are made up of C20 steel. The safe stresses are as follows :
   - Tensile stress = 60 N/mm^2
   - Compressive stress = 100 N/mm^2
   - Shear stress = 40 N/mm^2

   (**Ans.** d = 12 mm, d_2 = 14 mm, d_1 = 20 mm, modified d_2 = 16 mm, t = 4 mm, a = 5 mm, d_3 = 20 mm, t_1 = 3 mm, d_1 = 22 mm, d_4 = 32 mm, c = 6 mm, b = 20 mm)

2. A simple cotter joint is subjected to an axial load of 100 kN, which alternatively changes from tensile to compressive. Allowable stresses for the material are 80 N/mm^2, 35 N/mm^2 and 100 N/mm^2 in tension, shear and compression. The joint is subjected to 30% overload. **(S-02)**

   (**Ans.** d = 46 mm, d_2 = 56 mm, modified d_2 = 74 mm, t = 18.5 mm, a = 26 mm, d_3 = 90 mm, t_1 = 16 mm, d_1 = 90 mm, d_4 = 146 mm, b = 102 mm, c = 26 mm, l = 184 mm).

3. A knuckle joint is required to withstand a tensile load of 25 kN. Design the joint, if the permissible stresses are

    - Tensile stress = 56 MPa

    - Shear stress = 46 MPa and compressive stress = 70 MPa.   **(W-05)**

    (**Ans.** d = 24 mm, d_1 = 24 mm, t = 30 mm, d_2 = 48 mm, d_3 = 36 mm, t_1 = 22.5 mm, t_2 = 15 mm)

4. Design a turn buckle subjected to pull of 5 kN. The rod and nut are made of FeE380 and the factor of safety is 5.   **(S-04)**

    (**Ans.** d_c = 9.1523 mm, modified d_o = 22 mm, p = 5 mm, d_c = 17 mm, D = 26 mm, D_1 = 28 mm, D_2 = 30 mm)

5. Design a turn buckle to carry a load of 100 kN. The tie rod and nut are made of same material having permissible tensile stress as 75 N/mm^2 and permissible shear stress as 30 N/mm^2. Draw the neat sketch of joint.   **(S-05)**

    (**Ans.** d_c = 46.97 mm, modified d_o = 62 mm, p = 9 mm, d_c = 51 mm, l = 77.5 mm, D = 78 mm, D_1 = 68 mm, D_2 = 84 mm)

6. Design a hand lever having a length 1100 mm from the center of shaft to the point of application 800 N load. Effective overhang from nearest bearing is 150 mm. Find :

    (a) Diameter of shaft. (b) Section of lever, if $\dfrac{t}{b}$ = 0.5.

    The allowable tensile stress is 73 MPa and allowable shear stress is 60 MPa.
    Also design the key by using the same stress for key material.   **(W-04)**

    (**Ans.** d = 43 mm, w = 11 mm, t_1 = 7.33 mm, t = 27 mm, b = 54 mm)

7. The effective length of hand lever is 1 m. The effective overhang from nearest bearing is 150 mm. The lever is made of alloy steel, for which, permissible tensile stress is 115 N/mm^2 and shear stress is 57.5 N/mm^2. Maximum force exerted on handle is 300 N. Design the lever and shaft. Assume b = 3t.   **(W-06)**

    (**Ans.** d = 30 mm, d_2 = 46 mm, t_2 = 9 mm, l_2 = 37.5 mm, w = 7.5 mm, t_1 = 5 mm, t = 12 mm, b = 36 mm)

8. A foot lever is 1 m long from centre of shaft to point of application of 800 N load. Find : (1) Diameter of shaft (2) Dimensions of key and (3) Dimensions of rectangular arm of foot lever. Take overhang from nearest bearing = 100 mm. Allowable tensile stress and shear stress are taken as 70 N/mm^2.   **(S-11)**

9. A right angle bell crank lever is having one arm, 700 mm and other 400 mm long. The load of 175 kN is to be raised acting on a pin at the end of 700 mm arm and effort is applied at the end of 400 mm arm. The lever consist of a steel forgings, turning on a point at the fulcrum. The permissible stresses for the pin and lever are in tension and compression as 60 N/mm^2 and in shear as 80 N/mm^2. The bearing pressure on the pin is not to exceed 6 N/mm^2. Find :

    (a) Diameter and length of fulcrum pin.

    (b) Thickness (t) and depth (b) of rectangular cross-section of lever (assume b = 3t).   **(S-06)**

    (**Ans.** d_F = 218 mm, l_F = 272.5 mm, t = 124 mm, b = 372 mm)

10. A C-frame subjected to a force of 15 kN is shown in Fig. 2.63. It is made of grey cast iron FG300 with ultimate tensile strength of 300 MPa. The factor of safety is 2.5. Determine the dimension of cross-section.

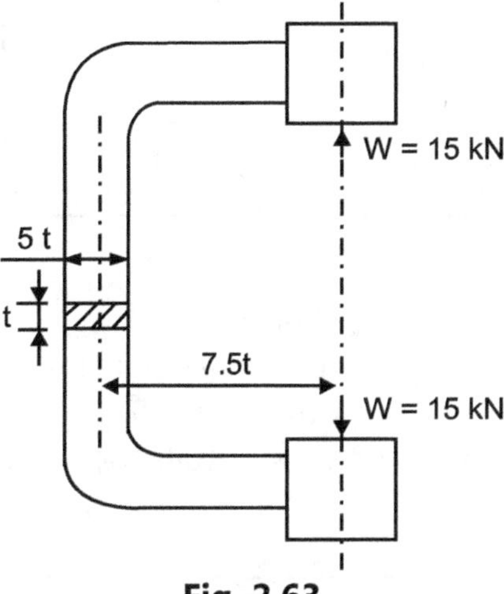

Fig. 2.63

(**Ans.** t = 15.81 mm $\cong$ 16 mm (say), b = 80 mm)

11. Fig. 2.64 shows a C-clamp, which carries a load of 25 kN. The cross-section of the clamp is rectangular and the ratio of width to thickness (b/t) is 2 : 1. The clamp is made of cast steel having S_{ut} = 400 N/mm^2 and the factor of safety is 4. Determine the dimensions of the cross-section of the clamp.

(**Ans.** t = 38.5 mm, b = 77 mm)

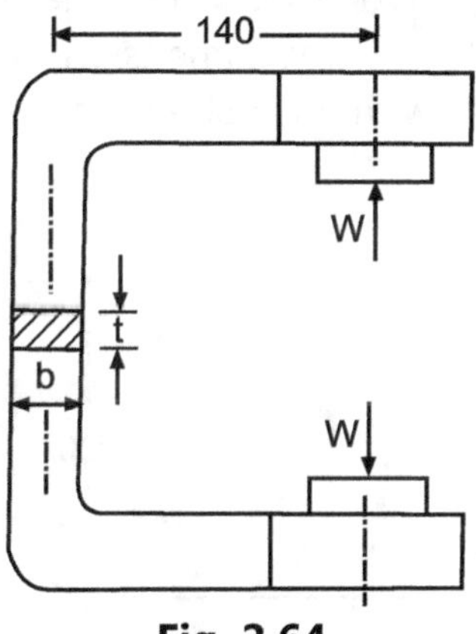

Fig. 2.64

12. The spindle of drilling machine is subjected to a maximum load of 10 kN during operation. Determine the diameter of solid C.I. column machine, if tensile stress is limited to 40 N/mm^2. The distance between axis of spindle and axis of column is 330 mm. Also, find the direct stress and stress due to bending in the column. **(S-08)**
(**Ans.** σ_b = bending stress = 37.98 N/mm^2, d = 96 mm, σ_o = 1.3812 N/mm^2)

13. A frame of hacksaw is shown in Fig. 2.65. The initial tension in the blade is 300 N. The frame is made of plain carbon steel with tensile yield strength 400 N/mm^2. Take factor of safety as 3. Determine the size of cross-section of the frame. **(S-05)**

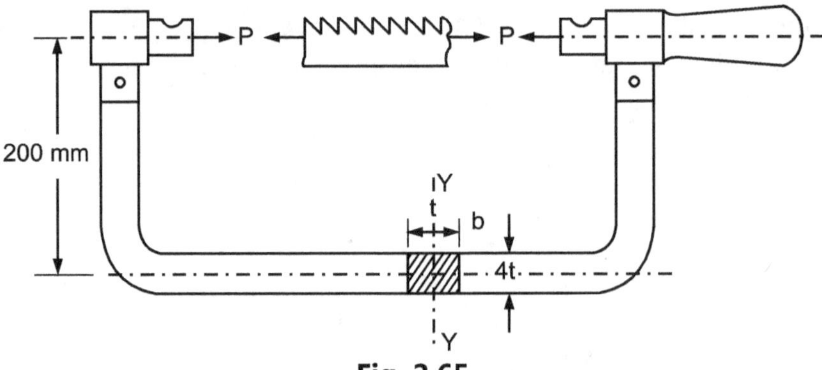

Fig. 2.65

(**Hint :** Assume b = 4t, **Ans.** t = 6 mm, b = 24 mm)

14. A M.S. link is shown in Fig. 2.66. It transmits a pull of 80 kN. Find the maximum stress included in it and the factor of safety available, if the yield point in tension is 200 N/mm^2.

(W-07)

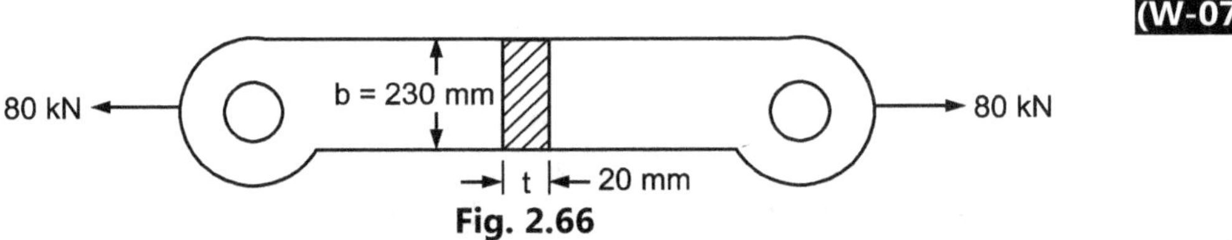

Fig. 2.66

(**Ans.**   F.O.S. = 2.87, σ_{max} = 69.56 N/mm^2)

15. A mild steel bracket shown in Fig. 2.67 is subjected to a force of 5 kN at an angle of 30° with horizontal axis. The cross-section of the bracket is rectangular with ratio of depth to thickness as 3 : 1. Find the dimension of the cross-section of bracket. The bracket is made of cast steel with σ_{yt} = 300 MPa. Use factor of safety as 5.

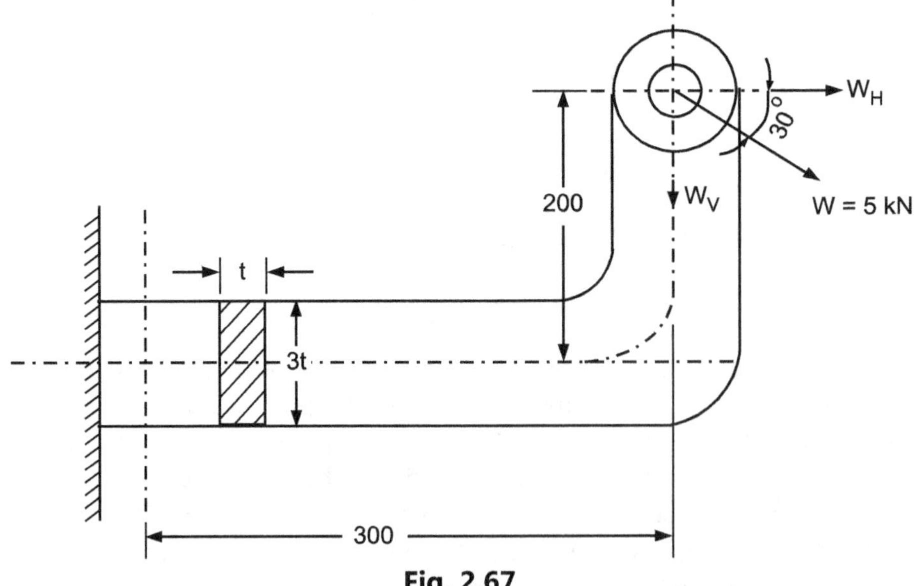

Fig. 2.67

(**Ans.**   t = 27 mm, b = 81 mm)

16. An overhang crank shown in Fig. 2.68 carries a tangential load of 10 kN at the centre of the crank pin. Find the maximum principal stress and maximum shear stress at the centre of the crankshaft.

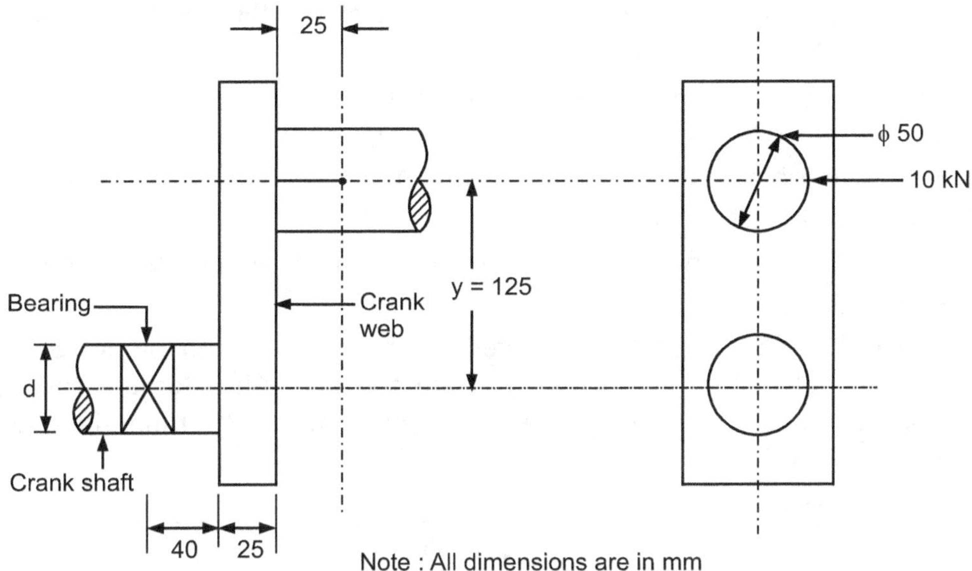

Fig. 2.68

(**Ans.** τ_{max} = 62.74 N/mm², $\sigma_{b\ max}$ = 99.41 N/mm²)

MSBTE Questions and Answers

Summer 2013

1.   Why taper is provided to cotter?   **(2 M)**

Ans. Refer Article 2.2.5.1.

2.   State the function of split pin in knuckle joint.   **(2 M)**

Ans. Refer Article 2.3.7.

3.   Draw a neat labelled diagram of a hand lever and state how diameter of shaft and boss is calculated.   **(4 M)**

Ans. Refer Article 2.5.2.

4.   Explain "Failure of Cotter in Bending".   **(4 M)**

Ans. Refer Article 2.2.5.

5.   State the design procedure of a knuckle joint with neat sketch.   **(8 M)**

Ans. Refer Article 2.3.4.

6.   A foot lever is 1 m from the centre of the shaft to the point of application of 800 N load. Find diameter of shaft. f_s = 70 MPa.   **(4 M)**

Ans. Refer Problem 2.7.

Winter 2013

1. Design a foot brake lever from the following data :   **(8 M)**

    (i)   Length of lever from the centre of gravity of the spindle to the point of application of load = 1 m.

    (ii)   Maximum load on the foot plate = 800 N.

    (iii)   Overhang from nearest bearing = 100 mm.

    (iv)   Permissible tensile and shear stress = 70 MPa.

Ans. Refer Problem 2.7.

2. Write the strength equations considered in design of turn buckle with neat sketch.

Ans. Refer Article 2.4.3.

3. Two C-40 rods of 40 mm diameter are to be connected by cotter joint. The thickness of cotter is 12 mm. Calculate the dimensions of the socket, if the maximum permissible stresses are 46 N/mm^2 in tension 35 N/mm^2 in shear and 70 N/mm^2 in crushing.   **(8 M)**

Ans. Refer Problem 2.2.

Summer 2014

1. Design a "C" clamp frame for a total clamping force of 20 kN. The cross-section of the frame is rectangular and width to thickness ratio is 2. The distance between load line and neutral axis of rectangular section is 12 mm and gap between two faces is 180 mm. The frame is made of cast steel. The permissible tensile stress for cast steel is 100 N/mm^2.   **(6 M)**

Ans. Refer Problem 2.11.

2. Explain the design procedure of hand lever with suitable sketch.   **(8 M)**

Ans. Refer Article 2.5.2.

3. Two mild steel rods of 40 mm diameter are to be connected by cotter joint. The thickness of cotter is 12 mm. Calculate the dimensions of the socket, if the maximum permissible stresses are 46 N/mm^2 in tension, 35 N/mm^2 in shear and 70 N/mm^2 in crushing.   **(8 M)**

Ans. Refer Problem 2.2.

❑❑❑

Chapter 3

DESIGN OF SHAFTS, KEYS AND COUPLINGS

About This Chapter

This chapter carries weightage of 24 marks and assigned duration is 14 hours. In this chapter, we will study types, materials and design of shafts, ASME code, different types of keys and their advantages, design of various types of couplings. Also we will study design considerations and procedure of gear, power transmission capacity, gear tooth failure modes etc.

Statistical Analysis

Examination	Weightage of questions asked
S-09	22 Marks
W-09	22 Marks
S-10	20 Marks
W-10	20 Marks
S-11	20 Marks
W-11	20 Marks
S-12	24 Marks
W-12	30 Marks
S-13	24 Marks
W-13	28 Marks
S-14	32 Marks

3.1 INTRODUCTION TO SHAFT

- Shaft is a rotating element, usually of circular cross-section.
- Shaft is used to transmit power, from one place to another.
- Power is delivered to the shaft by means of tangential force and resultant torque is set up within the shaft. To transfer the power from one shaft to another, the various components such as pulleys, gears etc., are mounted on it, by means of keys and splines.
- Generally, the power transmitting shafts are subjected to bending moment and twisting moment (or torque). Hence, bending and torsional shear stresses are induced in the shafts.
- Bending moment is caused due to mounting of pulleys, gears, sprockets etc.

(3.1)

3.1.1 Essential Characteristics of Shaft Material

The essential characteristics of the shaft material are :

(a) High strength.

(b) Good heat treatment properties.

(c) Good machinablity

(d) Low notch sensitivity factor.

(e) High wear resistant properties

(f) Ductility.

(g) High resilience

(h) High fatigue strength.

3.1.2 Materials used for Shaft

The commonly used materials for shaft are :

(a) For *ordinary use*, carbon steels are used. For example : 40C8, 45C8 and 50C4.

(b) For *high strength*, alloy steel such as nickel, nickel-chromium or chrome vanadium steel are used. For example : 40Cr1Mo28, 40Ni1Cr1Mo15 etc.

3.1.3 Manufacturing Processes used for Shaft

- The basic method of production of shaft is by hot rolling and then finished to size by cold drawing or turning and grinding.
- Cold drawing produces a stronger shaft than hot rolling. However, cold drawn shafts have certain disadvantages. Cold drawing produces residual stresses at and near the surface of shaft.
- During machining operations like slotting and milling, required to make the key slot, the residual stresses are partially released causing distortion of shaft. The straightening of this distorted and twisted shaft is very difficult and expensive operation.
- Therefore, most of the transmission shafts are turned and ground after hot rolling.
- Shafts of larger diameter are generally forged and turned to required size. In order to increase the wear resistance and toughness, heat treatment is done on the shaft material.

3.1.4 Types of Shafts

Shafts are classified into following types :

(a) Transmission shafts :

- It is used to transmit power from one point to another, i.e. from source of power to power absorrbing device. For example : Electric motor (source) and water pump (power absorbing device).
- They support transmission elements like gears, pulleys, sprockets etc.
- Examples : Line shafts, counter shafts and overhead shafts etc.
- Line shaft consists of number of shafts, which are connected in axial direction by means of couplings.
- Counter shaft is a secondary shaft, which is driven by main shaft and from which, power is supplied to a machine component.

(b) Spindle :

- A spindle is a short rotating shaft, which forms the integral part of machine.
- It is used in all machine tools, such as lathe spindle, drilling machine, grinding machine spindle etc. It imparts motion either to a cutting tool or workpiece.

(c) Axle :

- An axle is a non-rotating element.
- It supports a rotating element like wheel, hoisting drum or rope sheave, which is fitted to the housing by means of bearings.
- Axle does not transmit any torque. Therefore, axle is subjected to only bending moment due to transverse loads like bearing or support reactions.
- For example : rear axle of railway wagon.

(d) Machine shafts :

- They are an integral part of a machine itself.
- For example : Crank shaft.

3.1.5 Distinguish between Shaft and Axle

Question

1. Distinguish between shaft and axle. **(S-14)**

Sr. No.	Shaft	Axle
1.	Shaft is a rotating member.	Axle is non-rotating member.
2.	The purpose of a shaft is to transmit the torque and to support the transmission elements like gears, pulleys etc.	The purpose of an axle is only to support the transmission elements like wheels, pulleys etc.
3.	Shaft is subjected to torque, bending moment, and/or axial force.	Axle is subjected to bending moment and/or axial force.

3.1.6 Difference between Shaft, Axle and Spindle **(S-13)**

Shaft	Axle	Spindle
1. It is a rotating element, transmitting power from one place to other.	1. It is a stationary element, used to support a rotating body.	1. It is a short shaft imparting motion either to a cutting tool or workpiece.
2. It is subjected to torque, bending moment or axial force.	2. It is subjected to only bending moment.	2. It is subjected to torque, bending moment or axial force.
3. Example : Propeller shaft.	3. Example : Front and rear axles of motorcycle.	3. Example : Drill spindle.

3.1.7 Standard Sizes of Shafts

- The standard length of shafts are 5 m, 6 m and 7 m.
- The length of shafting should not be more than 7 m.
- The following are the common sizes of transmission shafts :
  - (a) 25 to 60 mm by 5 mm increments.
  - (b) 60 to 110 mm by 10 mm increments.
  - (c) 110 to 140 mm by 15 mm increments.
  - (d) 140 to 500 mm by 20 mm increments.   (Dimensions are in millimetres)

3.1.8 Design of Shaft on the Basis of Strength

- Shafts may be designed on the basis of (a) strength, (b) rigidity and (c) stiffness.
- While designing the shafts on the basis of strength, the following cases may be considered :
  - (a) Shafts subjected to twisting moment only.
  - (b) Shafts subjected to bending moment only.
  - (c) Shafts subjected to combined twisting and bending moments.

(a) Design of Shafts Subjected to Twisting Moment (Torque) Only :

- Here, the diameter of shaft can be determined by using basic torsion equation.

We know that,

$$\frac{T}{J} = \frac{\tau}{r} \qquad \text{.... (3.1)}$$

where, T = Twisting moment (or torque) acting on the shaft in N.mm

       J = Polar moment of inertia (Polar M.I.) of shaft about axis of rotation in mm^4

       τ = Torsional shear stress in N/mm^2

       r = Distance of neutral axis to outermost fiber in mm

$$= \frac{d}{2} \qquad \text{(for solid shaft)}$$

$$= \frac{d_o}{2} \qquad \text{(for hollow shaft)}$$

We have, $J = \dfrac{\pi}{32} \times d^4 \qquad \text{(for solid shaft)}$

$$= \frac{\pi}{32} \times (d_o^4 - d_i^4) \qquad \text{(for hollow shaft)}$$

Therefore, for solid shaft, equation (3.1) becomes,

$$\frac{T}{\dfrac{\pi}{32} d^4} = \frac{\tau}{\dfrac{d}{2}}$$

i.e. $T = \dfrac{\pi}{16} \cdot \tau \cdot d^3$

From this equation, we can find diameter of shaft.

Similarly, for **hollow shaft**, equation (3.1) becomes,

$$\frac{T}{\frac{\pi}{32}[d_o^4 - d_i^4]} = \frac{\tau}{\frac{d_o}{2}}$$

$$T \times \frac{d_o}{2} = \tau \times \frac{\pi}{32} \cdot [d_o^4 - d_i^4]$$

$$\therefore \quad T = \frac{\pi}{16} \cdot \tau \cdot \frac{(d_o^4 - d_i^4)}{d_o} = \frac{\pi}{16} \cdot \tau \cdot \frac{d_o^4}{d_o}\left[1 - \left(\frac{d_i}{d_o}\right)^4\right]$$

$$T = \frac{\pi}{16} \cdot \tau \cdot d_o^3 \, (1 - k^4)$$

where, $k = \dfrac{d_i}{d_o}$ = Ratio of inside diameter to outside diameter

(b) Design of Shafts Subjected to Bending Moment Only :

- Here, the diameter of shaft can be determined by using bending equation (flexural formula).

$$\frac{M}{I} = \frac{\sigma_b}{y} \qquad \qquad \text{... (3.2)}$$

where, M = Maximum bending moment on the shaft in N.mm

           I = Moment of inertia of cross-sectional area of shaft about axis of rotation in mm^4

           σ_b = Bending stress in N/mm^2

           y = Distance from neutral axis to outermost fibre in mm

For solid shaft, $I = \dfrac{\pi}{64} d^4$

and $y = \dfrac{d}{2}$

$\therefore$ Equation (3.2) becomes,

$$\frac{M}{\frac{\pi}{64} d^4} = \frac{\sigma_b}{\frac{d}{2}}$$

$$\therefore \quad M = \frac{\pi}{32} \cdot \sigma_b \cdot d^3$$

From this equation, diameter of solid shaft can be determined.

For hollow shaft, $I = \dfrac{\pi}{64} [(d_o)^4 - (d_i)^4]$

$$= \frac{\pi}{64} \cdot d_o^4 \, [1 - k^4] \qquad \qquad \left[\because k = \frac{d_i}{d_o}\right]$$

and $y = \dfrac{d_o}{2}$

$\therefore$ Equating (3.2) becomes,

$$\frac{M}{\frac{\pi}{64} \cdot d_o^4 \, (1 - k^4)} = \frac{\sigma_b}{\frac{d_o}{2}}$$

$\therefore$

$$M = \frac{\pi}{32} \cdot \sigma_b \cdot d_o^3 \, (1 - k^4)$$

From this equation, diameters of hollow shaft can be determined.

(c) Design of Shafts Subjected to Combined Twisting and Bending Moment :

When the shaft is subjected to combined twisting and bending moment, then the shaft must be designed on the basis of two moments simultaneously.

(1) According to maximum shear stress theory :

We have, τ_{max} = Maximum shear stress = $\dfrac{1}{2}\sqrt{\sigma_b^2 + 4(\tau)^2}$ ... (3.3)

We know that, $T = \dfrac{\pi}{16} \cdot \tau \cdot d^3$

$\therefore$ $\tau = \dfrac{16T}{\pi d^3}$

Also, $M = \dfrac{\pi}{32} \cdot \sigma_b \cdot d^3$

$\therefore$ $\sigma_b = \dfrac{32\,M}{\pi \cdot d^3}$

Put the values of τ and σ_b in equation (3.3),

$$\tau_{max} = \frac{1}{2}\sqrt{\left(\frac{32\,M}{\pi d^3}\right)^2 + 4\left(\frac{16T}{\pi d^3}\right)^2}$$

$$\tau_{max} = \frac{1}{2} \cdot \left(\frac{32}{\pi d^3}\right)\sqrt{M^2 + T^2}$$

$\therefore$

$$\sqrt{M^2 + T^2} = \frac{\pi}{16}\,\tau_{max} \cdot d^3$$

The expression $[\sqrt{M^2 + T^2}]$ is called as **equivalent twisting moment** and denoted by T_e. By limiting the maximum shear stress τ_{max} equal to allowable shear stress τ, we have,

$$T_e = \sqrt{M^2 + T^2} = \frac{\pi}{16}\,\tau \cdot d^3$$

(2) According to maximum normal stress theory :

The maximum normal stress in the shaft is,

$$\sigma_{b\ max} = \frac{1}{2}\,\sigma_b + \frac{1}{2}\sqrt{\sigma_b^2 + 4(\tau)^2}$$

$\therefore$

$$\sigma_{b\ max} = \frac{1}{2} \cdot \left(\frac{32M}{\pi d^3}\right) + \frac{1}{2}\sqrt{\left(\frac{32M}{\pi d^3}\right)^2 + 4 \cdot \left(\frac{16T}{\pi d^3}\right)^2}$$

$$\therefore \qquad \sigma_{b\,max} = \frac{1}{2}\left(\frac{32M}{\pi d^3}\right) + \frac{1}{2} \cdot \left(\frac{32}{\pi d^3}\right) \cdot \sqrt{M^2 + T^2}$$

$$\therefore \qquad \sigma_{b\,max} = \frac{32}{\pi d^3}\left[\frac{1}{2} \cdot M + \frac{1}{2} \cdot \sqrt{M^2 + T^2}\right]$$

$$\therefore \qquad \sigma_{b\,max} = \frac{32}{\pi d^3}\left[\frac{1}{2}(M + \sqrt{M^2 + T^2})\right]$$

$$\therefore \qquad \frac{1}{2}(M + \sqrt{M^2 + T^2}) = \frac{\pi}{32}\,\sigma_{b\,max}\,d^3$$

The expression $\frac{1}{2}\{M + \sqrt{M^2 + T^2}\}$ is called as **equivalent bending moment** and is denoted by M_e. By limiting the maximum normal stress (σ_{bmax}) equal to the allowable bending stress σ_b, we have, $M_e = \frac{1}{2}[M + \sqrt{M^2 + T^2}] = \frac{\pi}{32} \cdot \sigma_b \cdot d^3$

Thus, we can find diameter of shaft using above expression.

Similarly, for hollow shaft, we can derive,

$$T_e = \frac{\pi}{16} \cdot \tau_{max} \cdot d_o^3 \cdot (1 - k^4) = \sqrt{M^2 + T^2}$$

and

$$M_e = \frac{\pi}{32} \cdot \sigma_{b\,max} \cdot d_o^3\,(1 - k^4) = \frac{1}{2}(M + \sqrt{M^2 + T^2})$$

3.1.9 Design of Shaft on the Basis of Rigidity

- In some applications, torsional deformation of shaft (torsional rigidity) and lateral deflection (lateral rigidity) may not be tolerated.
- Insufficient rigidity or stiffness can result in poor performance of various shaft mounted elements such as bearings, clutches, gears etc.
- For such cases, rigidity or stiffness of shaft is very important.

Torsional Rigidity :

- The torsional rigidity refers to resistance to the angular deflection of a shaft.
- The torsional stiffness or rigidity of the shaft is given by,

$$S = \frac{\text{Torque}}{\text{Torsional deflection or angle of twist}} = \frac{T}{\theta} \qquad \ldots (3.4)$$

- The torsional deflection may be obtained by using the torsion equation.

$$\frac{T}{J} = \frac{G\theta}{L}$$

or

$$\theta = \frac{T \cdot L}{G \cdot J} \qquad \ldots (3.5)$$

where,

θ = Torsional deflection or angle of twist in radians

T = Twisting moment or torque in N.mm

$$J = \text{Polar M.I.}$$

$$= \frac{\pi}{32} \cdot d^4 \qquad \text{(for solid shaft) in mm}^4$$

$$= \frac{\pi}{32} \cdot [(d_o)^4 - (d_i)^4] \qquad \text{(for hollow shaft) in mm}^4$$

$$L = \text{Length of shaft in mm}$$

$$G = \text{Modulus of rigidty in N/mm}^2$$

- Therefore, equation (3.4) becomes

Torsional stiffness or rigidity of the shaft, $\;S = \dfrac{T}{\theta} = \dfrac{T}{\dfrac{T \cdot L}{G \cdot J}} = \dfrac{GJ}{L}$.   [Refer equation 3.5]

- The torsional rigidity should be high. It means that, the angle of twist should not be more than 0.25° per metre length of shafts, in case of I.C. engine, where timing of valves would be affected.

- The widely used deflection for shafts is limited to 1° for a length of 20 times the diameter of shaft.

- The various steps taken to reduce the deflection of shaft are :

  (a) Parts such as pulleys, gears mounted on shaft should be arranged very close to the bearings.

  (b) Pulleys, gears and other parts mounted should be lighter in weight.

3.1.9.1 Lateral Rigidity

- Lateral rigidity refers to the lateral deflection of shaft.

- In case of shaft running at high speed, where a small deflection would cause huge out of balance of forces, lateral rigidity is very important.

- In case, if shaft is of uniform cross-section, then the lateral deflection of a shaft may be obtained by using deflection formulae as in strength of materials.

- But, when the shaft is of variable cross-section, then the lateral deflection may be determined from fundamental equation of elastic curve of a beam.

$$\frac{d^2y}{dx^2} = \frac{M}{E \cdot I}$$

- Lateral deflection should not exceed *0.85 mm per metre of length of shafts*.

- The maximum permissible lateral deflection for transmission shafts is taken as,

$$\delta = 0.001 \text{ to } 0.003 \, L$$

where, $L = \text{Length of shaft in mm}$

- The product 'E · I' represents **lateral rigidity**.

- Lateral rigidity of shaft $= \dfrac{\text{Force}}{\text{Maximum deflection}} = \dfrac{F}{\delta}$

3.1.10 ASME Code for Design of Shaft Subjected to Fluctuating Load

- Transmission shafts or line shafts or overhead shafts are meant for transmitting power from one end to the other.

- A prime mover such as a constant speed electric motor is used to supply necessary power to the shaft. The power is taken out at various points from the shaft through various machine elements like belts and pulleys, chains and sprocket, gear pairs etc., directly mounted on it. The various shaft lengths are coupled together by using rigid coupling, thus, forming required length of the line shafting. These shafts are supported on sleeve bearings or pedestal bearings. These shafts are thus subjected to combined bending and twisting moments. Since, the loads on most of the shafts in connected machinery are not constant, it is necessary to make proper allowance for the harmful effects of load fluctuations.

- According to ASME (American Society of Mechanical Engineering) code, this effect is compensated by introducing two factors 'k_m' and 'k_t' in the usual design equations used for design of transmission shafts on the basis of maximum principal shear stress theory (Guest's theory) as follows.

  Maximum principal shear stress,

$$\tau_{max} \;=\; \frac{16}{\pi d^3}\sqrt{(k_m \cdot M)^2 + (k_t \cdot T)^2}$$

where, $k_m = k_b$ = Combined shock and fatigue factor in bending

k_t = Combined shock and fatigue factor in twisting

- The recommended values of k_m and k_t are given in the Table 3.1.

Table 3.1 : Recommended (ASME Code) values for k_m and k_t

Types of load	k_m or k_b	k_t
1. Stationary shaft		
(a) Gradually applied load	1.0	1.0
(b) Suddenly applied load	1.5 to 2.0	1.5 to 2.0
2. Rotating shafts		
(a) Gradually applied or steady load	1.5	1.0
(b) Suddenly applied with minor shocks	1.5 to 2.0	1.5 to 2.0
(c) Suddenly applied load with heavy shocks	2.0 to 3.0	1.5 to 3.0

- According to ASME code, permissible shear stress for shaft without keyway is taken as 30% of yield strength or 18% of ultimate tensile strength, whichever is minimum.

$\therefore$ τ_{max} = 0.30 τ_{yt}

or τ_{max} = 0.18 τ_{ut}

- If keyways are present, these values are to be reduced by 25 %.

3.1.11 Advantages of Hollow Shaft

Question

1. State the reasons for using hollow shaft rather than solid shaft for large power transmission. **(S-14)**

The hollow shafts have the following advantages over the solid shaft :

(1) The hollow shaft has higher torque transmitting capacity than the solid shaft of same weight. i.e. hollow shaft is lighter in weight than the solid shaft for same torque transmission capacity.

(2) The hollow shaft has higher torsional as well as lateral rigidity than the solid shaft of same weight.

3.1.12 Applications of Hollow Shaft

The hollow shafts are used in :

(1) Machine tools.

(2) Marine applications.

3.1.13 Comparison of Solid Shaft and Hollow Shaft

Question

1. Give any two differences between solid shaft and hollow shaft. **(S-09, 10)**

Solid shaft	Hollow shaft
1. Design equations : (a) $T = \dfrac{\pi}{16} \cdot \tau \cdot d^3$ (b) $M = \dfrac{\pi}{32} \cdot \sigma_b \cdot d^3$	1. Design equations : (a) $T = \dfrac{\pi}{16} \cdot \tau \cdot d_o^3 \cdot (1 - k^4)$ (b) $M = \dfrac{\pi}{32} \cdot \sigma_b \cdot d_o^3 (1 - k^4)$
2. Weight of solid shaft is more than hollow shaft for same torque transmitted.	2. Weight of hollow shaft is less. So material cost is reduced.

Additional Formulae

(1) Power,		$P = \dfrac{2\pi NT}{60}$ in watts

where,		T = Torque or twisting moment in N.m,

N = Speed of shaft in r.p.m.

(2) Torque transmitted by a pulley,

$T = (T_1 - T_2) \times R$

where,		T_1 = Tension in tight side of belt in 'N'

T_2 = Tension in slack side of belt in 'N'

R = Radius of pulley in 'mm'

Numerical Type No. 1 : "Shafts Subjected to Twisting Moment Only"

Problem 3.1 : *A solid shaft is transmitting 1 MW at 240 r.p.m. Determine the diameter of shaft, if the maximum torque transmitted exceeds the mean torque by 20%. Take the maximum allowable shear stress as 60 N/mm².* **(S-06)**

Solution : Given data : $P = 1$ MW $= 1 \times 10^6$ W, N $= 240$ r.p.m., $\tau = 60$ N/mm².

Procedure :

We have,

$$\text{Power transmitted} = P = \frac{2\pi N \cdot T_{mean}}{60}$$

$$\text{Torque transmitted, } T_{mean} = \frac{P \times 60}{2\pi N} = \frac{1 \times 10^6 \times 60}{2 \times \pi \times 240} = 39788.73 \text{ N-m}$$

It is given that : T_{max} exceeds more than T_{mean} by 20%.

$\therefore \qquad\qquad\qquad T_{max} = 1.2 \times T_{mean} = 1.2 \times 39788.73 = 47746.47$ N-m

$\therefore \qquad\qquad\qquad T_{max} = 47746.47 \times 10^3$ N-mm

The shaft is designed on the basis of strength from the torsion equation.

We have, $\qquad\qquad T_{max} = \pi/16 \times \tau \times d^3$

$\qquad\qquad 47746.47 \times 10^3 = \pi/16 \times 60 \times d^3$

$\therefore \qquad\qquad\qquad d = 159.43$ mm $\cong$ **160 mm (say)**

Problem 3.2 : *A hollow shaft of a rotary compressor is to be designed to transmit a maximum torque of 4750 N-m. The shear stress in the shaft is limited to 50 N/mm². Determine the inside and outside diameters of the shafts, if the ratio of inside to outside diameter is 0.4.*

Solution : Given data : $T = 4750$ N-m $= 4.75 \times 10^6$ N-mm, $\tau = 50$ N/mm².

$$(d_i/d_o) = k = 0.4$$

Procedure : The hollow shaft is designed on the basis of strength from the derived torsion equation,

$$T = \frac{\pi}{16} \times \tau \times d_o^3 (1 - k^4)$$

$$\therefore \qquad 4.75 \times 10^6 = \frac{\pi}{16} \times 50 \times d_o^3 \{1 - (0.4)^4\}$$

Thus, $d_o = 79.18$ mm $\approx$ **80 mm (say)** and $d_i = 0.4 \times d_o = 0.4 \times 80 = $ **32 mm**

Problem 3.3 : *A line shaft rotating at 250 r.p.m. is to transmit 25 kW. The shaft is having an allowable shear stress 42 MPa and bending stress 65 MPa. Find diameter of shaft.* **(S-13)**

Solution : Given data : $P = 25$ kW $= 25 \times 10^3$ W, N $= 250$ r.p.m., $\tau = 42$ N/mm², $\sigma_b = 65$ N/mm².

Procedure : We have, $\qquad P = \dfrac{2\pi NT}{60}$

$$\therefore \qquad 25 \times 10^3 = \frac{2\pi \times 250 \times T}{60}$$

$$\therefore \qquad\qquad T = 954.93 \text{ N.m} = 954.93 \times 10^3 \text{ N.mm}$$

As shaft is subjected to only twisting moment,

$$T = \frac{\pi}{16} \cdot \tau \cdot d^3$$

$$\therefore \quad 954.93 \times 10^3 = \frac{\pi}{16} \times 42 \times d^3$$

$$\therefore \quad d = \textbf{48.74 mm} \cong \textbf{50 mm (say)}$$

Problem 3.4 : *Find the diameter of solid shaft to transmit 20 kW at 200 r.p.m. The ultimate shear stress for steel may be taken as 360 MPa and F.S. = 8. If a hollow shaft is used in place of solid shaft, find inside and outside diameter. Ratio of outside to inside diameter for hollow shaft is 2.*   **(W-07)**

Solution : Given data : P = 20 kW = 20×10^3 W, N = 200 r.p.m.,

$$\tau_{ut} = 360 \text{ MPa}, \quad \text{F.O.S.} = 8$$

Procedure : We have,

$$\text{Working stress} = \frac{\text{Ultimate shear stress}}{\text{Factor of safety}} = \frac{360}{8} = 45 \text{ N/mm}^2$$

Given that,
$$\frac{d_o}{d_i} = 2$$

$$\therefore \quad k = \frac{d_i}{d_o} = \frac{1}{2} = 0.5$$

We know that,
$$P = \frac{2\pi NT}{60}$$

$$\therefore \quad T = \frac{P \times 60}{2\pi N} = \frac{20 \times 10^3 \times 60}{2 \times \pi \times 200}$$

$$\therefore \quad T = 954.92 \text{ N.m} = 954.92 \times 10^3 \text{ N.mm}$$

(1) For solid shaft : Torque transmitted,

$$T = \frac{\pi}{16} \times \tau \times d^3$$

$$\therefore \quad 954.92 \times 10^3 = \frac{\pi}{16} \times 45 \times d^3$$

$$\therefore \quad d = 47.63 \text{ mm} \cong \textbf{48 mm (say)}$$

(2) For hollow shaft : Torque transmitted,

$$T = \frac{\pi}{16} \times \tau \times d_o^3 \times [1 - k^4]$$

$$\therefore \quad 954.92 \times 10^3 = \frac{\pi}{16} \times 45 \times d_o^3 \times [1 - 0.5^4]$$

$$\therefore \quad d_o = 48.66 \text{ mm} \cong \textbf{50 mm (say)}$$

Also,
$$k = \frac{d_i}{d_o} = 0.5$$

$$\therefore \quad d_i = 0.5 \times d_o = 0.5 \times 50 = \textbf{25 mm}$$

Problem 3.5 : *A steel spindle transmits 1 MW at 240 r.p.m. The shaft must not twist more than $1°$ in a length of 15 times the diameter. If the modulus of rigidity for the material of the spindle is 84 kN/mm^2, find the diameter of the spindle and the shear stress induced in the spindle.*

Solution : Given data : $P = 1$ MW $= 1 \times 10^6$ W, $N = 240$ r.p.m., $\theta = 1°$, $L = 15 \times d$, $G = 84$ kN/mm$^2 = 84 \times 10^3$ N/mm^2.

Procedure : We have,

$$\text{Power transmitted, P} = \frac{2\pi N \cdot T_{mean}}{60}$$

$$\therefore \quad \text{Torque, } T_{mean} = \frac{P \times 60}{2\pi N} = \frac{1 \times 10^6 \times 60}{2 \times \pi \times 240}$$

$$= 39.788 \times 10^3 \text{ N-m} = 39.788 \times 10^6 \text{ N-mm}$$

Also, angle of twist, $\theta = 1° = \dfrac{\pi}{180} \times 1 = 0.0174$ radian.

If the shaft is designed on the basis of torsional rigidity, then we have,

$$\frac{T_{mean}}{J} = \frac{G\theta}{L} \quad \text{i.e.} \quad \frac{39.788 \times 10^6}{\pi/32 \times d^4} = \frac{84 \times 10^3 \times 0.0174}{15 \times d}$$

$$\therefore \quad d = 160.82 \text{ mm} \cong \textbf{162 mm (say)}$$

Also, $\qquad T_{mean} = \dfrac{\pi}{16} \times \tau \times d^3$

$$\therefore \qquad 39.788 \times 10^6 = \frac{\pi}{16} \times \tau \times (162)^3$$

$$\therefore \qquad \tau = \textbf{47.66 N/mm}^2$$

Problem 3.6 : *A shaft is required to transmit 1 MW power at 240 r.p.m. The shaft must not twist more than $1°$ on a length of one metre. If the modulus of rigidity for the material of the shaft is 80 kN/mm^2, find diameter of shaft and shear stress induced in it.* **(W-13)**

Solution : Given data : $P = 1$ MW $= 1 \times 10^6$ W, $N = 240$ r.p.m., $\theta = 1°$, $L = 1000$ mm, $G = 80 \times 10^3$ N/mm^2.

Procedure : We have, power transmitted, $P = \dfrac{2\pi N \cdot T_{mean}}{60}$

$$\text{Torque, } T_{mean} = \frac{P \times 60}{2\pi N} = \frac{1 \times 10^6 \times 60}{2 \times \pi \times 240} = 39.788 \times 10^3 \text{ N-m} = 39.788 \times 10^6 \text{ N-mm}$$

Also, angle of twist, $\theta = 1° = \dfrac{\pi}{180} \times 1 = 0.0174$ radian

(1) Diameter of shaft : If the shaft is designed on the basis of torsional rigidity, then we use,

$$\frac{T_{mean}}{J} = \frac{G\theta}{L} \quad \text{i.e.} \quad \frac{39.788 \times 10^6}{\pi/32 \times d^4} = \frac{80 \times 10^3 \times 0.0174}{1000}$$

$$\therefore \qquad d = 130.62 \text{ mm} \cong \textbf{132 mm (say)}$$

(2) Induced shear stress :

$$T_{mean} = \frac{\pi}{16} \times \tau \times d^3$$

$$39.788 \times 10^6 = \frac{\pi}{16} \times \tau \times (132)^3$$

$$\therefore \quad \tau = \mathbf{88.104\ N/mm^2}$$

Numerical Type No. 2 : "Shaft Subjeced to Bending Moment Only"

Problem 3.7 : *A pair of wheels of a railway wagon carries a load of 50 kN on each axle box acting at a distance of 100 mm outside the wheel base. The gauge of the rails is 1.4 m. Find the diameter of axle between the wheels, if the stress is not to exceed 100 MPa.*

Solution : Given data : $\quad W = 50\ kN = 50 \times 10^3\ N,\ L = 100\ mm$

$$L_1 = 1.4\ m = 1400\ mm,\ \sigma_b = 100\ MPa = 100\ N/mm^2$$

Procedure :

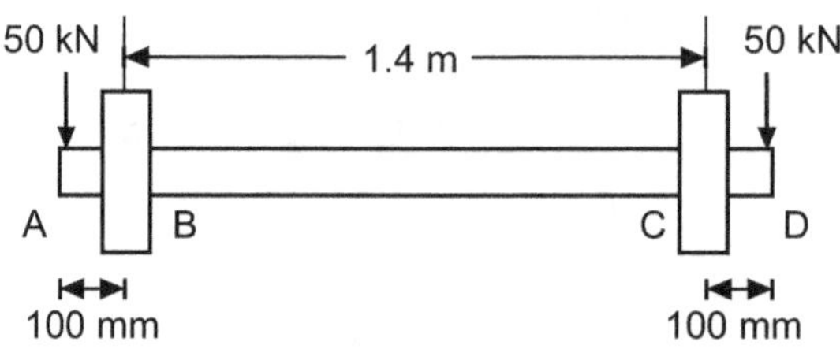

Fig. 3.1

Finding maximum B.M. :

B.M. at A, $\qquad M_A = 0$

B.M. at B, $\qquad M_B = W \times L = 50 \times 10^3 \times 100 = 50 \times 10^5\ N\text{-}mm$

B.M. at C, $\qquad M_C = W \times L = 50 \times 10^3 \times 100 = 50 \times 10^5\ N\text{-}mm$

B.M. at D, $\qquad M_D = 0$

$\therefore$ Maximum B.M. acting at B and C $= 50 \times 10^5\ N\text{-}mm$

We have, $\qquad M = \frac{\pi}{32} \cdot \sigma_b \cdot d^3$

$\therefore \qquad 50 \times 10^5 = \frac{\pi}{32} \times 100 \times d^3$

$\therefore \qquad d = \mathbf{79.85\ mm \cong 80\ mm\ (say)}$

Problem 3.8 : *An axle 1 m long is supported in bearings at its ends and carries a flywheel weighing 30 kN at centre. If the bending stress is not to exceed 60 MPa, find diameter of axle and sketch arrangement.*

Solution : Given data : $\quad W_B = 30\ kN = 30 \times 10^3\ N,\ \sigma_b = 60\ MPa = 60\ N/mm^2$

Procedure :

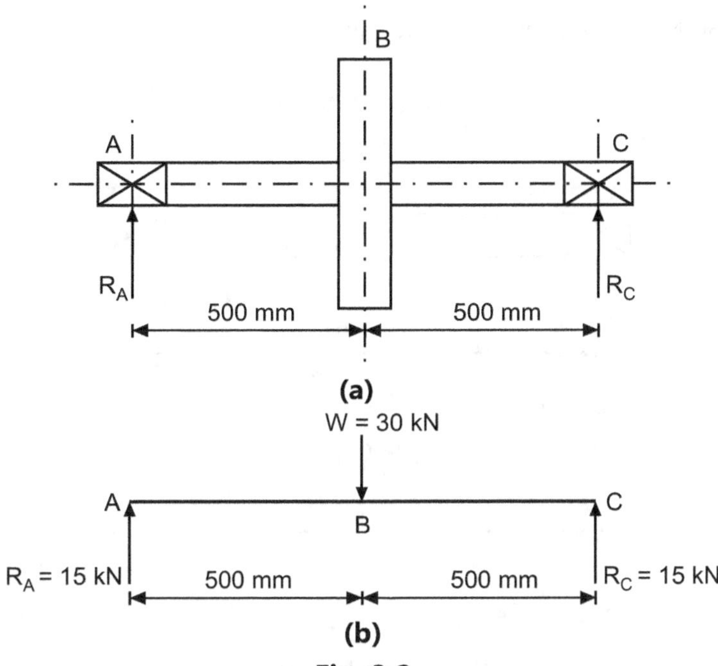

Fig. 3.2

Considering the vertical load diagram, $R_A + R_C = 30 \times 10^3$ N.

To find R_C, taking moment about point A, $\Sigma M_A = 0$.

$\therefore \qquad 30 \times 10^3 \times 500 - R_C \times 1000 = 0$

$\therefore \qquad\qquad\qquad\qquad R_C = 15 \times 10^3$ N

and $\qquad\qquad R_A = 30 \times 10^3 - R_C = 30 \times 10^3 - 15 \times 10^3$

$\therefore \qquad\qquad\qquad\qquad R_A = 15 \times 10^3$ N

$\therefore \quad$ Bending moment at point B $= M_B = 15 \times 10^3 \times 500 = 7500 \times 10^3$ N-mm

Axles are subjected to bending moment only. Therefore, the axle can be designed by using the equation,

$$M = \frac{\pi}{32} \cdot \sigma_b \cdot d^3$$

$$7500 \times 10^3 = \frac{\pi}{32} \times 60 \times (d)^3$$

$\therefore \qquad\qquad\qquad d = \textbf{108.38 mm} \cong \textbf{110 mm (say)}$

Numerical Type No. 3 : "Shaft Subjected to Both Twisting and Bending Moments"

Problem 3.9 : *A mild steel shaft transmits 20 kW at 200 r.p.m. It carries a central load of 900 N and is simply supported on bearings 2.5 metres apart. Determine the size of the shaft, if the allowable shear stress is 42 MPa and maximum tensile or compressive stress is not to exceed 56 MPa.* **(S-12)**

Solution : Given data : P = 20 kW, N = 200 r.p.m., τ = 42 MPa, $\sigma_t = \sigma_c$ = 56 MPa

Assume, σ_b = 56 MPa, Central load = 900 N

Procedure :

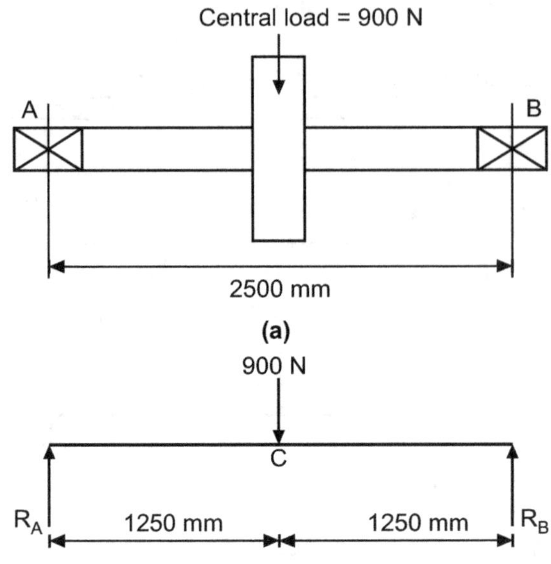

Fig. 3.3

From the figure, $R_A = R_B = \dfrac{900}{2} = 450$ N

We have, $P = \dfrac{2\pi NT}{60}$

$\therefore$ $T = \dfrac{P \times 60}{2\pi N} = \dfrac{20 \times 10^3 \times 60}{2\pi \times 200} = 954.92$ N.m

$\therefore$ $T = \mathbf{954.92 \times 10^3}$ **N.mm**

Also, maximum bending moment occurs at point C.

$\therefore$ $M_{max} = M_C = R_A \times 1250 = 450 \times 1250 = \mathbf{562.5 \times 10^3}$ **N.mm**

As the shaft is subjected to both twisting moment and bending moment, then

(1) According to maximum shear stress theory,

Equivalent twisting moment $= T_e = \dfrac{\pi}{16}\, \tau_{max} \cdot d^3$

$\therefore$ $\sqrt{M^2 + T^2} = \dfrac{\pi}{16}\, \tau_{max} \cdot d^3$

$\sqrt{(562.5 \times 10^3)^2 + (954.92 \times 10^3)^2} = \dfrac{\pi}{16} \times 42 \times d^3$

$d = \mathbf{51.22}$ **mm**

(2) According to maximum normal stress theory,

Equivalent bending moment, $M_e = \dfrac{1}{2}\left\{M + \sqrt{M^2 + T^2}\right\} = \dfrac{\pi}{32} \cdot \sigma_{b\ max} \cdot d^3$

$$\dfrac{1}{2}\left\{562.5 \times 10^3 + \sqrt{(562.5 \times 10^3)^2 + (954.92 \times 10^3)^2}\right\} = \dfrac{\pi}{32} \times 56 \times d^3$$

$\therefore$ $\qquad\qquad\qquad\qquad\qquad$ d $=$ **53.36 mm**

Taking larger value of two, $\qquad$ d $=$ 53.36 mm $\cong$ **54 mm (say)**

Problem 3.10 : *A solid circular shaft is subjected to a B.M. of 3000 N-m and T = 10,000 N-m. Shaft is made of 46C8 steel having yield tensile stress of 700 MPa and ultimate shear stress of 500 MPa. Assuming F.S. = 6, determine diameter of shaft.*

Solution : Given data : $\qquad$ M $=$ 3000×10^3 N.mm $=$ 3×10^6 N.mm

$\qquad\qquad\qquad\qquad\qquad\qquad$ T $=$ 10000×10^3 N-mm $=$ 10×10^6 N-mm

$\qquad\qquad\qquad\qquad\qquad\quad$ σ_{yt} $=$ 700 MPa, τ_{ut} $=$ 500 MPa, F.S. $=$ 6

Procedure :

Working bending stress, $\sigma_b = \dfrac{\sigma_{yt}}{\text{F.O.S.}} = \dfrac{700}{6} = 116.66 \ \text{N/mm}^2$ $\qquad \begin{bmatrix} \text{Assumed} \\ \sigma_b = \sigma_t \end{bmatrix}$

Working shear stress, $\tau = \dfrac{\tau_{ut}}{\text{F.O.S.}} = \dfrac{500}{6} = 83.33 \ \text{N/mm}^2$

Equivalent Twisting Moment :

$\qquad\qquad\qquad\qquad\qquad$ $T_e = \sqrt{M^2 + T^2} = \sqrt{(3 \times 10^6)^2 + (10 \times 10^6)^2}$

$\therefore$ $\qquad\qquad\qquad\qquad\qquad$ $T_e = 10.44 \times 10^6$ N-mm

We know that, $\qquad\qquad\quad$ $T_e = \dfrac{\pi}{16} \cdot \tau \cdot d^3$

$\therefore$ $\qquad\qquad$ $10.44 \times 10^6 = \dfrac{\pi}{16} \times 83.33 \times d^3$

$\therefore$ $\qquad\qquad\qquad\qquad\qquad$ d $=$ **86.09 mm**

Equivalent Bending Moment :

$\qquad\qquad\qquad$ $M_e = \dfrac{1}{2}\left[M + \sqrt{M^2 + T^2}\right] = \dfrac{1}{2}\left[M + T_e\right]$

$\therefore$ $\qquad\qquad\qquad$ $M_e = \dfrac{1}{2}\left[3 \times 10^6 + 10.44 \times 10^6\right] = 6.72 \times 10^6$ N-mm

We know that, $\qquad\qquad$ $M_e = \dfrac{\pi}{32} \times \sigma_b \times d^3$

$\therefore$ $\qquad\qquad$ $6.72 \times 10^6 = \dfrac{\pi}{32} \times 116.66 \times d^3$

$\therefore$ $\qquad\qquad\qquad\qquad\qquad$ d $=$ **83.71 mm**

Comparing both and taking larger value, d $=$ **86.09 mm** $\cong$ **88 mm (say)**

Problem 3.11 : *A shaft supported at the ends in the ball bearings carries a straight tooth spur gear and is required to transmit 7.5 kW at 300 r.p.m. The P.C.D. of gear is 150 mm. The distance between the centre line of the bearings and gear are 100 mm each. If the shaft is made of steel and allowable shear stress is 45 MPa, determine the diameter of shaft. Show the arrangement of the gear mounted on the shaft and bearings with a neat sketch. Pressure angle of gear is 20°.*

Solution : Given data : P $= 7.5$ kW $= 7.5 \times 10^3$ W, N $= 300$ r.p.m.,

  Diameter of gear, D $= 150$ mm, $\tau = 45$ MPa, L $= 200$ mm, $\alpha = 20°$

Procedure :

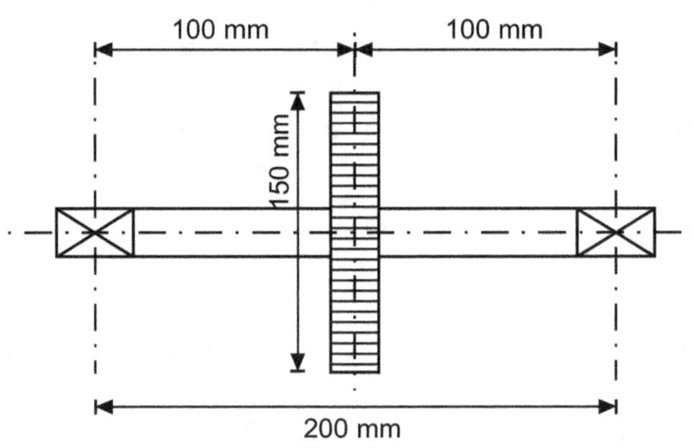

Fig. 3.4

Torque transmitted by the gear,

$$T = \frac{P \times 60}{2\pi N} = \frac{7.5 \times 10^3 \times 60}{2 \times \pi \times 300} = 238.73 \text{ N-m}$$

$\therefore$ $T = \mathbf{238.73 \times 10^3}$ **N-mm**

Tangential force acting on gear,

$$F_t = \frac{T}{\dfrac{D}{2}} = \frac{238.73 \times 10^3}{\dfrac{150}{2}} = 3.18 \times 10^3 \text{ N}$$

Normal load acting on tooth of gear,

$\therefore$ $W = \dfrac{F_t}{\cos \alpha} = \dfrac{3.18 \times 10^3}{\cos (20°)} = 3.38 \times 10^3$ N

Gear is mounted in the middle, therefore bending moment is,

$\therefore$ $M = \dfrac{WL}{4} = \dfrac{3.38 \times 10^3 \times 200}{4} = \mathbf{169 \times 10^3}$ **N-mm**

Equivalent Twisting Moment : $T_e = \sqrt{M^2 + T^2} = \sqrt{(169 \times 10^3)^2 + (238.73 \times 10^3)^2}$

$\therefore$ $T_e = \mathbf{292.49 \times 10^3}$ **N-mm**

We have, $T_e = \dfrac{\pi}{16} \tau d^3$

$\therefore$ $292.49 \times 10^3 = \dfrac{\pi}{16} \times 45 \times d^3$

$\therefore$ $d = \mathbf{32.10}$ **mm** $\cong$ **34 mm (say)**

Numerical Type No. 4 : "Shafts with One Pulley Subjected to Both Twisting and Bending Moments"

Problem 3.12 : *A mild steel shaft is supported in two bearings 1 metre apart and transmits 15 kW at 300 r.p.m. to a pulley of 200 mm diameter at a distance of 300 mm from left hand bearing. The belt passing over the pulley is vertical and the ratio of belt tension is 2 : 1. Pulley weighs 500 N. Design the diameter of shaft. Take* σ_t = 70 N/mm^2 *and* τ = 56 N/mm^2.   **(S-14)**

Solution : Given data : P = 15 kW = 15×10^3 W, N = 300 r.p.m., D = 200 mm.

$$\therefore \quad R = \frac{200}{2} = 100 \text{ mm}, \quad \sigma_t = 70 \text{ N/mm}^2, \quad \sigma_b = 70 \text{ N/mm}^2 \text{ (Assumed)}, \quad \tau = 56 \text{ N/mm}^2,$$

$$W_p = 500 \text{ N}, \quad \frac{T_1}{T_2} = 2.$$

Procedure :

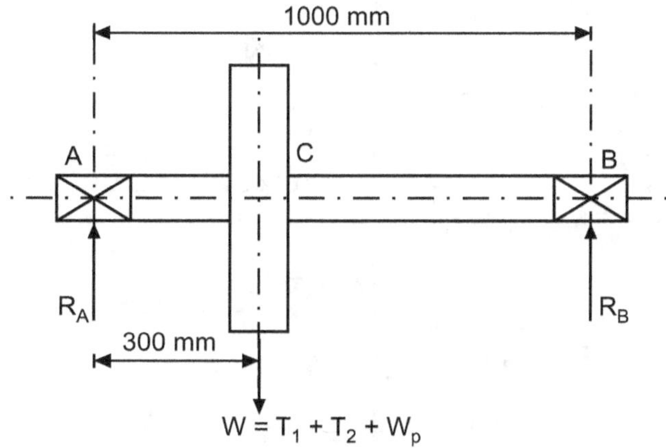

Fig. 3.5

We know that, power transmitted,

$$P = \frac{2\pi NT}{60}$$

$$15 \times 10^3 = \frac{2\pi \times 300 \times T}{60}$$

$$\therefore \quad T = 477.46 \text{ N-m} = 477.46 \times 10^3 \text{ N-mm}$$

Tension ratio for belt passing over pulley is given as,

$$\frac{T_1}{T_2} = 2; \quad T_1 = 2T_2$$

We know that, Torque transmitted (T) by pulley,

$$T = (T_1 - T_2) \cdot R$$

$$\therefore \quad 477.46 \times 10^3 = (2\,T_2 - T_2) \times 100 \qquad [\because T_1 = 2T_2]$$

$$\therefore \quad T_2 = \textbf{4774.6 N}$$

$$T_1 = 2 \times T_2 = 2 \times 4774.6 = \textbf{9549.2 N}$$

Therefore, total load acting at point 'C' = $T_1 + T_2 + W_p$

$$= 9549.2 + 4774.6 + 500 = 14823.8 \text{ N}$$

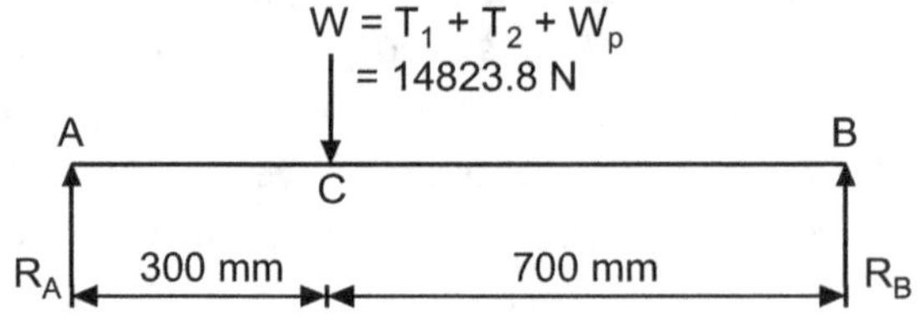

$$W = T_1 + T_2 + W_p$$
$$= 14823.8 \text{ N}$$

Fig. 3.6 : Vertical load diagram

Taking moment about point A,

$$\Sigma M_{@A} = 14823.8 \times 300 - R_B \times 1000 = 0$$

$$\therefore \quad R_B = 4447.14 \text{ N}$$

Also,

$$\Sigma F_y = 0$$

$$R_A + R_B = 14823.8 \text{ N}$$

$$\therefore \quad R_A + 4447.14 = 14823.8 \text{ N}$$

$$\therefore \quad R_A = \mathbf{10376.66 \text{ N}}$$

Maximum bending moment at point C,

$$M_C = R_A \times 300$$

$$\therefore \quad M = 10376.66 \times 300 = 3.113 \times 10^6 \text{ N.mm}$$

Considering maximum shear stress theory,

$$T_e = \sqrt{M^2 + T^2} = \frac{\pi}{16} \cdot \tau_{max} \cdot d^3$$

$$\therefore \sqrt{(3.113 \times 10^6)^2 + (477.46 \times 10^3)^2} = \frac{\pi}{16} \times 56 \times d^3$$

$$\therefore \quad d = \mathbf{65.91 \text{ mm}}$$

Considering maximum principal stress theory,

$$M_e = \frac{1}{2}\left\{M + \sqrt{M^2 + T^2}\right\} = \frac{\pi}{32} \cdot \sigma_{b\,max} \cdot d^3$$

$$\therefore \quad \frac{1}{2} \times \left[3.113 \times 10^6 + \sqrt{(3.113 \times 10^6)^2 + (477.46 \times 10^3)^2}\right] = \frac{\pi}{32} \times 70 \times d^3$$

$$\therefore \quad d = \mathbf{76.94 \text{ mm}}$$

Taking larger value of two, we have,

$$d = \mathbf{76.94 \text{ mm} \approx 78 \text{ mm (say)}}$$

Problem 3.13 : *A transmission shaft is supported on two bearings which are 1 m apart. Power is supplied to the shaft by means of flexible coupling, which is located to the left of the left hand bearing. Power is transmitted from the shaft by means of a belt pulley, 250 mm diameter, which is located at a distance of 300 mm from the left hand bearing. The mass of the pulley is 20 kg and the ratio of belt tension is 2 : 1. The belt tensions act vertically downward. The shaft is made of steel FeE 300 (S_{yt} = 300 N/mm^2) and the factor of safety is 3. Determine the shaft diameter, if it transmits 10 kW power at 360 r.p.m. from coupling to the pulley.*

(W-10)

Solution : Given data :

$$D_p = 250 \text{ mm}; \quad \therefore R_p = \frac{D_P}{2} = \frac{250}{2} = 125 \text{ mm}$$

$$W_p = 20 \text{ kg} = 20 \times 9.81 = 196.2 \text{ N}$$

$$\frac{T_1}{T_2} = 2; \quad \therefore T_1 = 2T_2$$

$$S_{yt} = 300 \text{ N/mm}^2, \quad \text{F.O.S.} = 3$$

$\therefore$ Permissible stress,

$$\sigma_t = \frac{S_{yt}}{\text{F.O.S.}} = \frac{300}{3} = 100 \text{ N/mm}^2$$

$$\sigma_b = 100 \text{ N/mm}^2 \text{ (Assumed)}$$

$$P = 10 \text{ kW} = 10 \times 10^3 \text{ W}, \quad N = 360 \text{ r.p.m.}$$

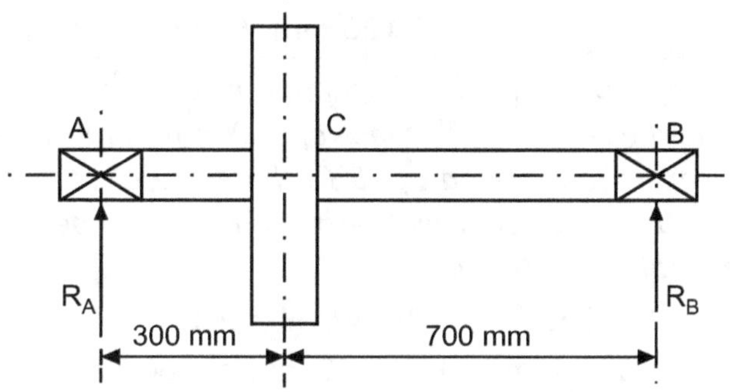

Fig. 3.7

Procedure : We have,

$$P = \frac{2\pi NT}{60}$$

$\therefore$

$$T = \frac{P \times 60}{2\pi N} = \frac{10 \times 10^3 \times 60}{2 \times \pi \times 360}$$

$$= 265.258 \text{ N.m} = \mathbf{265.258 \times 10^3 \text{ N.mm}}$$

Torque transmitted by pulley, $T = (T_1 - T_2) \times R_p$

$\therefore \qquad 265.258 \times 10^3 = (2T_2 - T_2) \times 125$

$\therefore \qquad T_2 = 2122.065 \text{ N}$

$\therefore \qquad T_1 = 2T_2 = 2 \times 2122.065 = 4244.13 \text{ N}$

Therefore, total load acting on pulley $= T_1 + T_2 + W_p$

$$= 4244.13 + 2122.065 + 196.2 = 6562.395 \text{ N}$$

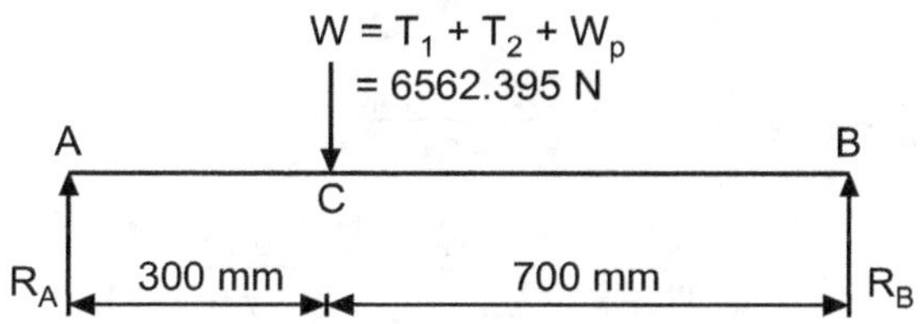

$$W = T_1 + T_2 + W_p$$
$$= 6562.395 \text{ N}$$

A   C   B

R_A 300 mm   700 mm R_B

Fig. 3.8 : Vertical load diagram

Taking moment @ point A, $\sum M_{@A} = 0$

$\therefore \qquad 6562.395 \times 300 - R_B \times 1000 = 0$

$\therefore \qquad R_B = 1968.71 \text{ N}$

Also, $\qquad\qquad\qquad \sum F_y = 0$

$\therefore \qquad\qquad\qquad R_A + R_B = 6562.395$

$\therefore \qquad\qquad\qquad R_A = 6562.395 - 1968.71 = 4593.685$ N

Maximum bending moment at point C,

$M_C = R_A \times 300 = 4593.685 \times 300 = \mathbf{1.378 \times 10^6}$ **N.mm**

According to maximum principal stress theory,

$$M_e = \frac{1}{2}\left\{M + \sqrt{M^2 + T^2}\right\} = \frac{\pi}{32}\, \sigma_{b\,max} \cdot d^3$$

$$\therefore \; \frac{1}{2}\times\left\{1.378\times10^6 + \sqrt{(1.378\times10^6)^2 + (265.258\times10^3)^2}\right\} = \frac{\pi}{32}\times 100 \times d^3$$

$$\therefore \qquad\qquad d = \mathbf{52.128\ mm} \cong \mathbf{54\ mm\ (say)}$$

Problem 3.14 : *A shaft 800 mm long is supported between two bearings. A 200 mm diameter pulley is keyed to the shaft at a distance of 300 mm from the left bearing. The pulley receives 5 kW at 900 r.p.m. Take overload of 25%. The angle of contact of pulley and belt is 180°. The pulley weighs 300 N. The coefficient of friction between belt and pulley is 0.14. Find suitable diameter of shaft. Take τ = 60 MPa.*

Solution : Given data : $P = 5$ kW $= 5 \times 10^3$ W, $N = 900$ r.p.m,

D_p = diameter of pulley = 200 mm; $\therefore R_p = 100$ mm, $\tau = 60$ N/mm^2, $W_p = 300$ N, $\mu = 0.14$,

$\theta = 180° = \pi^c$

Procedure :

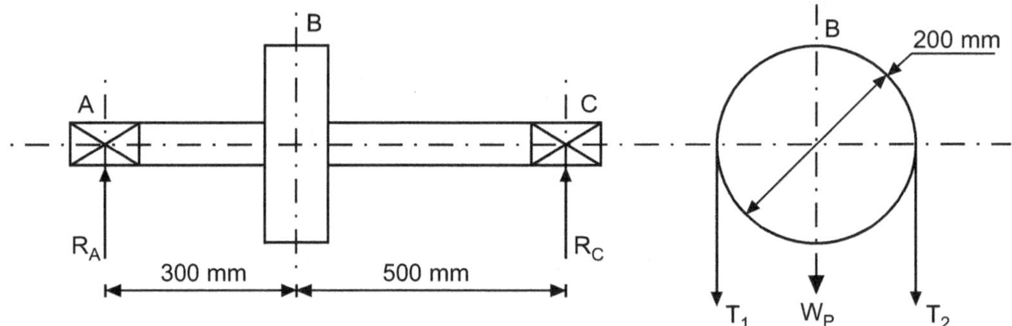

Fig. 3.9

We have,

$$\text{Power transmitted} = P = \frac{2\pi N\, T_{mean}}{60}$$

$$\therefore \qquad \text{Torque, } T_{mean} = \frac{P \times 60}{2\pi N} = \frac{5 \times 10^3 \times 60}{2 \times \pi \times 900}$$

$$= 53.051 \text{ N-m} = \mathbf{53051\ N\text{-}mm}$$

Taking overload of 25%, $\qquad T_{max} = 1.25 \times T_{mean} = 1.25 \times 53051$

$$= \mathbf{66313.75\ N\text{-}mm} \qquad\qquad \dots (1)$$

We know that,
$$\frac{T_1}{T_2} = e^{\mu\theta} = e^{0.14 \times \pi} = 1.552$$

$\therefore \qquad T_1 = 1.552 \times T_2$

Torque transmitted by pulley,

$$T = (T_1 - T_2) \times R_p = (1.552 \times T_2 - T_2) \times R_p = 0.552 \, T_2 \times 100$$
$$\dots (2)$$

On equating (1) and (2), we get,

$$66313.75 = 0.552 \, T_2 \times 100$$

$\therefore \qquad T_2 = 1201.33 \text{ N and } T_1 = 1.552 \times 1201.33 = 1864.46 \text{ N}$

Thus, total load acting on pulley B $= T_1 + T_2 + W_p = 1864.46 + 1201.33 + 300$
$$= 3365.79 \text{ N}$$
$$W = T_1 + T_2 + W_p = 3365.79$$

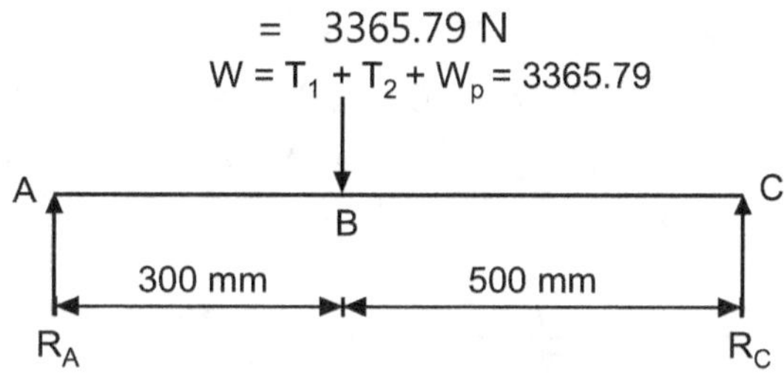

Fig. 3.10 : Vertical load diagram

Considering the vertical load diagram, $R_A + R_C = 3365.79$ N.

To find R_C, Take moment about point A, such that, $\Sigma M_A = 0$.

$\therefore \quad 3365.79 \times 300 - R_C \times 800 = 0$.

$\therefore \quad R_C = 1262.17$ N and $R_A = 3365.79 - R_C = 3365.79 - 1262.17 = 2103.62$ N

$\therefore \quad$ Bending moment at point B $= M = R_A \times 300 = 2103.62 \times 300 = \mathbf{631.09 \times 10^3}$ **N-mm.**

As the shaft is subjected to both twisting and bending moment, then according to maximum shear stress theory, the equivalent twisting moment is given by,

$$T_e = \frac{\pi}{16} \times \tau_{max} \times (d)^3 = \sqrt{M^2 + T^2}$$

$\therefore \qquad \dfrac{\pi}{16} \times 60 \times (d)^3 = \sqrt{(631.09 \times 10^3)^2 + (66313.75)^2}$

$\therefore \qquad d = \mathbf{37.76 \text{ mm}} \simeq \mathbf{38 \text{ mm (say)}}$

Numerical Type No. 5 : "Shaft with an Overhanging Pulley"

Problem 3.15 : *Determine the diameter of a hollow shaft having inside diameter 0.6 times outside diameter. The maximum allowable shear stress for the shaft is 60 MPa. The shaft is driven by a 900 mm diameter overhang pulley placed vertically below it. The weight of the pulley is 600 N. The tensions on the tight and slack side of the belt are 2900 N and 1000 N respectively. The overhang is 250 mm. Assume angle of lap of the belt on the pulley to be 180°.*

Solution : Given data : $d_i = 0.6 \, d_o$, $\therefore k = d_i/d_o = 0.6$, $D_p = $ Diameter of pulley $= 900$ mm,

$\therefore \quad R_p = 450$ mm, $\tau = 60$ N/mm^2, $W_p = 600$ N, $T_1 = 2900$ N, $T_2 = 1000$ N.

Procedure :

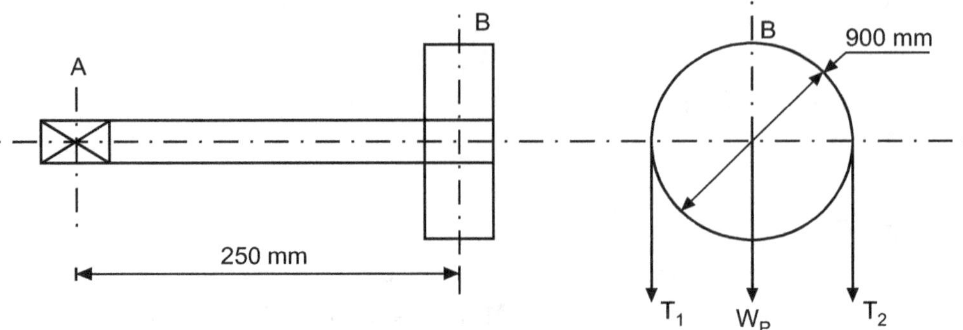

Fig. 3.11

Torque transmitted by pulley, $T = (T_1 - T_2) \times R_p$

$$= (2900 - 1000) \times 450 = \textbf{855} \times \textbf{10}^3 \textbf{ N.mm}$$

Thus, total load acting on pulley B $= T_1 + T_2 + W_P = 2900 + 1000 + 600 = 4500$ N

$$W = T_1 + T_2 + W_P = 4500 \text{ N}$$

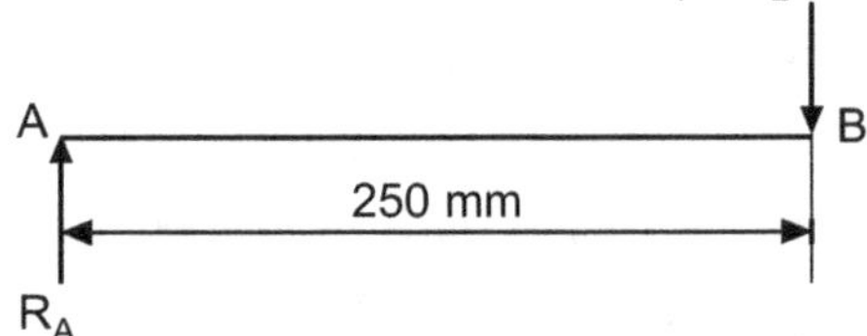

Fig. 3.12 : Vertical load diagram

Bending moment at point B = 0 (free end)

$\therefore$ Bending moment at point A = M = W $\times$ 250 = 4500 $\times$ 250 = **1.125 $\times$ 10^6 N-mm.**

As the shaft is subjected to both twisting and bending moment, then for hollow shaft, according to maximum shear stress theory, the equivalent twisting moment is given by,

$$T_e = \sqrt{M^2 + T^2} = \frac{\pi}{16} \times \tau \times d_o^3 (1 - k^4)$$

$\therefore$ $\sqrt{(1.125 \times 10^6)^2 + (855 \times 10^3)^2} = \dfrac{\pi}{16} \times 60 \times d_o^3 \{1 - (0.6)^4\}$

$\therefore$ $d_o = 51.65$ mm $\cong$ **52 mm (say)** and $d_i = 0.6 \times d_o = 0.6 \times 52 =$ **31.2 mm**

Problem 3.16 : *Design a shaft to transmit power from an electric motor to a lathe headstock through a pulley by means of a belt drive. The pulley weighs 200 N and is located at 300 mm from the centre of bearing. The diameter of the pulley is 200 mm and the maximum power transmitted is 1 kW at 120 r.p.m. The angle of lap of the belt is 180° and coefficient of friction between the belt and pulley is 0.3. The allowable shear stress in the shaft may be taken as 35 N/mm².* **(W -12)**

Solution : Given data : $W_p = 200$ N; $D_p = 200$ mm; $\therefore$ $R_p = \dfrac{200}{2} = 100$ mm

$P = 1$ kW $= 1000$ W, N $= 120$ r.p.m., $\theta = 180° = \pi^c$, $\mu = 0.3$, $\tau = 35$ N/mm².

Procedure : We know that, power transmitted,

$$P = \frac{2\pi NT}{60}$$

$$\therefore \quad 1000 = \frac{2\pi \times 120 \times T}{60}$$

$$\therefore \quad T = 79.58 \text{ N.m} = \mathbf{79.58 \times 10^3 \text{ N.mm}}$$

Ratio of belt tensions is given by following relation,

$$\frac{T_1}{T_2} = e^{\mu\theta} = e^{(0.3 \times \pi)} = 2.566$$

$$\therefore \quad T_1 = 2.566\, T_2$$

Also, torque transmitted by pulley,

$$T = (T_1 - T_2) \times R_p$$

$$\therefore \quad 79.58 \times 10^3 = (2.566\, T_2 - T_2) \times 100$$

$$\therefore \quad T_2 = 508.17 \text{ N}$$

$$\therefore \quad T_1 = 2.566\, T_2 = 2.566 \times 508.17 = 1303.96 \text{ N}$$

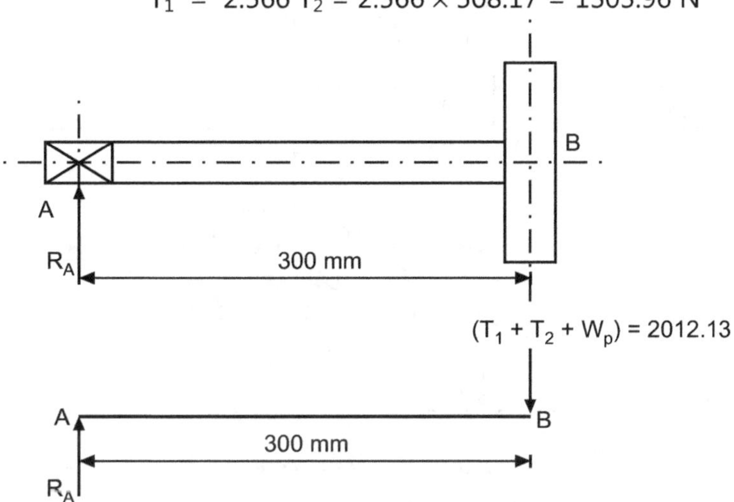

Fig. 3.13 : Vertical load diagram

Therefore, total load acting at point B = $T_1 + T_2 + W_P$

$$= 1303.96 + 508.17 + 200 = 2012.13 \text{ N}$$

Bending moment at point A is,

$$M_A = (T_1 + T_2 + W_P) \times 300 = 2012.13 \times 300 = 603639 \text{ N.mm}$$

Also, $M_B = 0$ (free end)

$\therefore$ Maximum bending moment occurs at point A.

$$\therefore \quad M = M_A = \mathbf{603639 \text{ N.mm}}$$

According to maximum shear stress theory,

$$T_e = \sqrt{M^2 + T^2} = \frac{\pi}{16} \cdot \tau_{max} \cdot d^3$$

$$\therefore \quad \sqrt{(603639)^2 + (79.58 \times 10^3)^2} = \frac{\pi}{16} \times 35 \times d^3$$

$$\therefore \quad d = \mathbf{44.58 \text{ mm}} \cong \mathbf{46 \text{ mm (say)}}$$

Numerical Type No. 6 : "Shaft with Two Pulleys Subjected to Both Twisting and Bending Moments"

Problem 3.17 : *A shaft made of mild steel is required to transmit 100 kW at 300 r.p.m. The supported length of the shaft is 3 metres. It carriers two pulleys each weighing 1500 N supported at a distance of 1 metre from each end respectively. Assuming the safe value of stress, determine the diameter of the shaft.* **(S-11)**

Solution : Given data : $P = 100$ kW, $N = 300$ r.p.m., $W_C = W_D = 1500$ N.

Procedure :

We have,
$$P = \frac{2\pi NT}{60}$$

$$\therefore \quad T = \frac{P \times 60}{2\pi N} = \frac{100 \times 10^3 \times 60}{2\pi \times 300} = 3183.09 \text{ N.m}$$

$$\therefore \quad T = \mathbf{3183.09 \times 10^3 \text{ N.mm}}$$

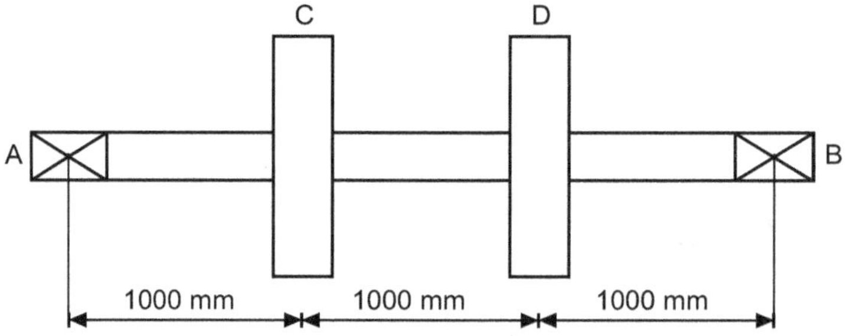

Fig. 3.14

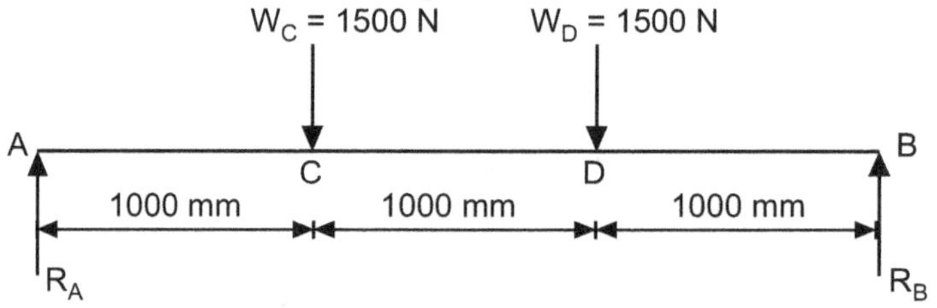

Fig. 3.15 : Vertical load iagram

We know, $\quad \sum F_y = 0$

$$\therefore \quad R_A + R_B = 1500 + 1500 = 3000 \text{ N} \qquad \dots (1)$$

Also $\quad \sum M_A = 0$

$$\therefore \quad 1500 \times 1000 + 1500 \times 2000 = R_B \times 3000$$

$$\therefore \quad R_B = 1500 \text{ N}$$

From equation (1), $\quad R_A + 1500 = 3000$

$$\therefore \quad R_A = 1500 \text{ N}$$

Bending moment at point C = $M_C = R_A \times 1000 = 1500 \times 1000 = 15 \times 10^5$ N.mm

Bending moment at point D = $M_D = R_B \times 1000 = 1500 \times 1000 = 15 \times 10^5$ N.mm

$\therefore$ Maximum bending moment = $M = \mathbf{15 \times 10^5 \text{ N.mm}}$

Assume safe shear stress, τ = 42 MPa. Due to combined twisting and bending moments, use maximum shear stress theory. The equivalent twisting moment is given by,

$$T_e = \sqrt{M^2 + T^2} = \frac{\pi}{16}\, \tau_{max} \cdot d^3$$

$$\sqrt{(15 \times 10^5)^2 + (3183.09 \times 10^3)^2} = \frac{\pi}{16} \times 42 \times d^3$$

$$\therefore \qquad d = \textbf{75.28 mm} \cong \textbf{76 mm (say)}$$

Problem 3.18 : *Fig. 3.16 shows a shaft of uniform diameter supported in two self aligning bearings at C and D. The two pulleys A and B are mounted having belt tensions 1800 N and 800 N respectively. The shaft transmits 10 kW power at 300 r.p.m. The pulleys weigh 200 N and 400 N respectively. Take safe working stress as 40 MPa.*

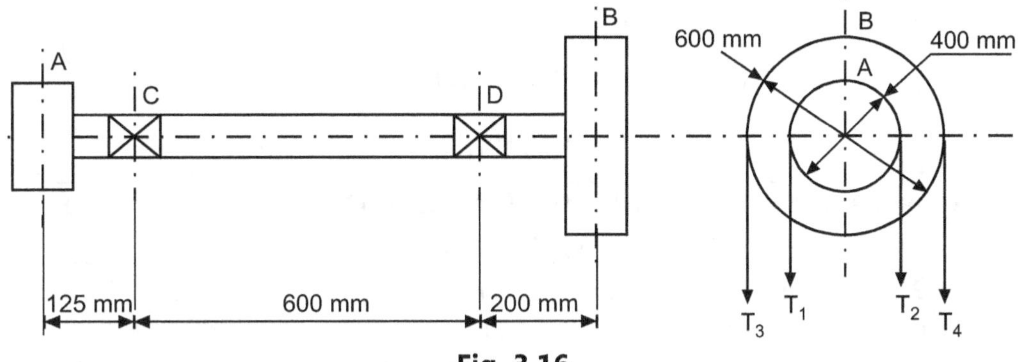

Fig. 3.16

Solution : Given data : P $= 10 \times 10^3$ W, N = 300 r.p.m., W_A = 200 N, W_B = 400 N, τ = 40 N/mm^2, D_A = diameter of pulley 'A' = 400 mm, $\therefore R_A$ = 200 mm, D_B = Diameter of pulley 'B' = 600 mm, $\therefore R_B$ = 300 mm.

Procedure : We have, Power transmitted, $P = \dfrac{2\pi N\, T_{mean}}{60}$

$\therefore$ Torque, $T = \dfrac{P \times 60}{2\pi N} = \dfrac{10 \times 10^3 \times 60}{2 \times \pi \times 300} = 318.31$ N-m $= 318.31 \times 10^3$ N-mm.

Belt tension in pulley A $= 1800$ N

$\therefore$ Load acting at pulley A $= 1800 + W_A = 1800 + 200 = 2000$ N

Belt tension in pulley B $= 800$ N

$\therefore$ Load acting at pulley B $= 800 + W_B = 800 + 400 = 1200$ N

$$T_1 + T_2 + W_A = 2000 \text{ N} \qquad\qquad\qquad T_3 + T_4 + W_B = 1200 \text{ N}$$

Fig. 3.17 : Vertical load diagram

Bending moments at extreme ends is zero.

$$\therefore \qquad M_A = 0 \quad \text{and} \quad M_B = 0$$

Now, Bending moment at point C = M_C = 2000×125 = 250×10^3 N-mm

And Bending moment at point D = M_D = 1200×200 = 240×10^3 N-mm

Thus, maximum bending moment occurs at point C.

$$\therefore \qquad M = 250 \times 10^3 \text{ N-mm.}$$

As the shaft is subjected to both twisting and bending moment, then according to maximum shear stress theory, the equivalent twisting moment is given by,

$$T_e = \frac{\pi}{16} \cdot \tau_{max} \cdot d^3 = \sqrt{M^2 + T^2}$$

$$\therefore \qquad \frac{\pi}{16} \times 40 \times d^3 = \sqrt{(250 \times 10^3)^2 + (318.31 \times 10^3)^2}$$

$$\therefore \qquad d = \textbf{37.21 mm} \cong \textbf{38 mm (say)}$$

Numericals Type No. 7 : "Shafts Subjected to Both Twisting and Bending Moments with Shock Loading"

Problem 3.19 : *Shaft is transmitting 25 kW at 1500 r.p.m, when it is subjected to bending moment of magnitude 150 N-m due to gear mounted on it, find the diameter of shaft. Take shock and fatigue factors, k_m = 1.5 and k_t = 1.2. Take yield strength of material as 300 MPa.*

Solution : Given data : P = 25 kW = 25×10^3 W, N = 1500 r.p.m., σ_y = 300 MPa, k_m = 1.5 and k_t = 1.2.

Procedure : We have, power transmitted, $P = \dfrac{2\pi N\, T_{mean}}{60}$

$$\therefore \quad \text{Torque, } T = \frac{P \times 60}{2\pi N} = \frac{25 \times 10^3 \times 60}{2 \times \pi \times 1500} = 159.15 \text{ N-m} = \textbf{159.15} \times \textbf{10}^\textbf{3} \textbf{ N-mm}$$

Bending moment due to gear = M = 150 N-m = $\textbf{150} \times \textbf{10}^\textbf{3}$ **N-mm** (Given)

Assume factor of safety = 5. The permissible bending is calculated as,

$$\sigma_b = \frac{\sigma_y}{\text{F.O.S.}} = \frac{300}{5} = 60 \text{ MPa.}$$

As the shaft is subjected to both twisting and bending moment, then according to maximum normal stress theory, the equivalent bending moment is given by,

$$M_e = \frac{1}{2}\{(k_m M) + \sqrt{(k_m M)^2 + (k_t T)^2}\} = \frac{\pi}{32} \times \sigma_{b\,max} \times (d)^3$$

$$\therefore \quad \frac{1}{2}\{1.5 \times 150 \times 10^3 + \sqrt{(1.5 \times 150 \times 10^3)^2 + (1.2 \times 159.15 \times 10^3)^2}\} = \frac{\pi}{32} \times 60 \times (d)^3$$

$$\therefore \quad d = 35.34 \text{ mm} = \textbf{36 mm (say)}$$

Problem 3.20 : *A mild steel shaft transmits 30 kW at 300 r.p.m. It carries a central load 1000 N and is simply supported between the bearings 3 m apart. Determine the size of the shaft, if allowable shear stress and tensile stress are 42 MPa and 56 MPa respectively. What change would you observe in the diameter of the shaft, if same shaft is subjected to suddenly applied load ? Take $k_m = k_t = 2.5$.*   **(S-13)**

Solution : Given data : $P = 30$ kW $= 30 \times 10^3$ W, $N = 300$ r.p.m., $W = 1000$ N, $\tau = 42$ N/mm², $\sigma_t = 56$ N/mm², $k_m = k_t = 2.5$.

Procedure : We have,

$$P = \frac{2\pi N\, T_{mean}}{60}$$

$$\therefore \quad T = T_{mean} = \frac{P \times 60}{2\pi \times N} = \frac{30 \times 10^3 \times 60}{2\pi \times 300}$$

$$\therefore \quad T = 954.93 \text{ N·m} = \mathbf{954.93 \times 10^3 \text{ N·mm}}$$

Free body diagram of the shaft carrying central load 'W' with two bearings 3 m apart is as shown below.

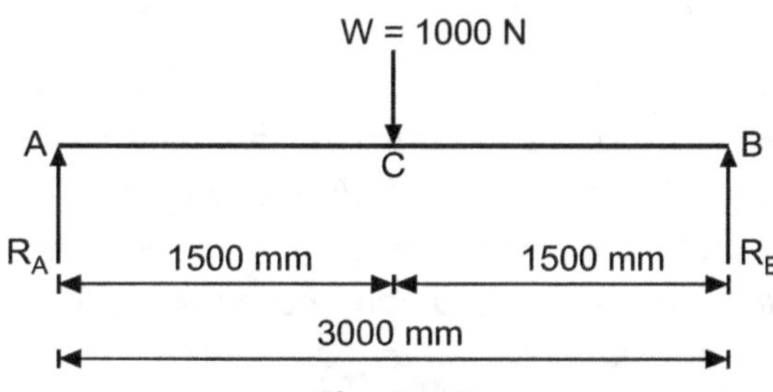

Fig. 3.18

As the shaft is centrally loaded between two end bearings, the support reactions are,

$$R_A = R_B = \frac{W}{2} = \frac{1000}{2} = 500 \text{ N}$$

$\therefore$ Bending moment, $M_C = M = R_A \times 1500 = 500 \times 1500 = \mathbf{750 \times 10^3 \text{ N·mm}}$

(1) Considering maximum shear stress theory,

$$T_e = \sqrt{M^2 + T^2} = \frac{\pi}{16}\,\tau_{max} \cdot d^3$$

$$\sqrt{(750 \times 10^3)^2 + (954.93 \times 10^3)^2} = \frac{\pi}{16} \times 42 \times d^3$$

$$\therefore \quad d = 52.80 \text{ mm} \cong \mathbf{54 \text{ mm (say)}} \quad\quad \dots (1)$$

If the same shaft is subjected to suddenly applied load, then

$$T_e = \sqrt{(k_m \times M)^2 + (k_t \times T)^2} = \frac{\pi}{16}\,\tau_{max} \cdot d^3$$

$$\therefore \quad \sqrt{(2.5 \times 750 \times 10^3)^2 + (2.5 \times 954.93 \times 10^3)^2} = \frac{\pi}{16} \times 42 \times d^3$$

$$\therefore \quad d = 71.66 \text{ mm} \cong \mathbf{72 \text{ mm (say)}} \quad\quad \dots (2)$$

(2) Considering maximum normal stress theory,

$$M_e = \frac{1}{2}\left[M + \sqrt{M^2 + T^2}\right] = \frac{\pi}{32}\,\sigma_{max} \cdot d^3$$

$$\therefore \ \frac{1}{2} \times \left[750 \times 10^3 + \sqrt{(750 \times 10^3)^2 + (954.93 \times 10^3)^2}\right] = \frac{\pi}{32} \times 56 \times d^3$$

$$d = 56.31 \cong \textbf{58 mm (say)} \qquad\qquad \ldots (3)$$

And for sudden loading,

$$M_e = \frac{1}{2}\left[k_m \cdot M + \sqrt{(k_m + M)^2 + (k_t \times T)^2}\right] = \frac{\pi}{32}\,\sigma_{max}\, d^3$$

$$\therefore \ \frac{1}{2} \times \left[2.5 \times 750 \times 10^3 + \sqrt{(2.5 \times 750 \times 10^3)^2 + (2.5 \times 954.93 \times 10^3)^2}\right] = \frac{\pi}{32} \times 56 \times d^3$$

$$d = 76.43 \text{ mm} \cong \textbf{78 mm (say)} \qquad\qquad \ldots (4)$$

Thus, by comparing values of diameter in equations (1) and (2) as well as in (3) and (4), we observed that, the required diameter of shaft increases, if it is subjected to suddenly applied load conditions.

Problem 3.21 : *Fig. 3.19 shows a shaft carrying a pulley A and gear B and supported in two bearings C and D. The shaft transmits 20 kW at 150 r.p.m. The tangential force F_t on the gear B acts vertically upwards as shown. The pulley delivers the power through a belt to another pulley of equal diameter vertically below the pulley A. The ratio of tensions (T_1/T_2) is equal to 2.5. The weights of gear and pulley are 900 N and 2700 N respectively. The permissible shear stress may be taken as 63 MPa. Assuming the weight of shaft to be negligible in comparison to other loads, determine its diameter. Take $k_b = k_m = 2$ and $k_t = 1.5$.*

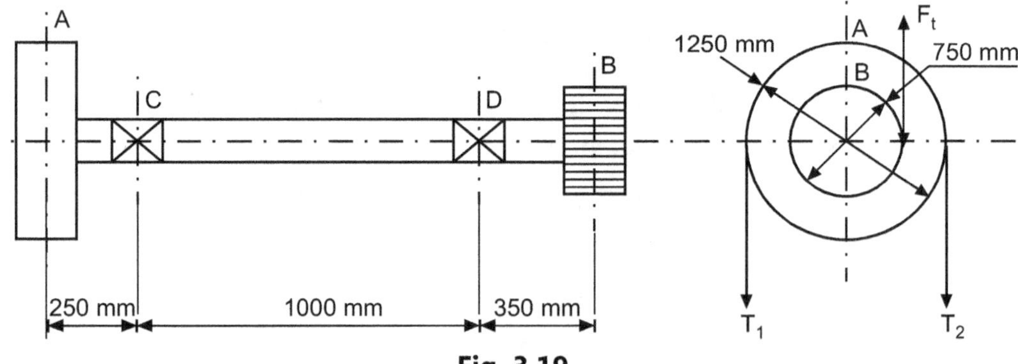

Fig. 3.19

Solution : Given data : P = 20 kW = 20×10^3 W, N = 150 r.p.m, (T_1/T_2) = 2.5

$\therefore \ T_1 = 2.5\ T_2$, D_A = diameter of pulley 'A' = 1250 mm, $\therefore \ R_A = \dfrac{1250}{2} = 625$ mm,

D_B = diameter of gear 'B' = 750 mm, $\therefore \ R_B = \dfrac{750}{2} = 375$ mm, $W_A = 2700$ N, $W_B = 900$ N,

$k_b = k_m = 2$ and $k_t = 1.5$, $\tau_{max} = 63$ MPa.

Procedure : We have, Power transmitted $= P = \dfrac{2\pi N\, T_{mean}}{60}$

Torque, $T = \dfrac{P \times 60}{2\pi N} = \dfrac{20 \times 10^3 \times 60}{2 \times \pi \times 150} = 1273.24$ N-m $= \mathbf{1273.24 \times 10^3}$ **N-mm**

Given that, $\qquad\qquad\qquad\qquad T_1 = 2.5 \times T_2$

Torque transmitted by pulley, $T = (T_1 - T_2) \times R_A$

$\therefore\qquad\qquad 1273.24 \times 10^3 = (2.5 \times T_2 - T_2) \times 625$

$\therefore\ T_2 = 1358.12$ N and $T_1 = 2.5 \times 1358.12 = 3395.3$ N

Thus, total load acting on pulley A $= T_1 + T_2 + W_A = 3395.3 + 1358.12 + 2700 = 7453.42$ N

Also, Torque transmitted by gear, $T = F_t \times R_B = F_t \times 375$

$\therefore\ 1273.24 \times 10^3 = F_t \times 375$

$\therefore\ F_t = 3395.30$ N (Acting vertically upward)

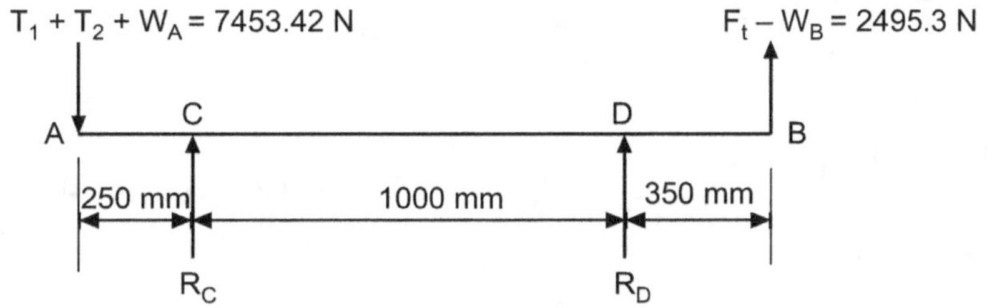

Also, $W_B = 900$ N (Acting vertically downward)

$\therefore\ $ Net load acting at point B $= F_t - W_B = 3395.30 - 900 = 2495.3$ N

Fig. 3.20 : Vertical load diagram

Bending moments at extreme end points are zero.

$\therefore\qquad\qquad\qquad M_A = 0$ and $M_B = 0$

Now, Bending moment at point C $= M_C = 7453.42 \times 250 = 1.863 \times 10^6$ N-mm

And, Bending moment at point D $= M_D = 2495.3 \times 350 = 873.35 \times 10^3$ N-mm

Thus, maximum bending moment occurs at point C.

$\therefore\ $ **M = $\mathbf{1.863 \times 10^6}$ N-mm**

As the shaft is subjected to both twisting and bending moment with shock loading then according to maximum shear stress theory, the equivalent twisting moment is given by,

Equivalent twisting moment $= T_e = \sqrt{(k_m M)^2 + (k_t T)^2} = \dfrac{\pi}{16} \times \tau_{max} \times (d)^3$

$\therefore\ \sqrt{(2 \times 1.863 \times 10^6)^2 + (1.5 \times 1273.24 \times 10^3)^2} = \dfrac{\pi}{16} \times 63 \times (d)^3$

$\therefore\ $ d $= \mathbf{69.69}$ **mm** $\cong$ **70 mm (say)**

Numerical Type No. 8 : "Comparison of Hollow Shaft and Solid Shaft"

Problem 3.22 : *Compare the weight, strength and stiffness of a hollow shaft of the same external diameter as that of solid shaft. The inside diameter of the hollow shaft is half the external diameter. Both the shafts have the same material and length.*

Solution : Given data : $d = d_o$, $d_i = 0.5 \times d_o$, $k = \dfrac{d_i}{d_o} = 0.5$, $L_h = L_s$.

As same material is used for solid and hollow shaft, the properties like weight density, permissible stress values, modulus of rigidity will be same.

Procedure : (i) Comparison of weight :

We have, Weight = Weight density $\times$ Volume = Weight density $\times$ Area $\times$ Length

For solid shaft, W_s = Weight density $\times$ $(\pi/4) \times d^2 \times L_s$ $\qquad$ ... (1)

For hollow shaft, W_h = Weight density $\times$ $(\pi/4) \times (d_o^2 - d_i^2) \times L_h$

$$= \text{Weight density} \times (\pi/4) \times d_o^2 \, (1 - k^2) \times L_h \qquad \left[\because k = \frac{d_i}{d_o}\right]$$

$$= \text{Weight density} \times (\pi/4) \times d_o^2 \, [1 - (0.5)^2] \times L_h$$

$$= 0.75 \times \text{Weight density} \times (\pi/4) \times d_o^2 \times L_h \qquad \text{... (2)}$$

Dividing (2) by (1),

$$\frac{W_h}{W_s} = \frac{0.75 \times \text{Weight density} \times (\pi/4) \times d_o^2 \times L_h}{\text{Weight density} \times (\pi/4) \times d^2 \times L_s} = \mathbf{0.75} \qquad (\because d = d_o \text{ and } L_h = L_s)$$

(ii) Comparison of strength :

The strength is given by,

For solid shaft, $\qquad T_s = \dfrac{\pi}{16} \times \tau_s \times d^3$ $\qquad$ ... (3)

For hollow shaft, $\qquad T_h = \dfrac{\pi}{16} \times \tau_h \times d_o^3 \, (1 - k^4) = \dfrac{\pi}{16} \times \tau_h \times d_o^3 \, [1 - (0.5)^4]$

$$= 0.9375 \times \pi/16 \times \tau_h \times d_o^3 \qquad \text{... (4)}$$

Dividing equation (4) by (3), we get,

$$\frac{T_h}{T_s} = \frac{0.9375 \times (\pi/16) \times \tau_h \times d_o^3}{(\pi/16) \times \tau_s \times d^3} = \mathbf{0.9375} \qquad (\because \tau_h = \tau_s \text{ and } d = d_o)$$

(iii) Comparison of stiffness :

Stiffness is given by, $\qquad S = \dfrac{T}{\theta}$

We have, $\qquad \dfrac{T}{J} = \dfrac{G\theta}{L}$

$\therefore \qquad S = \dfrac{T}{\theta} = \dfrac{G \cdot J}{L}$

For solid shaft,
$$S_s = \frac{G \times \pi/32 \times d^4}{L_s}$$

For hollow shaft,
$$S_h = \frac{G \times \pi/32 \times [(d_o)^4 - (d_i)^4]}{L_h} = \frac{G \times \pi/32 \times d_o^4 \, [1 - k^4]}{L_h}$$

$$= \frac{0.9375 \times G \times \pi/32 \times d_o^4}{L_h} \qquad \text{[Put } k = 0.5\text{]}$$

Thus,
$$\frac{S_h}{S_s} = \frac{(0.9375 \times G \times \pi/32 \times d_o^4)/L_h}{(G \times \pi/32 \times d^4)/L_s} = \mathbf{0.9375}$$

$$[\because d_o = d \,\&\, L_h = L_s]$$

Problem 3.23 : *The internal diameter of hollow shaft is $2/3^{rd}$ of its external diameter. Compare the strength and stiffness of the shaft with that of a solid shaft of same weight and material.*

Solution : Given data : $d_i = (2/3) \times d_o$; $\therefore$ $k = d_i/d_o = 0.67$, $W_h = W_s$.

Procedure : For solid shaft,
$$W_s = \text{Weight density} \times (\pi/4) \times d^2 \times L_s$$

For hollow shaft,
$$W_h = \text{Weight density} \times (\pi/4) \times (d_o^2 - d_i^2) \times L_h$$

$$= \text{Weight density} \times (\pi/4) \times d_o^2 \, (1 - k^2) \times L_h$$

$$= \text{Weight density} \times (\pi/4) \times d_o^2 \, [1 - (0.67)^2] \times L_h$$

$$= 0.5511 \times \text{Weight density} \times (\pi/4) \times d_o^2 \times L_h$$

But,
$$W_s = W_h$$

$\therefore$ $\text{Weight density} \times (\pi/4) \times d^2 \times L_s = 0.5511 \times \text{Weight density} \times (\pi/4) \times d_o^2 \times L_h$

As the material for the shaft is same, weight density is same.

and Assuming, $L_h = L_s$, the above equation becomes,

$$d^2 = 0.5511 \times d_o^2$$

$\therefore$ $\qquad d = 0.7423 \times d_o$ $\qquad\qquad$ ... (1)

(i) Comparison of strength :

The strength is given by,

For solid shaft, $T_s = \pi/16 \times \tau_s \times d^3 = \pi/16 \times \tau_s \times (0.7423 \times d_o)^3$ $\quad$ [From equation (1)]

$$= 0.409 \times \pi/16 \times \tau_s \times d_o^3 \qquad\qquad ... (2)$$

For hollow shaft, $T_h = \pi/16 \times \tau_h \times d_o^3 \cdot (1 - k^4) = \pi/16 \times \tau_h \times d_o^3 \times (1 - (0.67)^4)$

$$= 0.7984 \times \pi/16 \times \tau_h \times d_o^3 \qquad\qquad ... (3)$$

Dividing equation (3) by (2), we get,

$$\frac{T_h}{T_s} = \frac{0.7984 \times \pi/16 \times \tau_h \times d_o^3}{0.409 \times \pi/16 \times \tau_s \times d_o^3} = \mathbf{1.952} \qquad (\because \text{For same material, } \tau_h = \tau_s)$$

(ii) Comparison of stiffness :

Stiffness is given by, $S = \dfrac{T}{\theta}$.

We have, $\qquad\qquad \dfrac{T}{J} = \dfrac{G\theta}{L}$

$\therefore \qquad\qquad S = \dfrac{T}{\theta} = \dfrac{GJ}{L}$

For solid shaft,

$$S_s = \frac{G \times \pi/32 \times d^4}{L_s} = \frac{G \times \pi/32 \times (0.7423 \times d_o)^4}{L_s} = \frac{0.3036 \times G \times \pi/32 \times d_o^4}{L_s}$$

For hollow shaft,

$$S_h = \frac{G \times \pi/32 \times [(d_o)^4 - (d_i)^4]}{L_h} = \frac{G \times \pi/32 \times d_o^4 [1 - k^4]}{L_h} = \frac{0.7984 \times G \times \pi/32 \times d_o^4}{L_h}$$

Thus, $\quad \dfrac{S_h}{S_s} = \dfrac{(0.7984 \times G \times \pi/32 \times d_o^4)/L_h}{(0.3036 \times G \times \pi/32 \times d_o^4)/L_s} = \mathbf{2.6297}$ $\qquad [\because L_h = L_s]$

Problem 3.24 : *For an axial flow compressor, design the shaft from the following data :*

Torque on shaft : 1000 kN-mm

Bending moment on shaft : 250 N-m

Allowable shear stress : 50 N/mm^2

The load is applied gradually.

Find :

(a) Diameter of shaft considering it to be solid.

(b) Diameter of hollow shaft, when inner diameter is 0.5 times outer diameter.

Calculate % saving in material in case of hollow shaft.

For gradually applied load, take $k_b = 1.5$ and $k_t = 1.0$.

Solution : Given data : $T = 1000$ kN-mm $= 1000 \times 10^3$ N-mm,

$M = 250$ N-m $= 250 \times 10^3$ N-mm, $\tau = 50$ N/mm^2, $k_b = k_m = 1.5$ and $k_t = 1.0$.

Procedure : Case I : For solid shaft :

Equivalent twisting moment $= T_e = \sqrt{(k_m M)^2 + (k_t T)^2} = \dfrac{\pi}{16} \times \tau_{max} \times (d)^3$

$\therefore \quad \sqrt{(1.5 \times 250 \times 10^3)^2 + (1 \times 1000 \times 10^3)^2} = \dfrac{\pi}{16} \times 50 \times (d)^3$

$\therefore \quad d = 47.73$ mm $\cong$ **48 mm**

Case II : For hollow shaft : $d_i = 0.5\, d_o$, $k = d_i/d_o = 0.5$

Equivalent twisting moment is given by,

$$T_e = \sqrt{(k_m M)^2 + (k_t T)^2} = \frac{\pi}{16} \times \tau_{max} \times (d_o)^3 \{1 - (k)^4\}$$

$$\therefore \quad \sqrt{(1.5 \times 250 \times 10^3)^2 + (1 \times 1000 \times 10^3)^2} = \frac{\pi}{16} \times 50 \times (d_o)^3 \{1 - (0.5)^4\}$$

$$\therefore \quad d_o = 48.77 \text{ mm} \cong \textbf{50 mm} \text{ and } d_i = 0.5 \times 50 = \textbf{25 mm}$$

Weight of solid shaft = Weight density × Volume = W_s = Weight density $\times \frac{\pi}{4} \times d^2 \times L_s$

$$\therefore \quad W_s = \text{Weight density} \times \frac{\pi}{4} \times (48)^2 \times L_s = 2304 \times \text{Weight density} \times \frac{\pi}{4} \times L_s \qquad \ldots (1)$$

Similarly, Weight of hollow shaft = W_h = Weight density $\times \frac{\pi}{4} \times (d_o^2 - d_i^2) \times L_h$

$$\therefore \quad W_h = \text{Weight density} \times \frac{\pi}{4} \times d_o^2 (1 - k^2) \times L_h = \text{Weight density} \times \frac{\pi}{4} \times (50)^2 \times [1 - (0.5)^2] \times L_h$$

$$= 1875 \times \text{Weight density} \times \frac{\pi}{4} \times L_h \qquad \ldots (2)$$

Dividing (2) by (1),

$$\frac{W_h}{W_s} = \frac{1875 \times \text{Weight density} \times (\pi/4) \times L_h}{2304 \times \text{Weight density} \times (\pi/4) \times L_s} = 0.8138 \qquad (\text{assume } L_h = L_s)$$

$$\therefore \quad W_h = 0.8138 \ W_s$$

Percentage saving in material $= \dfrac{W_s - W_h}{W_s} \times 100 = \dfrac{W_s - 0.8138 \ W_s}{W_s} \times 100$

$\therefore$ Percentage saving in material = **18.62%**

3.2 INTRODUCTION TO KEY

Question

1. What is key ? State its function.   (W-12)

- A key can be defined as, *"a machine element, which is used to connect the transmission shaft to the rotating machine element like pulley, gear, sprocket or flywheel".*

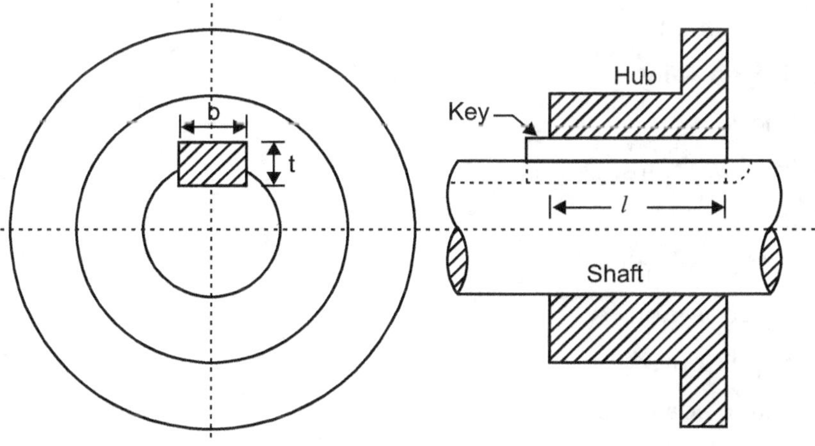

Fig. 3.21

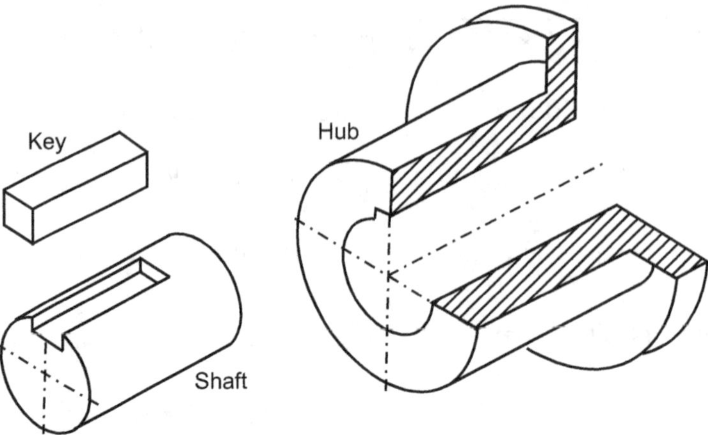

Fig. 3.22

- It is inserted between the shaft and hub or boss of pulley to connect them together in order to prevent relative motion between them.
- It is always inserted parallel to axis of shaft.
- It is used as temporary fastening.
- **A keyway** is a slot or recess in a shaft and hub of pulley to accommodate key.

3.2.1 Functions of Key, Advantages and Disadvantages of Keyed Joints

Functions of Key :

The two basic functions of the key are as follows :

(1) The primary function of the key is to transmit the torque from the shaft to the hub of mating element and vice versa.

(2) The second function of the key is to prevent relative rotational motion between the shaft and the joined machine element like gear or pulley. In most of the cases, key also prevents axial motion between two elements, except in case of feather key or splined connection.

Advantages of Keyed Joints :

1. Compactness.
2. No slip in power transmission.
3. Low cost.

Disadvantages of Keyed Joints :

1. Temporary conection.
2. Weak and fails quickly.
3. No protection against overload.
4. Shaft gets weakened, due to keyway (a slot).

3.2.2 Types of Keys

Questions

1. How keys are classified ? Draw neat sketches of different types of keys and state their applications. **(S-11)**
2. State board classification of keys. **(S-13)**

1. Sunk Keys :

- A sunk key is a key, in which, half the thickness of the key fits into the keyway on the shaft and the remaining half in the keyway on the hub. Therefore, keyways are required both on the shaft as well as on the hub of the mating element. The depth of keyway is uniform inside the shaft, but is tapering in the hub.
- Sunk key is suitable for heavy duty application, since, there is no possibility of the key to slip around the shaft. It is a positive drive.

Types of Sunk Keys : The sunk keys are of the following types :

(a) Rectangular sunk key :

- The usual proportions are, width (w) = $\dfrac{d}{4}$ and thickness of key (t) = $\dfrac{2w}{3}$ = $\dfrac{d}{6}$.

- It is rectangular cross-section and has taper on one face.

Application : For gears and pulleys mounted on shaft.

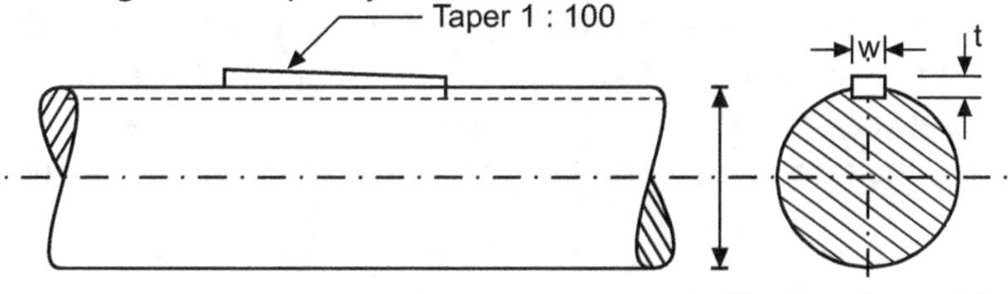

Fig. 3.23 : Rectangular sunk key

(b) Square sunk key :

- The only difference between a rectangular sunk key and square sunk key is that, its width is equal to thickness.

- Thus, w = t = $\dfrac{d}{4}$.

(c) Gib head key :

- It is rectangular sunk key with a head at one end called as *gib head*.
- It is usually provided to facilitate the easy removal of key.

- The usual proportions are, w = $\dfrac{d}{4}$ and t = $\dfrac{2w}{3}$ = $\dfrac{d}{6}$.

Advantages of Gib Headed Key :

- (i) The taper surface results in wedge action and increases frictional force and the tightness of the joint.

 (ii) The taper surface facilitates easy removal of the key, particularly with gib-head.

- However, machining taper on the surface increase the cost.

Application :

- It is used, where key is to be removed frequently.

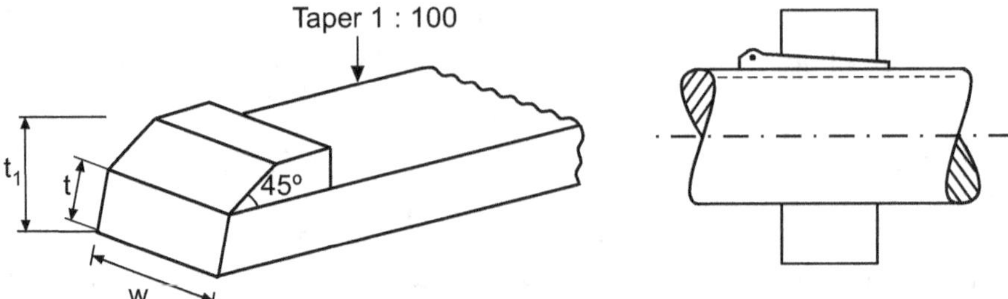

Fig. 3.24 : Gib headed key

(d) Feather key :

- A feather key is a parallel key, which is fixed either to the shaft or to the hub and which permits relative axial movement between them.

- The feather key is a particular type of sunk key with uniform width and height.

- There are number of methods to fix the key to the shaft or hub. Fig. 3.25 shows a feather key, which is fixed to the shaft by means of two cap-screws, having countersunk heads.

- There is a clearance fit between the key and the keyway in the hub. Therefore, the hub is free to slide over the key. At the same time, there is no relative rotational movement between the shaft and the hub. Therefore, the feather key transmits the torque and at the same time permits some axial movement of the hub.

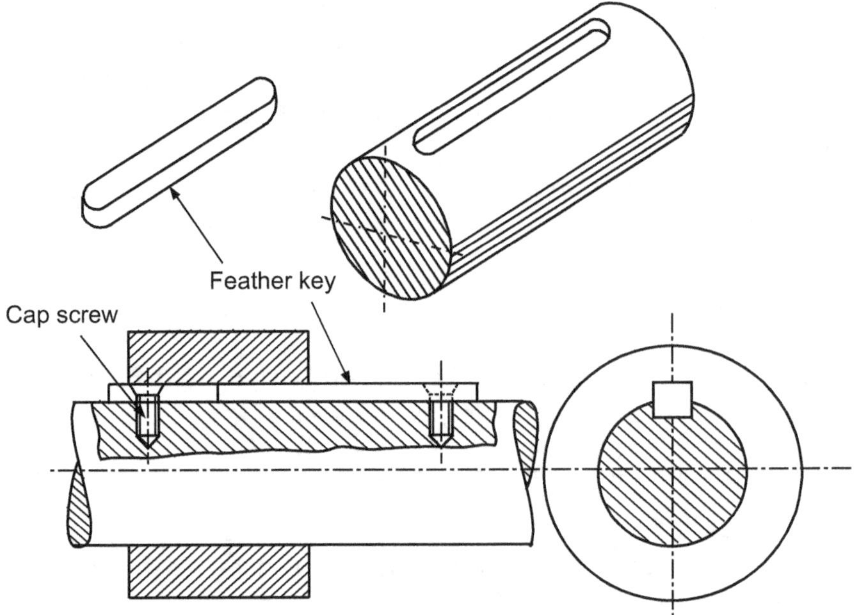

Fig. 3.25 : Feather key

Applications :

1. Feather keys are used, where the parts mounted on the shaft are required to slide along the shaft, such as clutches or gear shifting devices.

2. It is an alternative to splined connection. For example : Machine tools.

(e) Woodruff key :

- A woodruff key is a sunk key, in the form of an almost semi-circular disk of uniform thickness as shown in Fig. 3.26.

- The keyway in the shaft is in the form of a semi-circular recess with the same curvature, as that of the key.

- The bottom portion of the woodruff key fits into circular keyway in the shaft. The keyway in the hub is made in the usual manner. The projecting part of woodruff key fits into the keyway in the hub. Once placed in position, the woodruff key tilts and aligns itself on the shaft.

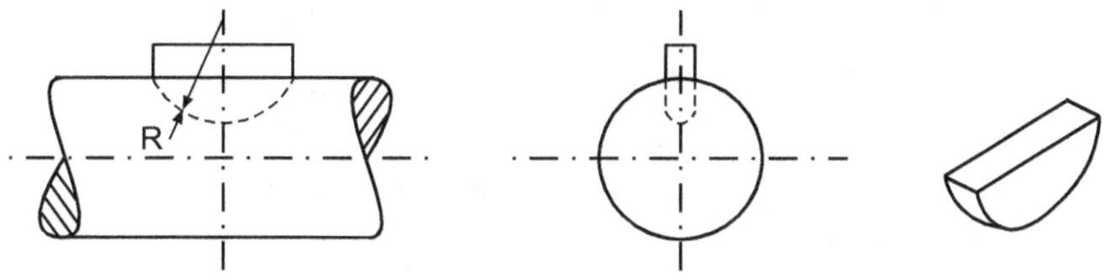

Fig. 3.26 : Woodruff key

Advantages of Woodruff Key :

(i) The woodruff key can be used on tapered shaft, because it can align itself by slight rotation in the seat.

(ii) The extra depth of key in the shaft prevents its tendency to slip over the shaft.

(iii) It permits easy removal of pulleys from shaft.

Disadvantages of Woodruff Key :

(i) The extra depth of keyway in the shaft increases stress concentration and reduces its strength.

(ii) The key does not permit axial movement between the shaft and the hub.

Applications :

- Woodruff keys are used on tapered shafts in machine tools and automobiles.

- It is used for transmitting moderate torques, especially in automotive engineering.

2. Saddle Keys :

- A saddle key is a key, which fits in the keyway of hub only. Here, keyway is absent on the shaft.

- There are two types of saddle keys,

(a) Flat saddle key :

- It is a taper key, which fits in the keyway in the hub and is flat on the shaft.

- It is likely to slip round the shaft under load.

(b) Hollow saddle key :

- It is a taper key, which fits in the keyway in the hub and concave surface bottom of key is shaped to fit the curved surface of the shaft.

Applications :

- They are suitable for light duty or low power transmission, as the power is transmitted due to friction.
- Saddle key is used as temporary fastening in fixing and setting eccentric parts, cams etc.

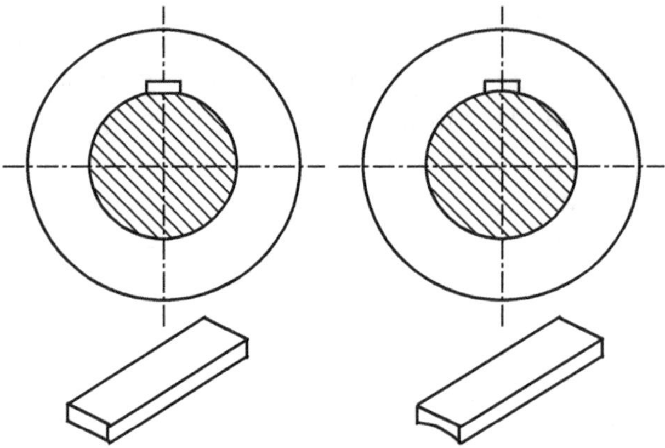

(a) Flat saddle key   **(b) Hollow saddle say**

Fig. 3.27 : Saddle key

3. Round keys :

- They are circular in section and fit into the holes drilled partly into the hub.

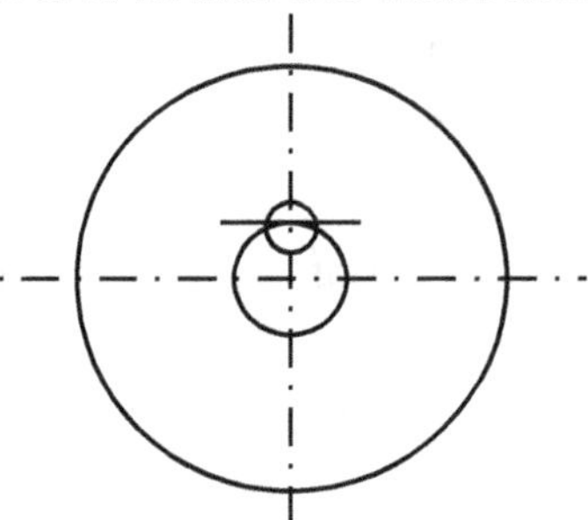

Fig. 3.28 : Round keys

Application :

- They are used for low power drive.

4. Splines :

- A spline is a group of keyways cut on the periphery of shaft. The remaining portion of the shaft material between the keyway forms a number of equidistant keys in-built with the shaft.
- In other words, the keys are made integral with the shaft, which fits in the keyways broached in the hub. Such shafts are called as *splined shafts*.

- They usually have four, ten or sixteen splines.

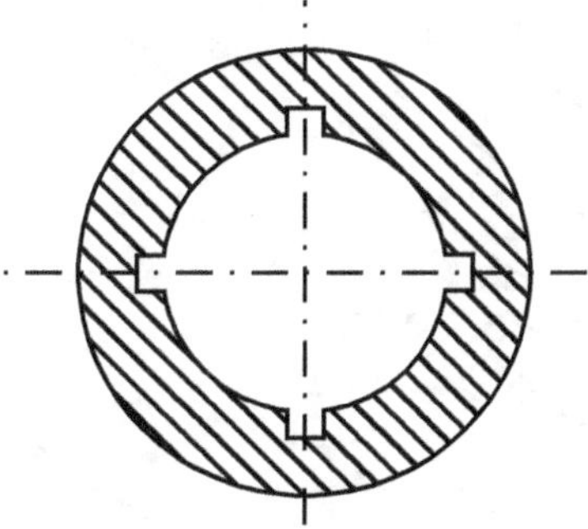

Fig. 3.29 : Splines

- The projections on the splined shaft engage with corresponding recesses in a splined hub.

Applications :

- These splines are used for power transmission of very high order and also provide axial movement between shaft and mounted member.
- Practical applications of splines may be seen in gear shifting mechanism used in automobile gear boxes.

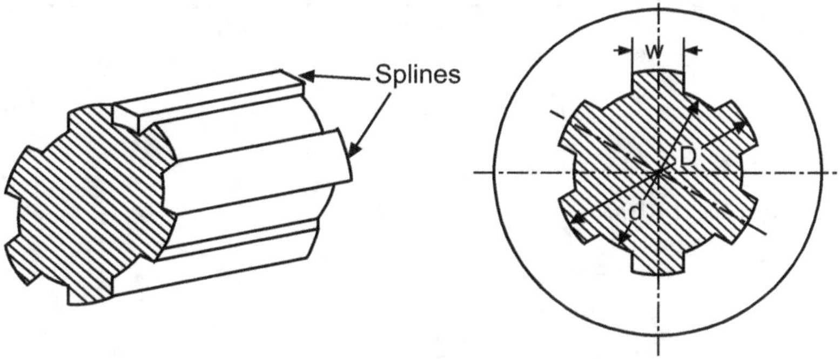

Fig. 3.30

3.2.2.1 Factors to be Considered While Selecting the Type of Key

(a) Power to be transmitted.   (b) Tightness of fit.
(c) Stability of the connection.   (d) Cost.

3.2.3 Design of Sunk Key

Strength of a Sunk Key or Different Types of Failure while Designing a Key :

Consider a rectangular key connecting the shaft and hub.

Let,

$$T = \text{Torque transmitted by shaft}$$
$$F = \text{Tangential force acting at the circumference of shaft}$$
$$d = \text{Diameter of shaft}$$
$$l = \text{Length of key}$$
$$w = \text{Width of key}$$
$$t = \text{Thickness of key}$$
$$\tau \text{ and } \sigma_{ck} = \text{Permissible shear and crushing stress for material of key}$$

A little consideration will show that due to power transmitted by the shaft, the key may fail due to either shearing or crushing.

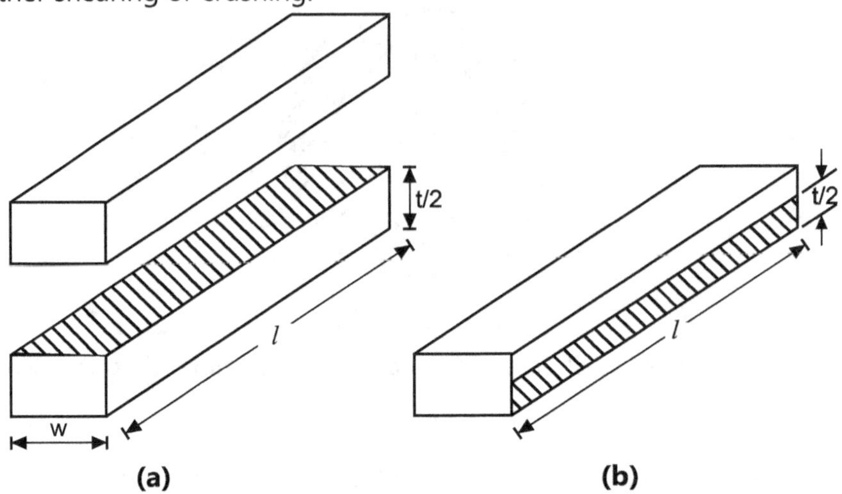

Fig. 3.31 : Rectangular sunk key

(1) Considering shearing of key, the shear stress induced can be given by,

$$\text{Shear stress} = \frac{\text{Tangential shearing force acting on shaft}}{\text{Area resisting shearing}}$$

$$\tau = \frac{F}{l \times w} \qquad \text{[Refer Fig. 3.31 (a)]}$$

$$\therefore \quad F = l \cdot w \cdot \tau$$

Therefore, torque transmitted,

$$T = F \times \frac{d}{2}$$

$$\therefore \quad T = l \cdot w \cdot \tau \cdot \frac{d}{2}$$

(2) Considering crushing of key, the crushing stress induced can be given by,

$$\text{Crushing stress} = \frac{\text{Tangential crushing force acting on the shaft}}{\text{Area resisting crushing}}$$

$$\sigma_{ck} = \frac{F}{l \times \dfrac{t}{2}} \qquad \text{[Refer Fig. 3.31 (b)]}$$

$$\therefore \quad F = l \cdot \frac{t}{2} \cdot \sigma_{ck}$$

Therefore, torque transmitted,

$$T = F \times \frac{d}{2}$$

$$\therefore \quad T = l \cdot \frac{t}{2} \cdot \sigma_{ck} \cdot \frac{d}{2}$$

3.2.3.1 Relation between Stresses for a Rectangular Key Equally Stronger in Crushing and Shearing

Considering a rectangular key connecting the shaft and hub.

Let,

T = Torque transmitted by shaft

F = Tangential force acting at the circumference of shaft

d = Diameter of shaft

l = Length of key

w = Width of key

t = Thickness of key

Let, τ and σ_{ck} be the permissible shear and crushing stress for key material respectively.

A little consideration will show that, due to power transmitted by the shaft, the key may fail either due to shearing or crushing.

Considering shearing of key, the tangential shear force acting on the shaft is,

$$F = \text{Area resisting shearing} \times \text{Shear stress}$$

$$= (l \times w) \cdot \tau$$

$$\therefore \quad \text{Torque transmitted,} \quad T = F \times \frac{d}{2} = l \cdot w \cdot \tau \cdot \frac{d}{2} \qquad \ldots (3.6)$$

Considering crushing of key, the tangential crushing force acting on the shaft,

$$F = \text{Area resisting crushing} \times \text{Crushing stress}$$

$$= l \cdot \frac{t}{2} \cdot \sigma_{ck}$$

$$\therefore \quad \text{Torque transmitted,} \quad T = F \times \frac{d}{2} = l \cdot \frac{t}{2} \cdot \sigma_{ck} \cdot \frac{d}{2} \qquad \ldots (3.7)$$

If key is equally strong in shearing and crushing, then on equating equations (3.6) and (3.7), we get,

$$l \cdot w \cdot \tau \cdot \frac{d}{2} = l \cdot \frac{t}{2} \cdot \sigma_{ck} \cdot \frac{d}{2}$$

$$\therefore \qquad \frac{\tau}{\sigma_{ck}} = \frac{t}{2w}$$

But, for rectangular key, put $w = \dfrac{d}{4}$ and $t = \dfrac{d}{6}$ (Using empirical relations)

$$\therefore \qquad \frac{\tau}{\sigma_{ck}} = \frac{\dfrac{d}{6}}{2 \times \dfrac{d}{4}}$$

$$\therefore \qquad \frac{\tau}{\sigma_{ck}} = \frac{1}{3} \quad \text{or} \quad \sigma_{ck} = 3\tau$$

3.2.3.2 Relation between Stresses for a Square Key Equally Strong in Crushing and Shearing

Questions
1. For a square key equally strong in shearing and crushing, show that, the permissible crushing stress is twice the shear stress. **(S-09, 12; W-09, 11)**
2. Prove that, for a square key, "crushing stress is twice shearing stress". **(S-13; W-13)**

Considering a square key connecting the shaft and hub.

Let,

$$T \; = \; \text{Torque transmitted by shaft}$$
$$F \; = \; \text{Tangential force acting at the circumference of shaft}$$
$$d \; = \; \text{Diameter of shaft}$$
$$l \; = \; \text{Length of key}$$
$$w \; = \; \text{Width of key}$$
$$t \; = \; \text{Thickness of key}$$

For square key, we have,

$$w \; = \; t$$

Let τ and σ_{ck} be the permissible shear and crushing stress for key material respectively.

A little consideration will show that due to power transmitted by the shaft, the key may fail either due to shearing or crushing.

Considering shearing of key, the tangential shearing force acting on the shaft is,

$$F \; = \; \text{Area resisting shearing} \times \text{Shear stress} \; = \; l \cdot w \cdot \tau$$

Also, Torque transmitted $= T = F \times \dfrac{d}{2} = l \cdot w \cdot \tau \cdot \dfrac{d}{2}$ ... (3.8)

Considering crushing key, the tangential crushing force acting on the shaft is,

$$F \; = \; \text{Area resisting crushing} \times \text{Crushing stress}$$
$$= \; l \cdot \dfrac{t}{2} \cdot \sigma_{ck}$$

$\therefore$ Torque transmitted $= T = F \times \dfrac{d}{2} = l \cdot \dfrac{t}{2} \cdot \sigma_{ck} \cdot \dfrac{d}{2}$ ... (3.9)

If key is equally strong in shearing and crushing, then on equating equations (3.8) and (3.9), we get,

$$l \cdot w \cdot \tau \cdot \dfrac{d}{2} \; = \; l \cdot \dfrac{t}{2} \cdot \sigma_{ck} \cdot \dfrac{d}{2}$$

$$\dfrac{\tau}{\sigma_{ck}} \; = \; \dfrac{t}{2w}$$

But, for square key, $w = t$

$$\dfrac{\tau}{\sigma_{ck}} \; = \; \dfrac{1}{2} \quad \text{or} \quad \sigma_{ck} \; = \; 2\tau$$

3.2.4 Effect of Keyways on Strength of Shaft

Question

1. What is the effect of keyway on the strength of shaft ? **(S-10, 12, 14)**

- Keyway is a slot machined either on the shaft or in the hub to accommodate the key.
- It is cut by vertical or horizontal milling cutter.
- A little consideration will show that, the keyway cut into the shaft reduces the load carrying capacity of shaft.
- This is due to stress concentration near the corners of the keyway and reduction in the cross-sectional area of shaft.
- In other words, the torsional strength of shaft is reduced.
- The following relation of reduction factor is used to analyze the weakening effect of keyway given by H. F. Moore.

$$e = 1 - 0.2\,(w/d) - 1.1(h/d)$$

Where, e = Shaft strength factor = $\dfrac{\text{Strength of shaft with keyway}}{\text{Strength of shaft without keyway}}$

w = Width of keyway,

d = Diameter of shaft,

h = Depth of keyway = $\dfrac{1}{2}$ × Thickness of key = $\dfrac{t}{2}$

- It is usually assumed that strength of keyed shaft is 75% of solid shaft.
- Thus, after finding out dimensions of key, the reduction factor 'e' is calculated and for safe design, its value should be less than **0.75**.

Numerical Type No. 9 : "Design of Key"

Problem 3.25 : *A 45 mm diameter shaft is made of steel with yield strength of 400 N/mm². A key of size 14 mm wide and 9 mm thick made of steel with yield strength of 340 N/mm² is to be used. Find the required length of key, if the shaft is loaded to transmit the maximum permissible torque. Use maximum shear stress theory and assume a factor of safety of 2.*

Solution : Given data : $d = 45$ mm, $\sigma_{yt} = 400$ N/mm²(for shaft), $\sigma_{yt} = 340$ N/mm²(for key), $w = 14$ mm, $t = 9$ mm.

Procedure : For key, $\sigma_{ck} = \dfrac{\sigma_{yt}}{\text{F.O.S.}} = \dfrac{340}{2} = \mathbf{170\ N/mm^2}$

According to maximum shear stress theory,

$$\tau_{max} = \frac{\sigma_{yt}}{2 \times \text{Factor of safety}}$$

∴   For shaft, $\tau_s = \dfrac{400}{2 \times 2} = \mathbf{100\ N/mm^2}$

And   For key, $\tau_k = \dfrac{340}{2 \times 2} = \mathbf{85\ N/mm^2}$

We know that, torque transmitted by shaft is given by,

$$T = \frac{\pi}{16} \times \tau_s \times d^3 = \frac{\pi}{16} \times 100 \times (45)^3 = 1.79 \times 10^6 \text{ N-mm}$$

Considering the key under shear failure,

$$T = l \times w \times \tau_k \times \frac{d}{2}$$

$$\therefore \quad 1.79 \times 10^6 = l \times 14 \times 85 \times \frac{45}{2}$$

$$\therefore \quad l = \text{Length of key} = \mathbf{66.85 \text{ mm}}$$

Considering the key under crushing failure,

$$T = l \times \frac{t}{2} \times \sigma_{ck} \times \frac{d}{2}$$

$$\therefore \quad 1.79 \times 10^6 = l \times \frac{9}{2} \times 170 \times \frac{45}{2}$$

$$\therefore \quad l = \text{Length of key} = \mathbf{103.99 \text{ mm}}$$

Taking the larger value of the two, **Length of key = l = 103.99 mm $\cong$ 104 mm (say)**

Problem 3.26 : *Design a rectangular key for shaft of 50 mm diameter. Shear and crushing stresses are limited to 42 Mpa and 70 Mpa respectively. Same material is used for shaft and key.*

Solution : Given data : d = 50 mm, τ = 42 N/mm^2, σ_{ck} = 70 N/mm^2

Procedure : We know that, torque transmitted by shaft is given by,

$$T = \frac{\pi}{16} \times \tau_s \times d^3 = \frac{\pi}{16} \times 42 \times (50)^3 = 1.03 \times 10^6 \text{ N-mm}$$

By empirical relations, w = Width of key = $\dfrac{d}{4}$ = $\dfrac{50}{4}$ = 12.5 mm

t = Thickness of key = $\dfrac{d}{6}$ = $\dfrac{50}{6}$ = 8.333 mm

Considering the key under shear failure,

$$T = l \times w \times \tau_k \times \frac{d}{2}$$

$$1.03 \times 10^6 = l \times 12.5 \times 42 \times \frac{50}{2}$$

$$\therefore \quad l = \text{Length of key} = \mathbf{78.47 \text{ mm}}$$

Considering the key under crushing failure,

$$T = l \times \frac{t}{2} \times \sigma_{ck} \times \frac{d}{2}$$

$$\therefore \quad 1.03 \times 10^6 = l \times \frac{8.333}{2} \times 70 \times \frac{50}{2}$$

$$\therefore \quad l = \text{length of key} = \mathbf{141.26 \text{ mm}}$$

Taking the larger of the two values, **Length of key = l = 141.26 mm $\cong$ 142 mm (say).**

Problem 3.27 : *A pulley is keyed to a shaft of diameter 100 mm by means of key of 20 mm width and 150 mm length. The allowable shear stress is 40 N/mm^2 and crushing stress 100 N/mm^2. The shaft is running at 250 r.p.m. Find the power transmission capacity and thickness of the key.*

Solution : Given data :

$$d = 100 \text{ mm} \qquad\qquad l = 150 \text{ mm}$$
$$\tau = 40 \text{ N/mm}^2 \qquad\qquad w = 20 \text{ mm}$$
$$\sigma_{ck} = 100 \text{ N/mm}^2 \qquad\qquad N = 250 \text{ r.p.m.}$$

Procedure : Consider shearing failure of key,

$$T = l \cdot w \cdot \tau \cdot \frac{d}{2} = 150 \times 20 \times 40 \times \frac{100}{2}$$

$$= 6000 \times 10^3 \text{ N-mm} = 6000 \text{ N-m}$$

(i) Power transmission capacity :

$$P = \frac{2\pi NT}{60} = \frac{2\pi \times 250 \times 6000}{60} = 157079 \text{ watt} = \mathbf{157.079 \text{ kW}}$$

(ii) Thickness of the key :

Consider crushing failure of key,

$$T = l \times \frac{t}{2} \times \sigma_{ck} \times \frac{d}{2}$$

$$\therefore \qquad 6000 \times 10^3 = 150 \times \frac{t}{2} \times 100 \times \frac{100}{2}$$

$$\therefore \qquad t = \mathbf{16 \text{ mm}}$$

3.3 INTRODUCTION TO COUPLINGS

- Shafts are usually available upto 7 metres length for easy handling and transportation. Therefore, when power is to be transmitted at a greater distance, two lengths of shaft or more are required to be connected by means of coupling.
- The shafts connected by the coupling, can be disengaged only after dismantling the coupling.

3.3.1 Functions of Coupling

Question

1. What is the function of shaft coupling ?　　　　　　**(W-12)**

Shaft couplings are used in machinery for different purposes, such as :

1. To provide the connection to shaft units that are manufactured separately, such as a motor shaft and a generator shaft. Also, to provide for disconnections for repairs or maintenance.
2. To provide for misalignment of the shafts or to introduce mechanical flexibility (such as in case of flexible coupling.)
3. To reduce the transmission of shock loads from one shaft to another.
4. To provide protection against overloads.
5. To alter the vibration characteristics of rotating members.

3.3.2 Requirements or Pre-requisites of A Good Coupling

Question

1. What are the pre-requisites of a good coupling ?   **(W-12)**
    1. Coupling should be easy to connect or disconnect.
    2. Coupling should transmit 100% power from one shaft to the other shaft without any losses.
    3. Coupling should hold the shafts in perfect alignment.
    4. Coupling should reduce the transmission of shock from one shaft to another shaft.
    5. Coupling should not have projected parts.

3.3.2.1 Factors to be Considered, While Selecting a Coupling
1. Misalignment of shafts.
2. Required torque and desired speed.
3. Operating conditions.
4. Protection against overload.
5. Duration or life.
6. Cyclic operations.
7. Direction of rotation.

3.3.3 Types of Couplings

Question

1. Write down classification of coupling and draw sketch of one coupling.   **(S-12)**

Shaft couplings are classified as,

1. **Rigid Coupling :**
    - It is used to connect two shafts, which are in perfect alignment.
    - It consists of two hubbed flanges, one keyed to the driving shaft and other to driven shaft. The two flanges are bolted together.
    - They are used in applications like,
        (i) When the required length of shaft is too long and is difficult to manufacture, then the shafts of suitable length are connected with the help of sleeve or muff couplings.
        (ii) For motor pump sets, motor gear box sets etc.
    - They can be classified as,
        a. Sleeve or muff coupling
        b. Spilt muff or compression coupling
        c. Flange coupling

2. **Flexible Coupling :**
    - It is used to connect two shafts having both lateral and angular misalignment.
    - Its construction is similar to that of a rigid coupling except that a resilient element such as rubber bush is inserted between the coupled parts.

- The rubber bush is provided with brass lining to avoid excessive wear. These bushes absorb the misalignment between the shafts.
- They are sub classified as,
    - d.   Bushed pin type coupling
    - e.   Universal coupling
    - f.   Oldham coupling

3.3.4 Applications of Shaft Couplings

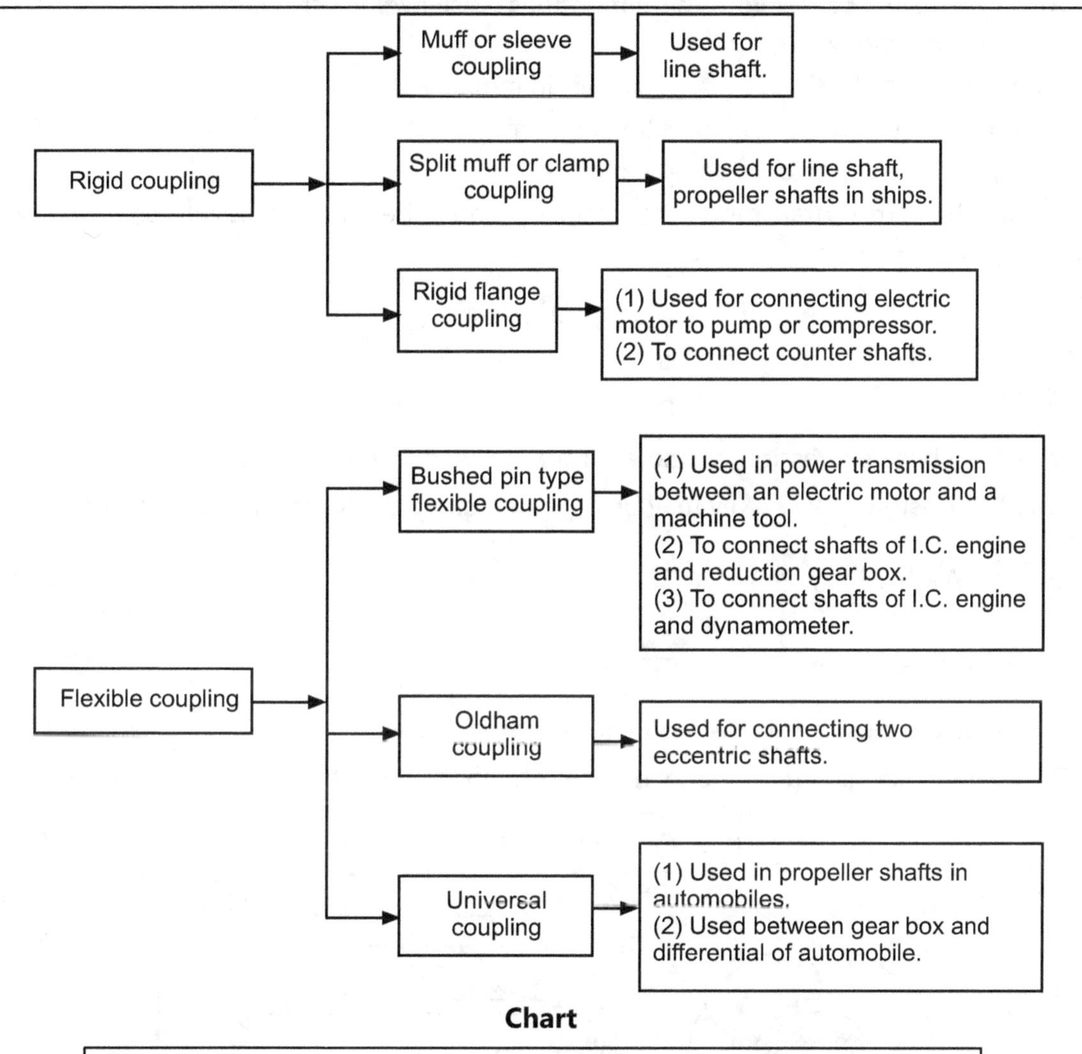

Chart

3.3.5 Design Procedure of Sleeve or Muff Coupling

Question

1.   Write down classification of coupling and draw sketch of one coupling.   **(S-12)**

- Sleeve or muff coupling consists of a hollow cylinder called as *sleeve or muff* having internal diameter equal to diameter of shafts.

- It is fitted at the ends of shafts to be connected with the help of gib headed key. Thus, the power is transmitted through the sleeve and key.
- It is generally used with small diameter shafts.

Step I : Design of shaft : Considering the shaft under twisting moment,

$$T = \frac{\pi}{16} \cdot \tau \cdot d^3$$

From above expression, diameter of the shaft can be determined.

Step II : Design of sleeve : The dimensions of sleeve are calculated by using standard proportions given below.

Outer diameter of sleeve, D $= (2d + 13)$ in mm

Length of the sleeve, L $= 3.5 \times d$ in mm

where, d is the diameter of shaft in mm.

If T be the torque transmitted by coupling and τ be the permissible shear stress for sleeve, then we have,

$$T = \frac{\pi}{16} \times \tau \times D^3 \, (1 - k^4)$$

where, $$k = \frac{d}{D}$$

From the above expression, diameter of the sleeve may be checked.

Step III : Design of key : Key may be designed using the following empirical relations.

$$\text{Width of key} = w = \frac{d}{4}$$

$$\text{Thickness of key} = t = \frac{2w}{3} = \frac{d}{6}$$

Length of key must be at least equal to length of sleeve.

The coupling key is usually made in two parts, so that, length of key in each shaft,

$$l = \frac{L}{2} = \frac{3.5\,d}{2}$$

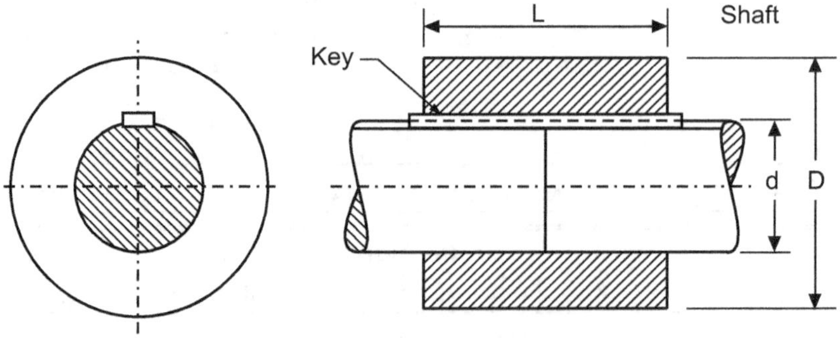

Fig. 3.32 : Muff or Sleeve coupling

After determining the dimensions of key, the crushing stress and shear stress induced in the key may be checked as follows :

Torque transmitted, $\qquad T = F \times \dfrac{d}{2} = l \times w \times \tau \times \dfrac{d}{2}$ $\qquad$ ... (In shear)

Torque transmitted, $\qquad T = F \times \dfrac{d}{2} = l \times \dfrac{t}{2} \times \sigma_{ck} \times \dfrac{d}{2}$ $\qquad$ ... (In crushing)

Numerical Type No. 10 : "Muff Coupling"

Problem 3.28: *Design a Muff coupling for connecting two shafts transmitting 50 kW at 450 r.p.m. The material for shaft and key is same, for which, allowable shearing and crushing stresses are 40 MPa and 80 MPa respectively.* **(S-13)**

Solution : Given data : $P = 50$ kW $= 50 \times 10^3$ W, $N = 450$ r.p.m., $\tau = 40$ N/mm^2, $\sigma_{ck} = 80$ N/mm^2

Procedure :

Step I : The power transmitted by shaft,

$$P = \frac{2\pi NT}{60}$$

$\therefore \qquad$ Torque, $T = \dfrac{P \times 60}{2\pi N} = \dfrac{50 \times 10^3 \times 60}{2 \times \pi \times 450}$

$$T = 1061.03 \text{ N-m} = \mathbf{1061.03 \times 10^3 \text{ N-mm}}$$

We know that, torque transmitted by shaft is given by,

$$T = \frac{\pi}{16} \times \tau \times d^3$$

$\therefore \qquad 1061.03 \times 10^3 = \dfrac{\pi}{16} \times 40 \times d^3$

$\therefore$ Diameter of shaft, $\quad d = 51.31$ mm $\cong$ **52 mm (say)**

Step II : Design of sleeve : The dimensions of sleeve are calculated by using standard proportions given below.

Outer diameter of sleeve, $D = 2d + 13 = 2 \times 52 + 13 =$ **117 mm**

$\qquad$ Length of sleeve, $L = 3.5\ d = 3.5 \times 52 =$ **182 mm**

We have, $\qquad k = \dfrac{d}{D} = \dfrac{52}{117} =$ **0.4444**

If $\qquad T =$ Torque transmitted by the coupling,

and $\qquad \tau =$ Permissible shear stress for the sleeve,

then, $\qquad T = \dfrac{\pi}{16} \times \tau \times D^3\ (1 - k^4)$

$\therefore \qquad \tau = \dfrac{T \times 16}{\pi \times D^3\ (1 - k^4)} = \dfrac{1061.03 \times 10^3 \times 16}{\pi \times (117)^3 \times [1 - (0.4444)^4]}$

$\therefore \qquad \tau = \mathbf{3.51 \text{ N/mm}^2 < 40 \text{ N/mm}^2}$

Thus, the induced stress is less than the given permissible shear stress. Hence, the design is safe.

Step III : Design of key : Key may be designed using the following empirical relations.

$$\text{Width of key (w)} \ = \ \frac{d}{4} \ = \ \frac{52}{4} \ = \ \textbf{13 mm}$$

$$\text{Thickness of key (t)} \ = \ \frac{2w}{3} \ = \ \frac{d}{6} \ = \ \frac{52}{6} \ = \ \textbf{8.67 mm}$$

Length of key must be at least equal to length of sleeve. The coupling key is usually designed into two parts.

$$\therefore \qquad \text{Length of key } (l) \ = \ \frac{L}{2} \ = \ \frac{182}{2} \ = \ \textbf{91 mm}$$

Checking the key under shear failure, we have,

$$\text{Torque transmitted} \ = \ T = l \times w \times \tau \times \frac{d}{2}$$

$$\therefore \qquad 1061.03 \times 10^3 \ = \ 91 \times 13 \times \tau \times \frac{52}{2}$$

$$\therefore \qquad \tau \ = \ \textbf{34.496 N/mm}^2 < \textbf{40 N/mm}^2$$

Thus, the induced shear stress in the key is less than permissible value. Hence, design of key is safe.

Checking the key under crushing failure,

$$T \ = \ l \times \frac{t}{2} \times \sigma_{ck} \times \frac{d}{2}$$

$$\therefore \qquad 1061.03 \times 10^3 \ = \ 91 \times \left(\frac{8.67}{2}\right) \times \sigma_{ck} \times \frac{52}{2}$$

$$\therefore \qquad \sigma_{ck} \ = \ \textbf{103.45 N/mm}^2 > \textbf{80 N/mm}^2$$

As the induced crushing stress (103.45 N/mm^2) is more than permissible value (80 N/mm^2), we will modify the value of 'l' by keeping the value of permissible crushing stress as follows :

$$T \ = \ l \times \frac{t}{2} \times \sigma_{ck} \times \frac{d}{2}$$

$$\therefore \qquad 1061.03 \times 10^3 \ = \ l \times \left(\frac{8.67}{2}\right) \times 80 \times \left(\frac{52}{2}\right)$$

$$\therefore \qquad l \ = \ 117.67 \text{ mm} \cong \textbf{118 mm}$$

Problem 3.29 : *Design muff coupling, which is used to connect two steel shafts transmitting 40 kW at 350 r.p.m.. The material for the shaft and key is plain carbon steel, for which, allowable stress may be assumed as 15 MPa. Assuming square key, find also dimensions of key.* **(S-14)**

Solution : Given data : P = 40 kW = 40 × 10^3 W,   N = 350 r.p.m., τ = 15 MPa = 15 N/mm^2

Procedure :

Step I : The power transmitted by shaft,

$$P = \frac{2\pi NT}{60}$$

$\therefore$ $\qquad$ Torque, $T = \dfrac{P \times 60}{2\pi N} = \dfrac{40 \times 10^3 \times 60}{2 \times \pi \times 350}$

$\therefore$ $\qquad$ $T = 1091.35$ N-m $= \mathbf{1091.35 \times 10^3\ N\text{-}mm}$

We know that, torque transmitted by shaft is given by,

$$T = \frac{\pi}{16} \times \tau \times d^3$$

$\therefore$ $\qquad$ $1091.35 \times 10^3 = \dfrac{\pi}{16} \times 15 \times d^3$

$\therefore$ $\qquad$ $d = 71.82$ mm $\approx \mathbf{72\ mm\ (say)}$

$\therefore$ $\qquad$ Diameter of shaft, $d = \mathbf{72\ mm}$

Step II : Design of sleeve : The dimensions of sleeve are calculated by using standard proportions given below.

$\qquad$ Outer diameter of sleeve, $D = 2d + 13 = 2 \times 72 + 13 = \mathbf{157\ mm}$

$\qquad\qquad$ Length of sleeve, $L = 3.5d = 3.5 \times 72 = \mathbf{252\ mm}$

We have, $\qquad$ $k = \dfrac{d}{D} = \dfrac{72}{252} = \mathbf{0.2857}$

Let, $\qquad$ $T = $ Torque transmitted by the coupling.

$\qquad\qquad$ $\tau = $ Permissible shear stress for the sleeve $= 15$ N/mm^{-2}

We have, $\qquad$ $T = \dfrac{\pi}{16} \times \tau \times D^3 (1 - k^4)$

$\therefore$ $\qquad$ $\tau = \dfrac{T \times 16}{\pi \times D^3 (1 - k^4)} = \dfrac{1091.35 \times 10^3 \times 16}{\pi \times (252)^3 [1 - (0.2857)^4]}$

$\qquad\qquad$ $\tau = \mathbf{0.35\ N/mm^2} < 15\ \mathbf{N/mm^2}$

Thus, the induced stress is less than the permissible stress value. Therefore, design of sleeve is safe.

Step III : Design of key : Key may be designed using the following empirical relations.

For square key to be used, we have, $w = t$.

$$\text{Width of key (w)} = \frac{d}{4} = \frac{72}{4} = \mathbf{18\ mm}$$

$\therefore$ $\qquad$ Thickness of key (t) $= w = \mathbf{18\ mm}$

Length of key must be at least equal to length of sleeve. The coupling key is usually desgined into two parts.

$\therefore$ $\qquad$ Length of key $(l) = \dfrac{L}{2} = \dfrac{252}{2} = \mathbf{126\ mm}$

Checking the key under shear failure,

$$\text{Torque transmitted} = T = l \times w \times \tau \times \frac{d}{2}$$

$$\therefore \qquad 1091.35 \times 10^3 = 126 \times 18 \times \tau \times \frac{72}{2}$$

$$\tau = \textbf{13.37 N/mm}^2 < \textbf{15 N/mm}^2$$

Thus, the induced shear stress in the key is less than permissible value. Hence, design of key is safe.

Checking the key under crushing failure,

$$T = l \times \frac{t}{2} \times \sigma_{ck} \times \frac{d}{2}$$

$$\therefore \qquad 1091.35 \times 10^3 = 126 \times \left(\frac{18}{2}\right) \times \sigma_{ck} \times \frac{72}{2}$$

$$\therefore \qquad \sigma_{ck} = \textbf{26.73 N/mm}^2$$

Value of permissible crushing stress is not given. Therefore, taking a square key ($w = t = 18$ mm), which is equally stronger in crushing and shearing, we have the relation,

$$\sigma_{ck} = 2\tau = 2 \times 15 = \textbf{30 N/mm}^2$$

Thus, the induced crushing stress ($\sigma_{ck} = 25.73$ N/mm^2) is less than permissible value (30 N/mm^2). Hence, design of key is safe.

3.3.5.1 Advantages of Muff Coupling

(1) It is the simplest form of coupling and easy to construct.

(2) It has no projection parts except the key head.

(3) The external surface of the sleeve is smooth.

3.3.5.2 Disadvantages of Muff Coupling

(1) It is difficult to assemble or dismantle, since the sleeve has to be either shifted over the shaft or ends of the shaft have to be drawn together.

(2) It cannot tolerate misalignment between the shaft axes.

(3) It cannot absorb shocks and vibrations.

(4) It require more axial space than flange coupling.

3.3.5.3 Clearance in Muff coupling

- Small clearance is provided at the joining surface of the coupling to create a pressure between the surface of the shaft and coupling.

- The pressure created by tightening the bolts causes friction on the surface of the shaft and these forces transmit the required torque.

3.3.6 Flange Coupling

Introduction :

- A flange coupling is a type of rigid coupling. It consists of two cast iron flanges, one mounted on the driving shaft and other on the driven shaft.
- The faces of couplings are turned upto right angles to the axis of shaft.
- The two flanges are connected together by means of four or six bolts arranged on a circle concentric with axes of shafts. Power is transmitted from the driving shaft to the left side flange through the key. It is then transmitted from the left side flange to the right side flange through the bolts. Finally, power is transmitted from the right side flange to the driven shaft through the key.
- There are two types of rigid flange couplings – unprotected and protected.
- Following Fig. 3.33 shows an un-protective type of coupling. The revolving bolt heads and nuts are dangerous to the operator and may lead to accidents.

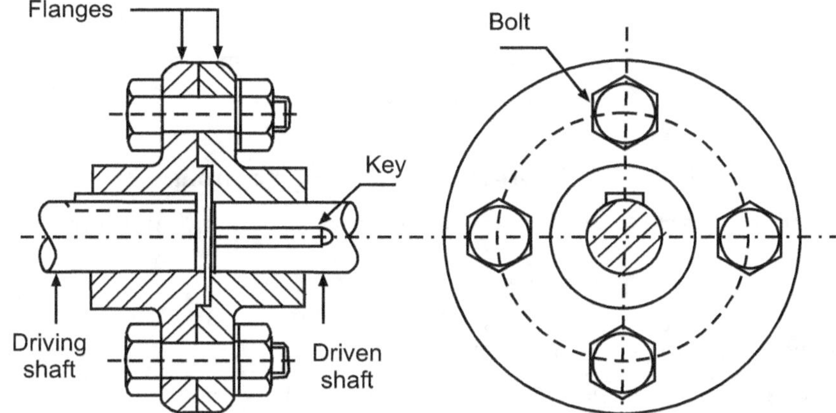

Fig. 3.33 : Unprotective type flange coupling

- Protected type flange coupling consists of two hubs keyed on the ends of two shafts. The hubs extend into the flanges, whose faces are brought together and connected by means of bolts. Bolts are guarded by giving projections at the flanges.

Design Procedure of Protected Type Flange Coupling :

Question
1. Sketch a protective type flange coupling and explain its design procedure.   **(S-10)**

Let,
$$d = \text{Diameter of shaft or inner diameter of hub}$$
$$D = \text{Outer diameter of hub}$$
$$d_c = \text{Core diameter of bolts}$$
$$D_1 = \text{Diameter of bolt circle}$$
$$n = \text{Number of bolts}$$
$$t_f = \text{Thickness of flange}$$

Let τ_s, τ_b, τ_k and τ_f be the permissible shear stresses for shaft, bolt, key and flange material, and σ_{ckb} and σ_{ckk} be the permissible crushing stresses for bolt and key material respectively.

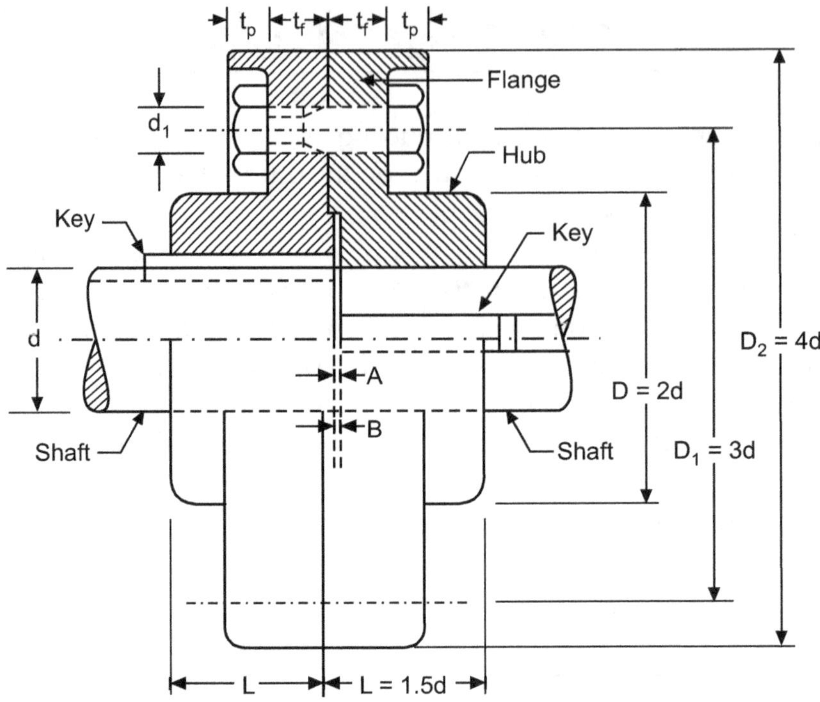

Fig. 3.34 : Protective type flange coupling

Step I : Design of shaft : Considering the shaft under twisting moment,

$$T \;=\; \frac{\pi}{16}\,\tau\,d^3$$

Hence, the diameter of shaft is determined.

Step II : Design of hub : Usual proportions are,

$$D \;=\; \text{Outer diameter of hub} = 2d$$

$$L \;=\; \text{Length of hub} = 1.5\,d$$

$$k \;=\; \frac{d}{D}$$

Considering hub as a hollow shaft, transmitting the same torque as that of shaft,

$$T \;=\; \frac{\pi}{16} \times \tau \times D^3 \,(1 - k^4) \qquad\qquad (\text{where, } k = d/D)$$

By putting the value of D in above expression, check the shear stress induced in hub.

Step III : Design of key : Key may be designed using the following empirical relations.

$$\text{Width of key} \;=\; w \;=\; \frac{d}{4}$$

$$\text{Thickness of key} \;=\; \frac{2w}{3} \;=\; \frac{d}{6}$$

Length of key must be atleast equal to length of hub. $\therefore\; l = L$

After determining the dimensions of key, the crushing stress and shear stress induced in the key may be checked as follows.

Torque transmitted, $\quad T = F \times \dfrac{d}{2} = l \times w \times \tau_k \times \dfrac{d}{2}$ $\qquad$ ... (In shearing)

Also, $\qquad T = F \times \dfrac{d}{2} = l \times \dfrac{t}{2} \times \sigma_{ckk} \times \dfrac{d}{2}$ $\qquad$ ... (In crushing)

Step IV : Design of flange : While transmitting the torque, the flange is under shear.

The torque transmitted, $\quad T =$ Circumference of hub $\times$ Thickness of flange

$\qquad\qquad\qquad\qquad\qquad\times$ Shear stress $\times$ Radius of hub

$\therefore \qquad T = (\pi \times D) \times t_f \times \tau_f \times \dfrac{D}{2}$

Taking $t_f = \dfrac{d}{2}$, shear stress induced in the flange may be checked.

(**Note :** For marine type of flange coupling, $t_f = d/3$).

Step V : Design of bolts : The bolts are subjected to shear stress due to torque transmitted.

$$\text{Load on each bolt} = \dfrac{\pi}{4} \times (d_c)^2 \times \tau_b$$

$\therefore \qquad$ Total load on all bolts $= n \times \dfrac{\pi}{4} \times (d_c)^2 \times \tau_b$

$\therefore \qquad$ Torque transmitted $=$ Force (or Load) $\times$ Radius $= n \times \dfrac{\pi}{4} \times (d_c)^2 \times \tau_b \times \dfrac{D_1}{2}$

Take $D_1 =$ Pitch circle diameter of bolts.

And, Number of bolts,

$\qquad\qquad n = 3$, for 'd' upto 40 mm

$\qquad\qquad\quad = 4$, for 'd' upto 100 mm

$\qquad\qquad\quad = 6$, for 'd' upto 180 mm

Putting the value of $D_1 = 3 \times d$ in the above equation, we can determine value of d_c.

The other proportions are, $D_2 = 4 \times d$

and thickness of protective circumferential flange $= t_p = 0.25$ d.

Numerical Type No. 11 : "Protective Type Flange Coupling"

Problem 3.30 : In a rigid flanged coupling to transmit 20 kW at 700 r.p.m., the flanges are of cast iron and other parts of C-40. Assume stresses for C.I., Tensile = 28 N/mm^2, Compressive = 60 N/mm^2, Shear = 10 N/mm^2

Stresses for C-40, Tensile = Compressive = 110 N/mm^2, Shear = 40 N/mm^2, Bearing = 25 N/mm^2.

Determine: Diameter of shaft, diameter of bolts, if 6 bolts are used and various flange dimensions. **(W-13)**

Solution : Given data : $\quad P = 20$ kW $= 20 \times 10^3$ W, $N = 700$ r.p.m.

$$\tau_s = 40 \text{ MPa} = 40 \text{ N/mm}^2 = \tau_k = \tau_b, \; \sigma_{ckk} = 110 \text{ N/mm}^2$$

$$\tau_{ci} = 10 \text{ N/mm}^2, \; \sigma_t = \sigma_{ck} = 100 \text{ N/mm}^2, n = 6$$

Procedure : The power transmitted by steel shafts,

$$P = \frac{2\pi NT}{60}$$

$\therefore \qquad$ Torque, $T = \dfrac{P \times 60}{2\pi N} = \dfrac{20 \times 10^3 \times 60}{2\pi \times 700}$

$\therefore \qquad\qquad\quad T = 272.84$ N-m $= \mathbf{272.84 \times 10^3}$ **N-mm**

We know that, torque transmitted by shaft is given by,

$$T = \frac{\pi}{16} \times \tau_s \times d^3$$

$\therefore \qquad 272.84 \times 10^3 = \dfrac{\pi}{16} \times 40 \times d^3$

$\therefore \qquad$ Diameter of shaft, d $= 32.63 \cong$ **33 mm (say)**

Step I : Design of hub : Usual proportions are,

$$D = \text{Outer diameter of hub}$$
$$= 2d = 2 \times 33 = \mathbf{66 \text{ mm}}$$
$$L = \text{Length of hub} = 1.5 \times d = 1.5 \times 33 = \mathbf{49.5 \text{ mm}}$$
$$k = \frac{d}{D} = \frac{33}{66} = \mathbf{0.5}$$

Considering hub as a hollow shaft transmitting the same torque as that of shaft, we have,

$$T = \frac{\pi}{16} \times \tau_{ci} \times D^3 \, (1 - k^4)$$

$\therefore \qquad 272.84 \times 10^3 = \dfrac{\pi}{16} \times \tau_{ci} \times (66)^3 \times [1 - (0.5)^4)]$

$\therefore \qquad\qquad\qquad \tau_{ci} = \mathbf{5.15 \text{ N/mm}^2 < 10 \text{ N/mm}^2}$

Thus, the induced shear stress in the cast iron hub is less than the given permissible shear stress. Hence, the design is safe.

Step II : Design of flange : Take $t_f = \dfrac{d}{2} = \dfrac{33}{2} = 16.5$ mm

While transmitting the torque, the flange is under shear.

The torque transmitted, $\quad T = $ Circumference of hub $\times$ Thickness of flange
$$\times \text{ Shear stress} \times \text{ Radius of hub}$$

$$T = (\pi \times D) \times t_f \times \tau_f \times \frac{D}{2}$$

$\therefore \qquad 272.84 \times 10^3 = \pi \times 66 \times 16.5 \times \tau_f \times \dfrac{66}{2}$

$\therefore \qquad\qquad\qquad \tau_f = \mathbf{2.42 \text{ N/mm}^2 < 10 \text{ N/mm}^2}$

Thus, induced shear stress is less than given permissible shear stress for flange material. Hence, the design is safe.

The other proportions are,

$$D_2 = 4 \times d = 4 \times 33 = \textbf{132 mm}$$

And thickness of protective circumferential flange

$$= t_p = 0.25 \times d = 0.25 \times 33 = \textbf{8.25 mm}$$

Step III : Design of bolts : The bolts are subjected to shear stress due to torque transmitted.

$$\therefore \qquad \text{Load on each bolt} = \frac{\pi}{4} \times (d_c)^2 \times \tau_b$$

$$\therefore \qquad \text{Total load on all bolts} = n \times \frac{\pi}{4} \times (d_c)^2 \times \tau_b$$

$$\therefore \qquad \text{Torque transmitted} = \text{Load} \times \text{Radius} = n \times \frac{\pi}{4} (d_c)^2 \times \tau_b \times \frac{D_1}{2}$$

Taking $D_1 = 3\,d = 3 \times 33 = 99$ mm and $n = 6$ (given), the above equation gives,

$$272.84 \times 10^3 = 6 \times \frac{\pi}{4} \times (d_c)^2 \times 40 \times \frac{99}{2}$$

$$\therefore \qquad d_c = 5.40 \text{ mm}$$

We have, $\qquad d_c = 0.84 \times d_o$

$$\therefore \qquad d_o = \frac{d_c}{0.84} = \frac{5.40}{0.84} = \textbf{6.428 mm} \cong \textbf{8 mm (say)}$$

$\therefore$ We will use M8 bolts. For safety reasons, we can increase the size of bolts upto M16.

Problem 3.31 : *Design and draw a protective type of cast iron flange coupling for a steel shaft transmitting 20 kW at 259 r.p.m. and having an allowable shear stress of 40 MPa. The working stress in the bolts should not exceed 90 N/mm^2. Assume that, the same material is used for shaft and key and that the crushing stress is twice the value of its shear stress. The maximum torque is 25% greater than the full load torque. The shear stress for cast iron is 14 N/mm^2.*

Solution : Given data : $P = 20$ kW $= 20 \times 10^3$ W, $N = 259$ r.p.m., $\tau_s = 40$ N/mm^2, $\tau_b = 90$ N/mm^2, $\tau_{ci} = 14$ N/mm^2. For key, $\sigma_{ck} = 2\tau_s = 2 \times 40 = 80$ N/mm^2

Procedure : The power transmitted by steel shafts $= P = \dfrac{2\pi NT}{60}$

$$\therefore \quad \text{Torque, } T = \frac{P \times 60}{2\pi \times N} = \frac{20 \times 10^3 \times 60}{2\pi \times 259} = 737.39 \text{ N-m} = \textbf{737.39}\times \textbf{10}^3 \textbf{ N-mm}$$

But, maximum torque is 25% greater than mean torque.

$$\therefore \qquad T_{max} = 1.25 \times T_{mean} = 1.25 \times 737.39 \times 10^3 = \textbf{921.73} \times \textbf{10}^3 \textbf{ N.mm}$$

We know that, torque transmitted by shaft is given by,

$$T = \frac{\pi}{16} \times \tau_s \times d^3$$

$$\therefore \qquad 921.73 \times 10^3 = \frac{\pi}{16} \times 40 \times d^3$$

$$\therefore \quad \text{Diameter of shafts} = d = 48.95 \text{ mm} \cong \textbf{50 mm (say)}$$

Step I : Design of hub :

Usual proportions are,

D = Outer diameter of hub = 2 × d = 2 × 50 = **100 mm**

L = Length of hub = 1.5 × d = 1.5 × 50 = **75 mm**

$$k = \frac{d}{D} = \frac{50}{100} = \textbf{0.5}$$

Considering hub as a hollow shaft, transmitting the same torque as that of shaft,

We have, $T = \dfrac{\pi}{16} \times \tau_{ci} \times D^3 (1 - k^4)$

$\therefore \quad 921.73 \times 10^3 = \dfrac{\pi}{16} \times \tau_{ci} \times (100)^3 \times \{1 - (0.5)^4\}$

$\therefore \quad \tau_{ci} = \textbf{5 N/mm}^2 < \textbf{14 N/mm}^2$

Thus, the induced shear stress in the cast iron hub is less than the given permissible shear stress. Hence, the design is safe.

Step II : Design of key :

Given data : As material for shaft and key is same. Take $\tau = 40$ N/mm^2 and

$$\sigma_{ck} = 2\tau = 2 \times 40 = 80 \text{ N/mm}^2$$

Thus, the crushing stress for key material is twice the shear stress, therefore a square key may be used, for which, t = w.

Key may be designed using the following empirical relations.

Width of key = $w = \dfrac{d}{4} = \dfrac{50}{4} = \textbf{12.5 mm}$

$\therefore \quad$ Thickness of key = t = **12.5 mm**

Length of key must be at least equal to length of hub. $\therefore l = \textbf{75 mm}$

Checking the key under shear failure,

Torque transmitted = $T = l \times w \times \tau \times \dfrac{d}{2}$

$\therefore \quad 921.73 \times 10^3 = 75 \times 12.5 \times \tau \times \dfrac{50}{2}$

$\therefore \quad \tau = \textbf{39.32 N/mm}^2 < 40 \text{ N/mm}^2$

Checking the key under crushing failure,

Torque transmitted = $T = l \times \dfrac{t}{2} \times \sigma_{ck} \times \dfrac{d}{2}$

$\therefore \quad 921.73 \times 10^3 = 75 \times \left(\dfrac{12.5}{2}\right) \times \sigma_{ck} \times \left(\dfrac{50}{2}\right)$

$\therefore \quad \sigma_{ck} = \textbf{78.65 N/mm}^2 < 80 \text{ N/mm}^2$

Hence, design of key is safe.

Step III : Design of flange :

Take $t_f = \dfrac{d}{2} = \dfrac{50}{2}$ = **25 mm**

While transmitting the torque, the flange is under shear. The torque transmitted is,

T = Circumference of hub × Thickness of flange × Shear stress × Radius of hub

$$\therefore \quad T = \pi \times D \times t_f \times \tau_f \times \frac{D}{2}$$

$$\therefore \quad 921.73 \times 10^3 = \pi \times 100 \times 25 \times \tau_f \times \frac{100}{2}$$

τ_f = **2.347 N/mm^2**, which is less than given permissible shear stress (14 N/mm^2) for flange material. So design is safe.

Step IV : Design of bolts :

Let us assume, n = number of bolts = 4 and

D_1 = diameter of bolt circle or pitch circle diameter = 3 × d = 3 × 50 = **150 mm**

The bolts are subjected to shear stress due to torque transmitted.

Load on each bolt $= \dfrac{\pi}{4} \cdot (d_c)^2 \cdot \tau_b$

$$\therefore \quad \text{Total load on all bolts} = n \times \frac{\pi}{4} \cdot (d_c)^2 \cdot \tau_b$$

$$\therefore \quad \text{Torque transmitted} = n \times \frac{\pi}{4} \cdot (d_c)^2 \cdot \tau_b \cdot \frac{D_1}{2}$$

$$\therefore \quad 921.73 \times 10^3 = 4 \times \frac{\pi}{4} \times (d_c)^2 \times 90 \times \left(\frac{150}{2}\right)$$

$\therefore \quad d_c$ = 6.59 mm.

$$\therefore \quad d_o = \frac{d_c}{0.84} = \frac{6.59}{0.84} = 7.84 \text{ mm} \cong \textbf{8 mm (say)}$$

Thus, we will use M8 bolts. For safer side, we may increase the size of bolt to M16.

Other proportions are, D_2 = 4 × d = 4 × 50 = **200 mm** and

Thickness of protective circumferential flange = t_p = 0.25 × d = 0.25 × 50 = **12.5 mm**

3.3.6.1 Advantages of Flange Couplings

(1) It has high torque transmitting capacity.

(2) It is easy to assemble and dismantle.

(3) It is simple in construction and easy to manufacture.

3.3.6.2 Disadvantages of Flange Couplings

(1) It cannot tolerate misalignment between the axes of two shafts.

(2) It can be used only, where the motion is free from shocks and vibrations.

(3) It requires more radial space as compared to muff coupling.

3.3.7 Flexible Coupling

- Flange coupling is rigid type of coupling. It can be used only, when there is perfect alignment between the axes of two shafts and the motion is free from vibrations and shocks.
- In practice, it is impossible to obtain perfect alignment of shaft.
- Misalignment exists due to the following reasons :
  - (i) Deflection of shafts due to lateral forces.
  - (ii) Error in shaft mounting due to manufacturing tolerances.
  - (iii) Use of two separately manufactured units such as an electric motor and a worm gear box.
  - (iv) Thermal expansion of the parts.
- If rigid coupling is used in such circumstances, the misalignment causes excessive bearing reactions resulting in vibrations and wear.
- To overcome this problem, flexible couplings are used.
- A flexible coupling employs a flexible element like rubber bush between the driving and the driven flanges. This flexible rubber bush not only accommodates for the misalignment, but also absorbs shocks and vibrations.

Construction of Flexible Coupling :

- The construction of the flexible coupling is shown in Fig. 3.35. It is similar to the rigid type of flange coupling except the provision of rubber bush and pins in place of bolts.
- The coupling consists of two flanges, one keyed to the input shaft and the other to the output shaft. The two flanges are connected together by means of four or six pins.
- At one end, the pin is fixed to the output flange by means of a nut. The diameter of the pin is enlarged in input flange, where a rubber bush is mounted over the pin. The rubber bush is provided with brass lining at the inner surface to avoid excessive wear of the rubber component.
- Power is transmitted from the input shaft to the input flange through the key. It is then transmitted from the input flange to the pin through the rubber bush. The pin then transmits the power to the output flange by shear resistance. Finally power is transmitted from the output flange to the output shaft through the key.

3.3.8 Bushed Pin Type Flexible Coupling

Introduction :

- A bushed pin type flexible coupling as shown in Fig. 3.35. It is a modification of the rigid type of flange coupling. The coupling bolts are known as *pins*. The rubber or leather bushes are used over the pins.

- The two halves (flanges) of the coupling are dissimilar in construction. A clearance of 5 mm is left between the faces of the two halves of the coupling. There is no rigid connection between them and the drive takes place through the medium of the compressible rubber or leather bushes.

- Flexible coupling is used to connect a machine to a prime mover for direct drive.

Purpose of Flexible Couplings :

(1) To prevent transmission of shock from one shaft to other.

(2) To eliminate stress reversals, when either shaft is subjected to deflection at or near the coupling.

Design Procedure of Flexible Coupling :

Question
1.   With neat sketch, explain the design procedure for bush pin type flexible coupling. **(W-10)**

- In designing the bushed pin type flexible coupling, the proportions of the rigid type flange coupling are modified. It involves reduction of bearing pressure on the rubber or leather bushes and it should not exceed 0.5 N/mm^2. For this, pitch circle diameter and number of pins are increased.

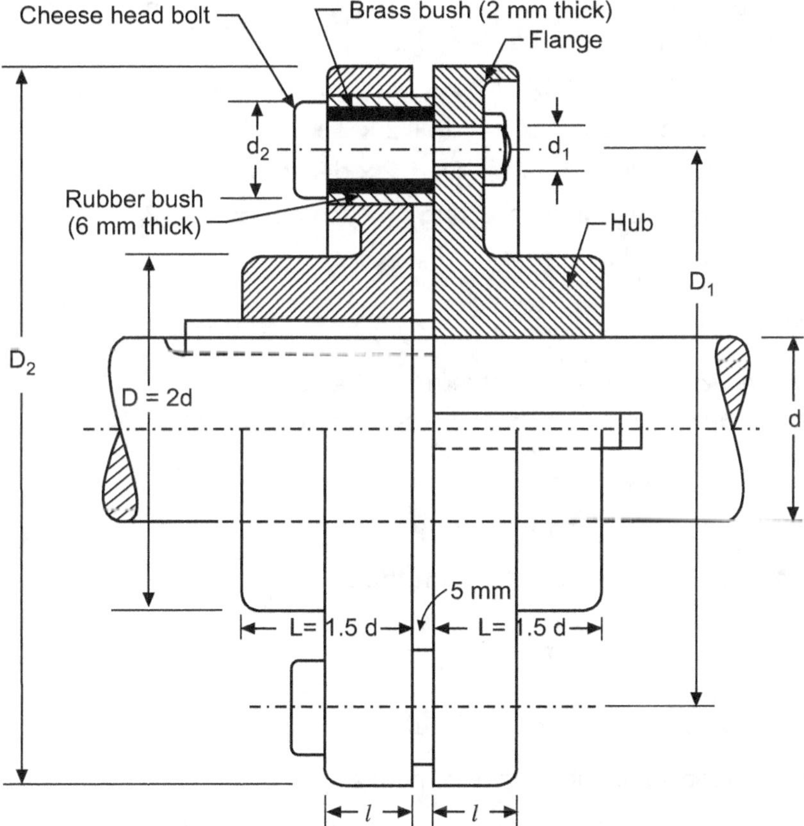

Fig. 3.35 : Bushed-pin type flexible coupling

Let,

$$l \ = \ \text{Length of bush in flange}$$
$$d_2 \ = \ \text{Diameter of bush}$$
$$P_b \ = \ \text{Bearing pressure on the bush or pin}$$
$$n \ = \ \text{Number of pins}$$
$$D_1 \ = \ \text{Diameter of pitch circle of pins}$$

Step I : Calculate diameter of shaft 'd', by using following equations.

Torque transmitted by shaft,

$$T \ = \ \frac{P \times 60}{2\pi N}$$

and

$$T \ = \ \frac{\pi}{16} \tau \, d^3$$

From these expressions, find 'd'.

Step II (a) : Calculate the diameter of pin,

$$d_1 \ = \ \frac{0.5 \, d}{\sqrt{n}}$$

where n can be assumed depending upon number of bolts.

The calculated diameter d_1 is modified and a brass bush of 2 mm thickness is fitted over the enlarged portion of pin.

Also the brass bush carries a rubber bush of 6 mm thickness.

$\therefore$ Diameter of rubber bush $= d_2 = d_1 + 2 \times 2 + 2 \times 6$

and   Diameter of pitch circle of pin $= D_1 = 2 \times d + d_2 + 2 \times 6$

Step II (b) : We have, bearing load acting on each pin $= W = P_b \times d_2 \times l$

$\therefore$ Total bearing load on all pins $= n \times P_b \times d_2 \times l$

$\therefore$ Torque transmitted by coupling $= W \times \left(\dfrac{D_1}{2}\right) = n \times P_b \times d_2 \times l \times \left(\dfrac{D_1}{2}\right)$

Using the above equation, we can determine the value of l.

Step II (c) : Calculate the direct shear stress in the coupling halves,

$$\tau \ = \ \frac{W}{\dfrac{\pi}{4}\,(d_1)^2}$$

Calculate the maximum bending stress on the pin,

$$\sigma_b \ = \ \frac{M}{Z}$$

where, $M = W \times \left(\dfrac{l}{2} + 5\right)$ and $Z = \dfrac{\pi}{32}\,(d_1)^3$

•   According to maximum shear stress theory,

$$\tau_{max} \ = \ \text{Maximum shear stress} \ = \ \frac{1}{2}\sqrt{\sigma_b^2 + 4\,(\tau)^2}$$

- According to normal stress theory,

$$\sigma_{b\,max} = \text{Maximum normal stress} = \frac{1}{2}\sigma_b + \frac{1}{2}\sqrt{\sigma_b^2 + 4\,(\tau)^2}$$

Check whether, the above maximum stresses are within the safe limits or not.

Step III : Design of hub :

Let, D = Diameter of hub, $D = 2d$

                        L = Length of hub, $L = 1.5\,d$

Considering the hub as a hollow shaft, check the induced shear stress for hub material (cast iron).

We have, $T = \dfrac{\pi}{16}\tau_c\,D^3\,(1 - k^4)$ $\left(\text{where, } k = \dfrac{d}{D}\right)$

Find $\tau_{c\,ind.}$

$\tau_{c\,ind.}$ should be less than $\tau_{c\,permissible}$ for safe design.

Step IV : Design for key :

Let, w = Width of key

                        t = Thickness of key

For rectangular key, $w = \dfrac{d}{4},\ t = \dfrac{d}{6}$

For square key, $w = \dfrac{d}{4},\ t = \dfrac{d}{4}$

Length of key l_1 is slightly greater than length of hub.

                        $l_1\ >\ L$

Now, check the induced stresses τ_k and σ_{ck} in key by considering shearing and crushing failure of key.

$$T = w \times l_1 \times \tau_k \times \frac{d}{2}$$ (Shearing of key)

Find $\tau_{ind.}$ It should be less than $\tau_{k\,permissible}.$

$$T = \frac{t}{2} \times l_1 \times \sigma_{ck} \times \frac{d}{2}$$ (Crushing of key)

Find $\sigma_{ck\,ind.}.$ It should be less than $\sigma_{ck\,permissible}.$

Step V : Design for flange :

Thickness of flange, $t_f = 0.5\,d$

Check the induced shear stress in the flange by considering the flange of the junction of hub in shear.

$$T = (\pi\,D\,t_f) \times \tau_c \times \frac{D}{2}$$

Find $\tau_{c\,induced}.$ It should be less than $\tau_{c\,permissible}$ for safe design of flange.

Numerical Type No. 12 : "Bushed Pin Type Flange Coupling"

Problem 3.32 : *Design a bushed pin type flexible coupling for connecting a motor shaft to pump shaft for the following service conditions :*

Power to be transmitted = 40 kW; speed of the motor shaft = 1000 r.p.m.; diameter of the motor shaft = 50 mm; diameter of the pump shaft = 45 mm; Allowable shear stress for C.I. = 15 MPa. The bearing pressure in the rubber bush and allowable shear stress in the pins are to be limited to 0.45 N/mm² and 25 N/mm²respectively.

The allowable shear stress and crushing stress for shaft and key material is 42 MPa and 84 MPa respectively.

Solution : Given data : $P = 40$ kW $= 40 \times 10^3$ W, $N = 1000$ r.p.m., $d = 50$ mm, $d_p = 45$ mm, $\tau_{ci} = 15$ N/mm², $P_b = 0.45$ N/mm², $\tau = 25$ N/mm².

Procedure :

Step I :

We have, power transmitted, $P = \dfrac{2\pi NT}{60}$

$\therefore$ Torque, $T = \dfrac{P \times 60}{2\pi N} = \dfrac{40 \times 10^3 \times 60}{2 \times \pi \times 1000} = 381.97$ N-m $= \mathbf{381.97 \times 10^3}$ **N-mm**

Step II (a) : Let n = number of pins = 6.

Calculate the diameter of pin as,

$$d_1 = \dfrac{0.5\,d}{\sqrt{n}} = \dfrac{0.5 \times 50}{\sqrt{6}} = \mathbf{10.206\ mm}$$

In order to permit the bending stress induced in the pin due to compressibility of brass bush, let us modify, diameter of pin from 10.206 mm to **20 mm**. This diameter is threaded and secured in right half coupling.

Let us take, diameter of the enlarged portion in the left half of coupling $d_1 = \mathbf{24\ mm.}$ A brass bush of 2 mm thickness is fitted over the enlarged portion of pin. Also the brass bush carries a rubber bush of 6 mm thickness.

$\therefore$ Diameter of rubber bush $= d_2 = d_1 + 2 \times 2 + 2 \times 6 = 24 + 4 + 12 = \mathbf{40\ mm}$

and Diameter of pitch circle of pins $= D_1 = 2 \times d + d_2 + 2 \times 6 = 2 \times 50 + 40 + 12 = \mathbf{152\ mm}$

Step II (b) :

We have, bearing load acting on each pin, $W = P_b \times d_2 \times l = 0.45 \times 40 \times l = 18 \times l$

$\therefore$ Total bearing load on all pins $= n \times W$

$\therefore$ Torque transmitted by coupling, $T = n \times W \times \dfrac{D_1}{2}$

$\therefore$ $\qquad\qquad 381.97 \times 10^3 = 6 \times (18 \times l) \times \dfrac{152}{2}$

$\therefore$ $\qquad\qquad l = \mathbf{46.54\ mm}$

$\therefore$ $\qquad\qquad W = 18 \times l = 18 \times 46.54 = \mathbf{837.72\ N}$

Step II (c) :

Calculate the direct shear stress in the coupling halves (taking minimum pin diameter).

$$\tau = \frac{W}{(\pi/4) \times (d_1)^2} = \frac{837.72}{\pi/4 \times (20)^2} = \textbf{2.67 N/mm}^2$$

Calculate the maximum bending stress on the pin,

$$\sigma_b = \frac{M}{Z} = \frac{W \times (l/2 + 5)}{\pi/32 \times (d_1)^3} = \frac{837.72 \times (\frac{46.54}{2} + 5)}{\pi/32 \times (20)^3} = \textbf{30.15 N/mm}^2$$

According to maximum shear stress theory,

$$\tau_{max} = \text{Maximum shear stress} = \frac{1}{2}\sqrt{\sigma_b^2 + 4(\tau)^2} = \frac{1}{2}\sqrt{(30.15)^2 + 4 \times (2.67)^2}$$

$$= \textbf{15.31 N/mm}^2$$

According to normal stress theory,

$$\sigma_{b\ max} = \text{Maximum normal stress} = \frac{1}{2}\sigma_b + \frac{1}{2}\sqrt{\sigma_b^2 + 4\,(\tau)^2}$$

$$= \frac{1}{2} \times 30.15 + \frac{1}{2}\sqrt{(30.15)^2 + 4 \times (2.67)^2} = \textbf{30.38 N/mm}^2$$

As the above maximum stresses are within the safe limits, design is safe.

Step III : Design for hub :

Diameter of hub, D = $2d$ = **100 mm**

Length of hub, L = $1.5\,d$ = **75 mm**

Considering hub as a hollow shaft, check the induced shear stress in the hub.

$$T = \frac{\pi}{16} \cdot \tau_{ci} \cdot D^3 \cdot (1 - k^4)$$

$\therefore \qquad 381.97 \times 10^3 = \frac{\pi}{16} \times \tau_{ci} \times 100^3\ [1 - (0.5)^4] \qquad\qquad (\because\ k = d/D = 0.5)$

$\therefore \qquad\qquad \tau_{c\ ind} = \textbf{2.075 N/mm}^2 < 15\ \text{N/mm}^2$

As induced shear stress is less than permissible stress, design is safe.

3.3.8.1 Advantages of Bushed Pin Type Flexible Coupling

(1) It is simple in construction.

(2) It can be used for transmitting high torques.

(3) It prevents transmission of shock from one shaft to the other shafts.

(4) It absorbs vibrations.

(5) It can tolerate 0.5 mm of lateral or 1.5° angular misalignment.

3.3.8.2 Disadvantages of Bushed Pin Type Flexible Coupling

(1) High cost.

(2) It requires more radial space as compared to other type of couplings.

Question

1. Why couplings are located near bearing ? Suggest suitable coupling for certain cases.

(S-06, 08)

Ans. : Couplings are provided near the bearing due to following reasons :

(1) It gives minimum vibrations.   (2) Bending load can be minimized.

Couplings Suggested for Specific Cases :

Case	Coupling suggested
(a) Shafts having parallel axes with small distance apart.	Oldham's coupling.
(b) Shafts with intersecting axes.	Universal coupling.
(c) Shafts having perfect alignment.	Rigid couplings like sleeve or muff and flange coupling.
(d) Shafts having both lateral and angular misalignment.	Universal coupling.
(e) Overhead crane shafts.	Protected type flange coupling.
(f) High speed pump and motor assembly.	Flexible coupling.

3.3.9 Comparison between Rigid and Flexible Coupling

Question

1. Compare rigid and flexible coupling on the following points :

    (i)   Purpose   (ii)   Alignment

    (iii)   Shock and vibrations   (iv)   Deflection

    (v)   Cost   (vi)   Suitability.   **(W-09, 11; S-13)**

Sr. No.	Comparative point	Rigid couplings	Flexible couplings
(i)	Purpose	It is used to connect two shafts, which are in perfect alignment.	It is used to connect two shafts, having both lateral and angular misalignment.
(ii)	Shock and vibrations	Due to absence of torsional flexibility, they cannot damp out vibrations.	Due to torsional flexibility they will damp out vibrations to certain extent.
(iii)	Rotational speeds	Relatively low.	Relatively high.
(iv)	Alignment	Rigid coupling cannot tolerate any misalignment between two shafts.	Flexible coupling can tolerate small amount of misalignment between two shafts.
(v)	Deflection	In rigid couplings, shaft deflection is less.	In flexible couplings, shaft deflection is more.

Sr. No.	Comparative point	Rigid couplings	Flexible couplings
(vi)	Cost	Rigid couplings are less expensive.	Flexible couplings are more expensive.
(vii)	Suitability	They are suitable for the applications like electric motor with pump or compressor.	They are suitable for high power transmission applications like electric motor and machine tool, shafts of I.C. engines with reduction gear box or dynamometer.

3.3.10 Difference between Coupling and Clutch (S-13)

Coupling	Clutch
1. It is used to make a permanent or semi-permanent connection between two shafts.	1. It permits rapid connection or disconnection as per the need of driver or operator.
2. Example: To connect an electric motor with a machine like pump.	2. Example: To connect or disconnect the engine shaft (driver shaft) to a driven shaft.

3.4 INTRODUCTION TO GEARS

- In case of belt or rope drives, slipping of belt or rope is a common phenomenon, which leads loss of power transmission between two shafts. It reduces the velocity ratio of the system.
- Gears transmit power positively *without slip* and at a *constant velocity ratio*.
- Gears are also called as *toothed wheels*. Fig. 3.36 shows a spur gear drive. The larger wheel is called as *spur gear*, whereas, smaller wheel is called as *spur pinion*.

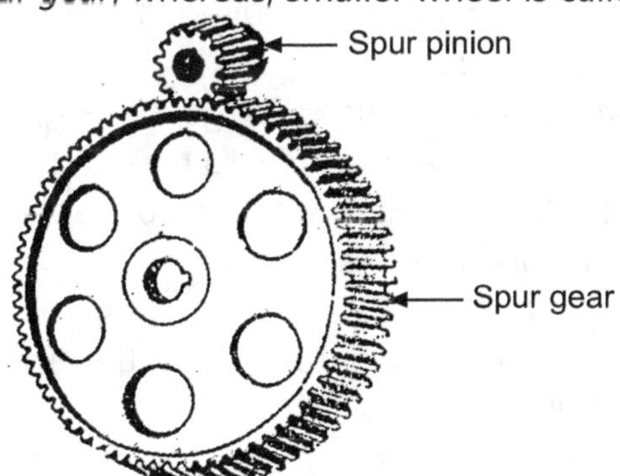

Fig. 3.36 : Spur gear drive

Applications of Gears :

(a) They are used in case of precise machines, where velocity ratio is of prime importance (e.g. watch mechanism).

(b) They are used, when the centre to centre distance between driver and driven shaft is small.

(c) Gears are used for heavy loads, such as in automobile gear boxes, in steam and gas turbines for speed reduction.

3.4.1 Classification of Gears

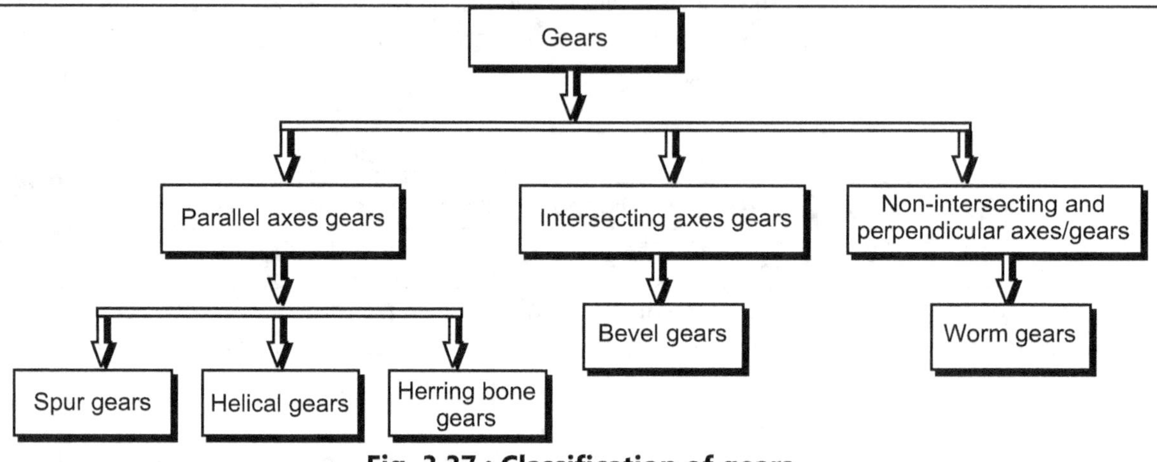

Fig. 3.37 : Classification of gears

3.4.2 Materials used for Gears

- The choice of material to be used for gears depends upon the strength and service conditions like wear, noise etc.
- The gears are manufactured from metallic and non-metallic materials.

1. Metallic Materials :

(a) Cast iron : It is commonly used due to its good machinability and good wear resistance properties.

(b) Steel :

- Steel is used, where high strength is required. It is heat treated, so as to have good toughness and tooth hardness.
- There are various types of steels used for gears ranging from plain carbon steel to highly alloyed steels and low carbon steel to high carbon steel.
- The plain carbon steels are used for medium duty applications, whereas, alloy steels are used for heavy duty applications.

(c) Non-ferrous metals :

- It is used in case of worm gears to reduce the effect wear, which is common problem in other metallic materials.
- The non-ferrous metals like copper, zinc, tin, aluminium and manganese are used in various combinations as gear materials.
- The most commonly used material is bronze. The various types of bronzes are used as gear material, because of their ability to withstand heavy-sliding loads, which are present in applications such as worm gear sets.

2. Non-metallic Materials :

(a) Wood (b) Nylon.

However, the non-metal gears are used only for light duty applications.

3.4.2.1 Criteria for Selection of Gear Materials

(1) Strength.

(2) Wear resistance.

(3) Service condition.

(4) Shock resistance.

(5) Speed.

(6) Degree of accuracy.

3.4.3 Gear Manufacturing Methods

The different types of gears are manufactured with the help of various methods such as casting, forming processes like rolling and extrusion, machining processes etc.

The different methods of machining used for gear manufacturing are :

1. Formed cutter method :

(a) Gear cutting on a milling machine by formed disc cutter.

(b) Gear cutting on a milling machine by formed end mill.

(c) Gear cutting by a formed single point cutting tool.

(d) Gear cutting on a broaching machine by formed cutter.

2. Template method

3. Generating method

(a) Gear planning method

(b) Gear shaping method

(c) Gear hobbing method.

3.4.4 Gear Terminology

1. **Pitch circle :** It is an imaginary circle, which by pure rolling action, would give the same motion as the actual gear.

2. **Pitch circle diameter :** It is the diameter of the pitch circle. The size of the gear is usually specified by the pitch circle diameter.

3. **Pitch point :** It is the common point of contact of two pitch circles of two different gears in mesh.

4. **Pressure angle :** It is the angle between the common normal to two gear teeths at the point of contact and the common tangent to the two pitch circles at the pitch point. The standard pressure angles are $14\frac{1}{2}°$ and $20°$.

5. **Addendum :** It is the radial distance of the tooth from the pitch circle to the top of the tooth.

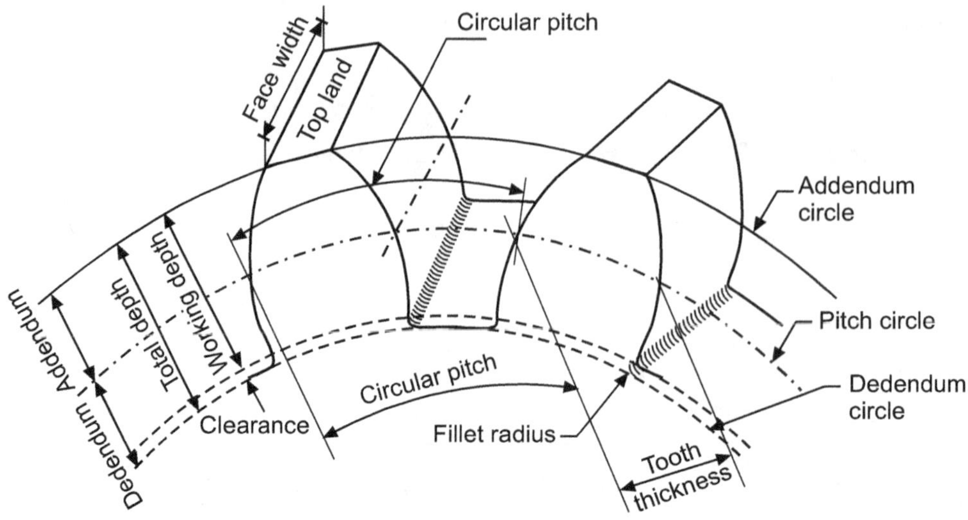

Fig. 3.38

6. **Dedendum :** It is radial distance of the tooth from pitch circle to the bottom of the tooth.

7. **Addendum circle :** It is the circle drawn through the top of the teeth and is concentric with the pitch circle.

8. **Dedendum circle :** It is the circle drawn through the bottom of the teeth.

9. **Circular pitch :** It is the distance measured on the circumference of the pitch circle from a point of one tooth to the corresponding point on the next tooth. It is usually denoted by p_c. Mathematically, $p_c = \dfrac{\pi D}{T}$

where   D = Diameter of the pitch circle and

     T = Number of teeth on the wheel.

10. **Diametral pitch :** It is the ratio of number of teeth to the pitch circle diameter in mm. Mathematically, $p_d = \dfrac{T}{D}$

11. **Module :** It is the ratio of pitch circle diameter to the number of teeth.

Module, $m = \dfrac{D}{T}$

12. **Clearance :** It is the radial distance from the top of tooth to the bottom of the tooth of a meshing gear.

13. **Total depth :** It is radial distance between the addendum and dedendum circle of a gear.

14. **Working depth :** It is radial distance from the addendum circle to the clearance circle.

15. **Tooth thickness :** It is the width of the tooth measured along the pitch circle.

16. **Tooth space :** It is the width of space between the two adjacent teeth measured along the pitch circle.

17. **Backlash :** It is the difference between tooth space and the tooth thickness, as measured on the pitch circle.

18. **Face of the tooth :** It is the surface of the tooth above the pitch surface.

19. **Top land :** It is the surface of the top of the tooth.

20. **Flank of the tooth :** It is surface of the tooth below the pitch surface.

21. **Face width :** It is the width of the gear tooth measured along a line parallel to axis.

22. **Profile :** It is the curve formed by the face and flank of tooth.

3.4.5 Advantages of Gear Drive

(1) Gear drives are *compact* as compared to belt or chain drives, because of small centre to centre distance.

(2) Gear drives can transmit *larger power* as compared to belt or chain drives.

(3) Gear drives can transmit power at *much higher speed* than belt or chain drives.

(4) It is a *positive drive* having *constant velocity ratio.*

(5) Gear drives give *higher speed ratio* than belt or chain drives.

(6) Gear drives can be used for *changing the speed ratios* over a wide range.

(7) It has more *efficient, reliable* and simple *operation.*

(8) It requires *low maintenance.*

3.4.6 Limitations of Gear Drive

(1) High cost as compared to belt or chain drive.

(2) Gear drives need continuous lubrication.

(3) Gear drives require precise alignment of shafts.

(4) Gear drives cannot be used for transmitting power over long distance.

3.4.7 Design Considerations for a Gear Drive

Question

1. State any four design considerations of gear drive. **(S-09, 11, 13; W-09, 11, 13)**

The following requirements must be met in the design of a gear drive :

(a) The gear teeth should have sufficient strength, so that, they will not fail during normal running condition.

(b) The gear teeth should have wear resistant property, so that, their life is satisfactory.

(c) The use of space and material should be economical.

(d) The alignment of the gears and deflection of the shafts must be considered to improve the performance of the gears.

(e) The gears should get satisfactory lubrication.

(f) High efficiency and speed ratio.

(g) Low cost.

In design of gear drive, the following data is usually given :

(1) The amount of power to be transmitted.

(2) The speed of driving gear.

(3) The speed of driven gear or the velocity ratio.

(4) The centre to centre distance between two shafts.

Objectives in design of gear drives :

(1) High power transmission.

(2) Compact in size.

(3) High efficiency.

(4) Less initial cost.

(5) Less maintenance and running cost.

(6) Noiseless and vibration free operation.

3.4.8　Beam Strength of Spur Gear Teeth – Lewis Equation

Question

1. Write Lewis equation for strength of gear tooth. Give the meaning of each term.

(S-09, 10, 11, 12, 14; W-10, 11, 13)

Solution :

- 'Lewis' derived an equation for determining the approximate stress in a gear tooth by considering it as a *cantilever beam of uniform strength*.

- Consider each tooth as a cantilever beam loaded by a normal load (W_N) as shown in Fig. 3.39.

- This normal load is resolved in two mutually perpendicular components.

  1. **Tangential component (W_T)** acting perpendicular to centerline of tooth : It induces a bending stress, which tends to break the tooth.

  2. **Radial component (W_R)** acting parallel to centerline of tooth : It induces a compressive stress of relatively smaller magnitude; therefore, its effect on the tooth may be neglected.

- Hence, bending stress is used as a basis for design calculations.

- The critical section or section subjected to maximum bending stress may be obtained by drawing a parabola passing through A and tangential tooth curves at B and C.

- The parabola outlines a beam of uniform strength i.e. there will be same stress at all sections of tooth.

- But, tooth is larger than parabola at every section except BC.

- Therefore, we can say that, section BC is section of maximum stress or critical section.

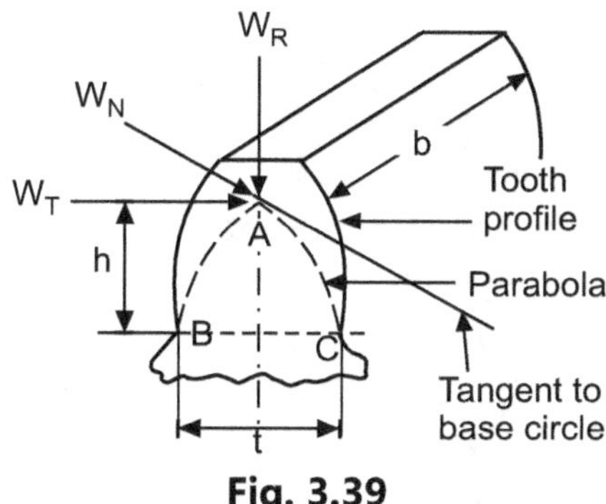

Fig. 3.39

Maximum value of bending stress at the section BC is given by,

$$\sigma_w = \frac{M}{I} \cdot y \qquad \qquad \text{... (3.10)}$$

where,

M = Maximum bending moment at critical section BC = $W_T \times h$

W_T = Tangential load acting at the tooth

h = Length of tooth

y = Half of tooth thickness = $\dfrac{t}{2}$

I = Moment of inertia about centerline of tooth = $\dfrac{1}{12} bt^3$

b = Width of gear face

Substituting the values of M, y and I in equation (3.10),

$$\sigma_w = \frac{(W_T \times h) \cdot \dfrac{t}{2}}{\dfrac{1}{12} \cdot b \cdot t^3} = \frac{6 \cdot W_T \cdot h}{b \cdot t^2}$$

$$\therefore \qquad W_T = \frac{\sigma_w \cdot b \cdot t^2}{6 \cdot h} \qquad \qquad \text{... (3.11)}$$

Here, t and h are the variables depending upon size of tooth and its profile.

Let, $t = x \cdot p_c$ and $h = k \cdot p_c$,

where, x and k are constants.

$\therefore$ Equation (3.11) gives,

$$W_T = \sigma_w \cdot b \cdot \frac{x^2 \cdot p_c^2}{6 \cdot k \cdot p_c} = \sigma_w \cdot b \cdot p_c \cdot \frac{x^2}{6 \cdot k}$$

Let,

$$y = \frac{x^2}{6 \cdot k} = \text{An another constant}$$

$$\therefore \qquad W_T = \sigma_w \cdot b \cdot p_c \cdot y$$

$$\therefore \qquad \mathbf{W_T = \sigma_w \cdot b \cdot \pi \cdot m \cdot y} \qquad \qquad (\because p_c = \pi \cdot m)$$

This is called as *Lewis equation*. It is applied to the gear or pinion, whichever is weaker element.

In the above equation,

$$m = \text{module}$$
$$b = \text{Width of gear face}$$
$$W_T = \text{Beam strength of tooth}$$
$$y = \text{Lewis form factor}$$

$$= 0.124 - \left(\frac{0.684}{T}\right) \quad \text{(for } 14\tfrac{1}{2}^{\circ} \text{ composite and full depth involute system)}$$

$$= 0.154 - \left(\frac{0.912}{T}\right) \quad \text{(for } 20^{\circ} \text{ full depth involute system)}$$

$$= 0.175 - \left(\frac{0.861}{T}\right) \quad \text{(for } 20^{\circ} \text{ stub system)}$$

Notes :

(a)   When both the pinion and the gear are made of same material, then pinion is the weaker.

(b) When both, the pinion and the gear are made of different material, then the product of $(\sigma_w \cdot y)$ or $(\sigma_o \cdot y)$ is deciding factor. The equation is applied (used) to that wheel, for which, $(\sigma_w \cdot y)$ or $(\sigma_o \cdot y)$ is less.

Permissible Working Stress :

It is given by,

$$\sigma_w = \sigma_o \times C_v$$

where, $\quad \sigma_o = \text{Allowable static stress}$

$$C_v = \text{Velocity factor}$$

3.4.9 Velocity Factor

Condition of gears	Value of velocity factor (C_v)
For ordinarily cut gears operating at velocity upto 12.5 m/s.	$C_v = \dfrac{3}{3 + V}$
For carefully cut gears operating at velocity upto 12.5 m/s.	$C_v = \dfrac{4.5}{4.5 + V}$
For accurately cut and ground metallic gears operating at velocity upto 20 m/s.	$C_v = \dfrac{6}{6 + V}$
For precision gears cut with high accuracy operating at velocity upto 12.5 m/s.	$C_v = \dfrac{0.75}{0.75 + \sqrt{V}}$
For metallic gears	$C_v = \left(\dfrac{0.75}{1 + V}\right) + 0.25$

Velocity ratio : $\text{V.R.} = \dfrac{T_G}{T_P} = \dfrac{D_G}{D_P} = \dfrac{N_P}{N_G}$

Power transmitted : $P = W_T \times V$

Pitch circle diameter : $D = m \times T$

Pitch line velocity : $V = \dfrac{\pi \cdot D \cdot N}{60}$

Circular pitch : $p_c = \pi \cdot m$

3.4.10 Design Procedure for Spur Gear

1. Design value of tangential tooth load is obtained from power transmitted and the pitch line velocity by using the following relation :

$$W_T = \frac{P}{V} \times C_s$$

where, W_T = Permissible tangential tooth load in 'N'

$\quad\ P$ = Power transmitted in 'watts'

$\quad\ V$ = Pitch line velocity in m/s = $\dfrac{\pi DN}{60}$

$\quad\ D$ = Pitch circle diameter in 'm'

$\quad\ N$ = Speed in r.p.m.

and C_s = Service factor

2. Apply Lewis equation to the weaker element (either pinion or gear)

i.e. $W_T = \sigma_w \cdot b \cdot p_c \cdot y$

$ = \sigma_w \times b \times \pi m \times y = \sigma_o \times C_v \times b \times \pi m \times y$ $[\because \sigma_w = \sigma_o \cdot C_v]$

Now, the deciding factor is $(\sigma_o \times y)$ or $(\sigma_w \times y)$.

Find $(\sigma_o \times y)_{gear}$ and $(\sigma_o \times y)_{pinion}$.

And apply Lewis equation to the wheel, for which, $(\sigma_o \times y)$ is less.

3. Calculate dynamic load (W_D) on the tooth by using Buckingham equation.

$$W_D = W_T + W_I$$

where, W_T = Steady load due to transmission of torque

$$= \frac{P}{V}$$

$\quad\ W_I$ = Increment load due to dynamic action

$$= \frac{21V\,(b \cdot C + W_T)}{21V + \sqrt{b \cdot C + W_T}}$$

4. Find static tooth load (i.e. beam strength or endurance strength of tooth),

$$W_s = \sigma_e \cdot b \cdot p_c \cdot y = \sigma_e \cdot b \cdot \pi m \cdot y$$

For safety against breakage, W_s should be greater than W_D.

5. Find the wear tooth load by using the relation

$$W_W = D \cdot b \cdot Q \cdot k$$

where, Q = Ratio factor

$$= \frac{2 \times V.R.}{V.R. + 1} = \frac{2T_G}{T_G + T_P} \qquad \text{[For external gearing]}$$

$$= \frac{2 \times V.R.}{V.R. - 1} = \frac{2T_G}{T_G - T_P} \qquad \text{[For internal gearing]}$$

$$V.R. = \frac{T_G}{T_P}$$

D = Pitch circle diameter in 'mm'

k = Load stress factor or material combination factor in N/mm^2

$$= \frac{(\sigma_{es})^2 \sin \phi}{1.4} \cdot \left(\frac{1}{E_P} + \frac{1}{E_G} \right)$$

σ_{es} = Surface endurance limit in N/mm^2

ϕ = Pressure angle in degrees

E_P = Young's modulus for pinion material

E_G = Young's modulus for gear material

Note : The wear load (W_w) should not be less than dynamic load (W_D) and should not be more than W_T.

3.4.11 Power Transmission Capacity of Spur Gear in Bending

Power transmission capacity can be calculated by the relation,

$$W_T = \frac{P}{V} \cdot C_s$$

where, W_T = Permissible tangential tooth load in 'N'

$$= \sigma_w \cdot b \cdot \pi \cdot m \cdot y$$

P = Power transmitted in watts

V = Pitch line velocity in m/s $= \dfrac{\pi D N}{60}$

D = Pitch circle diameter of gear in 'm'

C_s = Service factor

We have, circular pitch, $p_c = \dfrac{\pi D}{T} = \pi \cdot m$

$\therefore$ $D = mT$

where, m = Module in 'm'

T = Number of teeth

Also, $V = \dfrac{\pi D N}{60} = \dfrac{\pi \cdot m \cdot T \cdot N}{60}$ $\qquad (\because \ D = mT)$

$$= \frac{p_c \cdot T \cdot N}{60} \qquad (\because \ p_c = \pi \cdot m)$$

where, N = Speed in r.p.m.

3.5 MODES OF GEAR TOOTH FAILURE

Causes of Gear Tooth Failure:

The different modes of failure of gear teeth and their possible remedies to avoid the failure, are as follows:

1. **Bending failure:**
   - Every gear tooth acts as a cantilever. If the total repetitive dynamic load acting on the gear tooth is greater than the beam strength of the gear tooth, then the gear tooth with fail in bending, i.e., the gear tooth with break.
   - In order to avoid such failure, the module and face width of the gear is adjusted so that the beam strength is greater than the dynamic load.

2. **Pitting:**
   - It is the surface fatigue failure, which occurs due to many repetitions of contact stresses. The failure occurs, when the surface contact stresses are higher than the endurance limit of the material. The failure starts with the formation of pits, which continue to grow resulting in the rupture of the tooth surface.
   - In order to avoid the pitting, the dynamic load between the gear tooth should be less than wear strength of the gear tooth.

3. **Scoring :**
   - The excessive heat is generated, when there is an excessive surface pressure, high speed or supply of lubricant fails.
   - It is a stick-slip phenomenon, in which, alternate shearing and welding takes place rapidly at high spots.
   - This type of failure can be avoided by properly designing the parameters, such as, speed, pressure and proper flow of the lubricant, so that, the temperature at the rubbing faces is within the permissible limits.

4. **Abrasive wear:**
   - The foreign particles in the lubricants such as dirt, dust enter between the teeth and damage the form of tooth.
   - This type of failure can be avoided by providing filters for the lubricating oil or by using high viscosity lubricant oil, which enables the formation of thicker oil film and hence permits easy passage of such particles without damaging the gear surface.

5. **Corrosive wear:**
   - The corrosion of the tooth surfaces is mainly caused due to the presence of corrosive elements, such as additives present in the lubricating oils.
   - In order to avoid this type of wear, proper anti-corrosive additives should be used.

Practice Questions

1. Discuss the various types of shafts and standard sizes of transmission shafts.

2. What types of stresses are induced in shafts ?

3. What do you understand by torsional rigidity and lateral rigidity ?

4. "A hollow shaft has greater strength and stiffness than solid shaft of equal weight". Justify.

5. What is a key ? State its function.

6. How keys are classified ? Draw neat sketches of different types and state their application.

7. What is the effect of keyway cut into the shaft ?

8. Explain the strength equations of rectangular sunk key.

9. What are functions of coupling ?

10. Sketch a protective type flange coupling and explain its design.

11. Distinguish between rigid and flexible couplings.

12. Describe design procedure of bush-pin type flexible coupling with neat sketch.

13. How are the gears classified ?

14. Explain the design considerations for gear.

15. State the equation for beam strength of spur gear with important parametrers.

Problems for Practice

1. A mild steel shaft is transmitting 12.5 kW at 300 r.p.m. and is supported in two bearings 750 mm apart, to a pulley of 450 mm diameter fixed at a distance of 200 mm from one end. The belt passing over the pulley is vertical and tension ratio is 2. The safe working stresses for the shaft is F_t = 70 N/mm^2 and f_s = 56 N/mm^2. Design the diameter of shaft. The pulley weights 600 N.   (**Ans.** d = 52 mm) **(W-09)**

2. A mild steel shaft is supported on two bearings 1 metre apart. It transmits 15 kW at 300 r.p.m. to a pulley of diameter 200 mm mounted at a distance of 300 mm from one end. The belt passing over the pulley is vertical and the ratio of belt tension is 2 : 1. Pulley weighs 500 N. Design suitable diameter of shaft with following permissible stresses as σ_t = 70 N/mm^2, σ_s = 56 N/mm^2.

   (**Ans.** d = 49.1467 $\cong$ 50 mm (say) **(W-06)**

3. A shaft is required to transmit 100 kW at 1440 r.p.m. The outside diameter of shaft should not exceed 50 mm and maximum shear stress is 70 N/mm^2. Find the dimensions of hollow and solid shaft, which would just meet these requirements and compare the weights of the two.

   (**Ans.** W_H = 0.75 W_s, d_i = 44.36 mm, d = 36.40 mm) **(S-08)**

4. A line shaft is to transmit 25 kW at 150 r.p.m. It is driven by a motor placed directly under it by means of belt running on the 1000 mm diameter pulley keyed to the end of the shaft. The ratio of tight side to slack side tensions is 2.5 and the centre of pulley overhangs at 150 mm beyond the center line of end bearing. Determine diameter of shaft, if shear stress is 56 N/mm^2 and weight of pulley is 1.6 kN.

    (Ans. d = 59 mm)

5. Design of the diameter of a rotating shaft, which is subjected to a maximum torque of 200 N-m and bending moment of 350 N-m. Both the torque and bending moment are applied suddenly for following conditions :

    (a) Yield point value in shear = 300 N/mm^2.

    (b) Factor of safety = 3.

    (c) K_b = 2 and K_t = 1.5 are combined shock and fatigue load factor and twisting respectively.   **(Ans.** d = 36 mm)

6. A hollow shaft is required to transmit 600 kW at 110 r.p.m. The maximum torque being 20% greater than the mean. The shear stress is not to exceed 63 MPa and twist in a length of 3 m not to exceed 1.4°. Find external diameter of the shaft, if ratio of internal diameter to external diameter is 3/8. Take modulus of rigidity 84 GPa.

    (Ans. d_o = 176.2 mm)

7. A pulley is keyed to a shaft of diameter 100 mm by means of key of 20 mm width and 150 mm length. The allowable shear stress is 40 N/mm^2 and crushing stress is 100 N/mm^2. The shaft is running at 250 r.p.m. Find the power transmission capacity and (depth) thickness of the key.   **(Ans.** P = 157.079 kW; t = 16 mm)

8. Design a cast iron protective flange coupling to connect the shafts in order to transmit 7.3 kW at 500 r.p.m.

    (a) Allowable shear stress for shaft, bolt and key = 42 N/mm^2.

    (b) Allowable crushing stress for bolt and key = 82 N/mm^2.

    (c) Allowable shear stress for C.I. Flange = 8 N/mm^2.

    (Ans. d = 26 mm, w = 6.5 mm, l = 41 mm, M8 bolts)

9. A rigid C.I. flange coupling transmits 15 kW at 400 r.p.m. The maximum torque transmitted is 25% greater than the full load torque. Find the diameter and number of bolts required if :

    Shear stress for shaft = 40 N/mm^2.

    Shear stress for bolt = 30 N/mm^2.   **(Ans.** M16 bolts, n = 4) **(S-08)**

10. A sleeve coupling is to connect two shafts. The power transmitted is 38 kW at 200 r.p.m. If shear stress for the shaft and key material is 60 N/mm^2 and for muff 10 N/mm^2. Find : (i) diameter of shaft, (ii) diameter of sleeve and (iii) key dimensions.

    (Ans. d = 54 mm, D = 108 m, L = 81 mm, w = 13.5 mm, t = 9 mm) **(W-12)**

11. Design muff coupling, which is used to connect two shafts transmitting 30 kW at 300 r.p.m. The material for the shaft and key is plain carbon steel having allowable shear and crushing stresses as 35 MPa and 70 MPa respectively. The material for the muff is C.I., for which, allowable shear stress is assumed as 15 MPa.

(**Ans.** D = 117 mm, L = 182 mm, w = t = 13 mm, l = 91 mm)

MSBTE Questions and Answers

Summer 2013

1. State the difference between shaft, axle and spindle.   **(2 M)**

Ans. Article 3.1.6.

2. State broad classification of keys.   **(2 M)**

Ans. Refer Article 3.2.2.

3. State the difference between coupling and clutch.   **(2 M)**

Ans. Refer Article 3.3.10.

4. State four design considerations for a gear drive.   **(2 M)**

Ans. Refer Article 3.4.7.

5. Prove that for a square key, "Crushing stress is twice shearing stress".   **(4 M)**

Ans. Refer Article 3.2.3.2.

6. A line shaft rotating at 250 r.p.m. is to transmit 25 kW. The shaft is having an allowable shear stress 42 MPa and bending stress 65 MPa. Find diameter of shaft.

Ans. Refer Problem 3.3.

7. Design a Muff coupling for connecting two shafts transmitting 50 kW at 450 r.p.m. The material for shaft and key is same for which allowable shearing and crushing stresses are 40 MPa and 80 MPa respectively.   **(4 M)**

Ans. Refer Problem 3.28.

8. Compare rigid and flexible coupling on the basis of purpose, alignment, deflection and cost.   **(4 M)**

Ans. Refer Article 3.3.9.

9. A mild steel shaft transmits 30 kW at 300 r.p.m. It carries a central load 1000 N and is simply supported between the bearings 3 m apart. Determine the size of the shaft if allowable shear stress and tensile stress are 42 MPa and 56 MPa respectively. What change would you observe in the diameter of the shaft if same shaft is subjected to suddenly applied load? Take $k_m = k_t = 2.5$.   **(8 M)**

Ans. Refer Problem 3.20.

Winter 2013

1. Derive the relation between stress for square key equally strong in crushing and shearing. **(4 M)**

Ans. Refer Article 3.2.3.2.

2. In a rigid flanged coupling to transmit 20 kW at 700 r.p.m., the flanges are of cast iron and other parts of C-40. Assume stresses for C.I., Tensile = 28 N/mm^2, Compressive = 60 N/mm^2, Shear = 10 N/mm^2 and Stresses for C-40, Tensile = Compressive = 110 N/mm^2, Shear = 40 N/mm^2, Bearing = 25 N/mm^2. Determine: Diameter of shaft, Diameter of bolts, if 6 bolts are used and various flange dimensions. **(8 M)**

Ans. Refer Problem 3.30.

3. A shaft is required to transmit 1 MW power at 240 r.p.m. The shaft must not twist more than 1° on a length of one metre. If the modulus of rigidity for the material of the shaft is 80 kN/mm^2, find diameter of shaft and shear stress induced in it. **(8 M)**

Ans. Refer Problem 3.6.

4. (i) State any four design considerations for a spur gear. **(4 M)**

Ans. Refer Article 3.4.7.

   (ii) Write the Lewis equation for the strength of gear tooth. **(4 M)**

Ans. Refer Article 3.4.8.

Summer 2014

1. What is the effect of keyway on the strength of shaft? **(4 M)**

Ans. Refer Article 3.2.4.

2. Design muff coupling, which is used to connect two steel shafts transmitting 40 kW at 350 r.p.m. The material for the shaft and key is plain carbon steel, for which, allowable shear stress may be assumed as 15 MPa. Assuming square key, find also dimensions of key. **(8 M)**

Ans. Refer Problem 3.29.

3. Write Lewis equation for the strength of gear tooth. Give the meaning of each term. **(4 M)**

Ans. Refer Article 3.4.8.

4. State the reasons for using hollow shaft rather than solid shaft for large power transmission. **(4 M)**

Ans. Refer Article 3.1.11.

5. Distinguish between shaft and axle. **(4 M)**

Ans. Refer Article 3.1.5.

6. A mild steel shaft is supported on two bearings 1 metre apart and transmits 15 kW at 300 r.p.m. to a pulley of 200 mm diameter at a distance of 300 mm from left hand bearing. The belt passing over the pulley is vertical and the ratio of belt tension is 2 : 1. Pulley weighs 500 N. Design the diameter of shaft. Take $\sigma_t = 70$ N/mm^2 and $\tau = 56$ N/mm^2. **(8 M)**

Ans. Refer Problem 3.12.

Chapter 4

DESIGN OF POWER SCREWS

About This Chapter

This chapter has a weightage of 12 marks and assigned duration is 10 hours. In this chapter, we learn different types of thread profiles, their relative merits and demerits, self locking and overhauling property, torque required and efficiency for screw various types of stresses induced. Also, we learn design of screw jack and toggle jack.

Statistical Analysis

Examination	Weightage of questions asked
S-09	20 Marks
W-09	14 Marks
S-10	25 Marks
W-10	18 Marks
S-11	22 Marks
W-11	16 Marks
S-12	20 Marks
W-12	18 Marks
S-13	18 Marks
W-13	16 Marks
S-14	22 Marks

4.1 INRODUCTION TO POWER SCREWS

Question

1. State the meaning of power screw. **(S 13)**

- Power screws (translation screws) are used to convert rotary motion into linear motion (translatory motion), to transmit power.
- For example :
  (i) In *lead screw of lathe*, the rotary motion is available, but the tool has to be advanced axially in the direction of cut against cutting resistance of material.
  (ii) In *screw jack*, a small force applied in horizontal plane, is used to raise or lower a large load.
  (iii) Power screws are also used in *machine vices, testing machines, presses* etc.

- The main components of power screw are (i) screw and (ii) nut. Torque is applied to one of these components, causing it to rotate and move either itself or the other element in axial direction.

- One holding arrangement is necessary to hold either screw or nut in its place.

  Depending upon the holding arrangement, power screws operate in two different ways :

  (a) In case of lead screw of lathe, the screw rotates in its bearing, while the nut has axial motion.

  (b) In case of screw jack or machine vice, the nut is kept stationary and screw moves in axial direction.

4.1.1 Advantages of Power Screws 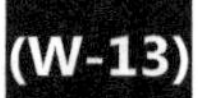 (W-13)

1. Large load carrying capacity.

2. Compact construction due to small overall dimensions.

3. Simple to design and manufacture.

4. Large mechanical advantage i.e. a load of 15 kN can be raised by applying an effort as small as 400 N.

5. Provides precisely controlled and highly accurate linear motion required in machine tool applications.

6. Low cost and more reliability due to less number of parts.

7. Smooth and noiseless service without any maintenance.

4.1.2 Disadvantages of Power Screws

1. Very poor efficiency as low as 40%. So it is not preferred in continuous power transmission elements like machine tools except lead screw of lathe.

2. Rapid wear of screw and nut due to high friction in threads.

4.1.3 Applications of Power Screws

- Power screws are mainly used for intermittent motion i.e. occasionally required for lifting the load or actuating any mechanism.

- Various types of power screws with practical application for each type are as under.

Type of Power Screw	Application
1. Screw jack	To raise the load.
2. Lead screw of lathe	To have accurate motion in machining operations.
3. Vice	To clamp a work piece.
4. Universal testing machine	To load specimen.

Material used for Screw and Nut :

- In case of square threads, the nut is usually made of soft material, which can be replaced when worn out.

Particular	Suitable Materials
1. Screw	Steel
2. Nut	Phosphor bronze or brass.

4.1.4 Terminology of Power Screw

1. Nominal diameter :

- It is defined as *'the largest diameter of the screw'*. It is also called as major diameter. It is denoted by letter d_o.

2. Core diameter :

- It is defined as *"the smallest diameter of screw thread"*. It is also called as minor diameter. It is denoted by letter d_c.

3. Pitch :

- It is defined as *'the distance, from a point on one thread to the corresponding point on adjacent thread, measured parallel to thread axis'*.
- It is denoted by **p**.
- For square threads, $d_c = d_o - p$

  i.e. $d_o = d_c + p$

4. Mean diameter :

- *'It is the average of nominal diameter d_o and core diameter d_c'*. It is also known as *pitch diameter*. It is denoted by letter **d**.

- Mathematically, Mean diameter, $d = \dfrac{d_o + d_c}{2}$

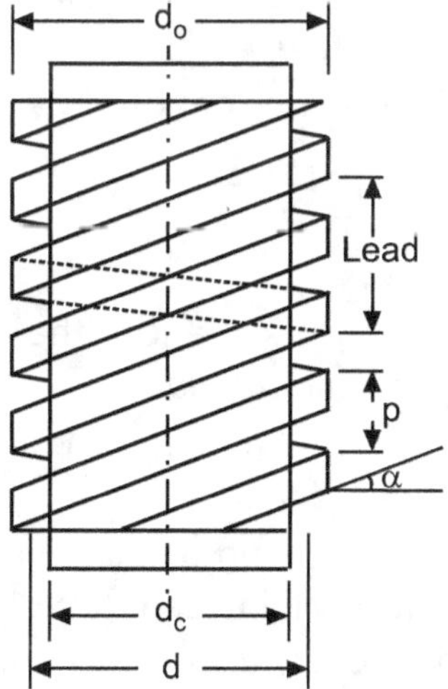

Fig. 4.1 : Terminology of power screw

- Mean diameter can also be expressed as,

(a)
$$d = \frac{d_o + d_c}{2}$$

$\therefore$
$$d = \frac{d_o + (d_o - p)}{2} \qquad \text{(As } d_o - d_c = p)$$

$\therefore$
$$d = \frac{2d_o - p}{2}$$

$\therefore$
$$\mathbf{d = d_o - \frac{p}{2}}$$

(b)
$$d = \frac{d_0 + d_c}{2}$$

$\therefore$
$$d = \frac{(d_c + p) + d_c}{2} \qquad [\text{As } d_o - d_c = p]$$

$\therefore$
$$d = \frac{2d_c + p}{2}$$

$\therefore$
$$\mathbf{d = d_c + \frac{p}{2}}$$

5. Lead :

- It is defined as '*the distance, through which, a screw advances axially in one revolution of nut*'.
- It is denoted by letter 'l'.
- For single start threaded screw, lead is equal to pitch, whereas for double start threaded screw, it is equal to twice the pitch and so on.
- For multiple threaded screws,

$$\text{Lead} = \text{Number of starts} \times \text{Pitch}$$

6. Helix angle :

- Helix angle is defined as '*the angle made by helix of thread with a plane perpendicular to the axis of screw*'.
- It is also called as *lead angle*. It is denoted by α.

Mathematically,
$$\tan \alpha = \frac{\text{Lead}}{\pi d}$$

7. Right hand and Left hand threads :

- When the axis of screw is vertical and if the thread slopes upward from left to right, it is known as *right hand thread*.
- When the axis of screw is vertical and if the thread slopes upward from right to left, it is known as *left hand thread*.
- For right hand threads, if the right hand fingers are kept in the direction of rotation of nut, the thumb will indicate the direction of an advancement of nut. Whereas for left hand threads, if the left hand fingers are kept in the direction of rotation of nut, the thumb will indicate the direction of advancement of nut.

- Right hand threads are most commonly used in power screws, lifting and clamping devices.

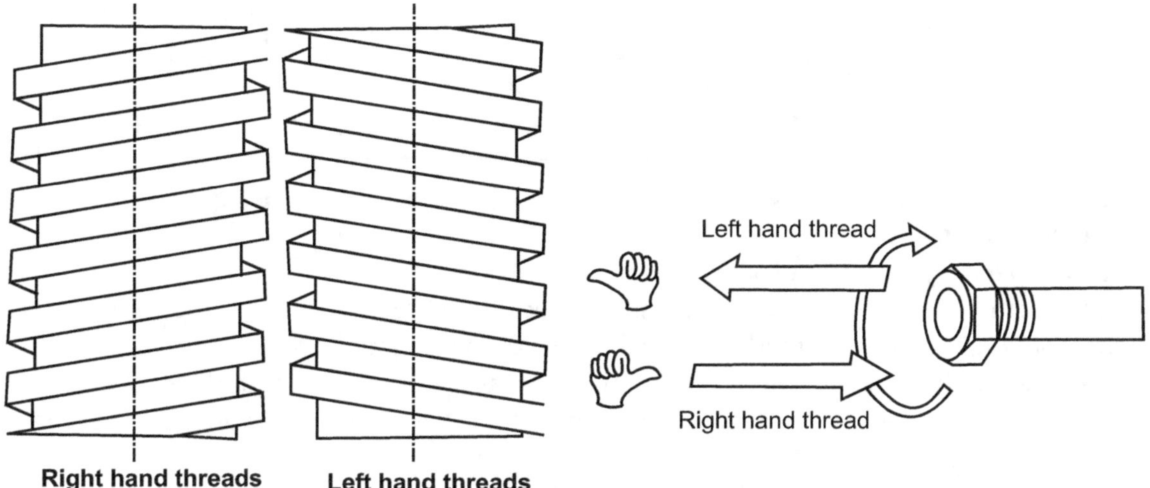

Fig. 4.2

4.2 VARIOUS THREAD PROFILES USED FOR POWER SCREWS

Questions

1. State two types of thread profiles used for power transmission. Draw neat sketch of any two. **(S-09, 12)**
2. State and explain with neat sketch, any four types of thread profiles used for power screws. **(S-10)**
3. What are the advantages of square thread profile ? Draw a thread profile used in power screw. **(S-12)**
4. What are the types of threads used in power screws ? **(W-12)**

1. Square Thread :

- It is a zero profile thread angle. It has flanks perpendicular to each other.
- Square threads are used, when force is to be applied in both directions.
- As they transmit power without any side thrust, they are used in screw jacks and clamping devices.

2. Trapezoidal Threads :

- In trapezoidal threads, the thread angle is 30°.
- They are manufactured on thread milling machine, with the help of multipoint cutting tool because machining with multipoint cutting tool is economical as compared to single point cutting tool used to machine square threads.
- Like square threads, the trapezoidal threads are used, when force is to be applied in both directions.
- They are used in lead screw and other power transmission devices used in machine tools.

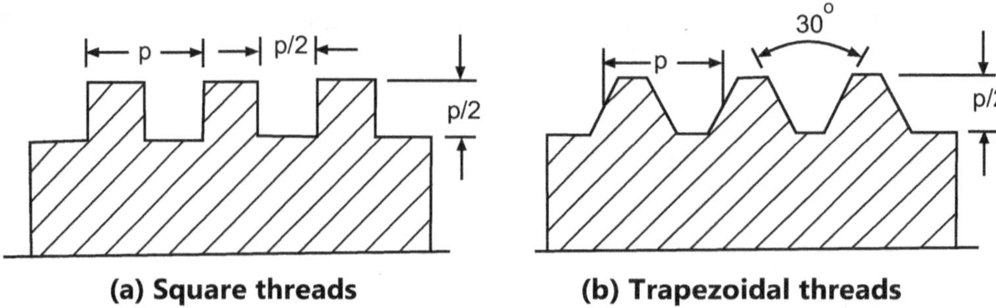

(a) Square threads   **(b) Trapezoidal threads**

3. Acme Threads :

- It is a special type of trapezoidal thread.
- Both acme and trapezoidal threads are identical in all respects except the thread angle. Thread angle in Acme threads is 29°, which is 30° in trapezoidal thread.
- Like square threads, they are used, when force is to be applied in both directions.
- Acme threads are used for lead screw and other power transmission devices used in machine tools.
- Acme threads can be cut by dies, therefore, they are easy to manufacture.
- Efficiency of acme threads is less than square thread, because of slight slope on the flanks.

4. Buttress Thread :

- Here, the flanks are inclined at angle of 45°.
- As they take unidirectional thrust, they are used in vices and clamping devices, where force is to be applied in one direction only.
- It is stronger than any other type of thread.

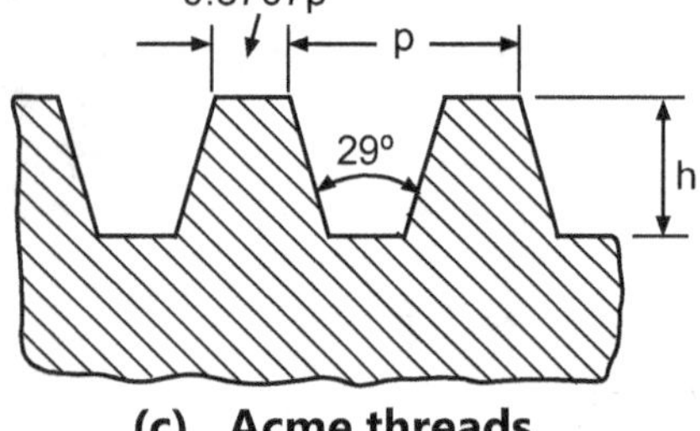

(c) Acme threads

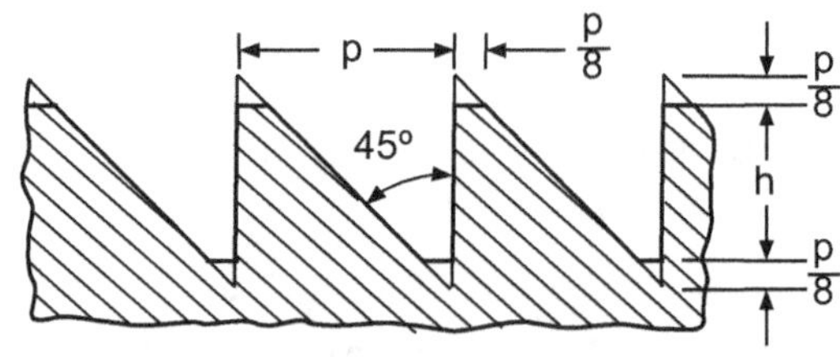

(d) Buttress thread

Fig. 4.3

4.2.1 Advantages, Disadvantages and Applications of Different Thread Profiles

1. Square Threads :

Advantages :

Question

1. What are advantages of square threads in power screw ?   **(S-10, 12)**

   (a) Maximum efficiency.

   (b) Minimum radial or bursting pressure on nut. As there is no side thrust, the motion of nut is uniform, which increases the life of nut.

Disadvantages :

   (a)   Low strength as compared to other thread profiles.

   (b)   Engagement and disengagement is difficult.

   (c)   Do not permit the use of split nut to compensate for wear.

   (d)   Difficult to manufacture.

   (e)   Machining with single point cutting tool is an expensive operation.

Applications :

   (a)   Screw jacks.   (b)   Mechanical presses.

   (c)   Clamping devices.   (d)   Feed screws.

2. Acme Threads :

Advantages :

   (a)   Permit the use of split nut, which can compensate the wear.

   (b)   Due to larger cross-section at the root, acme threads are stronger than square threads against shear.

Disadvantages :

   (a)   Lower efficiency than square threads, due to slope given to sides.

   (b)   Slope on the sides introduces some bursting pressure on the nut.

Applications :

   (a)   Lead screws of machine tools.

   (b)   Bench vices.

3. Trapezoidal Threads :

•   The relative advantages and disadvantages of trapezoidal threads are same as those of acme threads.

•   Applications of trapezoidal threads are same as those of acme threads.

4. Buttress Threads :

•   Buttress threads are used, where heavy axial force acts along the screw axis in one direction only.

Advantages :

   (a)   Due to largest cross-section at the root, threads are stronger than any other threads.

   (b)   They combine the advantages of square threads (high efficiency) and V-threads (high strength).

   (c)   They can be economically manufactured on thread milling machine.

Disadvantage :

   (a)   They can be used to transmit power in only one direction.

Applications :

   (a)   Machine vice.

   (b)   Screw jack.

4.2.1.1 Difference between Square Threads and Acme Threads

Square threads	Acme threads
1. The flanks are perpendicular to each other.	1. Roots and crests are straight and angle made by flanks of thread is 29°.
2. They are used for power transmission in either direction.	2. They are used for power transmission in only one direction.
3. More efficiency.	3. Less efficiency.
4. They are manufactured on lathe machine by single point cutting tool. So difficult to manufacture on mass scale.	4. They are cut by dies and therefore, easy to manufacture.

4.2.1.2 Difference between V-threads and Square Threads

Comparative point	V-threads	Square thread
1. Thread angle	60°	0°
2. Strength	As the thickness of V-threads at the base is equal to 'p', they are stronger than square threads. So less chances of thread failure.	As the thickness of square threads at the base is equal to p/2, they are weaker than 'V'-threads. So more chances of thread failure.
3. Load carrying capacity	Due to more strength, more is the load carrying capacity.	Due to comparatively low strength, less is load carrying capacity.
4. Efficiency	Less due to high friction.	High due to less friction.
5. Radial or bursting pressure	Due to thread angle (60°), the nut is subjected to radial or bursting pressure.	Due to zero thread angle, radial or bursting pressure is minimum or absent.
6. Manufacturing	Easy to manufacture on mass scale, as they can be easily cut on thread milling machine.	Difficult to manufacture on mass scale.
7. Cost	Cheaper due to low production cost.	Costlier due to high production cost.
8. Applications	*In case of fasteners*, due to high strength, low cost and easy availability.	*In case of power screws*, due to high power transmission efficiency.

4.2.1.3 Advantages and Disadvantages of 'V' Threads

Question
1. What are the advantages and disadvantages of 'V' thread over square thread?   **(S-14)**

Advantages of 'V' Threads over Square Threads:

(a) Strength: As the thickness of V-threads at the base is equal to 'p', they are stronger than square threads. So there are very less chances of thread failure. Whereas in case of square threads, the thickness of square threads at the base is equal to p/2, they are weaker than 'V'-threads. So there are more chances of thread failure.

(b) Application : Due to high friction, V-threads offer greater resistance to unscrewing and hence, they are used as fasteners. But, square threads are not used for fastening purpose, because of less friction involved.

(c) Load carrying capacity: In case of V threads, load carrying capacity is more due to more strength as compared to square threads having low strength.

(d) Mass production : As compared to square threads, 'V' threads are easy to manufacture on mass scale, as they can be easily cut on thread milling machine.

(e) Cost : 'V' threads are cheaper due to low production cost. In case of square threads, production cost is more due to necessity of machining with single point cutting tool, which is an expensive operation.

Disadvantages of 'V' Threads over Square Threads:

(a) Efficiency : Efficiency of V threads is less due to high friction as compared to square threads having less friction.

(b) Radial or bursting pressure : In case of 'V' threads, the nut is subjected to radial or bursting pressure due to 60° thread angle. This bursting pressure is minimum or absent in square threads due to zero (0°) thread angle.

(c) Power transmission : 'V' threads are not suitable for power transmission due of high profile angle, which reduces the efficiency. But, square threads are commonly used for power transmission, because zero profile angle gives greatest efficiency.

4.2.1.4 Reasons for using Square Threads in Transmission

Questions
1. Why square threads are used for power transmission ? Give reasons. **(S-09, 11)**
2. Why squared thread is preferred over V-thread for power transmission ? Name and sketch other thread profiles used for power transmission. **(W-09)**

- The square threads are preferred for power screws because,
    - (1) The efficiency of power screws depends on the profile angle. The square threads have the *greatest efficiency* as profile angle is zero.
    - (2) They produce *minimum bursting pressure* on the nut.
    - (3) Square threads *transmit power* without any side thrust in *either direction*.
    - (4) More power transmission efficiency, due to *less friction*.
    - (5) They are *smooth* and *noiseless* in operation.

4.2.1.5 Reasons for using 'V-Threads' for Fasteners

- 'V' threads are most suitable and commonly used for fastening purposes.

- V-threads offer greater resistance at the time of unscrewing due to high friction involved. Therefore, they are used in fasteners. For example: Screw and nut assembly.

- In addition to above, other factors permitting the use of V-threads as fasteners are,

    (a) High strength,

    (b) Low cost,

    (c) Easy manufacturing and

    (d) Large load carrying capacity.

- But, V-threads are not suitable for power transmission, because of high profile angle, which reduces the efficiency.

4.2.2 Multiple Threaded Screws

- Multiple threaded screws are used in certain applications, where higher travelling speed is required or comparatively large axial movement is required without much reduction in root area of threads.

- They are also called as *multiple start screws* such as double start, triple start or quadruple start screws.

- These screws have two or more threads cut side by side, around the rod.

- Multistart threads are used, when large lead with fine threads or high efficiency is required.

- Refer the Fig. 4.4, where pitch is denoted by p and lead is denoted by *l*.

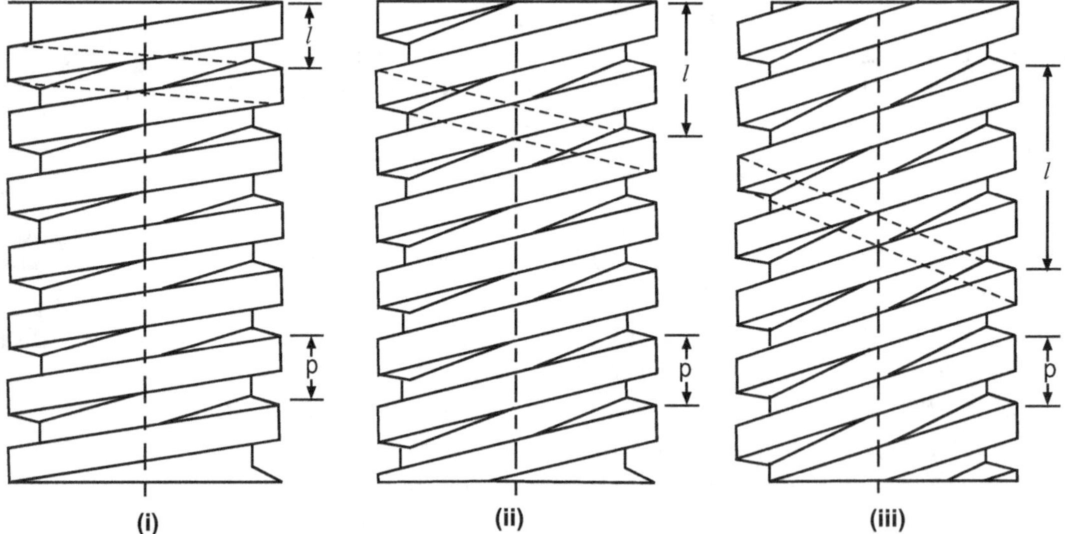

(i)   (ii)   (iii)

Fig. 4.4 : Multiple threaded screws

Single Start Thread :

- It is a single helical groove thread cut on the screws.

- For single start threads,

$$\text{Lead} = \text{Axial distance travelled by screw through one revolution}$$
$$= \text{Pitch}$$

Double Start Thread :

- When two threads are cut with equal spacing on the screw, threads are known as *double start threads*.

- For double start threads,

$$\text{Lead} = \text{Axial distance travelled by screw through one revolution}$$
$$= 2 \times \text{Pitch}$$

Similarly,   for triple start threads, Lead $= 3 \times$ pitch

for quadruple start threads, Lead $= 4 \times$ pitch

for multiple start threads, Lead $= n \times$ pitch

where, $n = $ Number of starts.

Advantages of Multiple Threaded Screw :

(1) Increased travelling speed due to large axial motion per revolution of screw.

(2) Efficiency of multi-threaded screw is more than single threaded screw due to increase in helix angle.

Disadvantages of Multiple Threaded Screw :

(1) Lower mechanical advantage as compared to single threaded screw.

(2) Chances of loosing self locking property.

4.3 EXPRESSION FOR TORQUE REQUIRED TO RAISE THE LOAD

- The load to be raised or lowered is placed on the head of the square threaded rod, which is rotated by the application of effort at the end of the lever for lifting the load.

- If one complete turn of screw is unwound and developed, it will form an inclined plane, as shown in Fig. 4.5 (a) and (b).

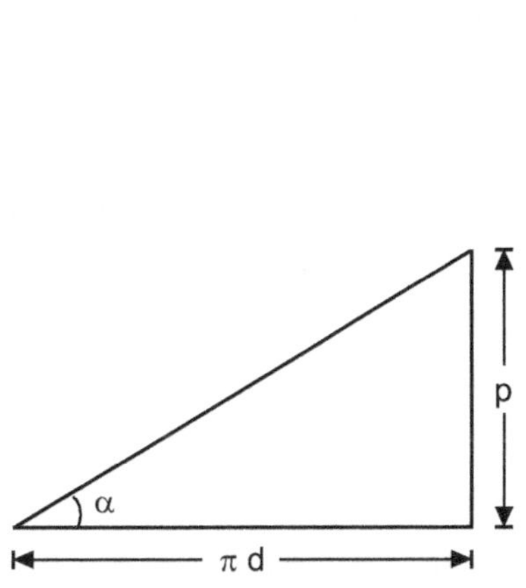

(a) Development of screw

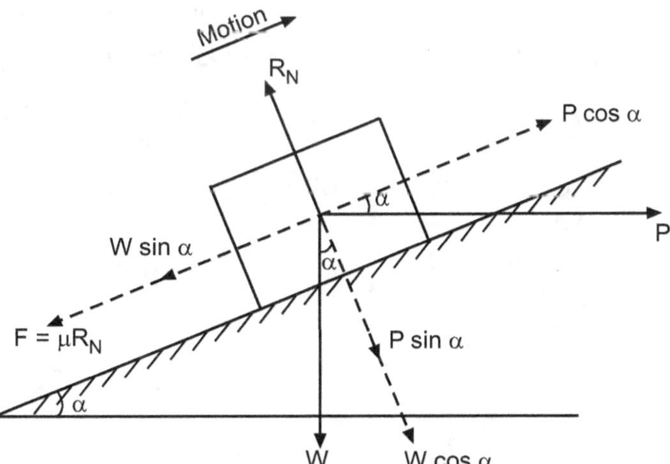

(b) Forces acting on screw, while raising the load

Fig. 4.5

Let, p = Pitch of screw

        d = Mean diameter of screw

        α = Helix angle

        P = Effort applied at the circumference of screw

        W = Load to be lifted

        μ = Coefficient of friction = $\tan\phi$

- From the development of screw,

$$\tan\alpha = \frac{p}{\pi d}$$

- Since the load is being lifted, therefore, the force of friction ($F = \mu \cdot R_N$) will act downward.

Resolving the forces along the plane,

$$\Sigma F_x = 0$$

$\therefore$ $P\cos\alpha - W\sin\alpha - \mu R_N = 0$

$\therefore$ $P\cos\alpha = W\sin\alpha + \mu R_N$ ... (4.1)

Resolving the forces perpendicular to the plane,

$$\Sigma F_y = 0$$

$\therefore$ $R_N - P\sin\alpha - W\cos\alpha = 0$

$\therefore$ $R_N = P\sin\alpha + W\cos\alpha$ ... (4.2)

Substituting the value of R_N in the equation (4.1), we have

$$P\cos\alpha = W\sin\alpha + \mu\,(P\sin\alpha + W\cos\alpha)$$

$\therefore$ $P\cos\alpha = W\sin\alpha + \mu\cdot P\sin\alpha + \mu\cdot W\cos\alpha$

$\therefore$ $P\cos\alpha - \mu\cdot P\sin\alpha = W\sin\alpha + \mu\cdot W\cos\alpha$

$\therefore$ $P\,(\cos\alpha - \mu\cdot\sin\alpha) = W\,(\sin\alpha + \mu\cdot\cos\alpha)$

$\therefore$

$$P = W\times\frac{(\sin\alpha + \mu\cdot\cos\alpha)}{(\cos\alpha - \mu\cdot\sin\alpha)}$$

By putting the value of μ = Coefficient of friction = $\tan\phi$ in above equation, we have,

$$P = W\times\frac{(\sin\alpha + \tan\phi\cdot\cos\alpha)}{(\cos\alpha - \tan\phi\cdot\sin\alpha)}$$

$\therefore$

$$P = W\times\frac{(\sin\alpha\cos\phi + \sin\phi\cos\alpha)}{(\cos\alpha\cos\phi - \sin\phi\sin\alpha)}$$

$\therefore$

$$P = W\times\frac{\sin(\alpha+\phi)}{\cos(\alpha+\phi)}$$

$\therefore$

$$P = W\tan(\alpha+\phi)$$

- Torque required to overcome friction between screw and nut,

$$T_1 \; = \; P \times \frac{d}{2} \; = \; W \cdot \tan(\alpha + \phi) \times \frac{d}{2} \qquad \text{... (4.3)}$$

- When the load is taken up by a thrust collar, so that, load should not rotate with screw, then torque required to overcome the friction at the collar will be,

$$T_2 \; = \; \frac{2}{3} \times \frac{\mu_1 \times W \times (R_1^3 - R_2^3)}{(R_1^2 - R_2^2)} \qquad \text{(Uniform pressure condition)}$$

or $$T_2 \; = \; \mu_1 \times W \times R \qquad \text{(Uniform wear condition)}$$

where, R_1 = Radius of head, R_2 = Radius of pin, and R = Mean radius = $\dfrac{R_1 + R_2}{2}$

- $\therefore$ **Total torque required to raise the load will be, T $=$ T$_1$ + T$_2$**

4.4 EXPRESSION FOR TORQUE REQUIRED TO LOWER THE LOAD

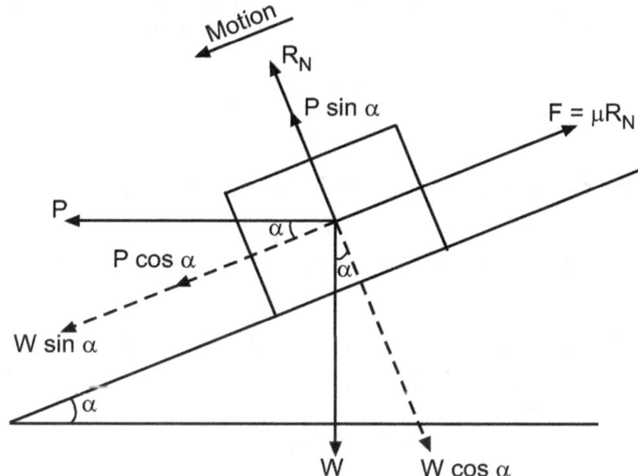

Fig. 4.6 : Forces acting on the screw, while lowering the load

- The load to be lowered is placed on the head of the square threaded rod, which is rotated by application of effort at the end of the lever for lowering the load. If one complete turn of screw is unwound and developed, it will form an inclined plane, as shown in Fig. 4.6.

- Resolving the forces along the plane,

$$\Sigma F_x \; = \; 0$$

$\therefore \quad - P \cos \alpha - W \sin \alpha + \mu \, R_N \; = \; 0$

$\therefore \quad P \cos \alpha + W \sin \alpha = \mu R_N \qquad \text{... (4.4)}$

- Resolving the forces perpendicular to the plane,

$$\Sigma F_y = 0$$

$\therefore \quad R_N + P \sin \alpha - W \cos \alpha = 0$

$\therefore \quad R_N = W \cos \alpha - P \sin \alpha \qquad \qquad \dots (4.5)$

Substituting the value of R_N in the equation (4.4),

$$P \cos \alpha + W \sin \alpha = \mu (W \cos \alpha - P \sin \alpha)$$

$$\therefore \quad P = W \times \frac{(\mu \cos \alpha - \sin \alpha)}{(\cos \alpha + \mu \sin \alpha)}$$

By putting the value of μ = Coefficient of friction = $\tan \phi$ in above equation,

$$P = W \times \frac{(\tan \phi \cos \alpha - \sin \alpha)}{(\cos \alpha + \tan \phi \sin \alpha)}$$

$$\therefore \quad P = W \times \frac{(\sin \phi \cos \alpha - \sin \alpha \cos \phi)}{(\cos \alpha \cos \phi + \sin \phi \sin \alpha)}$$

$$\therefore \quad P = W \times \frac{\sin (\phi - \alpha)}{\cos (\phi - \alpha)} = W \times \tan (\phi - \alpha)$$

- Torque required to overcome friction between screw and nut,

$$T_1 = P \times \frac{d}{2} = W \cdot \tan (\phi - \alpha) \times \frac{d}{2}$$

- When the load is taken up by a thrust collar, so that, load should not rotate with screw, then torque required to overcome the friction at the collar will be,

$$T_2 = \frac{2}{3} \times \frac{\mu_1 \times W \times (R_1^3 - R_2^3)}{(R_1^2 - R_2^2)} \qquad \text{(Uniform pressure conditions)}$$

or $\qquad T_2 = \mu_1 \times W \times R \qquad \qquad$ (Uniform wear conditions)

where R_1 = Radius of head, R_2 = Radius of pin, and R = Mean radius = $\dfrac{(R_1 + R_2)}{2}$

$\therefore$ Total torque required to lower the load will be, T = $T_1 + T_2$

- In both the cases (Raising and lowering the load), the torque applied at the end of handle of length L is given by,

$$T = P_1 \cdot L$$

where P_1 = Effort applied at the end of handle to rotate the screw.

4.5 DIFFERENCE BETWEEN SCREW FRICTION AND COLLAR FRICTION

Screw friction	Collar friction
1. It is the friction between screw and nut.	1. It is the friction between screw and collar.

2. Torque required to overcome the screw friction is,
 	
(a) $T_1 = W \tan(\alpha + \phi) \times d/2$
 	
    ... Raising the load
 	
(b) $T_1 = W \tan(\phi - \alpha) \times \dfrac{d}{2}$
 	
    ... Lowering the load.
	2. Torque required to overcome the collar friction is,
	
	(a) $T_2 = \dfrac{2}{3} \times \dfrac{\mu_1 \times W \times (R_1^3 - R_2^3)}{(R_1^2 - R_2^2)}$
	
	    (uniform pressure condition)
	Where, R_1 and R_2 are outer and inner radii of collar respectively.
	(b) $T_2 = \mu_1 \times W \times R$ (uniform wear condition)
	Where, R is mean radius of collar $= \dfrac{R_1 + R_2}{2}$
	
	and μ_1 = coefficient of friction between screw and collar surfaces.

4.6 VARIOUS TYPES OF STRESSES INDUCED IN POWER SCREW

1.   **Direct compressive stress due to axial load W :**

-
$$\sigma_c = \frac{W}{\frac{\pi}{4} \cdot d_c^2}$$

2.   **Torsional shear stress :**

- We know that, the torque transmitted by screw is given by,

$$T = \frac{\pi}{16} \times \tau \times d_c^3$$

$\therefore$ Shear stress, $\tau = \dfrac{16\,T}{\pi \times d_c^3}$

- When screw is subjected to both direct stress and torsional shear stress, then design must be based on,

    (a)   Maximum shear stress theory, according to which, maximum shear stress on minimum cross-section is,

$$\tau_{max} = \frac{1}{2}\sqrt{\sigma_c^2 + 4\tau^2}$$

(b) Maximum normal stress theory, according to which, maximum normal stress on minimum cross-section is,

$$\sigma_{c\,max} = \frac{1}{2}\sigma_c + \frac{1}{2}\sqrt{\sigma_c^2 + 4\tau^2}$$

3. Transverse shear stress due to axial load :

- Shear stress for screw,

$$\tau_{screw} = \frac{W}{\pi\, d_c \cdot n \cdot t}$$

- Shear stress for nut,

$$\tau_{nut} = \frac{W}{\pi\, d_o\, n \cdot t}$$

4. Bearing pressure :

In order to reduce the wear of screw and nut, the bearing pressure on thread surfaces must lie within limits. It is given by,

$$P_b = \frac{W}{\frac{\pi}{4}(d_o^2 - d_c^2)\,n} \quad OR \quad \frac{W}{\pi\, d\, n\, t}$$

where t = Thickness or width of screw = $\dfrac{p}{2}$

       n = Number of threads of screw in contact with the nut

$$= \frac{\text{Height of nut}}{\text{Pitch of threads}} = \frac{H}{p}$$

4.7 EFFICIENCY OF SCREW

- We know that, actual effort required at the circumference of screw to lift load is given by,

$$P = W \tan(\phi + \alpha)$$

where, W = Load to be lifted

      ϕ = Angle of friction

      α = Helix angle

- If there is no friction between the screw and nut, then $\phi = 0°$.

So the above equation reduces to give ideal effort as,

$$P_0 = W \tan\alpha$$

- Efficiency of screw is defined as, *'the ratio of ideal effort to actual effort'*.

 ∴ The efficiency of screw is given by,

$$\eta = \frac{P_0}{P} = \frac{W\tan\alpha}{W\tan(\phi + \alpha)} = \frac{\tan\alpha}{\tan(\phi + \alpha)}$$

- So we conclude that, the efficiency of screw is independent of load to be lifted (W), but is dependent of helix angle (α).

4.7.1 Overall Efficiency of Screw Jack

- The total torque required to raise the load comprises of torque required to overcome friction between screw and nut (T_1) and torque required to overcome collar or bearing friction (T_2).

$$\therefore \qquad \text{Total torque, } T = T_1 + T_2$$

where,

$$T_1 = W \tan(\alpha + \phi) \cdot \frac{d}{2}$$

and

$$T_2 = \mu_1 W R \qquad \text{(Assuming uniform wear condition)}$$

$$= \frac{2}{3} \mu_1 \cdot W \cdot \frac{(R_1^3 - R_2^3)}{(R_1^2 - R_2^2)} \qquad \text{(Assuming uniform pressure condition)}$$

where,

$$R_1 = \text{Outer radius of collar} = \text{Radius of head } (R_3) \text{ of screw jack}$$

$$R_2 = \text{Inner radius of collar} = \text{Radius of pin } (R_4) \text{ of screw jack}$$

$$R = \text{Mean radius} = \frac{R_1 + R_2}{2}$$

- Overall efficiency is given by,

$$\eta_o = \frac{\text{Ideal torque}}{\text{Actual torque}} = \frac{T_0}{T} \qquad \qquad \ldots (4.6)$$

- In case of ideal torque, friction will be absent. Therefore, $\phi = 0$ and thus $\mu_1 = \tan\phi = 0$. Thus, ideal torque is given by,

$$T_0 = W \tan(\alpha) \cdot \frac{d}{2} + 0 = W \tan\alpha \cdot \frac{d}{2}$$

- Equation (4.6) becomes,

$$\eta_o = \frac{W \tan\alpha \cdot \dfrac{d}{2}}{T_1 + T_2}$$

4.7.2 How to Improve Efficiency of Power Screws ?

Question

1. State and explain the influence of helix angle on efficiency of square threaded screw.

(S-11)

- We have,

$$\text{Efficiency of screw} = \eta = \frac{\tan\alpha}{\tan(\alpha + \phi)}$$

where, α is the helix angle.

Thus, efficiency of screw can be improved by increasing the helix angle. The efficiency is maximum for a helix angle between 40° to 45°.

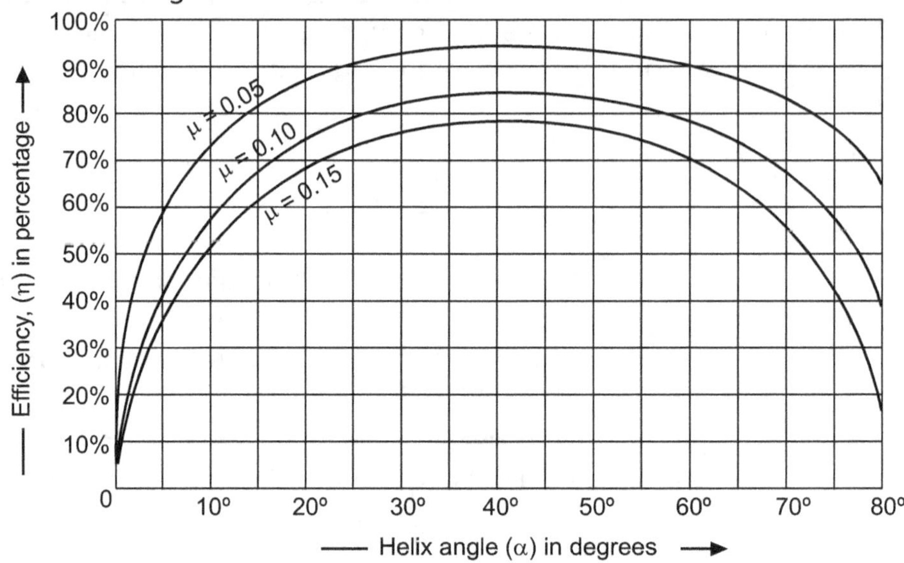

Fig. 4.7 : Graph of efficiency v/s helix angle

Conclusion of Graph :

    (a)   Efficiency is very less, when the value of α is close to 0° or 90°.

    (b)   Efficiency increases rapidly upto 20° helix angle and remains more or less constant for the value of helix angle between 30° to 60°.

    (c)   The efficiency is maximum for a helix angle between 40° to 45°.

    (d)   But, when the helix angle is increased beyond 60°, the efficiency drops, because the normal thread force increases, thereby increasing the force of friction.

4.7.3 Self-Locking and Overhauling of Screw

Questions

1. Explain the term self-locking of screw and overhauling of screw.

(S-09, 10, 12, 13, 14; W-10, 11)

2. (i) What is self locking property of threads ?

   (ii) Where it is necessary ?

   (iii) Show that, efficiency of self locking screw is less than 50%. **(S-11)**

3. What is self locking of screw ? What are the conditions of self locking ? **(W-13)**

    •   We know that the effort required at circumference of screw to lower the load is,

$$P = W \tan (\phi - \alpha)$$

    •   And torque required to lower the load is,

$$T = P \times \frac{d}{2} = W \tan (\phi - \alpha) \times \frac{d}{2}$$

- In the above expression, if ($\phi < \alpha$), then torque required to lower the load will be negative.

- In other words, the load will start moving downward without application of any torque. Such a condition is called as *overhauling*.

- However, if ($\alpha < \phi$), the torque required will be positive, indicating that an effort is applied to lower the load. Such a condition is called as *self-locking*.

- Efficiency of screw $= \eta = \dfrac{\tan \alpha}{\tan (\alpha + \phi)}$

- For self locking of screw, the condition is $\phi \geq \alpha$.

  $\therefore$ By substituting $\alpha = \phi$, efficiency for self-locking screw,

$$\eta = \frac{\tan \phi}{\tan 2\phi} = \frac{\tan \phi}{\dfrac{2 \tan \phi}{1 - \tan^2 \phi}} = \frac{1 - \tan^2 \phi}{2}$$

$\therefore \qquad \eta = \dfrac{1}{2} - \dfrac{\tan^2 \phi}{2} = 0.5 - \dfrac{\tan^2 \phi}{2}$

- This means that, efficiency will always come less than 50% for self locking screw.

- *Therefore, condition for self-locking is ($\phi > \alpha$), and efficiency is less than 50%.*

- *If efficiency is more than 50%, the screw is said to be overhauling.*

4.7.4 Maximum Efficiency of Square Threaded Screws

Question

1. Show that, efficiency of square threaded screw will be maximum, when helix angle, $\alpha = 45° - \dfrac{\phi}{2}$ and its maximum efficiency is given by,

$$\eta_{maximum} = \frac{1 - \sin \phi}{1 + \sin \phi}, \qquad \text{(where } \phi = \text{Angle of friction.)}$$

- We know that,

Efficiency of screw, $\qquad \eta = \dfrac{\tan \alpha}{\tan (\alpha + \phi)} = \dfrac{\sin \alpha \times \cos (\alpha + \phi)}{\cos \alpha \times \sin (\alpha + \phi)}$ $\qquad$ ... (4.7)

$\therefore \qquad 1 - \eta = 1 - \dfrac{\sin \alpha \times \cos (\alpha + \phi)}{\cos \alpha \times \sin (\alpha + \phi)}$

$\therefore \qquad 1 - \eta = \dfrac{\cos \alpha \times \sin (\alpha + \phi) - \sin \alpha \times \cos (\alpha + \phi)}{\cos \alpha \times \sin (\alpha + \phi)}$

$\therefore \qquad 1 - \eta = \dfrac{\sin [(\alpha + \phi) - \alpha]}{\cos \alpha \times \sin (\alpha + \phi)} = \dfrac{\sin \phi}{\cos \alpha \times \sin (\alpha + \phi)}$

$$\{ \because \sin A \cdot \cos B - \cos A \cdot \sin B = \sin (A - B) \}$$

$$\therefore \qquad 1 - \eta = \frac{2 \times \sin \phi}{2 \times \cos \alpha \sin (\alpha + \phi)} \qquad \text{(multiply and divide by 2)}$$

$$\therefore \qquad 1 - \eta = \frac{2 \times \sin \phi}{\sin (2\alpha + \phi) + \sin \phi}$$

$$\{\because\ 2 \sin A \cos B = \sin (A + B) + \sin (A - B)\}$$

- For greatest efficiency, value of $(1 - \eta)$ should be least. i.e. $\sin (2\alpha + \phi)$ should be greatest and we know, $\sin 90° = 1$. Therefore, $(2\alpha + \phi) = 90°$.

  It means, for maximum efficiency, helix angle $= \alpha = 45° - \dfrac{\phi}{2}$

- Put this value of α in equation (4.7), we have,

$$\eta_{maximum} = \frac{\sin (45° - \phi/2) \times \cos (45° - \phi/2 + \phi)}{\cos (45° - \phi/2) \times \sin (45° - \phi/2 + \phi)}$$

$$\therefore \qquad \eta_{maximum} = \frac{2 \times \sin (45° - \phi/2) \times \cos (45° - \phi/2 + \phi)}{2 \times \cos (45° - \phi/2) \times \sin (45° - \phi/2 + \phi)} \qquad \text{(Multiply \& Divide by 2)}$$

$$\therefore \qquad \eta_{maximum} = \frac{2 \sin (45° - \phi/2) \cdot \cos (45° + \phi/2)}{2 \cos (45° - \phi/2) \cdot \sin (45° + \phi/2)}$$

$$\therefore \qquad \eta_{maximum} = \frac{\sin 90° + \sin (- \phi)}{\sin 90° - \sin (- \phi)}$$

$$= \frac{1 - \sin \phi}{1 + \sin \phi}, \text{ Hence proved.}$$

4.7.5 Applications of Overhauling Screw

Question

Q. Justify the Statement, that, "Hand Presses are often provided with overhauling Power Screws".

- In case of hand presses, the torque required to lower the load should be negative. It is possible only, when $\phi < \alpha$.
- Thus, the load will start moving downward without any application of torque. Such condition is known as overhauling of screws.

Important Formulae

(1) Nominal diameter $=$ Core diameter + Pitch

$$d_o = d_c + p$$

(2) Mean diameter, $d = \dfrac{d_o + d_c}{2}$

$$d = d_o - \frac{p}{2}$$

$$d = d_c + \frac{p}{2}$$

(3)   Coefficient of friction between screw and nut = μ = tan ϕ.

(4)   Coefficient of friction between screw and collar = μ_1.

(5) $$\tan \alpha = \frac{\text{Lead}}{\pi \cdot d}$$

where,   Lead = Pitch 'p'   [For single start square thread]

$= 2 \times p$ [For 2-start square thread]

$= 3 \times p$ [For 3-start square thread]

$= 4 \times p$ [For quadruple start square thread]

(6)   (i)   Torque required to overcome friction between screw and nut at the time of lifting the load :

$$T_1 = W \tan (\alpha + \phi) \times \frac{d}{2}$$

(ii)   Torque required to overcome friction between screw and nut at the time of lowering the load

$$T_1 = W \tan (\phi - \alpha) \cdot \frac{d}{2}$$

(7)   Torque required to overcome collar friction :

(i) $T_2 = \mu_1 WR$ … [Assuming wear condition]

(ii) $$T_2 = \frac{2}{3} \mu_1 \cdot W \cdot \left[\frac{R_1^3 - R_2^3}{R_1^2 - R_2^2}\right]$$ [Assuming pressure condition]

where,   W = Load in 'N'

α = Helix angle in degrees

ϕ = Angle of friction in degrees

R_1 = External or outer radius of collar in mm

R_2 = Internal or inner radius of collar in mm

R = Mean radius of collar = $\dfrac{R_1 + R_2}{2}$ in mm.

(8)   Power required to rotate screw,

$$P = \frac{2\pi NT}{60} \text{ in watt}$$

where,   N = Number of revolutions made per minute

T = Torque in N.m

(9) $\left[\begin{array}{c}\text{Number of revolutions}\\\text{made by screw}\\\text{per minute}\end{array}\right] = N = \dfrac{\text{Linear speed/Cutting speed}}{\text{Pitch of screw}}$

(10) Efficiency of screw,

$$\eta = \frac{\text{Ideal torque } (T_0)}{\text{Actual torque } (T)}$$

(a)   When collar/bearing friction is neglected (i.e. $T_2 = 0$)

$$\eta = \frac{\tan \alpha}{\tan (\alpha + \phi)}$$

(b)   When collar/bearing friction is considered,

$$\eta = \frac{T_0}{T_1 + T_2} = \frac{W \tan \alpha \times \dfrac{d}{2}}{W \tan (\alpha + \phi) \times \dfrac{d}{2} + \mu_1 \cdot W \cdot R}$$

Note : To calculate overall efficiency, the same expression is used i.e. 10 (b), where η is nothing, but η_0.

(11) Stresses induced in various parts of screw jack,

(i)   For screw :

(a)   Compressive stress, $\sigma_c = \dfrac{W}{\dfrac{\pi}{4} d_c^2}$

(b)   Torsional shear stress, $\tau = \dfrac{16 T_1}{\pi d_c^3}$

(c)   Principal stresses :

    (i)   Maximum shear stress $= \tau_{max} = \dfrac{1}{2} \times \sqrt{\sigma_c^2 + 4\tau^2}$

    (ii)   Maximum normal stress theory $= \sigma_{c\ max} = \dfrac{1}{2} \sigma_c + \dfrac{1}{2} \times \sqrt{\sigma_c^2 + 4\tau^2}$

(d)   Transverse shear stress for screw,

$$\tau_{screw} = \frac{W}{\pi d_c \cdot n \cdot t}$$

(ii)   For nut :

(a)   Bearing pressure, $P_b = \dfrac{W}{\dfrac{\pi}{4} \cdot (d_o^2 - d_c^2) \times n}$

(b)   Transverse shear stress for nut, $\tau_{nut} = \dfrac{W}{\pi \cdot d_o \cdot n \cdot t}$

(12) Height of nut, $H = n \times p$

(13) Thickness of thread, $t = \dfrac{p}{2}$.

Numerical Type No. 1 : "Neglecting Bearing or Collar Friction"

Problem 4.1 : *A lead screw of lathe has square threads of 24 mm outside diameter and 5 mm pitch. In order to drive tool carriage, the screw exerts an axial pressure of 2.5 kN. Find the efficiency of screw and power required to drive the screw, if it rotates at 300 r.p.m. Neglect the bearing friction. Assume coefficient of friction for screw thread as 0.12.* **(S-08; W-11, 13)**

Solution : Given data : d_o = 24 mm, p = 5 mm, W = 2.5 kN = 2500 N, μ = 0.12, N = 300 r.p.m.

Procedure : We have,

$$d_c = 24 - 5 = 19 \text{ mm}$$

$$\therefore \quad d = \frac{d_o + d_c}{2} = \frac{24 + 19}{2} = \textbf{21.5 mm}$$

$$\therefore \quad \tan \alpha = \frac{p}{\pi d} = \frac{5}{\pi \times 21.5} = \textbf{0.07402}$$

$$\therefore \quad \alpha = \tan^{-1} (0.07402) = \textbf{4.233°}$$

Also, $\quad \mu = \tan \phi = 0.12$

$$\therefore \quad \phi = \tan^{-1} (0.12) = \textbf{6.843°}$$

Torque required to overcome the friction between screw and nut is given by,

$$T_1 = P \times \frac{d}{2} = W \tan (\alpha + \phi) \times \frac{d}{2}$$

$$= 2500 \times \tan (4.233 + 6.843) \times \frac{21.5}{2}$$

$$= 5260.97 \text{ N-mm} = \textbf{5.261 N-m}$$

As we have to neglect the bearing or collar friction, the torque required (T_2) to overcome friction between screw and collar, i.e. **T_2 = 0**.

$\therefore$ Total torque required to raise the load is,

$$T = T_1 + T_2 = 5.261 + 0 = \textbf{5.261 N-m}$$

(i) Efficiency of the screw :

$$\eta = \frac{\tan \alpha}{\tan (\alpha + \phi)} = \frac{\tan (4.233)}{\tan (4.233 + 6.843)} = \textbf{37.81\%}$$

(ii) Power required to rotate the screw :

$$P = \frac{2\pi N T}{60} = \frac{2 \times \pi \times 300 \times 5.261}{60} = 165.28 \text{ W} = \textbf{0.165 kW}$$

Problem 4.2 : *An electric motor driven power screw moves a nut in a horizontal plane against a force of 100 kN at a speed of 360 mm/min. Screw has pitch 8 mm on a major diameter of 50 mm. Coefficient of friction is 0.15.*

(i)   Estimate power of the motor.

(ii) State whether the screw is self-locking or over-hauling ?   **(S-13)**

Solution : Given Data : d_o = 50 mm, p = 8 mm,

$$W = 100 \text{ kN} = 100 \times 10^3 \text{ N}, \quad \mu = 0.15, \text{ Speed} = 360 \text{ mm/min.}$$

Procedure :

We have, $\qquad d_c = d_o - p = 50 - 8 = 42 \text{ mm}$

And, $\qquad d = \dfrac{d_o + d_c}{2} = \dfrac{50 + 42}{2} = \mathbf{46 \ mm}$

Also, $\qquad$ Speed = Pitch of screw $\times$ Number of revolutions per minute

$\therefore \quad$ Number of revolutions,

$$N = \frac{\text{Speed}}{\text{Pitch of screw}} = \frac{360 \text{ mm/min}}{8 \text{ mm}} = 45 \text{ r.p.m.}$$

We know, $\qquad \tan \alpha = \dfrac{p}{\pi d}$

$\therefore \qquad \alpha = \tan^{-1}\left(\dfrac{p}{\pi d}\right) = \tan^{-1}\left(\dfrac{8}{\pi \times 46}\right) = \mathbf{3.1685°}$

Also, $\qquad \mu = \tan \phi$

$\therefore \qquad \phi = \tan^{-1}(\mu) = \tan^{-1}(0.15) = \mathbf{8.5307°}$

Torque required to overcome the friction between screw and nut is given by,

$$T_1 = P \times \frac{d}{2} = W \times \tan(\alpha + \phi) \cdot \frac{d}{2}$$

$\therefore \qquad T_1 = 100 \times 10^3 \times \tan(3.1685 + 8.5307) \times \dfrac{46}{2}$

$\therefore \qquad \mathbf{T_1 = 476.27 \times 10^3 \ N.mm = 476.27 \ N.m}$

As we have to neglect the bearing or collar friction, the torque (T_2) required to overcome friction between screw and collar i.e. $T_2 = 0$.

$\therefore \quad$ Total torque required to raise the load, $T = T_1 + T_2$

$\therefore \qquad T = 476.27 + 0 = 476.27 \text{ N.m}$

(1) Power of the motor :

Power required to rotate the screw is given by,

$$P = \frac{2\pi NT}{60} = \frac{2 \times \pi \times 45 \times 476.27}{60} = 2244.36 \text{ W} = \mathbf{2.244 \ kW}$$

(2) Self locking or Overhauling :

Efficiency of the screw is,

$$\eta = \frac{\tan \alpha}{\tan(\alpha + \phi)} = \frac{\tan(3.1685)}{\tan(3.1685 + 8.5307)} = \mathbf{0.2673 = 26.73\%}$$

As the efficiency is less than 50%, therefore the screw is **self-locking**.

Problem 4.3 : *A double start square threaded power screw of nominal diameter 100 mm and pitch 12 mm is to be used to raise the load of 300 kN. The coefficient of friction at screw thread is 0.15. Neglect collar friction. Calculate :*

(i)   *Torque required to raise the load.*

(ii) *Efficiency of the screw.*   **(W-04; S-14)**

Solution : Given data : d_o = 100 mm, p = 12 mm, W = 300 kN = 300×10^3 N, μ = 0.15

Procedure : For double start square thread,

$$\text{Lead of the screw } (l) = 2 \times p = 2 \times 12 = \textbf{24 mm}$$

Also,
$$d_c = d_o - p = 100 - 12 = \textbf{88 mm}$$

$\therefore$ Mean diameter (d) $= \dfrac{d_o + d_c}{2} = \dfrac{100 + 88}{2} = \textbf{94 mm}$

We have,
$$\tan \alpha = \frac{\text{lead}}{\pi d}$$

$\therefore$
$$\alpha = \tan^{-1}\left(\frac{24}{\pi \times 94}\right) = \textbf{4.6463°}$$

Also,
$$\tan \phi = \mu$$

$\therefore$
$$\phi = \tan^{-1}(\mu) = \tan^{-1}(0.15) = \textbf{8.5307°}$$

(1) Torque required to raise the load :

Torque required to overcome the friction between screw and nut,

$$T_1 = P \times \frac{d}{2} = W \tan(\alpha + \phi) \cdot \frac{d}{2}$$

$$T_1 = 300 \times 10^3 \times \tan(4.6463 + 8.5307) \times \frac{94}{2}$$

$$= 3301154.225 \text{ N.mm} = 3301.15 \times 10^3 \text{ N.mm}$$

Neglect the torque required for collar friction, therefore $T_2 = 0$

$\therefore$ Total torque (T) required to raise the load = $T_1 + T_2$

$\therefore$
$$T = T_1 + T_2 = 3301.15 \times 10^3 + 0 = \textbf{3301.15} \times \textbf{10}^\textbf{3} \textbf{ N.mm}$$

(2) Efficiency of screw :

$$\eta = \frac{\tan \alpha}{\tan(\alpha + \phi)} = \frac{\tan(4.6463)}{\tan(4.6463 + 8.5307)} = \textbf{0.3471 or 34.71\%}$$

Numerical Type No. 2 : " Considering Bearing or Collar Friction"

Problem 4.4 : *The mean diameter of a square threaded screw having pitch of 10 mm is 50 mm. A load of 20 kN is lifted to a distance of 170 mm. Find the work done in lifting load and efficiency of screw, when (a) load rotates with screw, (b) load rests on loose head, which does not rotate with the screw.*

The internal and external diameters of bearing surface are 10 mm and 60 mm respectively and μ for all may be taken as 0.08.

Solution : Given data : $d = 50$ mm, $p = 10$ mm, $W = 20$ kN $= 20 \times 10^3$ N

$\mu = 0.08$, $\mu_1 = 0.08$, $D_1 = 60$ mm, $D_2 = 10$ mm

Procedure : We know, $d_o = d + \dfrac{p}{2} = 50 + \dfrac{10}{2} = \mathbf{55}$ **mm**

And, $d_c = d_o - p = 55 - 10 = \mathbf{45}$ **mm**

Also, $R_1 = \dfrac{D_1}{2} = \dfrac{60}{2}$ | $R_2 = \dfrac{D_2}{2} = \dfrac{10}{2}$

$\therefore$ $R_1 = \mathbf{30}$ **mm** | $\therefore$ $R_2 = \mathbf{5}$ **mm**

We have, $N = \dfrac{\text{Lift}}{\text{Pitch}} = \dfrac{170}{10} = \mathbf{17}$ **r.p.m.**

And, $\tan \alpha = \dfrac{p}{\pi d} = \dfrac{10}{\pi \times 50}$

$\therefore$ $\alpha = \tan^{-1}\left(\dfrac{10}{\pi \times 50}\right) = \tan^{-1}(0.0636) = \mathbf{3.6426°}$

Also, $\mu = \tan \phi$

$\therefore$ $\phi = \tan^{-1}(\mu) = \tan^{-1}(0.08) = \mathbf{4.5739°}$

Torque required to overcome the friction between screw and nut is given by,

$$T_1 = P \times \frac{d}{2} = W \times \tan(\alpha + \phi) \times \frac{d}{2}$$

$$= 20 \times 10^3 \times \tan(3.6426 + 4.5739) \times \frac{50}{2}$$

$\therefore$ $T_1 = \mathbf{72.198 \times 10^3}$ **N.mm**

Case I : As the load rotates with the screw, neglecting the bearing or collar friction, the torque required (T_2) to overcome friction between screw and collar will be zero.

i.e. $T_2 = 0$

$\therefore$ Total torque required to raise the load is,

$$T = T_1 + T_2 = (72.198 \times 10^3) + 0$$

$\therefore$ $T = \mathbf{72.198 \times 10^3}$ **N.mm** or **72.198 N.m**

(1) Work done in lifting load :

Work done in lifting load is the power required to rotate the screw, which is given by,

$$P = \frac{2\pi NT}{60} = \frac{2 \times \pi \times 17 \times 72.198}{60} = \mathbf{128.53}\ \mathbf{W} = \mathbf{0.128}\ \mathbf{kW}$$

(2) Efficiency of the screw :

$$\eta = \frac{\tan \alpha}{\tan(\alpha + \phi)} = \frac{\tan(3.6426)}{\tan(3.6426 + 4.5739)} = \mathbf{0.4409}\ \text{or}\ \mathbf{44.09\%}$$

Case II : As the load does not rotate with the screw, we must consider the torque required to overcome the bearing or collar friction. It is given by,

$$T_2 = \mu_1 \times W \times R \qquad \ldots \text{(Assuming uniform wear condition)}$$

We have,
$$R = \frac{R_1 + R_2}{2} = \frac{30 + 5}{2} = \textbf{17.5 mm}$$

$\therefore$
$$T_2 = 0.08 \times 20 \times 10^3 \times 17.5 = \textbf{28} \times \textbf{10}^3 \textbf{ N.mm}$$

$\therefore$ Total torque required to raise load is,
$$T = T_1 + T_2 = (72.198 \times 10^3) + (28 \times 10^3)$$

$\therefore$
$$T = \textbf{100.198} \times \textbf{10}^3 \textbf{ N.mm} = \textbf{100.198 N.m}$$

(1) Work done in lifting load :

Work done in lifting load is the power required to rotate the screw, which is given by,

$$P = \frac{2\pi NT}{60} = \frac{2 \times \pi \times 17 \times 100.198}{60} = \textbf{178.38 W} = \textbf{0.178 kW}$$

(2) Efficiency of the screw :

$$\eta = \frac{\text{Ideal torque}}{\text{Actual torque}} = \frac{T_o}{T} = \frac{W \times \tan \alpha \cdot \dfrac{d}{2}}{T}$$

$\therefore$
$$\eta = \frac{20 \times 10^3 \times \tan (3.6426) \times \dfrac{50}{2}}{100.198 \times 10^3} = \textbf{0.3176} \quad \text{or} \quad \textbf{31.76\%}$$

Problem 4.5 : *A vertical screw with single start square thread of 50 mm mean diameter and 12.5 mm pitch is raised against a load of 10 kN by means of hand wheel. The boss of wheel is threaded to act as a nut. The axial load is taken up by a thrust collar, which supports the wheel boss and has mean diameter 60 mm. The coefficient of friction is 0.15 for screw and 0.18 for collar. If tangential force applied by each hand of the wheel is 100 N, find suitable diameter of hand wheel.* **(W-07)**

Solution : Given data : $d = 50$ mm, $p = 12.5$ mm, $W = 10$ kN $= 10 \times 10^3$ N,
$$\mu = 0.15, \ \mu_1 = 0.18, \ D = 60 \text{ mm}$$

Procedure : We know, $d_u = d + \dfrac{p}{2} = 50 + \dfrac{12.5}{2} = 56.25$ mm,

$$d_c = d_o - p = 56.25 - 12.5 = 43.75 \text{ mm},$$

$$R = \frac{D}{2} = \frac{60}{2} = 30 \text{ mm}$$

And,
$$\tan \alpha = \frac{p}{\pi d} = \frac{12.5}{\pi \times 50} = 0.07957$$

$\therefore$
$$\alpha = \tan^{-1}(0.07957) = \textbf{4.5498°}$$

Also,
$$\mu = \tan \phi = 0.15$$

$\therefore$
$$\phi = \tan^{-1}(0.15) = \textbf{8.5307°}$$

Torque required to overcome the friction between screw and nut is given by,

$$T_1 = P \times \frac{d}{2} = W \tan(\alpha + \phi) \times \frac{d}{2}$$

$$= 10 \times 10^3 \times \tan(4.5498 + 8.5307) \times \frac{50}{2}$$

$$\therefore \qquad T_1 = \mathbf{58.087 \times 10^3 \ N.mm}$$

As the load does not rotate with the screw, the torque required to overcome the bearing or collar friction is given by,

$$T_2 = \mu_1 \cdot W \cdot R \qquad \text{(assuming uniform wear conditions)}$$

$$\therefore \qquad T_2 = 0.18 \times 10 \times 10^3 \times 30 = \mathbf{54 \times 10^3 \ N.mm}$$

$\therefore$ Total torque required to raise the load is,

$$T = T_1 + T_2 = 58.087 \times 10^3 + 54 \times 10^3 = \mathbf{112.087 \times 10^3 \ N.mm}$$

Diameter of handle (D_H) may be obtained by,

$$\text{Torque required} = \text{Effort applied by hand wheel} \times \text{Radius of hand wheel}$$

$$\therefore \qquad T = P_1 \times \frac{D_H}{2}$$

$$\therefore \qquad 112.087 \times 10^3 = 2 \times \left[100 \times \frac{D_H}{2} \right]$$

(Effort is taken as twice, as it is applied by each hand of wheel)

$\therefore$ Diameter of hand wheel $= D_H = \mathbf{1120.87 \ mm} \cong \mathbf{1122 \ mm}$ **(say)**

Problem 4.6 : *The spindle of a screw jack has single start square thread with outside diameter 45 mm and a pitch of 10 mm. The spindle moves in a nut. The load is carried on swivel head, but it is not free to rotate. The bearing surface of swivel has a mean diameter of 60 mm. Coefficient of friction between screw and nut is 0.2 and between the swivel head and spindle is 0.9. Calculate the load, which can be raised by effort of 100 N each applied at the end of two levers, each of effective length 350 mm. Also determine efficiency of lifting arrangement.*

Solution : Given data : $d_o = 45$ mm, $p = 10$ mm, $\mu = 0.2$, $\mu_1 = 0.9$,

$$D = 60 \text{ mm}, \quad P_1 = 100 \text{ N}, \quad L = 350 \text{ mm}$$

Procedure : We know,

$$d = d_o - \frac{p}{2} = 45 - \frac{10}{2} = \mathbf{40 \ mm}$$

$$d_c = d_o - p = 45 - 10 = \mathbf{35 \ mm}$$

$$R = \frac{D}{2} = \frac{60}{2} = \mathbf{30 \ mm}$$

We have,

$$\tan \alpha = \frac{p}{\pi d}$$

$$\therefore \qquad \alpha = \tan^{-1}\left(\frac{p}{\pi d}\right) = \tan^{-1}\left(\frac{10}{\pi \times 40}\right) = \mathbf{4.5498°}$$

Also,

$$\mu = \tan \phi$$

$$\therefore \qquad \phi = \tan^{-1}(\mu) = \tan^{-1}(0.2) = \mathbf{11.3099°}$$

(1) Load to be raised :

Torque required to overcome the friction between screw and nut is given by,

$$T_1 = P \times \frac{d}{2} = W \times \tan(\alpha + \phi) \times \frac{d}{2}$$

$$\therefore \qquad T_1 = W \times \tan(4.5498 + 11.3099) \times \frac{40}{2}$$

$$\therefore \qquad T_1 = \textbf{5.682 W in N.mm}$$

As the load is carried on a swivel head and not free to rotate, the torque required to overcome the bearing or collar friction is given by,

$$T_2 = \mu_1 \cdot W \cdot R \quad \text{(Assuming uniform wear condition)}$$

$$\therefore \qquad T_2 = 0.9 \times W \times 30 = \textbf{27 W in N.mm}$$

$\therefore$ Total torque required to raise the load is,

$$T = T_1 + T_2 = 5.682\,W + 27\,W = \textbf{32.682 W in N.mm}$$

We have, Torque required = Effort applied by each lever × Effective length of lever

$$T = P_1 \times L$$

$$32.682\,W = (2 \times 100) \times 350 \qquad\qquad \dots (\because \text{ there are two levers})$$

$$\therefore \qquad W = \text{Load raised} = \textbf{2141.85 N}$$

(2) Efficiency of the screw :

We have,
$$\eta = \frac{\text{Ideal torque}}{\text{Actual torque}}$$

$$= \frac{T_0}{T} = \frac{W \times \tan\alpha \times d/2}{32.862\,W} = \frac{\tan(4.5498) \times 40/2}{32.862}$$

$$\therefore \qquad \eta = \textbf{0.0484 or 4.84\%}$$

Problem 4.7 : *The cutter of broaching machine is pulled by square threaded screw of 55 mm external diameter and 10 mm pitch. The operating nut takes the axial load of 400 N on a flat surface of 60 mm and 90 mm internal and external diameter respectively. If μ is 0.15 for all contact surfaces, determine the power required to rotate the operating nut, when cutting speed is 6 m/min. Also find efficiency of screw.* **(W-09)**

Solution : Given data : W = 400 N, d_o = 55 mm, p = 10 mm, D_2 = 60 mm, D_1 = 90 mm, $\mu = \mu_1$ = 0.15, cutting speed = 6 m/min = 6000 mm/min.

Procedure : We know, $d_c = d_o - p = 55 - 10 = \textbf{45 mm,}$

$$d = \frac{d_o + d_c}{2} = \frac{55 + 45}{2} = \textbf{50 mm}$$

$$R_2 = \frac{D_2}{2} = \frac{60}{2} = 30 \text{ mm, and } R_1 = \frac{D_1}{2} = \frac{90}{2} = \textbf{45 mm}$$

$$\therefore \qquad R = \frac{R_1 + R_2}{2} = \frac{45 + 30}{2} = \textbf{37.5 mm}$$

We have, $\qquad \tan \alpha = \dfrac{p}{\pi d}$ $\qquad\qquad\qquad\qquad\qquad\qquad$ (single start)

$$\therefore \qquad \alpha = \tan^{-1}\left(\frac{p}{\pi d}\right) = \tan^{-1}\left(\frac{10}{\pi \times 50}\right) = \mathbf{3.6426°}$$

Also, $\qquad\qquad \tan \phi = \mu$

$$\therefore \qquad \phi = \tan^{-1}(\mu) = \tan^{-1}(0.15) = \mathbf{8.5307°}$$

Torque required to overcome the thread friction,

$$T_1 = W \tan(\alpha + \phi) \times \frac{d}{2}$$

$$= 400 \times \tan(3.6426 + 8.5307) \times \frac{50}{2}$$

$$\therefore \qquad T_1 = \mathbf{2157.19\ N.mm}$$

Torque required to overcome collar friction,

$$T_2 = \mu_1 \cdot W \cdot R = 0.15 \times 400 \times 37.5 = \mathbf{2250\ N.mm}$$

Total torque required to raise the load is given by,

$$T = T_1 + T_2$$

$$= 2157.19 + 2250 = 4407.19\ N.mm = 4.407\ N.m$$

Also, $\qquad$ Cutting speed = Pitch of screw × Number of revolutions per minute (N)

$$\therefore \qquad N = \frac{\text{Cutting speed}}{\text{Pitch (p)}} = \frac{6000}{10} = \mathbf{600\ r.p.m.}$$

(1) Power required : $\quad P = \dfrac{2\pi NT}{60} = \dfrac{2 \times \pi \times 600 \times 4.407}{60} = \mathbf{276.9\ Watt} = \mathbf{0.2769\ kW}$

(2) Efficiency of screw :

$$\eta = \frac{\tan \alpha}{\tan(\alpha + \phi)} = \frac{\tan(3.6426)}{\tan(3.6426 + 8.5307)} = 0.2951 = \mathbf{29.51\%}$$

Problem 4.8 : *A vertical 2-start square threaded screw of 120 mm mean diameter and 24 mm pitch, supports a vertical load of 20 kN. The axial thrust in screw is taken by collar bearing of 300 mm outside and 150 mm inside diameter. Find the force required at the end of the lever, which is 400 mm long in order to lift and lower the load. Coefficient of friction for screw and nut is 0.18 and for collar bearing is 0.25.* **(S-13)**

Solution : Given data : $d = 120$ mm, $p = 24$ mm, $\mu = 0.18$, $\mu_1 = 0.25$,
$W = 20$ kN $= 20 \times 10^3$ N, $L = 400$ mm, $D_1 = 300$ mm, $D_2 = 150$ mm.

Procedure :

We have, $\qquad R_1 = \dfrac{D_1}{2} = \dfrac{300}{2} = 150$ mm, $R_2 = \dfrac{D_2}{2} = \dfrac{150}{2} = 75$ mm,

$$\therefore \qquad R = \frac{R_1 + R_2}{2} = \frac{150 + 75}{2} = \mathbf{112.5\ mm}$$

We know that, for double start or two start square thread,

$$\tan \alpha = \frac{2 \times p}{\pi d} = \frac{2 \times 24}{\pi \times 120} = 0.1273$$

$$\alpha = \tan^{-1}(0.1273) = 7.2561°$$

Also, $\qquad \mu = \tan \phi = 0.18$

$\therefore \qquad \phi = \tan^{-1}(0.18) = \mathbf{10.2039°}$

Case I : For raising the load :

Torque required to overcome the friction between screw and nut is given by,

$$T_1 = P \times \frac{d}{2} = W \tan(\alpha + \phi) \times \frac{d}{2}$$

$$= 20 \times 10^3 \times \tan(7.2561 + 10.2039) \times \frac{120}{2}$$

$$= \mathbf{377.437 \times 10^3 \ N.mm}$$

As the load is not free to rotate, the torque required to overcome the bearing or collar friction is given by,

$$T_2 = \mu_1 \cdot W \cdot R \qquad \text{(Assuming uniform wear conditions)}$$

$\therefore \qquad T_2 = 0.25 \times 20 \times 10^3 \times 112.5 = \mathbf{562.5 \times 10^3 \ N.mm}$

$\therefore$ Total torque required to raise the load is,

$$T = T_1 + T_2 = 377.37 \times 10^3 + 562.5 \times 10^3$$

$$= \mathbf{939.937 \times 10^3 \ N.mm}$$

We know that,

Torque required $=$ Effort applied by lever $\times$ Effective length of lever

$$T = P_1 \times L$$

$\therefore \qquad 939.937 \times 10^3 = P_1 \times 400$

$\therefore \qquad \mathbf{P_1 = 2349.84 \ N}$

Case II : For lowering the load :

Torque required for lowering the load to overcome the friction between screw and nut is given by,

$$T_1 = P \times \frac{d}{2} = W \tan(\phi - \alpha) \times \frac{d}{2}$$

$\therefore \qquad T_1 = 20 \times 10^3 \times \tan(10.2039 - 7.2561) \times \dfrac{120}{2} = 61.793 \times 10^3 \ N$

From case (I), we have, the torque required to overcome the bearing or collar friction as,

$$T_2 = 562.5 \times 10^3 \ N.mm$$

$\therefore$ Total torque required to lower the load is given as,

$$T = T_1 + T_2 = 61.793 \times 10^3 + 562.5 \times 10^3$$

$\therefore \qquad \mathbf{T = 624.293 \times 10^3 \ N.mm}$

We know that,

$$\text{Torque required} = \text{Effort applied by lever} \times \text{Effective length of lever}$$

$$\therefore \qquad T = P_1 \times L$$

$$\therefore \qquad 624.293 \times 10^3 = P_1 \times 400$$

Thus, $\qquad P_1 = \textbf{1560.73 N}$

Problem 4.9 : *A square threaded bolt of mean diameter 24 mm and pitch 5 mm is tightened by screwing a nut, whose mean diameter of bearing surface is 50 mm. The load on the bolt is 10 kN. The coefficient of friction between nut and bolt is 0.1 and between nut and bearing surface is 0.16. Find the force required at the end of 0.5 m long spanner to tighten the nut.*

Solution : Given data : $d = 24$ mm, $p = 5$ mm, $D = 50$ mm, $\therefore\ R = \dfrac{50}{2} = 25$ mm

$W = 10 \times 10^3$ N, $\mu = 0.1$, $\mu_1 = 0.16$, $L = 0.5$ m $= 500$ mm

Procedure : We have,

$$\tan \alpha = \frac{p}{\pi d}$$

$$\therefore \qquad \alpha = \tan^{-1}\left(\frac{p}{\pi d}\right) = \tan^{-1}\left(\frac{5}{\pi \times 24}\right) = \textbf{3.7939}°$$

Also, $\qquad \tan \phi = \mu$

$$\therefore \qquad \phi = \tan^{-1}(\mu) = \tan^{-1}(0.1) = \textbf{5.7106}°$$

Torque (T_1) required to overcome the friction,

$$T_1 = P \times \frac{d}{2} = W \tan(\alpha + \phi) \times \frac{d}{2}$$

$$\therefore \qquad T_1 = 10 \times 10^3 \times \tan(3.7939 + 5.7106) \times \frac{24}{2}$$

$$= \textbf{20.091} \times \textbf{10}^3 \textbf{ N.mm}$$

Torque (T_2) required to overcome the collar friction,

$$T_2 = \mu_1 \cdot W \cdot R = 0.16 \times 10 \times 10^3 \times 25 = \textbf{40} \times \textbf{10}^3 \textbf{ N.mm}$$

$\therefore$ Total torque required to raise the load,

$$T = T_1 + T_2 = (20.091 \times 10^3) + (40 \times 10^3)$$

$$= \textbf{60.091} \times \textbf{10}^3 \textbf{ N.mm}$$

Now, torque required at the end of spanner,

$$T = P_1 \times L$$

where, P_1 is the effort or force applied at the end of spanner.

$$\therefore \qquad P_1 = \frac{60.091 \times 10^3}{500} = \textbf{120.18 N}$$

Problem 4.10 : *A machine vice has single start square threads with 22 mm nominal diameter and 5 mm pitch. The outer and inner diameter of the friction collar are 55 mm and 45 mm respectively. The coefficient of friction for thread and collar are 0.15 and 0.17 respectively. The machinist can comfortably exert a force of 125 N on the handle of mean radius of 150 mm. Assuming uniform wear for the collar, calculate :*

(i)   *The clamping force developed between jaws.*

(ii)   *The overall efficiency of the clamp.*   (W-10)

Solution : Given data : For screw, d_o = 22 m, p = 5 mm, D_1 = 55 mm, D_2 = 45 mm, μ = 0.15, P = 125 N, R_H = 150 mm, μ_1 = 0.17

Procedure : We have, $d_c = d_o - p = 22 - 5 =$ **17 mm**,

$$\therefore \qquad d = \frac{d_o + d_c}{2} = \frac{22 + 17}{2} = \textbf{19.5 mm},$$

Also, $\qquad R_1 = \dfrac{55}{2} =$ **27.5 mm** and $R_2 = \dfrac{45}{2} =$ **22.5 mm**

$$\therefore \qquad R = \text{Mean radius} = \frac{R_1 + R_2}{2} = \frac{27.5 + 22.5}{2} = \textbf{25 mm}$$

We have, $\qquad \tan \alpha = \dfrac{p}{\pi d}$

$$\therefore \qquad \alpha = \tan^{-1}\left(\frac{p}{\pi d}\right) = \tan^{-1}\left(\frac{5}{\pi \times 19.5}\right) = \textbf{4.666°}$$

And $\qquad \tan \phi = \mu$

$$\therefore \qquad \phi = \tan^{-1}(\mu) = \tan^{-1}(0.15) = \textbf{8.5307°}$$

(1) Clamping force :

Torque required to overcome the friction between screw and nut is given by,

$$T_1 = P \times \frac{d}{2} = W \times \tan(\alpha + \phi) \times \frac{d}{2}$$

$$\therefore \qquad T_1 = W \times \tan(4.666 + 8.5307) \times \frac{19.5}{2}$$

$$\therefore \qquad \textbf{T}_1 = \textbf{2.2862 W N.mm}$$

Also, torque required in overcoming collar friction,

$$T_2 = \mu_1 \cdot W \cdot R = 0.17 \times W \times 25$$

(Assuming uniform wear condition)

$$\therefore \qquad \textbf{T}_2 = \textbf{4.25 W N.mm}$$

Total torque required to raise the load, $T = T_1 + T_2$

$$\therefore \qquad T = 2.2862\,W + 4.25\,W = \textbf{6.5362 W N.mm} \qquad \dots(1)$$

The required torque is applied externally by handle,

$$\therefore \quad T = P \times R_H = 125 \times 150 = \textbf{18750 N.mm} \quad \dots (2)$$

Equating equations (1) and (2), we get

$$6.5362 \, W = 18750; \ W = \textbf{2868.64 N}$$

(2) Overall efficiency :
$$\eta_o = \frac{T_0}{T} = \frac{W \tan \alpha \cdot \dfrac{d}{2}}{T_1 + T_2} = \frac{2868.4 \times \tan (4.666) \times \dfrac{19.5}{2}}{18750}$$

$$= \textbf{0.1217} = \textbf{12.17\%}$$

Problem 4.11 : *The following data is given for a screw jack.*

- *Nominal diameter of screw = 40 mm,*
- *Pitch of square thread = 7 mm,*
- *Coefficient of thread friction = 0.15,*
- *Coefficient of collar friction = 0.1,*
- *Effective mean diameter of collar = 70 mm.*

The operator can comfortably exert a force of 150 N at a radius of 1.2 m to raise the load. Assuming single start threads, calculate:

(i)   The maximum load that can be lifted, (ii) The efficiency of the screw, and

(iii) The overall efficiency.

Solution : Given data : $d_o = 40$ mm, $p = 7$ mm, $\mu = 0.15$, $\mu_1 = 0.1$

$$D = 70 \text{ mm}, \ \therefore \ R = \frac{70}{2} = 35 \text{ mm}, \ P_1 = 150 \text{ N}, \ R_H = 1.2 \text{ m} = 1200 \text{ mm}$$

Procedure : We have, $\quad d_c = d_o - p = 40 - 7 = \textbf{33 mm}$

$$\therefore \quad \text{Mean diameter} = d = \frac{d_o + d_c}{2} = \frac{40 + 33}{2} = \textbf{36.5 mm}$$

We have, $\quad \tan \alpha = \dfrac{p}{\pi d}$

$$\therefore \quad \alpha = \tan^{-1}\left(\frac{p}{\pi d}\right) = \tan^{-1}\left(\frac{7}{\pi \times 36.5}\right) = \textbf{3.4933°}$$

Also, $\quad \tan \phi = \mu$

$$\therefore \quad \phi = \tan^{-1}(\mu) = \tan^{-1}(0.15) = \textbf{8.5307°}$$

(1) Maximum load lifted :

Torque required to overcome the friction between screw and nut, $T_1 = P \times \dfrac{d}{2}$

$$\therefore \quad T_1 = W \cdot \tan(\alpha + \phi) \times \frac{d}{2}$$

$$\therefore \quad T_1 = W \times \tan(3.4933 + 8.5307) \times \frac{36.5}{2} = \textbf{3.887 W in N.mm}$$

Assuming uniform wear conditions, torque (T_2) required to overcome the collar friction,

$$T_2 = \mu_1 \cdot W \cdot R = 0.1 \times W \times 35 = \textbf{3.5 W in N.mm}$$

∴   Total torque (T) required to raise a load,

$$T = T_1 + T_2 = 3.887\,W + 3.5\,W$$

∴ $\textbf{T = 7.387 W in N.mm}$ ... (1)

From the data, it is clear that, when effort or force (P_1) is applied tangentially at the other end of handle or lever, the lever moves along a circular path having radius of rotation 1200 mm. Therefore, length of handle or lever can be taken as, L = 1200 mm.

∴   Torque applied by the operator,

$$T = P_1 \times L = 150 \times 1200 = \textbf{180} \times \textbf{10}^3 \textbf{ N.mm} \qquad \text{... (2)}$$

Equating equations (1) and (2),

$$7.387\,W = 180 \times 10^3$$

∴ $W = \textbf{24367.13 N}$ or   **24.367 kN**

(2) Efficiency of screw :

$$\eta_s = \frac{\tan \alpha}{\tan (\alpha + \phi)} = \frac{\tan (3.4933)}{\tan (3.4933 + 8.5307)} = 0.2866 = \textbf{28.66\%}$$

(3) Overall efficiency :

$$\eta = \frac{T_0}{T} = \frac{W \cdot \tan \alpha \cdot \dfrac{d}{2}}{T}$$

$$= \frac{24367.13 \times \tan (3.4933) \times \dfrac{36.5}{2}}{180 \times 10^3} = 0.1508 = \textbf{15.08\%}$$

Problem 4.12 : *A sluice gate used in water pipeline consists of a gate raised by the spindle, which is operated by the hand wheel of radius 300 mm. The spindle has single start square threads. The nominal diameter of spindle is 36 mm and the pitch is 6 mm. The friction collar has inner and outer diameters of 32 mm and 50 mm respectively. The weight of the gate is 7.5 kN and the frictional resistance to open the valve due to water pressure is 2.75 kN. The coefficient of friction at threads and collar are 0.12 and 0.18 respectively. Using uniform wear theory, determine :*

(i)   The torque required to raise the gate,

(ii)   The overall efficiency.

Solution : Given data : $d_o = 36$ mm, p = 6 mm, $D_1 = 50$ mm; ∴ $R_1 = 25$ mm,

$D_2 = 32$ mm; ∴ $R_2 = 16$ mm, $W_G = 7.5 \times 10^3$ N, $F_R = 2.75 \times 10^3$ N, $\mu = 0.12$, $\mu_1 = 0.18$,

$R_H = 300$ mm.

Procedure :

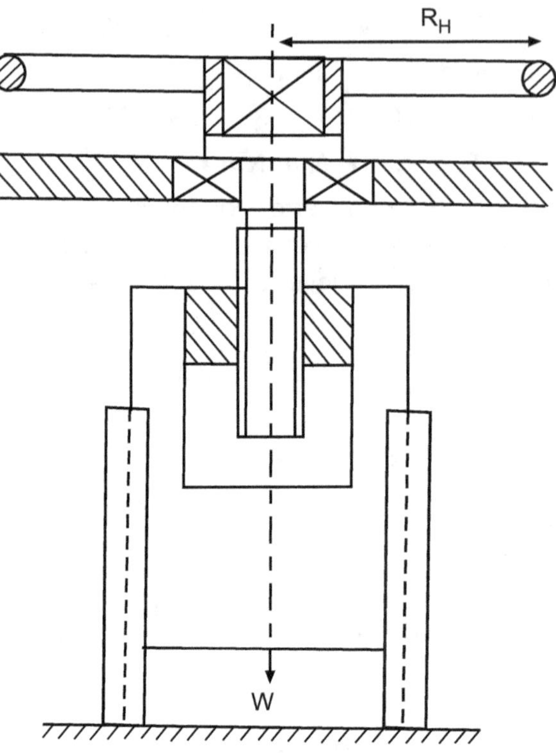

Fig. 4.8 : Sluice gate

$$\text{Mean radius of collar} = R = \frac{R_1 + R_2}{2} = \frac{25 + 16}{2} = \textbf{20.5 mm}$$

And,
$$d_c = d_o - p = 36 - 6 = \textbf{30 mm}$$

∴
$$d = \frac{d_o + d_c}{2} = \frac{36 + 30}{2} = \textbf{33 mm}$$

We have,
$$\tan \alpha = \frac{p}{\pi d}$$

∴
$$\alpha = \tan^{-1}\left(\frac{p}{\pi d}\right) = \tan^{-1}\left(\frac{6}{\pi \times 33}\right) = \textbf{3.3122°}$$

Also,
$$\tan \phi = \mu$$

∴
$$\phi = \tan^{-1}(\mu) = \tan^{-1}(0.12) = \textbf{6.8428°}$$

(1) Torque required to raise the gate :

$$W = W_G + F_R$$
$$= (7.5 \times 10^3) + (2.75 \times 10^3) = \textbf{10.25} \times \textbf{10}^3 \textbf{ N}$$

Torque (T_1) required to overcome the screw or thread friction,

$$T_1 = P \times \frac{d}{2} = W \times \tan(\alpha + \phi) \times \frac{d}{2}$$

$$T_1 = 10.25 \times 10^3 \times \tan(3.3122 + 6.8428) \times \frac{33}{2}$$

$$\therefore \qquad T_1 = \textbf{30293.3 N.mm}$$

Torque required to overcome the collar friction,

$$T_2 = \mu_1 \cdot W \cdot R = 0.18 \times 10.25 \times 10^3 \times 20.5 = \textbf{37822.5 N.mm}$$

$\therefore$ Total torque required, $T = T_1 + T_2$

$$T = 30293.3 + 37822.5 = \textbf{68115.8 N.mm}$$

(2) Force on hand wheel : Torque to be applied on hand wheel, $T = P_1 \times R_H$

$$\therefore \qquad P_1 = \frac{T}{R_H} = \frac{68115.8}{300} = \textbf{227.05 N}$$

(3) Overall efficiency : $\eta = \dfrac{T_0}{T} = \dfrac{W \cdot \tan\alpha \cdot \dfrac{d}{2}}{68115.8}$

$$= \frac{10.25 \times 10^3 \times \tan(3.3122) \times \dfrac{33}{2}}{68115.8} = \textbf{0.1437} = \textbf{14.37\%}$$

4.8 DESIGN OF SCREW JACK

Brief Description of Screw Jack :

- It is a portable device consisting of screw mechanism used to raise or lower the load.
- There are two types of jacks – Hydraulic and Mechanical.
- Mechanical jacks can be either hand operated or motor power driven.
- Hydraulic jack consists of cylinder and piston mechanism, where the movement of piston rod is used to lower or raise the load.

Construction of a Screw Jack :

- It consists of a screw and nut. The nut is fixed in cast iron frame and remains stationary.
- The rotation of the nut inside the frame is prevented by pressing a set screw against it.
- The screw is rotated in the nut by means of a handle, which passes through a hole in the head of a screw.
- The head carries a cup, which supports the load and remains stationary, while the screw is being rotated.
- There is a collar friction for the annular contacting surfaces between the cup and head of the screw.
- A washer is fixed to the other end of screw inside the frame, which prevents the screw to be completely turned out of the nut.

Design Procedure for Screw Jack :

Questions
1. Draw a neat sketch of screw jack. Give the design procedure of screw. **(S-10; W-10)**
2. Explain with necessary sketches and equations, how the screw spindle and nut of a screw jack is designed. **(W-12)**
3. Give the design procedure of screw and nut of a screw jack. **(S-14)**

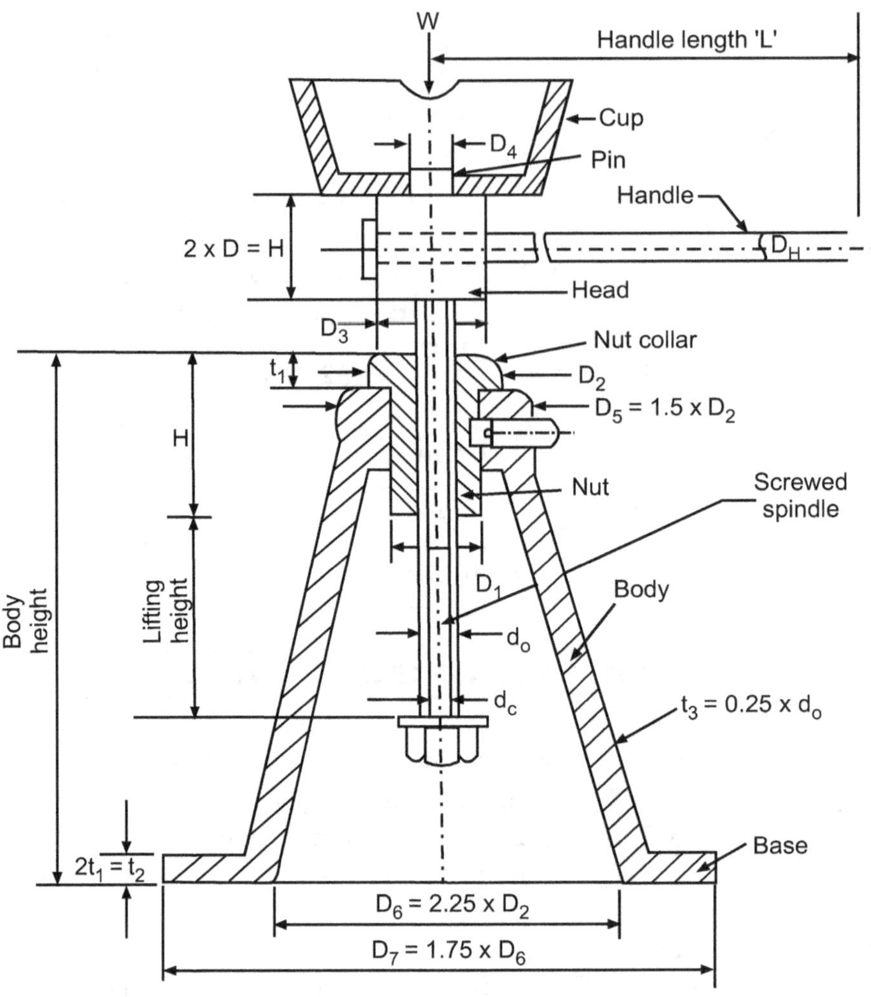

Fig. 4.9 : Screw jack

(A) Design of Screw:

(1) Find core diameter (d_c):

Considering the screw under pure compression, use the formula of direct compressive stress due to axial load to calculate value of d_c.

$$\sigma_c = \frac{W}{\frac{\pi}{4} \times d_c^2}$$

In addition to compressive stress, screw is also subjected to torsional shear stress. To account for this, increase the value of d_c considerably by referring the standard table of square threads, where, we get the values of d_o and p.

Now, calculate new 'd_c' using the formula, $d_c = d_o - p$.

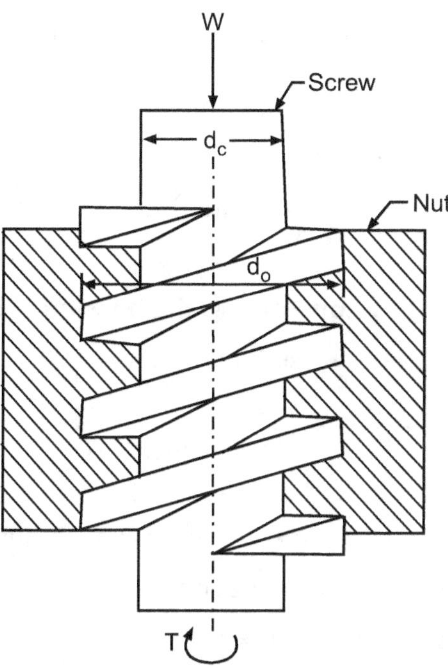

Fig. 4.10 : Screw and nut assembly

2.   Find torque T_1 required to rotate the screw and hence find the induced shear stress (τ) due to this torque :

$$T_1 \;=\; P \times \frac{d}{2} \;=\; W \tan(\alpha + \phi) \times \frac{d}{2}$$

where,   P = Effort required at circumference of screw

and   d = Mean diameter of screw

We know that, torque transmitted by screw,

$$T_1 \;=\; \frac{\pi}{16} \times \tau \times d_c^3$$

Find out the torsional shear stress due to torque T_1,

$$\tau \;=\; \frac{16\,T_1}{\pi \cdot d_c^3}$$

Also, find direct compressive stress (σ_c) induced due to axial load,

$$\sigma_c \;=\; \frac{W}{\dfrac{\pi}{4} \times d_c^2}$$

3.   Check maximum principal stresses : When screw is subjected to both direct stress (compressive) and torsional shear stress, then design must be based on,

   (a)   Maximum shear stress theory, according to which, maximum shear stress on minimum cross-section is,

$$\tau_{max} \;=\; \frac{1}{2} \times \sqrt{\sigma_c^2 + 4\tau^2}$$

(b) Maximum normal stress theory, according to which, maximum normal stress on minimum cross-section is,

$$\sigma_{c\ max} = \frac{1}{2}\sigma_c + \frac{1}{2} \times \sqrt{\sigma_c^2 + 4\tau^2}$$

Check whether the principal stresses are less than permissible limits.

(B) Design of Nut :

4. Find the height of nut by considering the bearing pressure acting on it :

By considering the bearing pressure on nut, we have

$$P_b = \frac{W}{\frac{\pi}{4}(d_o^2 - d_c^2) \times n}$$

where, n = Number of threads in contact with nut

(a) Calculate 'n' from the above equation.

(b) Calculate, Height of nut, $H = n \times p$

(c) Calculate, thickness or width of screw, $t = \dfrac{p}{2}$.

5. Check the transverse shear stresses in screw and nut as follows :

(a) Induced Transverse Shear stress for screw,

$$\tau_{screw} = \frac{W}{\pi \cdot d_c \cdot n \cdot t}$$

(b) Induced Transverse Shear stress for nut,

$$\tau_{nut} = \frac{W}{\pi \cdot d_o \cdot n \cdot t}$$

By using the above formulae, calculate τ_{screw} and τ_{nut} and verify that, these induced stresses are less than their permissible values.

6. Find inner diameter (D_1), outer diameter (D_2) and thickness (t_1) of collar :

(a) Inner diameter (D_1) : It is found by considering tensile failure of nut,

$$\sigma_t = \frac{W}{\frac{\pi}{4}(D_1^2 - d_o^2)}$$

(b) Outer diameter (D_2) : It is found by considering crushing failure of nut collar,

$$\sigma_{ck} = \frac{W}{\frac{\pi}{4}(D_2^2 - D_1^2)}$$

(c) Thickness of nut collar (t_1) : It is found by considering shearing failure of nut collar,

$$\tau = \frac{W}{\pi D_1 \, t_1}$$

7. Fix the diameter of head (D_3) and diameter of pin (D_4) fitted on top of screw :

Diameter of head $= D_3 = 1.75 \, d_o; \quad \therefore \; R_3 = \dfrac{D_3}{2}$

The cup is fitted with a pin.

Diameter of pin $= D_4 = \dfrac{D_3}{4}; \quad \therefore \; R_4 = \dfrac{D_4}{2}$

8. Find the torque required (T_2) to overcome friction at the top of screw :

$$T_2 = \frac{2}{3} \times \frac{\mu_1 \times W \times (R_3^3 - R_4^3)}{(R_3^2 - R_4^2)} \qquad \text{(uniform pressure condition)}$$

and $\qquad T_2 = \mu_1 \times W \times R \qquad\qquad\qquad$ (uniform wear condition)

where, $\quad R_3 =$ Radius of head, $\quad R_4 =$ Radius of pin, $\quad R = \dfrac{R_3 + R_4}{2}$

9. Find the total torque, to which, handle will be subjected :

$$T = T_1 + T_2$$

Assuming that a person can apply a force or effort of 300 N intermittently,

Find the length of handle required as, $L = \dfrac{T}{300} \qquad\qquad (\because \; T = P_1 \times L)$

10. Diameter of handle (D_H) may be obtained by considering bending moment :

Maximum bending moment $= M = \dfrac{\pi}{32} \times \sigma_b \times D_H^3$

Put the value of torque T as maximum bending moment (M) and calculate diameter of handle (D_H).

11. Height of head $= H = 2D$

12. Fix the diameter of body of screw jack as follows :

(i)   Diameter of body at top $= D_5 = 1.5 \times D_2$.

(ii)   Thickness of body $= t_3 = 0.25 \times d_o$.

(iii) Inside diameter at bottom $= D_7 = 2.25 \times D_2$.

(iv) Outside diameter at bottom $= D_7 = 1.75 \times D_6$.

(v)   Thickness of base, $t_2 = 2 \times t_1$.

(vi) Height of body = Maximum lift + Height of nut + 100 mm.

Table 4.1 : Reference table of square threads for nominal diameter and corresponding pitch

Nominal diameter (d_o) in mm	Pitch (p) in mm	Nominal diameter (d_o) in mm	Pitch (p) in mm
22		55	
24	5	58	9
26		60	
28		62	
30		65	
32	6	68	
34		70	
36		72	10
38		75	
40	7	78	
42		80	
44		82	
46		85	
48	8	88	12
50		90	
52		92	

Numerical Type No. 3 : "Design of Screw Jack"

Problem 4.13 : *A screw jack is to lift a load of 80 kN through a height of 400 mm. The elastic strength of screw material in tension and compression is 300 MPa and in shear is 120 MPa. The material for nut is phosphor bronze, for which, elastic limits are 150 MPa in tension, 135 MPa in compression and 160 MPa in shear. The bearing pressure between the nut and screw is not to be exceeding 18 N/mm². Design and draw the screw jack. Take μ = 0.15, μ_1 = 0.2.*

Solution : Given data : W = 80 kN = 80×10^3 N, μ = 0.15, μ_1 = 0.2, P_b = 18 N/mm²,

Maximum lift = 400 mm

Procedure : Let us assume factor of safety for screw and nut material as 5.

$\therefore$ For screw, $\sigma_c = \dfrac{300}{5}$ = **60 MPa**

$$\tau = \dfrac{120}{5} = \textbf{24 MPa}$$

$\therefore$ For nut, $\sigma_t = \dfrac{150}{5}$ = **30 MPa**

$$\sigma_{ck} = \dfrac{135}{5} = \textbf{27 MPa}$$

$$\tau = \dfrac{160}{5} = \textbf{32 MPa}$$

Design of Screw Jack :

(A) Design of Screw:

(1) Find core diameter (d_c) :

Considering the screw under pure compression, use the formula of direct compressive stress due to axial load.

$$\sigma_c = \frac{W}{\frac{\pi}{4} \times d_c^2}$$

$$\therefore \quad 60 = \frac{80 \times 10^3}{\frac{\pi}{4} \times d_c^2}$$

i.e. $\qquad$ **d_c = 41.20 mm**

In addition to compressive stress, screw is also subjected to torsional shear stress. Therefore, to account for this, the value of d_c is increased considerably and is taken from the standard table for square threaded screw.

Let us take **d_o = 68* mm** and **p = 10 mm**

*[**Note :** *For this, multiply the calculated d_c = 41.20 by 1.6 i.e. d_c = 41.20 $\times$ 1.6 = 65.92. Now, refer the standard table for square threads and choose the value of d_o higher than 65.92. Referring to the table, we get d_o = 68 mm and p = 10 mm.]*

$$\therefore \quad d_c = d_o - p = 68 - 10 = \textbf{58 mm}$$

$$\therefore \quad d = \frac{d_o + d_c}{2} = \frac{68 + 58}{2} = \textbf{63 mm}$$

(2) Find torque T_1 required to rotate the screw and find the shear stress (τ) due to this torque :

We have, $\qquad \tan \alpha = \dfrac{p}{\pi d} = \dfrac{10}{\pi \times 63}$

$\therefore \qquad \alpha = \tan^{-1}(0.05052) = \textbf{2.8924°}$

Also, $\qquad \mu = \tan \phi$

$\therefore \qquad \phi = \tan^{-1}(\mu) = \tan^{-1}(0.15) = \textbf{8.5307°}$

Torque (T_1) required to rotate the screw,

$$T_1 = P \times \frac{d}{2} = W \times \tan(\alpha + \phi) \times \frac{d}{2}$$

$$\therefore \quad T_1 = 80 \times 10^3 \times \tan(2.8924 + 8.5307) \times \frac{63}{2}$$

$$\therefore \quad T_1 = \textbf{509.178} \times \textbf{10}^\textbf{3} \textbf{ N.mm}$$

Torsional shear stress (τ) induced due to torque T_1 is,

$$\tau = \frac{16T_1}{\pi \times d_c^3} = \frac{16 \times 509.178 \times 10^3}{\pi \times (58)^3} = \textbf{13.29 MPa} < 24 \text{ MPa}$$

Direct compressive stress induced due to axial load,

$$\sigma_c = \frac{W}{\frac{\pi}{4} \times d_c^2} = \frac{80000}{\frac{\pi}{4} \times (58)^2} = \textbf{30.279 MPa} < 60 \text{ MPa}$$

The induced torsional shear and compressive stresses are less than permissible limits. So design is safe.

(3) Check maximum principal stresses : When screw is subjected to both direct stress (compressive) and torsional shear stress, then design must be based on,

(a) Maximum shear stress theory, according to which, maximum shear stress on minimum cross-section is,

$$\tau_{max} = \frac{1}{2}\sqrt{\sigma_c^2 + 4\tau^2} = \frac{1}{2}\sqrt{(30.279)^2 + 4\,(13.29)^2} = \textbf{20.145 MPa} < 24 \text{ MPa}$$

(b) Maximum normal stress theory, according to which, maximum normal stress on minimum cross-section is,

$$\sigma_{c\,max} = \frac{1}{2}\sigma_c + \frac{1}{2}\sqrt{\sigma_c^2 + 4\tau^2}$$

$$= \frac{1}{2} \times (30.279) + \frac{1}{2}\sqrt{(30.279)^2 + 4\,(13.29)^2} = \textbf{35.2845 MPa} < 60 \text{ MPa}$$

(B) Design of Nut :

(4) Find the height of nut, considering the bearing pressure on nut :

$$P_b = \frac{W}{\frac{\pi}{4}(d_o^2 - d_c^2) \times n}$$

$$\therefore \qquad n = \frac{W}{\frac{\pi}{4}(d_o^2 - d_c^2) \times P_b}$$

$\therefore$　　Number of threads of nut in contact with the screw,

$$n = \frac{80 \times 10^3}{\frac{\pi}{4}\,[(68)^2 - (58)^2] \times 18} = \textbf{4.491} \cong \textbf{5 (say)}$$

$\therefore$　　　　H = Height of nut = $n \times p$ = 5×10 = **50 mm**

and　　　　　　t = thickness of width of screw = $\dfrac{p}{2} = \dfrac{10}{2}$ = **5 mm**

(5) Check the transverse shear stresses induced in screw and nut as follows :

Transverse shear stress for screw,

$$\tau_{screw} = \frac{W}{\pi\,d_c\,n\,t} = \frac{80 \times 10^3}{\pi \times 58 \times 5 \times 5} = \textbf{17.56 MPa} < 24 \text{ MPa}$$

Transverse shear stress for nut,

$$\tau_{nut} = \frac{W}{\pi \, d_o \, n \, t} = \frac{80 \times 10^3}{\pi \times 68 \times 5 \times 5} = \textbf{14.98 MPa} < 32 \text{ MPa}$$

$\therefore$ The induced stresses are less than permissible limits. Hence, design of screw and nut is safe.

(6) Find inner diameter (D_1) and outer diameter (D_2) and thickness (t_1) of collar :

(a) Inner diameter (D_1) : It is found by considering tensile failure of nut,

$$\therefore \qquad \sigma_t = \frac{W}{\frac{\pi}{4}(D_1^2 - d_o^2)}$$

$$\therefore \qquad 30 = \frac{80 \times 10^3}{\frac{\pi}{4}[D_1^2 - (68)^2]}$$

$$\therefore \qquad D_1 = \textbf{89.55 mm} \cong \textbf{90 mm (say)}$$

(b) Outer diameter (D_2) : It is found by considering crushing of nut collar,

$$\sigma_{ck} = \frac{W}{\frac{\pi}{4}(D_2^2 - D_1^2)}$$

$$\therefore \qquad 27 = \frac{80 \times 10^3}{\frac{\pi}{4}[D_2^2 - (90)^2]}$$

$$\therefore \qquad D_2 = \textbf{108.96 mm} \cong \textbf{110 mm (say)}$$

(c) Thickness of nut collar (t_1) : It is found by considering shear failure of nut collar,

$$\tau = \frac{W}{\pi_1 \cdot D_1 \cdot t_1}$$

$$\therefore \qquad 32 = \frac{80000}{\pi \times 90 \times t_1}$$

$\therefore$ Thickness of nut collar, $t_1 = \textbf{8.842 mm} \cong \textbf{10 mm}$

(7) Fix the diameter of head diameter (D_3) and diameter of pin (D_4) fitted on top of screw :

$$\text{Head diameter} = D_3 = 1.75 \, d_o = 1.75 \times 68 = \textbf{119 mm}$$

$$\therefore \qquad R_3 = \frac{119}{2} = \textbf{59.5 mm}$$

The cup is fitted with a pin of diameter D_4.

$$\text{We have,} \qquad D_4 = \frac{D_3}{4} = \frac{119}{4} = \textbf{29.75 mm}$$

$$\therefore \qquad R_4 = \frac{D_4}{2} = \frac{29.75}{2} = \textbf{14.875 mm}$$

(8) The torque required (T_2) to overcome friction at the top of the screw :

We have,
$$R = \frac{R_3 + R_4}{2} = \frac{59.5 + 14.875}{2} = \mathbf{37.1875 \ mm}$$

Also, we know, $T_2 = \mu_1 \cdot W \cdot R$ (Assuming uniform wear condition)

$\therefore$ $T_2 = 0.2 \times 80000 \times 37.1875 = \mathbf{595 \times 10^3 \ N.mm}$

(9) Find the total torque, to which, handle will be subjected :

$$T = T_1 + T_2$$

$\therefore$ $T = (509.178 \times 10^3) + (595 \times 10^3) = \mathbf{1104.178 \times 10^3 \ N.mm}$

We have, $T = P_1 \times L$

Assuming that a person can apply a force of 300 N intermittently, length of handle required is calculated as,

$$T = 300 \times L$$

$\therefore$ $L = \dfrac{T}{300} = \dfrac{(1104.178 \times 10^3)}{300} = \mathbf{3680.59 \ mm} \cong \mathbf{3.68 \ m}$

(10) Diameter of handle (D_H) may be obtained by considering bending moment :

Maximum bending moment $= M = T = \dfrac{\pi}{32} \times \sigma_b \times D_H^3$

$\therefore$ $1104.178 \times 10^3 = \dfrac{\pi}{32} \times 30 \times D_H^3$ (Assume $\sigma_b = 30$ MPa)

$\therefore$ $D_H = \mathbf{72.10 \ mm} \cong \mathbf{74 \ mm}$ **(say)**

(11) Fix the dimensions of body of screw jack as follows :

Diameter of body at top $= D_5 = 1.5 \times D_2 = 1.5 \times 110 = \mathbf{165 \ mm}$

Thickness of body $= t_3 = 0.25 \times d_o = 0.25 \times 68 = \mathbf{17 \ mm}$

Inside diameter of body at bottom $= D_6 = 2.25 \times D_2 = 2.25 \times 110 = \mathbf{247.5 \ mm}$

Outside diameter of body at bottom $= D_7 = 1.75 \times D_6 = 1.75 \times 247.5 = \mathbf{433.125 \ mm}$

Thickness of base $= t_2 = 2 \times t_1 = 2 \times 12 = \mathbf{24 \ mm}$

Height of body $=$ Maximum lift + Height of nut + 100 mm

$= 400 + 50 + 100 = \mathbf{550 \ mm}$

Problem 4.14 : *A screw jack carries a load of 22 kN. If the coefficient of friction between screw and nut is 0.15, design the screw and nut. Neglect collar friction and column action.*

Take : $\sigma_c = 42$ N/mm^2 and $\tau = 28$ N/mm^2 for screw and take $\tau_{nut} = 21$ MPa. The permissible bearing pressure on the nut is 14 N/mm^2. **(S-11)**

Solution : Given data : $W = 22$ kN $= 22 \times 10^3$ N, $\mu = 0.15$, $P_b = 14$ N/mm^2

For screw : $\sigma_c = 42$ MPa $= 42$ N/mm^2, $\tau = 28$ MPa $= 28$ N/mm^2

For nut : $\tau = 21$ MPa $= 21$ N/mm^2

Procedure :

(A) Design of Screw :

(1) Find core diameter (d_c) :

Considering the screw under pure compression, use the expression of direct compressive stress due to axial load to find d_c.

$$\sigma_c = \frac{W}{\frac{\pi}{4} \times d_c^2}$$

$$42 = \frac{22 \times 10^3}{\frac{\pi}{4} \times d_c^2}$$

$$\therefore \quad d_c = \textbf{25.82 mm}$$

In order to take up torsional shear stress induced in the screw, the core diameter is increased considerably.

From the standard table for square threaded screw, let us take, d_o = **44 mm** and pitch (p) = **7 mm**

$$\therefore \quad d_c = d_o - p = 44 - 7 = \textbf{37 mm}$$

$$\therefore \quad d = \frac{d_o + d_c}{2} = \frac{44 + 37}{2} = \textbf{40.5 mm}$$

(2) Find torque T_1 required to rotate screw and find induced shear stress (τ) due to this torque :

We have, $\qquad \tan \alpha = \dfrac{p}{\pi d}$

$$\therefore \quad \alpha = \tan^{-1}\left(\frac{p}{\pi d}\right) = \tan^{-1}\left(\frac{7}{\pi \times 40.5}\right) = \textbf{3.1490}\degree$$

Also, $\qquad \mu = \tan \phi$

$$\therefore \quad \phi = \tan^{-1}(\mu) = \tan^{-1}(0.15) = \textbf{8.5307}\degree$$

Torque T_1 required to rotate the screw,

$$T_1 = P \times \frac{d}{2}$$

$$\therefore \quad T_1 = W \times \tan(\alpha + \phi) \times \frac{d}{2}$$

$$\therefore \quad T_1 = 22 \times 10^3 \times \tan(3.1490 + 8.5307) \times \frac{40.5}{2}$$

$$\therefore \quad T_1 = \textbf{92.094} \times \textbf{10}^3 \textbf{ N.mm}$$

Induced torsional shear stress due to torque T_1 is,

$$\tau = \frac{16 T_1}{\pi \times d_c^3} = \frac{16 \times 92.094 \times 10^3}{\pi \times (37)^3} = \textbf{9.26 N/mm}^2 < 28 \text{ N/mm}^2$$

Direct compressive stress induced due to axial load,

$$\sigma_c = \frac{W}{\frac{\pi}{4} \times d_c^2} = \frac{22 \times 10^3}{\frac{\pi}{4} \times (37)^2} = \textbf{20.46 N/mm}^2 < 42 \text{ N/mm}^2$$

The induced torsional shear and compressive stresses are less than permissible limits. So, design is safe.

(3) Check maximum principal stresses : When screw is subjected to direct stress (compressive) and torsional shear stress, then design must be based on,

(a) Maximum shear stress theory, according to which maximum shear stress on minimum cross-section is,

$$\tau_{max} = \frac{1}{2}\sqrt{\sigma_c^2 + 4\tau^2} = \frac{1}{2}\sqrt{(20.46)^2 + 4\,(9.26)^2}$$

$$= \textbf{13.79 N/mm}^2 < 28 \text{ N/mm}^2$$

(b) Maximum normal stress theory, according to which maximum normal stress on minimum cross-section is,

$$\sigma_{c\,max} = \frac{1}{2}\sigma_c + \frac{1}{2}\sqrt{\sigma_c^2 + 4\tau^2}$$

$$= \frac{1}{2} \times (20.46) + \frac{1}{2}\sqrt{(20.46)^2 + 4\,(9.26)^2}$$

$$= \textbf{24.028 N/mm}^2 < 42 \text{ N/mm}^2$$

Thus, principal stresses are less than permissible limits. Hence, design is safe.

(B) Design of Nut :

Considering the bearing pressure on nut, we have,

$$P_b = \frac{W}{\frac{\pi}{4}(d_o^2 - d_c^2)\,n}$$

$$\therefore \quad n = \frac{W}{\frac{\pi}{4}(d_o^2 - d_c^2)\,P_b}$$

$$\therefore \quad n = \frac{22 \times 10^3}{\frac{\pi}{4}[(44)^2 - (37)^2] \times 14} = \textbf{3.53} \cong \textbf{4 (say)}$$

We have, H = Height of nut = $n \times p = 4 \times 7 = \textbf{28 mm}$

and t = Thickness of screw = $\dfrac{p}{2} = \dfrac{7}{2} = \textbf{3.5 mm}$

Problem 4.15 : *A power screw having quadruple start square thread of nominal diameter 28 mm lifts a load of 10 kN. The outer and inner diameters of the screw collar are 50 mm and 20 mm respectively. The coefficient of thread friction and collar friction may be assumed as 0.21 and 0.14 respectively. Assuming uniform pressure condition of the collar, find (i) torque required to rotate the screw, (2) stresses developed in the screw, (3) height of the nut, if bearing pressure is limited to 15 N/mm², (4) power required to drive, if screw rotates at 14 r.p.m.*

Solution : Given data : $d_o = 28$ mm, $\mu = 0.21$, $\mu_1 = 0.14$, $W = 10 \times 10^3$ N,

$N = 14$ r.p.m., $D_1 = 50$ mm, $D_2 = 20$ mm, $P_b = 15$ N/mm^2

Procedure : *Pitch is not given in the problem.* Therefore, from standard table of square threads, for given nominal diameter (d_o) of 28 mm, pitch is taken as 5 mm. $\therefore$ p = **5 mm**.

$\therefore \qquad d_c = d_o - p = 28 - 5 = \textbf{23 mm}$

$\therefore \qquad d = \dfrac{d_o + d_c}{2} = \dfrac{28 + 23}{2} = \textbf{25.5 mm}$

Also, $\qquad R_1 = \dfrac{D_1}{2} = \dfrac{50}{2} = \textbf{25 mm}$

$\qquad R_2 = \dfrac{D_2}{2} = \dfrac{20}{2} = \textbf{10 mm}$

We know that for quadruple start square threads,

$$\tan \alpha = \frac{4 \times p}{\pi d} = \frac{4 \times 5}{\pi \times 25.5} = 0.24695$$

$\therefore \qquad \alpha = \tan^{-1}(0.24695) = \textbf{14.0176°}$

Also, $\qquad \mu = \tan \phi = 0.21$

$\therefore \qquad \phi = \tan^{-1}(0.21) = \textbf{11.8597°}$

(1) Torque required to rotate the screw : Torque required to overcome the friction between screw and nut is given by,

$$T_1 = P \times \frac{d}{2} = W \tan(\alpha + \phi) \times \frac{d}{2}$$

$$= 10 \times 10^3 \times \tan(14.0176 + 11.8597) \times \frac{25.5}{2}$$

$\therefore \qquad T_1 = \textbf{61.848} \times \textbf{10}^{\textbf{3}} \textbf{ N.mm}$

Torque required to overcome the bearing or collar friction is given by,

$$T_2 = \frac{2}{3} \times \frac{\mu_1 \times W \times (R_1^3 - R_2^3)}{(R_1^2 - R_2^2)} \qquad \text{(Uniform pressure condition)}$$

$\therefore \qquad T_2 = \dfrac{2}{3} \times \dfrac{0.14 \times 10 \times 10^3 \times [(25)^3 - (10)^3]}{[(25)^2 - (10)^2]} = \textbf{26} \times \textbf{10}^{\textbf{3}} \textbf{ N.mm}$

Total torque required to rotate the screw is,

$$T = T_1 + T_2 = (61.848 \times 10^3) + (26 \times 10^3)$$

$\therefore \qquad T = 87.848 \times 10^3 \text{ N.mm} = \textbf{87.848 N.m}$

(2) Stresses developed in the screw : Direct compressive stress induced due to axial load is given by,

$$\sigma_c = \frac{W}{\frac{\pi}{4} \times d_c^2} = \frac{10 \times 10^3}{\frac{\pi}{4} \times (23)^2} = \textbf{24.06 N/mm}^2$$

Torsional shear stress due to torque T_1 is,

$$\tau = \frac{16T_1}{\pi \times d_c^3} = \frac{16 \times 61.848 \times 10^3}{\pi \times (23)^3} = \textbf{25.88 N/mm}^2$$

According to maximum shear stress theory, maximum shear stress on minimum cross-section is,

$$\tau_{max} = \frac{1}{2} \times \sqrt{\sigma_c^2 + 4\tau^2}$$

$$= \frac{1}{2} \times \sqrt{(24.06)^2 + 4 \times (25.88)^2} = \textbf{28.54 N/mm}^2$$

According to maximum normal stress theory, maximum normal stress on minimum cross-section is,

$$\sigma_{c\,max} = \frac{1}{2}\sigma_c + \frac{1}{2} \times \sqrt{\sigma_c^2 + 4\tau^2}$$

$$= \frac{1}{2} \times (24.06) + \frac{1}{2} \times \sqrt{(24.06)^2 + 4 \times (25.88)^2}$$

$$= \textbf{40.57 N/mm}^2$$

(3) Height of nut : It can be obtained by considering bearing pressure on the nut,

$$P_b = \frac{W}{\frac{\pi}{4}(d_o^2 - d_c^2) \times n}$$

$$\therefore \quad n = \frac{W}{\frac{\pi}{4}(d_o^2 - d_c^2) \times P_b} = \frac{10 \times 10^3}{\frac{\pi}{4}[(28)^2 - (23)^2] \times 15}$$

$$\therefore \quad n = \textbf{3.3287} \cong \textbf{4 (say)}$$

$\therefore$ Height of nut, $H = n \times p = 4 \times 5 = \textbf{20 mm}$

(4) Power required to drive the screw :

We have, $$P = \frac{2\pi NT}{60} = \frac{2\pi \times 14 \times 87.848}{60} = \textbf{128.79 watts}$$

Problem 4.16 : *A triple start square threaded screw of nominal diameter 50 mm and pitch 8 mm is used to raise a load of 50 kN. The coefficient of friction between the screw and nut is 0.12, while there is no collar friction. If the height of the nut is 40 mm, find :*

(i)   Maximum shear stress induced in the screw.

(ii)   Transverse shear stress induced in the screw and nut thread.

(iii)   Bearing pressure between screw and nut.

Solution : Given data :

$$d_o = 50 \text{ mm}, \ p = 8 \text{ mm}, \ W = 50 \text{ kN} = 50 \times 10^3 \text{ N}$$

$$\mu = 0.12, \ H = 40 \text{ mm}$$

Procedure : We have, $d_c = d_o - p = 50 - 8 = \textbf{42 mm}$

For triple start square threaded screw,

$$\text{Lead} = 3 \cdot p = 3 \times 8 = \textbf{24 mm}$$

Also, Mean diameter (d) $= \dfrac{d_o + d_c}{2} = \dfrac{50 + 42}{2} = \textbf{46 mm}$

We have, $\alpha = \tan^{-1}\left(\dfrac{\text{Lead}}{\pi d}\right) = \tan^{-1}\left(\dfrac{24}{\pi \times 46}\right) = \textbf{9.4293°}$

Also, $\phi = \tan^{-1}(\mu) = \tan^{-1}(0.12) = \textbf{6.8427°}$

Torque required to overcome the thread friction,

$$T_1 = P \times \frac{d}{2} = W \tan(\alpha + \phi)\frac{d}{2}$$

$\therefore$ $\qquad T_1 = 50 \times 10^3 \times \tan(9.4293 + 6.8427) \times \dfrac{46}{2}$

$\therefore$ $\qquad T_1 = \textbf{335.673} \times \textbf{10}^{\textbf{3}} \textbf{ N.mm}$

Torque required to overcome collar friction,

$$T_2 = 0 \qquad\qquad (\because \text{There is no collar friction})$$

$\therefore$ Total torque required to raise the load,

$$T = T_1 + T_2$$
$$= (335.673 \times 10^3) + 0 = \textbf{335.673} \times \textbf{10}^{\textbf{3}} \textbf{ N.mm}$$

(i) Maximum shear stress in the screw :

Direct compressive stress induced in screw body is,

$$\sigma_c = \frac{W}{\dfrac{\pi}{4} \times d_c^2} = \frac{50 \times 10^3}{\dfrac{\pi}{4} \times (42)^2} = \textbf{36.09 N/mm}^{\textbf{2}}$$

Torsional shear stress induced in screw is,

$$\tau = \frac{16 T_1}{\pi d_c^3} = \frac{16 \times 335.673 \times 10^3}{\pi \times (42)^3} = \textbf{23.075 N/mm}^{\textbf{2}}$$

Maximum shear stress induced in a screw body :

$$\tau_{max} = \frac{1}{2}\sqrt{\sigma_c^2 + 4\tau^2} = \frac{1}{2}\sqrt{(36.09)^2 + 4(23.075)^2}$$

$$\tau_{max} = \textbf{29.29 N/mm}^{\textbf{2}}$$

(ii) Transverse shear stress in the screw and nut threads :

We know, Height of nut (H) $= n \times p$

$\therefore$ $\qquad n = \dfrac{H}{p} = \dfrac{40}{8} = \textbf{5}$

Also, $\qquad t = \dfrac{p}{2} = \dfrac{8}{2} = \textbf{4 mm}$

Transverse shear stress in the screw threads,

$$\tau_{screw} = \frac{W}{\pi\, d_c\, n\, t} = \frac{50 \times 10^3}{\pi \times 42 \times 5 \times 4} = \mathbf{18.947\ N/mm^2}$$

Transverse shear stress in the nut threads,

$$\tau_{nut} = \frac{W}{\pi\, d_o\, n\, t} = \frac{50 \times 10^3}{\pi \times 50 \times 5 \times 4} = \mathbf{15.91\ N/mm^2}$$

(iii) Bearing pressure between nut and screw :

$$P_b = \frac{W}{\dfrac{\pi}{4}\,(d_o^2 - d_c^2) \times n} = \frac{50 \times 10^3}{\dfrac{\pi}{4} \times (50^2 - 42^2) \times 5} = \mathbf{17.3\ N/mm^2}$$

Problem 4.17 : *The construction of a shaft straightener used on the shop floor is shown in Fig. 4.11. The screw has single start square threads of 80 mm nominal diameter and 10 mm pitch. The screw is required to exert a maximum axial force of 10 kN. The mean radius of the friction collar is 30 mm. The axial length of the nut is 40 mm. The coefficient of friction at the threads and the collar is 0.12. The mean diameter of the rim of the handweel is 500 mm.*

Calculate :

(i)   The force exerted at the rim to drive the screw.

(ii)   The efficiency of the straightener and

(iii)   The bearing pressure on the threads in the nut.

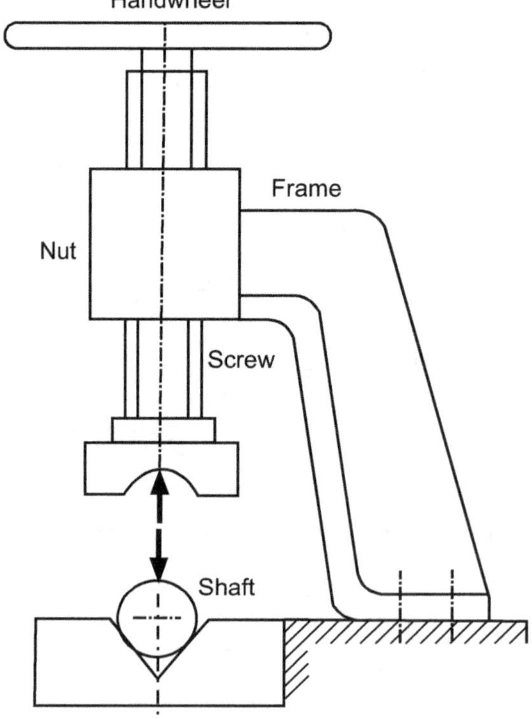

Fig. 4.11 : Shaft straightener

Solution : Given data : d_o = 80 mm, p = 10 mm, W = 10 kN = 10×10^3 N,

$\mu = \mu_1$ = 0.12, D_H = 500 mm, $\therefore$ R_H = 250 mm,

R = 30 mm, H = 40 mm

Procedure : We have, $d_c = d_o - p = 80 - 10 =$ **70 mm**

$\therefore$ Mean diameter (d) $= \dfrac{d_o + d_c}{2} = \dfrac{80 + 70}{2} =$ **75 mm**

Also, $H = n \cdot p$

$\therefore$ $n = \dfrac{H}{p} = \dfrac{40}{10} = 4$

We have, $\alpha = \tan^{-1}\left(\dfrac{p}{\pi d}\right) = \tan^{-1}\left(\dfrac{10}{\pi \times 75}\right) =$ **2.4302°**

Also, $\phi = \tan^{-1}(\mu) = \tan^{-1}(0.12) =$ **6.8427°**

Torque (T_1) required overcome the thread friction,

$$T_1 = P \times \dfrac{d}{2} = W \tan(\alpha + \phi) \times \dfrac{d}{2}$$

$$= 10 \times 10^3 \times \tan(2.4302 + 6.8427) \times \dfrac{75}{2}$$

$\therefore$ $T_1 =$ **61226.49 N.mm**

Torque (T_2) required to overcome the collar friction,

$$T_2 = \mu_1 \cdot W \cdot R = 0.12 \times 10 \times 10^3 \times 30 =$$ **36000 N.mm**

$\therefore$ Total torque required $= T_1 + T_2$

$\therefore$ $T = 61226.49 + 36000 =$ **97226.49 N.mm**

(i) The force exerted at the rim to drive the screw :

We know, Torque exerted on a screw,

$$T = P_1 \times R_H$$

$\therefore$ $97226.49 = P_1 \times 250$

$\therefore$ $P_1 = \dfrac{97226.49}{250} =$ **388.9 N**

(ii) The efficiency of the straightener :

Overall efficiency of screw,

$$\eta_o = \dfrac{T_0}{T} = \dfrac{W \cdot \tan \alpha \cdot \dfrac{d}{2}}{T}$$

$$= \dfrac{10 \times 10^3 \times \tan(2.4302) \times \dfrac{75}{2}}{97226.49} =$$ **0.1637 = 16.37%**

(iii) The bearing pressure on the threads in the nut :

$$P_b = \frac{W}{\frac{\pi}{4}(d_o^2 - d_c^2)\, n} = \frac{10 \times 10^3}{\frac{\pi}{4}(80^2 - 70^2) \times 4} = \textbf{2.122 N/mm}^2$$

Problem 4.12 : *Fig. 4.12 shows a screw clamp with a nut. Calculate :*

(1)   Diameter of screw.

(2)   Height of nut.

(3)   Dimensions of handle.

Maximum clamping force on the screw is 20 kN and the force required at the end of handle to operate the screw is 200 N. Bearing pressure is 20 N/mm². Allowable compressive stress for screw and nut is 80 MPa. Coefficient of friction between screw and nut is 0.15. Friction torque of screw pad is 40 N.m. Allowable bending stress for handle is 90 MPa. Dimensions of square threads (coarse series) in mm are given below :   **(S-07)**

Core diameter in mm	14	16	18	20	22	24
Nominal diameter in mm	22	24	26	28	30	32
Pitch in mm	8	8	8	8	8	8

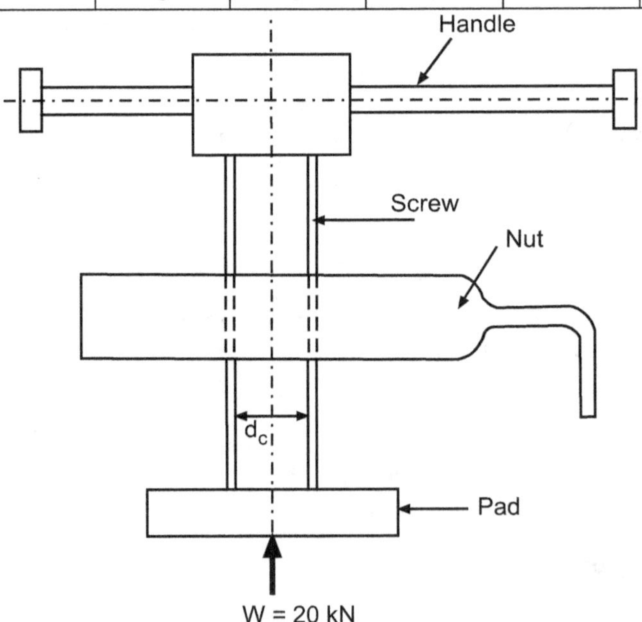

Fig. 4.12 : Screw and nut assembly with handle

Solution : Given data :   W = 20 kN = 20 × 10³ N, P_1 = 200 N,

σ_c = 80 MPa = 80 N/mm², P_b = 20 N/mm²,

μ = 0.15, T_2 = 40 N.m = 40 × 10³ N.mm,

σ_b = 90 MPa = 90 N/mm².

Procedure :

(1) Diameter of screw : Compressive stress in screw is given by,

$$\sigma_c = \frac{W}{\frac{\pi}{4} d_c^2}$$

$$\therefore \quad 80 = \frac{20 \times 10^3}{\frac{\pi}{4} \times d_c^2}$$

$$\therefore \quad d_c = \mathbf{17.84 \ mm}$$

In order to take torsional shear stress induced in the screw, value of d_c is considerably increased. From the standard table of square threads, let us assume,

$$d_o = \mathbf{30 \ mm} \quad \text{with } p = \mathbf{8 \ mm}$$

$$\therefore \quad d_c = d_o - p = 30 - 8 = \mathbf{22 \ mm}$$

$$\therefore \quad d = \frac{d_o + d_c}{2} = \frac{30 + 22}{2} = \mathbf{26 \ mm}$$

We have,
$$\tan(\alpha) = \frac{p}{\pi d}$$

$$\therefore \quad \alpha = \tan^{-1}\left(\frac{p}{\pi d}\right) = \tan^{-1}\left(\frac{8}{\pi \times 26}\right) = \mathbf{5.5937^\circ}$$

Also,
$$\tan \phi = \mu$$

$$\therefore \quad \phi = \tan^{-1}(\mu) = \tan^{-1}(0.15) = \mathbf{8.5307^\circ}$$

Torque required to overcome friction between screw and nut,

$$T_1 = P \times \frac{d}{2} = W \times \tan(\alpha + \phi) \times \frac{d}{2}$$

$$= 20 \times 10^3 \times \tan(5.5937 + 8.5307) \times \frac{26}{2}$$

$$= \mathbf{65.42 \times 10^3 \ N.mm}$$

$$\therefore \quad \text{Torsional shear stress, } \tau = \frac{16 T_1}{\pi d_c^3} = \frac{16 \times 65.42 \times 10^3}{\pi \times (22)^3} = \mathbf{31.29 \ N/mm^2}$$

Also, induced compressive stress,

$$\therefore \quad \sigma_c = \frac{W}{\frac{\pi}{4} d_c^2} = \frac{20 \times 10^3}{\frac{\pi}{4} \times (22)^2} = \mathbf{52.61 \ N/mm^2} < 80 \ N/mm^2$$

According to maximum normal stress theory,

$$\sigma_{c \ (max)} = \frac{52.61}{2} + \frac{1}{2}\sqrt{(52.61)^2 + 4\,(31.29)^2}$$

$$= \mathbf{67.18 \ N/mm^2} < 80 \ N/mm^2$$

As induced stresses are less than permissible stresses, hence design is safe.

Total torque required to overcome friction,

$$T = T_1 + T_2 \qquad [\because T_2 = 40 \text{ N.m given}]$$
$$= (65.42 \times 10^3) + (40 \times 10^3)$$
$$= \mathbf{105.42 \times 10^3 \ N.mm}$$

(2) Height of nut :

Considering bearing pressure on nut given by,

$$P_b = \frac{W}{\dfrac{\pi}{4}(d_o^2 - d_c^2) \times n}$$

$$\therefore \qquad 20 = \frac{20 \times 10^3}{\dfrac{\pi}{4} \times (30^2 - 22^2) \times n}$$

$$\therefore \qquad n = 3.06 \cong \mathbf{4 \ (say)}$$

We know,   Height of nut $(H) = n \times p = 4 \times 8 = \mathbf{32 \ mm}$

(3) Dimensions of handle :

(a) Length of handle :

Torque required at the end of handle is given by,

$$T = P_1 \times L$$
$$\therefore \qquad 105.42 \times 10^3 = 200 \times L$$
$$\therefore \qquad L = \mathbf{527.1 \ mm}$$

(b) Diameter of handle :

Considering bending stress induced in handle, we can write,

$$T = M = \frac{\pi}{32} \cdot \sigma_b \cdot D_H^3$$

$$\therefore \qquad 105.42 \times 10^3 = \frac{\pi}{32} \times 90 \times D_H^3$$

$$\therefore \qquad D_H = 22.85 \text{ mm} \cong \mathbf{23 \ mm \ (say)}$$

4.9 DESIGN OF SCREW HAVING ACME OR TRAPEZOIDAL THREADS

- In case of square threads, normal reaction is given by,

$$R_N = W \cos \alpha$$

where, α = Helix angle

- But, in case of Acme or trapezoidal threads, the normal reaction between screw and nut is increased, because the axial component of this normal reaction is equal to axial load (W).

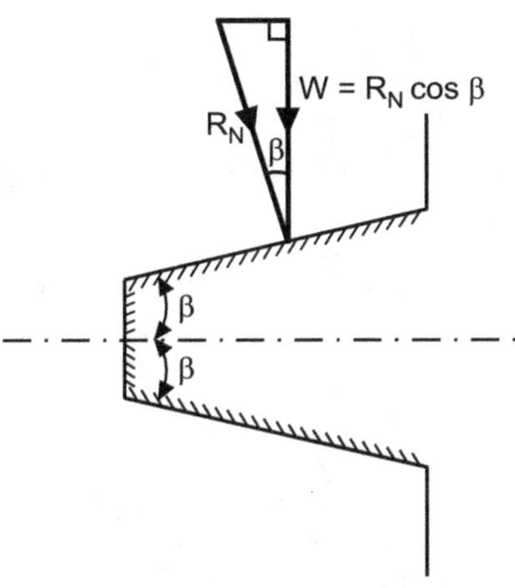

Fig. 4.13

- Let $\qquad$ 2β = Angle of Acme thread,

  and $\qquad$ β = Semi-angle of Acme thread

$\therefore \qquad W = R_N \cdot \cos \beta \quad$ or $\quad R_N = \dfrac{W}{\cos \beta}$ $\qquad\qquad$ ... (4.8)

$\therefore$ Frictional force, $\qquad F = \mu \cdot R_N = \mu \times \dfrac{W}{\cos \beta} = \mu' \cdot W$ $\qquad$ [From equation (4.8)]

where $\qquad \mu'$ = Virtual coefficient of friction $= \dfrac{\mu}{\cos \beta}$

- When virtual coefficient of friction μ' is considered, then acme thread becomes *equivalent* to a square thread.

- Therefore, in case of acme threads, μ' = **tan ϕ'** is substituted in place of μ = $tan\ \phi$.

  Thus, we have, $\qquad T_1 = W \tan (\alpha + \phi') \times \dfrac{d}{2}$

Note : *For Acme threads, $2\beta = 29°$ and for trapezoidal threads, $2\beta = 30°$.*

Numerical Type No. 4 : "Design of Acme Threads"

Problem 4.19 : *The lead screw of a lathe has Acme threads of 50 mm outside diameter and 8 mm pitch. The screw must exert an axial pressure of 2500 N in order to drive the tool carriage. The thrust is carried on a collar having 110 mm outside diameter and 55 inside diameter and lead screw rotates at 30 r.p.m. Determine :*

(i) The power required to drive the screw,

(ii) Efficiency of lead screw.

Assume $\qquad\qquad \mu = 0.15$ for screw

$\qquad\qquad\qquad\quad \mu = 0.12$ for collar $\qquad$ **(S-12; W-12)**

Solution : Given data : d_o = 50 mm, p = 8 mm, W = 2500 N, D_1 = 110 mm, D_2 = 55 mm, N = 30 r.p.m., μ = 0.15, μ_1 = 0.12.

Procedure :
$$R_1 = \frac{D_1}{2} = \frac{110}{2} = 55 \text{ mm} , \; R_2 = \frac{55}{2} = 27.5 \text{ mm}$$

$$R = \frac{R_1 + R_2}{2} = \frac{55 + 27.5}{2} = 41.25 \text{ mm}$$

And
$$d = d_o - \frac{p}{2} = 50 - \frac{8}{2} = 46 \text{ mm}$$

We have,
$$\tan \alpha = \frac{p}{\pi d}$$

$\therefore$
$$\alpha = \tan^{-1}\left(\frac{8}{\pi \times 46}\right) = 3.1685°$$

For acme threads,
$$2\beta = 29°$$

$\therefore$
$$\beta = 14.5°$$

We have,
$$\mu' = \frac{\mu}{\cos \beta} = \frac{0.15}{\cos (14.5°)} = 0.1549$$

But,
$$\mu' = \tan \phi'$$

$\therefore$
$$\phi' = \tan^{-1} (\mu') = \tan^{-1} (0.1549) = 8.8051°$$

Therefore, torque required to overcome friction between screw and nut is,
$$T_1 = W \tan (\alpha + \phi') \cdot \frac{d}{2}$$

$$= 2500 \times \tan (3.1685 + 8.8051) \times \frac{46}{2}$$

$$= \mathbf{12194.31 \text{ N.mm}}$$

Assuming uniform wear condition, torque required to overcome collar friction is given by,
$$T_2 = \mu_1 \cdot W \cdot R = 0.12 \times 2500 \times 41.25 = \mathbf{12375 \text{ N.mm}}$$

$\therefore$ Total torque required, $T = T_1 + T_2$
$$= 12194.31 + 12375$$
$$= 24569.31 \text{ N.mm} = \mathbf{24.569 \text{ N.m}}$$

(i) Power required to drive the screw,
$$P = \frac{2\pi NT}{60} = \frac{2\pi \times 30 \times 24.569}{60} = 77.18 \text{ W} = \mathbf{0.07718 \text{ kW}}$$

(ii) Efficiency of lead screw,
$$\eta = \frac{T_0}{T} = \frac{W \cdot \tan \alpha \cdot \dfrac{d}{2}}{T_1 + T_2}$$

$$= \frac{2500 \times \tan (3.1685) \times \dfrac{46}{2}}{24569.31} = 0.1295 = \mathbf{12.95\%}$$

4.10 DESIGN OF TOGGLE JACK

- Toggle jack is a type of screw jack, where maximum load is lifted with minimum effort.
- It consists of eight symmetrical links, two nuts and a screw having right hand-left hand threads.

Application :

(1)   Used for four wheelers to lift the punctured wheel.

Design Procedure :

Question

1.   Draw neat sketch of toggle jack and label its different parts.   **(W-09)**

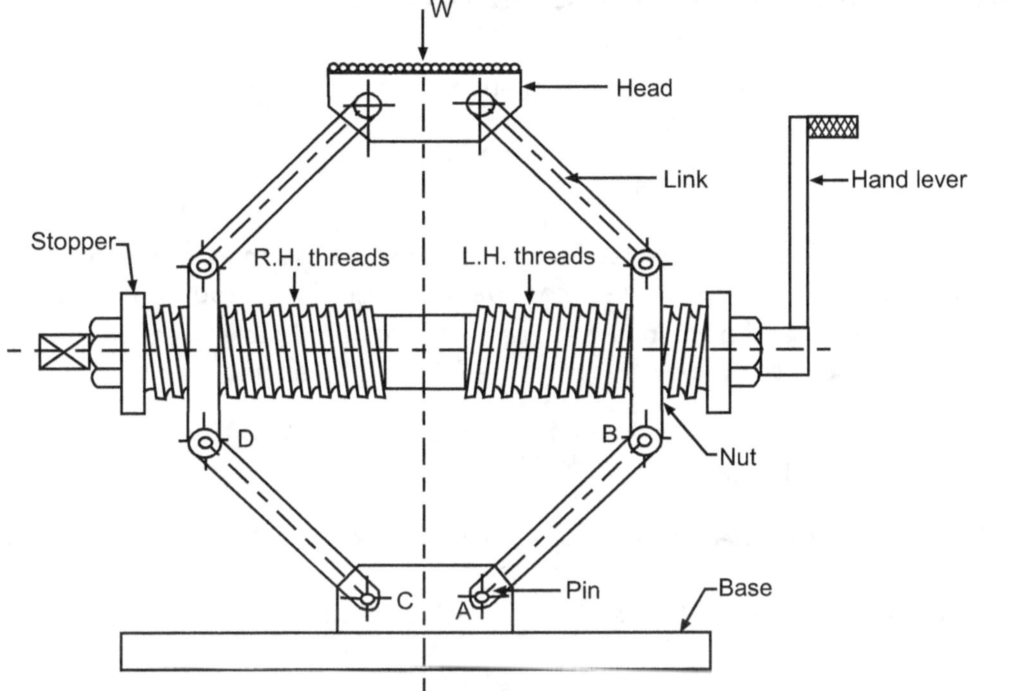

Fig. 4.14 : Toggle jack

(A) Design of Screw :

1. Find the value of W_1 :

- We know that, maximum load on the square threaded screw will occur, when the toggle jack is in its bottom position. The position of link CD is shown in Fig. 4.15.

- Suppose a pull F acts on the left nut, then another pull F of similar value will act on the other nut.

∴   Total tensile pull on the square threaded screw,

$$W_1 = 2F$$

where, $$F = \frac{W}{2 \times \tan \theta}$$

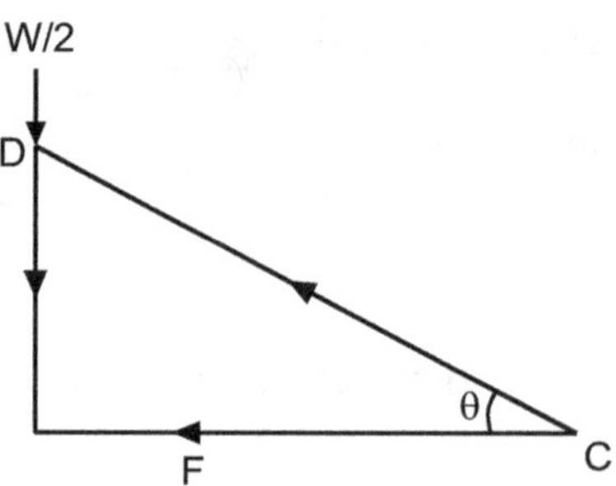

Fig. 4.15 : Position of link CD

2. Find the value of core diameter and mean diameter :

Let d_c = Core diameter of screw.

- Direct tensile or compressive stress due to axial load is given by,

$$\sigma_c = \frac{W_1}{\frac{\pi}{4} \times d_c^2}$$

- As the screw is also subjected to torsional shear stress, therefore to account for this, the value of d_c is increased considerably. For this purpose, values of nominal diameter 'd_o' and pitch 'p' are seleced from standard table of square threads. Then, find the increased value of d_c using the following relation.

$$d_c = d_o - p$$

Also, Mean diameter $= d = \dfrac{d_o + d_c}{2}$

3. Find the torsional shear stress induced due to torque 'T' required to rotate the screw :

Calculate the value of torque 'T' by following relation.

$$T = P \times \frac{d}{2} = W_1 \cdot \tan(\alpha + \phi) \times \frac{d}{2}$$

where, P = Effort required at the circumference of screw,

d = Mean diameter of screw.

Now to find the shear stress induced, use the following equation,

Torque transmitted by screw,

$$T = \frac{\pi}{16} \times \tau \times d_c^3$$

$\therefore$ Shear stress, $\tau = \dfrac{16\,T}{\pi \times d_c^3}$

4. Find the direct compressive stress induced due to axial load :

We have, $\sigma_c = \dfrac{W_1}{\frac{\pi}{4} \times d_c^2}$

5. Check maximum principal stresses :

When screw is subjected to both direct stress and (compressive) and torsional shear stress, then design is based on -

(a) Maximum shear stress theory, according to which, maximum shear stress on minimum cross-section is,

$$\tau_{max} = \frac{1}{2} \times \sqrt{\sigma_c^2 + 4\tau^2}$$

(b) Maximum normal stress theory, according to which, maximum normal stress on minimum cross-section is,

$$\sigma_{c\,max} = \frac{1}{2}\,\sigma_c + \frac{1}{2} \times \sqrt{\sigma_c^2 + 4\tau^2}$$

Check whether the principal stresses are less than permissible limits.

(B) Design of Nut :

Let n = Number of threads in contact with the nut.

To calculate the value of n, consider the bearing pressure on nut,

$$P_b = \frac{W_1}{\frac{\pi}{4}\,(d_o^2 - d_c^2) \times n}$$

$$\therefore \quad n = \frac{W_1}{\frac{\pi}{4}\,(d_o^2 - d_c^2) \times P_b}$$

To calculate the Height of nut, use following relation,

$$H = n \times p$$

Also, find thickness or width of screw, $t = \dfrac{p}{2}$

(C) Design of Pins in the Nuts :

If d_1 is the diameter of pins in the nuts, then considering the pins in double shear, we have,

Shear stress, $\quad \tau = \dfrac{F}{2 \times \left[\dfrac{\pi}{4} \times d_1^2\right]}$

From this equation, diameter of pin (d_1) can be determined.

Numerical Type No. 5 : "Design of Toggle Jack"

Problem 4.20 : *A toggle jack as shown in Fig. 4.16 is to be designed for lifting a load of 4 kN. When the jack is in its top position, the distance between the centerlines of nuts is 50 mm and in bottom position is 210 mm. The eight links of the jack are symmetrical and 110 mm long. The link pins in the base are set 30 mm apart. The links and pins are made up of mild steel, for which, the permissible stresses are 100 N/mm² in tension and 50 N/mm² in shear. The bearing pressure on the pins is limited to 20 N/mm². Assume, pitch of threads as 6 mm and coefficient of friction between threads as 0.2.*

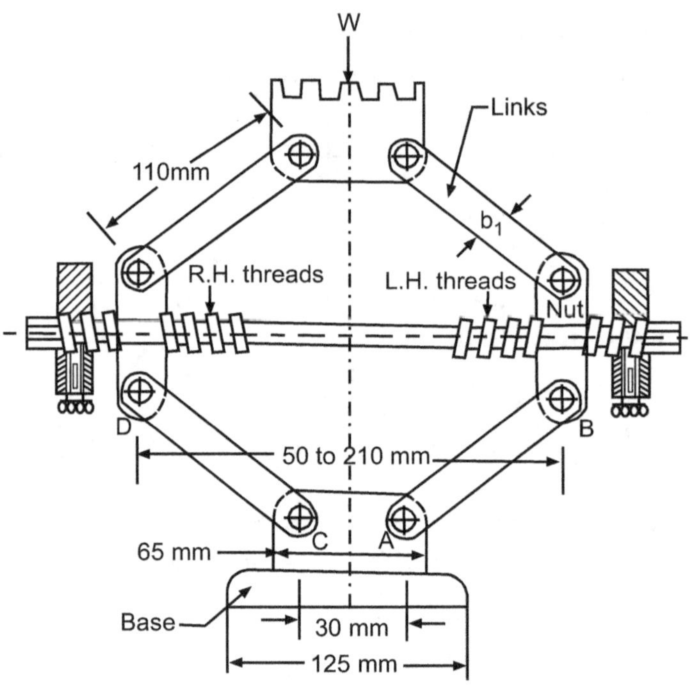

Fig. 4.16

Solution : Given data : W = 4 kN = 4000 N, l = 110 mm, p = 6 mm, μ = 0.2, σ_c = 100 N/mm², τ = 50 N/mm², P_b = 20 N/mm²

Procedure :

(1) Design of screw :

We know that, maximum load on the square threaded screw will occur, when the toggle jack is in its bottom position.

The position of link CD is shown in Fig. 4.17 (a).

Let θ = Angle of link CD made with horizontal.

$$\therefore \qquad \cos \theta \;=\; \frac{105 - 15}{110} \;=\; 0.8182$$

$$\therefore \qquad \theta \;=\; \cos^{-1}(0.8182) \;=\; \mathbf{35.094°}$$

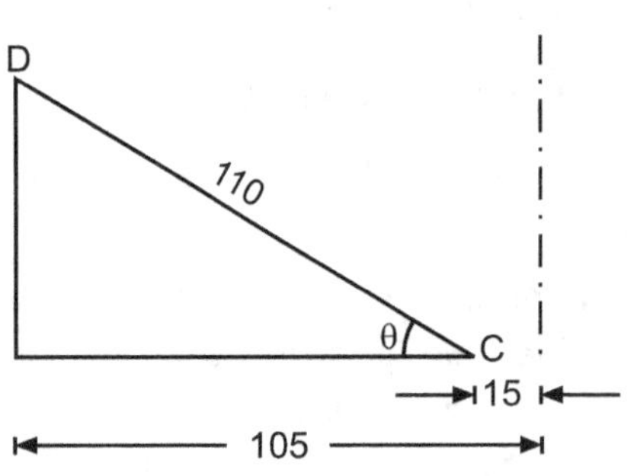

Fig. 4.17 (a)

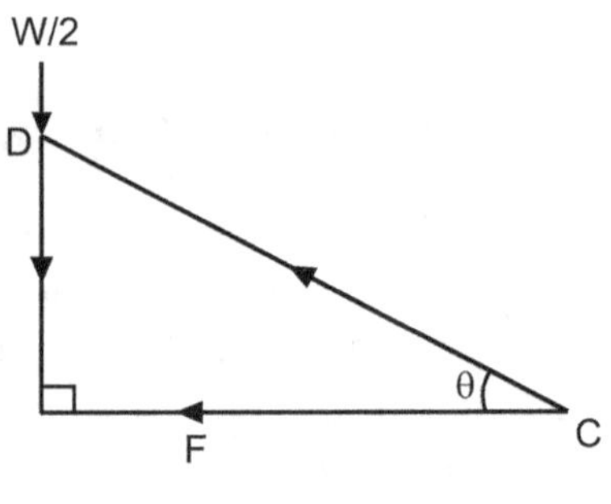

Fig. 4.17 (b)

Suppose a pull force 'F' acts on the left nut, due to which, link CD is in tension.

From Fig. 4.17 (b), we have,

$$\tan \theta = \frac{\frac{W}{2}}{F}$$

$$\therefore \quad F = \frac{W}{2 \tan \theta} = \frac{4000}{2 \times \tan (35.094)} = \textbf{2846.3 N}$$

Then another pull F of similar value will act on the other nut.

$\therefore$ Total tensile pull on the square threaded screw is given by,

$$W_1 = 2F = 2 \times 2846.3 = \textbf{5692.6 N}$$

Direct tensile or compressive stress due to axial load is given by,

$$\sigma_c = \frac{W_1}{\frac{\pi}{4} \times d_c^2}$$

$$\therefore \quad d_c^2 = \frac{W_1}{\frac{\pi}{4} \times \sigma_c} = \frac{5692.6}{\frac{\pi}{4} \times 100}$$

Thus, $d_c = 8.51$ mm $\cong$ **10 mm (say)**

As the screw is also subjected to torsional shear stress, therefore to account for this, the value of d_c is increased considerably.

$\therefore$ From standard table of square threads, let us take $d_o = 22$ mm and $p = 5$ mm

$$\therefore \quad d_c = d_o - p = 22 - 5 = \textbf{17 mm}$$

Mean diameter, $d = \dfrac{d_c + d_o}{2} = \dfrac{17 + 22}{2} = \textbf{19.5 mm}$

Also, $\tan \alpha = \dfrac{p}{\pi d}$; $\therefore$ $\alpha = \tan^{-1}\left(\dfrac{p}{\pi d}\right) = \tan^{-1}\left(\dfrac{5}{\pi \times 19.5}\right) = \textbf{4.666}°$

And, $\mu = \tan \phi$

$\therefore$ $\phi = \tan^{-1}(\mu) = \tan^{-1}(0.2) = \textbf{11.3099}°$

Torque required to rotate the screw,

$$T = P \times \frac{d}{2} = W_1 \tan (\alpha + \phi) \times \frac{d}{2}$$

$$= 5692.6 \times \tan (4.666 + 11.3099) \times \frac{19.5}{2}$$

$\therefore$ $T = \textbf{15.89} \times \textbf{10}^3 \textbf{ N-mm}$

We have,

Shear stress, $\tau = \dfrac{16\,T}{\pi \times d_c^3} = \dfrac{16 \times 15.89 \times 10^3}{\pi \times (17)^3} = \textbf{16.47 N/mm}^2 < 50 \text{ N/mm}^2$

And, Direct compressive stress, $\sigma_c = \dfrac{W_1}{\dfrac{\pi}{4} \times d_c^2} = \dfrac{5692.6}{\dfrac{\pi}{4} \times (17)^2} = $ **25.08 N/mm² < 100 N/mm²**

Also,

$$\tau_{max} = \frac{1}{2}\sqrt{\sigma_c^2 + 4\tau^2}$$

$$= \frac{1}{2}\sqrt{(25.08)^2 + 4 \times (16.47)^2} = \textbf{20.70 N/mm}^2 < 50 \text{ N/mm}^2$$

and

$$\sigma_{c\,max} = \frac{1}{2}\sigma_c + \frac{1}{2}\sqrt{\sigma_c^2 + 4\tau^2} = \frac{1}{2} \times 25.08 + \frac{1}{2}\sqrt{(25.08)^2 + 4 \times (16.47)^2}$$

$$= \textbf{33.24 N/mm}^2 < 100 \text{ N/mm}^2$$

As the induced stresses are less than permissible values, design of screw is safe.

(2) Design of nut :

We have,

$$P_b = \frac{W_1}{\dfrac{\pi}{4}(d_o^2 - d_c^2) \times n}$$

$\therefore$

$$20 = \frac{5692.6}{\dfrac{\pi}{4} \times (22^2 - 17^2) \times n}$$

$\therefore \qquad n = 1.85 \cong $ **4 (say)**

$\therefore$ Height of nut, $H = n \times p = 4 \times 5 = $ **20 mm**

(3) Design of pins : Considering failure of pins under double shear, we write,

$$\tau = \frac{F}{2 \times \dfrac{\pi}{4} d_1^2}$$

$\therefore$

$$d_1^2 = \frac{F}{2 \times \dfrac{\pi}{4} \times \tau} = \frac{2846.3}{2 \times \dfrac{\pi}{4} \times 50} = 36.24$$

$\therefore \qquad d_1 = $ **6.019 mm $\cong$ 7 mm (say)**

Practice Questions

1. Enlist the various types of power threads. Give at least one practical application for each type. Discuss their relative advantages and disadvantages.
2. Why are square threads preferable over V-threads for power transmission ?
3. What do you understand by overhauling of screws ?
4. What is self locking property of threads and where it is necessary ?
5. Explain "Efficiency of power screw".
6. Show that the efficiency of self locking screw is less than 50 %.
7. Explain "How to improve efficiency of power screw ?"
8. Obtain the expression for efficiency and maximum efficiency for square threaded screw.
9. Explain design procedure of screw jack with neat sketch.
10. Explain design procedure of toggle jack with neat sketch.

Problems for Practice

1. The lead screw of a lathe machine, having square thread is required to exert an axial force of 15 kN to the carriage. The coefficient of friction at the screw and collar are 0.1 and 0.15 respectively. Assume compressive stress and shear stress for screw material as 60 MPa and 33.33 MPa respectively, whereas bearing pressure on thread = 10 MPa. Design the screw and nut. If mean diameter of collar is 100 mm and screw rotates at 32 r.p.m., find power required to drive it. **(S-04)**

   (**Ans.** d_o = 30 mm, p = 6 mm, n = 6, H = 36 mm, P = 0.493 kW)

2. A screw jack carries a load of 25 kN. If the co-efficient of friction between screw and nut is 0.15, design the screw and nut. Neglect collar friction and column action. Take σ_c = 42 N/mm^2 and τ = 30 N/mm^2 for screw and take τ_{nut} = 20 N/mm^2. The permissible bearing pressure on the nut is 14 N/mm^2. (Use single start thread).

   (S-09)

   (**Ans :** d_o = 46 mm, p = 8 mm, d = 42 mm, n = 4, t = 4 mm, H = 32 mm)

3. A lead screw of a lathe has square threads of 24 mm outside diameter and 5 mm pitch. It supplies drive to a tool carriage, which needs an axial force of 2500 N. A collar bearing with inner and outer radii as 15 mm and 30 mm respectively is provided. The coefficient of friction for screw threads is 0.12 and for collar is 0.1. Find the torque required to drive the screw and the efficiency of the screw.

   If the lead screw rotates at 30 r.p.m., find the power required to drive the screw.

   (**Ans.** T = 10.886 N.m, P = 34.199 kW, η = 18.27%)

4. In a machine tool application, the tool holder is pulled by means of an operating nut mounted on a screw. The tool holder travels at a speed of 5 m/min. The screw has single start square threads of 48 mm nominal diameter and 8 mm pitch. The operating nut exerts a force of 500 N to drive the tool holder. The mean radius of the friction collar is 40 mm. The coefficient of friction at thread and collar surfaces is 0.15. Calculate :

   (i) Power required to drive the screw.

   (ii) The efficiency of the mechanism.   (**Ans.** (i) 0.35 kW, (ii) 12%)

5. A 50 kN capacity screw jack consists of a square threaded steel screw meshing with a bronze nut. The nominal diameter is 60 mm and the pitch is 9 mm. The permissible bearing pressure is 10 N/mm^2. Calculate :

   (i) The length of the nut.

   (ii) The transverse shear stress in the nut.   (**Ans.** (i) 63 mm, (ii) 8.42 N/mm^2)

6. A vertical double start square threaded screw of 80 mm outside diameter and 14 mm pitch, supports a vertical load of 1.5 kN. The axial thrust on screw is taken up by collar bearing having outside diameter as 200 mm and inside diameter as 73 mm. Assuming uniform pressure condition, find the force required at the end of lever 500 mm long to raise and lower the load. Take coefficient of friction as 0.15 for screw and 0.20 for collar.   (**Ans.** (i) P_1 = 74.29 N and (ii) P_1 = 47.41 N) **(W-06)**

MSBTE Questions and Answers

Summer 2013

1. State the meaning of power screw. **(2 M)**

Ans. Refer Article 4.1.

2. An electric motor driven power screw moves a nut in a horizontal plane against a force of 100 kN at a speed of 360 mm/min. Screw has pitch 8 mm on a major diameter 50 mm. Coefficient of friction is 0.15. Estimate power of the motor. **(4 M)**

Ans. Refer Problem 4.2.

3. A vertical 2-start square threaded screw of 120 mm mean diameter and 24 mm pitch supports a vertical load of 20 kN. The axial thrust on the screw is taken by a collar bearing of 300 mm outside diameter and 150 mm inside diameter. Find the force required at the end of the lever, which is 400 mm long in order to lift and lower the load. Coefficient of friction for screw and nut is 0.18 and for collar bearing is 0.25. **(8 M)**

Ans. Refer Problem 4.8.

4. State the meaning with respect to screw :(i) Overhauling, (ii) Self-locking.

Ans. Refer Article 4.7.3.

Winter 2013

1. Enlist four advantages of power screws. **(4 M)**

Ans. Refer Article 4.1.1.

2. The lead screw of lathe has square threads of 24 mm outside diameter and 5 mm pitch. In order to drive the tool carriage, the screw exerts an axial pressure of 2.5 kN. Find the efficiency of the screw and power required to drive the screw, if it is to rotate at 300 r.p.m. Neglecting bearing friction, assume coefficient of friction of screw threads as 0.12. **(8 M)**

Ans. Refer Problem 4.1.

3. What is self locking of screw? What are the conditions of self locking? **(4 M)**

Ans. Refer Article 4.7.3.

Summer 2014

1. Explain the meaning of self-locking and overhauling of screw. **(4 M)**

Ans. Refer Article 4.7.3.

2. A double start square threaded power screw of nominal diameter 100 mm and pitch 12 mm is to be used to raise a load of 300 kN. The coefficient of friction at screw thread is 0.15. Neglect collar friction. Calculate torque required to raise the load and efficiency of the screw. **(8 M)**

Ans. Refer Problem 4.3.

3. Give the design procedure of screw and nut of a screw jack. **(8 M)**

Ans. Refer Article 4.8.

4. What are the advantages and disadvantages of 'V' thread over square thread? **(4 M)**

Ans. Refer Article 4.2.1.3.

Chapter 5

DESIGN OF SPRINGS

About This Chapter

This chapter has a weightage of 12 marks and assigned duration is 8 hours. In this chapter, we learn functions and applications of springs, classification and advantages of springs, materials used for springs, different types of springs, stresses in springs, Deflection and energy stored in springs, construction of leaf spring and applications.

Statistical Analysis

Examination	Weightage of questions asked
S-09	08 Marks
W-09	12 Marks
S-10	08 Marks
W-10	04 Marks
S-11	08 Marks
W-11	12 Marks
S-12	16 Marks
W-12	18 Marks
S-13	18 Marks
W-13	20 Marks
S-14	16 Marks

5.1 INRODUCTION TO SPRING

- A *spring* is an elastic body, whose primary function is to deflect or distort under the application of load. When the load is removed, the spring restores its original shape.

5.1.1 Functions of Spring

Question

1. State any four functions of spring. **(W-09; S-14)**

   (a) To cushion, absorb or control energy due to either shock or vibration as in car spring, railway buffers, shock absorbers and vibration dampers.

   (b) To apply forces, as in brakes, clutches and spring loaded valves.

(c)	To measure forces, as in spring balances and engine.

(d)	To store energy, as in watches, toys etc.

(e)	To control motion by maintaining contact between two elements.

(f)	To change the vibration characteristics of a member as in flexible mounting of motors.

5.1.2 Applications of Springs

(a)	Car springs, railway buffers, shock absorbers, vibration dampers.

(b)	Brakes, clutches and spring loaded valves.

(c)	Watches, toys etc.

(d)	Spring balances, gauges, engines.

(e)	To provide clamping force in jigs and fixtures.

Sr. no.	Type of Spring	Applications
1.	Helical spring	Engine valve mechanism.
2.	Torsion spring	Clock and watches.
3.	Leaf springs	Automobiles.
4.	Belleville springs	Used, where high spring rates are needed.
5.	Conical and volute springs	Used, where increasing spring rate is desired with change in load.

5.1.3 Classification of Springs

Question

1.	How springs are classified ?	**(W-13)**

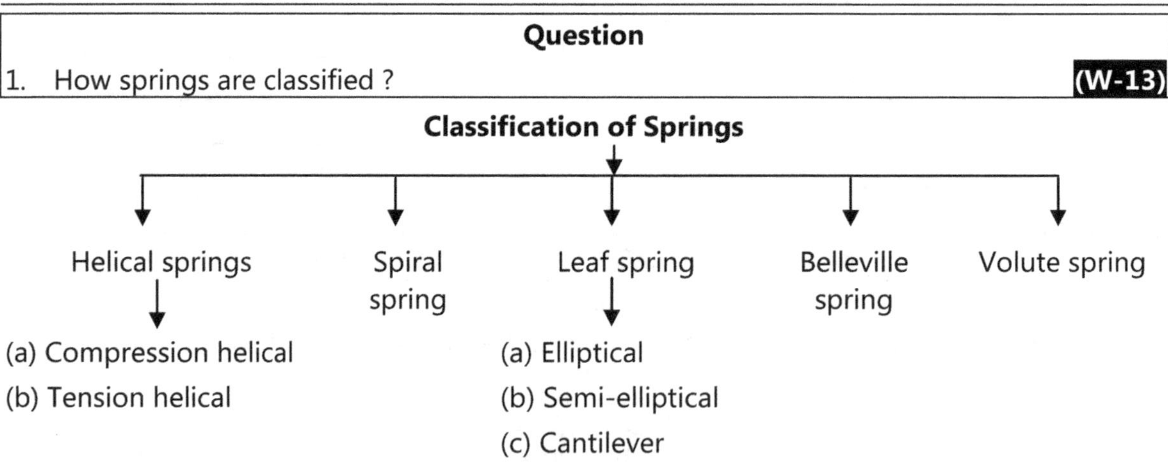

•	The various types of springs classified according to their shape are described below :

**1.	Helical Springs :**

•	They are made of a wire in the form of helix.

•	The cross-section may be circular, square and rectangular depending upon the type of loading and deflection required.

- The load applied on the spring is along the axis of helix. Here, the major stress induced is shear stress due to twisting.

- Depending on the type of axial force, the spring has to withstand, helical spring is further classified as :

(i) Helical Compression Spring :

- They take axial compressive load.

- The coils of spring are separate from each other.

Applications :

(a) Clutches.

(b) Brakes.

(c) Valve mechanisms of I.C. engines.

(d) Telescopic shock absorbers.

(ii) Helical Tension Spring :

- They take axial tensile load.

- The coils of spring are held closed to each other.

Applications :

(a) Spring loaded safety valve.

(b) Spring balances.

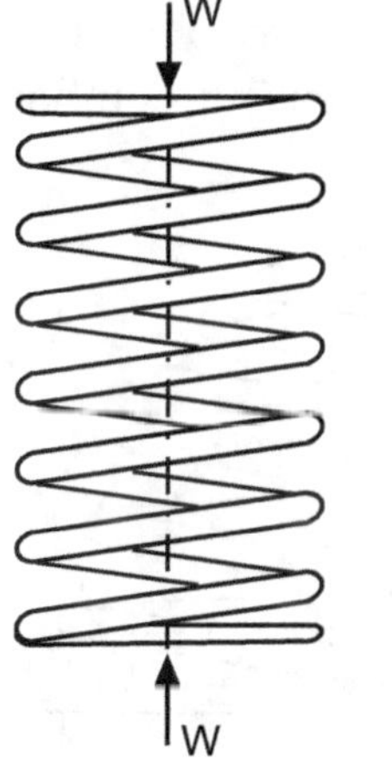

(a) Helical compression spring

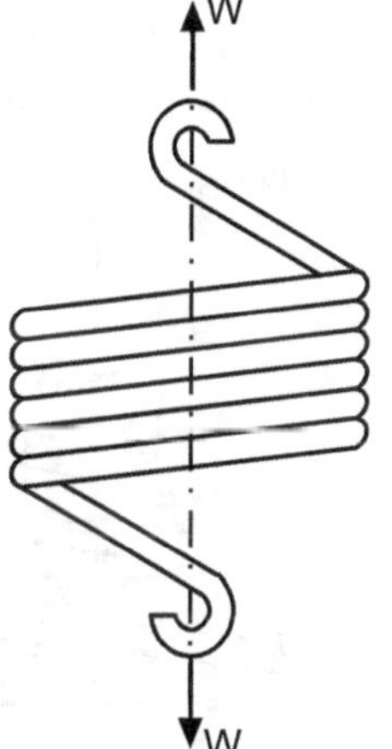

(b) Helical tension spring

Fig. 5.1

- Depending upon the value of helix angle, helical springs are also classified as :

(i) Closed Coiled Helical Springs :

- Here, the helix angle is very small. Usually its value is less than 10°. The plane containing each coil is nearly perpendicular to the axis of helix.

- The coils are so close that, there exists a small gap between the two adjacent coils.

(ii) Open Coiled Helical Springs :

- Here, the helix angle is more than 10°.
- The spring wire is so coiled that, there is a large gap between two adjacent coils.

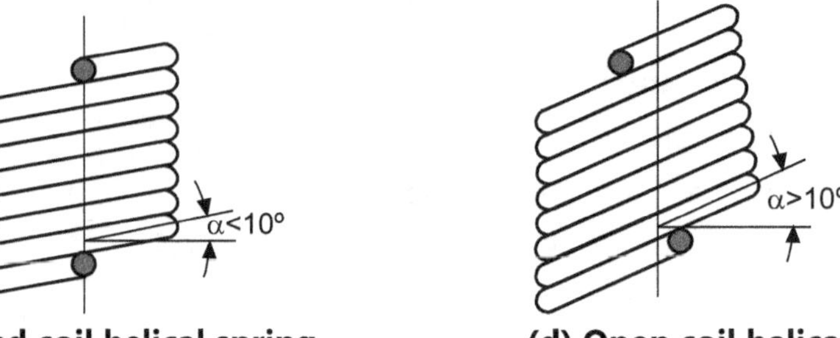

(c) Closed coil helical spring   **(d) Open coil helical spring**

Fig. 5.1

2. Conical and Volute Springs :

- Here, the coils are arranged in the shape of frustum of cone.
- They may be rectangular or round in section.
- When it is loaded axially, each element of spring behaves like a curved bar in tension.
- They are used, when increasing spring rate or stiffness is desired with the load.
- The conical spring is wound with uniform pitch, whereas the volute springs are wound in the form of parabolid (parabolic shape) with constant pitch and lead angles.
- The spring may be either partially or completely telescoping. In both cases, the number of active coils gradually decreases. The decreasing number of coils results in an increasing spring rate.

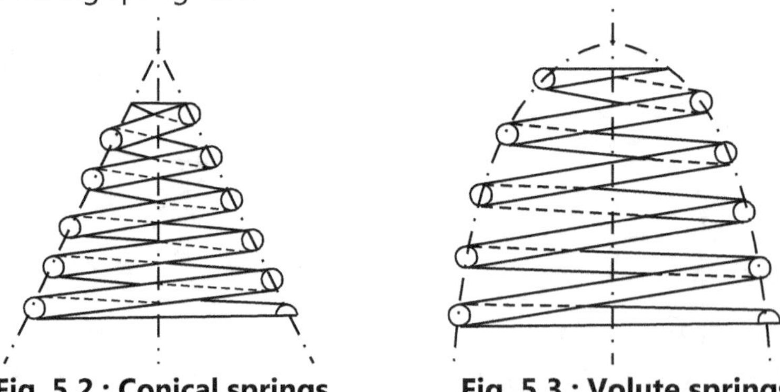

Fig. 5.2 : Conical springs   **Fig. 5.3 : Volute springs**

Applications :

- They are used to support a body, which has a varying mass, causing vibration problems.

3. Torsional Springs :

- They may be classified as helical or spiral type.
- Spiral springs are made of flat strip wound in the form of spiral and loaded in torsion.

- Helical torsional springs are manufactured by wounding a wire like compression spring and load is applied tangentially. They are subjected to torque about the central axis of spring coil. This induces bending stress in the wire.

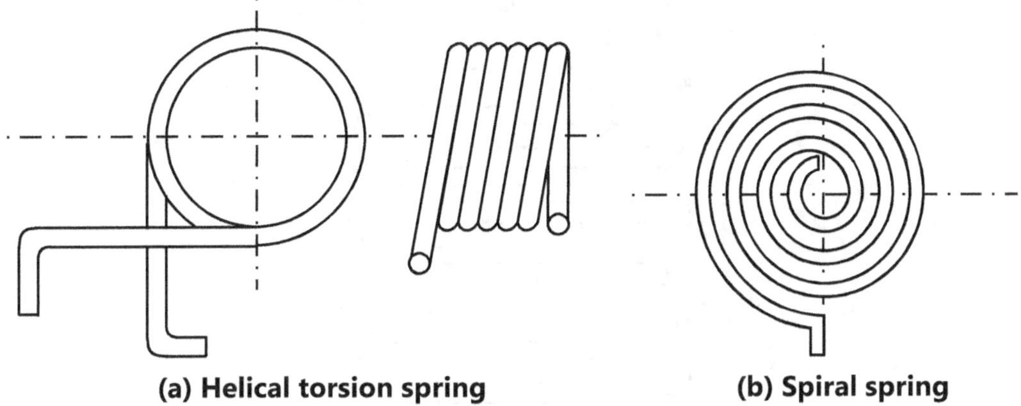

(a) Helical torsion spring   **(b) Spiral spring**

Fig. 5.4 : Torsional spring

Applications :

(1) Spiral torsional springs :

    (a) Mechanical watches.   (b) Clocks.

(2) Helical torsional springs :

    (a) Door hinges.   (b) Automobile starters.

4. Leaf Spring :

- A leaf spring is of semi-elliptical form and consists of number of leaves held together by means of clamps and bolts.

- These springs may carry lateral loads, brake torque, driving torque, in addition to shocks.

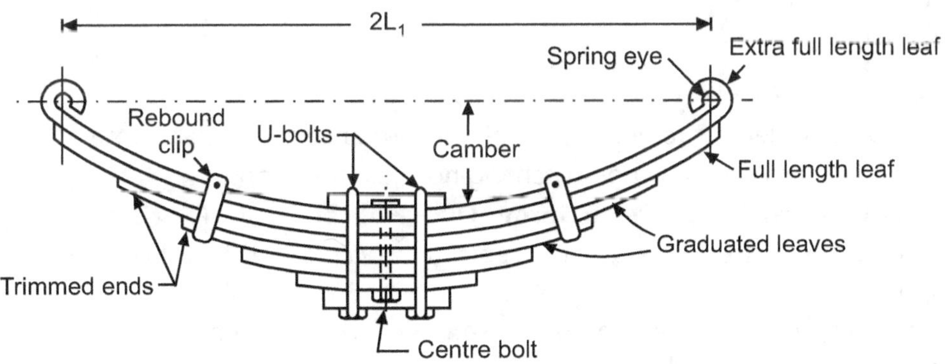

Fig. 5.5 : Leaf spring

Applications :

(S-12)

- Automobile suspension system.

- Shock absorber in railways.

5. Belleville Springs :

- It consists of several annular discs of conical shape.

Fig. 5.6 : Belleville spring

- They are stacked up one on top of other, in order to increase the deflection.
- The desired load deflection characteristics can be obtained by using number of conical discs.
- They are used, where high capacity compression springs must fit into small spaces i.e. higher spring stiffness is desired.

5.1.4 Advantages of Different Springs

Advantages of Helical Spring :

- Easy to manufacture.
- Available in wide range.
- Constant spring rate.
- Reliable and hence prediction of their performance is more accurate.
- Characteristics can be varied by changing the dimensions.

Advantages of Helical Compression Spring Over Helical Tension Spring :

(a) As no hook is used, very less concentration occurs at the end coils of compression spring.

(b) Tension springs are likely to be stressed beyond elastic limit. In case of compression springs, the coils touch each other.

Advantages of Torsional and Spiral Spring :

(a) They store more strain energy.

(b) They are used in transmission of small torque.

(c) Compact and occupy less space.

5.1.5 (a) Difference between a Close Coiled and Open Coiled Helical Spring

Close coiled helical spring	Open coiled helical spring
1. In this type of spring, the spring wire is coiled, so close that, the plane containing each turn is nearly right angles to the axis of helix.	1. In this type of spring, the spring wire is coiled, such that, there is considerable gap between two consecutive turns.
2. This type of spring is subjected to torsion.	2. This type of spring can take up compressive loads in addition to torsion.

5.1.5 (b) Difference between Tension Spring and Torsion Spring

Tension spring	Torsion spring
1. This type of spring is provided with hooks at the ends. The hooks may be made by turning whole coil or half of the coil.	1. This type of spring is wound in a similar way as tension spring, but the ends are shaped, so as to transmit torque.
2. This type of spring is primarily subjected to torsional shear stresses.	2. This type of spring is primarily subjected to bending stress.
3. They are used, where constant spring rate is required.	3. They are used for transmitting torques in door hinges, automobile starters etc.

5.1.6 Terms used in Helical Spring

Questions

1. Define spring index and spring stiffness. **(S-09; W-11, 12)**
2. Define : (a) Spring index, (b) Spring stiffness, (c) Free length, (d) Solid length. **(S-10, 11)**
3. Define : (a) Spring index, (b) Spring rate, (c) Free length, (d) Pitch. **(W-13)**

1. Solid height / Solid length :   **(S-10, 11)**
- When compression spring is compressed until the coils come in contact with each other, then spring is said to be solid.
- *"The solid length of a spring is the product of total number of coils and diameter of wire"*.
- Mathematically, Solid length $= L_s = n' \times d$

   where,

   n' = Total number of coils

   d = Diameter of spring wire.

2. Free length :   **(S-10, 11)**
- *"Free length is the length of spring, when the spring is in free or unloaded condition.*
- Free length = Solid length + $\begin{bmatrix} \text{Max. deflection} \\ \text{(Compression)} \end{bmatrix}$ + $\begin{bmatrix} \text{Clearance between} \\ \text{adjacent coils} \end{bmatrix}$
- $L_f = n' \cdot d + \delta_{max} + 0.15\, \delta_{max}$

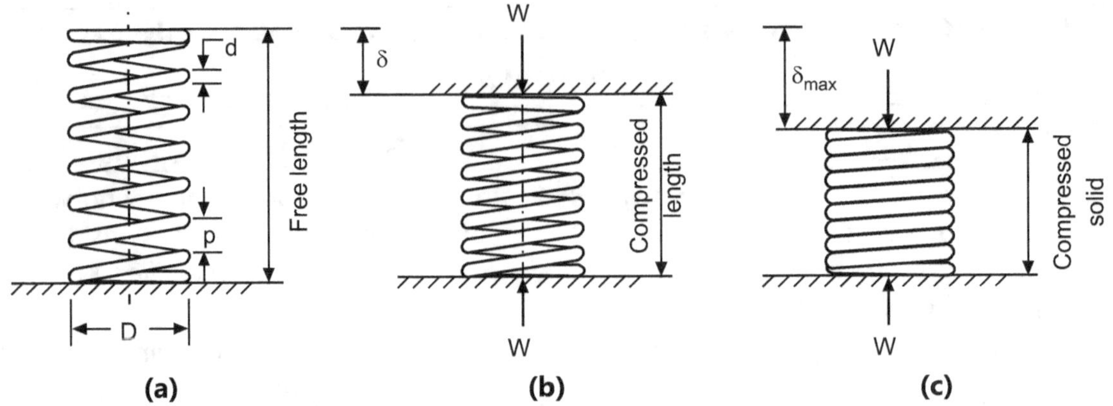

Fig. 5.7 : Nomenclature of helical compression spring

3. **Spring index :**

   - *Spring index is defined as "the ratio of mean diameter of coil to the diameter of spring wire".*

   - Mathematically, $\quad C = \dfrac{D}{d}$

   - Generally, the value of spring index is taken from 5 to 10.

4. **Spring rate / Stiffness / Spring constant :**

   - *Stiffness is defined as "the load required per unit deflection of the spring".*

   - Stiffness or Spring rate $= \dfrac{W}{\delta}$

5. **Pitch :**

   - *Pitch is defined as "the axial distance between adjacent coils in uncompressed state".*

   - Pitch of the coil $\quad = p = \dfrac{\text{Free length}}{n' - 1}$

5.1.7 (a) Material used for Springs

Question

1. State any two materials for helical spring. Write any two properties of these materials.

(W-04, 07)

   - The various materials used for spring are :

   (a) Plain carbon steel.

   (b) Alloy steels.

   (c) Corrosion resistant steel.

   (d) Non-ferrous spring materials such as phosphor bronze, brass, nickel alloys and beryllium copper.

   - The selection of material depends on the specific applications and service conditions, such as the static load and fluctuating load.

- Some of the spring steels are :

(a) Patented and cold drawn steel wires of Grade I, II, III and IV.

(b) Oil hardened and tempered spring steel wires :

    (i) Chromium – Vanadium spring steel with Cr-1.5%, V-0.2%, C-0.35% to 5%.

    (ii) Silicon – Manganese spring steel with Si-2%, Mn-1%, C-0.6 to 1.2%.

- The springs are commonly made from high carbon steel with carbon 0.7 to 1%, medium carbon alloy steels, phosphor bronze, brass.

5.1.7 (b) Desirable Properties of Spring Materials

Question

1. State four properties of a good spring material.   **(S-13)**

    (a) High resilience.

    (b) Ductile.

    (c) High static strength.

    (d) High fatigue strength.

    (e) Non-corrosive.

5.1.7 (c) Manufacturing of Springs

- Springs are manufactured either by hot or cold working processes, depending upon the size of the wire, spring index and the kind of properties desired.
- Small size springs are cold wound, while the large size springs are hot wound. During winding, residual stresses are induced in wires. A suitable heat treatment process like annealing is carried out to relieve these stresses. It should be remembered that, pre-hardened wire should not be used for springs with spring index, $C = \dfrac{D}{d} < 4$.
- Springs are heat treated in different ways, depending upon the final mechanical properties desired in the material, such as oil quenching followed by tempering to adjust the hardness of wire. Care must be taken to avoid formation of cracks due to quenching.
- For inducing greater resilience and toughness in the spring wire, special toughing treatments are carried out.

5.1.8 (a) Types of Spring Ends for Helical Compresion Springs

(S-07)

- The end connections for helical compression springs are suitably formed in order to apply the load. In springs, the end coils produce an eccentric application of load, increasing stress on one side of spring. When the length of spring is small, this effect must be taken into consideration.

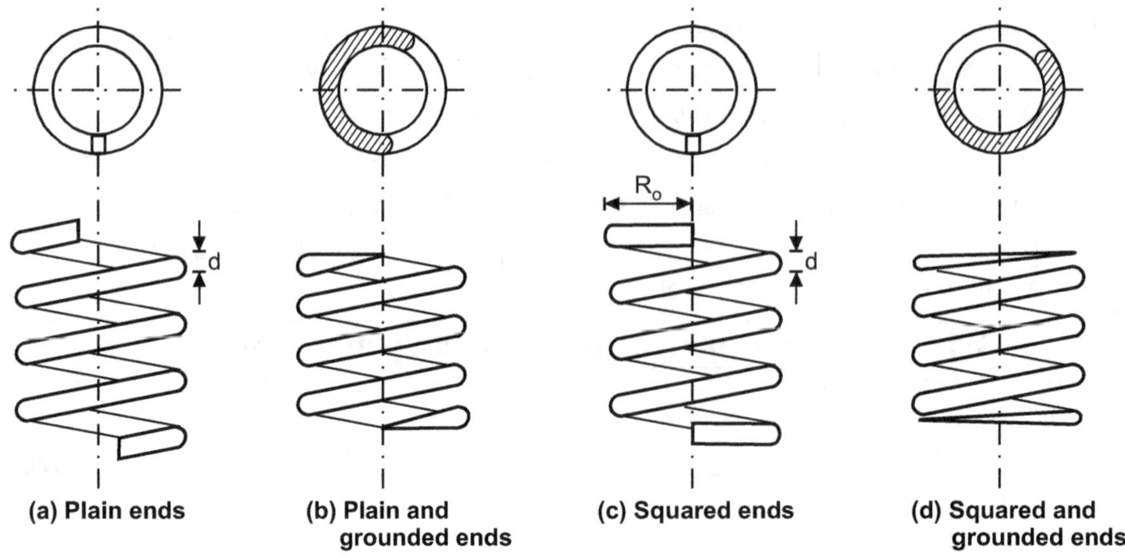

Fig. 5.8 : Types of ends

- The commonly used spring ends are of four types as under.

(a) Plain ends : In this, the load axis does not coincide with the axis of load. Hence, they are not much used in practice.

(b) Plain and grounded ends : In this, grounding the ends eliminates the drawback of plain ends. The total seat area is sufficient for the spring support.

(c) Squared ends : In this, the end coils are pressed, such that, they become square to the axis of spring. Due to this, total seat area for spring support increases. But, as the ends are not grounded, proper seating is not available.

(d) Squared and grounded ends : In this, nearest approach to axial loading is secured by the use of squared and grounded ends. Thus, they are widely used in helical compression springs.

Inactive turns : The part of coil, which is in contact with seat and do not contribute in spring action, is said to be inactive. The turns involved are called as *inactive turns*.

Active turns (n) : The turns, which take part in spring action, are called as *active turns*.

Types of end	Total number of turns (n')
Plain ends	n
Plain and grounded ends	n
Squared ends	n + 2
Squared and Grounded ends	n + 2

where, n = number of active turns or coils.

5.1.8 (b) Types of Ends for Helical Tension Spring

- The design of helical tension spring differs from design of helical compression due to,

    (a) Types of spring ends.

    (b) Bending stress in tension springs.

    (c) Initial tension in the springs.

- In case of helical tension springs, the ends are formed like hooks for applying the loads, so that, the stress concentration effects caused due to presence of bends are minimized.

- Fig. 5.9 shows different types of ends for tension loading.

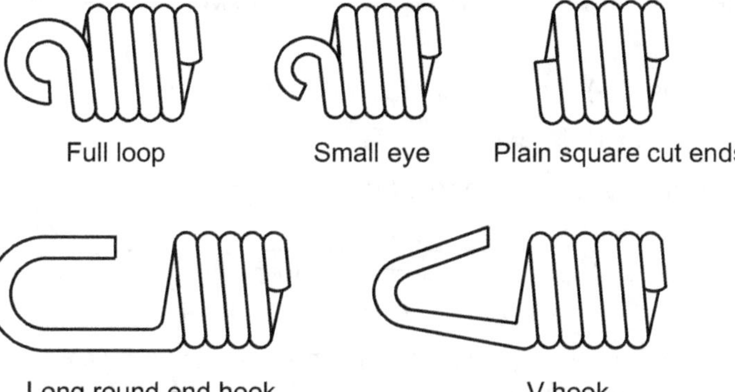

Fig. 5.9 : Spring ends for helical tension spring

- Here, all coils are active coils.

    Therefore, total number of coils (n') = Number of active coils (n).

5.2 DESIGN OF HELICAL SPRING

5.2.1 Stresses in Helical Springs

- Consider a helical compression spring of circular cross-section subjected to an axial load, as shown in Fig. 5.10.

    Let,

    D = Mean diameter of spring coil

    d = Diameter of spring wire

    n = Number of active coils

    G = Modulus of rigidity for spring material

    W = Axial load on the spring

    τ = Maximum shear stress induced in the wire

    C = Spring index = $\dfrac{D}{d}$

    p = Pitch of spring coil

    δ = Axial deflection of the spring

- The axial load 'W' tends to produce twisting moment in the wire, so torsional shear stress 'τ_1' is induced in the wire. The torsional moment or torque is given by,

$$T = W \times \frac{D}{2}$$

Also,

$$T = \frac{\pi}{16}\,\tau_1 d^3$$

Equating the above two equations, we get,

$$\tau_1 = \frac{8\,WD}{\pi d^3}$$

$$\dots \text{(Neglecting the stress due to curvature of wire)} \dots (5.1)$$

- In addition to the torsional shear stress (τ_1), the following stresses are also induced in the wire.

    (a) Direct shear stress (τ_2) due to axial load W.

    (b) Stress due to curvature of wire.

- The direct shear stress (τ_2) due to load W is given by,

$$\tau_2 = \frac{\text{Load}}{\text{Cross-sectional area}} = \frac{W}{\frac{\pi}{4}\cdot d^2} = \frac{4W}{\pi \cdot d^2} \qquad \dots (5.2)$$

- From equation (5.1) and (5.2), the resultant shear stress (τ) can be determined as, algebraic sum of two shear stresses.

$$\tau = \tau_1 + \tau_2$$

$$\therefore \qquad \tau = \frac{8\,WD}{\pi d^3} + \frac{4W}{\pi d^2} = \frac{8\,WD}{\pi d^3}\cdot\left(1 + \frac{d}{2D}\right)$$

$$= \frac{8\,WD}{\pi d^3}\cdot\left(1 + \frac{1}{2C}\right) \qquad\qquad \left(\because C = \frac{D}{d}\right)$$

$$\therefore \qquad \tau = K_s \cdot \frac{8\,WD}{\pi d^3} \qquad\qquad \dots (5.3)$$

where, $\qquad\qquad K_s$ = Shear stress factor = $1 + \dfrac{1}{2C}$

and $\qquad\qquad C$ = Spring index = $\dfrac{D}{d}$

- When the stress due to curvature of wire is to be considered, equation (5.3) is modified as,

$$\tau = K\cdot\frac{8\,WD}{\pi d^3} \;\text{ or }\; K\cdot\frac{8\,WC}{\pi d^2} \qquad\qquad \left(\because C = \frac{D}{d}\right)$$

where, $\qquad\qquad K$ = Wahl's stress concentration factor

and is given by, $\qquad\qquad K = \dfrac{4C-1}{4C-4} + \dfrac{0.615}{C}$

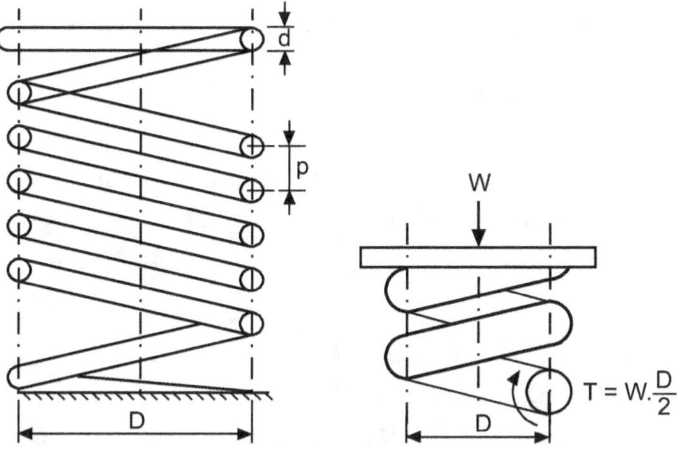

Fig. 5.10 : Stresses in helical springs

5.2.2 Wahl's Correction Factor

Questions

1. Explain Wahl's stress factor.   (S-09, 14)
2. State the significance of Wahl's correction factor.   (S-10, 12)

- In order to find the dimensions of spring, the maximum shear stress induced in the wire is considered, which is given by,

$$\tau = K_s \times \frac{8\,WD}{\pi d^3} \qquad \ldots (5.4)$$

where, K_s = Shear stress factor or shear multiplication factor

$$= 1 + \frac{1}{2C}$$

- In the above equation (5.4), we have taken into consideration the torsional shear stress and direct shear stress due to direct load W.
- But, we have neglected the stress due to curvature of wire.
- When a bar is bent in the form of helical coil, the curvature of coil increases stress on inside of the spring and at the same time, decreases stress on outside of spring. Thus, the length of inner fiber is less than the length of outer fiber.
- This results in stress concentration at the inside fiber of coil. And this curvature effect is considerably larger for high values of spring index. Therefore, a *Wahl's stress factor* is introduced in the equation (5.4).
- Equation (5.4) is modified as,

$$\tau = K \times \frac{8\,WD}{\pi d^3}$$

where,   K = Wahl's stress factor or Wahl's correction factor or spring stress factor

and is given by, $K = \dfrac{4C-1}{4C-4} + \dfrac{0.615}{C}$

- Wahl's correction factor may also be considered as composed of two sub-factors K_s and K_c, such that,

$$K = K_s \cdot K_c$$

where, K_s = Shear stress factor

K_c = Stress concentration factor due to wire curvature

Table 5.1 : Values of Wahl's stress factor for varying spring index

Spring index 'C'	Whal's stress factor
3	1.58
4	1.4
5	1.31
6	1.25
7	1.21
8	1.18
9	1.16
10	1.14

Note : Put the values of C as 3 to 16 and obtain the values of K from the formula,

$$K = \frac{4C - 1}{4C - 4} + \frac{0.615}{C} \text{ and plot accordingly.}$$

- Following graph shows the variation of Wahl's stress concentration factor with spring index.

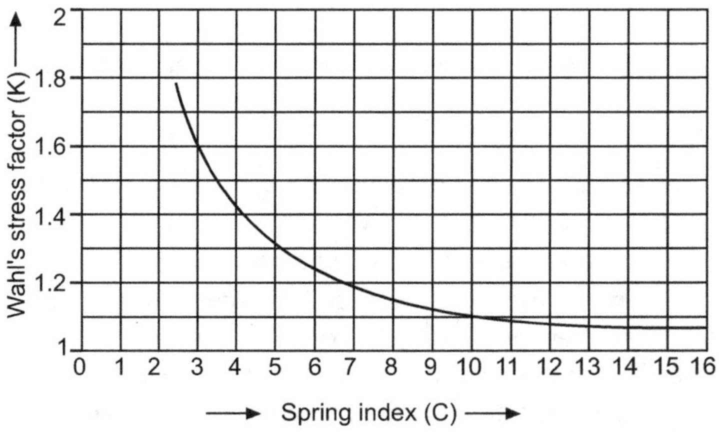

Fig. 5.11 : Graph of Wahl's stress factor versus spring index

5.2.3 Deflection of a Helical Compression Spring

Let,   D = Mean diameter of spring coil

n = Number of active coils

Therefore, Total active length of wire,

L = (Length of one coil) × (Number of active coils)

∴ $L = \pi D \cdot n$ ... (5.5)

- The twisting moment or torque developed due to axial load W is given by,

$$T = W \times \frac{D}{2} \qquad \qquad \text{... (5.6)}$$

- Let, $\qquad\qquad \theta$ = Angular deflection of wire, when subjected to torque T

Also, $\qquad\qquad J$ = Polar M.I. of spring wire $= \dfrac{\pi}{32} d^4 \qquad \qquad \text{... (5.7)}$

∴ Axial deflection of spring,

$$\delta = \theta \times \frac{D}{2} \qquad \qquad \text{... (5.8)}$$

- From basic torsion equation, we have,

$$\frac{T}{J} = \frac{G\theta}{L}$$

∴ $\qquad\qquad \theta = \dfrac{T \cdot L}{G \cdot J}$

∴ $\qquad\qquad \theta = \dfrac{W \times \dfrac{D}{2} \times \pi D n}{G \cdot \left(\dfrac{\pi}{32} d^4\right)} \qquad$ [From equations (5.5), (5.6) and (5.7)]

∴ $\qquad\qquad \theta = \dfrac{16\,WD^2 n}{Gd^4}$

Put this value of θ in equation (5.8),

$$\delta = \frac{16\,WD^2 n}{Gd^4} \times \frac{D}{2} = \frac{8\,WD^3 n}{Gd^4}$$

or $\qquad\qquad \delta = \dfrac{8\,WC^3 n}{Gd} \qquad\qquad \left(\because C = \dfrac{D}{d}\right)$

Note : If deflection per active turn is to be calculated, take $\dfrac{\delta}{n} = \dfrac{8WC^3}{G \cdot d}$.

5.2.4 Energy Stored in Helical Spring of Circular Wire

- If the spring material is not stored beyond the elastic limit, there will be a straight line load-deflection diagram as shown in Fig. 5.12.

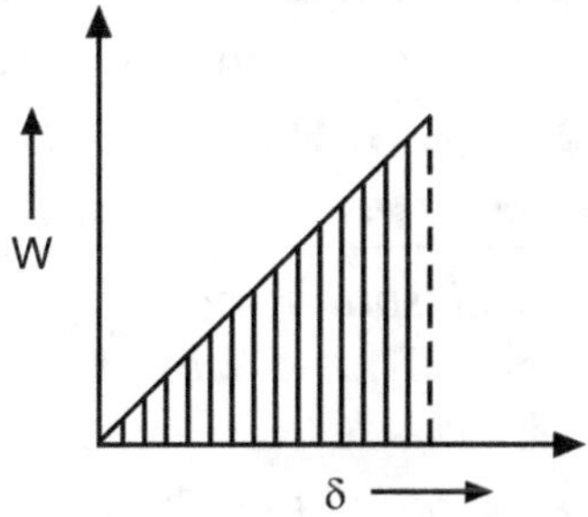

Fig. 5.12 : Energy stored in spring

- The energy stored in a spring is given by,

$$U = \frac{1}{2} \times W \times \delta \qquad \qquad \dots (5.9)$$

- We have, the maximum shear stress induced in the spring as,

$$\tau = K \times \frac{8\,WD}{\pi d^3}$$

$$\therefore \qquad W = \frac{\pi \cdot \tau \cdot d^3}{8 \cdot K \cdot D} \qquad \qquad \dots (5.10)$$

And deflection as, $\qquad \delta = \dfrac{8\,WD^3 n}{Gd^4} \qquad \qquad \dots (5.11)$

Put the values of W and δ in equation (5.9), we have,

$$U = \frac{1}{2} \times \frac{\pi \cdot \tau \cdot d^3}{8 \cdot K \cdot D} \times \frac{8\,WD^3 n}{Gd^4}$$

Again, put the value of W from equation (5.10) in the above expression, we have,

$$U = \frac{1}{2} \times \frac{\pi \cdot \tau \cdot d^3}{8 \cdot K \cdot D} \times \frac{8 \cdot \pi \cdot \tau \cdot d^3}{8 \cdot K \cdot D} \cdot \frac{D^3 n}{Gd^4}$$

$$= \frac{\tau^2}{4K^2 G} \cdot (\pi Dn) \cdot \left(\frac{\pi}{4} d^2\right)$$

$$= \frac{\tau^2}{4K^2 G} \cdot V$$

where, $\qquad V$ = Volume of spring wire

$\qquad$ = Length of spring $\times$ Cross-sectional area of wire

$\qquad$ = $(\pi Dn) \cdot \left(\dfrac{\pi}{4} d^2\right)$

- When a load (say P) falls on a spring through a height h, then the energy absorbed in a spring is given by,

$$U = P\,(h + \delta) = \frac{1}{2} \times W \times \delta$$

where, $\qquad W$ = Equivalent static load i.e. gradually applied load, which shall produce the same effect as by the falling load P, and

$\qquad \delta$ = Axial deflection produced in the springs.

Numerical Type No. 1 : "Design of Helical Spring Neglecting the Stress Concentration, Neglecting the Stress due to Curvature of Wire"

Problem 5.1 : *A compression coil spring made up of alloy steel is having following specifications : Mean diameter (D) = 50 mm, Wire diameter = 5 mm, Number of active coils = 20.*

If the spring is subjected to an axial load of 500 N, calculate the maximum shear stress, to which, the spring material is subjected. Neglect the curvature effect.

Solution : Given data : $D = 50$ mm, $d = 5$ mm, $n = 20$, $W = 500$ N

Procedure : We have, Spring index, $C = \dfrac{D}{d} = \dfrac{50}{5} = 10$

The axial load W tends to produce twisting moment in the wire, so torsional shear stress is induced in the wire.

The shear stress in the wire (neglecting the curvature effect) is given by,

$$\tau = \left(1 + \frac{1}{2C}\right) \times \frac{8\,WD}{\pi d^3} = \left(1 + \frac{1}{2 \times 10}\right) \times \frac{8 \times 500 \times 50}{\pi \times (5)^3} = \textbf{534.76 N/mm}^2$$

Problem 5.2 : *A closed coil helical spring is made of 10 mm diameter of steel wire. The coil consists of 10 complete turns with a mean diameter of 120 mm. The spring carries an axial pull of 200 N. Determine the shear stress induced in the spring, neglecting the effect of stress concentration. Determine also the deflection in the spring, its stiffness and strain energy stored by it, if the modulus of rigidity of the material is 60 kN/mm².* **(S-10)**

Solution : Given data : $D = 120$ mm, $d = 10$ mm, $n = 10$, $W = 200$ N, $G = 60 \times 10^3$ N/mm².

Procedure : (i) Shear stress induced :

The shear stress induced in the spring (neglecting the stress concentration) is,

$$\tau = \frac{8\,WD}{\pi d^3} = \frac{8 \times 200 \times 120}{\pi \times 10^3} = \textbf{61.115 N/mm}^2$$

(ii) Deflection in spring :

$$\text{Deflection, } \delta = \frac{8\,WD^3 n}{Gd^4} = \frac{8 \times 200 \times (120)^3 \times 10}{60 \times 10^3 \times 10^4} = \textbf{46.08 mm}$$

(iii) Stiffness :

$$\text{Stiffness, } S = \frac{W}{\delta} = \frac{200}{46.08} = \textbf{4.3402 N/mm}$$

(iv) Strain energy stored :

$$U = \frac{1}{2} \times W \times \delta = \frac{1}{2} \times 200 \times 46.08 = \textbf{4608 N.mm}$$

Numerical Type No. 2 : "Design of Helical Spring Considering Stress due to Curvature of Wire"

Problem 5.3 : *A helical spring is made from a wire of 8 mm diameter and has outside diameter 90 mm. If the permissible shear stress is 350 N/mm² and modulus of rigidity 84 kN/mm², find the axial load, which the spring can carry and the deflection per active turn.*

(i)   *Neglecting the effect of curvature.*

(ii) *Considering the effect of curvature.*

Solution : Given data : $d = 8$ mm, $D_o = 90$ mm, $\tau = 350$ N/mm²,

$$G = 84 \text{ kN/mm}^2 = 84 \times 10^3 \text{ N/mm}^2.$$

Procedure : We have, $\quad D = D_o - d = 90 - 8 = 82$ mm

$$C = \frac{D}{d} = \frac{82}{8} = 10.25$$

Case (I) : Neglecting the effect of curvature.

$$K_s = 1 + \frac{1}{2C} = 1 + \frac{1}{2 \times 10.25} = 1.0488$$

(i)   The shear stress induced in the spring is given by (neglecting the curvature effect),

$$\therefore \qquad \tau = K_s \times \frac{8\,WD}{\pi d^3}$$

$$\therefore \qquad 350 = 1.0488 \times \frac{8 \times W \times 82}{\pi \times 8^3}$$

$$\therefore \qquad W = \frac{350 \times \pi \times 8^3}{1.0488 \times 8 \times 82} = \textbf{818.26 N}$$

(ii)   Deflection per active turn is given by,

$$\frac{\delta}{n} = \frac{8\,WD^3}{Gd^4} = \frac{8 \times 818.26 \times 82^3}{84 \times 10^3 \times 8^4} = \textbf{10.49 mm}$$

Case (II) : Considering effect of curvature.

Wahl's stress concentration factor is,

$$K = \frac{4C - 1}{4C - 4} + \frac{0.615}{C} = \frac{4 \times 10.25 - 1}{4 \times 10.25 - 4} + \frac{0.615}{10.25} = \textbf{1.1411}$$

(i)   Shear stress induced in the spring is given by,

$$\tau = K \times \frac{8\,WD}{\pi d^3}$$

$$350 = 1.1411 \times \frac{8 \times W \times 82}{\pi \times 8^3}$$

$$\therefore \qquad W = \frac{350 \times \pi \times 8^3}{1.1410 \times 8 \times 82} = \textbf{752.073 N}$$

(ii)   Deflection per active turn is given by,

$$\frac{\delta}{n} = \frac{8\,WD^3}{Gd^4} = \frac{8 \times 752.073 \times 82^3}{84 \times 10^3 \times 8^4} = \textbf{9.6417 mm}$$

Problem 5.4 : *A helical compression spring carries a load of 500 N with a deflection of 25 mm. The spring index may be taken as 8. Assume permissible τ = 350 MPa. Modulus of rigidity = 84 kN/mm^2, Wahl's factor as $\dfrac{4C-1}{4C-4} + \dfrac{0.615}{C}$, where C is spring index. Find number of active turns of spring.*   **(W-09)**

Solution : Given data : $W = 500$ N, $\delta = 25$ mm, $C = 8$

$\tau = 350$ MPa $= 350$ N/mm^2, $\quad G = 84$ kN/mm$^2 = 84 \times 10^3$ N/mm^2

Procedure : Wahl's stress concentration factor is,

$$K = \frac{4C - 1}{4C - 4} + \frac{0.615}{C} = \frac{4 \times 8 - 1}{4 \times 8 - 4} + \frac{0.615}{8} = \mathbf{1.1840}$$

The maximum shear stress induced is given by,

$$\tau = K \times \frac{8\,WD}{\pi d^3} = K \times \frac{8\,WC}{\pi d^2} \qquad \dots\left(\because C = \frac{D}{d}\right)$$

$$\therefore \qquad d^2 = K \times \frac{8\,WC}{\pi \cdot \tau} = 1.1840 \times \frac{8 \times 500 \times 8}{\pi \times 350}$$

$$\therefore \qquad d = \mathbf{5.87\ mm}$$

and

$$D = C \times d = 8 \times 5.87 = \mathbf{46.96\ mm}$$

Number of active turns : It is calculated from the deflection formula.

$$\therefore \qquad \delta = \frac{8\,WD^3 n}{G d^4}$$

$$25 = \frac{8 \times 500 \times (46.96)^3 \times n}{84 \times 10^3 \times (5.87)^4}$$

$$\therefore \qquad n = \mathbf{6.0190 \cong 7\ (say)}$$

Total number of active turns = n = **7**.

Problem 5.5 : *The spring of spring balance elongates by 150 mm, when subjected to load of 400 N. The spring index is 6. Take permissible shear stress for the spring material as 540 N/mm². Consider the effect of direct shear and wire curvature. Take G = 8.4 × 10⁴ N/mm².*

Find : (i) Wire diameter and coil diameter.

(ii) Number of active turns required.

Solution : Given data : $\delta = 150$ mm, W = 400 N, C = 6,

$$\tau = 540\ \text{N/mm}^2,\ G = 8.4 \times 10^4\ \text{N/mm}^2$$

Procedure : Wahl's stress concentration factor is,

$$K = \frac{4C - 1}{4C - 4} + \frac{0.615}{C} = \frac{4 \times 6 - 1}{4 \times 6 - 4} + \frac{0.615}{6} = 1.2525$$

(i) Diameter of wire : The maximum shear stress induced is given by,

$$\therefore \qquad \tau = K \times \frac{8\,WD}{\pi d^3} = K \times \frac{8\,WC}{\pi d^2} \qquad \dots\left(\because C = \frac{D}{d}\right)$$

$$\therefore \qquad 540 = 1.2525 \times \frac{8 \times 400 \times 6}{\pi \times d^2}$$

$$\therefore \qquad \text{Wire diameter} = d = \mathbf{3.76\ mm}$$

The mean diameter of spring coil = D = C × d = 6 × 3.76 = **22.56 mm**

(ii) Number of active turns : It can be calculated from the deflection formula.

$$\delta \ = \ \frac{8\,WD^3 n}{Gd^4}$$

$$\therefore \qquad n \ = \ \frac{\delta \times G \times d^4}{8 \times W \times D^3} \ = \ \frac{150 \times 8.4 \times 10^4 \times (3.76)^4}{8 \times 400 \times (22.56)^3} \ = \ 68.541$$

$\therefore$ The number of active turns = n = **68.541** $\cong$ **69**

Problem 5.6 : *A closed coil helical spring is used for an automobile suspension system. The spring has stiffness 85 N/mm with squared and grounded ends. The load on the spring causes a total deflection of 9 mm. By taking permissible shear stress of 400 MPa,*

find : (i) Wire diameter of spring. (ii) Length of spring.

Take spring index = 6 and G = 80 $\times 10^3$ N/mm^2   **(S-09)**

Solution : Given data : S = 85 N/mm, δ = 9 mm, τ = 400 MPa = 400 N/mm^2,

$$C \ = \ 6, \ G = 84 \times 10^3 \ N/mm^2$$

To find :

Procedure : (i) Wire diameter of spring :

We have, Spring stiffness (S) $= \ \dfrac{W}{\delta}$

$\therefore$ W $= \ S \times \delta = 85 \times 9 = 765$ N

Wahl's stress concentration factor is,

$$K \ = \ \frac{4C-1}{4C-4} + \frac{0.615}{C} \ = \ \frac{4 \times 6 - 1}{4 \times 6 - 4} + \frac{0.615}{6} \ = \ 1.2525$$

The maximum shear stress induced is given by,

$$\tau \ = \ K \times \frac{8\,WD}{\pi d^3} \ = \ K \times \frac{8\,WC}{\pi d^2} \qquad\qquad \ldots\left(\because \ C = \frac{D}{d}\right)$$

$$\therefore \qquad d^2 \ = \ K \times \frac{8\,WC}{\pi \times \tau}$$

$$\therefore \qquad d^2 \ = \ 1.2525 \times \frac{8 \times 765 \times 6}{\pi \times 400}$$

$$\therefore \qquad d \ = \ \textbf{6.0497 mm}$$

and   D = C $\times$ d = 6 $\times$ 6.0497 = **36.29 mm**

$\therefore$ Diameter of spring wire = 6.0497 mm and Mean diameter of spring coil = 36.29 mm

(ii) Length of spring : Deflection is given by

$$\delta \ = \ \frac{8\,WD^3 n}{G \times d^4}$$

$$\therefore \qquad n \ = \ \frac{\delta \times G \times d^4}{8\,WD^3} \ = \ \frac{9 \times 80 \times 10^3 \times (6.0497)^4}{8 \times 765 \times (36.29)^3} \ = \ \textbf{3.29} \ \cong \ \textbf{4 (say)}$$

$\therefore$ Total number of active turns (n) = 4.

Given squared and grounded ends, therefore total number of turns is given by,

$$n' = n + 2 = 4 + 2 = 6$$

Solid length, $L_s = n' \times d = 6 \times 6.0497 = \mathbf{36.2982 \ mm}$

Free length, $L_f = n' \times d + \delta_{max} + 0.15 \times \delta_{max}$

$$= 6 \times 6.0497 + 9 + (0.15 \times 9) = \mathbf{46.648 \ mm}$$

Problem 5.7 : *Find the maximum shear stress and deflection induced in a helical spring, if it has to absorb 1000 N-m energy. Use the data as, D = 100 mm, d = 20 mm, n = 30, G = 84 kN/mm².*

Solution : Given data : $U = 1000 = N.m = 1000 \times 10^3$ N-mm, D = 100 mm, d = 20 mm, n = 30,

$G = 84 \times 10^3$ N/mm²

Procedure : (1) Maximum shear stress induced : We have,

$$\text{Spring index} = C = \frac{D}{d} = \frac{100}{20} = 5$$

∴   Wahl's stress concentration factor is,

$$K = \frac{4C-1}{4C-4} + \frac{0.615}{C} = \frac{4 \times 5 - 1}{4 \times 5 - 4} + \frac{0.615}{5} = 1.3105$$

From the expression of strain energy stored in a spring, we have,

$$U = \frac{\tau^2}{4K^2 \, G} \times V$$

where   V = Volume of wire = Cross-sectional area of spring wire × Length of wire

∴ $$U = \frac{\tau^2}{4K^2 \, G} \times \left(\frac{\pi}{4} \times d^2\right) \times (\pi D n)$$

∴ $$\tau^2 = \frac{U \times 4 \times K^2 \times G}{\left(\frac{\pi}{4} \times d^2\right) \times (\pi D n)} = \frac{1000 \times 10^3 \times 4 \times (1.3105)^2 \times 84 \times 10^3}{\left(\frac{\pi}{4} \times (20)^2\right) \times (\pi \times 100 \times 30)}$$

Thus, $\tau = \mathbf{441.46 \ N/mm^2}$

(2) Deflection : We have,

$$\tau = \frac{8 \times K \times W \times D}{\pi d^3}$$

∴ $$W = \frac{\tau \times \pi \times d^3}{8 \times K \times D} = \frac{441.46 \times \pi \times (20)^3}{8 \times 1.3105 \times 100} = 10582.88 \ N$$

Deflection is given by,

$$\delta = \frac{8 W D^3 \, n}{G \times d^4} = \frac{8 \times 10582.88 \times 100^3 \times 30}{84 \times 10^3 \times (20)^4} = \mathbf{188.98 \ mm}$$

Problem 5.8 : *A load of 2 kN is dropped axially on a close coil helical spring from a height of 250 mm. The spring has 20 effective turns and it is made of 25 mm wire diameter. The spring index is 8. Find the maximum shear stress induced in spring and amount of compression produced. Modulus of rigidity for material of the spring wire is 84 kN/mm².*

Solution : Given data : $P = 2$ kN $= 2 \times 10^3$ N, $h = 250$ mm, $C = 8$, $d = 25$ mm, $n = 20$, $G = 84 \times 10^3$ N/mm^2

Procedure : We have, spring index $= C = \dfrac{D}{d}$

$\therefore$ $D = C \times d = 8 \times 25 = 200$ mm

$\therefore$ Wahl's stress concentration factor is,

$$K = \frac{4C - 1}{4C - 4} + \frac{0.615}{C} = \frac{4 \times 8 - 1}{4 \times 8 - 4} + \frac{0.615}{8} = 1.184$$

Deflection is given by,

$$\delta = \frac{8WD^3 n}{G \times d^4} = \frac{8 \times W \times (200)^3 \times 20}{84 \times 10^3 \times (25)^4} = 0.039 \ W$$

We know that,

Energy stored by spring $=$ Work done by falling load

$\therefore$ $\dfrac{1}{2} \times W \times \delta = P \times (h + \delta)$

$\therefore$ $\dfrac{1}{2} \times W \times 0.039 \ W = 2 \times 10^3 \times (250 + 0.039 \ W)$

$\therefore$ $0.0195 \ W^2 - 78W - 500 \times 10^3 = 0$

$\therefore$ $W = \dfrac{-(-78) \pm \sqrt{(-78)^2 - (4 \times 0.0195 \times -500 \times 10^3)}}{2 \times 0.0195} = 7444.35$ N

(i)   The maximum shear stress induced is given by,

$$\tau = K \times \frac{8WD}{\pi d^3} = 1.184 \times \frac{8 \times 7444.35 \times 200}{\pi \times (25)^3} = \mathbf{287.295 \ N/mm^2}$$

(ii)   Maximum deflection, $\delta = 0.039 \ W = 0.039 \times 7444.35 = \mathbf{290.33 \ mm}$

Problem 5.9 : *A mechanism used in printing machinery consists of a tension spring assembled with a preload of 30 N. The wire diameter of spring is 2 mm and C = 6. The spring has 18 active coils. The spring wire is hard drawn and oil tempered having following material properties : $\tau = 680$ MPa, G = 80 kN/mm².*

Find (i) Initial τ, (ii) Spring rate, (iii) The force to cause the body of the spring to its yield strength.

Solution : Given data : $W_1 = 30$ N, $d = 2$ mm, $C = 6$, $n = 18$,

$$\tau = 680 \text{ MPa} = 680 \text{ N/mm}^2, \ G = 80 \times 10^3 \text{ N/mm}^2$$

Procedure :

(i)   Initial torsional shear stress in the wire (τ_1) :

We know, $K = \dfrac{4C - 1}{4C - 4} + \dfrac{0.615}{C} = \dfrac{4 \times 6 - 1}{4 \times 6 - 4} + \dfrac{0.615}{6} = 1.2525$

We have, $\tau_1 = K \times \dfrac{8W_1 C}{\pi d^2} = 1.2525 \times \dfrac{8 \times 30 \times 6}{\pi \times (2)^2} = \mathbf{143.5 \ N/mm^2}$

(ii) Spring rate :

We have,
$$\delta = \frac{8WD^3n}{Gd^4}$$

$\therefore$ Spring rate $= \dfrac{W}{\delta} = \dfrac{Gd^4}{8D^3n} = \dfrac{Gd}{8C^3n} = \dfrac{80 \times 10^3 \times 2}{8 \times (6)^3 \times 18} = \mathbf{5.144\ N/mm}$

(iii) Force required :

We have,
$$\tau = K \times \frac{8WC}{\pi d^2}$$

$\therefore$ $680 = 1.2525 \times \dfrac{8 \times W \times 6}{\pi \times (2)^2}$

$\therefore$ $W = \mathbf{142.134\ N}$

Numerical Type No. 3 : "Design of Helical Spring Operating between a Load Range"

Problem 5.10 : *Design a helical compression spring for maximum load of 800 N for a deflection of 25 mm. The spring index is 5 and Wahl's correction factor is 1.3. The maximum permissible shear stress for the spring wire is 400 MPa and modulus of rigidity is 84 kN/mm².*

(S-14)

Solution : Given data : $W = 800$ N, $C = 5$, $\delta = 25$ mm, $\tau = 400$ N/mm²,

$\qquad\qquad G = 84 \times 10^3$ N/mm², $K = 1.3$

Design of helical spring :

(1) Mean diameter of spring coil : The maximum shear stress induced is given by,

$$\tau = K \times \frac{8WD}{\pi d^3} = K \times \frac{8WC}{\pi d^2} \qquad \left(\because C = \frac{D}{d} \right)$$

$\therefore$ $d^2 - K \times \dfrac{8WC}{\pi \times \tau} = 1.3 \times \dfrac{8 \times 800 \times 5}{\pi \times 400}$

$\therefore$ $d = 5.75$ mm and $D = C \times d = 5 \times 5.75 = 28.75$ mm

Diameter of spring wire = d = **5.75 mm** and Mean diameter of spring coil = **28.75 mm**

(2) Number of turns : It is calculated from the deflection formula,

$$\delta = \frac{8WD^3\, n}{G \times d^4}$$

$\therefore$ $n = \dfrac{\delta \times G \times d^4}{8WD^3} = \dfrac{25 \times 84 \times 10^3 \times (5.75)^4}{8 \times 800 \times (28.75)^3} = 15.09 \cong \mathbf{16\ (say)}$

Total number of active turns = n = **16**

Assuming squared and grounded ends, total number of turns is given by,

$\qquad\qquad n' = n + 2 = 16 + 2 = \mathbf{18}$

(3) Solid length : $L_s = n' \times d = 18 \times 5.75 = \mathbf{103.5\ mm}$

(4) Free length : L_f $= n' \times d + \delta_{max} + 0.15 \times \delta_{max}$

$$= (18 \times 5.75) + 25 + (0.15 \times 25) = \textbf{132.25 mm}$$

(5) Pitch of the coil : $p = \dfrac{\text{Free length}}{n' - 1} = \dfrac{132.25}{18 - 1} = \textbf{7.7794 mm}$

Problem 5.11 : *Design a closed coil helical spring for a service load ranging from 2207 N to 2698 N. The axial deflection of spring is 6 mm. Assume spring index as 5. The permissible shear stress is 420 N/mm². Modulus of rigidity 84 × 10³ N/mm². Neglect the effect of stress concentration.* **(S-03; W-11)**

Solution : Given data : W_1 = 2207 N, W_2 = 2698 N, C = 5, τ = 420 N/mm²,

$$G = 84 \times 10^3 \text{ N/mm}^2$$

Procedure : Deflection for the load range, $W = (W_2 - W_1) = (2698 - 2207) = (491\ N)$ is 6 mm,

(i) Diameter of wire : The maximum shear stress induced due to maximum load W_2 = 2698 N, is given by,

$$\tau = \frac{8\ W_2 D}{\pi d^3} = \frac{8\ W_2\ C}{\pi d^2} \text{ (Neglecting effect of stress concentration)}$$

$$\therefore \qquad 420 = \frac{8 \times 2698 \times 5}{\pi d^2} \qquad \qquad \dots\left(\because C = \frac{D}{d}\right)$$

$$\therefore \qquad d = 9.0438 \text{ mm} \cong 9.05 \text{ mm (say)}$$

$\therefore$ Diameter of spring wire = d = **9.05 mm**

And Mean diameter of spring (D) $= C \times d = 5 \times 9.05 = $ **45.25 mm**

(ii) Number of turns : It is calculated from the deflection formula :

$$\delta = \frac{8\ WD^3 n}{G \times d^4}$$

$$\therefore \qquad n = \frac{\delta \times G \times d^4}{8 \times W \times D^3} = \frac{6 \times 84 \times 10^3 \times (9.05)^4}{8 \times 491 \times (45.25)^3}$$

$$\therefore \qquad n = 9.28 \cong \textbf{10 turns}$$

Assuming squared and grounded ends, total number of turns is given by,

$$n' = n + 2 = 10 + 2 = \textbf{12}$$

(iii) Maximum deflection : For a load range of 491 N, the deflection is 6 mm. Therefore, maximum deflection for maximum load of 2698 N can be calculated as follows :

For 491 N, $\qquad\qquad \delta = 6$ mm

For 2698 N, $\qquad\qquad \delta_{max} = \dfrac{(2698 \times 6)}{491}$

$$\therefore \qquad \delta_{max} = \textbf{32.97 mm}$$

(iv) Solid length : $\qquad L_s = n' \times d = 14 \times 9.05 = \textbf{126.7 mm}$

(v) Free length :

$$L_f = n' \times d + \delta_{max} + 0.15\,\delta_{max} = 12 \times 9.05 + 32.97 + 0.15\,(32.97)$$

$$L_f = \textbf{146.515 mm}$$

(vi) Pitch of the spring :

$$p = \frac{\text{Free length}}{n'-1} = \frac{146.515}{12-1} = \textbf{13.32 mm}$$

Problem 5.12 : *Design a close coiled helical compression spring for service load ranging from 2250 N to 2750 N. the axial deflection of the spring of the load range is 6 mm. Assume a spring index of 5. The permissible shear stress intensity is 420 N/mm² and modulus of rigidity, G = 84 kN/mm². Take design stress 25% excess of permissible stress for severe condition and intermittent operation.* **(W-12)**

Solution : Given data : W_1 = 2250 N, W_2 = 2750 N, C = 5,

Permissible stress = 420 N/mm², G = 84 × 10³ N/mm²

Deflection for the load range $(W_2 - W_1) = (2750 - 2250) = (500\ \text{N})$ is, δ = 6 mm.

Procedure : Wahl's stress concentration factor is,

$$K = \frac{4C-1}{4C-4} + \frac{0.615}{C} = \frac{4 \times 5 - 1}{4 \times 5 - 4} + \frac{0.615}{5} = 1.3105$$

For severe conditions and intermittent operations, take

Design stress $= 1.25 \times$ Permissible stress

$$\therefore \qquad \tau = 1.25 \times 420 = 525\ \text{N/mm}^2$$

(i) Diameter of spring wire : The maximum shear stress induced due to maximum load (W_2) is given by,

$$\tau = K \times \frac{8W_2 D}{\pi d^3} = K \times \frac{8W_2 C}{\pi d^2} \qquad \left(\because C = \frac{D}{d} \right)$$

$$\therefore \qquad d^2 = K \times \frac{8W_2 C}{\pi \times \tau} = 1.3105 \times \frac{8 \times 2750 \times 5}{\pi \times 525}$$

Thus,   d = 9.35 mm and D = C × d = 5 × 9.35 = 46.75 mm

$\therefore$ Diameter of spring wire, d = **9.35 mm**

And, Mean diameter of spring coil = **46.75 mm**

(ii) Number of turns : It is calculated from the deflection formula,

$$\delta = \frac{8WD^3\,n}{G \times d^4}$$

$$\therefore \qquad n = \frac{\delta \times G \times d^4}{8WD^3} = \frac{6 \times 84 \times 10^3 \times (9.35)^4}{8 \times 500 \times (46.75)^3} = 9.42 \cong 10\ \text{(say)}$$

Total number of active turns = **n = 10**

Assuming squared and grounded ends, total number of turns is given by

$$n' = n + 2 = 10 + 2 = \textbf{12}$$

(iii) Maximum deflection : For load range of 500 N, the deflection is 6 mm. Therefore, maximum deflection for maximum load of 2750 N can be calculated as follows :

For 500 N $\rightarrow$ $\delta = 6$ mm

For 2750 N $\rightarrow$ $\delta_{max} = \dfrac{2750 \times 6}{500} = $ **33 mm**

(iv) Solid length : $L_s = n' \times d = 12 \times 9.35 = $ **112.2 mm**

(v) Free length : $L_f = L_s + \delta_{max} + 0.15\, \delta_{max}$

$\therefore$ $\qquad\qquad L_f = 112.2 + 33 + 0.15 \times 33 = 150.15$ mm

(vi) Pitch of spring :

$$p = \frac{\text{Free length}}{n' - 1} = \frac{150.15}{12 - 1} = \textbf{13.65 mm}$$

Problem 5.13 : *Design a spring for balance to measure 0 to 1000 N over a scale of length 80 mm. The spring is to be enclosed in casing of 25 mm diameter. The approximate number of turns is 30. The modulus of rigidity is 85 kN/mm². Also calculate the maximum shear stress. The spring ends are grounded.*

Solution : Given data : $W = 1000$ N, $\delta = 80$ mm, $n = 30$, $G = 85 \times 10^3$ N/mm².

Procedure :

(1) Diameter of spring wire : As the spring is to be enclosed in a casing of 25 mm diameter, the outer diameter should be less than 25 mm. i.e. $D_o < 25$ mm.

By trial and error method, let us assume that, $d = 4.1$ mm

Thus, deflection produced is given by,

$$\delta = \frac{8WD^3 n}{G \times d^4}$$

$\therefore$ $\qquad\qquad D^3 = \dfrac{\delta \times G \times d^4}{8Wn} = \dfrac{80 \times 85 \times 10^3 \times (4.1)^4}{8 \times 1000 \times 30} = 8006.32$

Thus, $D = 20$ mm and $D_o = D + d = 20 + 4.1 = 24.1$ mm, which is less than 25 mm.

$\therefore$ Diameter of spring wire $= d = $ **4.1 mm is correct assumption.**

$\therefore$ Mean diameter of spring coil $= D = $ **20 mm**

and spring index $= C = \dfrac{D}{d} = \dfrac{20}{4.1} = $ **4.878**

(2) Total number of turns : As the ends are grounded, therefore total number of turns $= n' = n = 30$.

(3) Solid length : $L_s = n' \times d = 30 \times 4.1 = $ **123 mm**

(4) Free length : $L_f = n' \times d + \delta_{max} + 0.15 \times \delta_{max}$

$\qquad\qquad\qquad = (30 \times 4.1) + 80 + (0.15 \times 80) = $ **215 mm**

(5) Pitch of the coil : $p = \dfrac{\text{Free length}}{n' - 1} = \dfrac{215}{30 - 1} = $ **7.413 mm**

(6) Maximum shear stress : Wahl's stress concentration factor is,

$$K = \frac{4C-1}{4C-4} + \frac{0.615}{C} = \frac{4 \times 4.878 - 1}{4 \times 4.878 - 4} + \frac{0.615}{4.878} = 1.3194$$

The maximum shear stress induced is given by,

$$\tau_{max} = K \times \frac{8WD}{\pi d^3} = 1.3194 \times \frac{8 \times 1000 \times 20}{\pi \times (4.1)^3} = \mathbf{974.98 \ N/mm^2}$$

Numerical Type No. 4 : "Design of Spring for Safety Valves"

Problem 5.14 : *A safety valve of 60 mm diameter is to blow off at a pressure of 1.2 N/mm². It is held on its seat by a close coil helical spring. The maximum lift of valve is 10 mm. Design a suitable compression spring of spring index 5 with an initial compression of 35 mm. The shear stress is limited to 500 MPa. Take G = 80 kN/mm².*

Solution : Given data : $D_V = 60$ mm, $p = 1.2$ N/mm², $\tau = 500$ N/mm²,

$G = 80 \times 10^3$ N/mm², $C = 5$, Initial compression = 35 mm, Maximum lift of valve = 10 mm.

Procedure : Design of helical spring :

(i) Diameter of spring wire : The load, at which the valve blows off can be calculated as,

$$W_1 = \text{Pressure on valve} \times \text{Area of valve} = p \times \frac{\pi}{4} \times (D_V)^2$$

$$= 1.2 \times \frac{\pi}{4} \times (60)^2 = 3392.92 \ N$$

The maximum compression of spring = Initial compression + Maximum lift of valve

$$\delta_{max} = 35 + 10 = 45 \ mm$$

As the load $W_1 = 3392.92$ N keeps the valve on the seat with initial compression of 35 mm, therefore, maximum load on spring for maximum deflection, when valve is open, is given by,

Initial compression (35 mm) $\rightarrow W_1 = 3392.92$ N

Maximum compression (45 mm) $\rightarrow$ Maximum load,

$$W_2 = \frac{3392.92 \times 45}{35} = 4362.32 \ N$$

Wahl's stress concentration factor is,

$$K = \frac{4C-1}{4C-4} + \frac{0.615}{C} = \frac{4 \times 5 - 1}{4 \times 5 - 4} + \frac{0.615}{5} = 1.3105$$

The maximum shear stress is given by,

$$\tau = K \times \frac{8 W_2 D}{\pi d^3} = K \times \frac{8 W_2 C}{\pi d^2} \qquad \qquad \dots \left(\because C = \frac{D}{d} \right)$$

$$\therefore \quad d^2 = K \times \frac{8 W_2 C}{\pi \times \tau} = 1.3105 \times \frac{8 \times 4362.32 \times 5}{\pi \times 500}$$

Thus, $d = 12.06$ mm   and $D = C \times d = 5 \times 12.06 = 60.3$ mm

Diameter of spring wire $= \mathbf{d = 12.06\ mm}$

and Mean diameter of spring coil $= \mathbf{D = 60.3\ mm}$

(ii) Number of turns : It is calculated from the deflection formula,

$$\delta_{max} = \frac{8 W_2 D^3 n}{G \times d^4}$$

$$\therefore \qquad n = \frac{\delta_{max} \times G \times d^4}{8 W_2 D^3} = \frac{45 \times 80 \times 10^3 \times (12.06)^4}{8 \times 4362.32 \times (60.3)^3} = 9.95 \cong 10 \text{ (say)}$$

$\therefore$ Total number of active turns, $\mathbf{n = 10}$

Assuming squared and grounded ends, total number of turns is given by,

$$n' = n + 2 = 10 + 2 = \mathbf{12}$$

(iii) Solid length : $L_s = n' \times d = 12 \times 12.06 = \mathbf{144.72\ mm}$

(iv) Free length : $L_f = n' \times d + \delta_{max} + 0.15 \times \delta_{max}$

$$= (12 \times 12.06) + 45 + (0.15 \times 45) = \mathbf{196.47\ mm}$$

(v) Pitch of the coil : $p = \dfrac{\text{Free length}}{n' - 1} = \dfrac{196.47}{12 - 1} = \mathbf{17.86\ mm}$

Problem 5.15 : *Design a helical spring for a spring loaded safety valve for the following conditions :*

Operating pressure $= p_1 = 1$ N/mm^2

Maximum pressure, when the valve is blow-off freely $= p_2 = 1.075$ N/mm^2

Maximum lift of the valve, when the pressure is 1.075 N/mm$^2 = \delta = 6$ mm.

Diameter of valve seat $= D_v = 100$ mm.

Maximum shear stress $= \tau = 400$ N/mm^2.

Modulus of rigidity $= G = 86 \times 10^3$ N/mm^2

Spring index $= C = 5.5$.

Solution : Given data : $p_1 = 1$ N/mm^2, $p_2 = 1.075$ N/mm^2, $\delta = 6$ mm, $D_v = 100$ mm, $\tau = 400$ N/mm^2, $G = 86 \times 10^3$ N/mm^2, $C = 5.5$.

Procedure :

(i) To find diameter of wire and diameter of coil :

Initial tensile force acting on the spring is

$$W_1 = \frac{\pi}{4} D_v^2 \times p_1 = \frac{\pi}{4} \times 100^2 \times 1 = 7853.98 \text{ N}$$

Maximum tensile force is

$$W_2 = \frac{\pi}{4} \times D_v^2 \times p_2 = \frac{\pi}{4} \times 100^2 \times 1.075 = 8443.03 \text{ N}$$

$$\therefore \qquad \text{Load range} = W_2 - W_1 = 8443.030 - 7853.98 = 589.05 \text{ N}$$

Wahl's factor, $\quad K = \dfrac{4C-1}{4C-4} + \dfrac{0.615}{C} = \dfrac{4 \times 5.5 - 1}{4 \times 5.5 - 4} + \dfrac{0.615}{5.5} = 1.2785$

We have, $\quad \tau_{max} = K \times \dfrac{8\,W_2\,C}{\pi d^2}$

$\therefore \quad 400 = 1.2785 \times \dfrac{8 \times 8443.03 \times 5.5}{\pi \times d^2}$

$\therefore \quad d = \mathbf{19.44\ mm}$

$\therefore \quad$ Mean diameter, $D = C \times d = 5.5 \times 19.44 = \mathbf{106.92\ mm}$

(ii) To find active number of coils :

For load range, $W_{range} = 589.05 \to \delta_{range} = 6$ mm

For maximum load, $W_2 = 84403.03 \to \delta_{max} = \dfrac{8443.03 \times 6}{589.05} = \mathbf{85.99\ mm}$

We have, $\quad \delta_{max} = \dfrac{8\,W_{max} \times C^3 \times n}{G \cdot d}$

$\therefore \quad 85.99 = \dfrac{8 \times 8443.03 \times 5.5^3 \times n}{86 \times 10^3 \times 20}$

$\therefore \quad$ Active number of coils $= n = \mathbf{13.16} \cong \mathbf{14\ (say)}$

Total Number of coils, $n' = n + 2 = 14 + 2 = \mathbf{16}$

(iii) Free length of spring :

$$L_f = n' \times d + \delta_{max} + 0.15\,\delta_{max}$$

$$= (16 \times 20) + 85.99 + (0.15 \times 85.99) = \mathbf{418.88\ mm}$$

(iv) Pitch of coil : $\quad p = \dfrac{L_f}{n'-1} = \dfrac{418.88}{16-1} = \mathbf{27.92\ mm}$

Problem 5.16 : *The following particulars refer to the valve spring of a petrol engine.*

(1) Length of spring, when valve is opened = 40 mm

(2) Length of spring, when valve is closed = 50 mm

(3) Spring load, when valve is opened = 360 N

(4) Spring load, when valve is closed = 220 N

(5) Maximum inside diameter of spring = 25 mm

Calculate size of wire, number of active turns and pitch of coil for maximum operating stress of 400 N/mm² and G = 84 × 10³ N/mm².

Solution : Given data : $L_2 = 40$ mm, $L_1 = 50$ mm, $W_1 = 220$ N, $W_2 = 360$ N,

$$\tau = 400 \text{ N/mm}^2, \ G = 84 \times 10^3 \text{ N/mm}^2$$

Procedure :

(i) Diameter of spring wire :

It is given that, maximum inside diameter of spring = 25 mm

Let us assume that, D_i = 25 mm. Therefore, $D = D_i + d = 25 + d$

The maximum twisting moment is given by,

$$T = W_2 \times \frac{D}{2}$$

$$\therefore \quad T = 360 \times \frac{(25 + d)}{2} = 4500 + 180\,d \qquad \qquad \dots (1)$$

Also the twisting moment is given by,

$$T = \frac{\pi}{16} \times \tau \times d^3$$

$$\therefore \quad 4500 + 180\,d = \frac{\pi}{16} \times 400 \times d^3 \qquad \qquad \text{[referring equation (1)]}$$

$$\therefore \quad 4500 + 180\,d = 78.54\,d^3$$

By trial and error method, **d = 4.05 mm**,

$$\therefore \quad D = 25 + 4.05 = \textbf{29.05 mm}$$

$$\therefore \quad \text{Spring index} = C = \frac{D}{d} = \frac{29.05}{4.05} = 7.18$$

Wahl's stress concentration factor is,

$$K = \frac{4C - 1}{4C - 4} + \frac{0.615}{C} = \frac{4 \times 7.18 - 1}{4 \times 7.18 - 4} + \frac{0.615}{7.18} = 1.207$$

The maximum shear stress is given by

$$\tau = K \times \frac{8W_2 D}{\pi d^3} = K \times \frac{8W_2\,C}{\pi d^2} \qquad \dots \left(\because C = \frac{D}{d} \right)$$

$$\therefore \quad d^2 = K \times \frac{8W_2\,C}{\pi \times \tau} = 1.207 \times \frac{8 \times 360 \times 7.18}{\pi \times 400}$$

Thus, $\quad d = \textbf{4.46 mm}$

Taking larger value of two, (d = 4.05 mm and d = 4.46 mm), we have,

$\quad$ d = **4.46 mm** and D = 25 + 4.46 = **29.46 mm**

Diameter of spring wire = d = 4.46 mm and mean diameter of spring coil = 29.46 mm

(ii) Number of turns : Deflection of the spring for load range ($W_2 - W_1$ = 360 − 220 = 140 N) is $\delta = L_1 - L_2$ = 10 mm.

We have, $\quad \delta = \dfrac{8WD^3\,n}{G \times d^4}$

$$\therefore \quad n = \frac{\delta \times G \times d^4}{8WD^3} = \frac{10 \times 84 \times 10^3 \times (4.46)^4}{8 \times 140 \times (29.46)^3} = 11.60 \cong 12 \text{ (say)}$$

Total number of active turns = n = **12**

Assuming squared and grounded ends, total number of turns is given by,

$$n' = n + 2 = 12 + 2 = \mathbf{14}$$

(iii) Maximum deflection : For a load range of 140 N, the deflection is 10 mm. Therefore, maximum deflection for maximum load of 360 N can be calculated as follows.

For 140 N $\rightarrow$ $\quad \delta = 10$ mm

For 360 N $\rightarrow$ $\quad \delta_{max} = \dfrac{360 \times 10}{140} = \mathbf{25.71}$ **mm**

(iv) Solid length : $L_s = n' \times d = 14 \times 4.46 = \mathbf{62.44}$ **mm**

(v) Free length : $L_f = n' \times d + \delta_{max} + 0.15 \times \delta_{max}$

$$= (14 \times 4.46) + 25.71 + (0.15 \times 25.71) = \mathbf{92 \ mm}$$

(vi) Pitch of the coil : $p = \dfrac{\text{Free length}}{n' - 1} = \dfrac{92}{14 - 1} = \mathbf{7.08}$ **mm**

Problem 5.17 : *At the bottom of a main shaft, a group of 10 identical close coil helical springs are set in parallel to absorb the shock caused by falling of cage in case of failure. The loaded cage weighs 75 kN, while the counter weight is 15 kN. If the loaded cage falls through a height of 50 m, find the maximum stress induced in each spring, if it is made up of 50 mm steel rod. Take C = 6, n = 20, G = 80 $\times 10^3$ N/mm².*

Solution : Given data : $W_1 = 75$ kN $= 75 \times 10^3$ N, $W_2 = 15$ kN $= 15 \times 10^3$ N,

$h = 50$ m $= 50 \times 10^3$ mm, $d = 50$ mm, $C = 6$, $n = 20$, $G = 80 \times 10^3$ N/mm²

$$P = W_1 - W_2 = 75000 - 15000 = 60000 \text{ N}$$

Let W = Equivalent static load applied gradually, that shall produce same effect as by falling load P.

$$\delta = \frac{8WC^3 n}{G \cdot d} = \frac{8 \times W \times (6)^3 \times 20}{80 \times 10^3 \times 50}$$

$\therefore \qquad \delta = 8.64 \times 10^{-3} \, W$

Also, $\qquad$ Work done by falling load P = Energy stored by 10 springs

$\therefore \qquad P(h + \delta) = 10 \times \left(\dfrac{1}{2} \times W \times \delta \right)$

$\therefore \quad 60000 \, (50 \times 10^3 + 8.64 \times 10^{-3} \, W) = 5 \times W \times 8.64 \times 10^{-3} \, W \quad [\because \delta = 8.64 \times 10^{-3} \, W]$

$\therefore \qquad 3 \times 10^9 + 518.4 \, W = 0.0432 \, W^2$

$\therefore \qquad 0.0432 \, W^2 - 518.4 \, W - 3 \times 10^9 = 0$

$\therefore \qquad W = \mathbf{269591.43 \ N}$

Now, $\qquad K = \dfrac{4C - 1}{4C - 4} + \dfrac{0.615}{C} = \dfrac{4 \times 6 - 1}{4 \times 6 - 4} + \dfrac{0.615}{6} = \mathbf{1.2525}$

Maximum shear stress induced,

$$\tau = K \times \frac{8WC}{\pi d^2} = 1.2525 \times \frac{8 \times 269591.43 \times 6}{\pi \times (50)^2} = \mathbf{2063.64 \ N/mm^2}$$

Numerical Type No. 5 : "Design of Helical Spring Used for Railways"

Problem 5.18 : *A rail wagon of mass 20 tons is moving with a velocity of 9 kmph. It is brought to rest by using two buffer springs of 360 mm diameter. The maximum deflection of springs is 300 mm. An allowable shear stress for spring material is 800 MPa. Design the spring for buffers.* **(S-13)**

Solution : Given data : $m = 20$ tones $= 20 \times 10^3$ kg, $v = 9$ km/hr $= \dfrac{9 \times 10^3}{60 \times 60} = 2.5$ m/sec,

$\delta_{max} = 300$ mm, $\tau = 800$ N/mm², $D = 360$ mm

Procedure : Design of helical spring :

(1) Diameter of spring wire : Let W be the load acting on each spring, which causes a deflection of 300 mm. Since there are two springs, the energy stored in the two springs is given by,

$$U = 2 \times \frac{1}{2} \times W \times \delta = 2 \times \frac{1}{2} \times W \times 300 = 300\,W \qquad \dots (1)$$

Also, the kinetic energy of the railway wagon $= \dfrac{1}{2} \times m \times v^2$

$$K.E. = \frac{1}{2} \times 20 \times 10^3 \times (2.5)^2 = 62.5 \times 10^3 \text{ N-m} = 62.5 \times 10^6 \text{ N-mm} \dots (2)$$

Equating equations (1) and (2), we have,

$$300\,W = 62.5 \times 10^6$$

Thus, $\qquad\qquad W = 208.333 \times 10^3$ N

We know that, $\qquad T = W \times (D/2)$

$$= 208.333 \times 10^3 \times (360/2) = 37.5 \times 10^6 \text{ N-mm} \qquad \dots (3)$$

Also the twisting moment is given by,

$$T = \frac{\pi}{16} \times \tau \times d^3$$

$\therefore \qquad 37.5 \times 10^6 = \dfrac{\pi}{16} \times 800 \times d^3$ [Referring equation (3)]

$\therefore \qquad\qquad d = 62.03$ mm

Diameter of spring wire $= d = $ **62.03 mm**

(2) Number of turns :

$$\delta = \frac{8WD^3\,n}{G \times d^4} \qquad\qquad \text{[Assume } G = 84 \times 10^3 \text{ N/mm}^2]$$

$\therefore \qquad n = \dfrac{\delta \times G \times d^4}{8WD^3} = \dfrac{300 \times 84 \times 10^3 \times (62.03)^4}{8 \times 208.333 \times 10^3 \times (360)^3} = 4.79 \cong$ **5 (say)**

Total number of active turns $= n = $ **5**

Assuming squared and grounded ends, total number of turns is given by,

$$n' = n + 2 = 5 + 2 = \mathbf{7}$$

(3) Solid length : $L_s = n' \times d = 7 \times 62.03 = \mathbf{434.21\ mm}$

(4) Free length : $L_f = n' \times d + \delta_{max} + 0.15 \times \delta_{max}$

$$= (7 \times 62.03) + 300 + (0.15 \times 300) = \mathbf{779.21\ mm}$$

(5) Pitch of the coil : $p = \dfrac{\text{Free length}}{n' - 1} = \dfrac{779.21}{7 - 1} = \mathbf{129.87\ mm}$

Problem 5.19 : *A railway wagon weighing 50 kN and moving with a speed of 8 km/hr has to be stopped by 4 buffer springs, in which the maximum compression allowed is 220 mm. Find the number of turns in each spring having D = 150 mm, d = 25 mm, G = 84 kN/mm².*

Solution : Given data : Weight $= 50$ kN; $\therefore\ m = \dfrac{W}{g} = \dfrac{50 \times 10^3\ N}{9.81} = 5096.84$ kg

$$v = 8\ km/hr = \dfrac{8 \times 10^3}{3600} = 2.22\ m/s$$

$\delta = 220$ mm, $D = 150$ mm, $d = 25$ mm, $G = 84$ kN/mm² $= 84 \times 10^3$ N/mm²

Procedure :

$$\text{K.E.} = \dfrac{1}{2}\,mv^2 = \dfrac{1}{2} \times 5096.84 \times (2.22)^2$$

$$= 12559.63\ \text{N-m} = 12559.63 \times 10^3\ \text{N-mm}$$

This K.E. will be balanced by 4 springs.

$$\therefore \qquad \text{K.E.} = 4 \times \left(\dfrac{1}{2} \times W \times \delta\right)$$

$$\therefore \qquad 12559.63 \times 10^3 = 4 \times \left(\dfrac{1}{2} \times W \times 220\right)$$

$$\therefore \qquad W = \dfrac{12559.63 \times 10^3}{220 \times 2} = 28.544 \times 10^3\ \text{N}$$

To find number of active turns :

$$\delta = \dfrac{8WC^3 n}{G \cdot d} \qquad\qquad \left[\text{where, } C = \dfrac{D}{d} = \dfrac{150}{25} = 6\right]$$

$$\therefore \qquad 220 = \dfrac{8 \times 28.544 \times 10^3 \times (6)^3 \times n}{84 \times 10^3 \times 25}$$

$$\therefore \qquad n = 9.366 \cong \mathbf{10\ (say)}$$

5.3 SPRINGS IN SERIES AND PARALLEL

Springs in Series : Consider two springs connected in series as shown in Fig. 5.13.

Let, W = Load carried by the springs

       δ_1 = Deflection of spring 1

       δ_2 = Deflection of spring 2

       S_1 = Stiffness of spring 1 = $\dfrac{W}{\delta_1}$

and S_2 = Stiffness of spring 2 = $\dfrac{W}{\delta_2}$

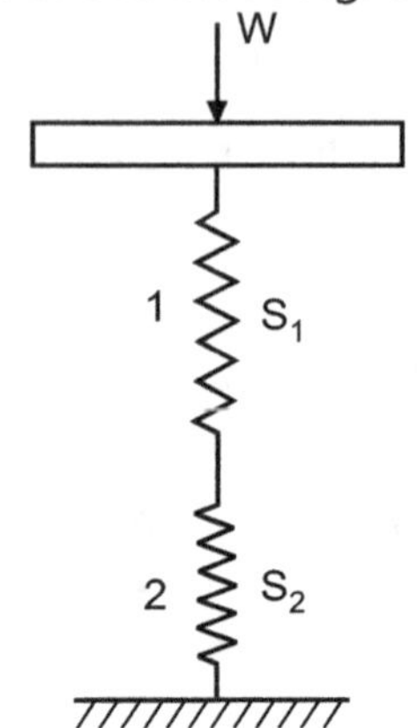

Fig. 5.13 : Springs in series

A little consideration will show that, *when springs are connected in series, then total deflection produced by the springs is equal to sum of the deflection of the individual springs.*

$\therefore$ Total deflection of the springs,

$$\delta = \delta_1 + \delta_2$$

$\therefore$
$$\frac{W}{S} = \frac{W}{S_1} + \frac{W}{S_2}$$

$\therefore$
$$\frac{1}{S} = \frac{1}{S_1} + \frac{1}{S_2}$$

where S = Combined stiffness of springs.

Springs in Parallel : Consider two springs connected in parallel as shown in Fig. 5.14.

Let, W = Load carried by the springs

       W_1 = Load shared by spring 1

       W_2 = Load shared by spring 2

       S_1 = Stiffness of spring 1

and S_2 = Stiffness of spring 2

A little consideration will show that, *when the springs are connected in parallel, then the total deflection produced by the springs is same as the deflection of the individual springs.*

i.e. $\delta = \delta_1 = \delta_2$

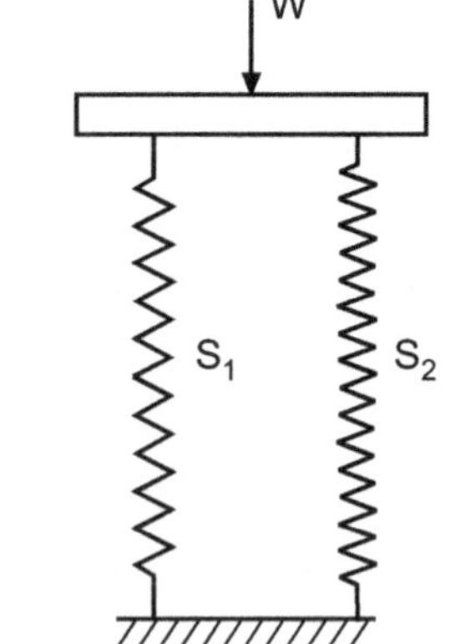

Fig. 5.14 : Springs in parallel

We know that,

$$W = W_1 + W_2$$

$\therefore$ $\delta \cdot S = \delta_1 \cdot S_1 + \delta_2 \cdot S_2$

$\therefore$ $S = S_1 + S_2$ $[\because \delta = \delta_1 = \delta_2]$

where, S = Combined stiffness of the springs and δ = Deflection produced.

Numerical Type No. 6 :
"Design of Helical Springs Arranged in Series or Parallel"

Problem 5.20 : *A helical spring of stiffness 12 N/mm is placed on the top of other spring having stiffness 8 N/mm. Find the force required to give a total deflection of 50 mm.*

Solution : Given data : $S_1 = 12$ N/mm, $S_2 = 8$ N/mm, $\delta = 50$ mm

Procedure : We know that, when the springs are connected in series,

$$\frac{1}{S} = \frac{1}{S_1} + \frac{1}{S_2} = \frac{1}{12} + \frac{1}{8}$$

$\therefore \qquad S = 4.8$ N/mm

Also, $\qquad S = \dfrac{W}{\delta}$

$\therefore \qquad W = S \times \delta = 4.8 \times 50 = \mathbf{240\ N}$

Problem 5.21 : *A closed coil helical spring of 12 active coils has a spring stiffness of K. It is cut into two springs having 5 and 7 turns. Determine the spring stiffness of resultant spring.*

(S-13)

Solution : Given data : $n_1 = 5$, $n_2 = 7$, $n = 12$

Procedure : We have, Stiffness $(S) = K = \dfrac{W}{\delta}$ [Here stiffness is termed as 'K' in question]

But, $\qquad \delta = \dfrac{8WD^3\,n}{G \times d^4}$

$\therefore \qquad K = \dfrac{G \times d^4}{8D^3\,n} = A \times \dfrac{1}{n} = A \times \dfrac{1}{12}$ $\left(\text{where, } A = \dfrac{G \times d^4}{8D^3}\right)$

Thus, $\qquad A = 12\,K$ ... (1)

Similarly, $\qquad K_1 = A \times \dfrac{1}{5} = 12\,K \times \dfrac{1}{5} = \mathbf{2.4\ K}$

and $\qquad K_2 = A \times \dfrac{1}{7} = 12\,K \times \dfrac{1}{7} = \mathbf{1.71\ K}$

Thus, K_1 and K_2 are the stiffness of resultant springs.

5.4 BUCKLING OF COMPRESSION SPRING

- It has been found experimentally that, when the free length of spring (L_f) is more than four times the mean or pitch diameter (D), then the spring behaves like a column and may fail by buckling at a comparatively low load as shown in Fig. 5.15.

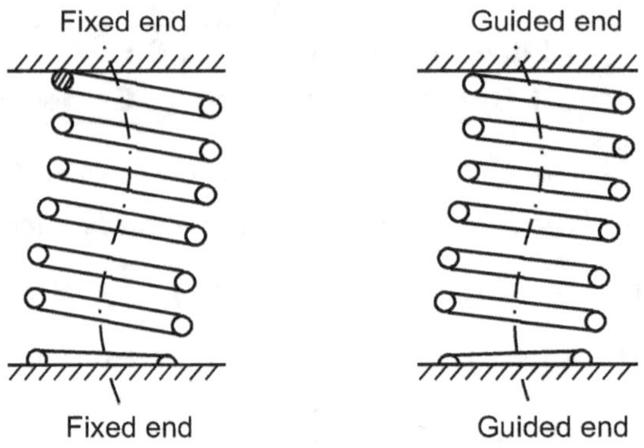

Fig. 5.15 : Buckling of springs

- The critical axial load (W_{cr}), that causes buckling, may be calculated by using the following relation, i.e.

$$W_{cr} = S \cdot K_b \cdot L_f$$

where, $\quad S =$ Spring rate or stiffness of the spring $= \dfrac{W}{\delta}$,

$\quad L_f =$ Free length of spring,

and $\quad K_b =$ Buckling factor depending upon the ratio $\left(\dfrac{L_f}{D}\right)$

- It may be noted that, a hinged end spring is one, which is supported on pivots at both ends (as in case of springs having plain ends), whereas a built-in end spring is one, in which, a squared and ground end spring is compressed between two rigid and parallel flat plates.

Method to Avoid the Tendency of Buckling of Compression Spring :

- In order to avoid the buckling of spring, it is either mounted on a central rod or located in a tube.
- When the spring is located in a tube, the clearance between the tube walls and the spring should be kept as small as possible, but it must be sufficient to allow for increase in spring diameter during compression.

5.5 SURGE IN SPRINGS

- When one end of a helical spring is resting on a rigid support and the other end is loaded suddenly, then all the coils of the spring will not suddenly deflect equally, because certain time is required for the propagation of stress along the spring wire.
- A little consideration will show that, in the beginning, the end of coils of the spring in contact with the applied load takes up whole of the deflection and then it transmits a large part of its deflection to the adjacent coils.
- In this way, a wave of compression propagates through coils to the supported end, from where, it is reflected back to deflected end. This wave of compression travels along the spring indefinitely.

- If the applied load is fluctuating type, as in case of valve spring in internal combustion engine and if the time interval between the load applications is equal to the time required for wave to travel from one end to other end, then resonance will occur.

- This results in very large deflection of coils and correspondingly very high stresses. Under this condition, it is just possible that the spring may fail. This phenomenon is called *surge*.

Methods to Avoid Surge in Springs :

(a) By using springs of high natural frequency.

(b) By using friction dampers on the center coils.

(c) By using springs having pitch of coil near the ends, different than, at the center to have different natural frequencies.

5.6 LEAF SPRING

5.6.1 Introduction

- Leaf springs or flat springs are made out of flat plates.

- The advantage of leaf spring over the helical spring is that the ends of spring may be guided along a definite path, as it deflects to act as a structural number, in addition to energy absorbing device.

- Thus, the leaf spring may carry lateral loads, brake torque, driving torque etc. in addition to shocks.

5.6.2 Construction

Questions

1. Sketch semi-elliptical leaf spring and name different parts on sketch. **(W-09)**
2. With neat sketch, explain the construction of leaf spring. **(W-10; S-11, 14)**
3. Explain with neat sketch constructional details of leaf spring. State any two applications. **(S-12)**

Construction :

- A leaf spring is of semi-elliptical form and consists of number of plates or leaves.

- The longest leaf is called as **master leaf** and has its ends formed in the shape of an eye, through which, bolts are passed to secure the spring to its supports.

- Usually the eyes, through which, spring is attached to shackle, are provided with bushings of anti-friction material.

- The other leaves are called as **graduated leaves**, which are arranged in the order of decreasing length and then clamped to the master leaf with the help of strips.

- Since master leaf has to withstand vertical bending loads as well as the loads due to sideways of vehicle, therefore, due to presence of stresses caused by these loads, it is usual to provide two full length leaves and rest as graduated leaves.

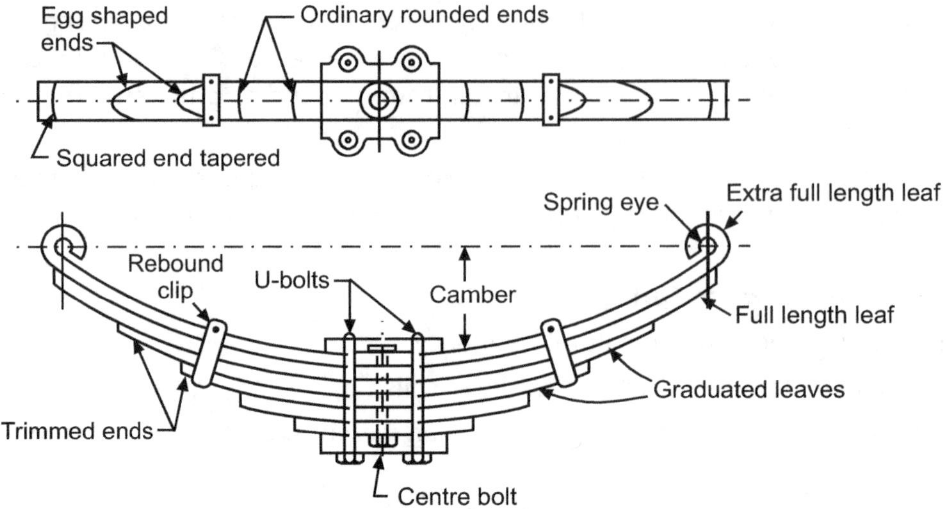

Fig. 5.16 : Semi-elliptical leaf spring

5.6.3 Utility of Centre Bolt, U-clamp, Rebound Clips and Camber in a Leaf Spring

Centre bolt : The leaf spring is made up of number of leaves. These leaves are held together by a bolt at the centre known as *centre bolt.*

U-clamp : The leaf spring is clamped to the axle by means of *U-clamp.*

Rebound clips : They are located at intermediate positions in the length of spring, so that, the graduated leaves can also share the stresses induced in the full-length leaves, when the spring rebounds.

Camber : The leaves are initially given curvature, so that, they will tend to straighten under the action of load. This is called as *camber.*

Material for Leaf Spring :

- The automobile leaf springs are made up of oil hardened and tempered alloy steels such as, 50 Cr 1, 50 Cr 1 V 23, 55 Si 2 Mn 90.

5.6.4 Advantages of Leaf Spring

(a)   In addition to an energy absorbing device, leaf spring acts as a structural member.

(b)   Leaf springs are used in automobile suspensions due to capability to take lateral loads, brake torque and driving torque in addition to shocks.

5.6.5 Expressions for Stresses and Deflections in Leaf Springs

Let, $2W$ = Central load

$2L$ = Effective length or Span of spring

b = Width of leaves

t = Thickness of leaves

$$n = \text{Total number of leaves}$$
$$l = \text{Length of central band}$$
$$n_f = \text{Number of full length leaves}$$
$$n_g = \text{Number of graduated leaves}$$

Then,

(1) Stress in leaf spring :

$$\sigma_b = \frac{6\,WL}{n\,b\,t^2}$$

where,

Effective length of spring $= 2L = 2L_1 - l$　　　　(when central band is used)

$$= 2L = 2L_1 - \frac{2}{3} \cdot l \qquad \text{(when U-bolt is used)}$$

(2) Deflection in leaf spring :

$$\delta = \frac{6\,WL^3}{n\,E\,b\,t^3}$$

(3) Stress in full length leaves :

$$\sigma_F = \frac{18\,WL}{bt^2\,(2n_g + 3n_f)}$$

(4) Stress in graduated leaves :

$$\sigma_G = \frac{12\,WL}{bt^2\,(2n_g + 3n_f)}$$

(5) Deflection in full length and graduated leaves :

$$\delta = \frac{12WL^3}{E\,b\,t^3\,(2n_g + 3n_f)}$$

5.6.6 Nipping in Leaf Springs

Question

1. Explain nipping in leaf springs.　　　　**(S-13)**

- We know that,

Stress in full length leaves:　$\sigma_F = \dfrac{18\,WL}{bt^2\,(2n_g + 3n_f)}$　and,

Stress in graduated leaves:　$\sigma_G = \dfrac{12\,WL}{bt^2\,(2n_g + 3n_f)}$

- It means that, stresses in full length leaves are 50% greater than the stresses in graduated leaves. In order to utilize the material to the best advantage, all the leaves should be equally stressed. This may be achieved by pre-stressing the leaves.

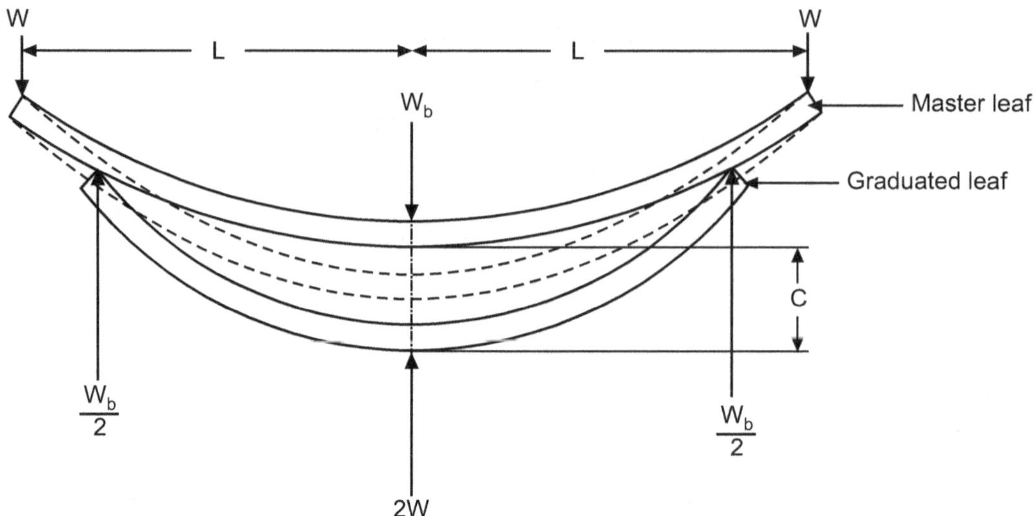

Fig. 5.17 : Nipping of leaf springs

- The pre-stressing of the spring can be done by giving greater radius of curvature to the full length leaves than the graduated leaves before assembly as shown in Fig. 5.17.
- The initial gap 'C' between full length leaf and graduated leaf before assembly is called as **nip**.
- When the central bolt holding leaves together is tightened, the extra full length leaf will bend back as shown by dotted lines and have an initial stress in a direction opposite to that of normal load.
- The graduated leaves will have an initial stress in the same direction as that of normal load.
- When the load is gradually applied to the spring, the extra full length leaves are first relieved of this initial stress and then stressed in opposite direction. Consequently the full length leaves will be stressed less than that without nip.
- This process of pre-stressing the spring by giving, different radii of curvature before assembly is known as **nipping.**
- The initial gap between the leaves (i.e. nip) is adjusted , so that, under the maximum load condition, the stresses in all leaves will be equal.
- Normally the nip is adjusted to give stress in full length leaves slightly less than the graduated leaves. This is desirable in automobile, because full length leaves are expected to take transverse forces in addition to bending load.

Numerical Type No. 7 : "Design of Numericals on Leaf Springs"

Problem 5.22 : *A semi-elliptical carriage spring of 1200 mm length withstand a load of 60 kN with maximum permissible deflection of 90 mm. Assume breadth to thickness ratio as 8. Design the spring, if σ_b = 540 MPa and E = 2 ×10⁵ N/mm².*

Solution : Given data : Central load on each spring = 2W = 60 kN,

W = 30 kN = 30×10^3 N, 2L = 1200 mm, L = 600 mm, δ = 90 mm, σ_b = 540 N/mm²,

E = 2×10^5 N/mm²

Procedure : We have, $\dfrac{b}{t}$ = 8, thus $b = 8t$

We know that, stress in leaf spring is given by,

$$\sigma_b = \frac{6WL}{nbt^2}$$

Thus, $\quad n \times b \times t^2 = \dfrac{6 \times W \times L}{\sigma_b} = \dfrac{6 \times 30 \times 10^3 \times 600}{540} = 200 \times 10^3 \qquad \text{... (1)}$

Also, $\quad \delta = \dfrac{6WL^3}{nEbt^3}$

Thus, $\quad n \times b \times t^3 = \dfrac{6 \times W \times L^3}{\delta \times E} = \dfrac{6 \times 30 \times 10^3 \times (600)^3}{90 \times 2 \times 10^5} = 2.16 \times 10^6 \qquad \text{... (2)}$

Dividing equation (2) by equation (1), we get,

$$t = \mathbf{10.8 \ mm}$$

$\therefore \qquad b = 8t = 8 \times 10.8 = \mathbf{86.4 \ mm}$

From equation (1),

$$n \times b \times t^2 = 200 \times 10^3$$

$\therefore \qquad n \times 86.4 \times (10.8)^2 = 200 \times 10^3$

$\therefore \qquad n = 19.84 \cong \mathbf{20 \ (say)}$

Problem 5.23 : *Design a leaf spring for the following specifications :*

(a) Total load = 16 kN

(b) Number of springs supporting the load = 4

(c) Maximum number of leaves = 10

(d) Span of the spring = 1000 mm

(e) Permissible deflection = 80 mm

(f) Young's modulus = 2×10^5 N/mm²

(g) Allowable stress in spring material = 600 N/mm²

Solution : Given data : Central load on each spring = $2W = \dfrac{16}{4}$ = 4 kN = 4×10^3 N

$\therefore \qquad W = 2 \times 10^3$ N $\qquad\qquad$ ($\because$ number of springs = 4),

$2L = 1000$ mm, $\delta = 80$ mm, $\sigma_b = 600$ N/mm², $n = 10$, $E = 2 \times 10^5$ N/mm²

Procedure : We have, $2L = 1000$ mm; $\quad \therefore L = 500$ mm

We know that, stress in leaf spring is given by,

$$\sigma_b = \frac{6 \times W \times L}{n \times b \times t^2}$$

Thus, $\quad n \times b \times t^2 = \dfrac{6 \times W \times L}{\sigma_b} = \dfrac{6 \times 2 \times 10^3 \times 500}{600} = 10 \times 10^3 \qquad \text{... (1)}$

Also, deflection in leaf spring is given by,

$$\delta = \frac{6 \times W \times L^3}{n \times E \times b \times t^3}$$

Thus,

$$n \times b \times t^3 = \frac{6 \times W \times L^3}{\delta \times E} = \frac{6 \times 2 \times 10^3 \times (500)^3}{80 \times 2 \times 10^5} = 93.75 \times 10^3 \qquad \text{... (2)}$$

Dividing equation (2) by equation (1), we get,

$$t = \textbf{9.375 mm}$$

From equation (1),

$$n \times b \times t^2 = 10 \times 10^3$$

$$\therefore \quad 10 \times b \times (9.375)^2 = 10 \times 10^3$$

$$\therefore \quad b = 11.37 \text{ mm} \cong \textbf{12 mm}$$

Problem 5.24 : *A semi-elliptical laminated spring 900 mm long and 55 mm wide is held together at the centre by a band 50 mm wide. If the thickness of each leaf is 5 mm, find the number of leaves required to carry a load of 4500 N. Assume a maximum working stress of 490 MPa.*

If the two of these leaves are full length leaves of spring, find the deflection of the spring. The Young's modulus for the spring is 210 kN/mm².

Solution : Given data : Central load = $2W$ = 4500 N, W = 2250 N, $2L_1$ = 900 mm, l = 50 mm, b = 55 mm, t = 5 mm, σ_b = 490 N/mm², E = 210 kN/mm² = 210×10^3 N/mm²

Procedure :

(i) Design of leaf spring : When central band is used, the effective length is,

$$2L = 2L_1 - l = 900 - 50 = 850 \text{ mm}$$

Thus,

$$L = 425 \text{ mm}$$

We know that, stress in leaf spring is given by,

$$\sigma_b = \frac{6 \times W \times L}{n \times b \times t^2}$$

$$\therefore \quad n = \frac{6 \times W \times L}{\sigma_b \times b \times t^2} = \frac{6 \times 2250 \times 425}{490 \times 55 \times (5)^2} = 8.515 \cong \textbf{10 turns (say)}$$

(ii) Deflection in leaf spring :

$$\delta = \frac{6 \times W \times L^3}{n \times E \times b \times t^3} = \frac{6 \times 2250 \times (425)^3}{10 \times 210 \times 10^3 \times 55 \times 5^3} = \textbf{71.78 mm}$$

Problem 5.25 : *A locomotive semi-elliptical laminated spring has overall length of 1 m and sustains a load of 70 kN at its centre. The spring has 3 full-length leaves and 15 graduated leaves with a central band of 100 mm wide. All leaves are to be stressed to 400 MPa, when fully loaded. The ratio of the total spring depth to that of width is 2.*

Take E = 200 kN/mm². Determine :

(1)   The thickness and width of the leaves.

(2)   The initial gap that should be provided between full length and graduated leaves.

(3)   The load exerted on band after spring is assembled.

Solution : Given data : Central load $= 2W = 70$ kN; $\therefore$ $W = 35$ kN $= 35 \times 10^3$ N,

$n_f = 3$, $n_g = 15$, $\therefore$ $n = n_f + n_g = 3 + 15 = 18$, $2L_1 = 1000$ mm, $l = 100$ mm,

$\sigma_b = 400$ N/mm^2, $E = 200$ kN/mm$^2 = 200 \times 10^3$ N/mm^2

Procedure : When central band is used, the effective length is,

$$2L = 2L_1 - l = 1000 - 100 = 900 \text{ mm} \quad \therefore \quad L = 450 \text{ mm}$$

Total spring depth $= 2 \times$ Width $= 2 \times b$ ... (1)

But, Spring depth $= n \times t = 18 \times t$ ... (2)

From (1) and (2),

$$18 \times t = 2 \times b; \quad \therefore \quad b = 9t$$

(i) The thickness and width of leaves :

We have, $\quad \sigma_b = \dfrac{6 \times W \times L}{n \times b \times t^2}$

$\therefore \quad 400 = \dfrac{6 \times 35 \times 10^3 \times 450}{18 \times 9t \times t^2}$

$\therefore \quad t = 11.34$ mm $= $ **12 mm (say)** and $b = 9t = 9 \times 12 = $ **108 mm**

(ii) The initial gap provided between full length and graduated leaves :

$$\text{Initial gap, } C = \frac{2 \times W \times L^3}{n \times E \times b \times t^3} = \frac{2 \times 35 \times 10^3 \times (450)^3}{18 \times 200 \times 10^3 \times 108 \times (12)^3} = \textbf{9.5 mm}$$

(iii) The load exerted on band after spring is assembled :

$$W_b = \frac{2 \times n_f \times n_g \times W}{n \times (2n_g + 3n_f)} = \frac{2 \times 3 \times 15 \times 35 \times 10^3}{18 \times (2 \times 15 + 3 \times 3)} = \textbf{4487.18 N}$$

Problem 5.26 : *A semi-elliptical laminated spring with a span of 600 mm carries a central load of 180 kN. The spring has 2 full-length leaves and 15 graduated leaves with thickness of 12 mm and width 96 mm. U-bolt of width 90 mm is used. Take E = 200 kN/mm². Determine the stress induced in full-length and graduated leaves. Also find the deflection produced.*

Solution : Given data : Central load $= 2W = 180$ kN $\therefore$ $W = 90$ kN $= 90 \times 10^3$ N,

$n_f = 2$, $n_g = 15$, $\therefore$ $n = n_f + n_g = 2 + 15 = 17$, $t = 12$ mm, $b = 96$ mm, $2L_1 = 600$ mm,

$l = 90$ mm, $E = 200$ kN/mm$^2 = 200 \times 10^3$ N/mm^2

Procedure : When U-bolt is used, the effective length is,

$$2L = 2L_1 - (2/3) \times l = 600 - (2/3) \times 90 = 540 \text{ mm} \quad \therefore \quad L = 270 \text{ mm}$$

(i) Stress induced in full-length leaves :

$$\sigma_F = \frac{18 \times W \times L}{b \times t^2 \times (2n_g + 3n_f)}$$

$$= \frac{18 \times 90 \times 10^3 \times 270}{96 \times (12)^2 \times (2 \times 15 + 3 \times 2)} = \textbf{878.91 N/mm}^2$$

(ii) Stress induced in graduated leaves :

$$\sigma_G = \frac{12 \times W \times L}{b \times t^2 \times (2n_g + 3n_f)}$$

$$= \frac{12 \times 90 \times 10^3 \times 270}{96 \times (12)^2 \times (2 \times 15 + 3 \times 2)} = \textbf{585.94 N/mm}^2$$

(iii) Deflection in full-length and graduated leaves :

$$\delta = \frac{12 \times W \times L^3}{E \times b \times t^3 \times (2n_g + 3n_f)}$$

$$= \frac{12 \times 90 \times 10^3 \times (270)^3}{200 \times 10^3 \times 96 \times (12)^3 \times (2 \times 15 + 3 \times 2)} = \textbf{17.79 mm}$$

Problem 5.27 : A truck spring has 12 number of leaves, two of which are full length leaves. The spring supports are 1.05 m apart and the central band is 85 mm wide. The central load is to be 5.4 kN with permissible stress 280 N/mm². Determine the thickness and width of the steel spring leaves. The ratio of the total depth to the width of the spring is 3. Also determine the deflection of the spring. **(S-05; W-05, 12)**

Solution : Given data : Central load = $2W$ = 5.4 kN, W = 2.7 kN = 2.7×10^3 N, n = 12, n_f = 2, n_g = 10, $2L_1$ = 1050 mm, l = 85 mm, σ_b = 280 N/mm², E = 2.1×10^5 N/mm² (Assumed).

Procedure : When central band is used, the effective length is,

$$2L = 2L_1 - l = 1050 - 85 = 965 \text{ mm}; \quad \therefore L = 482.5 \text{ mm}$$

Also, Total spring depth = 3 × Width = 3 × b $\qquad \qquad$ ... (1)

But, Spring depth = n × t = 12 × t $\qquad \qquad$ ... (2)

From (1) and (2),

$$12 \times t = 3 \times b$$

$$\therefore \qquad b = 4t$$

(1) The thickness and width of leaves : Assume that, the leaves are not initially stressed, the maximum bending stress for full length leaves is given by,

$$\sigma_F = \frac{18 \times W \times L}{b \times t^2 \times (2n_g + 3n_f)}$$

$$\therefore \qquad 280 = \frac{18 \times 2.7 \times 10^3 \times 482.5}{4t \times t^2 \times (2 \times 10 + 3 \times 2)}$$

$$\therefore \qquad 280 = \frac{225.47 \times 10^3}{t^3}$$

$$\therefore \qquad t = 9.303 \text{ mm} \cong \textbf{10 mm (say)}$$

and $\qquad b = 4t = 4 \times 10 = \textbf{40 mm}$

(2) Deflection in full length and graduated leaves :

$$\delta = \frac{12 \times W \times L^3}{E \times b \times t^3 \times (2n_g + 3n_f)}$$

$$= \frac{12 \times 2.7 \times 10^3 \times (482.5)^3}{2.1 \times 10^5 \times 40 \times (10)^3 \times (2 \times 10 + 3 \times 2)} = \textbf{16.66 mm}$$

Numerical Type No. 8 : "Design of Governor Spring"

Problem 5.28 : *In a spring loaded governor as shown in Fig. 5.18, the balls are attached to the vertical arms of the bell crank lever, the horizontal arms of which, lift the sleeve against the pressure exerted by a spring. The mass of each ball is 2.95 kg and the lengths of the vertical and horizontal arms of the bell crank lever are 150 mm and 112 mm respectively. The extreme radii of rotation of the balls are 100 mm and 150 mm and the governor sleeve begins to lift at 250 r.p.m. and reaches the highest position with a 7.5 % increase of speed. When effects of friction are neglected, design a suitable close coiled round section helical spring for the governor.*

Assume permissible stress in spring material as 420 MPa, modulus of rigidity as 84 kN/mm² and spring index 6.

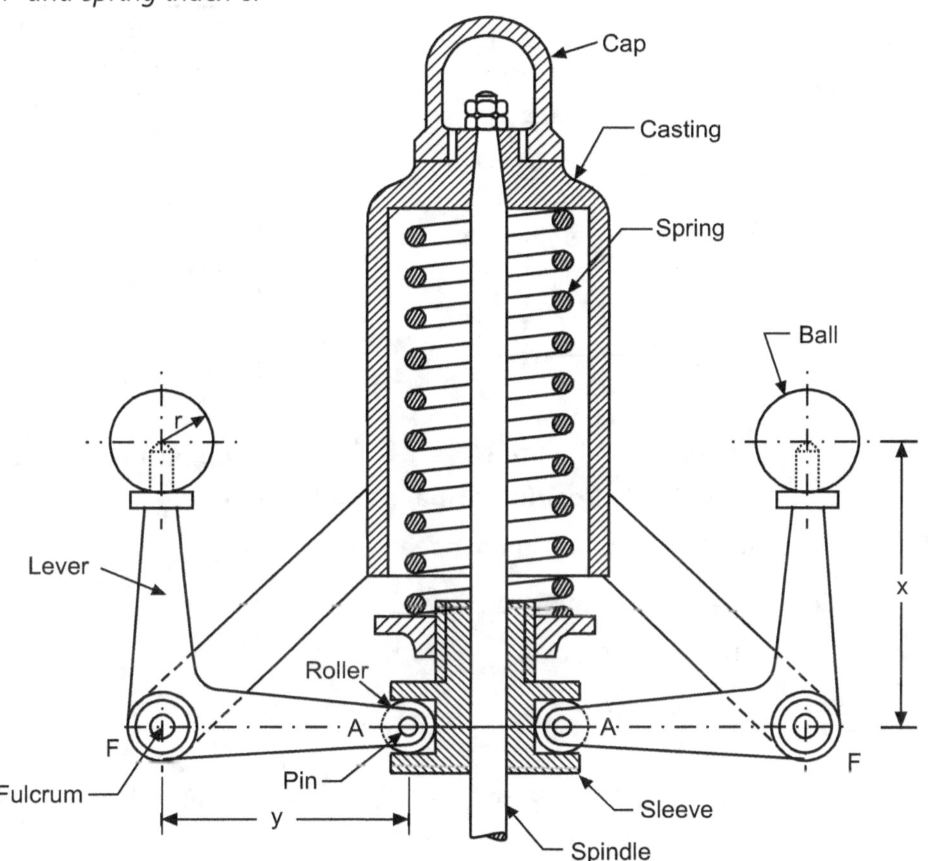

Fig. 5.18 : Governor spring

Solution : Given data : m = 2.95 kg, x = 150 mm = 0.15 m, y = 112 mm = 0.112 m,

r_2 = 100 mm = 0.1 m, r_1 = 150 mm = 0.15 m, N_2 = 250 r.p.m., τ = 420 MPa,

G = 84 × 10³ N/mm², C = 6

Figure 5.18 shows Hartnell type governor (centrifugal).

(1) To find compression of the spring : Minimum angular speed at which the governor sleeve begins to lift,

$$\omega_2 \;=\; \frac{2\pi N_2}{60} \;=\; \frac{2\pi \times 250}{60} \;=\; 26.179 \text{ rad/sec.}$$

Since increase in speed is 7.5%,

∴   Maximum speed,

$$\omega_1 \;=\; \omega_2 + \frac{7.5}{100} \times \omega_2 \;=\; 26.179 + \frac{7.5}{100} \times 26.179$$

∴ $\omega_1 \;=\; 28.142 \text{ rad/sec}$

The positions of the balls and the lever arms at the maximum and minimum speeds are shown in Fig. 5.19 (a) and (b).

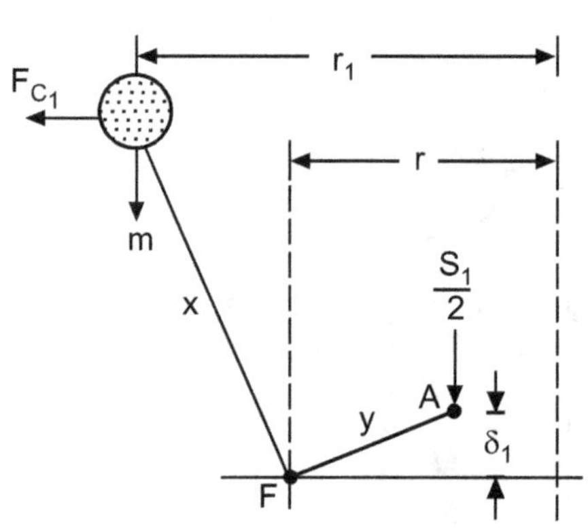

(a) Maximum position   **(b) Minimum position**

Fig. 5.19 : Position of balls and lever arms

Let F_{C_1} = Centrifugal force at maximum speed = $m\omega_1^2 \, r_1$

F_{C_2} = Centrifugal force at minimum speed = $m\omega_2^2 \, r_2$

Spring force at maximum speed (ω_1) :

$$S_1 \;=\; 2F_{C_1} \times \frac{x}{y} \;=\; 2m\omega_1^2 \, r_1 \times \frac{x}{y}$$

$$=\; 2 \times 2.95 \times (28.142)^2 \times 0.15 \times \frac{0.15}{0.112} \;=\; 938.69 \text{ N}$$

Spring force at minimum speed (ω_2) :

$$S_2 \;=\; 2F_{C_2} \times \frac{x}{y} \;=\; 2m\omega_2^2 \times r_2 \times \frac{x}{y}$$

$$=\; 2 \times 2.95 \times (26.179)^2 \times 0.1 \times \frac{0.15}{0.112}$$

∴ $S_2 \;=\; 541.54 \text{ N}$

Compression of spring will be equal to left of sleeve.

∴   Compression of spring,

$$\delta \; = \; \delta_1 + \delta_2 \; = \; (r_1 - r)\frac{y}{x} + (r - r_2)\frac{y}{x} \; = \; (r_1 - r_2) \cdot \frac{y}{x}$$

$$= \; (0.15 - 0.1) \times \frac{0.112}{0.15} \; = \; 0.03733 \text{ m} \; = \; \mathbf{37.33 \text{ mm}}$$

The compression of the spring is due to spring force $(S_1 - S_2)$

i.e. $S_1 - S_2 \; = \; (938.69 - 541.54) \; = \; 397.15$ N

(2) To find diameter of the spring wire :

Let d = Diameter of spring wire in mm.

∴   Wahl's stress factor,

$$K \; = \; \frac{4C - 1}{4C - 4} + \frac{0.615}{C} \; = \; \frac{4 \times 6 - 1}{4 \times 6 - 4} + \frac{0.615}{6} \; = \; 1.2525$$

∴   Maximum shear stress (τ),

$$\tau \; = \; K \times \frac{8WC}{\pi d^2}$$

∴ $420 \; = \; 1.2525 \times \dfrac{8 \times 938.69 \times 6}{\pi d^2}$ $(W = S_1 = \text{maximum spring force})$

∴ $d \; = \; 6.539$ mm $\cong$ **7 mm (say)**

(3) Mean diameter of the spring coil :

Let D = Mean diameter of coil $D = C \times d = 6 \times 7 =$ **42 mm**

(4) Number of turns of the coil :

Let n = Active number of turns of the coil

∴   Compression / deflection of spring is,

$$\delta \; = \; \frac{8WC^3 n}{Gd}$$

For $\delta_{range} = \delta_1 - \delta_2$, use $W = S_1 - S_2 = 397.15$ N

∴ $37.33 \; = \; \dfrac{8 \times 397.15 \times 6^3 \times n}{84 \times 10^3 \times 7}$

∴ $n \; = \; 31.98 \cong$ **32 turns**

Using squared and grounded ends,

Total number of turns, $n' = n + 2 = 32 + 2 =$ **34 turns**

(5) Free length of spring :

$$L_f \; = \; n'd + \delta_{max} + 0.15\,\delta_{max}$$

∴   To find δ_{max},

For load range $= 397.15$ N $\rightarrow$ Deflection $= 37.33$ mm

For maximum load $= 938.69$ N $\rightarrow \delta_{max} = ?$

∴ $\delta_{max} \; = \; 37.33 \times \dfrac{938.69}{397.15} \; = \; 88.23$ mm

∴ $L_f \; = \; (34 \times 7) + 88.23 + 0.15 \times (88.23) =$ **339.4645 mm**

(6) Pitch of coil : $p = \dfrac{\text{Free length}}{n' - 1} \; = \; \dfrac{339.4645}{33} \; = $ **10.286 mm**

Practice Questions

1. What is function of a spring ? State its applications.
2. Give practical application for each of following springs :
   (i) Helical tension spring.　　　　　(ii) Leaf spring.
   (iii) Helical torsion spring.　　　　(iv) Spiral tension spring.
3. List the material used in springs.
4. Explain the following terms of the spring :
   (a) Free length,　　　　　　　(b) Solid length,
   (c) Spring index,　　　　　　(d) Spring rate,
   (e) Spring stress factor,　　　(f) Pitch of coil.
5. Explain the stresses in helical springs of circular wire.
6. Explain what do you understand by A.M. Wahl's factor and state its importance in the design of helical springs.
7. Draw a graph of Wahl's stress factor versus spring index for helical compression spring and state the effect of curvature of coil on stress distribution.
8. Explain different end conditions for compression helical springs.
9. Explain springs in series and parallel.
10. Draw a neat sketch of semielliptical leaf spring with construction details. What is material used for leaf spring.

Problems for Practice

1. A helical spring is made from a wire of 6 mm diameter and has outside diameter of 75 mm. If the permissible shear stress is 350 MPa and modulus of rigidity is 84 kN/mm^2, find the axial load, which the spring can carry and deflection per active turn. Take Wahl's factor, $K = \dfrac{4C-1}{4C-4} + \dfrac{0.615}{C}$　　**(Ans.** 382.49 N, 9.233 mm) **(W-10)**

2. A helical spring is made from a wire of 6 mm diameter and has outside diameter of 75 mm. If the permissible shear stress is 350 MPa and modulus of rigidity is 84 kN/mm^2, find the axial load, which the spring can carry and deflection per active turn, neglecting effect and considering effect of curvature.

   (Ans. (i) 412.52 N, 9.958 mm (ii) 382.45 N, 9.232 mm)

3. Design a helical compression spring with squared and grounded ends for operating load range between 80 N and 145 N. The axial deflection of the spring is 6.5 mm, while spring index is 8. The permissible shear stress is 380 N/mm^2. Take design stress for intermittent operation of spring. **(S-04)**

   (Ans. d = 1.94 mm ≅ 2 mm, D = 16 mm, n = 5, n' = 7, L$_s$ = 14 mm, L$_f$ = 30.67 mm, p = 5.11 mm)

4. A helical spring is subjected to a load ranging from 2500 N to 3250 N. Axial compression for above load range is 5 mm. Design the spring, if C = 5 and τ = 400 N/mm^2 and G = 84 kN/mm^2.　　**(Ans.** d = 12 mm, D = 60 m, n = 6.52 ≅ 7, n' = 9, δ_{max} = 21.66 mm, L$_f$ = 132.90 mm, p = 16.61 mm)

5. Design a compression helical valve spring with squared and grounded ends for load range between 80 N to 145 N. The axial deflection of the spring is 6.5 mm. The spring index is 8. Permissible shear stress intensity is 380 N/mm^2. Take design stress 25% excess of permissible stress for severe condition and intermittent operating of spring. **(S-04)**

(**Ans.** d = 2.5 mm, D = 20 mm, n = 6, n' = 8, L_f = 36.6 mm, p = 5.21 mm)

6. Design a compression helical spring with squared and grounded ends for operating range 100 N to 135 N. The axial deflection of the spring is 5 mm. Spring index is 8. Permissible shear stress intensity is 330 N/mm^2. Take design stress 25% excess of permissible stress for severe condition and intermittent operation. **(S-04)**

(**Ans.** d = 2.81 mm, D = 22.48 mm, n = 9,

δ_{max} = 19.2857 mm, L_s = 30.91 mm, L_f = 53.09 mm, p = 5.309 mm)

7. A spring loaded safety valve for boiler is required to blow off at a pressure of 1.20 N/mm^2. Diameter of the valve is 65 mm. The maximum lift of the valve is 17.5 mm. Design a suitable compression spring for the safety valve. Assume C = 6 and provide initial compression of 30 mm. The maximum shear stress in the spring material = 450 N/mm^2 and G = 0.84×10^5 N/mm^2. **(S-06)**

(**Ans.** d = 16.35 mm, D = 98.10 mm, n = 6, n' = 8, L_f = 185.5 mm, p = 26.51 mm)

8. Design a helical spring using following data :
    - Valve seat diameter = 70 mm
    - Maximum pressure, when valve blows off freely = 0.73 N/mm^2
    - Valve lift, when pressure rises from 0.7 to 0.73 N/mm^2 = 3.5 mm
    - Maximum allowable stress = 500 N/mm^2
    - Spring index = 6.
    - Modulus of rigidity = 8.3×10^4 N/mm^2.

(**Ans.** d = 10.4 mm, D = 62.4 mm, δ_{max} = 88.14 mm,

n = 15.8 ≅ 16, n' = 18, L_f = 288.57 mm)

9. Design a valve spring of an I.C. engine with the following data :
    - Length of spring, when valve is closed = 4.5 cm
    - Length of spring, when valve is opened = 5.0 cm
    - Spring load when valve is open = 390 N
    - Spring load when valve is closed = 195 N
    - Maximum inside diameter of spring = 2.8 cm
    - Maximum shear stress for spring = 3.92×10^5 N/cm^2
    - Modulus of rigidity for spring material = 78×10^4 N/cm^2

(**Ans.** d = 4.65 mm, D = 32.65 mm, n = 4, n' = 6,

L_s = 27.9 mm, L_f = 42 mm, p = 8.41 mm)

10. Design a leaf spring for the following specifications.
    Total load = 140 kN,
    Number of springs supporting the load = 4,
    Maximum number of leaves = 10, span of spring = 1000 mm,
    Permissible deflection = 80 mm,
    Take Young's modulus (E) = 2×10^7 N/cm^2 and

    Allowable stress in spring material is 60 kN/cm^2. (**Ans.** t = 9.375 mm, b = 99.55 mm)

MSBTE Questions and Answers

Summer 2013

1. State four properties desirable for a good spring material.   **(2 M)**

Ans. Refer Article 5.1.7 (b).

2. A closed coiled helical compression spring of 12 active coils has a spring stiffness "K". It is cut into 2 springs having 5 and 7 turns. Determine the spring stiffness of resultant springs.   **(4 M)**

Ans. Refer Problem 5.21.

3. Explain "Nipping" in leaf springs.   **(4 M)**

Ans. Refer Article 5.6.6.

4. A rail wagon of mass 20 tons is moving with a velocity of 9 k.m.p.h. It is brought to rest by using two buffer springs of 360 mm diameter. The maximum deflection of springs is 300 mm. An allowable shear stress for spring material is 800 MPa. Design the spring for buffers.   **(8 M)**

Ans. Refer Problem 5.18.

Winter 2013

1. How springs are classified?   **(4 M)**

Ans. Refer Article 5.1.3.

2. The spring of spring balance, elongates by 150 mm, when subjected to load of 400 N. The spring index is 6. Take permissible shear stress for the wire material as 540 N/mm^2. Considering the effect of direct shear and wire curvature, find: (i) The wire diameter, (ii) The diameter of coil, (iii) Number of active turns. Take $G = 84$ kN/mm^2.   **(8 M)**

Ans. Refer Problem 5.5.

3. Define the term : (i) Spring index, (ii)Spring rate, (iii) Free length, (iv) Pitch.

Ans. Refer Article 5.1.6.

Summer 2014

1. Explain Wahl's correction factor for spring.   **(4 M)**

Ans. Refer Article 5.2.2.

2. Design a helical compression spring for maximum load of 800 N for a deflection of 25 mm. The spring index is 5 and Wahl's correction factor is 1.3. The maximum permissible shear stress for the spring wire is 400 MPa and the modulus of rigidity is 84 kN/mm^2.   **(4 M)**

Ans. Refer Problem 5.10.

3. Describe the construction of leaf spring with neat sketch.   **(4 M)**

Ans. Refer Article 5.6.2.

4. State any four functions of spring.   **(4 M)**

Ans. Refer Article 5.1.1.

DESIGN OF THREADED JOINTS

Chapter 6

About This Chapter

This chapter has a weightage of 06 marks and assigned duration is 04 hours. In this chapter, we learn about various types of fasteners & bolts of uniform strength, design of bolts subjected to eccentric loading.

Statistical Analysis

Examination	Weightage of questions asked
S-09	08 Marks
W-09	10 Marks
S-10	08 Marks
W-10	07 Marks
S-11	08 Marks
W-11	12 Marks
S-12	16 Marks
W-12	10 Marks
S-13	12 Marks
W-13	12 Marks
S-14	06 Marks

6.1 INTRODUCTION TO SCREWED JOINTS

- A screw thread is formed by cutting a continuous helical groove on a cylindrical surface.

- A screw made by cutting a single helical groove on the cylinder is known as *single start threaded screw*. When a second thread is cut in the space between the grooves of the first, it is known as *double start threaded screw*. Similarly, triple, quadraple threads may be made. The helical grooves cut on cylindrical surface may be either right hand or left hand.

- Screwed joint is mainly composed of two elements : Screw (bolt) and nut.

- These joints are used, where the machine parts are required to be readily connected or disconnected without causing any damage to the machine or fastening.

6.1.1 Applications or Uses of Screwed Joints

1. To connect the components together, which should be readily disassembled :

- For this purpose, the threads of high strength and low efficiency are required, so as to avoid the loosening during the service.
- Example : 'V' threads as fasteners.

2. To transmit power or energy :

- For this purpose, the threads of high efficiency are required, so as to reduce the power loss during power transmission.
- Example : Square threads.

Question

1. Give two examples, where screwed joints are preferred over welded joints.

(W-09; S-10, 12)

Answer :

1. Fasteners.
2. Automobile components, such as connecting rod and crank shaft assembly.

6.1.2 Advantages and Disadvantages of Screwed Joints

Question

1. Write down the advantages and disadvantages of screwed joints.   **(W-10, 12)**

Advantages of Screwed Joints :

1. They are convenient to assemble and dissemble in case of breakage or maintenance.
2. They are highly reliable in operation.
3. A wide range of screwed joints may be adopted to various operating conditions.
4. They are relatively cheap to produce because of standardization.
5. They give high clamping force.

Disadvantages of Screwed Joints :

1. The main disadvantage is *stress concentration* in the threaded portion, which is considerable under the conditions of variable loading.
2. The strength of screwed joints is less than that of welded joints due to presence of holes.

6.2 VARIOUS FORMS OF THREAD

The various forms of thread used in fasteners are :

(a) Whitworth thread.   (b) Acme thread.

(c) Buttress thread.   (d) Square thread.

(e) Knuckle thread.   (f) Unified thread.

Out of all above, the commonly used thread profiles are, 'V' threads and square threads.

Type of thread profile	Description	Sketch	Applications
British standard whitworth thread	1. It is symmetrical 'V'-thread. 2. They have fine pitches. 3. Angle between flanks = 55°	**Fig. 6.1 : B.S.W. thread**	Used for steel and iron pipes carrying fluids.
Square thread	1. They are used for transmission of power in either direction. 2. Width of thread = $\dfrac{\text{Depth of thread}}{2}$	**Fig. 6.2 : Square thread**	Mechanism of machine tools, valves, spindles, screw jacks etc. For example : feed screws, coupler screws.

6.2.1 Advantages and Disadvantages of 'V' Threads

Question

1. State advantages of 'V' threads over square threads.   **(W-11)**

Advantages of 'V' Threads :

 (i) 'V' threads are used in bolts, studs, nuts, tap bolts etc. to tighten the parts together.

 (ii) 'V' threads offer greater frictional resistance of motion than square thread and therefore better suited for fastening purpose.

 (iii) 'V' threads are stronger than square thread.

 (iv) 'V' threads are cheaper, because of easiness to cut by die or on machine.

Disadvantages of 'V' Threads :

 (i) 'V' threads are not suitable for power transmission.

 (ii) 'V' threads have a component of force, which acts perpendicular to the axis causing bursting action on the nut and increasing friction, whereas, square threads are ideal for power transmission, because they do not have any component of force perpendicular to axis.

6.3 TERMINOLOGY FOR SCREW THREADS

1. Major diameter :

 • *It is the largest diameter of an external or internal screw thread.*

 • The screw is specified by this diameter. It is also known as *outside* or *nominal diameter* (d_o).

2. Minor diameter :

 • *It is the smallest diameter of external or internal screw thread.*

 • It is also known as *root* or *core diameter* (d_c).

3. Pitch circle diameter :

- *It is the diameter of an imaginary cylinder, on a cylindrical screw thread, the surface of which would pass through thread at such points as to make equal width of thread and width of space between threads.*
- It is also known as *effective diameter.* It is denoted by d_p.

4. Pitch :

- *It is the distance between a point on one thread to corresponding point on next (adjacent) thread.*
- It is given by,

$$\text{Pitch} = \frac{1}{\text{No. of threads per unit length of screw}}$$

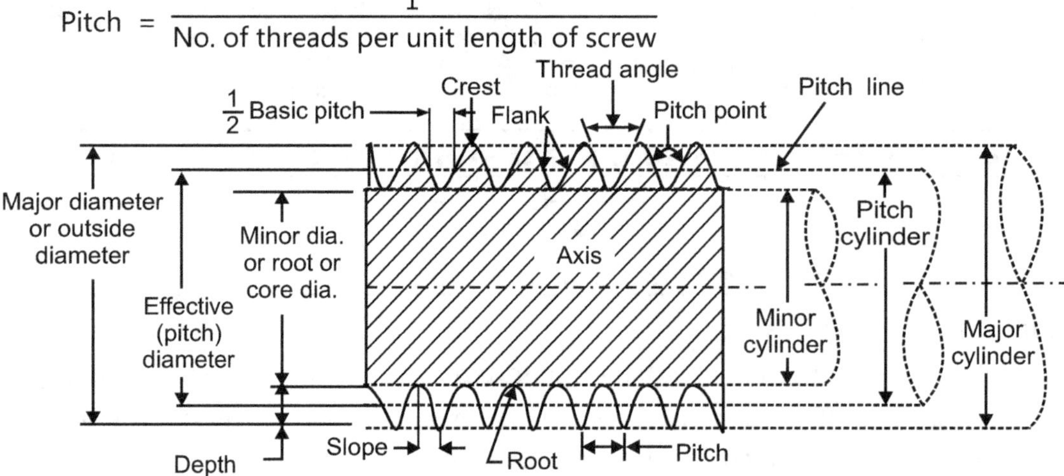

Fig. 6.3 : External thread

5. Lead :

- It is defined as '*distance through which, a screw advances axially in one rotation of nut'.*
- Lead = Pitch (in single start threads) = 2 × Pitch (in double start threads) and so on.

6. Hand of threads :

(a) Right hand threads : When the nut assembled on the screw is given clockwise rotation leading to tightening of the joint, then thread is called as **right hand thread.** On rotating in anticlockwise direction, it loosens the joint. The standard screwed joint employs right hand threads.

(b) Left hand threads : When the nut assembled on the screw is given clockwise rotation leading to loosening of the joint, then thread is called as **left hand thread.** On rotating in anticlockwise direction, it tightens the joint.

Fig. 6.4 : Hands of thread

6.3.1 Types of Screw Fastening 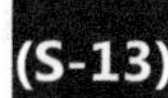 (S-13)

1. Through bolts :

- It is a cylindrical bar with threads at one end for the nut and head at the other end.
- The cylindrical part is shank.
- It is passed through drilled holes in the two parts to be fastened together and clamped them securely to each other, as the nut is screwed on to the thread end.

2. Tap bolt :

- A tap bolt or screw differs from a bolt.
- It is screwed into a tapped hole of one of the parts to be fastened without the nut.

3. Stud :

- Stud is a round bar threaded at both ends.
- One end of stud is screwed into tapped hole of parts to be fastened, while the other end receives nut on it.

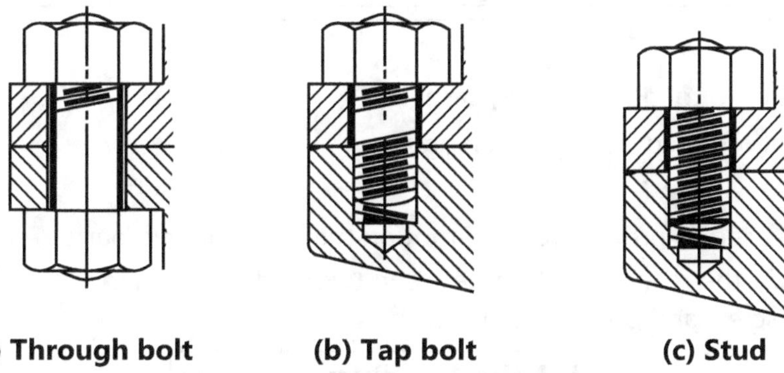

(a) Through bolt **(b) Tap bolt** **(c) Stud**

Fig. 6.5 : Use of bolt, stud and tap bolt

4. Cap screws :

- It is similar to tap bolts, that, it is screwed into a tapped hole of one of the parts to be fastened, without nut.
- They are of small size. A variety of shapes of heads are available as shown in figure.

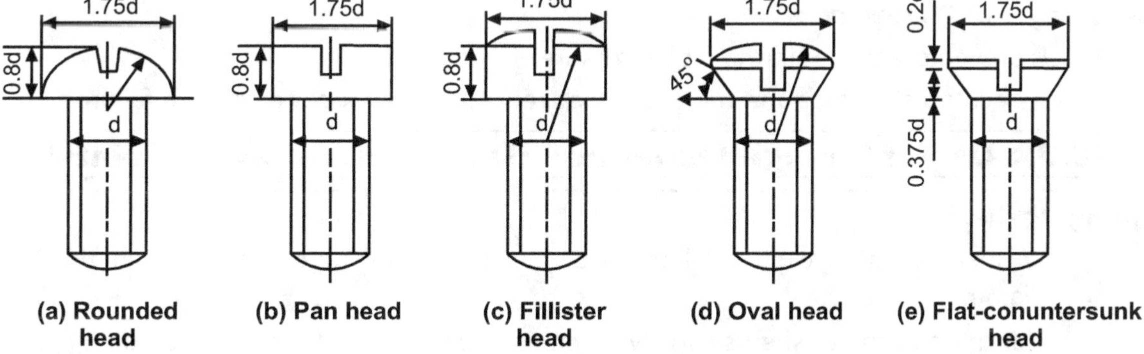

(a) Rounded head **(b) Pan head** **(c) Fillister head** **(d) Oval head** **(e) Flat-conuntersunk head**

Fig. 6.6 : Cap screws

5. Set screw :

- A set screw is screwed through a threaded hole in one part, so that, end of screw presses against the other part.

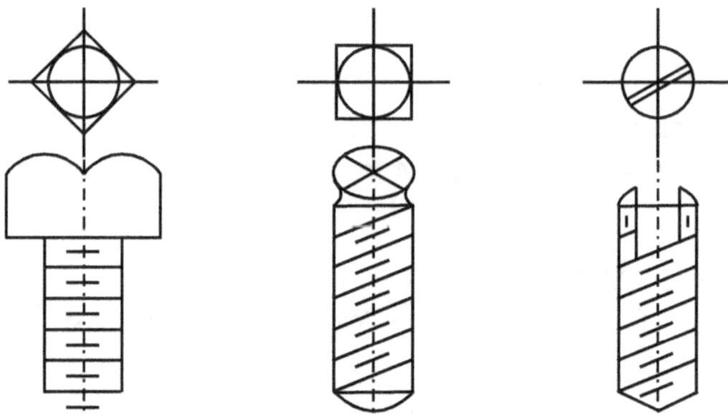

Fig. 6.7 : Set screws

6.3.2 Use of Cap Screws and Set Screws

Cap screws :

- They are used to fasten covers, cases etc.
- Nut is not required during fastening.

Set screws :

- They are used to prevent relative motion between the two parts.
- They resist the relative motion between two parts by means of friction between the point of screw and one of the parts.

6.3.3 Preloading of Bolts

- The material of bolt has elastic as well as plastic range of loading. The preloading of bolts means initial tightening of bolts, which gives strength to the joint.
- Good quality bolts can be preloaded into the plastic range to develop more strength.

Advantages of Preloading :

- It prevents leakages in the high-pressure vessels.
- It decreases fluctuations in loads, which reduces the chances of fatigue failure.

6.3.4 Use of Spring Washer and Gaskets in Screwed Joints

Spring Washers :

- Washers are thin circular plates with a central hole slightly large than the bolt diameter.
- Thickness of the washer is usually taken as equal to $0.15\,d_o$ and outside diameter of the washer is twice the nominal diameter.

- When nut and bolts secure thin material, washers increase the area, over which, the pressure of nut is distributed. It prevents the distortion of thin plate. On rough surface, washer provides a flat seat for nut.

- They are also used, when the hole, through which, bolt passes is much larger than the bolt, so as to provide sufficient bearing area.

Gaskets :

- Gaskets are made from material having lesser stiffness.

- When the screwed joint is to be made leak proof, a metal gasket or asbestos packing is inserted between the surfaces to be screwed.

6.4 STRESSES IN SCREWED FASTENING DUE TO STATIC LOADING

The following stresses in screwed fastening due to static loading are important :

1. Initial stresses due to screwing up forces,

2. Stresses due to external forces and

3. Stress due to combination of stresses at (1) and (2).

6.4.1 (a) Initial Stresses Due to Screwing Up Forces

The following stresses are induced in a bolt, screw or stud, when it is screwed up tightly.

1. Tensile stress due to stretching of bolt.

2. Torsional shear stress caused by the frictional resistance of the threads during its tightening.

3. Shear stress across threads.

4. Compression or crushing stress on threads.

5. Bending stress, if the surfaces under the head or nut are not perfectly parallel to the bolt axis.

Note : The core diameter (d_c) may be taken as $0.84\ d_o$, where d_o is the major diameter.

1. Tensile stress due to stretching of bolt :

- Since none of the above mentioned stresses are accurately determined, therefore bolts are designed on the basis of direct tensile stress with a large factor of safety, in order to account for the undetermined stresses.

- The initial tension in a bolt, based on experiments, may be found by the relation,

$$W_i = 2840\ d_o \text{ in 'N'}$$

where　　W_i = Initial tension in a bolt

and　　　d_o = Nominal diameter of bolt

- The above relation is used for making a joint fluid tight like steam engine cylinder cover, flanged joints etc.

- Sometimes, W_i is also denoted as W_1.

- When the joint is not required as tight as fluid-tight joint, then the initial tension in a bolt may be reduced. In such cases,

$$W_i \;=\; 1420 \, d_o$$

- The small diameter bolts may fail during tightening, therefore bolts of smaller diameter (less than M 16 or M 18) are not permitted in making fluid tight joints.

- If the bolt is not initially stressed, then the maximum safe axial load, which may be applied to it, is given by,

$$W \;=\; \text{Permissible stress} \times \text{Cross-sectional area at bottom of the thread}$$

(i.e. stress area)

- The stress area may be obtained by using the relation,

$$\text{Stress area} \;=\; \frac{\pi}{4}\left(\frac{d_p + d_c}{2}\right)^2$$

where, $\quad d_p \;=\;$ Pitch diameter or Mean diameter of screw

and $\qquad d_c \;=\;$ Core or minor diameter

2. Torsional shear stress caused by the frictional resistance of the threads during its tightening :

- The torsional shear stress caused by the frictional resistance of the threads during its tightening may be obtained by using the torsion equation.

- We know that,

$$\frac{T}{J} \;=\; \frac{\tau}{r}$$

$$\therefore \qquad \tau \;=\; \frac{T}{J} \times r \;=\; \frac{T}{\dfrac{\pi}{32}(d_c)^4} \times \frac{d_c}{2} \;=\; \frac{16\,T}{\pi\,(d_c)^3}$$

where, $\quad \tau \;=\;$ Torsional shear stress

$\qquad\quad J \;=\;$ Polar moment of inertia

$\qquad\quad T \;=\;$ Torque applied

and $\qquad d_c \;=\;$ Minor or core diameter of the thread

- It has been shown during experiments that, due to repeated unscrewing and tightening of the nut, there is a gradual scoring of the threads, which increases the torsional twisting moment (T).

3. Shear stress across threads :

- The average thread shearing stress for the screw (τ_s) is,

$$\tau_s \;=\; \frac{W}{\pi \, d_c \cdot t \cdot n}$$

where, $d_c =$ Core diameter, $\;\; t =$ Thickness of the thread section at the root

- The average thread shearing stress for the nut is,

$$\tau_n = \frac{W}{\pi \, d_o \cdot t \cdot n}$$

where,　　d_o　= Major diameter

　　　　　t　= Thickness of thread section at the root

4. Compression or Crushing stress on threads :

- The compression or crushing stress between the threads (σ_c) may be obtained by using the relation :

$$\sigma_c = \frac{W}{\frac{\pi}{4}\,[(d_o)^2 - (d_c)^2] \cdot n}$$

where,　　d_o　= Major diameter,

　　　　　d_c　= Minor diameter,

and　　　　n　= Number of threads in engagement

6.4.1 (b) Stresses Due to External Forces

The following stresses are induced in a bolt, when it is subjected to an external load.

1. Tensile stress
2. Shear stress
3. Combined tensile and shear stress

1. Tensile stress :

- The bolts, studs and screws usually carry a load in the direction of the bolt axis, which induces tensile stress in the bolt.
- If d_c = Root or core diameter of the thread and W = External load applied, then, permissible tensile stress for the bolt material (σ_t) is given by,

$$\sigma_t = \frac{W}{\frac{\pi}{4} \cdot (d_c)^2}$$

or　　　　$d_c = \sqrt{\dfrac{4W}{\pi \cdot \sigma_t}}$

- Now, the value of the nominal diameter of bolt corresponding to the value of d_c may be obtained from standard table or stress area $\left[\dfrac{\pi}{4}\,(d_c)^2\right]$ may be fixed.

Note :

(a)　If the external load is taken up by a number of bolts, then,

$$\sigma_t = \frac{W}{\frac{\pi}{4}\,(d_c)^2 \times n}$$

(b)　In case, the standard table is not available, then for coarse threads, $d_c = 0.84 \, d_o$, where d_o is nominal diameter of bolt.

2. Shear stress :

- Sometimes, the bolts are used to prevent the relative movement between two or more parts, as in case of flange coupling, then the shear stress is induced in the bolts.
- The shear stress should be avoided as far as possible. It should be noted that, when the bolts are subjected to direct shearing load, then they should be located, in such a way that, the shearing load comes upon the body (i.e. shank) of the bolt and not upon the threaded portion.
- In some cases, the bolts may be relieved of shear load by using shear pins.
- When a number of bolts are used to share the shearing load, the finished bolts should be fitted to the reamed holes.

Let, $\quad W_s$ = Load shared and carried by each bolt

$\quad\quad\quad d_o$ = Major diameter of the bolt

and $\quad\quad n$ = Number of bolts

then, shear stress (τ) is given by,

$$\tau = \frac{W_s}{\frac{\pi}{4} \cdot (d_o)^2 \times n}$$

or $\quad\quad d_o = \sqrt{\dfrac{4W_s}{\pi \cdot \tau \cdot n}}$

3. Combined tensile and shear stress :

- When the bolt is subjected to both tensile and shear loads, as in case of coupling bolts or bearing, then the diameter of the shank of the bolt is obtained from the shear load and that of threaded part from the tensile load.
- A diameter slightly larger than the required for either shear or tension may be assumed and stresses due to combined load should be checked for the following principal stresses.

(a) Maximum principal shear stress,

$$\tau_{max} = \frac{1}{2}\sqrt{(\sigma_t)^2 + 4\tau^2}$$

(b) Maximum principal tensile stress,

$$\sigma_{t\,max} = \frac{\sigma_t}{2} + \frac{1}{2}\sqrt{(\sigma_t)^2 + 4\tau^2}$$

- These stresses should not exceed the safe permissible values.

6.4.1 (c) Stress Due to Combined Forces

- The resultant axial load on a bolt depends upon the following factors :
  1. The initial tension due to tightening of the bolt,
  2. The external load, and
  3. The relative elastic yielding (springiness) of the bolt and the connected members.

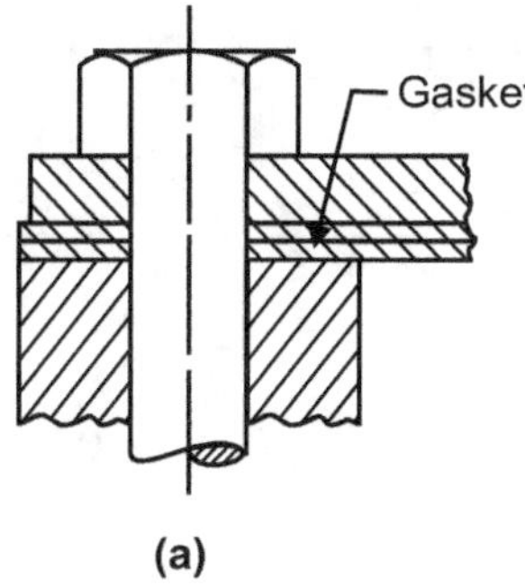

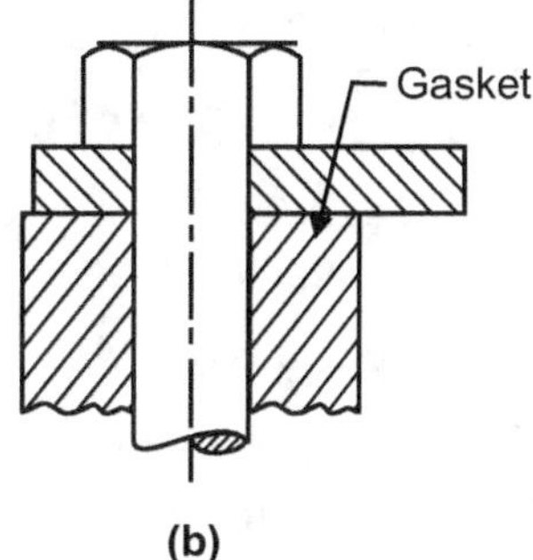

Fig. 6.8

- When the connected members are very yielding as compared with the bolt, which is a soft gasket, as shown in Fig. 6.8 (a), then the resultant load on the bolt is approximately equal to the sum of the initial tension and the external load.

- On the other hand, if the bolt is very yielding as compared with the connected members, as shown in Fig. 6.8 (b), then the resultant load will be either the initial tension or the external load, whichever is greater.

- The actual conditions usually lie between the two extremes. In order to determine the resultant axial load (W) on the bolt, the following equation may be used :

$$W = W_1 + \left(\frac{a}{1 + a}\right) \times W_2 = W_1 + K \cdot W_2 \quad \ldots \left(\text{Substituting } \frac{a}{1 + a} = K\right)$$

where, W_1 = Initial tension due to tightening of the bolt = W_i = 2840 d_o

          W_2 = External load on the bolt,

and   a = Ratio of elasticity of connected parts to the elasticity of bolt.

- For soft gaskets and large bolts, the value of 'a' is high and the value of $\frac{a}{1 + a}$ is approximately equal to unity, so that, the resultant load is equal to the sum of the initial tension and the external load.

- For hard gaskets or metal to metal contact surfaces and with small bolts, the value of 'a' is small and the resultant load is mainly due to the initial tension. In rare case, external load is greater than initial tension.

- The value of 'a' may be estimated by the designer to obtain an approximate value for the resultant load. The values of $\frac{a}{1 + a}$ (i.e. K) for various types of joints are shown in Table 6.1.

- The designer thus has control over the influence on the resultant load on a bolt by proportioning the sizes of the connected parts and bolts and by specifying initial tension in the bolt.

Table 6.1 : Values of 'K' for various types of joints

Type of joint	$K = \dfrac{a}{1+a}$
Metal to metal joint with through bolts	0.00 to 0.10
Hard copper gasket with long through bolts	0.25 to 0.50
Soft copper gasket with long through bolts	0.50 to 0.75
Soft packing with through bolts	0.75 to 1.00
Soft packing with studs	1.00

6.5 BOLTS OF UNIFORM STRENGTH

Question

1. Explain with neat sketch, the bolt of uniform strength.   **(S-09, 12, 13; W-10, 13)**

- In case of a cylinder head bolt of an internal combustion engine, when bolt is subjected to shock loading, the resilience of the bolt should be considered in order to prevent breakage at the thread.

- When ordinary bolt of uniform diameter is subjected to shock loads, stress concentration occurs at the weakest part of bolt i.e. threaded portion. This portion is of cross-sectional area at the root of threads.

- It means that, the stress induced in the threaded portion will be higher than that of shank.

- Therefore, a great portion of energy will be absorbed at the region of threaded part, which may cause fracture of threaded portion.

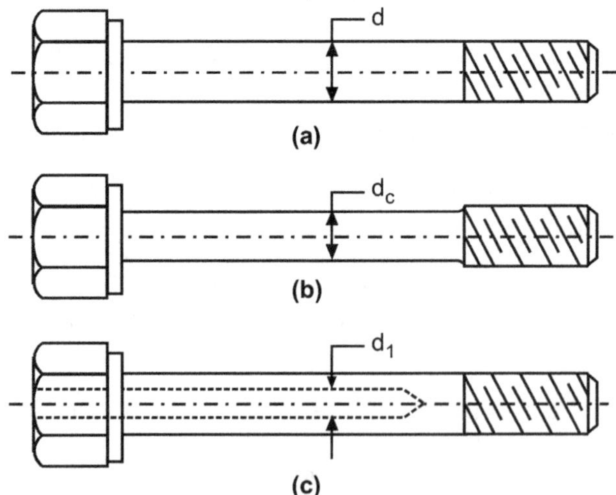

Fig. 6.9 : Bolts of uniform strength

- If the shank of the bolt is turned down to a diameter equal or even slightly lesser than the core diameter of the thread (d_c) as shown in Fig. 6.9 (b), then the shank of the bolt will undergo a higher stress. Thus, a shank will absorb a large portion of energy. The bolt in this way, becomes stronger and lighter and it increases the shock absorbing capacity of the bolt, because of an increased modulus of resilience. This gives *bolts of uniform strength*. The resilience of a bolt may also be increased by increasing its length.

- A second alternative method of obtaining the bolts of uniform strength is shown in Fig. 6.9 (c). In this method, an axial hole is drilled through the head as far as the threaded portion, such that, the area of the shank becomes equal to the root area of the thread.

If d_1 = Diameter of hole,

                 d_o = Outer diameter/nominal diameter of the thread,

and d_c = Root or core diameter of the thread,

then, for bolts of uniform strength, we write,

$$\frac{\pi}{4} d_1^2 = \frac{\pi}{4}\left(d_o^2 - d_c^2\right)$$

$$\therefore \quad d_1^2 = d_o^2 - d_c^2$$

$$\therefore \quad d_1 = \sqrt{d_o^2 - d_c^2}$$

Numerical Type No. 1 : "Design of bolts, if Bolts are not Initially Stressed"

Problem 6.1 : *Determine safe tensile load for bolts of M20 and M36. Assume the bolts are not initially stressed and take safe tensile stress as 200 MPa.*   **(S-11)**

Solution : Given data : σ_t = 200 MPa = 200 N/mm^2.

Procedure : Case (1) : For M20 bolts :

$$d_o = 20 \text{ mm}; \quad \therefore d_c = 0.84 \times d_o = 0.84 \times 20 = 16.8 \text{ mm}$$

Considering tensile stress,

$$\sigma_t = \frac{W}{\frac{\pi}{4} \cdot d_c^2}$$

$$\therefore \quad 200 = \frac{W}{\frac{\pi}{4} \cdot (16.8)^2}$$

$$\therefore \quad W = \mathbf{44334.15 \ N}$$

Case (2) : For M36 bolts :

$$d_o = 36 \text{ mm}; \quad \therefore d_c = 0.84 \, d_o = 0.84 \times 36 = 30.24 \text{ mm}$$

Considering tensile stress,

$$\sigma_t = \frac{W}{\frac{\pi}{4} \cdot d_c^2}$$

$$\therefore \quad 200 = \frac{W}{\frac{\pi}{4} \cdot (30.24)^2}$$

$$\therefore \quad W = \mathbf{143642.66 \ N}$$

Problem 6.2 : *A cylinder head of a steam engine is held in position by M20 bolts. The effective diameter of cylinder is 350 mm and steam pressure is 0.75 N/mm². If the bolts are not initially stressed, find the number of bolts required. Take working stress for the bolt material 20 N/mm².* **(S-09, 12)**

Solution : Given data : Diameter of cylinder = D = 350 mm

Pressure inside the cylinder = p = 0.75 N/mm²

Nominal diameter of bolts = d_o = 20 mm

Permissible stress = σ_t = 20 N/mm²

Procedure : We have,

$$d_c = 0.84 \ d_o = 0.84 \times 20 = 16.8 \ mm$$

Total load acting on the cylinder cover,

$$W_n = \text{Pressure inside the cylinder} \times \text{Area of cylinder}$$

$$\therefore \quad W_n = p \times \frac{\pi}{4} \times (D)^2$$

$$= 0.75 \times \frac{\pi}{4} \times (350)^2 = \mathbf{72.1584 \times 10^3 \ N}$$

This load is taken up by 'n' number of bolts.

$\therefore$ Load on each bolt,

$$W = \frac{W_n}{n} = \frac{72.1584 \times 10^3}{n}$$

Considering the failure of bolt in tension,

$$\sigma_t = \frac{W}{\frac{\pi}{4} \times (d_c)^2}$$

$$\therefore \quad 20 = \frac{72.1584 \times 10^3}{n \times \frac{\pi}{4} \times (16.8)^2}$$

$$\therefore \quad n = \frac{72.1584 \times 10^3 \times 4}{\pi \times (16.8)^2 \times 20} = 16.2760 \cong 18 \ (\text{say})$$

$\therefore$ **Number of bolts required = 18**

Problem 6.3 : *An engine cylinder is 30 cm in diameter and steam pressure is 1 N/mm² absolute with 0.3 N/mm² back pressure. If cylinder cover is held by 12 studs, find size of stud. Assume that, studs are not initially stressed. Take permissible stress for stud material as 28 MPa.*

Solution : Given data : D = 30 cm = 300 mm, n = 12, σ_t = 28 N/mm²

Pressure inside the cylinder, p = Absolute pressure − Back pressure = 1 − 0.3 = 0.7 N/mm²

Procedure : Total load acting on the cylinder is given by,

$$W_n = \text{Pressure} \times \text{Area of cylinder}$$

$$= p \times \frac{\pi}{4} \times (D)^2$$

$$= 0.7 \times \frac{\pi}{4} \times (300)^2 = 49.48 \times 10^3 \text{ N}$$

This load is taken up by 12 number of bolts.

$$\therefore \text{ Load on each bolt, } W = \frac{W_n}{n} = \frac{49.48 \times 10^3}{12} = 4123.34 \text{ N}$$

Considering the failure of bolt in tension,

$$\sigma_t = \frac{W}{\frac{\pi}{4} \times (d_c)^2}$$

$$\therefore \quad d_c^2 = \frac{4 \times W}{\pi \times \sigma_t} = \frac{4 \times 4123.34}{\pi \times 28}$$

$$\therefore \quad d_c = \textbf{13.69 mm}$$

But, $\quad d_c = 0.84\, d_o$

$$\therefore \quad d_o = \frac{13.69}{0.84} = 16.29 \text{ mm} \cong \textbf{18 mm (say)}$$

Therefore, $\quad d_c = 0.84\, d_o = 0.84 \times 18 = \textbf{15.12 mm}$

$\therefore$ **Bolts of size M 18 should be used, having core diameter 15.12 mm.**

Numerical Type No. 2 : "Design of the Bolts for Cylinder Cover Considering the Stress due to Combined Forces"

Problem 6.4 : *The cylinder head of steam engine is subjected to steam pressure of 0.7 N/mm². It is held in position by means of 12 bolts. A soft copper gasket is placed to make the joint leak proof. The effective diameter of cylinder is 300 mm. Find the size of bolts, so that, stress in the bolt is not to exceed 100 N/mm².*

Solution : Given data : $p = 0.7$ N/mm², $n = 12$, $D = 300$ mm, $\sigma_t = 100$ N/mm²

Procedure : The initial tightening load acting on each bolt $= W_1 = 2840\, d_o$

Also, total load acting on the cylinder cover due to steam pressure,

$$= p \times \frac{\pi}{4} \times (D)^2 = 0.7 \times \frac{\pi}{4} \times (300)^2 = 49.48 \times 10^3 \text{ N}$$

This load is taken up by 12 number of bolts.

$\therefore$ Load acting on each bolt due to steam pressure,

$$W_2 = \frac{49.48 \times 10^3}{12} = \textbf{4123.34 N}$$

We know, the resultant load,

$$W = W_1 + K \cdot W_2$$

where, K = ratio of elastic limits of connected parts = 0.6 for copper gasket. (Assumed)

$$\therefore \quad W = 2840\, d_o + (0.6 \times 4123.34) = 2840\, d_o + 2474.004$$

Considering the failure of bolt in tension,

$$\sigma_t = \frac{W}{\dfrac{\pi}{4} \times (d_c)^2}$$

$$\therefore \quad 100 = \frac{2840\, d_o + 2474.004}{\dfrac{\pi}{4} \times (0.84\, d_o)^2}$$

$$\therefore \quad (0.84\, d_o)^2 \times 100 \times \frac{\pi}{4} = 2840\, d_o + 2474.004$$

$$\therefore \quad 55.41\, d_o^2 - 2840\, d_o - 2474.004 = 0$$

$$\therefore \quad d_o = 52.11 \text{ mm} \cong \textbf{54 mm (say)}$$

$$\therefore \quad d_c = 0.84\, d_o = 0.84 \times 54 = \textbf{45.36 mm}$$

We should use bolt of size M 54, having core diameter 45.36 mm.

Problem 6.5 : *The cylinder head of steam engine is subjected to a steam pressure of 0.7 N/mm². It is held in position by means of 12 bolts. The bolts are tightened with an initial preload of 1.5 times the steam load. A soft copper gasket is used to make the joint leak proof. The effective diameter of cylinder is 300 mm. Find the size of bolts, so that, stress in bolts is not to exceed 100 MPa.* **(S-11)**

Solution : Given data : $p = 0.7$ N/mm², $n = 12$, $D = 300$ mm, $\sigma_t = 100$ MPa

Procedure : Steam load acting on cylinder head $= p \times \dfrac{\pi}{4} \times D^2$

$$\therefore \quad W_n = 0.7 \times \frac{\pi}{4} \times (300)^2 = 49.48 \times 10^3 \text{ N}$$

This load is taken up by 12 bolts.

$$\therefore \quad \text{Load on each bolt} = W_2 = \frac{W_n}{n} = \frac{49.48 \times 10^3}{12} = \textbf{4123.34 N}$$

Also, Initial preload on all 12 bolts due to tightening

$$= 1.5 \times \text{Steam load}$$
$$= 1.5 \times 49.48 \times 10^3 = 74220 \text{ N}$$

$$\therefore \quad \text{Initial preload on each bolt} = W_1 = \frac{74220}{12} = 6185 \text{ N}$$

We have, Resultant load,

$$W = W_1 + K \cdot W_2$$

where, $K = 0.6$ for soft copper gasket   (Assumed)

$$\therefore \quad W = 6185 + (0.6 \times 4123.34) = \textbf{8659 N}$$

Considering the failure of bolt in tension,

$$\sigma_t = \frac{W}{\frac{\pi}{4} \cdot d_c^2}$$

$$\therefore \quad d_c^2 = \frac{W \times 4}{\pi \times \sigma_t} = \frac{8659 \times 4}{\pi \times 100}$$

$$\therefore \quad d_c = 10.49 \text{ mm}$$

$$\therefore \quad d_o = \frac{d_c}{0.84} = \frac{10.49}{0.84} = 12.49 \text{ mm} \cong \mathbf{14 \text{ mm (say)}}$$

$\therefore$ **Bolts of size M 14 may be used.**

Problem 6.6 : *Determine the diameter of hole, that must be drilled in M 60 bolt, such that, the bolt becomes of uniform strength.*

Solution : Given data : $d_o = 60$ mm.

Procedure : We have, $\quad d_c = 0.84 \, d_o = 0.84 \times 60 = 50.4$ mm

For uniform strength of bolt, the diameter of hole,

$$d_1 = \sqrt{d_o^2 - d_c^2} = \sqrt{60^2 - (50.4)^2} = \mathbf{32.55 \text{ mm}} \cong \mathbf{33 \text{ mm (say)}}$$

Problem 6.7 : *Two machine parts are fastened together tightly by means of a 22 mm tap bolt. If the load tending to separate these parts is neglected, find the stress that is setup in the bolt by the initial tightening.*

Solution : Given data : $d_o = 22$ mm

Procedure :

We have, $\qquad\qquad d_c = 0.84 \, d_o = 0.84 \times 22 = 18.48$ mm

$\therefore$ Initial tension in the bolt,

$$W_1 = 2840 \, d_o = 2840 \times 22 = 62480 \text{ N}$$

We have, $\qquad\qquad W = W_1 + K \cdot W_2.$

It is given to neglect the value of W_2.

$$\therefore \qquad\qquad W = 62480 + (K \times 0)$$

$$= \mathbf{62480 \text{ N}}$$

Let, σ_t = Stress induced in the bolt, then initial tension in the bolt is,

$$W = \frac{\pi}{4} \, d_c^2 \times \sigma_t$$

$$\therefore \qquad 62480 = \frac{\pi}{4} \times (18.48)^2 \times \sigma_t$$

$$\therefore \qquad \sigma_t = \mathbf{232.94 \text{ N/mm}^2} = \mathbf{232.94 \text{ MPa}}$$

6.6 DESIGN OF BOLTS FOR CYLINDER COVER

The cylinder cover may be secured by means of bolts or studs.

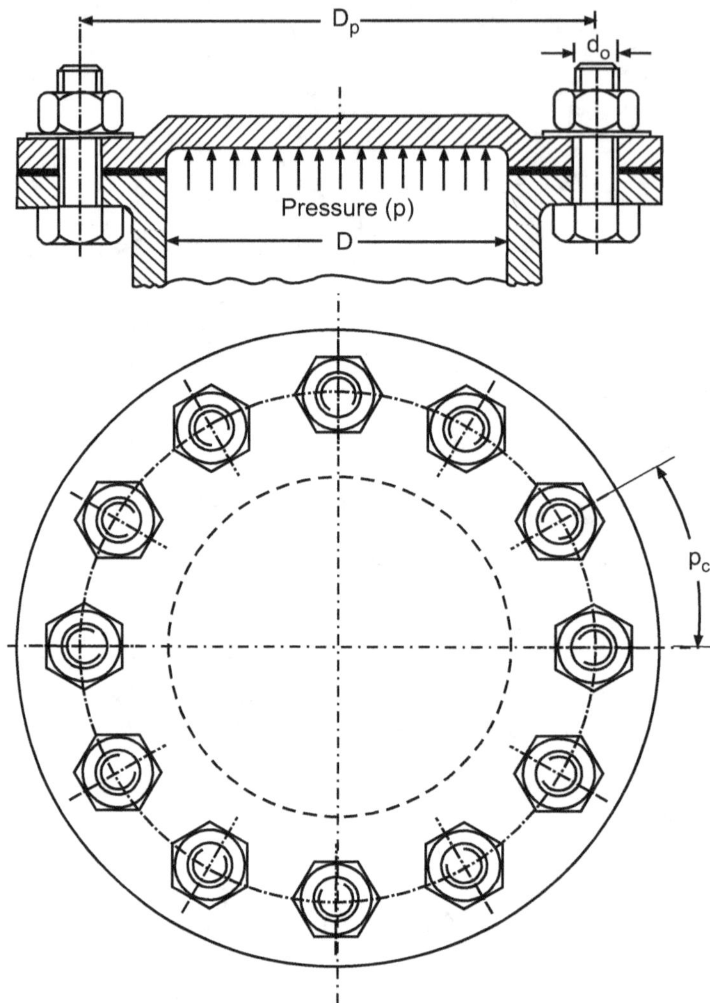

Fig. 6.10 : Cylinder bolts

Let d_c = Core diameter of bolt or stud,

n = Number of bolts,

D = Diameter of cylinder,

t = Thickness of cylinder cover,

p = Pressure in cylinder,

σ_t = Permissible tensile stress for bolt.

Step 1 : Upward force acting on cylinder cover,

$$W_n = \frac{\pi}{4}\, D^2 \times p \qquad\qquad\qquad \dots (6.1)$$

Step 2 : This force is taken up by 'n' number of bolts. Therefore, load taken by each bolt,

$$W \;=\; \frac{W_n}{n} \qquad\qquad \ldots (6.2)$$

Step 3 : Considering tensile stress induced in each bolt,

$$\sigma_t \;=\; \frac{W}{\frac{\pi}{4}\cdot d_c^2}$$

$$\therefore \qquad W \;=\; \sigma_t \cdot \frac{\pi}{4}\cdot d_c^2 \qquad\qquad \ldots (6.3)$$

Step 4 : Equate equations (6.2) and (6.3).

Step 5 : Usually size of bolt for safe design is 16-24 mm. This value is assumed and accordingly number of bolts are calculated.

Step 6 : P.C.D. of bolts,

$$D_p \;=\; D + 2t + 3d_1$$

where, values taken are,

$$d_1 \;=\; \text{Diameter of hole} = d_o + 1$$
$$t \;=\; \text{Thickness of cylinder cover} = 10 \text{ mm}$$

Step 7 : Calculate circumferential pitch, $p_c \;=\; \dfrac{\pi D_p}{n}$

Check whether p_c lies between $20\sqrt{d_1}$ to $30\sqrt{d_1}$. If yes, the assumption made in step number '5' is correct.

Numerical Type No. 3 : "Design of Bolts for Cylinder Cover (Number and Size of Bolts are Not Known)"

Problem 6.8 : A M.S. cover plate is to be designed in shell of pressure vessel. The hole is 120 mm in diameter. The pressure inside vessel is 6 N/mm². Design the bolts. Assume σ_t = 40 MPa. Take t = 10 mm.

Solution : Given data : D = 120 mm, t = 10 mm, p = 6 N/mm², σ_t = 40 MPa

Procedure :

$$W_n \;=\; \frac{\pi}{4}\, D^2 \times p = \frac{\pi}{4} \times (120)^2 \times 6 \;=\; \mathbf{67.858 \times 10^3 \ N}$$

This load is taken up by 'n' number of bolts.

$$\therefore \quad \text{Load on each bolt} = W = \frac{W_n}{n} = \frac{67.858 \times 10^3}{n}$$

Here, size of bolt and number of bolts are not known for leakproof joint. Therefore, let us assume d_o = 24 mm.

$$\therefore \qquad\qquad d_c \;=\; 0.84\, d_o = 0.84 \times 24 = 20.16 \text{ mm}$$

Considering tensile failure of bolt material,

$$\sigma_t \;=\; \frac{W}{\frac{\pi}{4}\cdot d_c^2}$$

$$\therefore \qquad 40 \;=\; \frac{67.858 \times 10^3}{n \times \dfrac{\pi}{4} \times (20.16)^2}\; ;\;\; \therefore n = \textbf{5.31} \cong \textbf{6 say)}$$

Also, d_1 = size of hole = $d_o + 1$ = 24 + 1 = 25 mm

P.C.D. of bolts, D_p = D + 2t + 3d_1

$$= 120 + (2 \times 10) + (3 \times 25) = \textbf{215 mm}$$

Circumferential pitch, $p_c = \dfrac{\pi D_p}{n} = \dfrac{\pi \times 215}{6} = \textbf{112.57 mm}$

Now, p_c should lie in range $20\sqrt{d_1}$ to $30\sqrt{d_1}$.

$$20\sqrt{d_1} \;=\; 20\sqrt{25} = \textbf{100} \text{ and } 30\sqrt{d_1} = 30\sqrt{25} = \textbf{150}$$

As p_c lies between 100 and 150, assumption is correct. $\therefore$ **M24 bolts can be used.**

Problem 6.9 : *A steam engine cylinder has effective diameter of 200 mm. It is subjected to maximum steam pressure of 1.75 N/mm². Calculate the number and size of studs required to fix the cylinder cover onto the cylinder flange. Assume the permissible stress as 30 MPa. Take P.C.D. of studs as 320 mm and total load on studs as 20% higher than external load on the joint. Also, check circumferential pitch of studs so as to give leak-proof joint.*

Solution : Given data : p = 1.75 N/mm², D = 200 mm, σ_t = 30 N/mm², D_p = 320 mm

Procedure : Total load acting on cylinder cover

$$= p \times \frac{\pi}{4} \times (D^2) \;=\; 1.75 \times \frac{\pi}{4} \times (200)^2 \;=\; 54.977 \times 10^3 \text{ N}$$

Taking the load 20% higher, we have,

$$W_n \;=\; 54.977 \times 10^3 + 20\% \text{ of } 54.977 \times 10^3$$

$$= 54.977 \times 10^3 + 10.995 \times 10^3 \;=\; 65.973 \times 10^3 \text{ N}$$

This load is taken up by 'n' number of studs.

$$\therefore \qquad \text{Load on each stud} \;=\; W \;=\; \frac{W_n}{n} = \frac{65.973 \times 10^3}{n}$$

Let us assume that, M 24 bolts are used.

$$\therefore \qquad d_o \;=\; 24 \text{ mm}$$

$$\therefore \qquad d_c \;=\; 0.84\, d_o \;=\; 0.84 \times 24 \;=\; 20.16 \text{ mm}$$

Considering the failure of bolt in tension,

$$\sigma_t \;=\; \frac{W}{\frac{\pi}{4} \times (d_c)^2}$$

$$\therefore \qquad 30 \;=\; \frac{65.973 \times 10^3}{n \times \dfrac{\pi}{4} \times (20.16)^2}$$

$$\therefore \qquad n \;=\; 6.889 \;\cong\; \textbf{8 (say)}$$

Now, we have, pitch circle diameter of bolts $= D_p = 320$ mm and

$\qquad d_1 = $ Diameter of hole for bolts $= d_o + 1 = 24 + 1 = 25$ mm

$$\therefore \quad \text{Circumferential pitch of bolts} \;=\; p_c \;=\; \frac{\pi \times D_p}{n} \;=\; \frac{\pi \times 320}{8} \;=\; \textbf{125.67 mm}$$

Calculating, $\qquad 20\sqrt{d_1} \;=\; 20 \times \sqrt{25} \;=\; \textbf{100}$

$$\qquad\qquad 30\sqrt{d_1} \;=\; 30 \times \sqrt{25} \;=\; \textbf{150}$$

As p_c lies between $20\sqrt{d_1}$ and $30\sqrt{d_1}$, therefore, the assumed size of bolts is correct.

$\therefore$ **We should use 8 bolts of size M 24.**

6.7 DESIGN OF JOINTS SUBJECTED TO ECCENTRIC LOADING

Consider the following two cases of bolted joints subjected to eccentric loading, when eccentric load is,

1. Parallel to the axis of bolts.
2. Perpendicular to the axis of bolts.

6.7.1 Bolted Joints Subjected to Eccentric Load Acting Parallel to Axis of Bolts

Consider a bracket having a rectangular base bolted to a wall by means of four bolts.

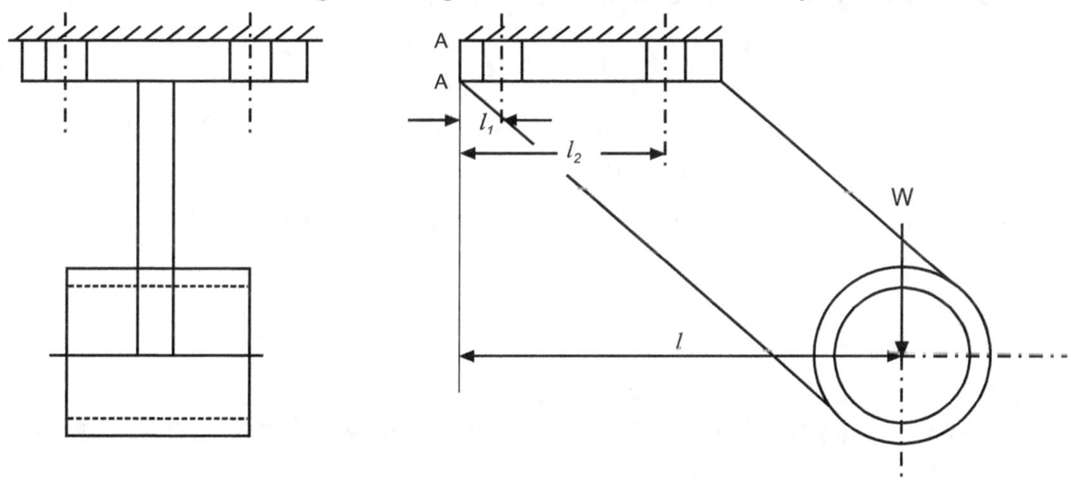

Fig. 6.11 : Bolted joints subjected to eccentric load acting parallel to bolt axis

Each bolt is subjected to a direct tensile load of

$$W_{t1} \;=\; \frac{W}{n} \;=\; \frac{W}{4} \qquad\qquad\qquad\qquad \ldots (6.4)$$

where $\qquad\qquad n = $ Number of bolts

Now, the load 'W' tends to rotate the bracket about the edge A-A.

Let 'w' be the load in a bolt per unit distance due to turning effect of bracket and let W_1 and W_2 be the loads on each of the bolts at distance l_1 and l_2 from tilting edge A-A.

$\therefore$ Load on each bolt at distance l_1,

$$W_1 \;=\; w \times l_1$$

and moment of this load about this tilting edge $= w \times l_1 \times l_1 \;=\; w \times (l_1)^2$

Similarly, load on each bolt at distance l_2,

$$W_2 \;=\; w \times l_2$$

and moment of this load about this tilting edge $= w \times l_2 \times l_2 \;=\; w \times (l_2)^2$

$\therefore$ Total moment of load on 4 bolts about tilting edge

$$= \; 2w \times (l_1)^2 + 2w \times (l_2)^2 \qquad \text{... (6.5)}$$

Also, moment due to load 'W' $= W \times l \qquad \text{... (6.6)}$

From equations (6.5) and (6.6),

$$W \times l \;=\; 2w \times (l_1)^2 + 2w \times (l_2)^2$$

$\therefore$ Load, $w \;=\; \dfrac{W \times l}{2\,[(l_1)^2 + (l_2)^2]}$

Most heavily loaded bolts are those, which are situated at greatest distance from tilting edge. Here, bolts at distance l_2 are most heavily loaded bolts.

Therefore, tensile load on each bolt at distance l_2 is,

$$W_{t2} \;=\; W_2 \;=\; w \times l_2 \;=\; \frac{W \times l \times l_2}{2\,[(l_1)^2 + (l_2)^2]} \qquad \text{... (6.7)}$$

From equations (6.4) and (6.7), total tensile load on most heavily loaded bolt is,

$$W_t \;=\; W_{t1} + W_{t2}$$

If d_c is core diameter of bolt and σ_t is tensile stress for bolt material, then considering tensile stress,

$$\sigma_t \;=\; \frac{W_t}{\dfrac{\pi}{4} \cdot d_c^2}$$

$\therefore$ Value of d_c may be obtained. From core diameter, size of bolt (nominal diameter) is obtained.

6.7.2 Bolted Joints Subjected to Eccentric Loading Acting Perpendicular to Axis of Bolts   (W-04)

- A wall bracket carrying eccentric load perpendicular to axis of bolt is shown in Fig. 6.12.
- In this case, the bolts are subjected to direct shearing load, which is equally shared by all the bolts.

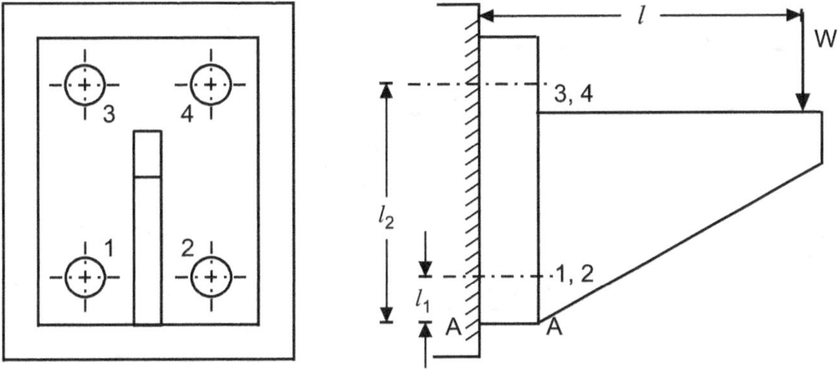

Fig. 6.12 : Bolted joints subjected to eccentric load acting perpendicular to axis of bolt

- Therefore, direct shear load on each bolt,

$$W_s = \frac{W}{n} , \quad \text{where n is number of bolts} \qquad \text{... (6.8)}$$

- Eccentric load 'W' will try to tilt the bracket in the clockwise direction about edge A-A, and the bolts will be subjected to tensile stress due to turning moment.

- The maximum tensile load on a heavily loaded bolt (W_t) may be obtained as follows :

$$W_t = w \times l_2 = \frac{W \times l \times l_2}{2 \left[(l_1)^2 + (l_2)^2\right]} \qquad \text{... (6.9)}$$

- When the bolts are subjected to shear as well as tensile loads, then equivalent loads may be determined by,

$$W_{te} = \text{Equivalent tensile load} = \frac{1}{2}\left[W_t + \sqrt{(W_t)^2 + 4\,(W_s)^2}\right]$$

$$W_{se} = \text{Equivalent shear load} = \frac{1}{2}\left[\sqrt{(W_t)^2 + 4\,(W_s)^2}\right]$$

- Knowing the value of load, size of bolt may be determined for the given allowable stress from the following equations.

$$\sigma_t = \frac{W_{te}}{\frac{\pi}{4} \times (d_c)^2} \quad \text{and} \quad \tau = \frac{W_{se}}{\frac{\pi}{4} \times (d_c)^2}$$

Numerical Type No. 4 : "Design of Bolted Joints Subjected to Eccentric Load Acting Parallel to Axis of Bolt"

Problem 6.10 : *A bracket carrying a vertical load of 25 kN as shown in Fig. 6.13. The load is taken up by 4 bolts for fixing the bracket. Determine the size of bolt for permissible tensile stress of 80 N/mm².* **(S-14)**

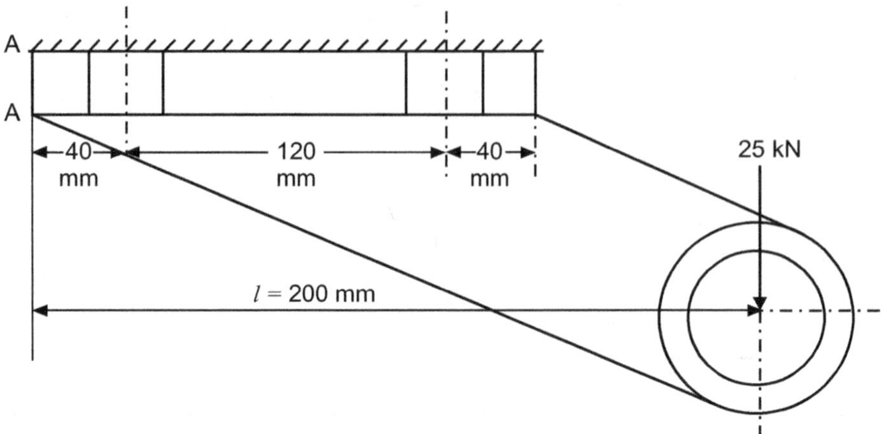

Fig. 6.13

Solution : Given data : $W = 25$ kN $= 25 \times 10^3$ N, $\sigma_t = 80$ N/mm², $l_1 = 40$ mm, $l_2 = 40 + 120 = 160$ mm, $l = 200$ mm

Procedure : Consider a bracket as shown, having a rectangular base bolted to a wall by means of 4 bolts. Each bolt is subjected to a direct tensile load of

$$W_{t1} = \frac{W}{n} = \frac{W}{4} = \frac{25 \times 10^3}{4} = 6250 \text{ N} \qquad \ldots (1)$$

Now, the load 'W' tends to rotate the bracket about the edge A-A.

Let 'w' be the load in a bolt per unit distance due to turning effect of bracket, then

$$\text{Load, } w = \frac{W \times l}{2\,[(l_1)^2 + (l_2)^2]}$$

Most heavily loaded bolts are those, which are situated at greatest distance from tilting edge. Here bolts at distance l_2 are most heavily loaded bolts.

$\therefore$ Tensile load on each bolt at distance l_2,

$$W_{t2} = w \times l_2$$

$$= \frac{W \times l \times l_2}{2 \times [(l_1)^2 + (l_2)^2]} = \frac{25 \times 10^3 \times 200 \times 160}{2 \times [(40)^2 + (160)^2]} = 14705.88 \text{ N} \ldots (2)$$

$\therefore$ Total tensile load on most heavily loaded bolts is

$$W_t = W_{t1} + W_{t2} = 6250 + 14705.88 = 20955.88 \text{ N}$$

If d_c is core diameter of bolt and σ_t is tensile stress for bolt material, then,

$$\sigma_t = \frac{W_t}{\frac{\pi}{4} \times (d_c)^2}$$

$\therefore$

$$(d_c)^2 = \frac{W_t}{\frac{\pi}{4} \times \sigma_t} = \frac{20955.88}{\frac{\pi}{4} \times 80}$$

$\therefore$

$$d_c = \textbf{18.26 mm}$$

$$\therefore \quad d_o = \frac{d_c}{0.84} = \frac{18.26}{0.84} = \textbf{21.73 mm} \cong \textbf{22 mm (say)}$$

Taking d_o = 22 mm, we have, $d_c = 0.84\, d_o = 0.84 \times 22 = 18.48$ mm

∴   **We will use bolts of size M 22 having core diameter 18.48 mm.**

Problem 6.11 : *Fig. 6.14 shows a C.I. bracket to carry a shaft and belt pulley. The bracket is fixed to the main body by means of standard bolts. The tensions in the slack side and tight side are 5000 N and 10000 N respectively. The safe stress for the bolt is 60 N/mm². Determine the size of bolts.*

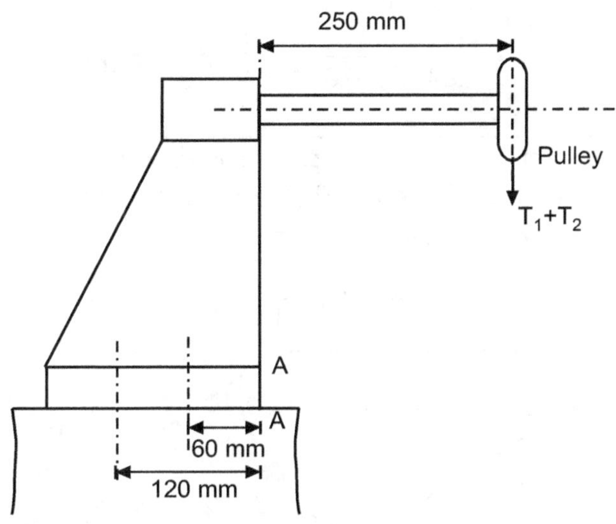

Fig. 6.14

Solution : Given data : Tension in slack side = T_2 = 5000 N,

Tension in tight side = T_1 = 10000 N,

Safe stress, σ_t = 60 N/mm², l_1 = 60 mm, l_2 = 120 mm, l = 250 mm.

Procedure :

Total tension in pulley is acting in downward direction. It is given by,

$$T = T_1 + T_2 = 10000 + 5000 = 15000 \text{ N}$$

Due to tension in belt, the bracket will try to tilt about tilting edge A-A.

And, Tilting moment, $M = T \times l = 15000 \times 250 = 375 \times 10^4$ N-mm   ... (1)

Let 'w' be the load in each bolt per unit distance from tilting edge.

Assuming 4 bolts,

Total resisting moment = $2w\,[l_1^2 + l_2^2] = 2w\,[60^2 + 120^2] = 36000\,w$ ... (2)

Equating equations (1) and (2),

$$375 \times 10^4 = 36000\,w$$

$$\therefore \quad w = \textbf{104.167 N/m}$$

The maximum tensile load on heavily loaded (W_t) may be obtained as follows :

$$W_t = w \times l_2 = 104.167 \times 120 = \mathbf{12500\ N}$$

If d_c is core diameter of bolt and σ_t is tensile stress for bolt material, then,

$$\sigma_t = \frac{W_t}{\frac{\pi}{4} d_c^2}$$

$$\therefore \quad 60 = \frac{12500 \times 4}{\pi \times d_c^2}$$

$$\therefore \quad d_c = 16.28\ mm$$

$$\therefore \quad d_o = \frac{d_c}{0.84} = \frac{16.28}{0.84} = 19.38 \cong \mathbf{20\ mm}$$

We will use bolt of size M 20.

Problem 6.12 : *A bracket as shown in Fig. 6.15 is used to support a load of 'P' N. It is fastened to the wall with 4 bolts of size M 30. The distances are l = 600 mm, l_1 = 50 mm, l_2 = 300 mm. Determine the load P, if allowable stress is 60 MPa.*

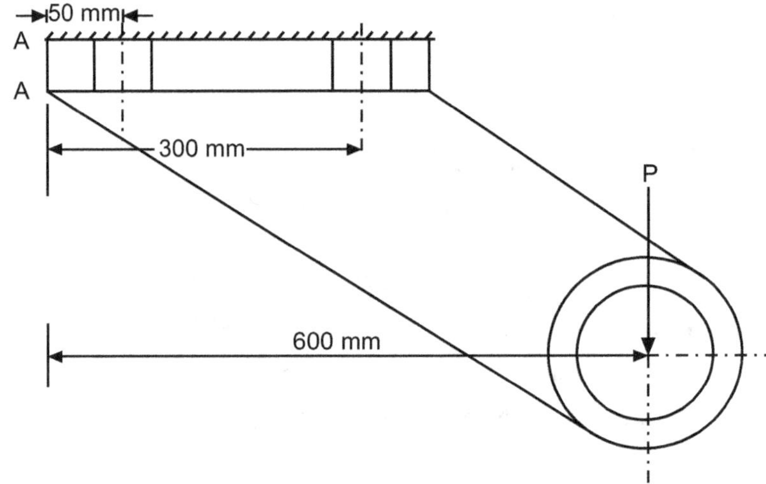

Fig. 6.15

Solution : Given data : σ_t = 60 N/mm², l_1 = 50 mm, l_2 = 300 mm, l = 600 mm, d_o = 30 mm

Procedure : We have, $d_c = 0.84\ d_o = 0.84 \times 30 = 25.20\ mm$.

Consider a bracket as shown in Fig. 6.15 having a rectangular base bolted to a wall by means of four bolts.

Each bolt is subjected to a direct tensile load, $W_{t1} = \dfrac{W}{n} = \dfrac{P}{4} = 0.25\ P$　　　... (1)

Now, the load 'P' tends to rotate the bracket about the edge A-A.

Let 'w' be the load in a bolt per unit distance due to turning effect of bracket. We have,

$$\text{Load, } w = \frac{W \times l}{2\,[l_1^2 + l_2^2]}$$

Most heavily loaded bolts are those, which are situated at greatest distance from tilting edge. Here bolts at distance l_2 are most heavily loaded bolts.

$\therefore$ Tensile load on each bolt at distance l_2 is

$$W_{t2} = w \times l_2 = \frac{W \times l}{2 \, [l_1^2 + l_2^2]} \times l_2$$

$$= \frac{P \times 600 \times 300}{2 \times [50^2 + 300^2]} = 0.9729 \, P \qquad \qquad ... (2)$$

From equations (1) and (2), total tensile load on most heavily loaded bolt is given by,

$$W_t = W_{t1} + W_{t2} = 0.25 \, P + 0.9729 \, P = 1.2229 \, P$$

If d_c is core diameter of bolt and σ_t is tensile stress for bolt material, then

$$\sigma_t = \frac{W_t}{\frac{\pi}{4} \times d_c^2}$$

$\therefore$

$$60 = \frac{1.2229 \, P}{\frac{\pi}{4} \times (25.20)^2}$$

$\therefore$ $$P = \mathbf{24470.97 \, N}$$

Numerical Type No. 5 : "Design of Bolted Joints Under Eccentric Loading, When Eccentric Load is Perpendicular to Bolt Axis"

Problem 6.13 : *A wall bracket is attached to a wall by means of four bolts, two at a distance of 50 mm from the lower edge and remaining two at a distance of 450 mm from the lower bolts. It supports a load of 50 kN at a distance of 500 mm from the wall. Sketch the arrangements and estimate the diameter of bolts. Assume working in stress in stress in tension as 80 N/mm².*   **(W-13)**

Solution : Given data : $W = 50 \text{ kN} = 50 \times 10^3 \text{ N}$, $\sigma_t = 80 \text{ N/mm}^2$, $l_1 = 50 \text{ mm}$

$l_2 = 50 + 450 = 500 \text{ mm}$, $l = 500 \text{ mm}$, $n = 4$.

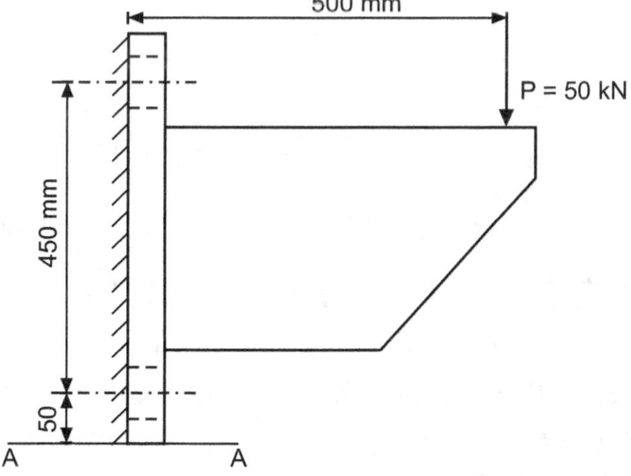

Fig. 6.16

Procedure : In this case, the bolts are subjected to direct shearing load, which is equally shared by all the bolts.

$$\therefore \quad \text{Direct shear load on each bolt, } W_s = \frac{W}{n} = \frac{50 \times 10^3}{4} = 12500 \text{ N} \qquad \ldots (1)$$

Eccentric load 'W' will try to tilt the bracket in the clockwise direction about edge A-A. Therefore, the bolts will be subjected to tensile stress due to turning moment.

The maximum tensile load on heavily loaded (W_t) may be obtained as follows :

$$W_t = w \times l_2 = \frac{W \times l \times l_2}{2 \, [l_1^2 + l_2^2]} = \frac{50 \times 10^3 \times 500 \times 500}{2 \, [50^2 + 500^2]} = 24752.47 \text{ N} \qquad \ldots (2)$$

When the bolts are subjected to shear as well as tensile load, then from (1) and (2), equivalent tensile load may be determined by,

$$W_{te} = \frac{1}{2} \left[W_t + \sqrt{(W_t)^2 + 4 \, (W_s)^2} \right]$$

$$= \frac{1}{2} \left[24752.47 + \sqrt{(24752.47)^2 + 4 \, (12500)^2} \right] = 29966.61 \text{ N}$$

If d_c is core diameter of bolt and σ_t is tensile stress for bolt material, then

$$\sigma_t = \frac{W_{te}}{\frac{\pi}{4} \times d_c^2}$$

$$\therefore \qquad 80 = \frac{29966.61}{\frac{\pi}{4} \times d_c^2}$$

$$\therefore \qquad d_c = 21.83 \text{ mm}$$

$$\therefore \qquad d_o = \frac{d_c}{0.84} = \frac{21.83}{0.84} = \textbf{25.99 mm} \cong \textbf{26 mm (say)}$$

Taking $d_o = 26$ mm, we have, $d_c = 0.84 \, d_o = 0.84 \times 26 = 21.84$ mm

$\therefore$ **We will use bolt of size M 26 having core diameter 21.84 mm.**

Problem 6.14 : *A bracket for crane is as shown in Fig. 6.17. Load of 20 kN is acting vertically at a distance of 500 mm from the face of the column. The vertical face of the bracket is secured to a column by 4 bolts, in two rows (2/row) at a distance of 50 mm from the lower edge of the bracket. Determine size of bolt, if permissible tensile stress for bolt material is 90 MPa.* **(S-13)**

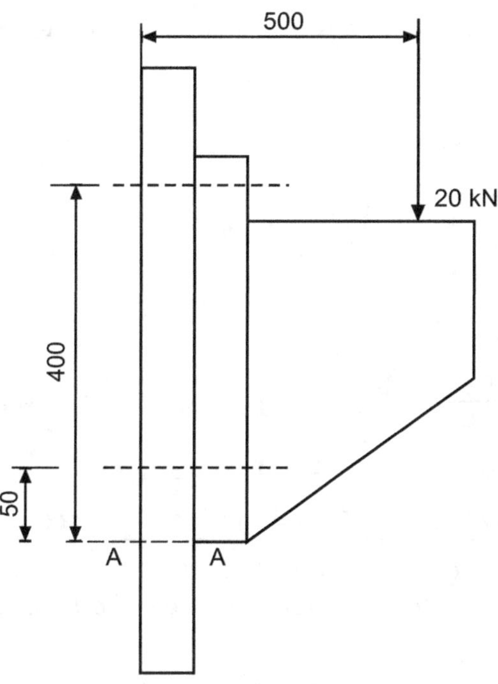

All dimensions are in mm

Fig. 6.17

Solution : Given data : $W = 20$ kN $= 20 \times 10^3$ N, $\sigma_t = 90$ N/mm², $l_1 = 50$ mm,

$l_2 = 400$ mm and $l = 500$ mm, $n = 4$

Procedure : In this case, the bolts are subjected to direct shearing load, which is equally shared by all the bolts. Therefore, direct shear load on each bolt,

$$W_s = \frac{W}{n} = \frac{20 \times 10^3}{4} = 5 \times 10^3 \text{ N} \qquad \text{... (1)}$$

where n is number of bolts.

Eccentric load W will try to tilt the bracket in the clockwise direction about edge A-A, then the bolts will be subjected to tensile stress due to turning moment.

The maximum tensile load on a heavily loaded bolt (W_t) may be obtained as follows :

$$W_t = w \times l_2 = \frac{W \times l \times l_2}{2\,[(l_1)^2 + (l_2)^2]} = \frac{20 \times 10^3 \times 500 \times 400}{2 \times [(50)^2 + (400)^2]} = 12307.69 \text{ N} \quad \text{... (2)}$$

When the bolts are subjected to shear as well as tensile loads, then from equations (1) and (2), equivalent tensile load may be determined by,

$$W_{te} = \frac{1}{2} \left[W_t + \sqrt{(W_t)^2 + 4\,(W_s)^2} \right]$$

$$= \frac{1}{2} \left[12307.69 + \sqrt{(12307.69)^2 + 4\,(5 \times 10^3)^2} \right] = 14082.89 \text{ N}$$

If d_c is core diameter of bolt and σ_t is tensile stress for bolt material, then

$$\sigma_t = \frac{W_{te}}{\frac{\pi}{4} \times (d_c)^2}$$

$$\therefore \qquad (d_c)^2 = \frac{W_{te}}{\frac{\pi}{4} \times \sigma_t} = \frac{14082.89}{\frac{\pi}{4} \times 90}$$

$$\therefore \qquad d_c = 14.11 \text{ mm}$$

We have, $\qquad d_o = \dfrac{d_c}{0.84} = \dfrac{14.11}{0.84} = 16.8 \text{ mm} \cong \textbf{18 mm (say)}$

$$\therefore \qquad d_c = 0.84\, d_o = 0.84 \times 18 = 15.12 \text{ mm}$$

$\therefore$ **We will use bolts of size M18 having core diameter 15.12 mm**

Problem 6.15 : *Write the design procedure of designing the bolts used to fix the wall bracket. Number of bolts is 3. Two are at top and one at bottom. The load W acts vertically at distance 'l' from the wall.*

Solution : A wall bracket carrying eccentric load perpendicular to axis of bolt is shown in Fig. 6.18.

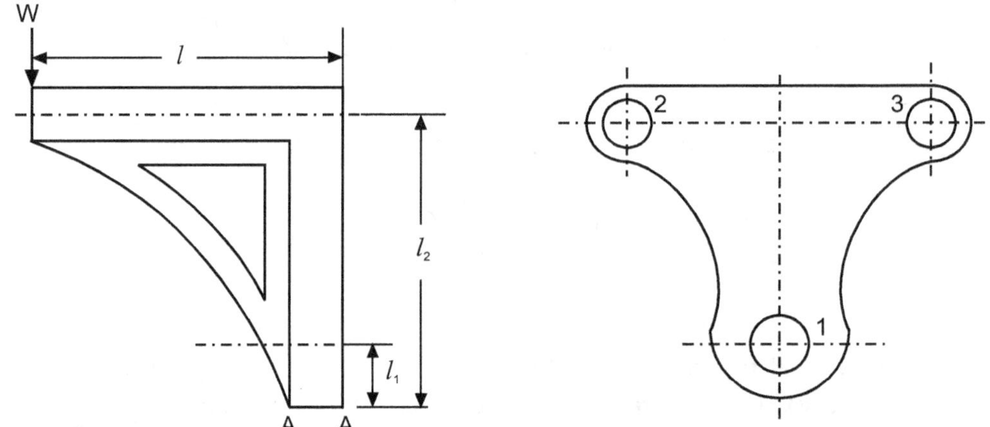

Fig. 6.18

- In this case, the bolts are subjected to direct shearing load, which is equally shared by all the bolts.

  $\therefore$ Direct shear load on each bolt,

$$W_s = \frac{W}{n} = \frac{W}{3} \text{ , where n is number of bolts} \qquad \dots (1)$$

- Now, the load W tends to rotate the bracket about the edge A-A.

  Let 'w' be the load in a bolt per unit distance due to turning effect of bracket and let W_1 be the load on single bolt at a distance l_1 from tilting edge and W_2 be the loads on two bolts at distance l_2 from tilting edge.

$\therefore$ Load on single bolt at distance l_1 is, $W_1 = w \times l_1$

and moment of this load about this tilting edge $= w \times l_1 \times l_1 = w \times (l_1)^2$ ... (2)

Similarly, load on each bolt at distance l_2 is, $W_2 = w \times l_2$

and moment of this load about this tilting edge $= w \times l_2 \times l_2 = w \times (l_2)^2$

Total moment of load on two bolts about tilting edge $= 2 \times w \times (l_2)^2$

$\therefore$ Total moment of load on 3 bolts about tilting edge $= w \times (l_1)^2 + 2w \times (l_2)^2$ ... (3)

Also, total moment due to load $W = W \times l$ ... (4)

From equations (2), (3) and (4),

$$W \times l = w \times (l_1)^2 + 2w \times (l_2)^2$$

$\therefore$ Load, $w = \dfrac{W \times l}{(l_1)^2 + 2 \times (l_2)^2}$

- Most heavily loaded bolts are those, which are situated at greatest distance from tilting edge. Here, bolts at distance l_2 are heavily loaded bolts.

- Eccentric load W will try to tilt the bracket in the clockwise direction about edge A-A, then the bolts will be subjected to tensile stress due to turning moment.

- The maximum tensile load on a heavily loaded bolt (W_t) may be obtained as follows :

$$W_t = w \times l_2 = \dfrac{W \times l \times l_2}{(l_1)^2 + 2 \times (l_2)^2} \qquad \text{... (5)}$$

When the bolts are subjected to shear as well as tensile loads, then equivalent loads may be determined by,

$$W_{te} = \text{Equivalent tensile load} = \frac{1}{2}\left[W_t + \sqrt{(W_t)^2 + 4\,(W_s)^2}\right]$$

$$W_{se} = \text{Equivalent shear load} = \frac{1}{2}\left[\sqrt{(W_t)^2 + 4\,(W_s)^2}\right]$$

Knowing the value of load, size of bolt may be determined for the given allowable stress, using following equations.

$$\sigma_t = \dfrac{W_{te}}{\dfrac{\pi}{4} \times (d_c)^2} \quad \text{and} \quad \tau = \dfrac{W_{se}}{\dfrac{\pi}{4} \times (d_c)^2}$$

Problem 6.16 : *A wall bracket is fixed to the wall by means of three bolts, one at distance of 25 mm from the lower edge and remaining two at a distance of 175 mm from lower bolt. It supports a load of 7.5 kN at a distance of 250 mm from the wall. The bolts are made of plain carbon steel 45C8 with tensile yield strength of 380 N/mm². If the factor of safety is 2.5, estimate the size of bolts. Sketch the arrangement.*

Solution :

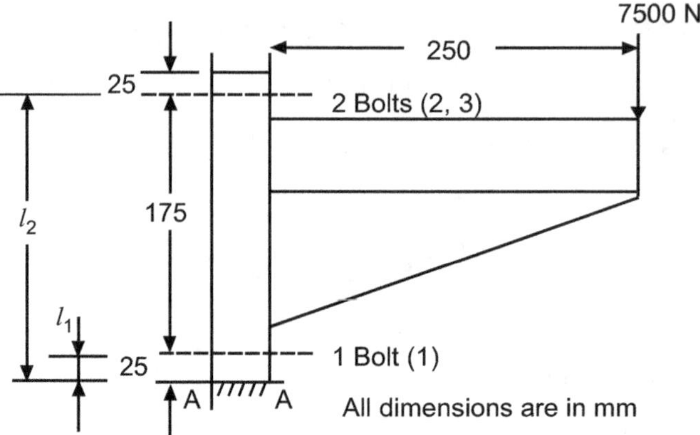

Fig. 6.19

Given data : W = 7500 N, l_1 = 25 mm, $l_2 = l_3$ = 25 + 175 = 200 mm, l = 250 mm, S_{yt} = 380 N/mm^2, F.O.S. = 2.5

Procedure : We have,

$$\therefore \quad \sigma_t = \frac{S_{yt}}{F.O.S.} = \frac{380}{2.5} = 152 \text{ N/mm}^2$$

Direct shear load on each bolt,

$$W_s = \frac{W}{n} = \frac{7500}{3} = 2500 \text{ N}$$

Also, the maximum tensile load on a heavily loaded bolt (W_t) may be obtained as follows :

$$W_t = w \times l_2 = \frac{W \times l \times l_2}{l_1^2 + 2l_2^2} = \frac{7500 \times 250 \times 200}{25^2 + 2 \times (200)^2} = 4651.16 \text{ N}$$

When bolts are subjected to shear as well as tensile load, then equivalent tensile load may be determined by,

$$W_{te} = \frac{1}{2}\left[W_t + \sqrt{(W_t)^2 + 4\,(W_s)^2}\right]$$

$$= \frac{1}{2}\left[4651.16 + \sqrt{(4651.16)^2 + 4\,(2500)^2}\right] = 5740 \text{ N}$$

Knowing the value of load, size of bolt may be determined for the given allowable stress.

$$\sigma_t = \frac{W_{te}}{\frac{\pi}{4} \times d_c^2}$$

$$\therefore \quad 152 = \frac{5740}{\frac{\pi}{4} \times d_c^2}$$

$$\therefore \qquad d_c = 6.93 \text{ mm}$$

$$\therefore \qquad d_o = \frac{d_c}{0.84} = \frac{6.93}{0.84} = 8.25 \text{ mm} \cong 10 \text{ mm (say)}$$

∴   **We will use bolts of size M 10.**

Problem 6.17 : *A wall bracket as shown in Fig. 6.20 is fixed to a wall using six bolts. Find the size of the bolt required, if allowable tensile and shear stresses in bolt material are 42 N/mm² and 35 N/mm² respectively.*

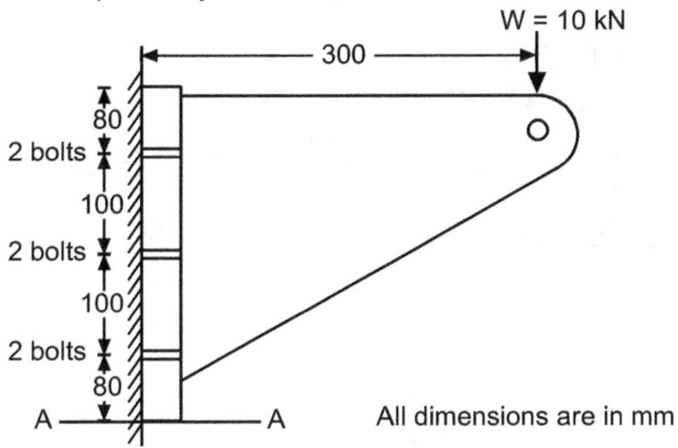

Fig. 6.20

Solution : Given data : $W = 10 \text{ kN} = 10 \times 10^3 \text{ N}$, $l_1 = 80 \text{ mm}$, $l_2 = 80 + 100 = 180 \text{ mm}$, $l_3 = 80 + 100 + 100 = 280 \text{ mm}$, $l = 300 \text{ mm}$, $n = 6$, $\sigma_t = 42 \text{ MPa}$, $\tau = 35 \text{ MPa}$.

Procedure : In this case, bolts are subjected to direct shear load, which is equally shared by all the bolts.

Direct shear load on each bolt, $W_s = \dfrac{W}{n} = \dfrac{10 \times 10^3}{6} = 1666.67 \text{ N}$ ... (1)

Eccentric load 'W' will try to tilt the bracket in the clockwise direction about the edge A-A, then the bolts will be subjected to tensile stress due to turning moment.

∴   The maximum tensile load on heavily loaded bolts (W_t) may be obtained as follows :

$$W_t = \frac{W \cdot l \cdot l_3}{2 \, [l_1^2 + l_2^2 + l_3^2]} = \frac{10 \times 10^3 \times 300 \times 280}{2 \times [(80)^2 + (180)^2 + (280)^2]} = 3583.62 \text{ N} \qquad ... (2)$$

When the bolts are subjected to shear as well as tensile load, then from equations (1) and (2), equivalent tensile load may be determined by,

$$W_{te} = \frac{1}{2} \left[W_t + \sqrt{(W_t)^2 + 4 \, (W_s)^2} \right]$$

$$= \frac{1}{2} \times \left[3583.62 + \sqrt{(3583.62)^2 + 4 \, (1666.67)^2} \right] = \mathbf{4238.92 \ N}$$

If d_c is core diameter of bolt and σ_t is the tensile stress for bolt material then,

$$\sigma_t = \frac{W_{te}}{\frac{\pi}{4} d_c^2}$$

$$\therefore \qquad d_c^2 = \frac{W_{te}}{\frac{\pi}{4} \times \sigma_t} = \frac{4238.92 \times 4}{\pi \times 42} = 128.50$$

$$\therefore \qquad d_c = 11.33 \text{ mm}$$

$$\therefore \qquad d_o = \frac{d_c}{0.84} = \frac{11.33}{0.84} = \textbf{13.49 mm} \qquad \qquad \dots (3)$$

Also, equivalent shear load may be obtained by,

$$W_{se} = \frac{1}{2} \left[\sqrt{(W_t)^2 + 4\,(W_s)^2} \right]$$

$$= \frac{1}{2} \times \left[\sqrt{(3583.62)^2 + 4 \times (1666.67)^2} \right] = \textbf{2447.11 N}$$

If τ is the permissible shear tress, then,

$$\tau = \frac{W_{se}}{\frac{\pi}{4} \cdot d_c^2}$$

$$\therefore \qquad d_c^2 = \frac{W_{se} \times 4}{\pi \times \tau} = \frac{2447.11 \times 4}{\pi \times 35} = 89.02$$

$$\therefore \qquad d_c = 9.435 \text{ mm}$$

$$\therefore \qquad d_o = \frac{d_c}{0.84} = \frac{9.435}{0.84} = \textbf{11.23 mm} \qquad \qquad \dots (4)$$

From equations (3) and (4), taking the larger value of d_o,

i.e. $\qquad d_o = 13.49 \text{ mm} \cong \textbf{14 mm (say)}$

So, bolts of size M14 may be used.

Problem 6.18 : *A bearing bracket is to be bolted to vertical surface and supports a load of 30 kN at an eccentricity of 300 mm from the wall; the two top bolts are 120 mm apart and at 100 mm from single bottom bolt, which is 40 mm away from bottom edge of bracket. Design the suitable diameter of steel bolts. Take σ_t = 100 MPa and τ = 40 MPa.*

Solution : Given data : $W = 30 \text{ kN} = 30 \times 10^3 \text{ N}$, $\sigma_t = 100 \text{ N/mm}^2$, $\tau = 40 \text{ N/mm}^2$, $n = 3$,

$l_1 = 40 \text{ mm}$, $l_2 = 40 + 100 = 140 \text{ mm}$ and $l = 300 \text{ mm}$

Procedure : A wall bracket carrying eccentric load perpendicular to axis of bolt is shown in Fig. 6.21.

In this case, the bolts are subjected to direct shearing load, which is equally shared by the three bolts.

$$\therefore \quad \text{Direct shear load on each bolt, } W_s = \frac{W}{n} = \frac{W}{3} = \frac{30 \times 10^3}{3} = 10 \times 10^3 \text{ N} \qquad \dots (1)$$

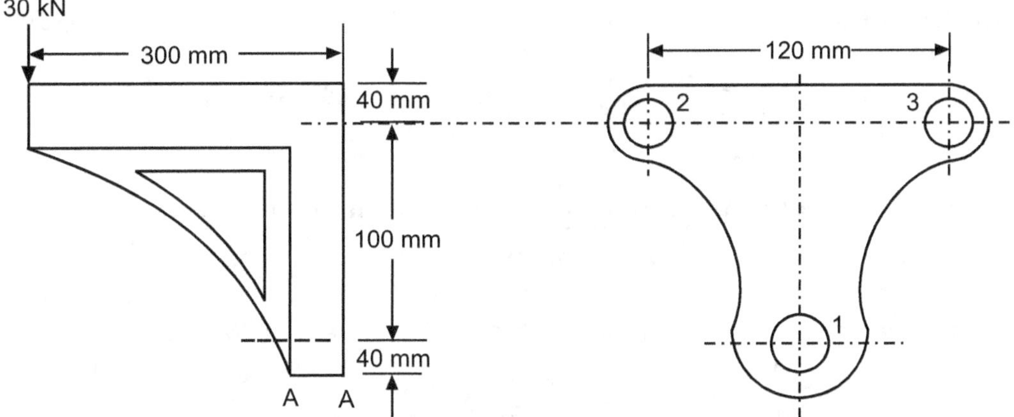

Fig. 6.21

The maximum tensile load on a heavily loaded bolt (W_t) may be obtained as follows :

$$W_t = w \times l_2 = \frac{W \times l \times l_2}{(l_1)^2 + 2 \times (l_2)^2} = \frac{30 \times 10^3 \times 300 \times 140}{(40)^2 + 2 \times (140)^2}$$

$$= 30882.35 \text{ N} \qquad \qquad \dots (2)$$

When the bolts are subjected to shear as well as tensile load, then equivalent loads may be determined by,

$$W_{te} = \text{Equivalent tensile load} = \frac{1}{2}\left[W_t + \sqrt{(W_t)^2 + 4\,(W_s)^2}\right]$$

$$= \frac{1}{2}\left[30882.35 + \sqrt{(30882.35)^2 + 4\,(10 \times 10^3)^2}\right] = \textbf{33837.64 N}$$

And, $\qquad W_{se} = \text{Equivalent shear load} = \frac{1}{2}\left[\sqrt{(W_t)^2 + 4\,(W_s)^2}\right]$

$$= \frac{1}{2}\left[\sqrt{(30882.35)^2 + 4\,(10 \times 10^3)^2}\right] = \textbf{18396.46 N}$$

We have, $\qquad \sigma_t = \dfrac{W_{te}}{\dfrac{\pi}{4} \times (d_c)^2}$

$\therefore \qquad (d_c)^2 = \dfrac{W_{te}}{\dfrac{\pi}{4} \times \sigma_t} = \dfrac{33837.64}{\dfrac{\pi}{4} \times 100}$

$\therefore \qquad d_c = \textbf{20.76 mm} \qquad \qquad \dots (3)$

Also, $\qquad \tau = \dfrac{W_{se}}{\dfrac{\pi}{4} \times (d_c)^2}$

$\therefore \qquad (d_c)^2 = \dfrac{W_{se}}{\dfrac{\pi}{4} \times \tau} = \dfrac{18396.46}{\dfrac{\pi}{4} \times 40}$

$\therefore \qquad d_c = \textbf{24.19 mm} \qquad \qquad \dots (4)$

Taking larger value of two, d_c = 24.19 mm   [From (3) and (4)]

$$\therefore \quad d_o = \frac{d_c}{0.84} = \frac{24.19}{0.84} = 28.80 \text{ mm} \cong \textbf{30 mm (say)}$$

$$\therefore \quad d_c = 0.84\, d_o = 0.84 \times 30 = 25.2 \text{ mm}$$

$\therefore$ **We will use bolts of size M30, having core diameter of 25.2 mm.**

Problem 6.19 : Fig. 6.22 shows a bracket of jib crane. It is connected to the crane by using 4 bolts. The bracket carries a maximum load of 30 kN inclined at 30° to horizontal. Calculate the size of bolts required to fix the bracket. Assume σ_t = 70 MPa.

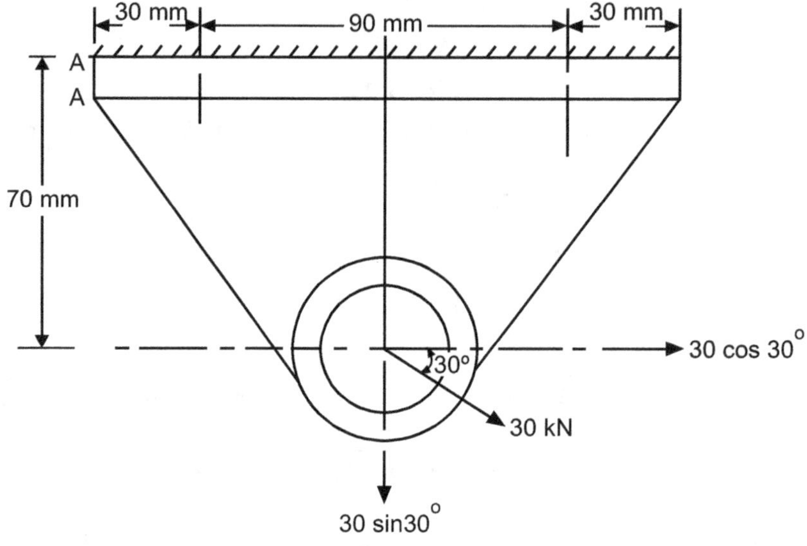

Fig. 6.22

Solution : Given data : W = 30 kN = 30 × 10³ N at an angle of 30° to horizontal, σ_t = 70 N/mm², n = 4.

Procedure : Resolving the inclined load into two perpendicular components.

$$W_x = 30 \times 10^3 \times \cos 30° = 25980.76 \text{ N}$$

$$W_y = 30 \times 10^3 \times \sin 30° = 15000 \text{ N}$$

In this case, due to vertical load W_y, the bolts will be subjected to direct tensile load.

$$\therefore \quad W_{t1} = \frac{W_y}{n} = \frac{15000}{4} = \textbf{3750 N} \qquad \text{... (1)}$$

Also, due to horizontal load W_x, the bolts are subjected to direct shearing load as well as tensile load.

$\therefore$ Direct shear load on each bolt,

$$W_s = \frac{W_x}{n} = \frac{25980.76}{4} = \textbf{6495.19 N} \qquad \text{... (2)}$$

where n is number of bolts.

Eccentric load W_x will try to tilt the bracket in the clockwise direction about edge A-A and then the bolts will be subjected to tensile stress due to turning moment.

$\therefore$ $l_1 = 30$ mm, $l_2 = 30 + 90 = 120$ mm and $l = 70$ mm

The maximum tensile load on a heavily loaded bolt (W_{t2}) may be obtained as follows :

$$W_{t2} = w \times l_2 = \frac{W \times l \times l_2}{2\,[(l_1)^2 + (l_2)^2]} = \frac{25980.76 \times 70 \times 120}{2 \times [(30)^2 + (120)^2]} = \textbf{7131.97 N} \quad \dots (3)$$

$\therefore$ Total tensile load $= W_t = W_{t1} + W_{t2} = 3750 + 7131.97 = \textbf{10881.97 N}$

$$\dots \text{[From (1) and (3)]} \dots (4)$$

When the bolts are subjected to shear as well as tensile load, then from equations (2) and (4), equivalent tensile load may be determined by,

$$W_{te} = \frac{1}{2}\left[W_t + \sqrt{(W_t)^2 + 4\,(W_s)^2}\right]$$

$$= \frac{1}{2}\left[10881.97 + \sqrt{(10881.97)^2 + 4\,(6495.19)^2}\right] = \textbf{13913.98 N}$$

If d_c is core diameter of bolt and σ_t is tensile stress for bolt material, then

$$\sigma_t = \frac{W_{te}}{\frac{\pi}{4} \times (d_c)^2}$$

$\therefore$
$$(d_c)^2 = \frac{W_{te}}{\frac{\pi}{4} \times \sigma_t} = \frac{13913.98}{\frac{\pi}{4} \times 70}$$

$\therefore$ $d_c = 15.90$ mm

$\therefore$
$$d_o = \frac{d_c}{0.84} = \frac{15.90}{0.84} = 18.93 \text{ mm} \cong \textbf{20 mm}$$

$\therefore$ $d_c = 0.84\,d_o = 0.84 \times 20 = 16.8$ mm

$\therefore$ **We will use bolts of size M20, having core dimeter 16.8 mm.**

Practice Questions

1. Give advantages and disadvantages of screwed joints.

2. Sketch and explain any two threaded profiles used for screwed joints.

3. Explain the method of determining the size of the bolt, when the bracket carries an eccentric load perpendicular to the axis of the bolt.

4. Explain the method of determining of the size of the bolt, when the bracket carries an eccentric load parallel to the axis of the bolt.

5. Define the following terms related to screwed joints :

   (i) Major diameter, (ii) Minor diameter, (iii) Pitch and (iv) Lead.

6. What are the bolts of uniform strength ? Explain any two methods of obtaining bolts of uniform strength.

7. What are different stresses occurring in screwed fastening ?

Problems for Practice

1. Determine the safe tensile load for a bolt of M 30, assuming a safe tensile stress of 45 MPa. **(Ans.** W = 22444.16 N)

2. The effective diameter of cylinder is 400 mm. The maximum pressure of steam acting on the cylinder cover is 1.12 N/mm^2. Find the number of M 24 size studs required to fix the cover. Stress in bolts should not exceed 33 MPa. Assume bolts are not initially stressed. **(Ans.** n = 14) **(W-09)**

3. The cylinder head of a steam engine is head in position by M 20 bolt, the effective diameter of cylinder is 300 mm and steam pressure is 0.6 N/mm^2. Assuming that the bolts are not initially stressed, find the number of bolts required, if working stress for the bolt material is not to exceed 20 MPa. **(Ans.** n = 10) **(S-10)**

4. A double acting steam engine cylinder having 360 mm cylinder diameter works on maximum steam pressure in cylinder of 1 N/mm^2 absolute with 0.03 N/mm^2 back pressure. Determine the diameter of screwed end of piston rod, where permissible safe stress in tension is 60 MPa. **(Ans.** M 56 size)

5. A steam engine cylinder of 300 mm diameter is supplied with steam at 1.5 N/mm^2. The cylinder cover is fastened by means of 8 bolts of size M 20. The joint is made leak-proof by means of suitable gaskets. Find stress produced in bolts.

    (Ans. σ_t = 202.85 N/mm^2)

6. A steam engine cylinder has effective diameter of 200 mm. It is subjected to maximum steam pressure of 1.8 N/mm^2. Calculate the number and size of studs required to fix the cylinder cover onto the cylinder flange. Assume the permissible stress as 35 N/mm^2. Take P.C.D. of studs as 325 mm. Also, check the circumferential pitch of studs so as to give leak-proof joint. **(Ans.** 8 bolts of size M 24)

7. Fig. 6.23 shows a bracket carrying vertical load of 20 kN. The load is taken up by 4 bolts. Determine size of bolts for permissible tensile stress of 75 N/mm^2.

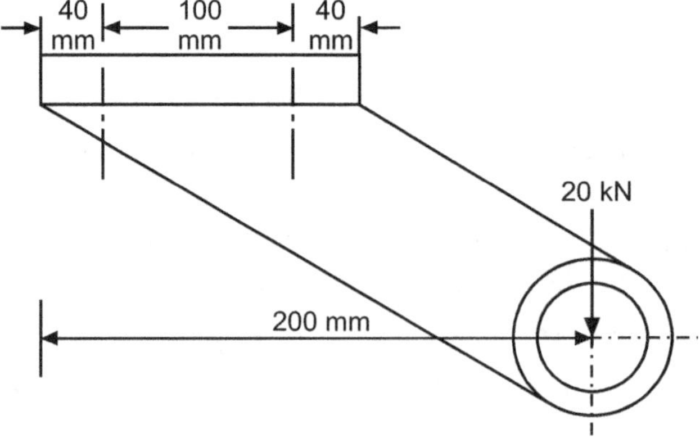

Fig. 6.23

(Ans. M 22)

8. A cast iron cylinder head is fastened to the cylinder having bore 400 mm with 6 studs. The maximum pressure inside cylinder is 2 MPa. The ratio of elasticity of connected parts to elasticity of bolt is 3. What should be the initial tightening load on the bolt, so that, the joint is leak proof at maximum pressure ? Take permissible stress = 35 MPa.

$$\textbf{(Ans. } W_1 = 448.72 \times 10^3 \text{ N)} \textbf{ (Hint : } \text{Given } a = 3, \ \therefore \ K = \frac{a}{1+a} = \frac{3}{1+3} = 0.75\text{)}$$

9. A bracket supports a load of 30 kN at a distance of 50 cm from one end of its rectangular base, bolted to a wall by means of four bolts. The distance of centerline of two bolts from the same end of base is 8 cm, while centerline of remaining two bolts is at a distance of 25 cm from the same end. Determine the size of bolts, if maximum allowable tensile stress in the bolt is not to exceed 6000 N/cm^2.

(Ans. Bolts of size M30)

Summer 2013

1. Explain with a neat sketch "Bolts of Uniform Strength".   **(4 M)**

Ans. Refer Section 6.5.

2. Explain with neat sketch : (i)Through bolt, (ii)Tap bolt.   **(4 M)**

Ans. Refer Section 6.3.1.

3. A bracket for crane is as shown in Fig. 6.24. Load of 20 kN acting vertically at a distance of 500 mm from the face of the column. The vertical face of the bracket is secured to a column by 4 bolts, in two rows (2/row) at a distance of 50 mm form the lower edge of the bracket. Determine size of bolt if permissible tensile stress for bolt material is 90 MPa.   **(4 M)**

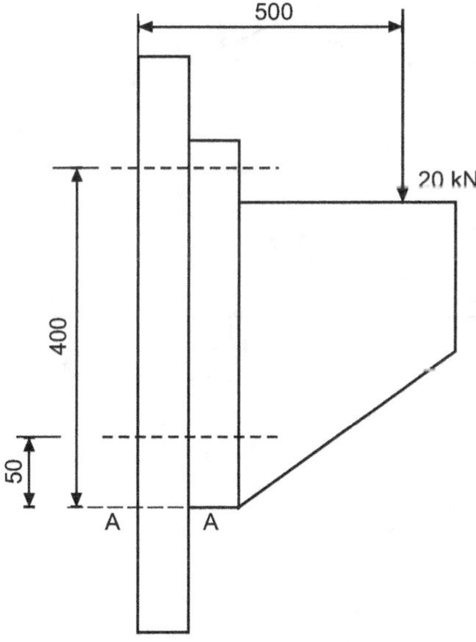

Fig. 6.24

Ans. Refer Problem 6.14.

Winter 2013

1.   What do you understand by bolt of uniform strength? Explain with neat sketch.

(4 M)

Ans. Refer Section 6.5.

2.   A wall bracket is attached to a wall by means of four bolts, two at a distance of 50 mm from the lower edge and remaining two at a distance of 450 mm from the lower bolts. It supports a load of 50 kN at a distance of 500 mm from the wall. Sketch the arrangements and estimate the diameter of bolts. Assume working in stress in tension as 80 N/mm^2. **(8 M)**

Ans. Refer Problem 6.13.

Summer 2014

1.   A bracket carrying a vertical load of 25 kN as shown in figure. The load is taken up by 4 bolts for fixing the bracket. Determine the size of bolts for permissible tensile stress of 80 N/mm^2. **(6 M)**

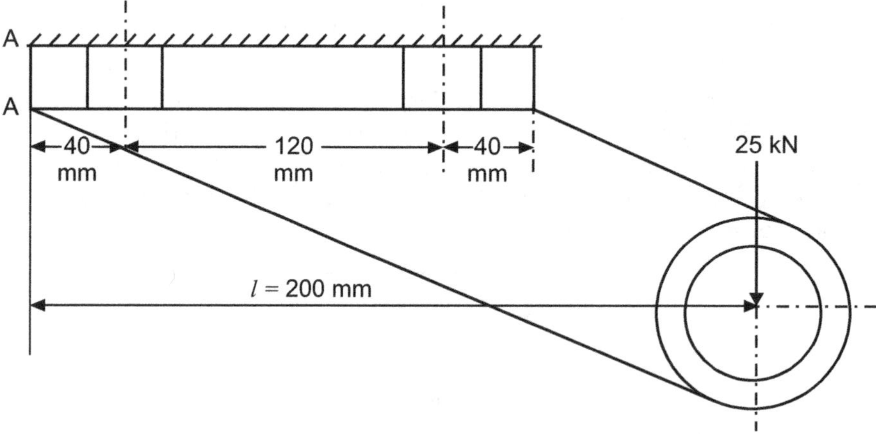

Fig. 6.25

Ans. Refer Problem 6.10.

DESIGN OF WELDED JOINTS

About This Chapter

This chapter has a weightage of 6 marks and assigned duration is 4 hours. Here we learn about the various types of welded joints, their advantages, disadvantages and applications, I.S. symbols, design of transverse and parallel fillet welds.

Statistical Analysis

Examination	Weightage of questions asked
S-09	04 Marks
W-09	04 Marks
S-10	– Marks
W-10	07 Marks
S-11	04 Marks
W-11	04 Marks
S-12	04 Marks
W-12	08 Marks
S-13	06 Marks
W-13	04 Marks
S-14	06 Marks

7.1 INTRODUCTION TO WELDED JOINTS

- A welded joint is a permanent joint, which is obtained by the fusion of the edges of two parts to be joined together with or without the application of pressure and a filler material.

- The heat required for the fusion of the material may be obtained by burning of gas or by an electric arc.

- Welding is extensively used in fabrication as an alternative method for casting or forging and as replacement for bolted and riveted joints.

- It is also used as a repair medium. e.g. to reunite metal at a crack, to build up a small part that has broken off, such as gear tooth or to repair a worn surface such as a bearing surface.

7.1.1 Advantages and Disadvantages of Welded Joints

Question

1. Write down the advantages and disadvantages of welded joint. **(W-10)**

Advantages of Welded Joints :

(1) They have 100% efficiency.

(2) They have more strength and rigidity.

(3) Changes and additions to the existing structures are easy.

(4) It is possible to weld any part of structure to any point.

(5) Process of welding takes very less time.

(6) Welded assembly results in lighter construction.

(7) The cost of welded assembly is lower than that of bolted joints.

(8) The design of welded assemblies can be easily and economically modified to meet the changing product requirements.

(9) Welded joints are tight and leak proof as compared to other joints.

(10) When two parts are joined by threaded joints, holes are drilled in the parts to accommodate the screws. The holes reduce the cross-sectional area of the members and result in stress concentration. There is no such problem in welded connection.

(11) The strength of the welded joint is higher. Very often, the strength of the weld is more than the strength of the plates that are joined together.

(12) Machine components of certain shape such as circular steel pipe, can be easily welded.

Disadvantages of Welded Joints :

(1) Due to heating required for fusion, the member to be joined may get distorted and stresses may be developed.

(2) The quality and the strength of the welded joint depend upon the skill of the welder. It requires high skilled labour.

(3) It is very difficult to inspect.

(4) It cannot be used to join two dis-similar materials, as in case of riveting.

(5) Welded joints are poor in damping out the vibrations.

7.1.2 Applications of Welded Joints

(1) Welding is extensively used in fabrication as an alternate method of casting or forging and as a replacement of bolted and riveted joint.

(2) Welding is also used as repair medium e.g. to reunite metal at a crack to build up a small part, that has broken off, such as gear tooth or to repair a worn surface such as bearing surface.

(3) Welded steel structures like bridges, industrial shades, towers, crane and material handling equipments.

(4) Solid beams and frame beams under dynamic loads.

(5) Pressure vessels :

    (a) Unfired pressure vessels like storage tanks, reservoirs, process equipments in chemical, paper and sugar industries.

    (b) Fired pressure vessels like boilers and furnaces.

(6) Welded machine components like flywheels, gears, jigs and fixtures, machine structures, automobile chassis etc. and press machine frames and many heavy duty machine frames can be welded suitably.

7.1.3 Advantages of Welded Joints over Riveted Joints

(1) Permanent joint.

(2) Longer life.

(3) Higher reliability.

7.1.4 Classification of Welded Joints

Question

1. State the classification of welded joints. **(S-13)**

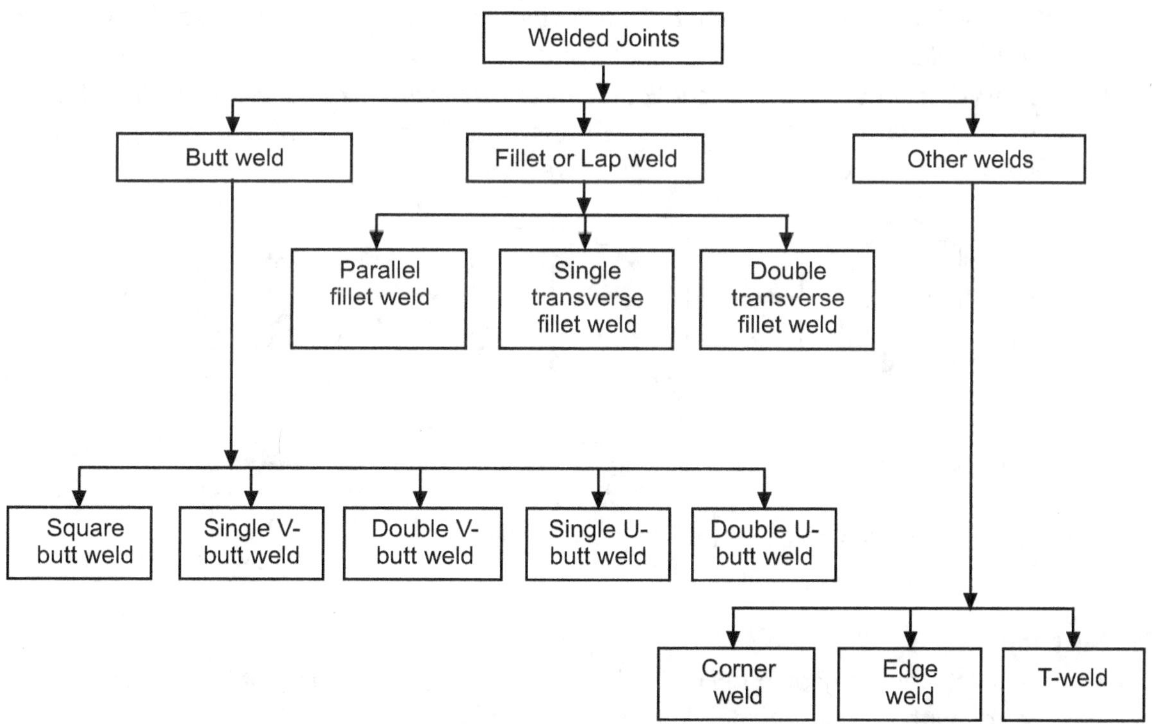

Classification/Types of welded joints

7.2 VARIOUS TYPES OF FREQUENTLY USED WELDED JOINTS

(a) Lap joint or fillet joint :
- (i)   Single transverse fillet joint.
- (ii) Double transverse fillet joint.
- (iii) Parallel fillet joint.

(b) Butt joint :
- (i)   Square butt joint.
- (ii) Single V-butt joint.
- (iii) Double V-butt joint.
- (iv) Single U-butt joint.
- (v)   Double U-butt joint.

(c) Other joint :
- (i)   Corner joint.
- (ii) Edge joint.
- (iii) T-joint.

1. Lap Joint:

- It is a joint between two overlapping components.
- It consists of fillet welds.
- Fillet weld is having triangular cross-section joining two surfaces at right angles to each other.
- The examples of lap joint are single transverse fillet, double transverse fillet, parallel fillet welds.
- Based on the relative positions of the load axis with respect to the fillet axis, the fillet welds are classified into two types.

(a) Parallel fillet weld : *"If the load axis is parallel to the axis of the fillet, it is known as parallel fillet weld"*.

(b) Transverse fillet weld : *"If the load axis is perpendicular to the axis of the fillet, it is known as transverse fillet weld"*. The transverse fillet weld can be a single transverse fillet weld or a double transverse fillet weld.

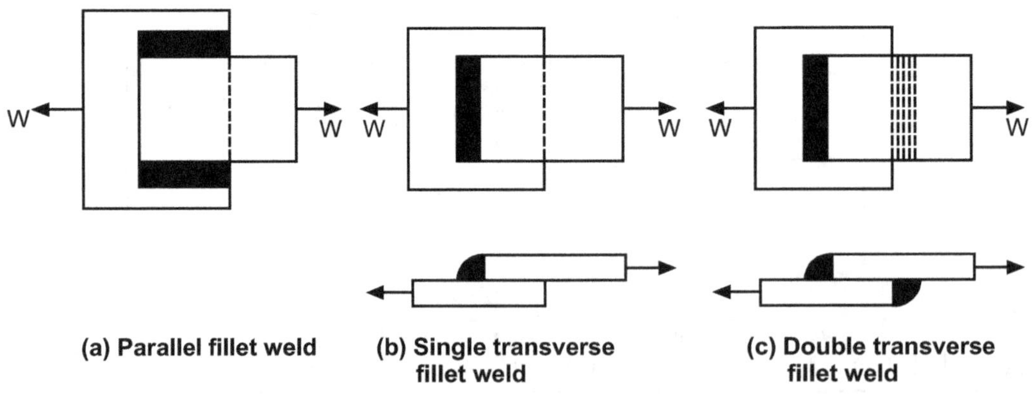

Fig. 7.1 : Fillet welds

2. Butt Joint :

- The butt weld as shown in Fig. 7.2 is obtained by placing the plates to be joined side by side with their edges nearly touching each other.
- The small gap is maintained between the edges for the filler material.

- The examples of lap joints are square butt, single V-butt, single U-butt, double V-butt and double U-butt.

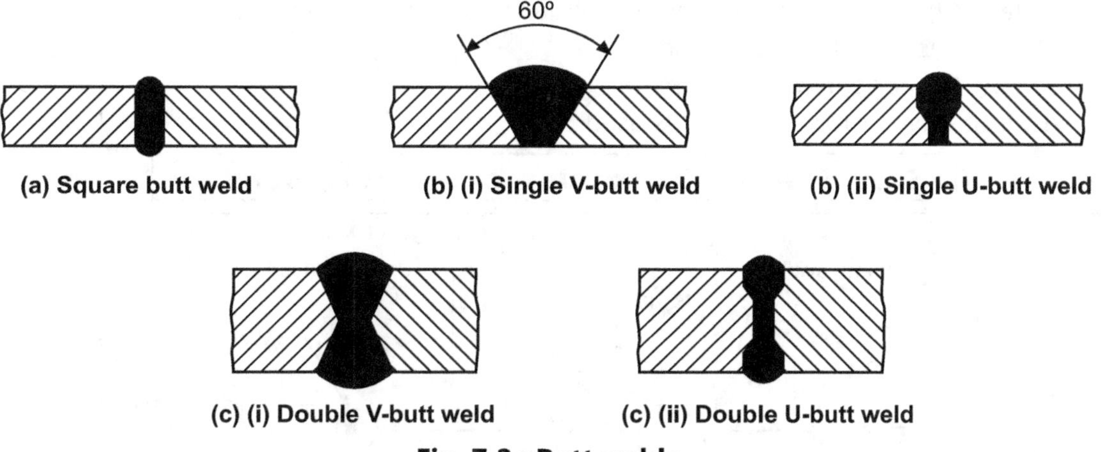

(a) Square butt weld   **(b) (i) Single V-butt weld**   **(b) (ii) Single U-butt weld**

(c) (i) Double V-butt weld   **(c) (ii) Double U-butt weld**

Fig. 7.2 : Butt welds

(a) Square butt weld : If the thickness of the plates is less than 5 mm, the edge of the plates do not require bevelling and hence the joint used is known as square butt weld.

(b) Single V-butt weld or single U-butt weld : If the thickness of the plates is in between 5 and 12.5 mm, the edges are bevelled to 'V' or 'U' groove and accordingly single V-butt or single U-butt weld may be used.

(c) Double V-butt weld or Double U-butt weld : If the thickness of the plates is more than 12.5 mm, it is necessary to bevel and weld the plates from both sides. In such cases, double V-butt or double U-butt welds are used.

3. Other Welded Joints :

- In addition, the other types of welded joints used are :
  Corner weld, Edge weld and T-weld.

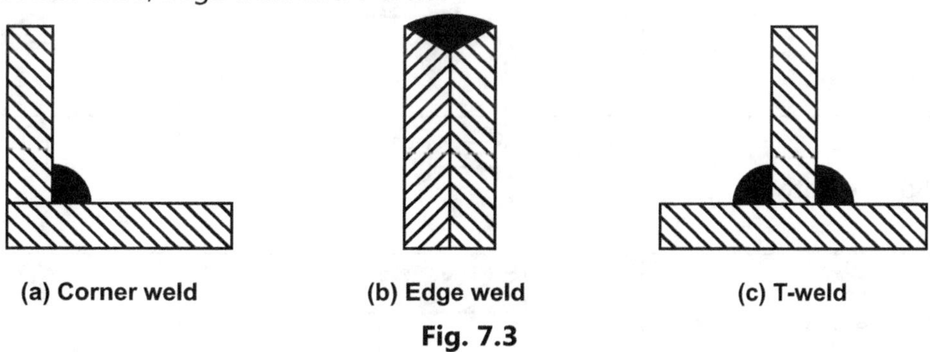

(a) Corner weld   **(b) Edge weld**   **(c) T-weld**

Fig. 7.3

7.2.1 Assumptions Made in Designing Welded Joints

(i) The load is distributed uniformly along the entire length of the weld.

(ii) The stress is spread over the effective section uniformly.

(iii) Suitable stress concentration factors and factors of safety are employed to account for the unknown factors like,

   (a)   Change in physical properties due to high rate of cooling.

   (b)   Thermal stresses in welds.

   (c)   Homogeneity of weld metal.

(iv) Proper type of welded joint is used.

7.2.2 Standard Location of Welding Symbols

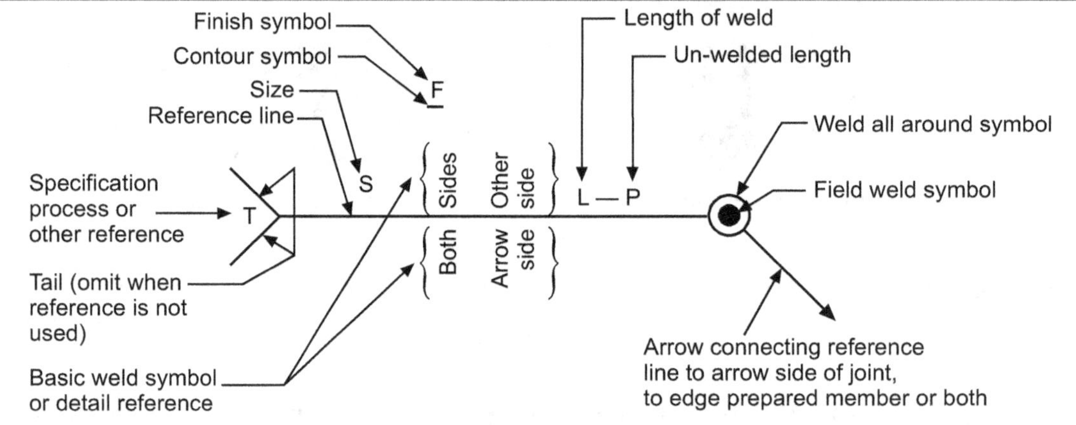

Fig. 7.4 : Standard location of welding symbols

7.2.3 Various I.S. Symbols Representing Welded Connections

Question
1.   Draw symbolic representation of following types of weld :
(i)   Weld all around, (ii) Double 'V' but joint.   **(W-13)**

Sr. No.	Form of weld	Sectional representation	Symbol
1.	Fillet		
2.	Square butt		
3.	Single V butt		
4.	Double V butt		

Sr. No.	Form of weld	Sectional representation	Symbol
5.	Single U butt		
6.	Double U butt		
7.	Single bevel butt		
8.	Double bevel butt		
9.	Single J butt		
10.	Double J butt		
11.	Stud		
12.	Sealing run		
13.	Spot		
14.	Seam		
15.	Plug		

Sr. No.	Form of weld	Sectional representation	Symbol
16.	Projection		△
17.	Flash		

7.2.4 Supplementary I.S. Symbols Representing Welded Connections

Sr. No.	Particulars	Drawing representation	Symbol
1.	Weld all round		○
2.	Field weld		
3.	Flush contour		—
4.	Convex contour		
5.	Concave contour		
6.	Grinding finish		G
7.	Machining finish		M
8.	Chipping finish		C

- Welds used in any component, must be precisely specified on working drawing. Therefore, welding symbols are used.

7.3 DESIGN OF TRANSVERSE FILLET OR LAP JOINTS

- The fillet or lap joint is obtained by overlapping the plates and then welding the edges of plates.

- Please refer to the diagrams of single and double transverse fillet joints. (Fig. 7.5 and 7.6)

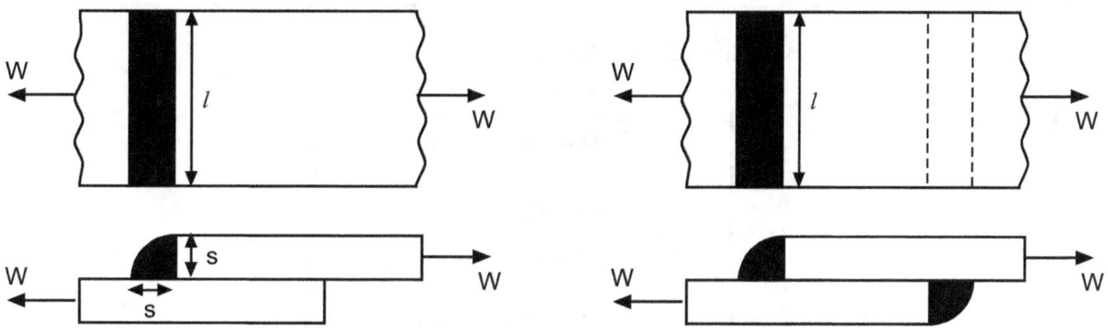

Fig. 7.5 : Single transverse fillet weld   **Fig. 7.6 : Double transverse fillet joint**

- Let us assume that, section of fillet is a right angled triangle ABC with hypotenous AC making equal angles with other two sides AB and BC.

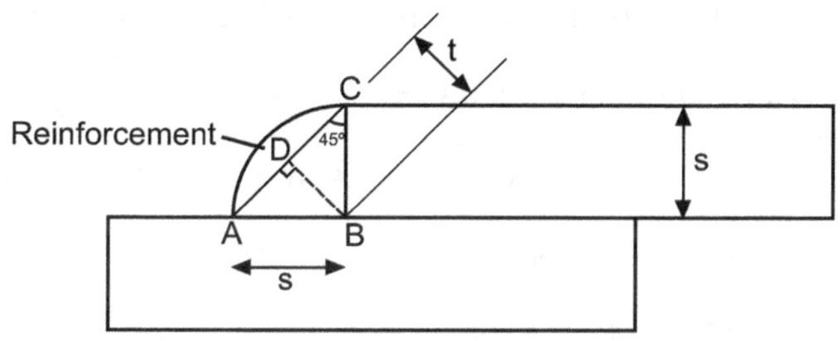

Fig. 7.7

The length of each side = AB = BC = Leg or size of weld

Perpendicular distance of AC from point B = BD = Throat thickness

- Let,   t = Throat thickness

                     s = Size of weld = Thickness of plate

                     l = Length of weld

Referring Fig. 7.7, we have, throat thickness = t = s $\times$ sin 45° = 0.707 s

$$\therefore \begin{bmatrix} \text{Minimum area of} \\ \text{weld or throat area} \end{bmatrix} = \text{Throat thickness} \times \text{Length of weld}$$

$$= t \times l = 0.707 \, s \times l$$

- The transverse fillet joints are designed on the basis of tensile strength.

- If σ_t is the permissible tensile stress induced in the weld metal, then tensile strength of the joint is,

(a) For single transverse fillet weld, $W = 0.707 \cdot s \cdot l \cdot \sigma_t$

(b) For double transverse fillet weld, $W = 2 \times 0.707 \cdot s \cdot l \cdot \sigma_t = 1.414 \cdot s \cdot l \cdot \sigma_t$

7.4 DESIGN OF SINGLE AND DOUBLE PARALLEL FILLET WELD

- Fig. 7.8 shows double parallel fillet welds.

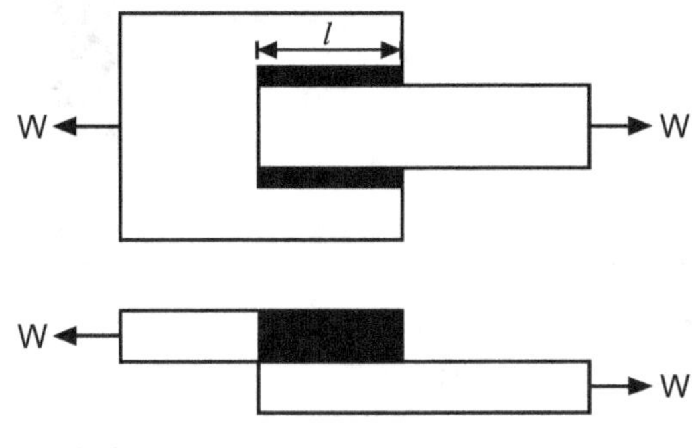

Fig. 7.8

- The parallel fillet welds are designed on the basis of shear strength.

- Minimum area of weld or throat area $= 0.707 \times s \cdot l$

- If τ = Permissible shear stress induced in weld metal, then

(a) For single parallel fillet weld,

Shear strength, $W = 0.707 \times s \cdot l \cdot \tau$

(b) For double parallel fillet weld,

Shear strength, $W = 2 \times 0.707 \times s \cdot l \cdot \tau = 1.414 \times s \cdot l \cdot \tau$

7.5 DESIGN OF COMBINATION OF PARALLEL AND TRANSVERSE FILLET WELDS

Question

1. Write the strength equations for designing a symmetrically loaded parallel and transverse weld along with neat sketches. **(W-12)**

- The combined double parallel and single transverse fillet weld is shown in Fig. 7.9. It is subjected to tensile stress and shear stress.

$$\text{Tensile strength} = W_t = \sigma_t \cdot A$$
$$= \sigma_t \cdot (0.707 \times s \cdot l_1)$$
$$= 0.707 \cdot s \cdot l_1 \cdot \sigma_t$$
$$\text{Shear strength} = W_s = \tau \cdot A$$
$$= \tau \cdot (2 \times 0.707 \times s \cdot l_2)$$
$$= 1.414 \cdot s \cdot l_2 \cdot \tau$$

$\therefore$ Total strength of weld $= W_t + W_s$

$$W = 0.707 \cdot s \cdot l_1 \cdot \sigma_t + 1.414 \cdot s \cdot l_2 \cdot \tau$$

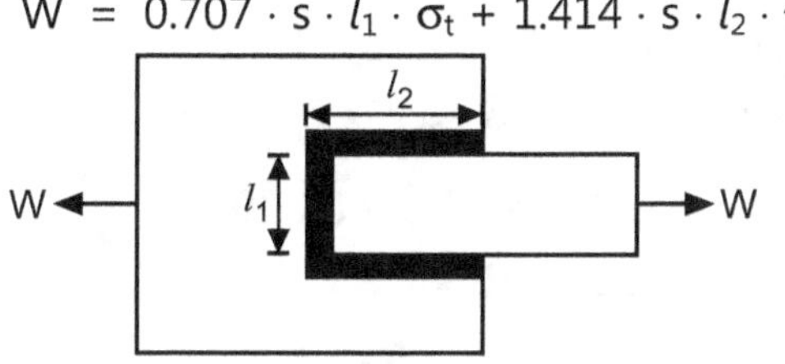

Fig. 7.9

7.6 STRESS CONCENTRATION FACTOR FOR WELDED JOINTS

- Stress concentration gets developed at the junction of weld and the parent metal. Therefore, stress concentration factor should be taken into account in case of fatigue (dynamic or variable) loading.

- Obtain permissible stresses for fatigue loading by dividing given permissible stresses by respective stress concentration factor.

Type of joint	Stress concentration factor
Transverse fillet weld	1.5
Parallel fillet weld	2.7

Note : In order to avoid starting and stopping of weld run, 12.5 mm should be added to length of each weld.

Numerical Type No. 1 :

"Design of Double Transverse Fillet Weld (Static Loading)"

Problem 7.1 : *Two steel plates 120 mm wide and 12.5 mm thick are to be connected together by double transverse fillet weld. The maximum tensile stress for the plate and welding material is not to exceed 70 N/mm². Find the length of weld required for maximum static loading.* **(W-06, 09)**

Solution : Given data : Thickness of plate = Size of weld = s = 12.5 mm,

     σ_t = 70 N/mm², width = 120 mm

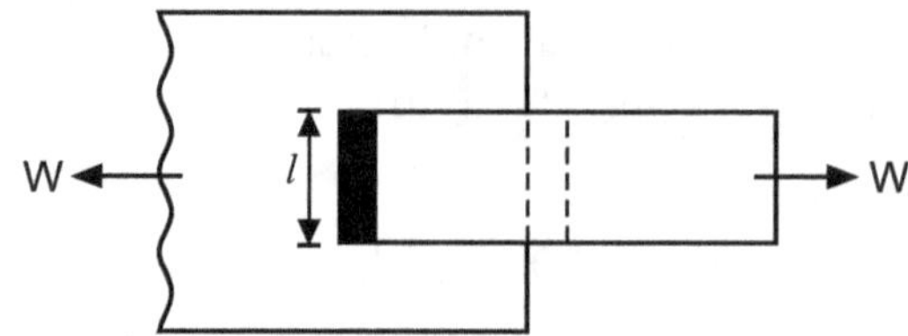

Fig. 7.10

Procedure : Maximum load, which plate can carry is,

$$W = \text{Area} \times \text{Maximum stress} = (\text{Width} \times \text{Thickness}) \times \sigma_t$$
$$= (120 \times 12.5) \times 70$$
$$W = \mathbf{105 \times 10^3 \ N} \qquad \qquad \qquad \text{... (1)}$$

For double transverse fillet weld,

$$W = 2 \times 0.707 \times s \times l \times \sigma_t$$
$$= 1.414 \times 12.5 \times l \times 70$$
$$W = \mathbf{1237.25 \times l} \qquad \qquad \qquad \text{... (2)}$$

On equating equations (1) and (2),

$$105 \times 10^3 = 1237.25 \times l$$
$$\therefore \qquad l = \mathbf{84.86 \ mm}$$

For starting and stopping of weld run, 12.5 mm is added to the length of weld.

$$\therefore \qquad l = 84.86 + 12.5$$
$$l = \mathbf{97.36 \ mm}$$

Numerical Type No. 2 :
"Design of Double Transverse Fillet Weld (Static and Dynamic Loading)"

Problem 7.2: *Two steel plates 10 cm wide and 1.25 cm thick are to be connected together by double transverse fillet weld. For static and dynamic loading, take stress concentration factor = 1.5 and tensile stress as 7000 N/cm². Find the length of weld.*

Solution : Given data : Thickness of plate = Size of weld = s = 1.25 cm = 12.5 mm,

$\sigma_t = 7000 \ N/cm^2 = 70 \ N/mm^2$,   Width = 10 cm = 100 mm, $K_f = 1.5$

Procedure : Case I : For static loading :

Maximum load, which plate can carry is,

$$W = \text{Area} \times \text{Maximum stress}$$
$$= \text{Width} \times \text{Thickness} \times 70$$
$$= 100 \times 12.5 \times 70 = 87.5 \times 10^3 \ N \qquad \qquad \text{... (1)}$$

For double transverse fillet weld,

$$W = 2 \times 0.707 \, s \times l \times \sigma_t$$
$$= 1.414 \times 12.5 \times l \times 70 = 1237.25 \times l \qquad \qquad \text{... (2)}$$

On equating equations (1) and (2),

$$87.5 \times 10^3 \ = \ 1237.25 \times l$$

$$\therefore \qquad l \ = \ \textbf{70.72 mm}$$

For starting and stopping of weld run, 12.5 mm is added to the length of weld.

$$\therefore \qquad l \ = \ 70.72 + 12.5 \ = \ \textbf{83.22 mm}$$

Case II : For dynamic loading :

$$\text{Allowable tensile stress} \ = \ \frac{70}{K_f} \ = \ \frac{70}{1.5} \ = \ 46.67 \ \text{N/mm}^2$$

For double transverse fillet weld,

$$W \ = \ 2 \times 0.707 \ s \times l \times \sigma_t$$

$$= \ 1.414 \times 12.5 \times l \times 46.67 \ = \ 824.9 \times l \qquad \qquad \text{... (3)}$$

On equating equations (1) and (3),

$$87.5 \times 10^3 \ = \ 824.9 \times l$$

$$\therefore \qquad l \ = \ \textbf{106.07 mm}$$

For starting and stopping of weld run, 12.5 mm is added to the length of weld.

$$\therefore \qquad l \ = \ 106.07 + 12.5 \ = \ \textbf{118.57 mm}$$

Numerical Type No. 3 :

"Design of Double Parallel Fillet Weld (Static Loading)"

Problem 7.3: *A plate 100 mm wide and 10 mm thick is to be welded to another plate by means of double parallel fillet welds. The plates are subjected to a static load of 80 kN. Find the length of weld, if the permissible shear stress in the weld does not exceed 55 N/mm².*

Solution : Given data : Thickness of plate = Size of weld = s = 10 mm,

$$W = 80 \ \text{kN} = 80 \times 10^3 \ \text{N}, \ \tau = 55 \ \text{N/mm}^2, \ \text{width} = 100 \ \text{mm}$$

Procedure : For double parallel fillet weld, the shear strength is given by

$$W \ = \ 2 \times 0.707 \times s \times l \times \tau$$

$$\therefore \qquad 80 \times 10^3 \ = \ 1.414 \times 10 \times l \times 55$$

$$\therefore \qquad l \ = \ \textbf{102.86 mm}$$

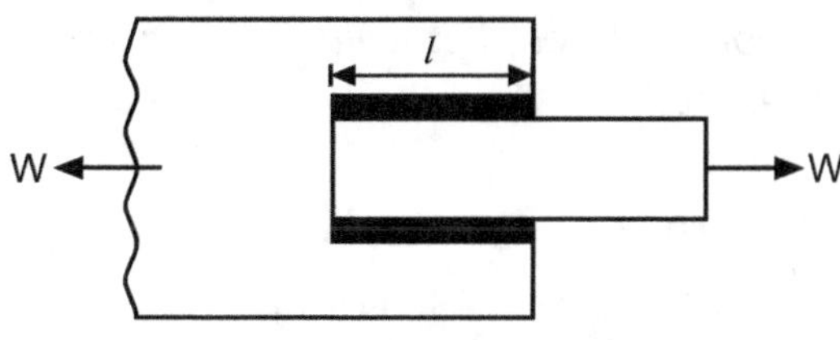

Fig. 7.11

For starting and stopping of weld run, 12.5 mm is added to the length of weld.

$$\therefore \qquad l \ = \ 102.86 + 12.5 \ = \ \textbf{115.36 mm}$$

Numerical Type No. 4 : "Design of Double Parallel Fillet Weld (Static and Dynamic/Fatigue Loading)"

Problem 7.4 : *A plate 100 mm wide and 12.5 mm thick is to be welded to another plate by means of double parallel fillet welds. The plates are subjected to a load of 50 kN. Find the length of weld, so that, the maximum stress does not exceed 56 N/mm². Consider the joint first under static loading and then under fatigue loading. Take stress concentration factor for parallel fillet welding as 2.7.*　**(S-13)**

Solution : Given data : Thickness = size of weld = s = 12.5 mm, W = 50×10^3 N,

$\tau = 56$ N/mm², width = 100 mm

Procedure : Case I : For static loading,

$\therefore$ 　　　　　　　$W = 1.414 \times s \times l \times \tau$

$\therefore$ 　　　　$50 \times 10^3 = 1.414 \times 12.5 \times l \times 56$

$\therefore$ 　　　　　　　$l = 50.51$ mm

Adding 12.5 mm for starting and stopping of weld run.

$\therefore$ 　　　　　　　$l = 50.51 + 12.5$

　　　　　　　　$= \mathbf{63.01}$ **mm**

Case II : For fatigue loading, stress concentration factor for parallel fillet weld is 2.7.

$\therefore$ 　Permissible shear stress,

$$\tau = \frac{56}{2.7} = 20.74 \text{ N/mm}^2$$

We have, 　　　　　$W = 1.414 \times s \times l \times \tau$

$\therefore$ 　　　　$50 \times 10^3 = 1.414 \times 12.5 \times l \times 20.74$

$\therefore$ 　　　　　　　$l = \mathbf{136.39}$ **mm**

Adding 12.5 mm for starting and stopping of weld,

　　　　$l = 136.39 + 12.5 = \mathbf{148.89}$ **mm**

Numerical Type No. 5 : "Design of Combined Single Transverse and Double Parallel Fillet Weld (Static Loading)"

Problem 7.5 : *A plate 75 mm wide and 12.5 mm thick is to be joined with another plate by a single transverse and double parallel fillet weld. The maximum tensile and shear stresses are 70 N/mm² and 56 MPa respectively. Find the length of each parallel fillet weld, if joint is subjected to 90 kN.*　**(S-09, 12)**

Solution : Given data : $W = 90$ kN $= 90 \times 10^3$ N, $\sigma_t = 70$ N/mm²

　　　　　　$\tau = 56$ MPa $= 56$ N/mm², Size of weld $= s = 12.5$ mm

Procedure : Effective length of single transverse filled weld is,

　　　　　$l_1 = 75 - 12.5 = 62.5$ mm

Let 　　　　　　　$l_2 = $ Length of each parallel fillet weld

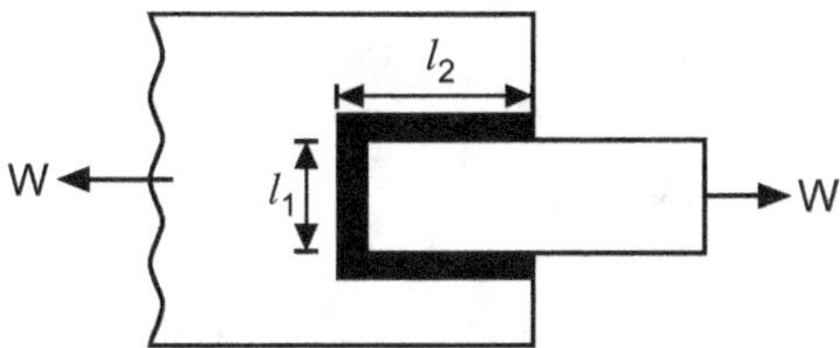

Fig. 7.12

The load carried by single transverse fillet weld,

$$W_1 = 0.707 \times s \times l_1 \times \sigma_t$$

$\therefore \qquad W_1 = 0.707 \times 12.5 \times 62.5 \times 70 = 38664.06 \text{ N}$

The load carried by double transverse fillet weld,

$$W_2 = 2 \times 0.707 \times s \times l_2 \times \tau$$

$\therefore \qquad W_2 = 1.414 \times 12.5 \times l_2 \times 56 = 989.8\, l_2$

$\therefore \quad$ Total strength of weld,

$$W = W_1 + W_2$$

$\therefore \qquad 90 \times 10^3 = 38664.06 + 989.8\, l_2$

$\therefore \qquad l_2 = 51.86 \text{ mm}$

For starting and stopping of weld run, 12.5 mm is added to the length of weld,

$$l_2 = 51.86 + 12.5$$

$$l_2 = \textbf{64.36 mm}$$

Problem 7.6 : *A steel plate 100 mm wide and 10 mm thick, is joined with another steel plate by means of a single transverse and double parallel fillet welds, as shown in Fig. 7.13. The strength of the welded joint should be equal to the strength of plates to be joined. The permissible tensile and shear stresses for the weld material and the plates are 70 and 50 N/mm² respectively. Find the length of weld. Assume tensile force acting on the plates as static.*

(W-10)

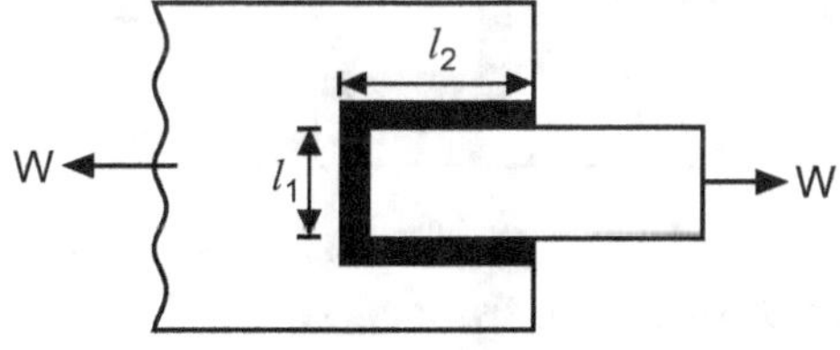

Fig. 7.13

Solution : Given data : Thickness of plate $= s = 10$ mm, Width $= 100$ mm

$$\sigma_t = 70 \text{ N/mm}^2, \quad \tau = 50 \text{ N/mm}^2$$

Procedure : The effective length of weld for the single transverse weld is obtained by,

$$l_1 = \text{Width} - 12.5 = 100 - 12.5 = 87.5 \text{ mm}$$

Let, $\qquad\qquad l_2 = $ Length of each parallel fillet weld

Total strength of weld, $W = $ Area $\times$ Maximum stress $= (100 \times 10) \times 70 = 70 \times 10^3 \text{ N} \ldots(1)$

The load carried by single transverse fillet weld is,

$$W_1 = 0.707 \times s \times l_1 \times \sigma_t = 0.707 \times 10 \times 87.5 \times 70$$

$$\therefore \quad W_1 = 43303.75 \text{ N} \quad\quad\quad \dots (2)$$

The load carried by double parallel fillet weld is,

$$W_2 = 1.414 \times s \times l_2 \times \tau = 1.414 \times 10 \times l_2 \times 50 = 707 \cdot l_2 \quad\quad \dots (3)$$

We have, $\quad\quad W = W_1 + W_2$

$$\therefore \quad 70 \times 10^3 = 43303.75 + 707 \cdot l_2 \quad\quad \text{[From equations (1), (2) and (3)]}$$

$$\therefore \quad l_2 = 37.76 \text{ mm}$$

For starting and stopping of weld run, 12.5 mm is added to length of weld.

$$l = 37.76 + 12.5 = \textbf{50.26 mm}$$

Numerical Type No. 6 : "Design of Combined Single Transverse and Double Parallel Fillet Weld (Dynamic Loading)"

Problem 7.7 : *Find the length of the weld run for a plate of size 120 mm wide and 15 mm thick to be welded by means of single transverse weld and double parallel fillet weld, when subjected to dynamic loading. Take $\sigma_t = 75$ N/mm^2 and $\tau = 60$ N/mm^2.*   **(S-14)**

Solution : Given data : Thickness of plate = Size of weld = s = 15 mm, Wdith = 120 mm,

$$\sigma_t = 75 \text{ N/mm}^2 \text{ and } \tau = 60 \text{ N/mm}^2$$

Procedure :

We have, $\quad\quad$ Load = Area $\times$ Maximum stress

$$\therefore \quad W = (120 \times 15) \times 75 = 135 \times 10^3 \text{ N} \quad\quad \dots (1)$$

As the joint is subjected to variable loading, assume and take stress concentration factor as 1.5 and 2.7 for transverse fillet weld and parallel fillet weld respectively.

Therefore, Allowable tensile stress $= \dfrac{75}{k_f} = \dfrac{75}{1.5} = 50 \text{ N/mm}^2$

and Allowable shear stress $= \dfrac{60}{K_f} = \dfrac{60}{2.7} = 22.22 \text{ N/mm}^2$.

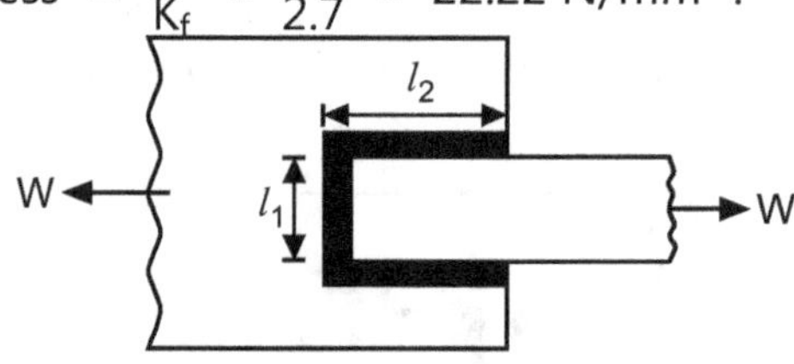

Fig. 7.14

The effective length of weld for single transverse filled weld is,

$$l_1 = \text{Width} - 12.5 = 120 - 12.5 = 107.5 \text{ mm},$$

Let, l_2 = Length of each parallel filled weld.

The load carried by single transverse filled weld,

$$W_1 = 0.707 \times s \times l_1 \times \sigma_t = 0.707 \times 15 \times 107.5 \times 50$$

$$= 57001.875 \text{ N} \quad\quad \dots (2)$$

The load carried by double parallel filled weld,

$$W_2 = 2 \times 0.707 \times s \times l_2 \times \tau$$

$$= 1.414 \times 15 \times l_2 \times 22.22 = 471.28 \, l_2 \quad\quad \dots (3)$$

We have, $W = W_1 + W_2$

∴ $135 \times 10^3 = 57001.875 + 471.28\, l_2$ [From equations (1), (2) and (3)]

          $l_2 = \textbf{165.5 mm}$

For starting and stopping of weld run, 12.5 mm is added to length of weld. Therefore, new length of weld is,

∴ $l_2 = 165.5 + 12.5 = \textbf{178 mm}$

Practice Questions

1. Give merits and demerits of welded joints.
2. Explain strength equations for transverse fillet welds with sketch.
3. Explain strength equations for double parallel fillet welds with neat sketch.
4. State the strength equation of double parallel fillet weld and single transverse fillet weld with sketches.

Problems For Practice

1. Find the length of the weld run for a plate of size 120 mm wide and 15 mm thick to be welded by means of single transverse weld and double parallel fillet weld, when subjected to dynamic loading. Take $\sigma_t = 75\ \text{N/mm}^2$ and $\tau = 60\ \text{N/mm}^2$.

   (**Ans.** l = 178.5 mm)

2. Fig. 7.15 shows a plate 70 mm wide and 12 mm thick joined with another plate by a single transverse weld and a double parallel weld. Determine the length of parallel fillet weld of the joint subjected to both static and fatigue loading. Given $\sigma_t = 80\ \text{MN/m}^2$, $\tau = 50\ \text{MN/m}^2$ and stress concentration factor 1.4 for transverse weld and 2.5 for parallel weld.

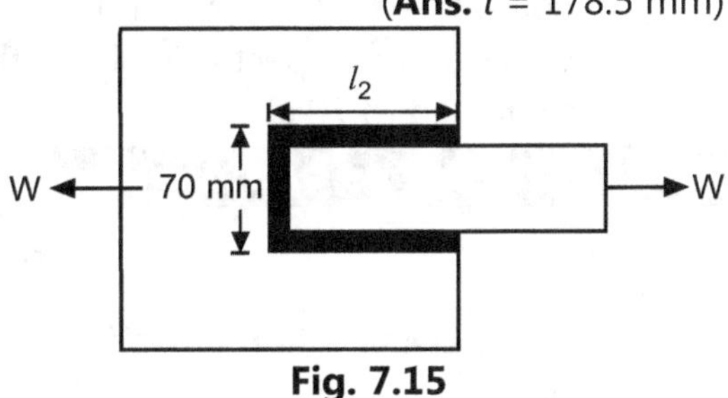

Fig. 7.15

   (**Note :** $\sigma_t = 80\ \text{MN/m}^2 = \dfrac{80 \times 10^6}{10^3 \times 10^3\ \text{mm}^2} = 80\ \text{N/mm}^2$)

   (**Ans.** (i) l_2 = 45.3 mm (ii) l_2 = 110.38 mm)

3. A plate, 75 mm wide and 10 mm thick, is joined with another steel plate by means of single transverse and double parallel fillet welds, as shown in Fig. 7.16. The joint is subjected to maximum tensile force of 55 kN. The permissible tensile and shear stresses in the weld material are 70 and 50 N/mm^2 respectively. Determine the required length of each parallel fillet weld.

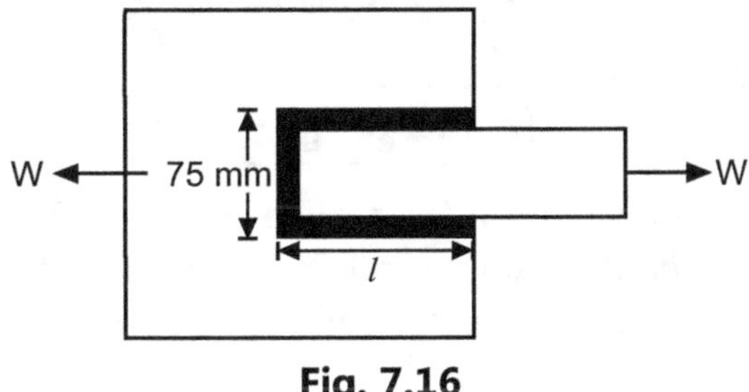

Fig. 7.16

   (**Ans.** l_2 = 46.55 mm)

4.   A plate of 100 mm wide and 12.5 mm thick is to be welded to another plate by means of parallel fillet welds. The plates are subjected to load of 50 kN. Find the length of the weld so that the maximum stress does not exceed 56 MPa. Consider the joint under fatigue loading.

(Ans. l = 148.896 mm)

5.   Two steel plates 120 mm wide and 12.5 mm thick are to be connected together by double transverse fillet weld. The maximum tensile stress for plate and welding not to exceed 70 N/mm^2. Find the length of weld for maximum static loading.   **(W-06)**

(Ans. 97.36 mm)

6.   Determine the length of the weld run for a plate of size 120 mm wide and 15 mm thick to be welded to another plate by means of a single transverse weld and double parallel fillet welds when the joint is subjected to variable load.   **(S-11)**

(Ans. l_2 = 178 mm)

7.   A plate 90 mm wide and 10 mm thick is to be joined with a single transverse and double parallel fillet weld. The maximum tensile and shear stress are 70 N/mm^2 and 55 N/mm^2 respectively. Find the length of each parallel fillet weld, if joint is subjected to 70 kN.   **(Ans.** 53.19 mm) **(W-11)**

MSBTE Questions and Answers

Summer 2013

1.   State classification of welded joints.   **(2 M)**

Ans. Refer Article 7.1.4.

2.   A plate 100 mm wide and 12.5 mm thick is to be welded to another plate by parallel fillet welds. It is subjected to a load of 50 kN. Find length of the weld so that maximum stress should not exceed 56 MPa. Consider first static loading and then fatigue loading. Stress concentration factor is 2.7.   **(4 M)**

Ans. Refer Problem 7.4.

Winter 2013

1.   Draw symbolic representation of following types of weld :   **(4 M)**
     (i) Weld all around. (ii) Double 'V' butt joint.

Ans. Refer Article 7.2.3.

Summer 2014

1.   Find the length of the weld run for a plate of size 120 mm wide and 15 mm thick to be welded by means of single transverse weld and double parallel fillet weld, when subjected to dynamic loading. Take σ_t = 75 N/mm^2 and τ = 60 N/mm^2.   **(6 M)**

Ans. Refer Problem 7.7.

Chapter 8

ANTIFRICTION BEARINGS

About This Chapter

This chapter has weightage of 08 marks and assigned duration is 04 hours. In this chapter, we will study about classification of bearings into sliding and rolling contact. We also study about terminology of ball bearings, life load relationship, basic static load rating and basic dynamic load rating, limiting speed, selection of ball bearings using manufacturer's catalogue.

Statistical Analysis

Examination	Weightage of questions asked
S-09	04 Marks
W-09	06 Marks
S-10	06 Marks
W-10	06 Marks
S-11	04 Marks
W-11	04 Marks
S-12	04 Marks
W-12	08 Marks
S-13	12 Marks
W-13	12 Marks
S-14	08 Marks

8.1 INTRODUCTION TO BEARINGS

- A bearing is a mechanical element, that permits relative motion of the two parts, such as shaft and housing (journal), with minimum friction.
- Due to relative motion between the contact surfaces, certain amount of power is wasted in overcoming frictional resistance and if the rubbing surfaces are in direct contact, there will be rapid wear.
- To reduce frictional resistance and wear and in some cases to carry away the heat generated, a layer of fluid (as a lubricant) may be provided.
- The lubricant used to separate the journal and bearing is usually a mineral oil refined from petroleum. In addition, vegetable oil, silicon oil, greases etc. may be used.

8.1.1 Functions of Bearings

(1) The bearing is used to support the shaft or axle and to hold it in correct position with respect to frame or casing.

(2) The bearing ensures free rotation of the shaft or axle with minimum friction.

(3) The bearing is used to take up the forces acting on the shaft or axle and to transmit them to the frame or the casing.

8.1.2 Desirable Properties of Bearing Material

The desirable properties of bearing material are :

(1) Compressive strength to withstand high pressures without distortion.

(2) Corrosion resistance, because excessive temperature causes oxidation of lubricating oils and forms corrosive acids.

(3) Thermal conductivity.

(4) Bondability.

(5) Compatibility.

(6) Sufficient surface endurance strength and fatigue resistance to avoid fatigue, when subjected to fluctuating stresses.

8.2 CLASSIFICATION OF BEARINGS

Question

1. Give classification of bearings.   **(S-10, 13; W-12)**

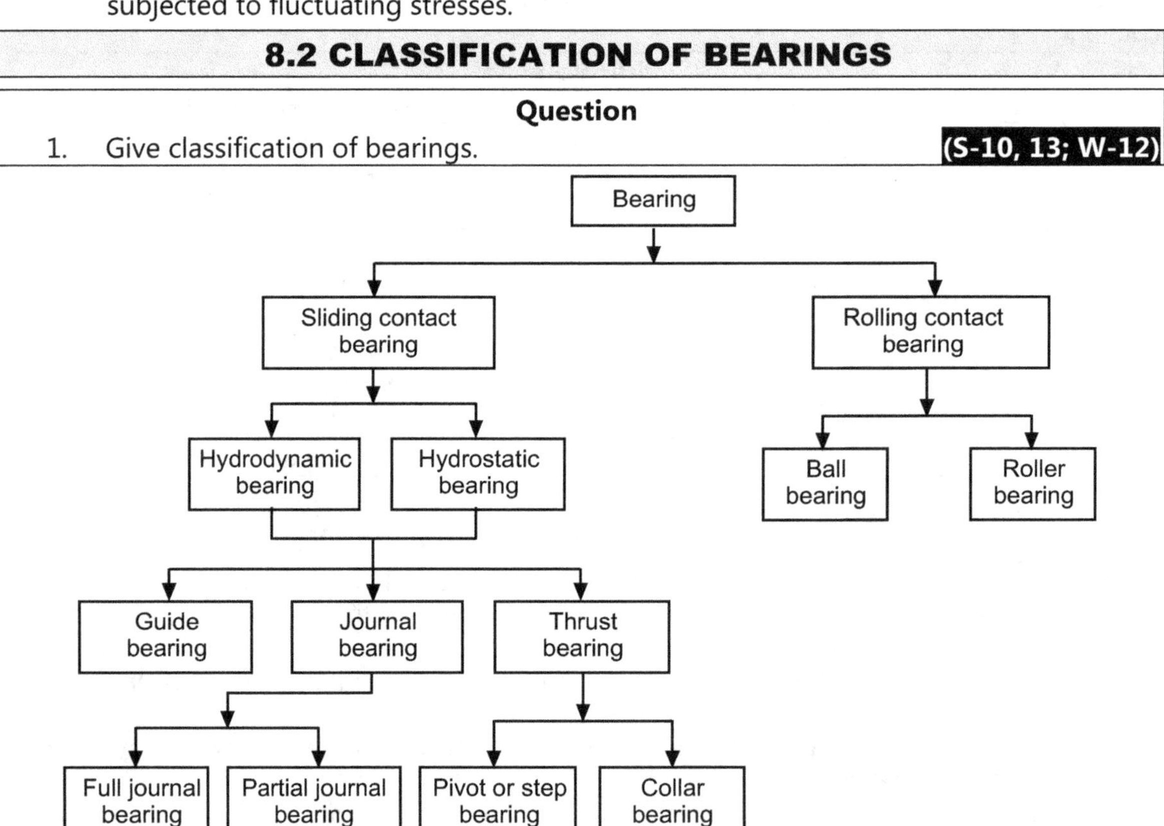

(A) Bearings are classified, according to direction of force acting upon them, into two categories :

(a) Radial bearing : A radial bearing supports the load, which is perpendicular to the axis of the shaft and the bearing.

(b) Thrust bearing : A thrust bearing supports the load, which acts along the axis of the shaft and bearing.

- The most important criteria to classify the bearings is, *"the type of the friction between the shaft and the bearing surface"*. Depending upon the type of friction, bearings are classified into two main groups – sliding contact bearings and rolling contact bearings.

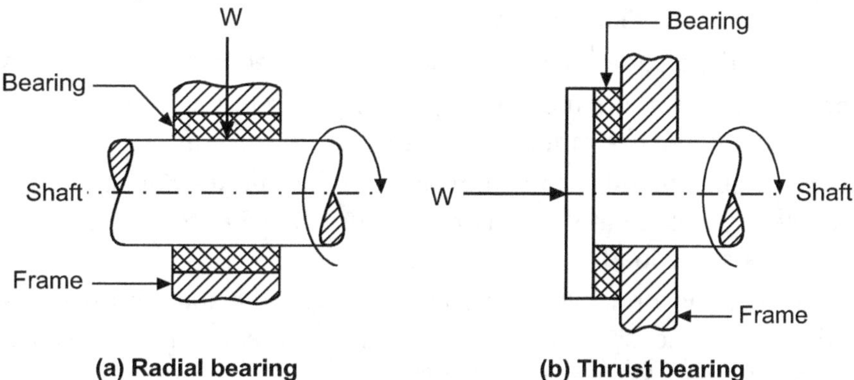

(a) Radial bearing   **(b) Thrust bearing**

Fig. 8.1

(B) Based on the nature of relative motion between the contacting surfaces, the bearings are mainly classified into two types :

I. Sliding contact bearing :

- They are also called as plain bearings, journal or sleeve bearing.
- Here, the contacting surfaces makes a sliding contact.
- The surface of shaft slides over the surface of bush resulting in friction and wear.
- The contacting surfaces may also be separated by a film of lubricant, in order to reduce friction.

II. Rolling contact bearing :

- Here, the contacting surfaces have rolling contact.
- Rolling elements, such as balls or rollers are introduced between the shaft and outer race fixed to the frame.
- Due to low friction offered by rolling contact bearings, they are also known as *antifriction bearings.*
- Here, sliding friction is replaced by rolling friction.

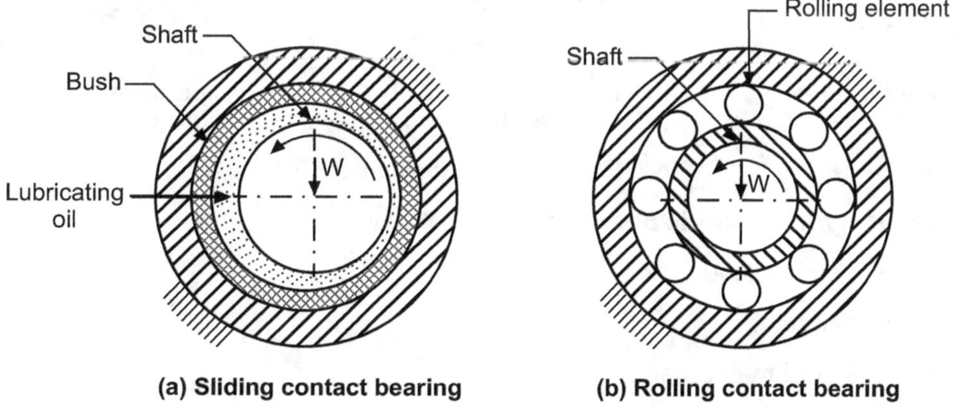

(a) Sliding contact bearing   **(b) Rolling contact bearing**

Fig. 8.2

8.2.1 Classification of Sliding Contact Bearings Based on Thickness of Layer of Lubricant between Journal and Bearing or Mode of Lubrication

1. Hydrodynamic or Thick Film Bearings :

- In this, the working surfaces are completely separated from each other by lubricant.
- In hydrodynamic bearing, the load supporting high pressure fluid film is created due to the shape and relative motion between the two surfaces.
- The moving surface pulls the lubricant into a wedge-shaped zone at a velocity sufficiently high to create the high pressure film necessary to separate the two surfaces against the load.
- Fig. 8.3 shows the principle of working of hydrodynamic journal bearing. Initially when the journal (i.e. shaft) is at rest, it makes contact with the bearing at its lowest point A due to load 'W' [Refer Fig. 8.3 (a)].
- When the journal starts rotating in clockwise direction, it will climb the bearing surface and contact is made at point B. [Refer Fig. 8.3 (b)].
- As the speed of the journal is further increased, the lubricant is pulled into the wedge-shaped region and forces the journal to the other side.
- The converging wedge film between points C and D supports the journal.
- Thus, in hydrodynamic bearings, it is not necessary to supply the lubricant under pressure and the only requirement is to ensure sufficient and continuous supply of the lubricant.

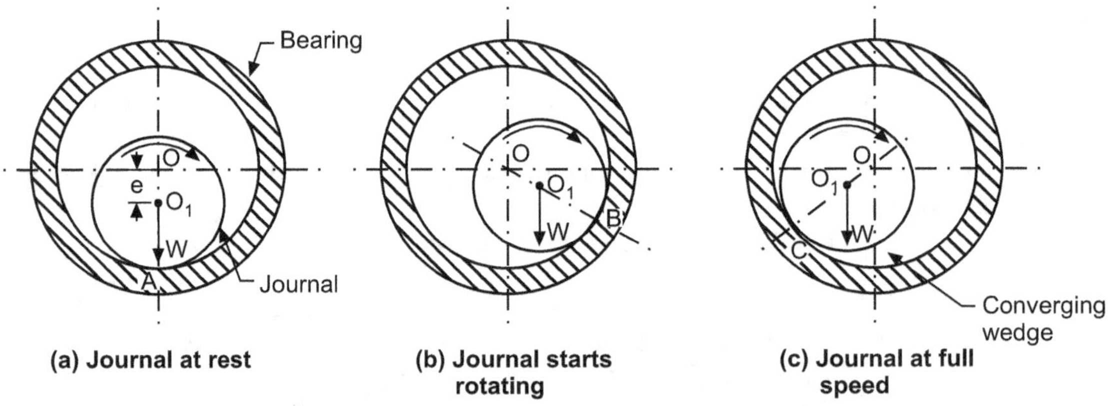

(a) Journal at rest   **(b) Journal starts rotating**   **(c) Journal at full speed**

Fig. 8.3 : Hydrodynamic bearing

Advantages of Hydrodynamic Bearings :

(1) Simple in construction.

(2) Easy to maintain.

(3) Low initial and maintenance cost.

(4) Do not require auxiliary equipments such as pumps.

Disadvantages of Hydrodynamic Bearings :

(1) They produce high friction at low speeds.

(2) Cannot be used for low speed applications.

(3) Less accurate in positioning.

(4) They offer high starting friction.

Applications of Hydrodynamic Bearings :

(1) In engines to support crankshaft.

(2) In centrifugal pumps.

(3) In hydraulic turbines.

2. Hydrostatic or Externally Pressurized Bearings :

- They can support steady loads without any relative motion between the journal and bearing.

- This is achieved by means of forcing the external pressurized lubricant between the members.

- In hydrostatic bearings, the load supporting high pressure fluid film is created by an external source, like pump.

- The pressurized lubricant is supplied between the two surfaces externally.

- So, unlike the hydrodynamic bearings, the hydrostatic bearings do not require motion of one surface relative to another.

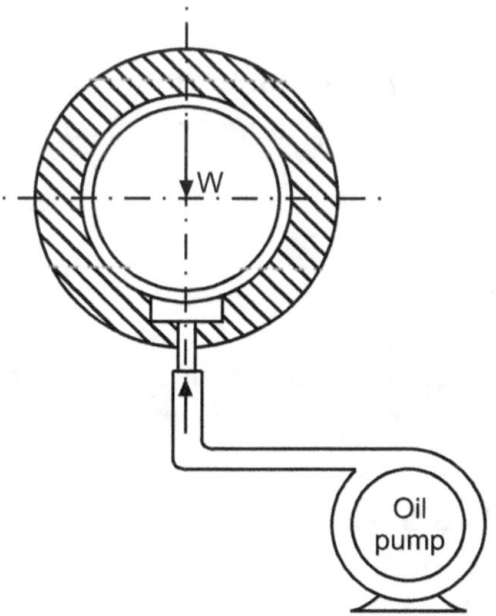

Fig. 8.4 : Hydrostatic bearing

8.2.1.1 Difference between Hydrodynamic & Hydrostatic Bearings

Hydrodynamic bearings	Hydrostatic bearings
1. Shape and relative motions of the sliding surfaces create the load supporting the fluid film.	1. The load supporting the fluid film is created by an external source, like a pump supplying fluid under pressure.
2. Since the pressure is created within the system due to rotation of shaft, this type of bearing is called as *self-acting bearing*.	2. Since the pressure is created by external source, it is known as *externally pressurized bearing*.
3. They are simple in construction.	3. They are complex in construction.
4. Low initial as well as maintenance cost.	4. Comparatively costlier.
5. Less load carrying capacity.	5. High load carrying capacity even at low speeds.
6. **Applications :** Bearings mounted on engines and centrifugal pumps.	6. **Applications :** Bearings mounted on turbo generators, centrifuges and ball mills.

3. Boundary Lubrication or Thin Film Bearings :
- In this, the working surfaces are partially in contact with each other at least part of time, through which, lubricant is present.

4. Zero Film Bearings :
- They operate without any presence of lubricant.

Advantages of Hydrostatic Bearings :
(1) High load carrying capacity even at low speeds.
(2) No starting friction.
(3) No rubbing action at any operating speed or load.
(4) The load carrying capacity is independent of speed.
(5) More accuracy in positioning.

Disadvantages of hydrostatic bearings :
(1) High initial cost.
(2) High maintenance cost.
(3) Require auxillary equipments like pump, filter, pipes carrying oil, so cost increases, as well as, system becomes complicated.
(4) Power is lost in friction as well as in pumping.

Applications of Hydrostatic Bearings :
(1) In vertical turbo-generators.
(2) In ball-mills.
(3) In centrifuges.

8.2.2 Classification of Sliding Contact Bearings on the Basis of Angle of Contact of Bearing with Journal OR Relative Motion between Two Surfaces

Based on relative motion between the two surfaces, the sliding contact bearings are classified into three types :

1. Guide Bearings :

- In guide bearings, the relative sliding motion between the two parts is linear.
- Examples: Guide ways of machine tools, piston-cylinder cross-head of steam engine etc.

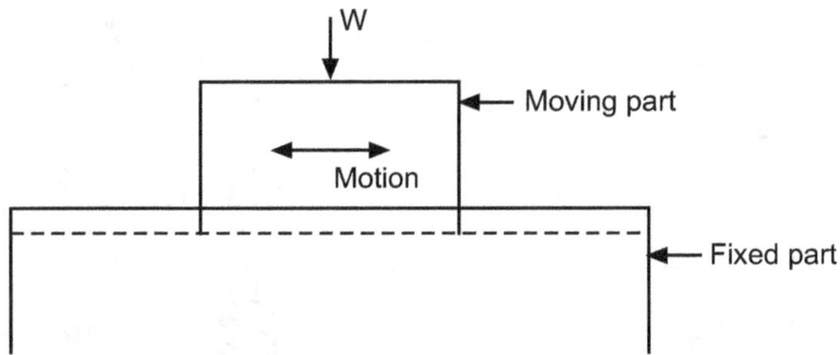

Fig. 8.5 : Guide bearing

2. Journal (Sleeve) Bearings :

- If the relative sliding motion between two parts is of rotation and the pressure on the bearing is perpendicular to the axis of the shaft, the bearing is known as *journal or sleeve bearing*.
- The part, which is enclosed is called as *journal* and the part, which encloses the journal is called as *bearing*. Normally, the journal rotates in the fixed bearing.
- Journal bearing supports the radial load, which is perpendicular to the axis of the shaft and bearings.

Classification of Journal Bearings :

(a) **Full journal bearing** : When the angle of contact of the bearing with the journal is 360°, the bearing is called as full journal bearing.

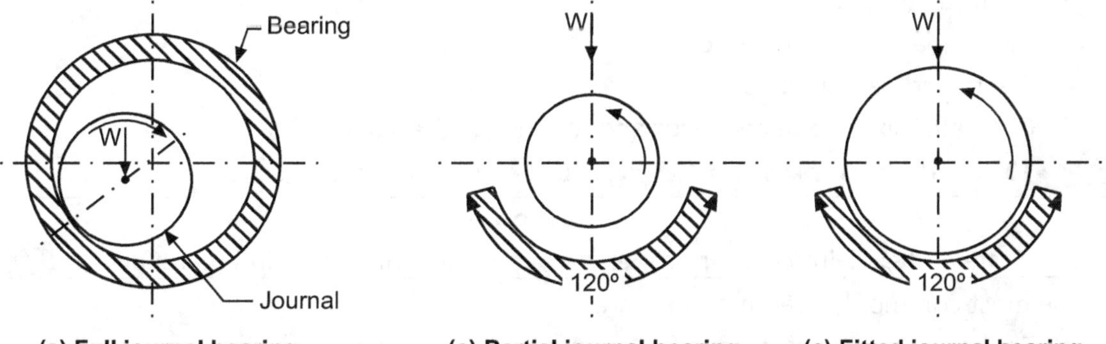

(a) Full journal bearing   (a) Partial journal bearing   (c) Fitted journal bearing

Fig. 8.6 : Journal bearings

(b) Partial journal bearing : When the angle of contact of the bearing with the journal is 120°, the bearing is called as partial journal bearing.

(c) Fitted journal bearing : When a partial journal bearing has no clearance i.e. the diameters of journal and bearing are same, it is said to be fitted journal bearing.

3. Thrust Bearing :

- If the relative sliding motion between the two parts is of rotation and the pressure on the bearing is parallel to the axis of the shaft, the bearing is called as *thrust bearing*.

- In the thrust bearing, if the shaft terminates at the bearing surface, as shown in it, is called pivot bearing [Refer to Fig. 8.7 (a)].

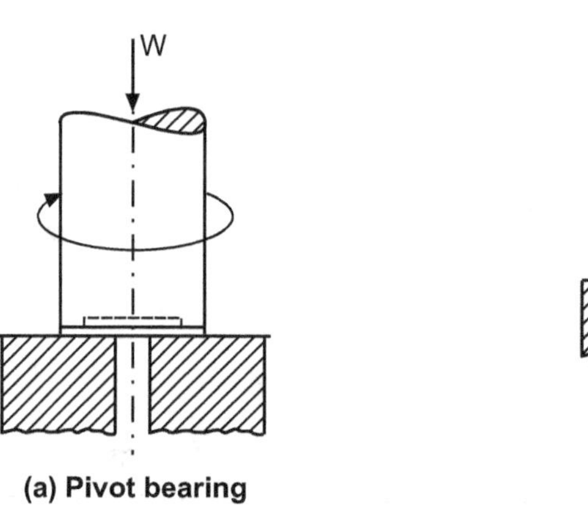

    (a) Pivot bearing   **(b) Collar bearing**

Fig. 8.7

- If the shaft extends through and beyond the bearing, it is called as collar bearing [Refer Fig. 8.7 (b)].
- The thrust bearing supports axial or thrust load, which is along the axis of the shaft and the bearing.

Applications of Sliding Contact Bearings :

(1) Crankshaft bearings in petrol and diesel engines.

(2) Centrifugal pumps.

(3) High capacity electric motors.

(4) Steam and gas turbines.

(5) Concrete mixer, rope conveyor and marine installations.

8.2.2.1 Materials used for Sliding Contact Bearings

Question
1.   State and explain any four properties of sliding contact bearing material.   **(S-13)**

The most commonly used materials are :

(1) Tin base babbit due to *excellent conformability* and *embed-ability, bond-ability* and *better corrosion resistance property*.

(2) Lead bronze due to excellent casting and machining properties, *higher strength* and *ability to withstand high pressures, excellent corrosion resistance property*.

In addition to these, other materials used are :

(a) Copper leads.

(b) Aluminium.

(c) Silver.

(d) Silver lead deposited.

8.2.3 Classification of Rolling Contact Bearings

- Here, the contact between the bearing surfaces is rolling. It consists of four parts, i.e. inner and outer race, rolling element and a cage.

- The steel balls or rollers are interposed between the moving and fixed elements, i.e. inner race and outer race.

Types of Rolling Contact Bearings :

- There are two types of rolling contact bearings.
    1. Ball bearings
    2. Roller bearings

- The ball and roller bearings consist of an inner race, which is mounted on the shaft and an outer race, which is carried by the housing.

- Balls or rollers are placed between the inner and outer race. The number of balls and rollers are held at proper distances by retainers, so that, they do not contact each other.

- The retainers are the thin strips made up of two parts.

- When the balls are properly spaced, the two parts of retainer strips are assembled.

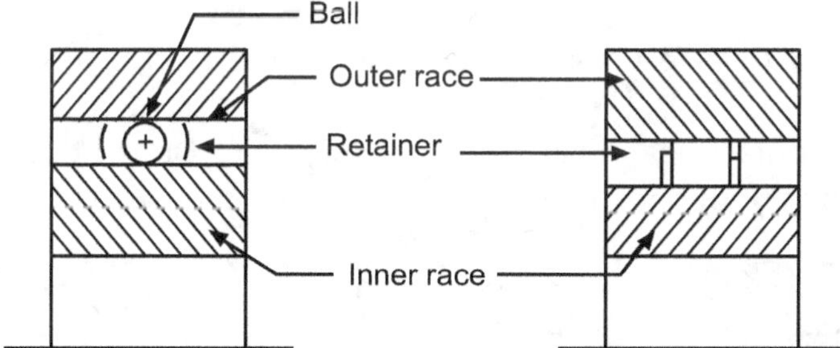

Fig. 8.8 : Ball bearings   **Fig. 8.9 : Roller bearings**

The rolling contact bearings can also be classified on the basis of type of load into,

1. **Radial bearings :** The bearing supports a radial load and the plane of rotation of ball is normal to the centre line of the bearing.

2. **Thrust bearings :** The bearing supports a thrust load and action of load is to shift the plane of rotation of balls.

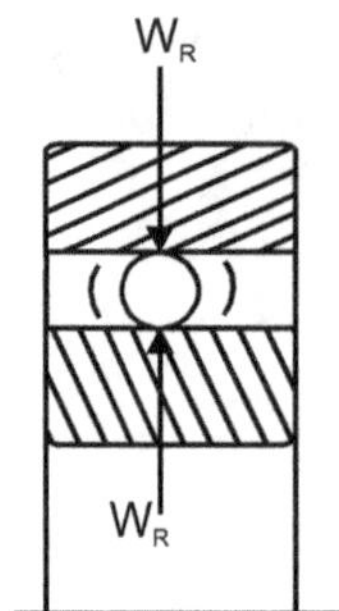

Fig. 8.10 : Radial bearing   **Fig. 8.11 : Thrust ball bearings**

8.2.3.1 Types of Radial Ball Bearing   (W-13)

Following are the various types of radial ball bearing :

(a) Single row deep groove bearing :

- During assembly of this bearing, the races are eccentric and the balls are inserted between the races.
- Balls are symmetrically located with the help of a retainer or cage after the centering of races.
- The deep groove ball bearings are used due to their high load carrying capacity and suitability for high running speeds.

(b) Filling notch bearings :

- They have notches in the inner and outer races due to which, maximum number of balls can be inserted in deep groove ball bearings.
- The notches do not extend to the bottom of the race way and therefore the ball inserted through the notches should be forced in position.

(c) Angular contact bearings :

- In this, one side of the outer race is cut away, due to which, more number of balls can be inserted than a deep groove ball bearing without having a notch cut into both races.
- They are used to take up a relatively large axial load in one direction alongwith radial load.
- The angular contact bearing is usually used in pairs. Due to this, it is possible to take up axial load in both directions.

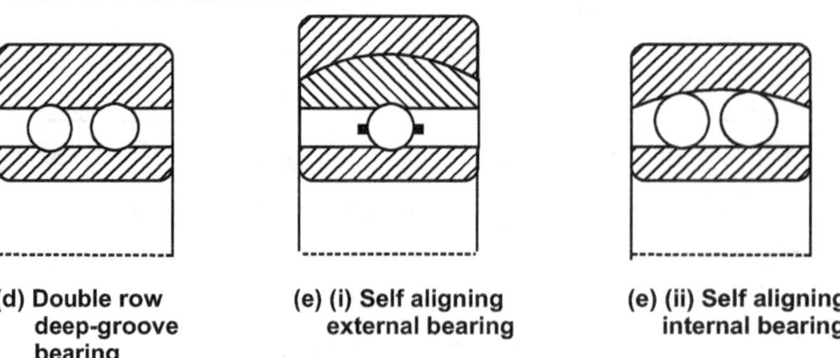

(d) Double row deep-groove bearing   **(e) (i) Self aligning external bearing**   **(e) (ii) Self aligning internal bearing**

Fig. 8.12 : Types of radial ball bearings

(d) Double row bearings :

- These bearings can be made with radial or angular contact between the balls and races.

(e) Self-aligning bearings :

- They are called as self-aligning bearings, because they allow the shaft to deflect through 2 to 3 degrees.
- They are of two types :
    - **(i) Externally self-aligning bearing :** The outer surface of the outer race is ground to a spherical surface, which fits, in a mating spherical surface in a housing.
    - **(ii) Internally self-aligning bearing :** The inner surface of the outer race is ground to a spherical surface.

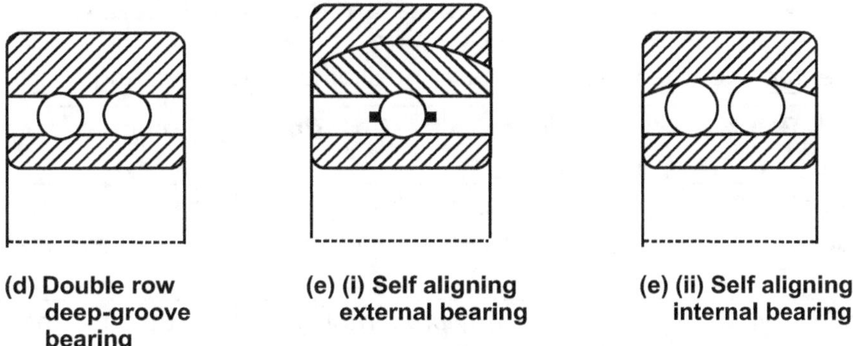

<table>
<tr><td>(d) Double row
    deep-groove
    bearing</td><td>(e) (i) Self aligning
    external bearing</td><td>(e) (ii) Self aligning
    internal bearing</td></tr>
</table>

Fig. 8.13 : Different types of ball bearings

8.2.3.2 Types of Roller Bearings

(a) Cylindrical roller bearings :

- They have short cylindrical rollers guided in raceways or cage.
- They are comparatively more rigid against radial motion.
- They are used in case of *high speeds*.

(b) Spherical roller bearings :

- They are also called as *self-aligning bearings*. The self-aligning feature is achieved by means of grinding one of the races in the form of sphere.
- Smaller angular misalignments are permissible.

(c) Needle roller bearings :

- No retainer or cage is required in this type of bearing.
- They are used as piston pin bearings in heavy-duty diesel engines, where heavy loads are to be carried with an oscillatory motion.

(d) Tapered roller bearings :

- In this type of bearing, rollers and raceways are in the form of truncated cone.
- These types of bearings can carry radial as well as thrust loads. The elements of conical surfaces of rollers and raceways intersect at a common point.

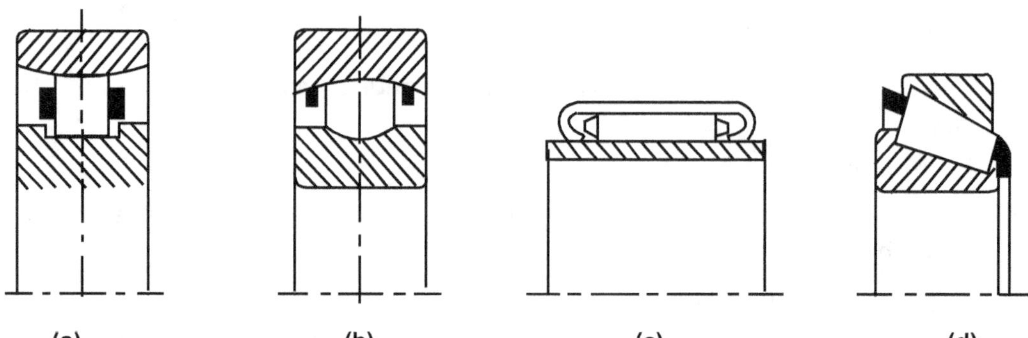

Fig. 8.14 : Types of roller bearings

8.2.4 Distinguish between Sliding Contact and Rolling Contact Bearings

Question

1. Differentiate between rolling contact and sliding contact bearings.   **(W-13)**

Sr. No.	Points	Sliding contact bearing	Rolling contact bearing
(a)	Size of bearing (space)	Sliding contact bearing requires more *axial space*.	Rolling contact bearing requires considerable *radial space*.
(b)	Load carrying capacity	It is *linearly proportional to the speed*. Therefore, sliding contact bearings are suitable for *high load-high speed condition*.	On the other hand, rolling contact bearing has *fixed load carrying capacity* depending upon its size. The load carrying capacity of rolling contact bearing is given in manufacturer's catalogue. It is independent of speed.
(c)	Shock load	Sliding contact bearing can absorb shock load due to damping of the oil film between the journal and the bearing.	Rolling contact bearing is subjected to shock loads due to poor damping capacity.
(d)	Starting torque	Comparatively high.	Comparatively low.
(e)	Noise	Comparatively less noise.	Comparatively high noise.
(f)	Housing design feature	Simple housing design.	Complicated housing design.

Sr. No.	Points	Sliding contact bearing	Rolling contact bearing
(g)	Cost	The initial cost of sliding contact bearing is much higher than that of rolling contact bearing due to additional accessories like pump, filter and pipelines.	Rolling contact bearing is cheaper.
(h)	Axes of the journal and bearing	In sliding contact bearing, working on hydrodynamic principle, the axes of the journal moves eccentrically with respect to the axis of the bearing.	In case of rolling contact bearing, the axes of the journal and bearing are co-liner.

8.2.5 Advantages and Disadvantages of Rolling Contact Bearings over Sliding Contact Bearings

Advantages of Rolling Contact Bearings :

(1) Rolling contact bearings need **low starting torque** as compared to sliding contact bearing.

(2) Rolling contact bearings can carry **combined radial and axial loads** without any complications, whereas sliding contact bearing can take load only in one direction.

(3) Rolling contact bearing requires **less axial space** as compared to sliding contact bearings. It does not require lubrication system consisting of pipelines, sump and filter. This results in compact construction. (i.e. Small Overall Dimensions).

(4) Rolling contact bearings maintain accurate **alignment** of the shaft. The axis of the shaft and the bearing are co-linear, which results in precise positioning of the shaft.

(5) The **lubrication** of rolling contact bearing is simple and requires little or no attention. This is particularly true for low speed grease lubricated bearings. The grease is retained in bearing by means of oil seals. Many times, the initial supply of grease lasts for the entire life of the bearing. On the other hand, sliding contact bearing requires continuous and adequate supply of lubricating oil. The oil needs replacement at regular intervals.

(6) Selection of rolling contact bearing from the manufacturer's catalogue is relatively simple.

(7) Easy mounting.

(8) Reliability of service.

Disadvantages of Rolling Contact Bearings :

(1) Rolling contact bearing has poor damping capacity. The balls and races are permanently deformed under shock loads resulting in excessive **heat, noise** and **friction**.

(2) Rolling contact bearing requires **more radial space**, which increases the diameter of the housing.

(3) Rolling contact bearings are **noisy** in operation due to metal to metal contact.

(4) Rolling contact bearing is very sensitive to air, dust and foreign particles.

(5) Design of bearing housing is complicated.

(6) Low resistance to shock loads.

(7) More initial cost.

Advantages of Sliding Contact Bearings :

(1) Sliding contact bearing can carry **heavy load at high rotational speed**. The load carrying capacity of sliding contact bearing increases with increasing speed.

(2) Sliding contact bearing can **absorb shock and vibrations** due to excellent damping capacity.

(3) In running condition, the surfaces of the journal and the bearing are separated by the film of lubricating oil. There is **no metal to metal contact** resulting in almost noiseless operation.

(4) The **service life** of sliding contact bearing is **independent of speed**.

Disadvantages of Sliding Contact Bearings :

(1) At rest, in sliding contact bearing, there is **metal to metal contact** between the surfaces of the journal and the bearing at the starting. This results in higher starting torque.

(2) Sliding contact bearings **require additional accessories** like sump, filter, pipeline and pump, which increases the cost.

(3) The axis of the shaft rotates eccentrically with respect to the axis of the bearing. The eccentricity varies with speed and load. Therefore, it is **not possible to maintain precise alignment** of the shaft, in case of sliding contact bearings.

(4) Their **maintenance cost is higher**, because of the replacement of lubricating oil at regular intervals.

(5) There is **no standardization** of sliding contact bearings. It is not possible to select sliding contact bearing from different manufacturer's catalogue. Their replacement is also difficult.

8.2.6 Comparison between Ball and Roller Bearings

Sr. No.	Comparison parameters	Ball bearing	Roller bearing
1.	**Rolling element**	In ball bearings, **spherical balls** are used as the rolling elements.	In roller bearings, **cylindrical rollers**, **taper rollers**, or **spherical rollers** are used as the rolling elements.
2.	**Nature of contact**	In ball bearings, the contact between the inner race and ball or the outer race and ball is **point contact**.	In roller bearings, the contact between the inner race and roller or the outer race or roller is **line contact**.
3.	**Load carrying capacity**	Because of point contact, the load carrying capacity of the ball bearings is **low**.	Because of line contact, the load carrying capacity of the roller bearings is **high**.
4.	**Radial dimensions**	For ball bearings, the radial dimension is **more**.	For roller bearings, the radial dimension is **less**. Hence roller bearings are used, where compactness is required in radial direction.
5.	**Axial dimensions**	**Less.**	**More.**
6.	**Cost**	Comparatively **cheaper**.	**Costly** as compared to ball bearings.
7.	**Coefficient of friction**	Independent of load and speed. Its value is 0.0015.	Its value is five times larger.

8.2.7 Applications of Rolling Contact Bearings

Rolling contact bearings are used in following applications :

(i)   Machine tool spindles.

(ii)   Automobile front and rear axles.

(iii)   Gear boxes.

(iv)   Small size electric motors.

(v)   Rope sheave, crane hook and hoisting drum.

8.2.8 Applications of Bearings with Reasons

1. State the applications of following bearings with suitable reasons :
   (i) Deep groove ball bearing.   (ii) Taper roller bearing.
   (iii) Thrust roller bearing.   (iv) Needle roller bering.
   (v) Solid bush type journal bearing   **(S-09, 10, 12, 14; W-11)**

Bearing	Application	Reason
Deep groove ball baring	Electric motor.	Capacity to take heavy axial load with high rotational speed.
Taper roller bearing	Axle housing of automobile.	Ability to take high radial as well as thrust load.
Thrust collar bearing	Clutch of an automobile.	Ability to combine radial and axial load with medium speed.
Needle roller bearing	Differential of an automobile.	It takes less radial space. Also, it has high radial load carrying capacity.
Solid bush type journal bearing	Steam and gas turbines	Ability to take radial load.

8.3 EQUIVALENT BEARING LOAD

- In many practical applications, bearing has to carry both radial and axial loads. In addition, they are sometimes required to operate with a rotating outer race condition resulting into an hypothetical equivalent load, which can satisfy the above conditions.

- **An equivalent load** is that stationary radial load, which, if applied to the bearing with the rotating inner race and stationary outer race, would give the same life as a bearing operating under actual conditions.

- The equivalent dynamic load W, which is applicable to ball and roller bearings, is given by,

$$W = X \cdot V \cdot F_r + Y \cdot F_a$$

where, F_r = Radial load

               F_a = Axial load

               V = Rotation factor

               V = 1.0 for inner race rotating = 1.2 for outer race rotating

                     = 1.0 for self aligning bearings

               X = Radial load factor

               Y = Thrust load factor

8.4 LIFE LOAD RELATIONSHIP

Question

1. How do you express life of bearings ? **(W-12)**

The relationship between the dynamic load carrying capacity, the equivalent dynamic load and the bearing life is given by,

$$L = \left(\frac{C}{W}\right)^a$$

where, W = equivalent dynamic load

L = bearing life (in million revolutions)

C = dynamic load capacity (N)

and a = constant

a = 3 (for ball bearings)

$a = \dfrac{10}{3}$ (for roller bearings)

The relationship between *"life in million revolutions"* and *"life in working hours"* is given by,

$$L = \frac{60\ N\ L_h}{10^6}$$

where, L_h = bearing life (hours) and N = speed of rotation in r.p.m.

8.5 BASIC STATIC LOAD RATING

Question

1. State the meaning for ball bearings :
    (i) Basic static load rating, (ii) Basic dynamic load rating **(S-13)**

- A static load is the load carried by a non-rotating bearing.
- **The basic static load rating** is defined as, *'the static radial load (for radial ball or roller bearings), or axial load (for thrust ball or roller bearings), which corresponds to a total permanent deformation of ball/roller and race, at the most heavily stressed contact, equal to 0.0001 times the ball/roller diameter.*
- In a single row angular contact ball bearing, the basic static load relates to the radial component of the load, which causes a purely radial displacement of the bearing rings in relation to each other.

According to IS : 3823 - 1984, the basic static load rating (C_o) in Newton for different ball and roller bearings may be calculated as shown below :

1. **For radial ball bearings :** The basic static radial load rating (C_o) is given by,

$$C_o = f_o \cdot i \cdot Z \cdot D^2 \cdot \cos \alpha$$

where, f_o = A factor depending upon the type of bearing.

The values of factor (f_o) for bearing made of hardened steel are taken as,

f_o = 3.33 for self-aligning ball bearings.

= 12.3 for radial contact and angular contact groove ball bearings.

i = Number of rows of balls in any one bearing.

Z = Number of balls per row.

D = Diameter of balls, in mm.

α = Nominal angle of contact i.e. the nominal angle between the line of action of the ball load and a plane perpendicular to the axis of bearing.

2. **For radial roller bearings :** The basic static radial load rating is given by,

$$C_o = f_o \cdot i \cdot Z \cdot l_e \cdot D \cdot \cos \alpha$$

where, f_o = 21.6 for bearings made of hardened steel.

i = Number of rows of roller in bearing.

Z = Number of rollers per row.

l_e = Effective length of contact between one roller and that ring (or washer), where the contact is the shortest (in mm). It is equal to the overall length of roller minus roller chamfers or grinding undercuts.

D = Diameter of roller in mm (It is the mean diameter in case of tapered rollers)

and α = Nominal angle of contact i.e. the nominal angle between the line of action of the roller resultant load and a plane perpendicular to the axis of the bearing.

8.6 BASIC DYNAMIC RATING OF ROLLING CONTACT BEARINGS

(S-13)

- **The basic dynamic load rating** is defined as, *'the constant stationary radial load (in case of radial ball or roller bearings) or constant axial load (for thrust ball or roller bearings), that can be carried for a minimum life of one million revolutions'.*

- The minimum life (in the definition) is the life, which 90% of the bearings will reach or exceed before fatigue failure.

- The dynamic load carrying capacity is based on the assumption that, the inner race is rotating, while the outer race is stationary.

- When the bearing starts rotating, the load is more evenly distributed amongst balls and races, thereby sustaining more permanent deformation than in static conditions.

- The dynamic capacity of bearing is based on the fatigue life of the material.

- *One million revolutions life is equivalent to 500 hours of operation at 33.3 rpm.*

If C = Dynamic load rating

and W = Load

Then,   Rating life, $L = \left(\dfrac{C}{W}\right)^3$ millions of revolutions

$$\therefore \qquad W = C \times \left(\frac{1}{L}\right)^{1/3}$$

If $\qquad N = $ r.p.m.

and $\qquad L = $ Life in hours

then, the value of equivalent load is found from the following relation :

$$W = C \left(\frac{10^6}{60 \, N \cdot L}\right)^{1/3}$$

Also, $\qquad \dfrac{C}{W} = $ Loading ratio

Bearing life is generally referred to as L_{10} life on a 10% of failure or 90% survival rate. A bearing with 5 L_{10} life means, life is 5×10^6 revolutions.

$$C = \left(\frac{L}{L_{10}}\right)^{1/a} \times W$$

where, $\qquad L_{10} = $ Life of bearing for 90% survival at one million revolution

and $\qquad a = 3$ $\qquad\qquad$ (for ball bearings)

$$\qquad\quad = \frac{10}{3} \qquad\qquad \text{(for roller bearings)}$$

8.7 SELECTION OF BEARING FROM MANUFACTURER'S CATALOGUE

Questions

1. What is the procedure for selection of bearings from manufacturer's catalogue. **(W-09, 10, 13; S-11)**
2. How will you select ball bearing from manufacturer's catalogue ? **(W-12)**
3. Explain the selection procedure of bearings from manufacturer's catalogue. **(S-14)**

Steps Involved in Selection of Bearing :

1. Calculate radial and axial forces acting on bearing and determine diameter of shaft, where bearing is to be mounted.
2. Select the type of bearing for the given application.
3. Calculate the values of X (radial factor) and Y (thrust factor), from the catalogue. These values depend upon two ratios (F_a/F_r) and (F_a/C_o), where C_o is the static load capacity. Therefore, bearing is selected by trial and error method.
4. Calculate equivalent dynamic load by, $W = X \cdot F_r + Y \cdot F_a$.
5. Express the life in million revolutions.
6. Calculate dynamic load capacity, $L = (C/W)^a$.
7. Check whether the selected bearing has required dynamic capacity or not. If not, bearing of next series is selected and procedure is repeated.

In the above equation,

$$a = \text{constant}$$
$$= 3 \qquad \text{(for ball bearing)}$$
$$= \frac{10}{3} \qquad \text{(for roller bearing)}$$

Following chart shows the method to select bearing from manufacturer's catalogue.

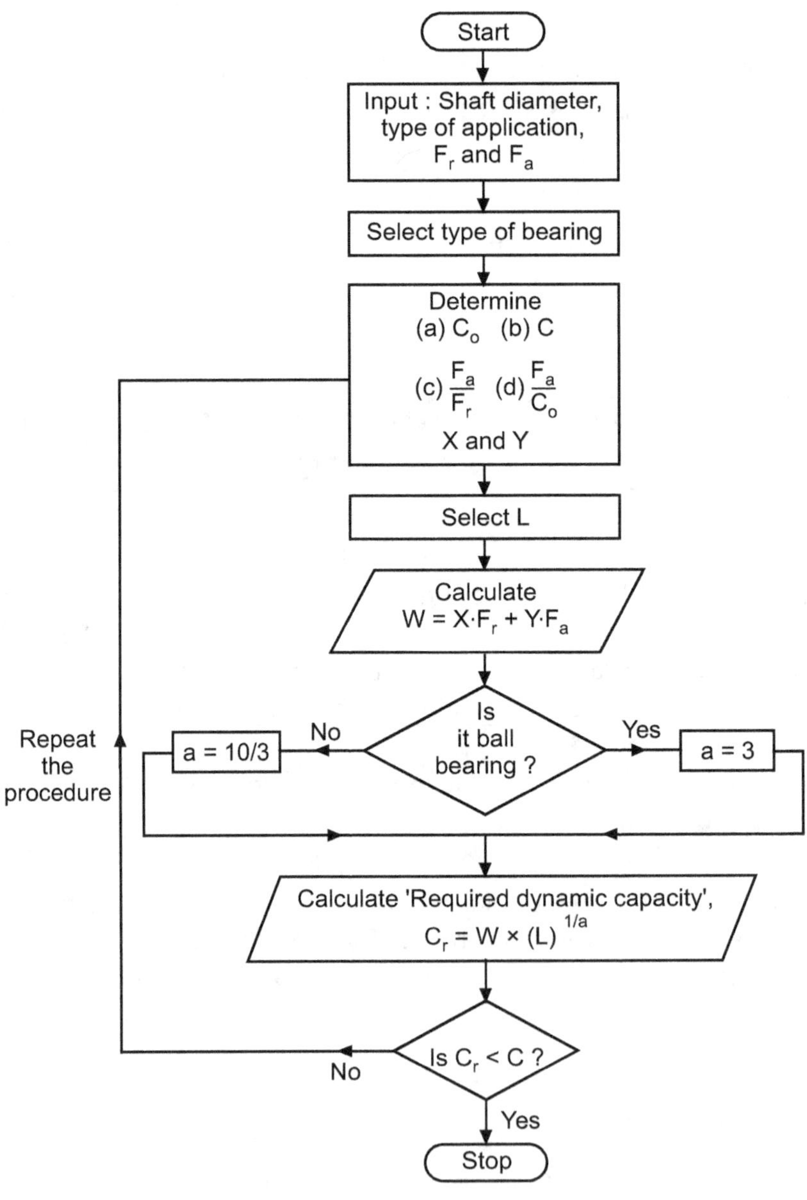

8.8 FACTORS AFFECTING THE SELECTION OF BALL BEARING

(i) Mechanical requirements such as :

    (a) Load

    (b) Speed

    (c) Starting friction

    (d) Space requirements

(ii) Environmental conditions :

    (a) Temperature

    (b) Pressure

(iii) Economics :

    (a) Life

    (b) Maintenance

    (c) Cost

(iv) Type of application.

8.9 LIMITING SPEED

- *"The maximum speed, at which, it is possible for the bearing to continuously operate without the generation of excessive heat beyond specified limits is called as **limiting speed** (rev/min)".*

- As bearing speed increases, the temperature of the bearing also increases due to frictional heat generated in the interior of bearing.

- If the temperature continues to rise and exceeds certain limits, the efficiency of the lubricant drastically decreases and the bearing can no longer continues to operate in a stable manner.

- In other words, the limiting speed of a bearing is considered to be the maximum continuous speed, at which, there will be no risk of gripping due to temperature rise or excessive heat dissipation of the bearing.

- The limiting speed of a bearing depends on the mechanical or thermal constraints such as

    (a) Type of bearing

    (b) Bearing size

    (c) Quantity and viscosity of the lubricant

    (d) Cooling conditions

    (e) Type of cage

    (f) Operating clearance.

Practice Questions

1. Explain 'classification of bearings'.
2. Differentiate between 'Hydrodynamic and Hydrostatic bearings'.
3. Give classification of rolling contact bearings.
4. Differentiate between rolling contact and sliding contact bearings.
5. Give advantages and disadvantages of rolling contact bearings over sliding contact bearings.
6. Give relation between life and load.
7. Explain basic static load rating of R.C.B.
8. Discuss basic dynamic load rating of Rolling Contact Bearing.
9. Explain the procedure for selection of ball bearings using manufacturer's catalogue.

MSBTE Questions and Answers

Summer 2013

1. State the classification of bearings.	**(4 M)**
Ans. Refer Article 8.2.
2. State and explain any four properties of sliding contact bearing materials.	**(4 M)**
Ans. Refer Article 8.2.2.1.
3. State the meaning for ball bearings.	**(4 M)**
   (i) Basic static load rating.
   (ii) Basic dynamic load rating.
Ans. Refer Articles 8.5 and 8.6.

Winter 2013

1. Explain the procedure of selection of ball bearings using manufacturer's catalogue.	**(4 M)**
Ans. Refer Article 8.7.
2. Enlist different types of Radial ball bearings.	**(4 M)**
Ans. Refer Article 8.2.3.1.
3. Differentiate between rolling contact and sliding contact bearing.	**(4 M)**
Ans. Refer Article 8.2.4.

Summer 2014

1. State the applications of the following bearings with suitable reasons: (i) Deep groove ball bearing (ii) Thrust roller bearing, (iii) Taper roller bearing (iv) Solid bush type journal bearing.	**(4 M)**
Ans. Refer Article 8.2.8.
2. Explain the selection procedure of bearings from manufacturer's catalogue.	**(4 M)**
Ans. Refer Article 8.7.

Reference Table for Nominal Diameter and Pitch of Square Threads

Nominal diameter in mm	Pitch in mm	Nominal diameter in mm	Pitch in mm
22	5	55	9
24		58	
26		60	
28		62	
30	6	65	10
32		68	
34		70	
36		72	
38	7	75	
40		78	
42		80	
44		82	
46	8	85	12
48		88	
50		90	
52		92	

(T.1)

1. (A) Attempt any THREE of the following :   **(12)**

(a)   State the steps involved in general design procedure.

Ans. Refer Section 1.2.

(b)   State maximum shear stress theory with their use.

Ans. Refer Section 1.28.

(c)   List different types of keys.

Ans. Refer Section 3.2.2.

(d)   Explain the term self locking of screw.

Ans. Refer Section 4.7.3.

(B) Attempt any ONE of the following :   **(6)**

(a)   Design 'C' clamp frame for a total clamping force of 20 kN. The cross-section of the frame is rectangular and width of thickness ratio is 2. The distance between the load line and neutral axis of rectangular section is 120 mm and gap between two faces is 180 mm. Frame is made of cast steel. The permissible tensile stress for cast steel is 100 N/mm^2.

Ans. Refer Problem 2.11.

(b)   A wall bracket shown in Fig. 1 is fixed to a wall by means of four bolts. Find the size of bolts. The permissible tensile stress for bolt material is 70 N/mm^2.

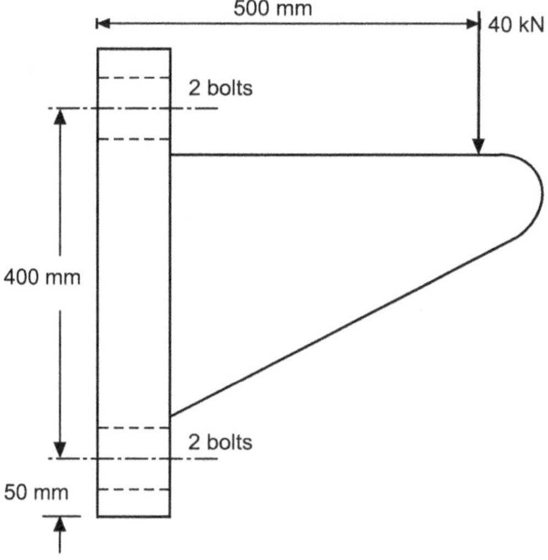

Fig. 1

Ans. Refer Similar Problem 6.13.

2. Attempt any TWO of the following :   **(16)**

(a) Draw a neat sketch of hand lever and write various strength equations for its complete design.

Ans. Refer Section 2.5.2.

(b) A simple cotter joint is subjected to an axial load of 100 kN which alternately changes from tensile to compressive. Allowable stresses for the material are 80 N/mm^2, 35 N/mm^2 and 100 N/mm^2 in tension, shear and compression respectively. The joint is subjected to 30% overload due to tighting. Design spigot cotter.

Ans. Refer Similar Problem 2.1.

(c) Design a muff coupling which is used to connect two steel shaft transmitting 40 kW at 350 rpm. The material for shaft and key is plain carbon steel for which allowable shear and crushing stresses may be taken as 40 N/mm^2 and 80 N/mm^2 respectively. The allowable shear stress for muff is 15 N/mm^2 and the material for muff is cast iron.

Ans. Refer Problem 3.29.

3. Attempt any FOUR of the following :   **(16)**

(a) Write any four factors to be considered while selecting the factor of safety.

Ans. Refer Section 1.14.1.

(b) Explain the causes of stress concentration.

Ans. Refer Section 1.15.

(c) Write the Lewis equation for strength of a gear tooth with usual notation.

Ans. Refer Section 3.4.8.

(d) Why hollow shaft is preferred over solid shaft for large power transmission ?

Ans. Refer Problem 3.23.

(e) List four advantages of rolling contact bearing.

Ans. Refer Section 8.2.5.

4. (A) Attempt any THREE of the following :   **(12)**

(a) Explain :

(i) Transverse shear stress. (ii) Tortional shear stress.

Ans. (i) Refer Article 1.7 (4).

     (ii) Refer Article 1.7 (5).

(b) Designate the following matrials : (i) Fe 500. (ii) X 20 Cr 18 Ni 2.

Ans. (i) Refer Section 1.21 (3).

     (ii) Refer Section 1.21 (7).

(c)　Design the shaft subjected to combine bending moment and twisting moment by maximum shear stress theory.

Ans. Refer Section 3.1.8 [(c) 1].

(d)　Define the following term with reference to spring design :

　　(i)　Solid length. (ii) Free length. (iii) Spring rate. (iv) Spring index.

Ans. (i)　Refer Section 5.16 (1).

　　(ii)　Refer Section 5.16 (2).

　　(iii)　Refer Section 5.16 (4).

　　(iv)　Refer Section 5.16 (3).

(B)　Attempt any ONE of the following :　　　　　　　　　　　　　　　　**(6)**

(a)　Show the efficiency of self blocking is screw less than 50%.

Ans. Refer Section 4.7.3.

(b)　A cylinder head of a steam engine is held in position by M20 bolts. The effective diameter of the cylinder is 300 mm and steam pressure of 0.6 N/mm^2. Assume bolts are not initially stressed. Find the number of bolts required, if working stress for bolt material is not to exceed 20 N/mm^2.

Ans. Refer Problem 6.2.

5.　Attempt any TWO of the following :　　　　　　　　　　　　　　　　**(16)**

(a)　A lathe machine receives the power from a overhang shaft situated exactly above the lathe pulley by means of belt drive. Pulley weighing 400 N and of diameter 270 mm is fixed on the shaft at a distance of 300 mm to the right of the left hand bearing. The centre to centre distance between two shaft supported bearing is 900 mm. Maximum power transmitted is 5 kW at 200 rpm, belt tension ratio is 2.5. If permissible shear stress is 40 N/mm^2, determine the diameter of shaft.

Ans. Refer Problem 3.12.

(b)　The lead screw of a lathe has acme thread of 60 mm outside diameter and 8 mm pitch. It supplies drive to the tool carriage which requires an axial force of 300 kg. A collar bearing with diameter 12 cm and 6 cm is provided to take up the thrust if the lead screw rotated at 50 rpm and coefficient of friction for screw thread is 0.18 and for collar is 0.14. Find power required to drive screw and efficiency.

Ans. Refer Problem 4.19.

(c)　A spring loaded safety valve for boiler is required to blow at a pressure of 1.20 N/mm^2. Diameter of valve is 65 mm. The maximum lift of valve is 17.5 mm. Design a suitable compression spring for the safety valve. Assume C = 6 and provide initial compression of 30 mm. The maximum permissible shear stress in the spring material is 450 N/mm^2 and G = 0.84×10^5 N/mm^2.

Ans. Refer Problem 5.14.

6. **Attempt any FOUR of the following :**   **(16)**

(a)   Differentiate between sliding contact bearing and rolling contact bearing.

Ans. Refer Section 8.2.4.

(b)   Give the importance of shape and size in aesthetic design.

Ans. Refer Section 1.37.

(c)   State any four advantages of 'V' thread over square thread.

Ans. Refer Section 4.2.1.3.

(d)   Sketch semi-elliptic leaf spring and name different part on sketch.

Ans. Refer Section 5.6.

(e)   Write any four functions of spring.

Ans. Refer Section 5.1.1.

Time : 4 Hrs.   **SUMMER 2015**   **Marks : 100**

1. **Attempt any FIVE :**   **(5 × 4 = 20)**

(a)   Define 'machine design'. Enlist the various phases involved in the process of machine design.

Ans. Refer Section 1.1.

(b)   State the various theories of elastic failure. Explain maximum distortion energy theory.

Ans. Refer Section 1.28.

(c)   Prove that for a square key, 'crushing stress is twice shearing stress'.

Ans. Refer Section 3.2.3.2.

(d)   State the types of thread profile used in power transmission. Draw neat sketches of any two profiles.

Ans. Refer Section 4.5.

(e)   Draw an eccentrically loaded offset link of rectangular cross-section and show load, eccentricity and neutral axis on it.

Ans. Refer Section 2.7.2.

(f)   Explain with neat sketch 'bolt of uniform strength'.

Ans. Refer Section 6.5.

(g)   State aesthetic considerations in design regarding size and surface finish.

Ans. Refer Section 1.37.

2. **Attempt any TWO :**   **$(2 \times 8 = 16)$**

(a)   Te maximum pull of 100 kN acts on the round tie bar of the roof truss. If the safe tensile and shearing stress in the rod are 80 N/mm^2 and 30 N/mm^2 respectively. Design the turn buckle joint. Draw sketch.

Ans. Refer Similar Problem 2.4.

(b)   Design a bell-crank lever used to lift a load of 2200 N acting at the end of 125 mm long vertical arm. The effort is applied at the end of 150 mm horizontal arm. The arms of rectangular cross-section with width to thickness ratio of 2.5 have permissible bending stress of 100 N/mm^2. The fulcrum pin is made of C20 with permissible bearing and shearing stress as 10 MPa and 30 MPa respectively.

Ans. Refer Problem 2.8.

(c)   Design a muff coupling for connecting two shafts transmitting 35 kW at 200 rpm. The shear stress for shaft and key material is 60 N/mm^2 and for muff 10 N/mm^2. The crushing stress for key material is 100 N/mm^2.

Ans. Refer Similar Problem 3.28.

3. **Attempt any FOUR :**   **$(4 \times 4 = 16)$**

(a)   Define 'factor of safety'. State the conditions where higher value of 'factor of safety' is chosen.

Ans. Refer Sections 1.14, 1.14.2 and 1.14.4.

(b)   State any two causes for stress concentration. Draw sketches and explain any two remedial measures to control the effect of stress concentration.

Ans. Refer Sections 1.15 and 1.16.

(c)   Write the expressions for static and dynamic load for spur gears and explain various terms used in it.

Ans. Refer Section 3.4.10.

(d)   Prove that, the hollow shaft has higher torque transmitting capacity than the solid shaft of same weight.

Ans. Refer Problem 3.23.

(e)   Distinguish between sliding contact and rolling contact bearing.

Ans. Refer Section 8.2.4.

(f)   A lead screw of lathe has square threads of 24 mm outside diameter and 5 mm pitch. In order to drive tool carriage, the screw exerts an axial pressure of 2 kN. Find the efficiency of a single threaded screw, if coefficient of friction for square screw thread is 0.12. Neglect bearing friction.

Ans. Refer Problem 4.1.

4. Attempt any FOUR :   (4 × 4 = 16)

(a) Draw stress-strain diagram for ductile and brittle materials. Name the salient points on the diagrams.

Ans. Refer Sections 1.6.1 and 1.6.2.

(b) State any four advantages of standardization.

Ans. Refer Section 1.25.

(c) An axle of 1 m long is supported in bearings at its ends and carries a flywheel of 30 kN at the centre. If the maximum stress in axle material is 50 MPa, find the diameter of the axle.

Ans. Refer Problem 3.8.

(d) State the significance of Wahl's correction factor used in springs.

Ans. Refer Section 5.2.2.

(e) Draw a neat sketch of toggle jack and name the various parts.

Ans. Refer Section 4.10.

(f) A bracket shown in Fig. 1, supports a load of 35 kN. Determine the size of bolts if allowable tensile stress is 60 MPa. Four bolts are used.

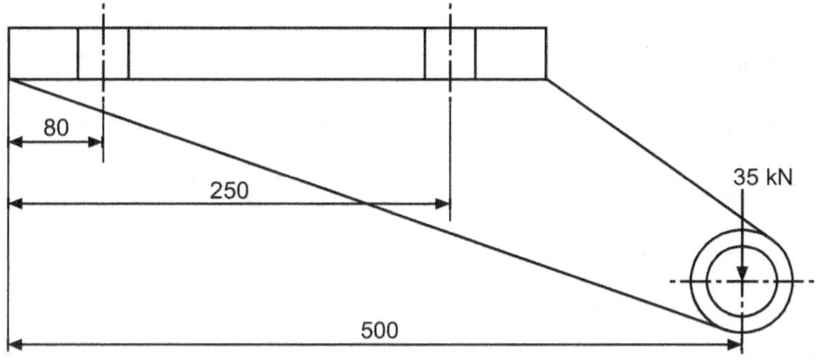

All distances are in mm.

Fig. 1

Ans. Refer Similar Problem 6.10.

5. Attempt any FOUR :   (4 × 4 = 16)

(a) A hollow shaft from a rotary compressor is to be designed to transmit a maximum torque of 4500 N.m. The limiting shear stress in shaft material is 60 MPa. Determine inside and outside diameters of shaft, if the ratio of inside to outside diameter is 0.4.

Ans. Refer Problem 3.2.

(b) Write the expressions to determine :

    (i) Direct compressive stress. (ii) Torsional shear stress.

    (iii) Shear stress due to axial load. (iv) Bearing pressure, induced in power screws.

Ans. Refer Section 4.6.

(c)   A railway wagon of mass 20 tonnes is moving with a velocity of 3 m/sec. It is brought to rest by two buffers with spring of 300 mm diameter. The maximum deflection in the spring is 250 mm. The allowable shear stress is 700 MPa. Find the diameter of spring wire.

Ans. Refer Problem 5.18.

(d)   Draw a neat sketch of 'Woodruff key'. State its application.

Ans. Refer Section 3.2.2. [1 (e)].

(e)   State the meaning with respect to screw : (i) Overhauling. (ii) Self-locking.

Ans. Refer Section 4.7.3.

(f)   A helical compression spring carries a load of 500 N with 25 mm deflection. The spring index is 8. Maximum shear stress is 350 MPa and modulus of rigidity for spring material is 84 kN/mm^3. Assuming Wahl's factor as $\dfrac{4C-1}{4C-4} + \dfrac{0.615}{C}$, find the number of turns if C is the spring index.

Ans. Refer Problem 5.4.

6. Attempt any FOUR :   **(4 × 4 = 16)**

(a)   State the meaning for ball bearings :

   (i)   Basic static load rating. (ii) Basic dynamic load rating.

Ans. Refer Section 8.17 and 8.18.

(b)   Define the terms : (i) Aesthetic. (ii) Ergonomics.

Ans. Refer Section 1.34.

(c)   Write the equations used to find the tensile and shear stresses included in a bolt, with meaning of each term.

Ans. Refer Section 6.4.1 (b).

(d)   Sketch semi-elliptical leaf spring and name different parts.

Ans. Refer Section 5.6.

(e)   State any four applications of spring.

Ans. Refer Section 5.1.2.

(f)   List any four applications of welded joints.

Ans. Refer Section 7.1.2.

Time : 4 Hrs.   **WINTER 2015**   **Marks : 100**

1. (a) Attempt any THREE of the following :   **(12)**

(i) What are the steps involved in general design produce ? Explain.

Ans. Refer Section 1.2.

(ii) Differentiate between Knuckle joint and Cotter joint (any four points of difference).

Ans. Refer Section 2.3.8.

(iii) Write Lewis equation for strength of gear tooth. State the meaning of each term.

Ans. Refer Section 3.4.8.

(iv) State four different thread profiles used in power transmission. Draw neat sketches of any two of them.

Ans. Refer Section 4.2.

(b) Attempt any ONE of the following :   **(6)**

(i) What is stress concentration ? Explain any four methods to reduce it.

Ans. Refer Sections 1.15 and 1.16.

(ii) A shaft 1000 mm long is supported between two bearings. A pulley of 250 mm diameter is keyed at 400 mm distance away from left hand bearing. The power transmitted by shaft is 10 kW at 800 r.p.m. The pulley gives power to another pulley vertically below it having an angle of contact between pulley and belt as 180°. The weight of pulley is 300 N. The coefficient of friction between belt and pulley is 0.15. Take shear stress for shaft material as 60 MPa. Find the diameter of the shaft.

Ans. Refer Similar Problem 3.12.

2. Attempt any TWO of the following :   **(16)**

(a) Explain the design procedure of hand lever with neat sketch.

Ans. Refer Section 2.5.2.

(b) Explain the design procedure of bush pin type flexible coupling with neat sketch.

Ans. Refer Section 3.3.8.

(c) (i) Explain with neat sketch, the stress-strain diagram for ductile material.

Ans. Refer Section 1.6.1.

    (ii) Design "C" clamp frame for a total clamping force of 20 kN. The cross-section of the frame is rectangular and width of thickness ratio is 2. The distance between the load line and natural axis of rectangular cross-section is 120 mm and the gap between two faces is 180 mm. The frame is cast steel for which maximum permissible tensile stress is 100 N/mm^2.

Ans. Refer Problem 2.11.

3. **Attempt any FOUR of the following :**　　　　　　　　　　　　　　　**(16)**

   (a)　State the composition of following materials :

   　　(i)　Fe E 230. (ii) X 20 Cr 18 Ni 2. (iii) 35 C 8. (iv) 40 Ni 2 Cr 1 Mo 28.

   Ans. (i)　Refer Section 1.21 (3).

   　　(ii)　Refer Section 1.21 (9).

   　　(iii)　Refer Section 1.21 (4).

   　　(iv)　Refer Section 1.21 (6).

   (b)　Design an offset link for a load of 1000 N. Maximum permissible stress in tension for link material is 60 N/mm^2. Assume b = 3t for rectangular cross-section of the link.

   Ans. Refer Problem 2.15.

   (c)　Prove that for square key equally strong in shear and crushing, the permissible crushing stress is twice the permissible shear stress.

   Ans. Refer Section 3.2.3.2.

   (d)　Explain with neat sketch the bolts of uniform strength.

   Ans. Refer Section 6.5.

   (e)　How keys are classified ? Give detailed classification of keys with neat sketches; also state their applications.

   Ans. Refer Section 3.2.2.

4. **(a)**　**Attempt any THREE of the following :**　　　　　　　　　　　**(12)**

   (i)　State the meaning of following colour codes in aesthetic consideration while designing the product : (1) Red. (2) Orange. (3) Green. (4) Blue.

   Ans. Refer Section 1.37 (3).

   (ii)　Define the following terms with respect to springs :

   　　(1)　Spring index. (2) Spring stiffness. (3) Free length of spring.

   　　(4)　Solid length of spring.

   Ans. (1)　Refer Section 5.1.6 (3).

   　　(2)　Refer Section 5.1.6 (4).

   　　(3)　Refer Section 5.1.6 (2).

   　　(4)　Refer Section 5.1.6 (1).

   (iii)　State the effect of keyway on the strength of the shaft.

   Ans. Refer Section 3.2.4.

   (iv)　A cylinder head of steam engine is held in position by M20 bolts. The effective diameter of cylinder is 350 mm and the steam pressure is 0.75 N/mm^2. If the bolts are not initially stressed, find the number of bolts required. Take working stress for bolt material as 20 N/mm^2.

   Ans. Refer Problem 6.2.

(b)   Attempt any ONE of the following :   **(6)**

(i)   State the different modes of failure of gear teeth and their possible remedies to avoid the failure.

Ans. Refer Section 3.5.

(ii)   Explain the following types of stresses :

    (1)   Transverse shear stress. (2) Compressive stress. (3) Torsional shear stress.

Ans. (1)   Refer Section 1.7 (4).

    (2)   Refer Section 1.7 (2).

    (3)   Refer Section 1.7 (5).

5. Attempt any TWO of the following :   **(16)**

(a)   A vertical double start square threaded screw of 120 mm mean diameter and 24 mm pitch supports a vertical load of 20 kN. The axial thrust in screw is taken by collar bearings of 300 mm outside and 150 mm inside diameter. Find the force required at the end of the lever which is 400 mm long in order to lift and lower the load. The coefficient of friction for screw and nut is 0.18 and for collar bearings it is 0.25.

Ans. Refer Problem 4.8.

(b)   A safety valve of 60 mm diameter is to blow off at a pressure of 1.2 N/mm^2. It is held on its seat by a close coiled helical spring. The maximum lift of the valve is 10 mm. Design a suitable compression spring of spring index 5 with an initial compression of 35 mm. The shear stress for spring material is limited to 500 MPa. Take $G = 80$ kN/mm^2.

Ans. Refer Problem 5.14.

(c)   (i)   Differentiate between sliding contact and rolling contact bearings. (any four points of difference).

Ans. Refer Section 8.2.4.

    (ii) Explain the terms self locking and overhauling of screw.

Ans. Refer Section 4.7.3.

6. Attempt any FOUR of the following :   **(16)**

(a)   State the strength equations of double parallel fillet weld and single transverse filled weld with neat sketches.

Ans. Refer Section 7.5.

(b)   A semi-elliptical carriage spring of 1200 mm length withstands a load of 60 kN with maximum deflection of 90 mm. Assume breadth to thickness ratio as 8. Design the spring if bending stress of spring material is 540 MPa and $E = 2 \times 10^5$ N/mm^2.

Ans. Refer Problem 5.22.

(c)   A wall bracket is fixed to the wall by means of three bolts, one bolt at a distance of 25 mm from the lower edge and remaining two bolts at a distance of 175 mm from the lower bolts. It supports a load of 7.5 kN at a distance of 250 mm from the wall. The bolts are made from plain carbon steel 45C8 with tensile yield strength of 380 N/mm². If factor of safety is 2.5, estimate the size of the bolts. Sketch the arrangement.

Ans. Refer Problem 6.16.

(d)   Explain the selection procedure of bearings from manufacturer's catalogue.

Ans. Refer Section 8.7.

(e)   State the applications of following bearings with suitable reasons :

    (i)   Deep grove ball bearing. (ii) Taper roller bearing. (iii) Thrust coller bearing.

    (iv) Needle roller bearing.

Ans. Refer Section 8.2.8.